MW00935327

ASCENDED

THE LIGHTBEARER CHRONICLES
BOOK 3

DAN KENNER

AKEWNON BOOKS

First published by Akewnon Books 2022 *Copyright © 2022 by Dan Kenner*

All rights reserved. No part of this publication may be reproduced, stored or transmitted in any form or by any means, electronic, mechanical, photocopying, recording, scanning, or otherwise without written permission from the publisher. It is illegal to copy this book, post it to a website, or distribute it by any other means without permission.

This novel is entirely a work of fiction. The names, characters and incidents portrayed in it are the work of the author's imagination. Any resemblance to actual persons, living or dead, events or localities is entirely coincidental.

First edition

Editing by Jana @ The Writer's Assistant

❀ Created with Vellum

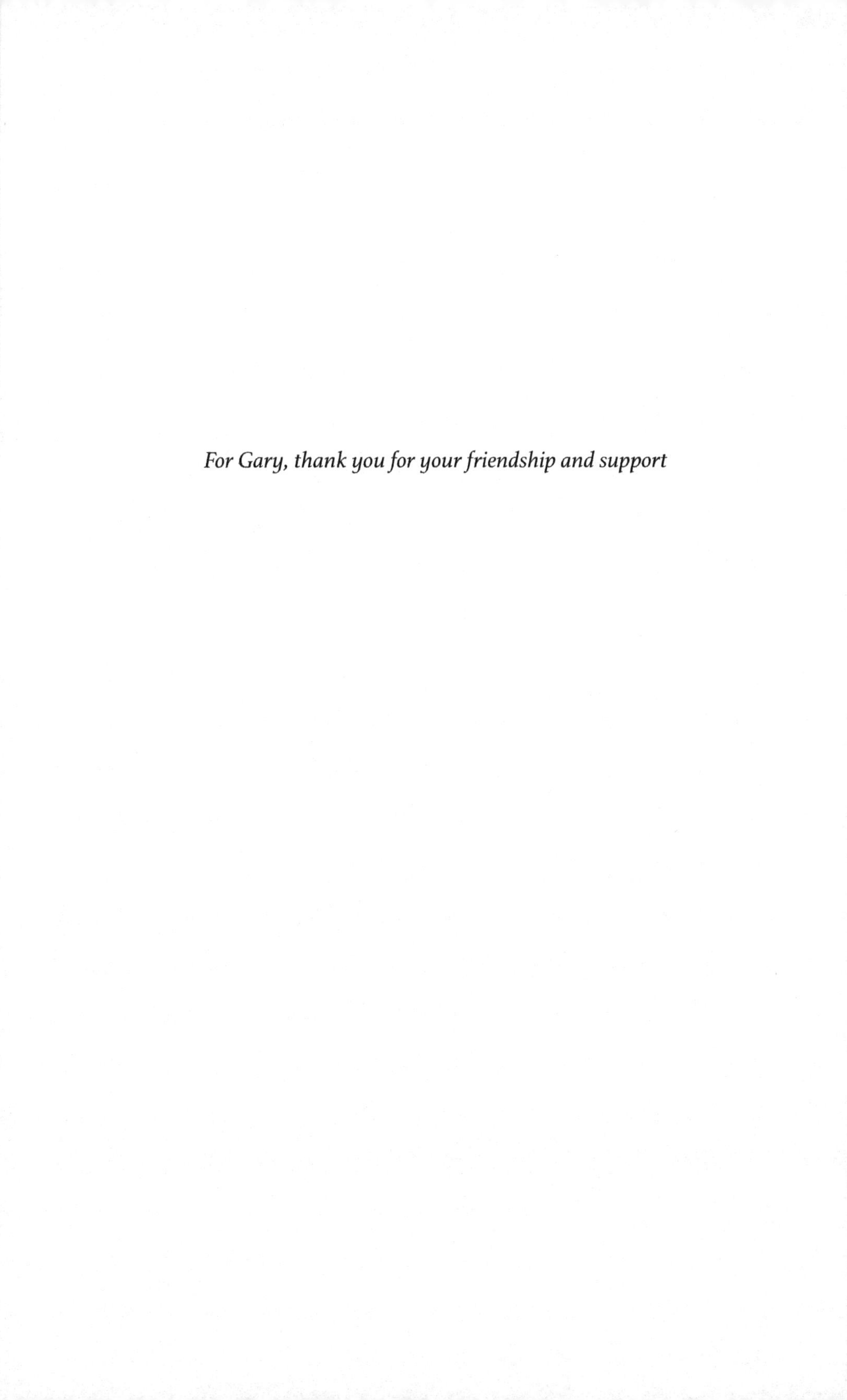

For Gary, thank you for your friendship and support

MAP OF LINDRAD

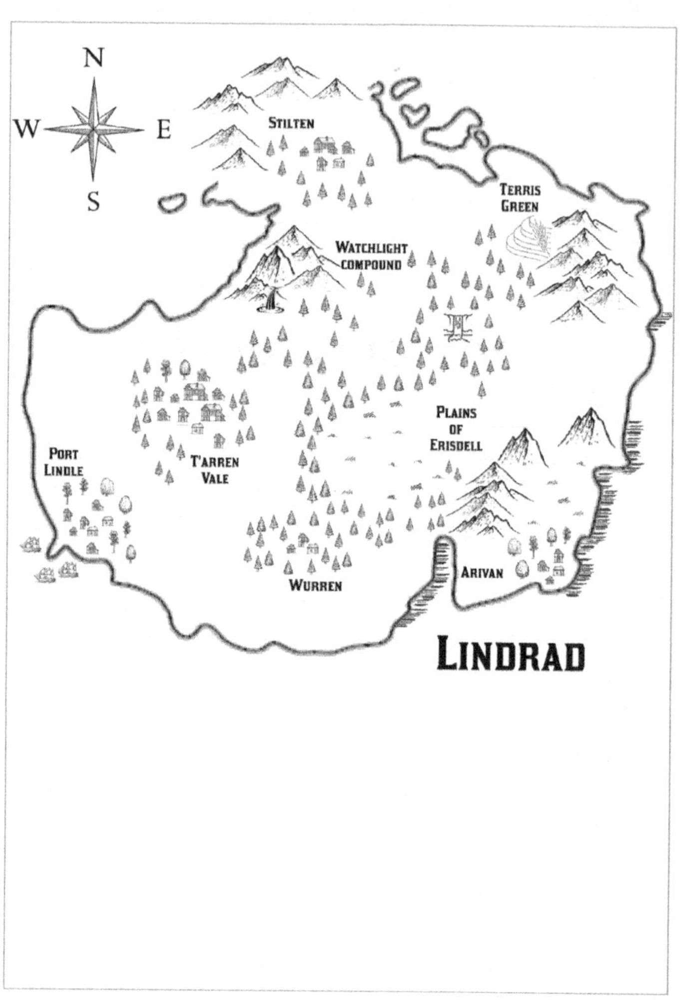
N
W
E
S
STILTEN
TERRIS
GREEN
WATCHLIGHT
COMPOUND
PLAINS
OF
ERISDELL
PORT
LINDLE
T'ARREN
VALE
WURREN
ARIVAN
LINDRAD

LIGHTBEARING SYMBOLIC SYSTEM

Shielder - Creates a dome-like barrier which is invunerable to most things. Protects from Seeing abilities.

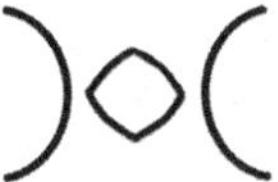

Mover - Move objects and people to and away from themselves using Light

Fixer - Mends or fixes any object or wound back to its perfect state

Destroyer - Breaks down or disintegrates objects or people using small orbs of Light or by touch

Seer - Sees future and past events by entering the vision realm or 'in-between'

Conjurer - Creates objects from Light that possess all the physical qualities of the true object

Lighter - Forms orbs to illuminate large areas and enhance the abilities of others

Voidbearer - One who is immune to effects of all Lightbearing classes

PROLOGUE

Dust continued to settle from the shattered ceiling above him. He tried to focus on what had just happened. Yet his mind still couldn't grasp anything besides the pain he felt throughout his entire body. As he tried to sit up, his chest throbbed and he couldn't breathe.

Fog it, how did she of all people become a Lightbearer? he thought.

Until now, Macks hadn't considered where his previous ward had gone. He'd heard rumblings of an assassin woman who caused trouble for some of their allies, but Luden hadn't ever mentioned who it was.

In truth, he hadn't cared.

Sure, he'd suspected it was Janis they spoke of, but he never expected to cross paths with her again. In fact, his Seeing had been handy in keeping it that way. Now, not only did she know he worked for Luden but she'd aligned herself with one of the groups in this ridiculous power war between Watchlight and Evenir.

Macks closed his eyes, trying once again to breathe deeply. This time, his lungs complied, though the thick dust in the air made him choke. He coughed, his throat rejecting the debris it brought in. Everything hurt, so he couldn't pinpoint exactly what was wrong with his body.

Opening his eyes once more, he looked up through the massive hole in the roof. He didn't know how long he'd been unconscious. An explosion sounded from somewhere outside, causing his body to tense. There were other sounds, men shouting, bowstrings swishing, and other signs of a fight. He also noticed how the sun still hadn't set. Macks knew then that he must have only been unconscious for a short time.

He clenched his teeth and focused on rising. Given that he'd already been able to roll over, albeit slowly, he hoped that he'd have enough in him to at least sit up.

He was disappointed in that assumption. His body didn't respond favorably.

I have to try something. Janis probably knows that I'm not dead. She'll be back for me, he thought, frustrated.

This made everything become more urgent. Instead of focusing on moving his whole body, he moved his right arm over himself, pleased that it didn't ache too badly. Whether it was because the heavy pain in the rest of him drowned out this pain or because his arm was unhurt, he didn't know. Still, he positioned the hand over his chest, trying to breathe gently. To his relief, he felt his chest, which was likely broken in a few places, suck in air.

His lungs filled with air and he couldn't help but sigh in relief, despite the pain. Macks still knew little of Lightbearing, but based on what he'd been able to learn, every Lightbearer had the potential to develop a second power. He'd been a Seer for years with only the minor appearance of other powers but recently learned that he now had the ability to Shield. His skills still hadn't advanced much, but they'd been enough to hide him from other Seers.

Flexing his abdominal muscles, he pulled himself upward, surprised that he could do so. His body still hurt in most places, but he was able to move with quick and painful jolts.

Another explosion cracked through the hole in the roof and Macks tensed, his eyes shifting up. He expected to see Janis there, or another Lightbearer, but the space was empty. His employer, Luden, had dragged him into this mess. If it weren't for the fool's blind rage, Macks would have been paid and far away from the whole conflict. That was how he worked, after all. Now he was beaten in the middle of Stilten, a place he'd avoided for so many years.

As the sounds of fighting continued, Macks worked on inspecting his other injuries. Though there were many, he didn't feel that any were fatal. He knew he'd have to be careful with that. Sometimes the most serious injuries were those hidden from plain sight. Once he had the major breaks and cuts accounted for, Macks stopped. His breathing still labored, he felt that he could drift off to sleep. Instead, he let the pain in the various parts of his body keep his mind aware.

Just as he got to his feet, a loud crack rang through the air. Macks jumped to the side of the room he'd been lying in, causing his injuries to twinge in pain. He sucked in a breath but didn't have time to recover before shouting from the road put him on alert once more.

I need to get out of here, he thought.

Peering upward, he noted that he couldn't make the leap back up to the roof. Not without his full strength. Instead, he searched the dim room. The only light filtering in came from the setting sun through the broken ceiling. Macks opted to use one of the other abilities he still knew little about. Holding out his hand, he summoned a small ball of red. Though minuscule, it pierced the darkness of the room with ease.

He'd fallen into a bedroom of sorts, though it was bare save for a bed and a set of drawers. He remembered Luden had strong-armed the owner of the bar below to let them enter. It wasn't uncommon for bars to have a set of rooms for guests to quarter. Macks was glad his fall hadn't been farther. Noticing a door for the first time, he angled toward it and slowly cracked it open. Just beyond, a short hallway ended at a set of stairs. He moved toward it, keeping his Light illuminated.

Inspecting the stairs, Macks paused. It appeared as if something heavy had dropped from above, shattering the steps in a direct line to the bottom of the spirals. Adrenaline coursed through his body and he shifted his eyes around, expecting to see an enemy somewhere.

For a moment, Macks thought to go back to the room to think, but the shouting outside intensified, and he feared what would happen if one of the groups decided to enter the building. They might not be searching for him, but if they found him, he didn't expect it would be good.

The moment I get somewhere quiet, I'll need to summon—him, Macks thought. For the past year, the anti-god had visited Macks. He shuddered, trying not to think or say his name out loud. It never felt right, but Macks didn't regret what he'd learned. Reaching down to his belt, he tried to grab the small book he used to say the right words.

He froze. Empty.

Resisting the urge to erupt in loud cursing, Macks shuffled back to the room, holding the Light aloft to search for the small book. The simple room bore no true hiding places where the small text could have fallen. His chest filled with dread. If it wasn't here, then it meant something worse.

Janis, he thought.

Part of him felt that her taking it from him was deserved, so to speak, for his betrayal. Did he deserve this though? That book had become his everything. It was how he could manipulate Luden; it was how he could tempt the anti-god into helping him. Ugglyn had mentioned that his limited power was waning, but Macks guessed it was just a lie. He believed he could get more from the being.

Macks shook his head and moved as quickly as he could back to the stairs. He gripped the wood railing and deliberately made his way down the spirals. Meanwhile, he noticed the sounds outside had become quieter. Where there were explosions and shouting before, now there was only distant yelling and clashing metal.

But something wasn't right.

Trying to move more quickly, he breathed through the pain and made it to the ground level. There he cautiously moved into the main bar. It was empty. Before, the bartender had been hiding with his crossbow. Macks was relieved that this obstacle wasn't a problem. He moved to the door, exiting onto the street, but froze.

A column of swirling clouds spun upward into the darkening sky. His eyes widened as he followed the trail with his gaze. It extended far enough that he couldn't see the end. Something ran through the air, an energy that made his hairs stand. He recognized the feeling. It was the same he would get every time he summoned Ugglyn. His body started quivering in fright and he felt locked in position.

No, no, it can't be. He was supposed to be sealed by Yrillnan. He can't be free,

Macks thought.

Until a year ago, Macks had no idea that his Awakening as a Lightbearer was part of something larger. The anti-god had explained it all to him. The being told him that Macks was the way out. It was then that he noticed his Light turning red. That part hadn't been explained to him, but Macks guessed it had something to do with Ugglyn's influence.

Macks knew something was wrong. He tried to step backward, to retreat somewhere until this passed, but part of him knew he couldn't get away. If Ugglyn was free, he would find him.

Cursing, Macks instinctively reached to where the book should be. He suspected the anti-god would be very displeased with his loss of the book. If Ugglyn knew Janis had taken it, Macks assumed the anger would be far more severe.

After a few moments, the smoke cleared, two forms appearing within the torrent.

Prost, the very man Macks had seen before Janis blasted him through the roof, stood rigidly in the road, a look of shock on his face. A pale corpse lay on the road before him. Macks realized it was the one who headed up the red-Light crew. Riln. Blood pooled outward from the body. It was obvious he was dead. Macks knew their names only from Luden's insistence that he learned of Watchlight and their leaders.

One thing he'd learned: these two men were the Yrillnan. At least, before his former ward had become involved. Macks stood there, unsure of what to do. Prost turned his direction, his eyes filled with silvery smoke.

Macks fell backward, hiding himself behind the wall beneath the window. Panting, he counted to twenty before peeking back over the sill. The larger man was gone, likely run away from the corpse of his master. A glint of something caught Macks's attention near the ground, and he squinted to see a dark pommel protruding from the man's neck. Even from here, the weapon was unmistakable.

Janis's favorite dagger. Though his gut wrenched at the thought of rushing into the open, commotion on the city wall suggested the retreating Lightbearers were distracting the city guard. Gritting his teeth, he slipped along the wall to the doorway, readying himself there. With a determined breath, Macks burst through the door, dashing across the now empty street to stand over the body. Grimacing at the mess there, he reached down and grabbed the handle, yanking it free. He winced at the sound it made as it was withdrawn.

"Hey! You there! Stop!" a voice rang out from the wall above.

Cursing, Macks dashed back to the entrance to the bar, pushing through the doors and diving behind the sill. He could hear other guards shouting about what they'd seen. Some had been ordered to come fetch him.

Muttering various curses, he crawled away from the window to the rear of the bar. He'd been to bars like this before, and if he was right, then there should be a way out the back.

There.

Macks saw through the portal to the stairs that another door led somewhere else. Based on what he'd remembered, that should lead to a stable. That meant horses he could take. Wiping Janis's weapon on the leg of his pants, he slipped the dagger into his belt to keep it out of the way.

When he reached a safe distance from the window, he got up and shuffled quickly to the door. He breathed out a sigh of relief when he saw three horses tied there. The animals were agitated, so he moved slowly toward the beasts. Knowing his time was short, he sized up the horses and selected the mid-sized one. He may have gone for the larger, expecting it to run faster, but there was a nervous energy from the creature. Macks guessed he'd have a rough time taming the beast.

Despite the lack of saddle, Macks hefted himself onto the animal and used its mane to direct it toward the stall door.

With a kick to the side, he urged the horse out into the back alley.

Macks didn't know where he was supposed to go or what he should do. He'd never received his last payment from Luden. A loss for sure, but he'd just seen his former employer skewered on a sword. His only choice was to collect what he could and get as far from Stilten as possible.

Part of him knew he needed to get away. If Ugglyn truly was free, Macks needed to leave. He hadn't ventured out of Lindrad yet, but now was looking like a good time to try.

Then again, if Ugglyn was free, he doubted he could escape, and without the book—Macks knew his death was imminent.

1

Stepping into Wurren was nothing like Marric would have expected. When he'd last been here, three men had been searching for him. He remembered how terrified he'd been, waiting for the men to find out who he was and do something terrible. All because Jord had been kidnapped years before, never to be seen again.

Except he had seen him, standing with Watchlight, his hands bearing the destructive red Light that could deteriorate anything, living or not.

Marric's mind spiraled through all the things that had happened since he'd last left his little town. He might have expected the memories to flow in some semblance of order, but they came in waves with no organization at all.

He recalled seeing himself kneel on the ground next to Arrant Falls, pain exploding from inside as he awakened into a Lightbearer. Then he was in his home in Wurren, watching as Janis's dagger slammed into Tins's gut. He recalled the blood on the floor making him ill.

Seeing blood didn't affect him anymore.

A flashback brought him to Terris Green, where Janis blew up her quarters, demolishing a stone wall and almost killing herself.

I wonder how they are doing with their journey, Marric thought.

"'Ey, Mar, ya all right there? Ye've been Seeing a bunch fer the last bit," Shrell said next to him.

Marric jumped at the voice and let himself fall back into reality. They'd only spotted the distant borders of Wurren moments ago, and he'd already slipped back into reliving the past few months through his Seer visions.

"Yeah, sorry, I don't mean to be rude. Seeing my old town again distracted me," Marric replied.

Shrell cocked his head, though his face held a smile. His wavy hair now hung down to his shoulders. Apparently, he wasn't in any hurry to cut it.

"No worries, I can' imagine 'avin all tha' 'appen in a short bit o' time." Shrell glanced behind him, sizing up the group that had come with them. "Best keep them eyes dim, though, once we get into town. We don' wanna bring too much attention to us."

Marric nodded, but his thoughts once again drifted to Janis and the others. He couldn't help but wonder how their journeys were going. He knew they had further to go to get to his town, but he knew they hadn't missed the Awakening. The first day or two they'd had to push their horses to the maximum to have the chance of making it.

Just to be sure, Marric eyed his companion apologetically, then allowed his mind to slip into a vision. He opened up his mind's eye and felt his physical eyes stretch open, the blue Light likely filling them.

Shrell sighed next to him.

"An' 'ere 'e goes again. No worries, I like talkin' to myself," Shrell commented.

Marric chuckled and he would have rolled his eyes if he weren't preoccupied.

"I'm just checking up on Janis. Give me a moment."

He turned off his hearing for a moment and allowed his consciousness to materialize next to Janis. She sat atop a horse, looking displeased. All around her were men and women dressed in Evenir clothing. Magness sat regally atop her own horse in front.

"Speak of Ugglyn himself, there they are," Magness said. Her jaw hardened.

Marric shifted his vision gaze forward, following the direction the Evenir leaders looked. There, a few dozen black-clad people stood down the street. He didn't recognize the place but could only assume it was Stilten, knowing that was where they were headed for their Awakening.

Watchlight is already there? Marric thought.

He did a quick internal check to verify that what he was Seeing was the present.

It was.

A flash of blue to his left startled him. He could feel his physical body far away flinching in surprise.

He watched as a spear of blue Light flew toward Prost, skewering the horse he was riding. The creature crumpled to the ground, its rider almost getting caught beneath it.

"By Lanser's name, Janis! Did you have to just go at it?!" Magness said, clearly as shocked as he was.

Janis didn't answer. Marric's vision eyes trained on her face and all he could see was determination. She dismounted and barreled toward the group of Watchlight men and women.

Magness ordered a Shield raised, and the blue wall sprung up just behind Janis. A red one covered Watchlight at the same moment.

The world spun again, leaving Marric reeling. He didn't want to pull away, but a thought jolted him back to reality.

"Watchlight is there already," he said with no context.

"*Wha*'?!" Shrell's head spun right and left as he scanned the town border just ahead.

Nostalgia for the street entrance pushed its way into Marric's chest and he sucked in a breath.

He realized he was trying to cope with coming back to this place by losing himself in visions.

Shaking his head, Marric turned toward Shrell.

"No, Watchlight is already in Stilten. Janis just rushed their group as if it was nothing," he explained.

Shrell relaxed a little, then nodded.

"Let's 'ope they can deal wif 'em right quickly, then. Fer now, we better be ready fer anythin'," Shrell said, narrowing his eyes forward.

Just then, they entered the town border, wooden houses and shops on both sides. After Seeing what he just had, Marric expected black-dressed men and women to appear around them. His memory flashed again to when they'd been trying to leave Wurren months ago and were ambushed by others then. Movement to his right made him jump. He breathed out when he realized it was just a boy running down the street.

Marric scanned the surrounding area, two-story wood buildings on either side. The street wasn't overly populated, given that it wasn't a market day, but there were people about. Despite the impending sunset, Isllan was still far away, so there would be citizens on the streets for longer. The hooves of their horses clacked noisily on the road, the sound echoing off of the close buildings on either side. As they approached, people stared in awe at them and backed away. These people were likely astounded by the horses and the size of the group.

Was that truly so long ago? Marric thought.

Now he was with the men he formerly feared, going to retrieve his friend Crents.

"So 'ow close are yeh to this fellow? Right lucky tha' yeh get to see 'is Awakening 'f 'yeh ask me," Shrell commented.

Marric smiled, thinking about seeing Crents again.

"Crents is like a brother to me. We worked together for so long, and I was stealing money for—" Marric stopped, gritting his teeth.

Shrell perked up at the words.

"Wait, did yeh just say tha'—" Shrell cut off when they heard a scream down the street.

Marric might have blushed at his admission of stealing for Crents and his family, but the high-pitched sound set everyone in motion.

"This way!" Marric shouted, pushing his horse forward toward Crents's home. Normally, Crents would be working at this time, but with Narim gone and the shop burned, Marric wasn't sure the boy had work to be done.

Marric shook his head, not wanting to remember the loss of his home.

Dust sprang up everywhere as the pack of Evenir people pushed their horses forward. More shouts came from the locals as they dove out of the way, Shrell yelling at them to move.

Marric's heart raced, the energy clearing his mind. He didn't remember when he'd gained the ability to focus more in stressful situations, but he was grateful. As the corner approached, Marric yanked on the reins of his horse, causing it to neigh restlessly. The animal reacted and turned sharply to the right.

There, ahead, he saw Crents's home, and a handful of black-cloaked people facing them.

Marric didn't think; instead, he rushed his horse forward and threw his hands outward, scattering the men and women, their bodies glowing blue from his Lightbearing.

"Shrell! Check above!" Marric yelled, pulling his horse to a stop and Conjuring a bow, an arrow already nocked.

"Shield! Watch th' roofs!" Shrell commanded.

A blue translucent Shield appeared above them just as arrows descended from the rooftops, each clattered harmlessly against the surface. Marric could hear shouting from above as they realized they couldn't get their arrows through the Shield.

"This can' be Watchligh', I don' see any red Light. Mus' be th' others, then," Shrell said, pulling his horse up to Marric.

Dread set into Marric's chest at the words.

If they aren't Riln's people, then— Marric thought.

An image of Turrin writhing in pain, dark veins full of poison, forced its way into his mind. Just before he could shout out a warning, more arrows rained from above. Instead of clattering on the Shield, they pierced through, the tips glowing with a silver hue.

Men and women cursed as the arrows struck half a dozen down, the arrows taking them off their horses.

"Take cover! Stay close t' the 'ouses!" Shrell yelled.

The Shield repaired itself, but the Evenir men and women pushed up against the buildings to either side. Without line of sight, the archers couldn't hit them. Still, they tried, the silver-tipped arrows bouncing off the road.

"I need to get in there," Marric said through gritted teeth.

"Mar, yeh can' jus'—"

Before Shrell could continue, Marric jumped from his horse and ran full force at the door to Crents's home. Shrell cursed. Marric hoped his mad rush took their enemy by surprise, keeping his head down as he sprinted.

Many still recovered from his Lightbearing shove moments ago, but a few were up, their eyes trained on him.

To his left, he could see two figures intending to cut off his entry to the house. One of his Light arrows pierced one woman in the chest. Her falling body tripped her companion, whose shout cut short as his face slammed into the ground. Three others approached from the right, but Marric threw his hand out, Moving them into the building behind.

Air whisked past his ear as an arrow almost found its way into his head. Marric gritted his teeth, determined to make it. Without hesitation, he threw his body weight into the door, the wood shattering. Pain erupted in his shoulder from the contact, but he ignored it.

Gasping from exertion, Marric thanked Lanser that the door gave as easily as he'd thought it would.

Shrell and a couple other Lightbearers flew through the opening after him.

"Mar! Yeh can' jus' run off like tha'! If I don' get yeh back to Terris Green safely, Avryn'll kill me right good," Shrell complained. "Not to mention Janis."

Shrell shivered then.

Though he heard the words, Marric ignored them. Adrenaline still coursed through him. The urgency of knowing they hadn't found Crents before the others kept him going.

The front hallway into the home was narrow and long. Wood slats decayed on either side, the structure not well-kept. Sounds of fighting and flashes of blue Light carried on in the street behind them. Marric cautiously walked forward, seeing an empty armchair by the hearth. The red upholstery was torn in numerous places, and it held stains everywhere.

Marric knew this was where Crents's father normally sat. Stuck in his alcoholism, there wasn't a time he remembered Crents's father not sitting there.

Voices further in the home prompted Marric to hurry in that direction. As he rounded the corner, he gasped as he tripped on something heavy on the ground. Tumbling forward, Marric saw the ground rush up to his face, then pain lanced up his wrist.

"Fog it, what the—" Marric said, rolling over to see what he'd tripped on.

His stomach turned.

It was a body. The body of Crents's father.

"Mar, yeh all right?" Shrell whispered, eyeing the corpse.

Marric nodded, then rose quickly. He could still hear the voices in the next room. It sounded like two men were arguing. Then a younger voice pleaded.

That's him, Marric thought.

As they moved closer, Marric could make out the words.

"Just kill him and get out of here! Why are you—"

Crashing from behind made Marric spin. Two figures ran at them, shouting in anger. One of the Evenir companions threw up a Shield, the enemy skittering to a stop just before the barrier.

Shrell cursed at the noise, knowing that they'd be discovered. The door they'd just been about to enter casually opened, the hinges creaking.

"Well, well, here they are now," an evil-looking man said. "Told you they would get here soon."

The man's black hood was back, showing strawberry-blond hair cropped close to his head. His wicked grin sat below a sharp nose and wide eyes.

"Luden did say to take as many of you as we could, so let's get started," he said, holding up his sword.

The hair rose on Marric's neck as he saw the blade laced with the mercuric poison that had almost killed Turrin.

"Shrell, that's what they got Turrin with. The Shield won't work—"

Before he could continue, the two men behind them slashed with their swords, the blades cutting through the blue Shield easily. The Shielder gasped in shock as he was cut down with the sword. Shrell was there at once, slashing swiftly as he killed one of the men. The other engaged him in battle. The woman who had accompanied Marric came and stood next to him, her back straight, a short sword stretched outward.

Marric glanced at her, realizing it was Narinda, one of the Lighters who kept Terris Green lit. Even with her large spectacles and the memory of her poring over a large book, she looked far more imposing than she had the first time Marric met her.

"Give us the boy," she said, her voice firm.

The man chuckled, holding his sword up higher.

"You think we'll just listen to you? No, I think we'll just kill the lot of you," he said.

"Have it your way," Narinda said. She flipped her sword forward, her blade clanging into his. He cursed, not prepared for her speed.

Narinda pushed into the sword, knocking the man off balance. He apparently expected this, as he leaned into it, crouched down, and spun around to face them again.

"A wench with parlor tricks. Lucky me," he said.

Narinda scoffed, then spoke to Marric.

"Get the boy," she said, still looking at the man in front of her.

Marric heard Crents's whimper again in the other room, but he didn't move immediately.

"*Go*," Narinda said, more forcefully.

Marric jumped into motion, pressing himself against the wall, away from the man.

"You won't get him!" the man said, jumping toward Marric. Narinda slid between them and held up her hand. A flash of Light made the man scream in confusion. He backed up against the wall, his hand covering his eyes. The other hand flipped his sword back and forth in a frenzy, causing Marric and Narinda to jump backward.

Instinctively, Marric pushed his hand outward, Moving the man's sword until it smashed into the wall, where it wedged itself. Their assailant cursed, yanking as hard as he could on the sword, to no avail.

A curse from Shrell behind made Marric tense. He pushed both hands out this time, and the man in front of him glowed blue before being slammed into the wall. He fell forward and lay still.

"Help Shrell!" Marric yelled to Narinda, who turned and engaged the black-clad figures there. By now, a few more had shown up. Seeing her short sword parry a few blows from the pursuers, Marric Conjured his bow, aiming the Light-created arrow at one of the figures. His arm held taut, he tried to aim around Narinda and the others' moving forms, but he didn't trust himself to not hit his ally.

For a moment, he stood in awe, watching as the woman who he'd thought was a harmless Lighter fly through the enemies like a storm. Movement to her left made Marric shift his gaze there, where Shrell nursed his arm. Blood trickled from a wound under his sleeve. One of the black-clad figures had slipped past Narinda and was about to drop his sword over Shrell's neck. Before he could, Marric let his arrow fly, the tip piercing through their stomach.

A woman's voice cursed before Shrell thrust his sword upward, finishing her off.

"Go! I can Fix him in a moment," Narinda yelled, her voice masked slightly by the clanging of the swords and the grunting of the fighters.

Nodding resolutely, Marric spun around and pushed through the decaying door. Dark lines ran from the top to the bottom, showing where a leak in the roof must have allowed rainwater to drip.

Marric froze as his eyes adjusted. The Light from his bow illuminated the surrounding area, but it was dark in the room. A slight sound from his right made him tense before his reflexes pushed him to the left. Air whooshed past his ear, followed closely by the thunking of a blade in the door behind him.

Rolling onto his knees, Marric let an arrow fly back to where he came from. It thudded into the wall.

"Blast yeh foggin' Lightbearers. We'll kill the lot of yeh!"

The voice was husky and came from the dark of the room to his left. Squinting his eyes, Marric could barely make out a form in the dim Light from his bow.

"'Elp! Summon 'elp! They'll kill me—" Crents's voice was muffled by something being shoved over his mouth.

Marric heard heavy breathing to his front right, but Crents's voice had come from the left. That meant—

Stinging pain erupted in Marric's side as a knife sliced through his tunic and cut open his flesh.

Cursing, he shot another arrow right at the first person who attacked him, causing the man to yell and duck out of the way.

"Git 'im, yeh idiot! The poison will kill 'em all!"

The poison— Marric's stomach rolled, images of the thick veins on Turrin's legs forcing into his mind once more.

"'E's a crafty git! I'm tryin'!"

Marric launched a few arrows toward the right again. A squelching sound was followed by a howl of pain. His body was sweating profusely, and the musty smell of the room overwhelmed him. Another knife flew from the darkness, this one just between his legs. Gasping, Marric dropped his bow, plunging the room into darkness once more.

"Think yeh can hide, huh?" the voice from the left growled.

The sounds of the man he struck with his knife disappeared as the man died. Marric stood there, afraid to move for fear they would hear him. Crents screamed, his voice muffled by what sounded like cloth over his mouth.

Reaching right, Marric imagined the hilt of the short sword he'd tried to fight with at Terris Green. He knew his skill wasn't great, but he also knew he couldn't use his Conjured bow. He could guess the size of the room only by how far away Crents's crying was. The whimpering came from the floor, perhaps ten paces in front of him. Marric couldn't tell if the man was still there, but he knew he had to act fast.

Knowing the man's eyes would adjust soon, Marric sucked in a deep breath and jumped forward. Just before he got to where Crents was, he summoned a ball of Light, putting everything he could into it to make it bright.

The ball itself was small, only the size of his thumbnail, but in the dimness of the room, it made him squint. A man shouted from his right, and Marric tossed the Light that way. He swung his arm, Conjuring a short sword while he moved. The blade whisked in the air, but the man was too far away.

Turning his body, Marric dropped his sword and Conjured his bow, an arrow already nocked. Just as he let his arrow fly, he felt a sharp pain in his upper leg as a knife slid inward.

His arrow flew true, however, piercing the man's chest. He fell to the ground, lifeless.

Gasping in pain, Marric reached down and looked at the knife sticking from his leg. His stomach turned as the red blood bubbled from the wound. Gritting his teeth, he yanked it out. The pain made his vision blur and his Conjured weapons had snuffed out, but his Light ball remained, giving him just enough visibility to work. Placing his hand over his leg, he focused, trying not to pass out.

A slight blue glow pulsed under his palm. Though the pain didn't subside, the bleeding did. Marric moved his hand to inspect the wound, fearing the worst. He sighed in relief when he saw no signs of poison.

Fighting continued out in the hallway, blue Light flashing here and there. Marric could hear Narinda and Shrell shouting to each other between the flashes.

Marric thought for a moment to go out and help them, but Crents's muffled scream reminded him of their goal. He crawled over to where he could see his friend cowering on the ground. Adrenaline still coursed through his veins, and he breathed hard, trying to ward off the pain of the internal bleeding that remained.

"Crents, are you ok?" Marric said through his haggard breaths.

His friend stared at him, confused.

Crents said something that sounded like his name, but Marric couldn't be sure. He reached for his sword and realized he, like other Conjurers, didn't carry a steel sword.

"Foggin' Light, can you just come over here?" Marric said, mostly to himself.

When the Light ball didn't move, Marric just let it snuff into nothing, awarding him with another small squeal from his friend. He held up his hand again, another ball forming there.

Marric's body was getting cold, but he didn't know if it was from the blood loss or from coming off the intense fight. It felt strange, considering that the air was still and stuffy, the heat from the day caught inside. He gritted his teeth, wondering why this room didn't have a window.

"Don't panic. It's me, Marric. I'm going to do something that might seem scary, but I won't hurt you," he said.

Crents nodded, though Marric knew his words were ironic considering what his friend must be thinking about what he'd just seen.

Marric focused again and Conjured a dagger. As he moved it closer to his friend, Crents flinched.

"I won't hurt you, just—" Marric slipped the dagger along the cloth covering Crents's mouth and pushed upward. As the cloth fell away, Crents started speaking.

"They jus' came in 'ere an' grabbed me. My da', is 'e aight? Wha' is 'appenin'?"

Just before Marric could answer, the door behind them slammed open, someone breathing hard.

"Watchligh' is 'ere! We need t'get outta 'ere *now*," Shrell said.

Marric was relieved to see his friend standing there. His arm didn't look injured at all. As if to confirm his words, flashes of red Light illuminated Shrell's form.

"Ah, Mar, yeh're all hurt. Narinda will 'ave to fix yeh up, come on!"

Shrell gestured to the two boys. Crents looked back and forth between Marric and Shrell, fear clear on his face.

"We can trust him, we just need to get out of here before we're caught. I'll have to explain later, but you—" Marric was saying when Crents fell to the ground.

Oh no, Marric thought.

Shrell's eyes widened, and he shouted for Marric to back away. Everything slowed down then. Even though he knew what was happening, his stomach clenched in terror. Turning sharply, Marric tried to run through the door. Shrell held out his hand, trying to reach him. Before he could grab the hand, a force of blue Light slammed into his back.

Marric smashed into Shrell, who also was thrown backward. The two hit the wall outside of the room and crumpled to the ground. Pain erupted in Marric's head and on his right shoulder. Shrell groaned on the ground next to him.

Knowing it was coming again, Marric Moved the door, which had been blown off the hinges, and positioned it in front of them. Another blast of force hit the object, and it flew toward them. Marric pushed outward to keep it from connecting.

A third blast of the power rocked the walls of the house, one of the inner walls breaking outward, the wood splintering.

Dust thickened the surrounding air. Splintered wood covered both Marric and Shrell everywhere.

It took each of them a few moments to get their bearings. There wasn't anyone else in the room, except for the bodies of the men they'd fought just before. Marric could hear Narinda shouting from down the hall, where she must have retreated when Crents Awakened.

"Mar, yeh all right?" Shrell asked before trying to stand. He groaned in pain.

"I'm fine, but Crents—" Marric couldn't see or hear his friend. He stood, pain lancing down his arm. He felt his shoulder and realized it had been dislocated in the blow.

Marric pushed back into the room and found Crents unconscious on the floor. Kneeling by the boy, Marric summoned his ball of light once more. He sighed in relief when he could see the boy's chest rising and falling.

"Oh, fog it," Shrell cried out behind him. Marric turned to see a sword through Shrell's chest, the metal of the blade writhing with a mercuric liquid.

Marric heard himself scream, the sound inhuman and full of grief. Shrell fell to his knees, the blade sliding out of him. Behind him stood the man Marric had Moved into the wall.

Rage filled him, and Marric pushed outward with all his might. The man's eyes widened as he was thrown backward, crashing into the wall. Without hesitation, Marric Conjured his bow and shot an arrow into the fallen man's back.

He lay still.

Marric fell to his knees, tears streaming. He could hear himself yelling for help, but he sounded muffled, even to himself. Narinda appeared, worry in her eyes. She looked rough, having been engaged in battle herself.

They both watched, hopeless, as Shrell stopped moving.

2

Wind rustled the trees of the forest as the group of horses barreled down the dirt pathway away from Stilten. Men shouted from the tops of the walls, calling orders to their fellow guards or to townspeople to take cover. An arrow slammed into the ground to the side of Janis's horse as they sped away.

"Blasted guards! If they knew who we were, they might not be so apt to kill us!" Avryn shouted next to her over the clapping of the horses' hooves.

Janis scoffed at his words, though she was sure he wouldn't hear.

"I don't think anyone could see the damage we caused and think we were people they should trust," Janis shouted.

Avryn's face fell into something like consternation. She didn't mean to be a downer in the already stressful situation, but his comment wasn't well founded considering their position.

She had to give him credit, however, because their leader, Magness, had been killed. The sun was almost down over the horizon. The surrounding trees plunged them into a deeper darkness. Squinting, Janis allowed her eyes to adjust as quickly as they could so she wouldn't lead her mount into a tree or boulder. The dirt road still glowed slightly in the waning sunlight, the dirt just brighter than the surrounding brush and trees.

Right as her eyes were adjusting to the darkness, a flash of brilliant blue appeared from above. Janis flinched from the brightness and looked over at Avryn. The man turned back and nodded gratefully to another Evenir operative behind. Janis assumed Avryn had given the order for a Lighter to create orbs for them, though she'd been too distracted to hear any verbal command. The single orb which hovered above their large entourage split into half a dozen and spread in a tight circle around their group. The new Light source cast odd shadows from the trunks of the trees surrounding them on each side. As such, Janis had to adjust her mind's ability to track all movement, now that most of the movement they would detect were just shadows.

"I think we can slow our pace!" Avryn said to Janis, who studied him.

He continued to stare as they led the pack of Evenir men and women down the road. When Janis didn't do anything, Avryn held up his hand and shouted for them to slow.

She pulled on the reins of her horse until it was a quick trot. Avryn did the same, causing the rest of the horses behind them to reduce their speed. When they'd left Stilten, Janis hadn't expected to be one of those at the head of the group, but Avryn insisted she stay forward with him. Looking sideways, Janis noted that Avryn stared at her.

"What?" she asked in an annoyed tone.

He furrowed his brows.

"What happened back there? What happened to Magness? What happened to you?" Avryn asked, his mouth open after his last question. He seemed to want to ask more but he stopped there.

Janis stared back for a moment before facing forward.

"I made a mistake, and it cost Magness her life," Janis admitted. Under normal circumstances, her assassin self wouldn't feel so guilty saying those words, but after tonight, things had changed.

I don't know if I can handle guilt. I was living happily without it for so many years, Janis thought.

Avryn grimaced at her words.

"Janis, that makes no sense. Magness was a skilled fighter. She couldn't have gone down." Avryn was more assertive this time.

Ever since she'd met Avryn, she'd never heard him speak this way. In some ways, it was encouraging, proving that the "soft" man she'd seen all this time could be hardened after all. Watching his skill with sword and Lightbearing felt out of place with his upbeat personality.

Janis sighed, steeling herself for the conversation. She lamented internally that she had to speak about it.

"The new Lightbearer was in the middle of our group when she began Awakening. I remembered only just before that she was a Destroyer. In my haste, I covered the girl with a Shield, something to hopefully keep the power contained. It worked—just not well enough." Janis looked forward and focused on the tree line to their left. "Magness was right next to her when the girl exploded."

Avryn's eyes carried something more than just shock. There was more going through his mind, and it was obvious by the way he stared at her.

"I see," he said, continuing to stare. "I assume that's why the new Lightbearer isn't with you as well."

Janis nodded, hoping it would be enough for him.

It was.

They fell silent, the only sounds around them the rustling of nature in the wind and the horses. Her heart still pounded from the fight they'd just left, but there was more. Janis's mind reeled at what she'd seen. Magness's death had unfortunately affected her more than she was willing to admit, but there were also more losses she was trying to process. Janis had gone back for her prized dagger, the one she'd had all these years, but her instinct told her to run and leave it. Prost had driven it into the neck of Evenir's former enemy, Riln.

As far as losing a prized weapon goes, there were worse ways to lose them, but Janis still regretted not being able to retrieve it. Yet it wasn't destroyed, so there was a possibility she'd see her old weapon again.

Then there was Macks. She'd left him broken and bleeding on the top floor of the bar. Janis didn't know what she'd intended to do with him when she'd planned to go back for him, but she assumed he wasn't dead. The man had a way of living through the worst. Janis feared not knowing what the man planned to do now. Macks had paired up with Luden, aiding the man in killing Lightbearers. Who knew what other schemes he had up his sleeve?

"You never answered my question," Avryn said in a hard tone.

She looked up at him.

"You asked about Magness, and I answered. What more do you want?" Janis replied. Avryn narrowed his eyes at her response. She realized she had been harsher in her response than she intended, but she didn't correct herself.

"The other question," Avryn gritted his teeth as he spoke.

Janis focused forward again, annoyed that her former response hadn't made him forget what he'd asked before. When she said nothing, Avryn spoke again, though in quieter tones this time.

"Janis, what happened to *you*?" he whispered. "Something's changed, I know it. What happened back there with Watchlight?"

She continued to lead her horse forward, not wanting to delve into the complexity of the last few hours. She hadn't even had a moment to think on everything that had occurred. Janis wasn't sure she had a proper response.

The air filled with tension, and Janis turned to see it came from Avryn, whose eyes bore into her soul. It was at that moment that she was glad Avryn wasn't a Seer.

"I don't know how else to say it, so I'll just be frank. My Lightbearing came out with a passion. My powers are no longer half-formed. I'm a full-fledged Lightbearer, just like you." She gripped her reins and looked away from him.

Avryn's mouth fell open, then he too turned forward.

"I suppose it's time for you to take your place as the leader of Evenir," he replied.

Janis's chest ached at the words.

"You can't be serious," she said. "What makes you think that I—"

Before she could continue, Avryn put his finger to his mouth and hushed her. Anger flared up in her chest, but she stifled it as quickly as she could. She observed Avryn, his long light-brown hair blowing around his face in the wind. He raised his eyebrows and pointed his thumb behind him, then shook his head. Though he'd said nothing, she understood his message.

Here wasn't the place to talk about leadership rights. Any indication of wavering or confusion with leadership could cause chaos among the men and women whom they led. Janis had infiltrated enough groups in her time as an assassin that she knew taking out a leader of a group could bring the organization to its knees.

"Men, Janis and I will scout ahead. Continue the course along this road for another few hours, then set for camp. There aren't any signs of pursuit from Stilten, so we should be safe."

The few people behind them nodded in approval, then continued leading their horses at the same pace.

"'Ey!" a voice came from behind.

Janis winced at the sound. Even before the man moved closer she recognized who it was.

"Yeh ain' gonna leave me outta this, are yeh? Oi fink oi 'ave as much a say in wha' 'appens as this lady 'ere," Harmel said, beaming at her.

Janis rolled her eyes.

Harmel's ability to bother her in the most tense of moments was unlike anything she'd experienced before. He knew that putting her on a pedestal drove her mad, yet he did it. Janis knew he was fond of her, but her own feelings for him were—too complicated.

Avryn smiled at their new companion, but there was no mirth. It was merely a reaction to a familiar friend. Assuming that Avryn thought to put the man off as well, Janis eyed Harmel with a critical eye. Yet neither Janis nor Avryn felt they had good reason to turn their friend away.

Clicking at his horse, Avryn sped up to pull a few hundred paces ahead of the rest of the group. Janis and Harmel followed until they caught up with him.

The moment they arrived, Avryn spoke.

"Janis, you can't appear so insecure in front of the people you lead. It won't bode well for you *or* them," Avryn said.

Janis stared blankly at him.

"What are you talking about? I don't *lead* anyone. I'm an assassin. I work alone. You know that," she said, narrowing her eyes at him.

Avryn pressed his lips together.

"You really believe that? After all that's happened? I knew the moment you and Livella spoke of your—status that you were the rightful leader of Evenir. Fog, Magness knew, but Evenir needed to be told of the reasons before anything changed—"

Janis held out her hand, trying hard not to shout. She noticed his pause before using the word "status" but chose not to dwell on it further.

"Stop. Now."

Avryn obeyed, which made her feel both grateful and uneasy. Whenever she'd interrupted him before, he normally hadn't listened right away. That he listened now drove deeper the evidence that he thought her higher than him.

"I'm not replacing Magness. *You* are. I can't lead these people. I'm not cut out for a job like that."

Janis's mind shifted to the column of swirling silvery-black smoke she saw just before they'd fled Stilten.

"Just because Lanser gave me some parlor tricks doesn't make me fit to lead anyone. *You* are fit to lead. You are Magness's second, so that means it's you," Janis said.

Narrowing his eyes, Avryn took a moment to consider his response. Before he could, however, Harmel spoke.

"Ah lass, yeh know tha' ain' it at all. 'Course S'ren is roit fit to lead, but it's yous tha' we need. Ugglyn's tail—" Harmel paused after saying that. "Lanser, forgive me. Ye've got t'see tha' yous are the one to lead."

Avryn smiled, this time with more happiness at his friend's support.

Janis stared at Harmel flatly.

"When did you become the expert in leadership? Even *you* could lead Evenir better than I can." Janis shook her head.

A strong gust of wind rustled the trees and caused the three of them to turn away from the flow of the air. The loudness of the rustling foliage irked Janis to no end. It impeded her sense of hearing.

Avryn stared at her for a moment longer before shaking his head.

"This war has become so much more complex than I could have imagined. Little did I know when I met you in Wurren months ago that you would be put in this position. While I can't make you accept anything, know that the people of Evenir would accept you. It would take some time, yes, but they would."

At that, Avryn pulled the reins of his horse and turned back to the rest of the entourage. Harmel smiled at her, his usual cheeriness giving her no other sign of what he was truly thinking.

"Don't look so pleased with yourself," she told him.

Harmel, apparently amused with the comment, grinned before shrugging.

"Yeh'll see, lass. Yeh're a better person than yeh think."

Janis doubted that. Still, the conversation lapsed and the rest of the group soon caught up to her. She couldn't help but wonder why she had been brought into all of this. Tryvv had told her she had changed, and Janis could see it. She could *feel* it. As much as she wanted to deny it, she cared more for these people than before. She had, after all, defended them against the tyrant Riln earlier that evening, which went against all she was used to. Under normal circumstances, she'd have just run away, escaped and hid herself.

An image of Marric slipped into her mind and she pressed her lips together. He reminded her of her brother, the one she'd lost years ago. As regret crept into her chest, she pushed it out.

No emotions today. There's been too much going on, Janis thought.

Their group continued on the pathway until Avryn called for a rest. Janis wished to keep moving, pushing until just before the fog rolled in, but she deferred to Avryn, fearing that by saying anything she might draw others to consider her as having any authority. With Avryn's assessment that they weren't being followed, he thought the rest necessary. Avryn led the group off the pathway and into the trees, where a few fires were lit, people grouping around each of them. Around their own fire sat Avryn, Harmel, Alsry, Livella, and a couple others Janis didn't know well.

The spindly Livella sat far closer to Janis than she would normally have allowed. Given what had just happened with Riln and Prost in Stilten, the woman made Janis even more uncomfortable than she had before. Janis recounted seeing Prost plunge that dagger—*her* dagger, of all things—into the other Prime Lightbearer. The fact that Riln was dead didn't bother her too much. She suspected he'd had it coming for a long time. What irked her was how easily he'd been killed by the one person who was immune to his powers.

Livella was still immune to hers as well.

The smaller woman turned to look at Janis, her timing eerie considering how Janis's thoughts were on her at the moment. Rather than look away, Janis held her gaze and gave a strained smile. Livella didn't appear to sense anything off and just smiled back, her own look more genuine than Janis's felt.

They stared for a moment, an awkward air between them, before Janis thought to talk to her.

"Are you okay? That was—an intense fight back there," Janis said.

The words felt strange in her mouth. Before now she hadn't cared that much if someone was "okay" during fights. While the question might not have been entirely sincere, Janis could feel it was closer to the sentiment than she'd ever shown before.

Livella smiled again, this one more jovial.

"Oh, I'm all right. I didn't get to see much of the fighting. I was pushed into the closest shop as soon as the first javelin flew," Livella replied.

The woman spoke the words with a kind of reverence. Janis resisted the urge to cringe at the almost admiring tone of the woman's reference to Janis engaging with a Conjured javelin.

The others by the fire were busy with a conversation of their own, so none of them noticed Livella's comment. Janis, however, couldn't miss it.

Was that a joke? Janis thought. Before now, the two women hadn't had anything but an obligatory connection. She'd not once heard Livella say anything other than comment on how terrified she was. The smile with the comment was nothing Janis had experienced with Livella before now.

Taking a moment to soak it in, Janis looked back at the fire.

"Well, Conjured Light javelins are not the normal arsenal of an assassin. Unless they want to have a brief career, at least," Janis said.

To her surprise, Livella chuckled. Janis smiled to herself. It was a dark joke, but Livella had picked up on it, which made her think the woman might actually be capable of something other than fear.

"I will say that I am disappointed to have missed your fight. After you chased after them, I missed everything. The music you created was far more interesting than anything I'd heard in Arivan growing up," Livella said, picking at her skirt.

Another joke, Janis thought. *Who is this strange creature we call Livella?*

Janis smiled, then spoke again.

"As with all music, I am glad there won't be an encore. Now that Riln's gone, at least."

Janis felt Livella tense next to her.

"Wait—*what*?"

Janis furrowed her brow and looked over at the Voidbearer. It was then that she realized there had been no mention of what happened with Riln back in the city. Leveling her eyes with Livella, Janis nodded.

"Prost, the other"—Janis hesitated, not wanting to use the term for what Livella was—"person like you took a knife to Riln's throat. Looks like you and I will be the only ones holding the pact together."

Livella paled. Her earlier mirth drained from her.

"Then the column of smoke that we saw—was that—no."

The mousy-haired woman seemed to be talking to herself, so Janis just turned away. Avryn's focus had shifted almost completely to who would lead Evenir. He'd dropped the conversation about what had happened back in Stilten.

Her thoughts shifted to the fight she'd had with Riln. The man had been overwhelmingly powerful, something she'd previously assumed but hadn't seen firsthand. At this point, she was just grateful she'd come into her Lightbearing powers. It disappointed another part of her that Prost had been the one to kill Riln, rather than her.

This thought brought her back to when Ugglyn appeared to them in the Evenir war room.

What was it he'd said? Janis thought.

A picture of the man formed in her mind, tight-fitting black clothes, the handsome face of an aging man, silver beard cut close to his chin and equally silver hair. Besides the fact that he'd been handsome, he also had an air of pride. Janis packed that impression away, hoping she might utilize the knowledge should he appear again.

She remembered him demanding Livella kill her, to end it all so that he could be free. At the time, Livella was still the bumbling and confused girl from when they'd first found her. Janis wondered if he had shown up later, perhaps after Livella started opening up like she had today, what would she have done?

A thought struck Janis hard, a jolt of energy running up and down her arms.

He said if Livella killed me, he'd be free, but Prost killed Riln.

Livella noticed her reaction and reached over, touching Janis on the arm. Surprising even herself, Janis didn't recoil at the touch. Instead, Janis said nothing, narrowing her eyes forward and trying to process the information. In all her life she'd not seen any weather anomalies like the one they'd seen in Stilten, let alone something which held a man at the center.

"What is it? Why did you flinch like that?" Livella asked.

Knowing it wasn't a good time for her to explain anything to Livella, Janis shrugged. It was uncharacteristic for her to do so, and Livella clearly picked up on it but didn't comment.

"I'm just thinking about Watchlight. Somehow, both of our groups came out of that fight without leaders. I'm just hoping without leadership they will fall into chaos."

Livella pressed her lips together, considering the statement. "Hmmm," she hummed, seemingly unsure of what to say.

The two women lapsed into silence as the other members of the group continued to eat and laugh.

Suddenly, Janis recalled the book that she'd taken from Macks on the roof of the bar. Before she reached down to touch the book, she scanned over the others to make sure they weren't watching. She decided that, despite their merriment, she would rather review what she'd found privately.

"I have some business to take care of. I'll be back," Janis offered to Livella, who appeared to be the only one listening. She was wrong, however, as Avryn looked over from the other side of the fire.

"What business? You can't go after Watchlight, not alone," Avryn spoke harshly.

Under normal circumstances, his presumption might have made her angry, but she just smirked.

"I appreciate your worry for my well-being, Avryn, but I meant that I have to relieve myself. If you think you need to come with me to do that, by all means."

Avryn blushed deeply enough that anyone could see even with just the firelight.

"Oh, erm—sorry," he replied, turning back to his conversation.

The damage was done, however, as Harmel burst out laughing and began poking fun at their companion. Janis rolled her eyes, then turned to the forest. The darkness of the trees felt even more imposing with the residual feeling left over from her thoughts about her encounter with Ugglyn. The breeze rustling the trees picked up, as if the wind was responding to her discomfort as well. She allowed her eyes to adjust to the darkness after leaving the camp. As she walked, Janis let her hand slide down to the small book stuffed into her waistband. The moment the skin of her fingertips touched the object, a tingling sensation spread up her hand like wildfire. Janis gritted her teeth, pulling her hand away sharply and trying not to make any other noises that might alert the others. While she dreaded having to inspect the book, she knew it had to be done. Especially knowing now that she'd not just imagined what she felt from the book back in Stilten. One thing was obvious to her.

Macks had mixed himself up in something. Now she'd been dragged into it.

3

The sky was lightening rapidly, telling Prost that the sun would be up in full force soon. Trees surrounded them on all sides, the dull light casting fuzzy shadows from each of the sturdy trunks. Fresh air ruled the morning, as it often did, and Prost tried to take it in to calm his mind. Despite his efforts, the image of Riln dying in front of him still plagued his thoughts. Inside, he felt the satisfaction he'd always longed for. He'd finally gotten the revenge he'd wanted for the past five years.

But Riln's death meant something else. A part of Prost lamented Riln's death for this reason.

Oh, there isn't any need to mourn the loss of that man. He was going to die eventually, be it by your hand or the wench's, Ugglyn's voice roared in his mind.

Prost clenched his teeth, trying to not let the sound get the better of him. He'd just ordered the Watchlight envoy to move out from their resting place in the forest. Most had grumbled, saying they were exhausted from the previous battle, but Prost didn't care. He couldn't allow them to get ambushed by any roaming soldiers from Evenir, or even operatives who worked for Luden.

Yes, that man had been annoying, hadn't he? He deserved the sword in the chest, Ugglyn pressed into his mind.

Prost shifted his gaze to look at Vint.

"Vint, did you get a count of the loss?" he asked.

Vint shifted in his saddle, turning to look at Prost. The man's glowing eyes dimmed as he left a vision.

"Based on what I See, we lost about one third of those that we came with. I haven't had the chance to gather all the information. But I've learned that of these, more than half were lost to Evenir, the other part to the strange poison. I can't be sure what it was, but I will keep looking."

Grunting, Prost returned to facing forward.

Ah yes, the poison. I put a dent in your wretched Lightbearers, didn't I? Ugglyn sounded amused.

"Will you shut up?!" Prost shouted, grabbing his temple.

Vint, whose eyes had glowed again, jumped. All at once, his eyes dimmed and he stared at Prost, confused.

"Sir, I had said nothing yet," Vint said through a tight jaw.

Prost shook his head, then steeled himself. "My thoughts have gotten the better of me today. Continue your work."

How am I supposed to function with this whispering in my head? Prost thought.

Something within his mind snapped. It felt as if his consciousness lost touch with his body. Something took control of his arms, his face, everything.

What in Lanser's name?! he thought.

Don't use that wretch's name, even in here, Ugglyn replied.

As the thought came, Prost felt his hand move up to his head, his pointer finger tapping his temple.

Let us see how dedicated these followers are to you.

Just then, Prost's foot kicked the side of his horse, spurring the creature to motion. His mouth let out a whoop as the horse launched into a full-speed run. Shouts of surprise sounded behind him. Prost tried to look back, to shout to them to hold their pace, but he couldn't. His horse ran forward on the rough dirt of the road, its hooves pounding. Prost tried not to panic. Instead, he focused on the sensation he'd had only moments before this. All he could feel was the pressure of something else in his mind. Something was forcing him back.

Suddenly, he found what he looked for in his mind.

Unsure of what to do, Prost focused on pushing back against the force that held his consciousness at bay. A man screamed in his skull. At that moment, Prost felt his body snap back into his control. Prost pulled on the reins of his horse to slow the creature. He was grateful he had many years' experience riding. Any beginner trying to ease the stress of a horse would likely have been forced from its back.

The sound of other horses came from behind him, and he turned to see that just a few of his men had run to catch up. One of them was Vint.

"Sir! What is happening?! Did you spot Evenir men?" he asked, his eyes shifting among the trees.

Well, they do trust you. More than you think in this empty head of yours, Ugglyn teased.

Prost once again ignored the voice.

"No, though I thought for a moment there was up ahead," Prost said, thinking how he should proceed. "I hoped to distract them for a time so you and the others could get away. I don't believe we are fit for another fight."

The lie felt hollow, completely uncharacteristic of his normally brazen nature. But without the plague of Riln, Prost felt freed. He tried not to shiver at the immediate change from the man's death. Eyeing the newcomers, his gut wrenched as he assumed they'd not believe his words.

To his surprise,Vint and the other two who had followed him looked around, fear in their eyes. After a moment, Vint looked at Prost.

Prost could see it. There was something there that the man would undoubtedly deny. It looked like a mixture of respect and gratitude.

"That was—kind of you," Vint replied, though there was skepticism in his tone, "but I think there are better ways to handle an ambush."

Ugglyn's voice cackled within Prost's head, and he resisted the urge to flinch at the horrendous noise. Prost already felt that his announcement of Riln giving him the rule over Watchlight was tenuous. If he appeared mentally unstable or incapable of leading in any other way, it wouldn't be long before their loyalty would vanish.

Prost feared saying anything for fear of Ugglyn interrupting him. He feared losing control once more, yet remaining silent wouldn't bode well for a leader.

"Agreed. You know that my sole priority is to get everyone back to our lair. We may have lost the other three Lightbearers, but we got the one. It's important that we all make it back," Prost explained.

The answer must have been an acceptable one, for Vint nodded in return. Prost's stomach writhed as he spoke the words. He felt the anger, the annoyance at having to deal with his soldiers, something he'd felt for years. Yet so much bitterness, so much anger, had diffused with the death of that pale man.

Prost wasn't sure he liked it.

"But, sir," another man said. Prost couldn't recall his name, but he recognized his face. "What is the plan if we were to get attacked by Evenir? They could be out roaming for us as we speak."

By now the rest of their group had almost caught up to their position on the road. Dust lightly kicked up from the mass of horse hooves and feet. They hadn't lost too many more of their mounts despite all the fighting within Stilten. Horses had a way of escaping perilous situations and securing themselves in safe places. Still, Prost could see that they had many on foot, their haggard expressions showing their sentiment toward the trip.

Prost shifted his eyes back to the man who'd asked the question. Until now he'd had no wish to lead anyone. Ever since he'd been with Watchlight, he'd only sought to undermine Riln, to pull control from him in the smallest ways, just in case there was an uprising against him someday. He contained his shock at how many appeared to look to him now. Prost hoped there were no true witnesses to what he'd done to their former master. As of yet, no one had mentioned anything. The same feelings he'd had only days ago—to escape, to get back to his normal life in T'Arren Vale—crept into his thoughts, but something pushed them away.

It was him again.

No, no, we need them. I can't rule Lindrad without an army, now can I?

In response to the unwanted opinion of the anti-god, and as a way to show contemplation to Vint and the others outside of his mind, Prost sucked in a deep breath.

Then he gave the answer he knew best.

"We'll kill them, as we always have."

Vint furrowed his brow as if he detected something off with their new leader. The other two men stared at him in shock.

"But sir—we're all exhausted from Stilten despite what our Fixers have done. How can we threaten them?"

Whether Vint agreed with the soldier's words, Prost didn't know, but he didn't argue. He also didn't defend Prost. Instead, the man's green eyes gazed upon him, waiting for an answer.

If you think you're an all-powerful being, then prove it, Prost countered in his mind.

Though Ugglyn didn't respond, he felt pride blossom in his chest, as if it came from somewhere else.

Recalling when Ugglyn had first taken control of him, Prost held up his hand. It felt unwise to put his trust in the anti-god. It was the very being who countered his religion, the god he'd always worshiped and believed in. Yet Prost felt he didn't have a choice. Ugglyn inhabited him despite everything, and there was no way out.

The moment his palm reached his shoulder, a sword formed there, made of swirling silvery smoke. It was the same as he'd seen before, yet Prost expected it this time, so he inspected it more closely. Narrowing his eyes, he noted it was light for a weapon. His own sword weighed more than double what this smoke-sword did. Yet somehow he knew it was just as sharp and deadly.

"We have something we didn't have before," Prost said. He knew little of the power he now held from Ugglyn's presence within, but it felt like the exact tool that Evenir wouldn't be able to expect.

The men gasped, one of them pulling his horse away, eyes wide. Vint stared at the sword.

"You hold a power we don't understand. This is no Lightbearing. How can we know that this—new power will hold up to Evenir? What even is this magic?" Vint's voice was mixed with malice. Prost assumed the man was just as scared of the power as the others, but his companions wouldn't admit it.

Prost squeezed the handle of the sword, feeling the hardness of the weapon despite its insubstantial appearance. He didn't know exactly what it was, but it felt powerful.

"For years, Riln has called upon the power of one greater than Lanser, and we have followed. Ugglyn has answered our loyalty, and he's granted me this power in Riln's stead. With it, we can strike down Evenir and those who lead them," Prost said, his voice rising loud enough that the rest of their group could now hear.

The black-clad men and women collectively stared at the sword in his grasp, most with fear in their eyes. The darkness of the blade appeared more potent in the increasing light from the rising sun. Just as Lightbearing pierced the darkness of night, so did this sword appear stark in the light of day. A tingling sensation tickled Prost's skin where he held the Conjured weapon. It wasn't painful, but it was unpleasant.

"What is this power called, sir? How can it help us?"

One woman walking next to the group of horses looked upward at him. There was a hardness in her eyes, a hardness that spanned years. Prost knew he wasn't the only one who had lived a rough life. Truthfully, Prost didn't know the answer to her question, but even as she asked it, a thought formed in his mind, something to call this power.

"Voidweaving, a gift from the anti-god himself," he answered.

Ah, so you accept me being here, then? It will work better with cooperation anyway. I—

Ugglyn's voice cut off as Prost forced it away. A feeling of resentment and anger, one that was not his own, accompanied it. Prost breathed evenly, trying not to focus on the energy it took to internally push away the unwanted inhabitant inside of him.

"And with it, we will rule Lindrad as we are meant," Prost declared, holding his pseudo-Conjured sword above his head.

Shouts of agreement came from the crowd of Watchlight allies, but only a few.

And with it, I can kill Janis, Prost thought.

This time, he felt the resentment from Ugglyn change to pure satisfaction.

4

Marric held Shrell, tears streaming down his face.

"Marric! We need to leave!" Narinda said. "Watchlight is here and we need to get out before—"

An explosion rocked the side of the house and Narinda ducked her head. The sound snapped Marric out of the sorrow. Deep sadness lingered inside, but he knew he had to do something about Crents. The boy lay unconscious on the ground a few paces away. It was then that Marric realized he could see. Until now, he'd fought the men in the darkness. Looking up, he could see a few large blue orbs hovering in the corners of the room.

That's right, Narinda is a Lighter, he thought.

His mind was fuzzy still, the grief of seeing Shrell lifeless on the ground still affecting him. The sounds of swords clashing and men shouting outside Crents's home helped him to focus on something else. Another explosion rang out from outside the walls. Gritting his teeth, Marric turned to Crents and hefted the boy up onto one shoulder. He felt surprisingly light. Marric's body was toned and strong from months of training. Narinda stood poised, facing the broken hallway behind them.

"Is there another way out?" Narinda asked, her voice tense. "They've seen us come in this way. They'll be waiting for us."

Marric shook his head, then realized she wasn't watching him.

"I don't know. I've never been in his house before," Marric replied.

Narinda's head snapped around and she gave him an odd look.

"I thought you knew this boy. Yet you haven't been in his home?"

Marric blushed. He hadn't thought about the oddity. Now that they were trapped inside the house, he regretted not taking the time to go into Crents's home. When they were younger, Marric was too scared of Crents's father, the drunk, to come inside.

His eyes drifted to the hallway where the corpse of the man who had scared him so much laid. His stomach twisted at the sight.

So many dead, he thought.

"Let's try the back. There must be some way out," Marric yelled over the noises outside.

Narinda nodded and gestured for him to lead the way. Just before he could leave, he turned back, looking at his friend. It wasn't logical, but he knew he couldn't just leave Shrell here. Already carrying Crents over his shoulder, Marric knew he couldn't hold the larger man too. Narinda glanced over at Marric, her face softening.

"We can't carry him with us. I can't risk losing you too. If we need to fight our way out of here, I'll need to be unburdened by the weight," she said, answering the question he hadn't voiced.

Narrowing his eyes, Marric recalled what Alsry had shown him back in Terris Green. Movers could carry objects much larger than themselves. Taking a deep breath, he held out his hand and focused on the body of his friend. Shrell glowed with blue Light, his body lifting off of the ground.

"Marric, we can't move fast enough—" Narinda said.

Marric shot her a dark glare. She clenched her jaw, knowing it wouldn't be worth her time to argue.

"You lead, I'll guard us from behind," she said.

It took a lot of concentration for Marric to lead the hovering body of Shrell through the narrow hallways of the deteriorating house. He was grateful for the orbs of Light that Narinda created. Glancing upward, he could see that one of the blue orbs followed at the same pace he walked. Though he couldn't explain how, he knew his Moving abilities were being bolstered by the unwavering Light from above.

They reached the end of the hallway in moments. The home of Crents was small; smaller than most in Wurren. Marric promptly saw a boarded-up doorway to his left. A few nails had been hammered through the boards and into the frame behind. Narinda turned the corner and saw, cursing.

"Blast. Where is a Destroyer when you need one?" she said, peering back down the hallway. "We will have to turn back."

Marric gritted his teeth. He knew if they turned back, the likelihood of him being able to bring Shrell would be gone. They couldn't face Watch-light with him in tow.

An idea formed in his mind, one that likely wouldn't work. He knew he still had to try.

He gently lowered Shrell to the ground, the man's lifeless head alighting softly on the dirt floor. It wasn't until then that Marric realized most of the floors here were dirt, the single bedroom being the only one made of wood.

"I'm going to try using my Destroying," Marric said. Even as the words came from his mouth, they sounded desperate.

Narinda must have thought the same, for she looked at him with skepticism.

"You aren't a Destroyer, that won't work—we don't have time for this," she replied.

Marric's hardened look landed on her once more and she rolled her eyes.

"I don't remember you being this stubborn when I first met you," she said, moving to his side.

Until now, Marric hadn't tried to use his limited Destroying. He bent down, carefully setting the unconscious form of Crents on the ground next to Shrell. Unsure exactly how to do it, he imagined Conjuring a ball of something that would explode at the touch. A small orb of blue Light formed in his hand. He looked up, hoping the extra power from the surrounding Lighting orbs would help. With a grunt, he threw the ball at the planks of wood.

The ball thudded into the wood and fell to the ground as if it were made of wood itself. Marric cursed, then tried again with shaky hands, focusing on putting more into the ball. This also thudded into the wall and rolled away. It sounded as if it was made of metal.

"You're Conjuring, not Destroying," Narinda said, nudging him aside. "Let me try."

The woman closed her eyes and opened her palm. A small ball of blue light formed there. Her eyes snapped open and she threw the ball at the planks. A loud crack split the surrounding air, the plank splintering down the middle.

Narinda cursed again.

"It's not going to work, Marric," she said, gripping her sword more tightly.

Frustration built within him. His limited Lighting ability had given Avryn enough of a boost to help him Fix Turrin in the forest, yet this hadn't worked. The sound of metal thudding into wood came from behind them in the hall. A woman's voice shouted a warning, followed by clashing steel.

"They're in the house, Marric. Fog it, we should have just gone out the other way," Narinda said, angling herself to engage whoever was moving down the hallway.

The frustration piqued in Marric and he let out a shout. He pulled backward with his Moving, putting as much into it as he could. The planks on the door glowed with brilliant blue Light, the nails creaking. With one last roar, the wood snapped through the nails and flew past him. One piece of wood flew toward him and he ducked. It slammed into his elbow, pain lancing up his arm. Marric sucked in a breath, trying to cope with the pain. Fresh air blew past his face, telling him he'd been successful in breaking through all the wood.

Despite the pain, he felt triumphant. He looked at the now open door and turned toward Narinda. His body went stiff when he saw a sword swinging at him instead. Gasping, he fell to the ground just as the sword slammed into the wall next to him. Narinda fought a woman wielding twin Conjured daggers. The red Light cast eerie shadows on the enclosed space. The man who'd just missed Marric growled and turned toward him. Marric Moved the man, throwing his arms outward. The man's eyes went wide as his body flung backward down the hallway and toward a surprised Narinda, who twisted just enough that the warrior flipped over her back, landing just short of his ally.

Without hesitation, Narinda righted herself and thrust her sword into the fallen man, his body becoming still. His companion let out a roar of her own and dashed toward Marric with her wicked daggers. Before she could slip by, Narinda was there, cutting the woman down easily.

Marric's heart raced as he desperately scanned the space behind them. No others followed.

Narinda eyed him, her own breath labored.

"Next time, can you try to Move them *away* from me? That could have ended a lot differently," Narinda said.

He nodded, blushing at his mistake.

"Um, I got the door open."

Her eyes shifted to the door and she looked confused. Marric assumed she'd been too preoccupied with the approaching shouts to see what he'd done.

"How—never mind, let's go."

The woman reached out her hand and grasped Marric by the forearm. He was shocked by the strength of her grip as she lifted him off the ground. He was again surprised at what a capable fighter she was.

"I'll go first to make sure there isn't anyone waiting for us out there," Narinda offered.

Nodding, Marric stepped aside to let her pass. He took the moment to bend down and heft Crents back over his shoulder. It started aching from the weight of the boy the moment he was settled.

Narinda slipped out the door, her short sword held aloft. Only a moment passed before she returned, gesturing for Marric to follow. He concentrated on Shrell again and Moved the man's body back into the air.

Exiting the home, Marric breathed in the fresh air, trying to focus past the pain in his shoulder and arm. The sun was behind the surrounding buildings, casting the street into shadows.

"Come, this way!" Narinda hissed to his right. He turned to see her pointing down a back alley. It was narrow, and he recalled this was the same place he'd slipped from the roof all those months ago to give Crents the money he'd pilfered.

So much has changed, he thought, moving toward her.

He reached the opening to the narrow alley and paused. Wind blew steadily through the small passageway. Wooden walls of the two-story buildings on either side appeared weathered and worn in places. He recalled the times when, as younger children, he and Jord would run through the alley, letting the strength of the wind push them through.

The thoughts of Jord made him pause. For years he'd thought his friend dead, only to learn that he'd allied himself with Watchlight. As more sorrow settled into Marric, he focused only on moving through the alley carefully. When they'd reached the other side, Narinda paused. Flashes of red and blue Light reflected off of the buildings in front of them. Villagers screamed and shouted, running left, away from the fighting Lightbearers.

"They'll be fighting around the corner to the right. The main exit is to the left. If we go that way, we should be out of here quickly," he said.

Narinda nodded, then stepped onto the dirt street. She angled herself right, allowing Marric to Move Shrell out of the alley and slide past while carrying Crents. The boy on his shoulder grumbled and shifted.

"Erm—what? What's happening?" Crents said.

Marric sighed in relief. He hoped that Crents would wake up soon so that he wouldn't have to carry him much longer. Once out of the alley, the two turned and began making their approach toward the main street.

"There, they have the boy," a voice sounded behind them.

Marric's body chilled.

"Good, now look for the rest of their crew. I'll take the boy and meet you there," a second voice spoke out behind them.

Narinda turned, holding her sword upward. Marric, sensing the danger, released his Moving on Shrell. The man's body fell to the ground, making Marric wince. He Conjured a sword in his free hand, the blue Light piercing and strong. At the same time, he gently leaned down and propped Crents against one of the buildings.

He knew the voice, yet the sound of it disturbed him more than it normally would.

"Well, Marric, 'ow ironic tha' we'd meet again 'ere in our ol' town," Jord said. He lifted his hands to his hood and pulled it back, his light hair cut close to his head.

"Jord," Marric said.

His former friend stood there, black cloak flowing in the wind. Two other men stood to either side of him. One held a Conjured sword of his own, the red Light shining on the walls of the building next to them. The other stood weaponless, though Marric knew that didn't mean he wouldn't be dangerous.

"Wasn't it that very alley we'd use to sneak away from those we'd stolen from?"

Marric stared at the other boy warily. His breathing increased as he considered what options they had. The way Jord had spoken to him showed that his former friend didn't care to reminisce. Marric guessed he was biding the time.

"Narinda, he's a Destroyer," Marric said.

Narinda breathed out next to him, then lifted her hand into the air, sending a few blue orbs overhead. The street illuminated with blue Light. Shadows cast from the surrounding buildings sat unwavering from the steadiness of the Lighting orbs.

"Don' feel like remembering, hm? Too bad, tha'. I see yeh 'ave a pet Lighter with yous. Too bad she'll be useless in this figh'," Jord said, baring his teeth.

Something inside Marric warned him that if he waited too long, they'd be surrounded and outnumbered. His chest burned in anticipation, adrenaline filling him. With little thought, he jumped forward with his Conjured sword, swinging it in a wide arc toward Jord.

His old friend, full of ego, hadn't expected the move. His eyes widened as he bent backward to avoid the sharp blade of the Light sword. Marric grunted as his sword overextended and moved toward one of Jord's companions. This one now held a red Conjured sword and wasn't as taken aback from the forward attack. He blocked Marric's sword and moved forward to stab him. Instinct told Marric to roll, so he ducked to the ground, his sword puffing into nothing.

Grunting from the hardness of the dirt road, Marric stopped himself and jumped up. Just as he got to his feet, he gasped, seeing the tip of the red sword coming for his gut. At the last moment, Narinda's sword was there, slamming the Conjured blade away from him. Marric breathed out and Conjured his bow. Narinda continued to engage the Conjurer, her face determined.

In quick succession, he Conjured an arrow, nocked it, then released it toward Jord and the other man. Jord appeared ready for something like this. Before Marric's arrow flew toward him, he'd summoned a small ball of Light. With a flick of his wrist, Jord's ball connected with Marric's arrow, an explosion of Light momentarily blinding Marric with the flash. The loud crack echoed down the wood of the buildings, and he heard a few screams from villagers likely watching from darkened windows.

Gritting his teeth, Marric Conjured arrow after arrow, launching them quickly toward the two Watchlight men. Narinda continued to fight the other man to the left. Her breathing was labored, and Marric wondered how much energy she had left after the Fixing she'd had to do already.

His arrows missed, but they kept Jord from throwing his Destroying powers at Marric and Narinda. Marric's arm tired as he continued to shoot arrows toward the attackers. Jord managed to Destroy arrows here and there, but he wasn't as quick as Marric's arrows could fly, some slipping past his defenses and hitting the surrounding areas. A flash of red in front of Marric made him gasp. The wall behind him exploded, wood splintering everywhere and slicing his face and arms.

He cursed, ducking and moving away from the wall.

"Too bad you didn't get any useful powers from your Awakening!" Jord taunted. Marric looked up to see another Destroying ball flying toward him. The world slowed down, and Marric felt his chest constrict. He couldn't breathe. Marric reached up and focused on the ball of power. He flung his empty hand outward, hoping it would work. Sure enough, the red ball gathered a bluish hue, the joint Lights making it look purple, before it flew off course, slamming into the ground.

Marric couldn't help but smile. He hadn't thought about Moving a Destroyer's powers. He was relieved to see that it worked well enough.

Jord growled, creating another orb.

Before he could throw it, Marric shot an arrow right toward his head. Jord yelled and ducked, the arrow flying harmlessly over him. Marric heard Narinda shouting, her voice roaring with each clash of her sword on the enemy's.

The other Watchlight man remained hooded, but he lifted his hands and pushed outward. Marric's body glowed red and flew backward. The world spun out of control for a moment until Marric felt his body slam into the ground. He slid a few more paces before he came to a stop. Pain shot up his left arm, and he had to focus to suck in another breath.

He was a Mover this whole time! Marric thought. He guessed that was why the arrows hadn't hit their marks. His aim wasn't perfect, but it was good enough that he should have hit either of them at least once.

"There, get the boy," Marric heard his former friend say.

Cursing, Marric jumped to his feet, ignoring the pain in his body. He turned to see the man moving toward Crents, who was watching the scene wide-eyed. Reacting at once, Marric tossed the man aside, Moving the person with ease.

The man recovered once he'd reached far enough that Marric's Moving couldn't reach him, then he stepped forward and pushed Marric back. The force slammed into Marric, threatening him off his feet, but instead of losing complete control, Marric went with the force and shuffled his feet. As expected, he went out of range of the man's Moving powers.

Then he smiled, Conjuring his bow. A Moving fight wouldn't be productive, so Marric thought he'd use range as his advantage. He hoped that the range of his Conjures would be further. Knowing his aim wasn't as good from afar, Marric sought only to keep the Mover away from Crents. He fired an arrow, the blue Light lighting up the street as it flew toward the enemy. The man Moved it away, the Light of the arrow turning purple before it thudded into the wooden door of the shop next to the man.

Just then, Narinda's assailant cried out just before Marric heard a heavy thud to his right. He turned to see Narinda standing over the man's body, a grim expression on her face. She turned, the blue orbs from above showing the glistening sweat on her brow. She focused on Jord, then the other man. With a slight nod, she barreled toward him.

"You take care of the Destroyer! I'll get this one," she shouted as she ran.

Marric opened his mouth to warn her, but it was too late. The man flung both arms outward and Narinda roared as she glowed red, her body flying sideways and smashing into a wall. She gasped as it pushed the air out of her lungs. When she didn't rise right away, Marric's mind went into a frenzy. His eyes flipped back and forth between Jord and the other man. It didn't take long before Jord was flinging more balls of red Light at him. Marric tried to Move them, but they came too fast for him to keep up. One of them landed at his feet, the dirt of the road exploding. The force knocked him on his backside. Dust filled his nostrils and the surrounding air. For a moment he lost sight of his attackers. Flashes of red announced more Destroying coming at him, and he scrambled backward to get away from them. After a few more explosions on the streets, the onslaught paused.

Marric knew he had to use their inability to see him to his advantage. If he stayed quiet, they might think him dead.

His stomach rolled. He couldn't believe that Jord, his childhood friend, could attack him this way. Even from the moment he'd learned of the power, Marric was disgusted by Destroying. He was grateful, even now, that he didn't awaken with the terrible power.

"Oh dear, did I finally get you? Nasty things, those Destroying orbs. They can make even a grown man disappear in mere moments."

Marric shook, but he remained quiet. He knew Jord was trying to bait him out, to test to see if he really was killed. Shifting his eyes left, Marric hoped Crents would stay still and that they couldn't see him or Shrell's body.

An idea struck Marric and he followed it. Focusing on the dust particles from the exploded road, he reached up his hands and tried to grab them. The sensation wasn't like it normally was. When Moving objects, Marric could feel some exertion in his body, as if part of his physical form was feeling the pressure of the object's weight. Now, however, the dust Moved quickly, with no feeling. The dust gathered in front of Marric, becoming so thick that it formed a column of dirt, swirling as if the wind had seized it. With his teeth clenched, he pushed outward, the dust flinging toward Jord and the other man. Each cursed, and Marric heard thumping as at least one body leapt out of the way.

Jord shouted as the dust particles flew right into his face. They were past the men quickly, now that they'd reached outside of Marric's Moving reach, but the damage was done. The Mover lay on the ground, his hand over his eyes. Jord stood, rubbing his eyes frantically to get the dust out of them.

Marric Conjured his bow and an arrow, pointing the shot at his friend's chest. His breathing quickened, and sweat dripped down the side of his face.

I—I can't kill him, Marric thought.

The fact that Jord's voice, his tone, sounded so much like Riln's, disturbed Marric to no end. It also reminded him of Riln's imperative to kill without thinking. Marric didn't know how Jord had become this way, but he wouldn't stoop to that level.

Still, Marric knew he couldn't leave Jord unharmed. He aimed for the boy's leg, but before he could release the arrow, Jord's eyes erupted in red beams of Light.

"Take my eyes. I can still See you," he said, creating a ball of power and lobbing it at Marric.

Marric's brain screamed at him to get out of the way, but it happened so fast that he didn't process it. On instinct, he fired his arrow at the ball. It wasn't a direct hit, but the Conjure skimmed the ball enough to make it explode. The power knocked him off his feet again.

Pain shot up his back from the force of the hard street.

That explains how he found us, Marric thought.

Marric hadn't had an encounter with his friend after his own Awakening. He had also forgotten about the second power. Most hid it until the last moment. Now he knew Jord was a Seer.

Jord smiled and began throwing more orbs, his eyes glowing red. Marric rolled left and right, cursing. He Moved a few, but he had to be careful not to Move them into shops or villagers cowering down the street.

Dust flew everywhere, hiding Jord once more in the mess. Marric could see the glowing red eyes for one last moment before the dust covered those as well.

He'd not had as much experience with Seeing as Jord likely had, but he knew he'd be dead if he didn't try. Focusing on his eyes, he allowed them to glow. Marric felt them expand, as if they'd opened to their maximum. He felt his body separate from his physical form, but he grunted, focusing on the present.

His vision-self settled back into his body and the situation. Time slowed down. Though he couldn't see through the dust, he could See where the red orbs would be.

In his mind, Marric knew that his breathing was normal, that the sweat still stuck his shirt to his back, but his eyes perceived everything more quickly. As each orb flew toward him, he grabbed them with his Moving and held them. When he'd gathered four or five, he pushed forward, focusing on sending them back toward Jord.

That didn't last long before Jord caught on. The Destroying orbs stopped flying.

"So—you have learned more than Riln thought," Jord said, his voice barely carrying over the fighting that had intensified behind Marric.

Marric focused his vision behind him, and this time his vision-self separated to look toward the crossroads. Men and women in black backed up toward him, fending off the blue Light of Evenir.

Panic rose inside him. He knew he had little time before he'd be stuck in the middle of them. Moving wouldn't help him here. And Conjuring likely would likewise fail.

"You are trapped, Marric. Give us Crents, and I'll kill you quickly," Jord said.

To his right, he heard Narinda sighing and shuffling, but he couldn't see her.

His mind reeled. The Watchlight men and women advanced toward him, and one of them spotted his back standing there.

Something snapped within him. A warmth spread through his chest and into his limbs. It felt familiar, reminiscent of his Awakening, without the sickness and pain. Somehow he knew something had changed within him. His stomach turned at the realization.

No—no, he thought.

He gritted his teeth once more, dreading what had just happened.

Yet he couldn't deny the help that had come. Sucking in a breath, Marric summoned a small ball of blue Light. He spun, tossing it at the feet of those advancing.

It slammed into the ground and exploded, tossing men and women in every direction.

5

Janis continued forward into the darkness of the forest. The trees came into focus as her eyes adjusted to the dim. She couldn't see completely, but the light from Stellan filtered through the eaves above. The red of the moon gave her enough to make out most of the foliage.

Janis knew she could create an orb of Light, but she didn't want anyone following her. Her feet stepped on fallen branches and leaves, the crunching louder to her ears than the slight breeze that blew through the trees. It was a warm night, an excellent night for sleeping outdoors. Still, her mind focused on the fact that Watchlight was out there. She'd been to their compound and knew it was south of Stilten, so they'd be moving in the same direction for some time.

Tuning her ears to her surroundings, she focused on continuing forward. Janis peeked back after a moment to ensure she could see the flickering of the fires. They were clear and visible in the darkness. At some point, they would need to extinguish them to sleep. Janis hoped it was sooner rather than later so they didn't stick out like feeble prey.

After wandering for a few more moments, Janis came to an especially thick section of brush. Putting both hands out, she spread the leaves carefully so as to not make much noise. Satisfied, she slipped through the brush and stood between two large trees.

She paused, listening for unusual noises. The breeze continued to blow through the forest, rustling the leaves. An animal crunched a branch to her left, but she knew the sound. It was too small to be anything dangerous.

Once she'd determined she was alone, she created a small Light orb, the size of her thumbnail. The Light was piercing and blue. Her chest buzzed, warning her of the danger of exposing herself, but she pressed it away. She kept her senses vigilant, knowing they'd warn her in time.

With her other hand, she reached into her sleeve, pulling out a handkerchief she kept there. She hadn't used it much, but having one on hand had proven useful. Amid a fight, sweat had occasionally obscured her vision enough that she'd needed to wipe it away with the cloth. Janis now used it to pull the small book out of her belt.

The cloth barrier prevented the same sensation from flowing up her arm as it had the previous times. Despite the protection, the moment her eyes landed on the book, her insides twisted and she felt alarmed. Janis didn't understand why, but it felt wrong. The cover of the small book was made of fine leather, and it had small words inscribed in silver ink. They reflected the blue Light of her orb back at her. The text was unreadable, for it was written in characters unfamiliar to her. Squinting and holding the Light closer, she could see that minuscule writing bordered the front and back covers of the book. It was thin, perhaps only fifty pages.

She paused, wanting to use both hands to inspect the words but knowing she held the ball of light in her palm. Janis recalled the times when she'd seen Lighters let orbs such as this fly free. Furrowing her brow, she dropped her palm slowly. The orb remained where it had been when she'd first created it. Satisfied, she reached her now empty hand over and lightly touched the cover. She sucked in a breath, expecting the odd sensation in her hand. Sure enough, the tingling erupted in her fingertips and spread up her arm. Despite the discomfort, she let it happen, analyzing the feeling as best as she could. After a few beats, she released a breath she hadn't realized she was holding. The sensation was strange, but it didn't hurt. It was as if she'd held her hand in a position for so long it had lost feeling. The moment she removed her hand, the tingling disappeared as quickly as it had come.

Once Janis realized it wouldn't hurt her, she pulled the cover of the book open. She was disappointed to find no writing on the dark pages of the book. Somehow the paper inside was a deep black, as if someone had taken normal parchment and rubbed it with ash. Suddenly, words appeared in sections, as if an invisible hand wrote them. The words were scrawled in the same reflective silver ink. She gasped, almost dropping the small book in surprise, only her pointer finger and thumb gripping the cover.

She gritted her teeth and righted the book, inspecting the appearing text. Janis hadn't done much reading in her life, but she knew that this was no normal paper and ink. While colored ink wasn't impossible, none glowed like this.

The sight of it reminded her of the poison she'd seen lacing the arrows of the men Luden stationed on top of the bar back in Stilten. She narrowed her eyes, trying to put pieces together. This felt familiar, but she couldn't place it.

Rustling sounded in the trees behind her and she spun, moving her free hand down to her belt where a small dagger still sat. She cursed internally, remembering that her favorite dagger was left behind, having been used by Prost to kill his former master.

"Blasted forest! How do you see in this mess?!"

It was Livella.

Janis relaxed, knowing it wasn't a danger behind her.

"You get used to it. The light from Stellan should be enough once you learn how to adjust to the dark," Janis replied, turning back to the book.

Of all the people she thought would come to check on her, Livella was the last she'd expected. She had almost forgotten they'd brought the woman with them until after the battle, when she saw Livella rattled by Janis's fight in the street with Prost and then Riln.

"I could use some time out of the forest. It's getting old," Livella spat. The woman squinted as Janis's orb pierced her vision, blinking until her eyes adjusted to the alternative source of brightness.

Janis raised an eyebrow, though she knew the newcomer wouldn't be able to see it. How Livella had become so outspoken and opinionated she didn't know. She thought perhaps that since Livella was coming to terms with the fact that she couldn't leave, she was learning to be more comfortable around them.

Janis couldn't say the change disappointed her.

Maybe she'll be able to defend herself if we get attacked again, Janis thought.

"We're still a week's time from Terris Green. You'd best get used to it to save yourself the grief," Janis noted.

She hadn't realized she'd hidden the small black book behind her back, but now that she knew it was Livella, Janis didn't feel the need to hide it. While she didn't think Livella was the kind of woman Janis could confide in, she knew that the two were equally caught up in this mess against their will.

"What's that?" Livella asked, noticing the small book once Janis pulled it out.

"I'm—not sure," Janis replied, eyeing the book once more. "I got it from one of the Watchlight men in Stilten."

It wasn't technically true, but Janis didn't want to broach the topic of Macks and Luden at the moment.

In the dim Light of her orb, Janis saw Livella make a disgusted face.

"Is that a book? Why do you have a book—"

The moment her eyes landed on the cover, Livella gasped.

"Why do you have *that*? Why does it have *his* name on it?!"

She was practically yelling, her tone of voice making Janis uncomfortable with their dark surroundings.

Janis was about to ask who she meant when the familiarity of the color hit her. The shining silver of the text matched that of the odd creatures they'd encountered in the war room back at Terris Green. If she overlooked the shining blue of her reflected Light, she realized it matched the smoke, save the dirt and debris the torrent had picked up, which had surrounded Riln and Prost in Stilten.

"You can read this?" Janis asked. She held the cover of the small book up in the air so that Livella could see it.

"Yes! Can't you read? Isn't that something assassins have to learn before they become professional?"

Livella sounded aghast.

Staring at her, Janis held it closer to her.

"It's not written in Lindradian, Livella," Janis told the woman.

Livella continued to stare at the book, her eyes wide.

"How can that be? I can read it just fine, at least, that word—" Livella paused.

Janis wasn't sure how it was possible for the woman to look even more scared, but she did. Janis gingerly opened the book, breathing evenly to cope with the intense tingling that spread up her arm as she grabbed the cover with her free hand. Stepping to the side, Janis positioned herself so that the hovering orb of Light would reflect the silver writing on the black pages of the book.

"This, can you read this too?" Janis asked.

Her companion squinted in the darkness, then shook her head.

"No, it's too dark. I can't—"

Janis reacted by looking at her orb of Light, willing it to expand. It did, growing to the size of her palm.

Livella jumped, obviously not expecting the change in the Light. She eyed the orb, then stepped closer again.

"Yes, it's written in Lindradian. Can't you see that?" The woman turned and looked at Janis curiously.

"No, it's in an unfamiliar language," she told Livella.

That the ink was like the odd creatures they'd seen, and that Ugglyn's name was written on the front, made her want to drop the book and bury it. Narrowing her eyes a bit, Livella's head started moving to the left and right as if she was reading what she saw.

"*—the power of the Void. This is within reach if one simply states the words—*"

"*NO!*" Janis shouted.

As Livella had read the book aloud, the surrounding air thickened, gathering as if the lingering darkness was concentrating in one place. With a quick movement, Janis slammed the book closed, making Livella jump.

"Don't read it, not now," Janis said through her teeth. "I don't think any good would come of it."

In the blue of the Light, Janis could see that Livella looked abashed.

"Sorry, I didn't realize I was doing anything wrong," she said.

Janis rolled her eyes.

"It's fine. If what you say is true, then this book might be connected to Ugglyn. I can't imagine that reading anything even partially influenced by him would be in our best interest," Janis continued.

She held the closed book in her right hand, looking at it hesitantly. Another gust of wind rustled the trees louder. Allowing the air to pass, she turned back to Livella. Janis had just a moment to think about their predicament before she thought to try something.

"Hold this for a moment," Janis said, handing the small book over to Livella. With a curious expression, she held out her hand and let Janis put it there. Trying not to show any reactions, Janis observed Livella as she pretended to reach into her holsters for something.

Livella gave no reaction at all. Janis gave up on her facade and turned to the woman.

"You didn't feel anything, did you?" Janis asked.

Livella cocked her head as if she was a child being given instructions that she couldn't handle or understand.

"It's—just a book. I don't know what you're looking for," Livella said, still confused.

Janis reached out with the cloth and pulled the book away. Her thoughts flipped through possibilities of where the text could have originated, but nothing felt right. She'd only been brought into this mess half a year ago, but she had to trust her instincts because they were all she had. When she didn't respond to Livella, the woman cleared her throat.

"Are you ok? You look angrier than usual," Livella asked. Her arms were now folded across her chest and she raised a brow at Janis.

"When my skin touches the book, it feels—wrong, as if the book is reacting to my touch. When you held it, you said you felt nothing. See the problem?" Janis asked.

Livella continued to stare at her. Gritting her teeth to get a hold of her frustration, Janis relaxed before explaining.

"You've been infused with Ugglyn's power, or so Tryvv said to us. If this text has any association with Ugglyn, it makes sense that it would react to you as it does to me. That you felt nothing just validates the origin of this," Janis said.

The woman paled, then she opened her mouth. It hovered open for a moment before she looked away.

"Oh," she responded.

Her eyes flitted to the book, then back to Janis's face. When she had stared for only a moment, Livella put one foot back and leaned slightly away from it.

"That is why I didn't want you to read from it," Janis said, wrapping the book gingerly in her handkerchief and replacing it in her belt.

Livella's eyes widened.

"Lanser—I was reading about the power of the Void—"

Janis didn't think it was possible for someone to pale even further, but Livella managed to in that moment. Something hung in the air between them, and it made Janis squirm from discomfort. Before she'd stopped Livella, something had formed in the surrounding space. Her skin crawled at knowing that Livella could have summoned something from Ugglyn, or perhaps even the anti-god himself.

In response to the thought, Janis increased the size of the Lighting orb she had summoned. The Light spread farther into the surrounding trees, the shadows from the trees and brush sharpening in the intensifying Light. Livella's eyes snapped to the Light, and she shivered.

"Do you *have* to do that? Those things are creepy," Livella said.

Janis smirked.

"Now you know how I felt when I first Awakened. It's completely unnatural and unnerving. Though for some reason seeing you squirm is amusing," Janis joked.

Livella glared at her. After they held each other's gaze for a moment, Livella sighed and turned around, her arms still folded on her chest.

She stepped toward the rest of the group before she paused.

"Actually—before we go back—" Livella said, her back still to Janis.

The sounds of their group settling in for the night drifted over the slight breeze through the eaves. Men and women talked, the fire crackled, horses whinnied and complained about needing food.

Livella's pause felt even more potent with these sounds present. The quiet between the two didn't bother her. Janis thrived on quiet. She thrived on leaving tension and silence in the air. It was an opportunity for her to assert her power over the other if she held still and kept her gaze.

She did this now, staring hotly at Livella's hair, waiting for the woman to turn around to see her looking. When she finally did, Janis wasn't disappointed.

In the shining Light of her orb, Livella's eyes widened and she jumped, seeing Janis's intense gaze. After a moment of recovery, Livella looked down.

"Mind if I try holding the book once more? I didn't know what you were looking for before now, but I would like to see it again."

Janis cocked her head. This was a whole new woman. Something about the exchange in Stilten had changed her. Livella never asked for anything, especially not from Janis. Though it was refreshing to hear her say anything, Janis didn't trust the changes.

"I don't think so, no. We know now that it's of Ugglyn. I think the best we can do is leave it alone until we are somewhere not in the open," Janis offered.

Livella pressed her lips together. She still looked at the ground, but Janis could see her reaction.

"If you think that's best, then sure."

She sounded dejected. Normally, emotions like that wouldn't bother Janis in the least, but something had changed in her during the vision she'd had atop the bar in the city. The emotion from Livella slammed into her, making her feel guilty, though she didn't believe she had any reason to.

Janis let out a loud breath. This got Livella's attention.

"Fine, but don't read it out loud. It would only mean trouble," Janis said.

Livella nodded but held out her hand as Janis reached to her belt and grabbed the book. As she did, the cloth fell free and her fingers touched the leather. The same intense tingling ran up her hand and she gritted her teeth.

It's like the book is trying to push my hand away, she thought.

Once her fingers left the leather, the feeling stopped. Livella smiled grimly, then opened the book. Janis watched as the woman turned so that the Light of the orb ran over the pages. Even as she did, Janis noticed a dark mist that hovered around the edge. When she'd seen the book before, she hadn't looked close enough to notice it. Now she could see tendrils twisting and writhing out of the book. She shivered as she remembered seeing a similar thing in the cave back at Terris Green.

They stood there in silence. Livella's eyes wandered to the page before she flipped the page over to the next one. The silence was once again palpable as Janis stared at the woman. A mostly translucent silver mist hovered, tendrils dancing from the book like grass in the wind.

Suddenly, a column of silvery black smoke erupted from Livella. A loud *whoosh* filled Janis's ears and she jumped back in alarm. The column shot through the canopy above and into the sky. Despite the darkness, the column reflected the red light of Stellan high above them. Janis's eyes shot to Livella, who kept observing the book. Janis's heart raced and she breathed shallowly. Sounds of alarm sounded from their camp through the forest.

Panicked, Janis reached out and grabbed her Light orb. In a swift motion, she flung the orb through the column. A sound like shattering glass echoed through the night before the column dissipated into nothing, extinguishing their Light with it. The forest plunged into dingy red darkness. This made Livella yelp and drop the book. It struck the ground with a sound that shouldn't have accompanied a text so small.

"What in Lanser's name was that?!" Livella said.

Her hands were clenched by her sides as she scanned the surrounding forest.

"*Were you reading it*?" Janis asked.

Her voice came out harsh, and she saw the effects of her tone in Livella's expression as she paled. But Janis didn't have time to feel bad right now.

"Umm, no, you were right there. You didn't hear me. I th-think—"

Janis shook her head.

"Not out loud, in your head?!" Janis snapped.

Livella's eyes widened.

"Yes. Did something happen? I didn't mean—"

Janis didn't allow the woman to finish her sentence. She rushed forward and grabbed Livella's hand. With a swift motion, she scooped up the book, wincing again at the tingling, and shoved it in her belt before marching

Livella to their camp. Livella began sputtering various things as Janis dragged her through the trees.

Bursting through the trees, many Evenir warriors looked in their direction. A few, though not as many as Janis would have preferred, armed themselves and faced them. If they were to be ambushed, Janis feared they'd be overtaken with a reaction like this.

"We need to move—*now*," Janis said.

She wasn't talking to anyone in particular; she was just saying it out loud to cause people to react. When no one did, she started to shout again but was stopped by Avryn's shuffling through the crowd.

"What is happening?" Avryn said. "What was that thing in the sky?" His tone was fierce but not forceful. There was fear in his eyes; it was obvious the moment she saw them.

"We don't have time to discuss it. Whatever it was, everyone in the area doubtless saw it. If Watchlight saw it, they may be on their way here now," Janis replied.

Avryn's eyes widened before he locked his jaw and nodded.

"We move," he agreed.

Turning sharply, Avryn threw his hands in the air and called for the group to move out as fast as they could.

Her mind reeled at the memory of the odd pillar of smoke they'd just seen. For a moment her eyes snapped to Livella, who had resumed her pale visage. Based on her reaction, Janis didn't think the woman intended foul play. Janis moved to the mount she'd been using and checked her things. For a moment she considered putting the small book in a pack so she wouldn't have it near her person any longer, but she kept it close.

As the group began moving through the night, Janis could only wonder how Macks had found the book, and how he'd wrapped himself in matters of Ugglyn.

Most of all, Janis knew they needed to get out of this place as soon as possible.

6

A flicker of something in the night caught Prost's attention. The moment he saw it in the corner of his eye, a burning sensation blossomed within him. It filled him with the thrill of a fight, the anticipation of overwhelming an enemy.

Before he could try to understand the feeling itself, Ugglyn's voice pressed into his mind.

Ah, there you are, my friend, Ugglyn whispered.

The voice, while imposing, came and went as if it was carried on a wind. Prost knew he was the only one who could hear the warbling of the anti-god, but he still had to resist the urge to look around to see if anyone else heard.

Prost closed his eyes, trying to focus. *What are you on about?* he pressed in his mind.

While he thought it, he turned to inspect the column of silver-black smoke that rose in the distance. Before Ugglyn could respond, the column broke and disappeared into nothingness. Prost's heart raced as he realized what he'd seen looked similar to the swirling smoke that had engulfed him earlier in Stilten.

That, my Voidbearer, is the way to my freedom, Ugglyn whispered to him. Satisfaction filled Prost's chest, along with images of innocent men and women scattering and running from the silvery smoke coalescing around them. Prost growled and shook his head, awarding him odd looks from those around him.

"Sir, wha' was tha'?" someone asked to his right.

He turned to see one of their companions staring behind him, pointing into the sky.

Watchlight continued to travel on the road south of Stilten, the sky only visible through the wide break in the canopy above. Though restricted, the column of smoke had been unmistakable from their vantage point.

"It is nothing of our concern. We march back to the compound—"

His words were cut off as Ugglyn tried to assume control. Instead of continuing his sentence, garbled sounds erupted from his mouth, causing more men and women around them to stare in confusion.

"Sir? Are you all right?" another woman asked.

Prost continued to fight until Ugglyn's force subsided. Straightening his back, Prost looked at the woman. He hadn't realized it was Lathe before now. The woman's cropped hair matched in color and style with her brother, Vint. Save for her chest, there would be little else showing she was a woman.

"I'm fine. I am just recovering still from the loss of Riln," he replied.

Lathe continued to stare, doubt visible in her face, but she nodded and returned to leading her horse.

No! That is the text I need! You will lead Watchlight there to retrieve it! Ugglyn screamed in Prost's head.

Prost gritted his teeth, forcing himself not to shout out loud. After a moment's concentration, Ugglyn receded once more.

"Vint!" Prost yelled.

When no one responded, Prost shouted the name once more.

A muffled reply sounded over the heads of the entourage. Though Prost didn't hear the words, he assumed it was Vint responding to his call. Moments later, the burly man's form slipped through the horses behind Prost. Vint guided his mount through those following behind to meet Prost.

"How far until we get back to our enclave?" Prost asked.

Vint narrowed his eyes, then looked past Prost into the trees. His eyes became wistful and then they glowed a steady red. After a beat, the man's eyes faded and he spoke.

"Four days, tha's all. Weather's fine, no storms brewin' far as I can tell," Vint said.

"Good," Prost replied, facing forward.

The group lapsed into silence as the horses' hooves clopped on the dirt road. His thoughts drifted to the feeling of the smoke-like sword he'd held earlier that day. Ugglyn had assumed control of his mouth during that moment, but he recalled the word the anti-god had used.

Voidweaving, Prost thought.

Ugglyn's presence pressed into his mind, causing Prost to suck in air.

You push me away, then dare revel in the power that I *wield? You shan't dare think of such things without allowing me the control I deserve*, Ugglyn said, contempt filling Prost's being.

As far as anti-gods went, Ugglyn was far more emotional than Prost could have ever imagined. He once again closed his eyes and breathed, trying to think of how to respond to the unwelcome inhabitant in his brain.

You entered my *body, not the other way around. I rule myself*, Prost pressed into his thoughts.

Amusement filled him.

Your rule is weak, then, Ugglyn whispered to him.

Prost felt his eyes expand, as if someone held them open by force. A coldness gathered there, making Prost shiver from the discomfort. Red orbs continued to hover in the air around them as they traveled. One of the Lighters, likely Neera, held them so they could travel with ease in the night. Dark smoke formed in the surrounding air. Prost shook in fear. The forest was still visible on either side. Watchlight operatives continued to travel on their horses next to him. None of them appeared to notice anything happening.

Prost watched as the silvery black smoke coalesced into two forms. His breath caught when he recognized one as himself. A statue form of him stood frozen while another formed next to it, of another man. Once this one had formed, Prost recognized it as the man he'd met in the fields of Erisdell months ago. His name eluded Prost, but it was soon exposed as voices filled his mind.

What is this sorcery? Prost thought.

Satisfaction blossomed in his chest, once again emotions that weren't his own pushing through his person, making Prost shiver.

You've always wanted to See, have you not? Ugglyn teased.

"I don't want apologies, Iridian. I want answers."

Prost's own voice echoed in the air. He noticed the mouth of the smoke form of himself moving in time with the words.

"We'll address your tardiness in a moment," the form of him spoke.

It felt so familiar. Prost's memory pressed backward through the past few months. The last time they'd visited the Plains of Erisdell, they'd been following Janis and Marric. They had stopped to visit one of their men there, a handler of creatures.

Why am I seeing this right now? Prost thought.

He looked to see if anyone else was hearing the same things. They continued to travel forward in silence.

"Where is the boy? Your first letter placed them here three days ago, but your next said they had moved on," the smoke Prost said.

Let us remember your self-control. This is a perfect example of it, I'd say, Ugglyn spoke again in his mind.

"Y-Yes sir. They went north, straight north without much deviation," the smoke form of the man Iridian replied.

Prost's skin chilled. He remembered the encounter now. He realized then why Ugglyn was dangling this scene in front of him.

The two smoke figures continued to talk, just the way Prost remembered it. Iridian had been tasked with stalling Marric and Janis and he'd failed. Marric and Janis had destroyed a herd of trained spine hogs with companions.

"And who is following them now?" Prost's smoke-form asked.

The feeling was odd, as if Prost was living a memory but carrying out his life in the present. He felt nauseous as he tried to process the past vision and the present all at once.

"I didn't send a person to follow them. I sent a bird!" Iridian's form said.

The movements of the smoke forms were exactly what they'd been when Prost had been there before. He couldn't remember each detail, but seeing them here laid out in front of him, he knew they were the same.

The hair on his neck stuck up as Prost continued to process what he was seeing.

"And what's the bird's name?"

His body ran cold as he remembered then what he'd done.

"Speeker, that's her. Why would you—?"

Iridian's words were interrupted as the smoke-Prost slashed with a knife, cutting the man's throat. The smoke-Iridian fell to the ground, the sound of him dying replaying before Prost. All at once, the forms puffed into the air, disappearing into nothing.

For a man who rules himself, you act instinctually, Ugglyn drawled in his mind. *Shall I call up another example?*

Prost stared forward. Rather than respond to the anti-god's taunts, Prost demanded Ugglyn explain what he'd just witnessed.

What is this sorcery? What have you done to me?

You've wanted to bear the Light for years now, but you don't want Lanser's poison as a power. I've given you something he can't. You can See just like any Seer can.

This got Prost's attention.

Show me Janis, then, he thought.

Ugglyn chuckled inside, the laugh echoing as if they stood within a stone cavern.

The dark smoke formed once again in front of him, a perfect image of Janis coalescing there. Another woman, one Prost didn't recognize, stood next to her. This one held a small book of some sort in her hand. Janis stared off past the woman at something else. The woman Prost didn't know was reading the contents of the pages, her smoky eyes moving across the small pages.

Prost watched as a pillar of smoke formed around them and shot into the sky.

The smoke-form of Janis held up her hand, creating a ball of what Prost assumed was Light shown in smoke form. In a flash, she launched it through the pillar, shattering it until it disappeared into nothing.

"What in Lanser's name was that?!" the unfamiliar woman exclaimed.

"*Were you reading it*?" Smoke-Janis asked. The stress was clear in her voice.

"Umm, no, you were right there. You didn't hear me. I th-think—"

The Janis form shook her head. "Not out loud, in your head?!" she snapped.

The smaller woman's eyes widened.

"Yes. Did something happen? I didn't mean—"

The smoke figures disappeared as quickly as they had appeared.

Yes, this was only moments ago. It seems the other Voidbearer attempted to summon me before that wench got in her way, Ugglyn sneered. *We must get that book. Lead the army toward them. I must have my power—*

Prost pressed back once again, forcing Ugglyn out of his mind. He hadn't realized it, but his fists were clenched.

No, he thought firmly, pressing back against the force in his mind, *I will not let you control me even with whatever power you've brought with you.*

An echoing hiss rang through Prost's mind then as Ugglyn receded into the depths of his mind. Prost knew the anti-god was there, but he wasn't pressing any longer.

"Sir? Is everything ok?" Vint's voice cut through Prost's thoughts.

He looked up sharply, struggling to keep the anger out of his voice, then realized he'd stopped his horse to watch the second scene of shadowy figures. Setting his jaw, Prost held his confidence and nodded.

"Yes, keep moving," he confirmed. "We have to get home before Evenir has the chance to ambush us." Vint, noticing Prost's resolve return, flipped his mount around and continued forward, the rest of the group following.

Prost focused forward, allowing his mind to recount what had just happened without allowing Ugglyn to take over again. He couldn't describe how he knew, but Ugglyn's voice disappeared somewhere deep in his mind, poised to return. Enjoying the quiet, Prost thought of the shadowy apparitions he'd seen just moments before. While they didn't have the detailed features of humans, the forms were strikingly accurate of the people in the memory. At least, the one of himself in the Plains of Erisdell. So the other images? The one of Janis and the unfamiliar woman?

Ugglyn mentioned the other Voidbearer. Could this be her? Prost wondered.

Voidweaving. That was what Ugglyn called this power inside him. The word had no familiarity to Prost at all. Then again, he hadn't been a religious person for most of his life. Only after being imprisoned in Watchlight had he started worshiping. Prost's parents, wealthy as they were, never mixed themselves up in any form of religion. Growing up, he'd not thought much about a deity at all. Still, he wondered if there were other texts that spoke of this power, this Voidweaving.

Shaking his head, Prost focused back on the images he'd seen of Janis and the other woman. If the memory he'd seen was correct, they'd been reading from the book, some text, which Ugglyn wanted desperately. The moment Prost had the thought, he felt Ugglyn stir inside his mind. Somewhat panicked, he pushed the thought away, instead focusing on the aspects of the powers he'd just seen. Prost recalled the sword of silvery smoke he'd created in Stilten. Though he'd never experienced Conjuring, that felt like what he'd seen Conjurers do. Ugglyn mentioned Seeing, and he had seen something he'd not experienced before.

Prost didn't know what it meant.

The best thing they could do was move, keep traveling to their base. They'd need to make a plan. Prost would need to share the news of Riln's death and his rise to leadership. He knew there would be opposition. Those who disagreed with him would die. Only after stabilizing Watchlight could they move forward.

While he knew logically this was what needed to happen, it irked Prost. The scene he'd just witnessed had awoken something inside. Even now, he felt a gravitational pull to the east. The feeling persisted, subtle but firm. If he let his mind lapse for too long, the pull became stronger, willing him to change directions. Prost kept vigilant, moving with his men and women south to their base. Despite his efforts, one thought kept lingering in his mind. Killing Janis.

Prost wasn't sure if the force came from Ugglyn or from himself.

7

Chaos erupted throughout the street.

Marric's stomach clenched as he witnessed the destruction of the road and surrounding houses at his hand. In his mind, he could See multiple things happening at once. A Watchlight man and woman collided together before slamming into the wall of a nearby shop. Another Watchlight man screamed in pain as his forearm was ripped by the cobblestones exploding upward from the Destroying blast. Jord glared at him from behind, holding his hand up and summoning a Destroying ball of his own. Eyes still filled with Seeing Light, Marric Saw all this happening at once. He'd not experienced this type of Seeing before. It was overwhelming—yet empowering.

For the first time since he'd left Wurren, Marric wasn't nervous. While his insides still writhed from the destruction he'd just brought around him with his new second-born power, he felt calm, collected. He'd Awakened with three abilities, which made him feel as if he'd be unable to develop another. Yet Avryn had mentioned that any Lightbearer could develop a another. Marric assumed he would never develop another, given that he'd started with three.

The world spun around him, his eyelids still closed, as he turned to face Jord. His former friend's eyes glowed a steady red, and Marric somehow knew he was Seeing the present in the same way. Images spun through his consciousness of Watchlight and Evenir operatives around fighting and citizens observing through windows. Marric felt this type of Sight should make him incapable of functioning, but he was processing it.

"So." Jord's voice was both far away and close as one of Marric's visions was affixed within feet of his opponent. "You've learned to use Seeing for combat. A pity you couldn't use it to save your *friend* over there."

Jord gestured to the body of Shrell lying facedown near Crents. Marric's mind buzzed, fury engulfing his frame. He held out his hand and created a Destroying ball, ready to Move it at Jord. Marric could See it, he could See that Jord wouldn't be able to react in time, his Seeing playing out the future. Yet Marric paused, not wanting to kill his friend. His mind continued to process the present and immediate futures around him. Despite the empowering feeling of Seeing everything, Marric could feel his energy draining.

"Don't speak disrespect of the dead," Marric spat, raising his hand with the blue orb still hovering there. The moment he did, Jord raised his own hand.

"Ah-ah-ah, watch where you toss that. I can See the future as well as you can. We wouldn't want to cause any unnecessary casualties," Jord taunted.

As the words came out, Marric's mind flashed forward in time. He witnessed his rage overcoming him, causing him to Move the orb at Jord. His former vision showed Jord getting ripped to shreds, but now Jord reacted as if he knew the trajectory of Marric's orb. The two collided midair, an explosion of red and blue Light rocking the surrounding air. Marric felt sick as he watched the wave ripple outward. The wave slammed into Narinda, the force disintegrating her. Crents and Jord's companion were killed similarly.

Teeth clenched, Marric's mind flipped back to the present. As if knowing his thoughts, Jord spoke.

"It's no use. We're at a stalemate. Your decisions affect my future and mine yours. While we both See all, we can't gain footing over the other. But even you can feel it now. It's draining you," Jord said smugly.

Marric's breathing sped up. He could see Narinda had slain her opponent and was Fixing her arm. His mind processed another future, Jord throwing his orb in her direction, the power ripping her to shreds while she focused on her wound. Air sucked through his teeth as Marric reacted.

As if in slow motion, Jord let his orb fly. Marric threw out his hand but also tossed his own orb left, toward the road between Crents and their enemies. Jord's face contorted as Marric assumed he Saw what would happen. Rather than rush toward Crents like he planned, he stepped back and covered his face with his hands. Everything came to fruition as Marric's Moving shoved Jord's red orb away from Narinda, the power exploding the side of a shop. Narinda's head snapped upward, eyes shocked at what had almost just killed her. At the same moment, Marric's orb slammed into the ground, stones and dirt exploding outward. Crents cried out in pain as debris pelted him. Jord was prepared, the debris slamming into his cloak and arms covering his exposed face and skin.

Jord's companion was not so lucky. Marric realized only then that though he and Jord communicated without words, the Watchlight man was not aware of the impending danger. The man had moved right on top of where the orb landed. He disappeared with a scream of pain. Tattered clothes and blood were all that remained.

Marric's stomach clenched as he realized what he'd just done. Somehow he knew this was one of the few options he had. He'd Seen them all within a small moment and knew this was what he had to do. His energy continued to be sucked away until his omniscient Seeing snuffed out. The last thing he Saw before it did was Narinda's horrified expression at what he'd just done.

Guilt swept over him.

Fortunately, Jord's own use of the Sight in this way ended at the same time. The two boys panted, staring at each other from twenty paces away.

Jord spoke first.

"This isn't over, Marric. Once Riln has taken over Lindrad, you'll be the first we come for. You and your friends will be our slaves or dead," he spat.

As if out of nowhere, a woman riding a stallion appeared from the road behind Jord. Hand outstretched, she reached down and grabbed Jord's hand, hefting him onto the horse. The next moment, they were speeding the other direction on the road. Marric cursed, Conjuring his bow and launching an arrow toward them. Unfortunately, summoning the object had taken longer than usual. It was as if his Lightbearing was sluggish and slower.

Marric's mind felt foggy, every movement somewhat slow. He jumped as Narinda stepped up beside him, a grim look on her face.

"We need to help the others and get the boy," she said.

Nodding, Marric turned around to see the destruction he'd caused. A few Watchlight men and women lay dead from his blast before. The others were calling for a retreat. They watched, weapons ready, as their enemies escaped through side alleys and down the street.

Shaking his head, Marric tried to dispel the fog.

He wasn't successful.

"I need to help. Looks like there are a lot of people injured," Narinda said. She eyed him, expecting something. Marric realized she was waiting for him to give her the go-ahead. He nodded, showing that she should go. As she moved down the street toward the fallen Evenir members, Marric turned and stumbled toward Crents.

The small boy stared at his hands, a few cuts there from the road debris that had pelted him just moments before.

"Crents," Marric croaked. His voice was weaker than normal.

When Crents didn't reply, Marric knelt. He fell harder than he expected, his energy still exhausted from the strange Seeing event. His knees ached from the sharp, hard stone, but he ignored it as he pushed on his friend's shoulder.

At first Marric thought the boy was completely unaware, but as he looked closer, he realized Crents was staring hard at the broken ground ten paces in front of him. Following his gaze, Marric noted the broken road. A Destroying orb—his or Jord's, Marric wasn't sure—had landed just short of where Crents was sitting against the wall of the wooden building. Marric pressed his lips together, thinking about how to respond. Before he could say anything, Narinda shouted to him. Alerted by her voice, Marric's head snapped in her direction, where a Watchlight member ran at him.

Without hesitation, he flung his hands outward, the figure glowing blue before flying backward and landing hard on his back. He groaned in pain, trying to stand. Before he could move, Marric held out his hand, holding the man in place. His body wreathed in the Moving Light, the man growled, unable to move.

Despite Marric's hold on the man, he was able to move his mouth.

Oddly, the man started laughing.

Marric's stomach twisted at the sound, his skin tingling from the eerie laughter.

"Thot Oi'd ge' the drop on yeh loik we did on yer mum," the man said.

The tingling intensified within Marric and he let go of the man out of shock. Without hesitation, the man barreled right at him, a sword materializing out of red Light. With a shout, the man lunged forward, slicing at Marric's arm. Gasping, Marric ducked out of the way, but just too late. The Conjured sword sliced his bicep, pain searing upward into his shoulder. As the blood trickled from Marric's arm, adrenaline flowed through him. He spun and pushed outward with his Moving. With a grunt, the man slid backward, the blue Light fading quickly from Marric's short burst of power.

"So—yeh ain't a Shielder, then? Makin' it easy fer me," the man drawled before advancing.

Before Marric could act, the man jumped forward, his sword coming right at Marric's chest. Marric's eyes exploded with Light, the world slowing almost to a stop. He could See the man's Conjured sword glowing red, sharp and as real as ever. Now that his mind could See what was happening, Marric prepared to Conjure a sword of his own to block the man's attack. Just before he could, however, the man's body slowly spread with blue Light. At that moment, Marric's Seeing stopped, his energy spent from the experience once more.

Roaring, the man flew backward and slammed hard into the wall. In an instant, Narinda was there, a fierce look on her face. With a grunt, she slipped her short sword into the man's shoulder, pinning him to the wood of the building behind him.

Marric fell to his knees, his exhaustion overwhelming him. Blood flowed from his arm still, soaking his sleeve and dripping to the ground. His mind swam from what had just happened. He'd just experienced this type of Seeing with Jord, but it still felt overwhelming.

How did that happen? Marric thought. *I didn't Move him. I was trying to Conjure something.* "That—worked," a timid voice said behind him.

Marric turned, his vision fuzzing somewhat as he moved too quickly.

Crents was looking past him at the man pinned to the wall. Narinda was speaking to him, but Marric couldn't hear what either of them was saying.

"That—was *you*?" Marric said.

Crents, still wide-eyed, just nodded. His eyes still focused on the scene on the other side of the road.

"No! Oi'll git the lot of yeh! Tha' boy will die loik 'is mother 'afore him. Terrible leader, she was. Leadin' Lightbearers to captivity, she was—"

The man grunted as Narinda punched him across the face.

"That's enough from you. If you won't be of any help, then we've no use for you," she spat, slipping a dagger out of a hidden sheath in her belt.

"Wait!" Marric called to her.

A wicked grin spread across the man's face as Narinda paused. She didn't turn away from the man, but she didn't kill him.

"What do you know of my mother? How do you know who I am?" Marric asked.

He could feel himself trembling. His whole life he'd known that his mother had died, only to find out she had lived until a mere six months before his own awakening. Rather than respond, the man continued to grin, blood staining his teeth, before spitting on the ground. The sight repulsed Marric, but another burst of anger and adrenaline was flowing through him. He had no attachment to his mother, having never met her, but his emotions were volatile after everything that had happened today.

"Tsk, tsk, tsk, asking fer infermation widout offerin' me anythin' such loik—"

Marric stopped the man by tossing a small ball of Light at the road a few paces away. A loud crack rang in their ears and echoed down the street as the road exploded there, pelting the man with debris. Narinda flinched as some hit her. Her eyes flicked to Marric. There was fear there.

A part of Marric felt bad at causing this in his friend, but he had to know.

"Tell—me—now," Marric said.

The man scowled, a few cuts dripping blood along his face. His clothes were ripped along his shoulders and sleeves from the same explosion.

"Nah, Oi fink not," the man said before jumping up and throwing his hands outward. Narinda yelled as she, glowing red, was flung backward down the street.

"Yeh'll die at Watchloit's blade jus' loik yer mum!"

Marric's mind moved quicker than he expected, but not fast enough. He Conjured a bow and shot an arrow right at the approaching man. Before it could strike its mark, the blue Light arrow flashed purple, the man's red Moving Light taking hold and flipping it away. This time, no help came from his small friend behind. The tip of the cloaked man's sword flew toward Marric, but it was deflected at the last moment by Marric's own Moving.

Breathing hard, Marric stumbled back, fear taking over. He glanced at Narinda, who was struggling to get up. The man had thrown her back at least fifteen paces before she landed on the hard dirt street. A roar brought his attention back to the horrific-looking Watchlight man. Instinctively Marric ducked. While it helped him avoid the brunt of the blow, the assailant's fist still came in contact with his head. Pain sprung through his skull and his vision fuzzed. Falling to the ground, Marric tried to look upward. He couldn't see anything clearly. Desperate, Marric pushed his hands outward, a flash of blue energy waving outward. A grunt came from somewhere in front of him, followed by a body thudding on the ground.

For a moment they each panted, trying to get their bearings. Marric's vision cleared just enough for him to see the man on the ground before him, shaking his head, disoriented. Marric stumbled backward, his hands aching from the rough dirt of the street below him. He was losing feeling in his arm, blood flowing.

"Yer mum was roit tricky t'kill too."

The man sniffled and wiped his nose. Marric heard the words and wanted to ask more, to pin the man down and get him to say why they'd wanted to kill his mother. Until now, he'd known little about his mother's death. Now this man was claiming he had information.

Why did you kill her?! Marric thought, trying to find the strength to yell it out loud. His mind flashed through the situation, knowing the brutish man would come at him once more and soon. He prepared himself, knowing his opponent was a Mover.

"Riln promised a fancy sum t' the one 'oo could take 'er down. Oi wasn't the lucky bloke t'git 'er, but Oi was there," the man said, standing unsteadily. "'Er Shield failed 'er in the end, as it will again, yeh Evenir scum! Yeh shouldn't 'ave meddled in Ulivar!"

He roared once more before running right at Marric. Sucking in a breath, Marric Conjured a few heavy rocks of Light and Moved them at the man. Sneering, the man easily Moved them away as he ran. Then his eyes widened in shock as his chest sprouted an arrow made of the same Light.

"Fog it all," he said before falling to his knees.

Marric stood strong, his Conjured bow strung with another arrow. Just after lobbing the Conjured rocks, he'd summoned his bow and shot right between them. The man hadn't seen it coming.

"Riln—will—git yeh—"

The man never finished his words as he fell dead to the road.

Marric's heart still raced, yet he stared at the man, tears forming there. Not once in this whole situation had he thought much about his mother and how she'd led Evenir until her death. Now questions of her burned in his mind, filling him with a new obsession. He scanned the road for more Watchlight men and women but found none. Instead, a few of their own stumbled in their direction.

His mind released the tension and Marric fell to the ground, his knees barely feeling the pain given that the rest of him hurt more. Shaking his head, he gazed at Narinda, who was finally rising. Her hand glowed brightly as she Fixed parts of her body that were injured. She looked haggard, dark circles under her eyes and a gaunt look to her face. Once her eyes landed on Marric, they opened wide. Shuffling, she moved to his side and began Fixing him.

Marric held up a hand, trying to stop her, but she kept working. He only realized then that he wasn't listening. He could hear her talking, but it was drowned out by the loud ringing in his ears from the intensity of the last hour.

After a few moments, her voice started reaching him.

"—blasted Watchlight. This was worse than any of us could have planned for." Narinda wiped her brow, her forehead shiny with sweat and dirt.

The night had come, the red light of Stellan shining on the walls of the buildings. It cast long shadows on the road where it peeked through the break in the rooftops above. The moon wasn't high in the sky yet, likely just coming over the horizon. Blue Light mixed with it from what Marric assumed were still Narinda's Lighting orbs hovering over the street.

She cursed. Marric tensed inside, but his normal outward reactions failed to activate. He was too tired.

"I'm exhausted. I can't get any more Fixing out of me," she said, collapsing on the road next to him. "I stopped the bleeding at least. Let's hope one of our other Fixers is still alive to help."

Marric nodded but said nothing else. His mind was still consumed by the only image of his mother he'd ever seen. The door to the Evenir war room filled his thoughts. His mind's eye moved close to the space in the carved tree where his mother's face sat. It wasn't until then that he could see the resemblance. Those were his eyes, his mouth. Marric needed to know why Riln wanted her dead.

More than anything, Marric was angry. Angry that Shrell had just died; angry that he never knew his mother; angry that he'd Awakened as a Destroyer.

He spoke before he could think more. "We need to get back to Terris Green. Something's wrong, I can feel it." For some reason, the mention of his mother and Watchlight's killing her discomforted him more than just the death of his mother.

Narinda nodded, looking at the ground.

"I'll be glad to be somewhere safe after this fog of a night," she replied.

Now that Watchlight had retreated, their allies moved in from the square to help the three of them, and Marric could still only focus on one thing.

He would never be the same after tonight.

8

Janis sat in a stone chair within the war room, facing the wall. Avryn was muttering to Varith and Alsry about the events of the past week. After the incident with the small book they'd found, the travels back had been quiet. Janis still couldn't believe they'd made it back without any problems, but she was grateful. She didn't expect how exhausted she'd feel after using her Lightbearing to fight Riln in Stilten.

And now he's dead, Janis thought.

She thought she should be happy that the man was gone, but something inside her squirmed at the realization. It had been only a few weeks since she'd seen Tryvv and found out about the pact sealing Ugglyn. Janis lamented the loss of her past life. Things had been much simpler when she only had herself to care for.

"Oi, yeh're lost in yer thoughts again. What yeh got goin' on in that noggin' o' yers?" Harmel said beside her.

Refocusing on the others, Janis eyed the man next to her. His hair was longer than it had been when she'd first met him, likely because he hadn't found the time to cut it with all that was going on. His eyes were full of mirth, as usual, but there was something else there. Crow's feet sank deep on either side of his eyes as he smiled his usual goofy grin.

"You wouldn't be interested in what goes on in this mind," Janis said, waving off the comment.

"Sure, sure. Yous just don't wanna tell me the truth, oi finks," Harmel said, leaning back in his chair.

Janis shook her head, looking to the other leaders in the middle of the room. Now that Magness was dead, Evenir didn't have a genuine leader. Her gut wrenched. She knew what Avryn's stance was on the matter. He had convinced the other leaders that Janis should step up and take their former leader's place.

Janis didn't want it.

Still, even she, the sole person wanting out of the whole mess, knew that it was logical. She'd Transformed, become the Prime Lightbearer that she was apparently meant to be.

Yet she still resisted this role.

Quiet laughter brought Janis from her thoughts, and she glanced back at Avryn and the others. He was smiling as he held Varith's shoulder, shaking it back and forth. He was the one laughing, but his eyes held no happiness. Pain was obvious in his gaze as he tore his eyes from the dark-skinned Fixer.

Something warm landed on her hand and Janis tensed, yanking her arm away. She Conjured a dagger of Light and spun toward Harmel. The man's eyes were wide, but his smile remained.

"Well, fer Lanser's sake, yeh aren't dyin' are yeh?" Harmel said, shaking his head.

Janis felt her body react, her face reddening, and she turned away, staring back at the wall. She cursed herself for getting embarrassed.

"Yeh know, even the strongest need summ'on to be there fer 'em," Harmel said to her side.

Despite knowing the words were well-intentioned, Janis hated hearing them. She'd been independent for so long that she didn't like the idea of needing anything other than her own skills.

Unsure of how to respond, she shrugged.

"Thank—you—" Janis said, still looking away.

When Harmel tried to reach out and hold her hand again, she shied away.

"What do you think happened in Stilten?" Janis asked to change the topic.

It was Harmel's turn to shrug.

"Dunno, Oi was with Avryn, 'member? I jus' saw the smoke swirling as we all ran outta there," Harmel said.

Janis's mind reeled as she recalled the events. Her fight with Riln had been the most intense of her life. Yet it didn't come close to the feeling of dread she felt when she'd seen the pillar of silvery smoke, almost mist, really, spinning around Prost and the corpse of Riln.

"—need to wait until we hear from the others," Avryn's voice broke through her thoughts.

She looked up at him. Ever since they'd arrived the day before, she'd been thinking about Marric and the others. They'd sent Rivelen to Arivan with a group to gather the Awakened Lightbearer there. As far as they knew, she'd been successful and would arrive soon. No one had heard from Marric or Shrell since they'd arrived at Wurren. Their greatest Seers had tried to communicate with them a number of times but hadn't had any success.

Her stomach twisted at the thought that something bad could have happened to them.

"What about our new leader?" Varith asked. The man's gaze darted toward Janis but moved away quickly.

Sighing, Avryn shook his head, holding his hand to his forehead.

"That will have to wait. We need every general to discuss that, and we aren't all here. For now, we need to get our bearings. Once Rivelen is back, we can talk about the hearings for the new leader. Based on the timing of our communication with her, that should be any moment now."

They'd been told by the Seers that Rivelen had appeared to them two days ago, showing their expected return to Terris Green.

Janis wasn't eager to see the woman again. She recalled the times when they'd conversed and how annoying she found the lanky blonde's voice. Still, Janis knew she had to at least try. With the recent events of her "Transforming," she felt the need to be nicer to everyone.

"Let's hope that she was successful in retrieving the Lightbearer there," Alsry said, voicing the thoughts Janis had. Before now, she had cared little about gathering Lightbearers, but something had changed. Her mind returned to the moment she'd run back for her dagger in Stilten. The spinning column of silvery smoke whirled in a torrent around Prost, Riln's limp body at his feet. The feeling she'd had when witnessing that was something she hoped she wouldn't feel again.

Dread.

Sheer dread ripped at her insides as she stared at the onslaught of strange smoke-mist. Her whole life she'd been able to keep that dagger, only to lose it to who-knows-what in Stilten.

Maybe Prost picked it up, she thought, hoping the man might want to keep a trophy from her.

Janis assumed Prost was that kind of person, but in this she felt little hope. Based on the events in Stilten, Prost had other things on his mind.

"Lanser, bless us that Rivelen was successful. Another Lightbearer in the hands of Watchlight would have meant trouble for us. Our scuffle with them has taken on a whole new meaning. We're at war now. Numbers mean more than they used to," Avryn said, leaning forward on the war room table with a grim look.

Turrin cleared his throat before speaking.

"Moit Oi speak, sir?" he asked, glancing from Avryn to Janis, then back again.

Janis squirmed at the reaction. It was evidence that the other generals still struggled with her being a leader despite her recent change.

"Speak, please. We are here as generals but also as friends. No need for formalities until a new leader is chosen," Avryn said as he pushed off the table to an upright position. His eyes bore the weight of many problems and people he'd not carried before.

"We need to foind Watchlight's lair an' attack 'em. With them wanderin' abou', Oi don't fink it'll be long 'afore they foind us 'ere," Turrin said.

Avryn looked grim at the words, but he was nodding.

"That is possible, though I doubt it. Our Shielders are very skilled at keeping us hidden from other Seers. We've stationed even more in active duty since the happenings in Stilten."

The conversation continued around her as Janis lapsed into memories. She recalled seeing Macks, broken and bleeding on the ground within the roof. Somehow Janis knew he wasn't dead. For a moment she thought of trying to See him. As far as she knew, Macks wasn't a Shielder. Then again, she only knew of his main Lightbearing skill of Seeing.

The hair on her arms raised as she thought about the possibility of him watching her right now. How many times had he Seen her, watched her without her knowing after he'd abandoned her for dead? Janis expelled the thought, remembering Avryn's words just moments before, that they had Shielders everywhere. Still, Janis resisted the urge to throw up her Shield now. She had the ability, and she was confident in it now, but she held off, only to avoid the questioning gazes of those around her.

Janis wasn't angry. She was past the point of pettiness and anger. More than anything, it intrigued her that her former mentor had hidden so long from her. Especially considering she had informants all over Lindrad.

Varith, the dark-skinned Fixer general, spoke next.

"Well, since we were successful in acquiring the Seer and the Conjurer from Stilten, I'd say the odds are better than we think," the austere man said.

"I am grateful that we were successful with these, but I fear the loss of the others will prove costly for us. We still need to train the two boys as quickly as possible. Even then, they will probably not be battle ready before Watchlight comes."

"Or something worse," Alsry said.

Trease scoffed at the comment. "Leave it ta Alsry t' be positive," she said, folding her arms across her large chest.

Trease's hair was cut so close to her head that you could see the contours of her skull. Janis thought the look was practical, though it did look terrible on her.

"Trease, you didn't see it. That was unnatural. I haven't seen or felt anything like it before in my life," Alsry said, shaking her head. "Something happened in Stilten, and I don't think it was a simple storm."

The room fell silent at the mention of the smoke column. Janis knew it was related to Ugglyn, but she didn't want to make any assumptions as to what it could really mean. In theory, the pact between her and Livella held strong, the anti-god locked away wherever he was.

"Ugglyn," she finally said, turning the heads of those in the room toward her.

"Excuse me?" Avryn replied.

A tension filled the air. Based on the look on Avryn's face, she knew he'd been thinking the same thing. Her voicing the words was different, and he knew it.

Varith scoffed and swirled the mug he held in his left hand. "Seems the assassin is spouting random thoughts again. What does the anti-god have to do with all this?" he asked before taking a slow drink.

"The column we saw in Stilten, it was him. Or it had something to do with him," Janis replied. Her voice was measured, without fear. When she'd seen Prost within the torrent of strange smoke, her dread melded with urgency. Though she couldn't describe the exact feeling, she knew it was the same she'd had when Ugglyn appeared for her and Livella in the very room weeks ago.

"Are you quite certain?" Avryn's voice was calm, yet firm.

Silence once more.

Janis stared the man down before nodding curtly. "Yes, it's related to him."

Trease cursed before making a clawed hand, swiping it through the air in front of her. Janis shook her head at the gesture. Religious people were something she could never understand. Devout followers of Lanserian truly believed that such a simple gesture could have an effect on a being like Ugglyn.

"For our sake, and for Lindrad's sake, I hope you are wrong," Avryn said. "For now, we'll have to hope that our Shielders have kept our location hidden. We need to gather the reports from the rescue parties before we can move forward with confidence."

The party lapsed into silence once more, Varith and Turrin holding a quiet conversation on their side of the room, while Alts and Trease had their own. Avryn continued to stare at the map set out on the war table, his brow tight and furrowed. Janis, after eavesdropping enough to know each of the pairs was not discussing anything of import, settled back into her chair. She allowed herself to be carried away in her Seeing, her vision shifting through blurred colors and arriving just outside of Terris Green.

The sun shone brightly along the terraced hills that covered the complex network of tunnels below. A ragged group of cloaked figures plodded toward a waterfall that slithered through the terraces. Even Janis could appreciate the beauty of what covered the compound Evenir used for refuge. By now she'd had much practice with her Seeing, so she focused more closely on the group approaching. Her mind's eye landed on the lead figure, cloak crimson red and long, covering the haunches of the mount she rode. Rivelen's clothing and hair looked perfect, especially compared to the rest of the group. Yet her face was gaunt and tired, as if she'd run out of energy.

It was clear these men and women had traveled long and hard. Janis knew this was the current time, and she opened her mouth, knowing that despite her vision being elsewhere, her companions in the war room could hear her without trouble. "Rivelen and her company are just without the walls of the compound. She'll be here within the hour."

She could feel her mouth moving and heard Avryn respond, despite still only Seeing the green terraces of the outside. Her vision moved closer until she was a few paces away from Rivelen. The woman looked grim as they rode, and Janis could tell that they'd encountered trouble in their trek to collect the Lightbearer.

For a moment Janis inspected the woman. Her blonde hair hung loose over her shoulders, contrasting the crimson robes in the sunlight. A majority of the party behind her rode quietly, save for a few men and women talking in hushed whispers. It had been a long time since Janis had been in Arivan, but she knew that Rivelen and the others should have been back by now. That they'd been delayed showed that something else had gone awry.

As of now, the other two parties sent to various parts of Lindrad had returned, both having lost their Lightbearers. Watchlight had secured one before Evenir could make it, the other lost to the same poison that killed the poor Fixer boy in T'Arren Vale weeks ago.

Janis balked at how long it had been since that experience. Time couldn't be reined in despite her wishes that it could. Passing time meant little to someone living and relying on their own. As an assassin, the passing of time was only relevant if she was on a job with a deadline. If not, she'd cared little about how quickly the days passed.

Now, each passing day felt like a countdown to something worse. She grimaced, not caring that her physical face on the outside showed the emotion. Under normal circumstances, she wouldn't want to reveal any bit of how she felt, but she knew the people. Janis had learned from Tryvv that she had to trust, so today she would.

As the world around her spun, Janis thought to try spying Marric and Shrell once more. Until now, no Seers had had any success Seeing the group. It was obvious that a Shielder or two was on constant work keeping them hidden. Janis assumed she'd run into the same black wall that always stopped someone trying to See through a Shield, but she inhaled as her vision formed into colors and a crisp scene. Marric rode on a mare at the head of the group, his face stricken with grief.

Janis's insides buzzed at the vision and she spoke out loud.

"I can See Marric, their Shield must have dropped, if only for a moment." Her voice sounded distant and muffled, as if she was under water.

"What do you See? Are they ok?" Avryn asked, his voice eager.

She went quiet, inspecting the group. Their convoy had taken a massive hit, evident by how few their numbers were. Of the ones sent to Wurren, only twenty remained. Sadness welled in Janis's chest, and she pushed it away, trying not to let it overcome her. She gritted her teeth subtly to cope but not show too much to those who watched her. No doubt the entire room was inspecting her.

Trease spoke then, validating her thoughts. "Well, out wif it, eh. What are yeh Seein' of 'em?" Her voice was hard, annoyed.

"They've been fighting, it looks like they've lost—" Janis paused, reluctant to give too much detail. "They've lost many."

Avryn cursed, a pounding on wood echoing in her ears. Janis recognized the sound of Avryn's fist crashing on the table in the middle of the war room.

He's been doing that a lot lately, Janis thought, feeling something like pity for the temporary leader of Evenir.

For a moment Janis tried to get her bearings. While she could still hear

Avryn, she could also hear the horses and sounds of the forest coming from Marric and his companions. Most of them looked rested, save for one woman who slept in her saddle. Spectacles askew, Janis watched the bouncing form of Narinda. Her brown hair was pulled back into a tail, but much of it had fallen out, making her look particularly disheveled.

Janis felt a bit of pride seeing Marric lead the group. He held his head high, but she couldn't help but stare in sadness at the obvious grief in his eyes. She noticed tear streaks down his cheeks that had dried but left the salt behind.

Furrowing her brow on her physical body, Janis looked around the group more, looking for Shrell. Her body went stiff when she looked through the faces. She didn't recognize all of them, not having met every Evenir operative in the compound, but she knew Shrell was missing.

It was then that she noticed the horse next to Marric empty, save for a tarp-covered form slung over the back of the beast.

Her blood chilled.

Oh no, she thought.

For the first time since she'd been abandoned by Macks, Janis felt her chest constrict with the pain of the thought of death. While she couldn't see the body that hung there, she knew it was their friend. Memories flashed through her mind, threatening to pull her vision away to witness the events of the past, but she pushed them away. Shrell wasn't a close friend, but he was a trusted ally, one she'd fought with many times in their short time together.

More than anything, she felt the pain of having to tell Harmel. The two brothers were insufferable, yet it was obvious they loved each other deeply.

Death was no stranger to Janis, but she loathed having to see it now. While she wanted to hold it back from Harmel, she knew she had to tell him.

"Foggin' assassin's holdin' it right good fer herself," Trease said grumpily.

Janis heard a tsking sound, followed by Varith's voice. "Now, now, dear, if you had Seeing abilities yourself, you might be more patient. It's a delicate art, I hear."

Varith sounded sarcastic, but Janis brushed it off.

"They've suffered losses, but they have the boy. I recognize him from my time protecting Marric in Wurren," Janis replied.

Just then, the vision went black. The Shielder must have resumed their duty. Why they'd taken a break, she didn't know. Still, she'd gathered enough information to know that they were a three days' ride away. They must have been traveling slower than normal, for Wurren should only be a week's ride away.

The world swirled around her once more before her vision returned to the war room.

"They have the boy? That's news we need to hear right now," Avryn said, a slight smile forming at the right edge of his lips.

Janis's eyes shifted to Harmel, grinning from ear to ear from where he stood. Despite her many experiences with death, she struggled to know what to say.

Fog it, this used to be so much easier to deal with. Is caring worth it if it means feeling like this? Janis thought, forcing the emotion out of her expression and her posture.

She leveled her eyes with Harmel. For a moment he continued laughing and speaking with Trease. His jokes weren't landing well with the brass woman, but he still cracked himself up with whatever he was saying.

"Harmel," she said, her voice firm.

Hearing her tone, his brows knit downward, making them appear even thicker than they were.

"Wa's tha'?" he answered, the smile remaining on his face. When his eyes locked on to hers, Janis felt the buzzing in her chest that had been making its appearance too often these days. A life full of dangerous situations and near-death experiences, and this man was beginning to make her feel more nervous than in any of those times. Janis shoved the feeling deep, just as she'd been doing since it'd begun weeks ago. As with any time she'd had to deal with death and loss, Janis decided to be forward with the news.

"Shrell fell in battle," she said. "They've brought his body with them so we can make sure he receives a proper burial."

A proper burial? Since when did I get so formal? Janis wondered, perturbed by her own words.

Harmel's face shifted ever so slightly yet extremely quickly through denial, shock, then desperate pain. Hands gripping his sides, he began shaking his head.

"Nah, nah, nah—tha' can't be roit. Shrell doesn't get 'imself into bits loik tha', yeh must've mistaken it," he replied.

The air thickened with sadness. Janis resisted the urge to inspect the others and their reactions, opting to focus her gaze directly on Harmel. She kept her eyes piercing and straight, not wanting to break the contact with Harmel. Despite her intent on focusing, Harmel took a step back and looked around the room.

"Nah, nah, he can't've doid," Harmel said, before noticing just how seriously Janis stared at him. "Are yeh sure—are yeh roit sure—"

Keeping her gaze measured, she nodded, allowing her expression to remain grim. Movement in her peripheral caught Janis's attention, but she held her eyes on Harmel. The movement was Avryn positioning himself between herself and Harmel. Without hesitation, the man embraced Harmel in a tight hug.

Janis couldn't help but feel jealous at the display. Since her Transformation in Stilten, she'd realized how much she'd cared about the people she'd fought with. Her care wasn't deep for every member of Evenir, yet the many experiences she'd had with those present bonded them. Even if she wouldn't admit it out loud, she knew it was true. The burning desire returned, reminding her of the growing fondness she had for the man, and she broke her gaze on Harmel.

When she looked back, the two men were parting. Janis didn't know how she expected Harmel to react, but he refrained from crying, save for a lone tear that slipped down his cheek. With a loud sniff, he stood up straight and nodded.

"A soldier's death ain' a bad one, bu' oi'll kill th' fogger tha' did this to 'im," Harmel declared.

Her respect for the man solidified at this comment. Just as she opened her voice to mention that she'd help him exact his revenge, Avryn cut in.

"Revenge for our dear friend won't bring him back," Avryn commented, still holding a firm hand on Harmel's shoulder. "We need to ensure the safe return of the others."

At that, he turned and faced the rest of the entourage.

"Varith, make sure that the stables and Fixers are ready to receive Rivelen and her company. See that we take care of their needs. Send Rivelen here when she arrives. Trease, gather a rescue group to meet Marric and the others halfway. Can you recall their location?"

Janis realized after a pause that Avryn was talking to her. For a moment she reflected on the vision she'd had of Marric and the others. Somehow she knew almost their exact location. A direct path to Terris Green should allow her to give a relative location for the group.

She nodded, pulling her eyes from Harmel once more to look at Avryn.

"Good. Show Alsry on these maps where they can expect them in a day's ride. We can move more quickly than them with our refreshed men and mounts," Avryn said.

Seeing Avryn's ability to take command wasn't surprising, but Janis admired it. It was obvious who should be the leader of Evenir in Magness's absence. She knew she wasn't the only one thinking it, especially as Varith, Trease, and the others moved to action immediately after his directives. In only moments, Harmel, Janis, and Avryn were the only ones remaining in the war room.

Once they'd left, Avryn sighed, then slammed his hands on the table.

"So many deaths. This crusade for new Lightbearers has to end. We can't keep sustaining these losses. With Watchlight and Luden's men opposing us, I fear we'll be extinct before we can make a difference for Lightbearers in Lindrad."

Avryn took a moment to let his head hang, a few quiet sobs escaping his mouth, his back bouncing with each suppressed cry. Irked once more at the brazen display of emotions, Janis stared awkwardly at Avryn, then looked back at Harmel. Grief was clear still on the man's face, but he stared at her, eyes sorrowful.

Her heart fluttered in her chest, the uncomfortable feeling making her breath come in short bursts. Thoughts of Macks swam in her mind, the love she'd felt for him when she was younger, vulnerable, crashing into her like a wave. The assassin in her screamed to back away, to leave him be. Death took them in the end, after all.

But the pain in the man's eyes struck her deep. Her instincts screamed at her to run, to not trust this man, yet her feet moved her toward him. His tearful eyes never left her own, and before she could realize what was happening, Harmel had his arms wrapped around her, his face buried in her neck.

The shiver of intense wanting washed through every inch of her, and her brain balked at the experience, yet something in her chest cracked, her emotional shell fracturing.

Desire, hatred, pleasure, mistrust. It exploded in her as Harmel sobbed into her shoulder.

Somehow both hesitantly and eagerly at the same time, she wrapped her own arms around the man's strong shoulders.

The assassin inside continued to scream.

9

Chaos.

That was all Prost had heard throughout the war room for the past few hours. Given the haphazard organization prior to Riln's death, contention had risen substantially. Riln hadn't named any successors in the case of his death, which had proven a perfect opportunity for Prost to put himself at their head.

No, not me. Ugglyn forced me into this, Prost insisted in his mind.

Don't pretend you don't want this power just as much as I do, Ugglyn whispered back, his deep voice echoing within Prost's mind.

While Prost didn't appreciate the anti-god within his mind, he'd been focusing on learning to cope with it. Ugglyn's words weren't untrue. There had been many times Prost wished he could kill Riln, take control, and return some of the terror he'd received from the others onto them.

Part of him wanted to leave.

We can't leave. Lindrad will finally change now that we are both close to freedom, Ugglyn reminded him.

Prost continued to steel himself. He'd learned this quickly. For the first days of the fusion between him and Ugglyn, Prost hadn't been able to keep his outward expressions free from the oddity of the possession by the anti-god. Now, Prost could hold it in. Any show of weakness and Prost expected he'd lose more control of Watchlight than he could afford.

Around two dozen black-robed figures yelled and fought with each other at the bottom of the steps to the throne. Prost sat on the throne, back straight, his expression serious, half listening to the mixed conversations.

Finally, a voice rang out louder than the rest.

"We need to vote, to decide together as an organization who should be in charge. You've no evidence that Riln named you his successor. There's nothing written, and there is no witness to said declaration. I posit we gather as a body and cast a vote," Vint declared.

This comment brought about more fighting and arguing from the others. Prost eyed the rest of the group. Many of them he didn't know well, save for having seen them around the compound, but there were some who he'd joined on many excursions. Alts, Neera, and Lathe, Vint's sister, were the key members present he knew well enough.

"Prost—sire—" a man's voice spoke.

Prost eyed the man. He wore his hair long and gathered in a ponytail at the back of his head. His voice shook as he spoke, but he kept his gaze measured.

"You must understand the position of the general populace within Watchlight. We've little knowledge of you or your interactions with Riln. How can we possibly trust that he named you his successor?" the man demanded. His shoulders pushed back ever so slightly, making his chest puff out in a show of confidence.

"See, that's what *I'm* trying to say. We can't trust you to tell us what he said. How do we know that Riln actually named you his second? We should *vote*."

Alts tsked from the side. "We all knows yeh want to be in charge 'ere, Vint. Yeh can' jus' come out and say it," she drawled before flicking something out of her hand. "But 'ere's the thing, Riln was all 'bout the power, 'bout the strongest among us. I think we outta 'ave a duel. Battle it out to see who's the top."

Ugglyn buzzed with satisfaction within his head. Prost once again resisted the urge to react to the oppressive and uncontrollable set of emotions from his possessor. While the anti-god was thrilled at the words from Alts, Prost's stomach twisted. The meshed emotions clashed within his chest and head, threatening to distract him too much from the conversation.

"Let's try it now, test it right well. Yeh think you'd beat 'im in a duel, Vint? Let's have a go," Alts commented, folding her arms defiantly.

The thrill flared in Prost's chest, but he shoved it away the best he could.

"Well—I—no, that's just not the best way to handle it," Vint sputtered, his eyes flashing between Alts and Prost.

Prost had to admit he was surprised at the impertinence of this man, to face a person who'd been immune to Lightbearing for years; to challenge his claim of leadership within the organization.

The rest of the group had fallen silent, fear-stricken eyes flitting to their companions, many of them landing only on Prost for a short time before flicking away in fear. They knew he was the most powerful, not only because of his history with immunity but also because of the strange displays of power Ugglyn had flaunted on their travels home.

They'd been back at the lair for less than an hour before this meeting had been forced into motion. Prost had retreated here to gather his thoughts, to converse with the unwelcome guest in his head, but the group had materialized almost instantly. As news ran through the compound that Riln was dead, Prost knew unrest grew within the ranks.

We'll just kill them all if we have to. With me we can hunt that wretched woman alone, Ugglyn mused.

Prost ignored the comment.

"That fight wouldn't be fair, as I'd win with no challenge," Prost said, his eyes wandering upward to the large orb of red Light hanging there. The pillars on the side cast their long, dark shadows, the single Light source above creating the effect.

"I never cared for the dimness of this place, Neera. Give us more Light, if you will," Prost ordered.

His voice wasn't loud, but it was firm. Vint scowled, though Prost wasn't sure if it was at his command to Neera or to his brazen claim to easily defeat Vint in a duel. Prost suspected the latter.

In reality, Prost wasn't sure he was immune to the Light any longer. Since the possession in Stilten, he'd had no battles with any Lightbearers.

His wounds had healed with the strange silvery substance from which he'd created a rough Conjure of a sword. There'd been no need to try Lightbearing on his wounds.

His stomach tightened at the thought that he might not be immune to Lightbearing any longer. Janis had thrown him off the roof of that bar with no trouble, and with Riln dead, the pact between them was broken. The fury within stoked up at the memory, and satisfaction blossomed in his chest, Ugglyn's oppressive emotions running free within him once more.

Yes, yes, remember the true motivation. We kill her, then we can both be free. Forget these squabbles, we can find her and kill her now and—

Quiet! You don't rule me, Prost cut Ugglyn off.

"Yes, sir," Neera replied, pulling Prost's attention back into the room with the rest of the group.

The dark-skinned woman placed her palms together, then spread them outward, a large red orb illuminating her face. The group fell silent as they watched her look upward, the orb moving with her gaze. The orb split into a dozen others, then zipped upward and outward to position themselves in the corners of the ceiling and behind the pillars. The shadows of the pillars melted away, leaving wisps of darkness from the various positions of the orbs around the lined stone columns on either side.

With the dimness gone, Prost felt something stir inside. For a moment he thought it was Ugglyn, but he realized it was himself. Somehow, illuminating the throne room in a way that Riln never had made Prost feel triumphant, like a small yet potent victory against his former oppressor.

I already did defeat him, and look how it's turning out for me, Prost thought grimly.

You should consider yourself lucky to be my host. I have given you power beyond anything you could have imagined before now. Before, you were just a dud—

Anger blossomed in Prost's chest, and this time he didn't hold back his facial expression. Gritting his teeth, Prost growled quietly and forced the anti-god back into the deep recesses of his mind. Prost knew this wouldn't last forever, but it would give him time to at least continue the conversation.

From one oppressor to another. I can't get away, Prost thought.

This reaction caught the attention of everyone in front of him. Some cowered in fear, some stared, but Vint looked skeptical. His eyes narrowed at Prost, detecting that something wasn't right.

"How can we expect someone with little control over their emotions, as made clear by what we just saw, to run Watchlight in an organized manner?" Vint spat.

This comment was intended to infuriate him, but Prost felt amused, a welcome emotion after the conflict within his mind over the past week. Leaning back casually in the throne, Prost let a smile spread on his face.

"You realize the irony of your comment, don't you? At what point could you say that our prior leader, Riln, had complete and utter control over his emotions? That man was more volatile than a blazing wildfire in the middle of the forest."

Vint's face flushed, and the color was emphasized by the shining red orbs floating above them. The mirth faded from Prost's face, and he stared Vint down as he spoke his next words. "Regardless of what you believe or don't believe, I am the new leader. Riln declared me second; I am in charge. You will obey or you will die."

Prost said the last part with chilling calmness. His stomach writhed at the tone, for it matched Riln's almost exactly.

I can't become like him, Prost thought.

Ugglyn threatened to come forward then, but Prost continued to hold the force at bay. Though Prost was effectively doing so, he could sense the invisible wall inside bowing, weakening with each moment.

"And what of these new powers you flouted before us? What is the meaning of these?" Vint accused. "How can we be sure that this isn't some destructive power intended to ruin us all?"

Interesting, Prost thought. Until now, he hadn't considered what the strange gifts could mean. Prost had witnessed Ugglyn's power manifest in ways similar to those of Lightbearers. He'd called it Voidweaving, but Prost didn't understand the details. Just before he could open his mouth, Prost paused.

"Those are of no concern to you. I am more powerful than even you. If you want to challenge my authority, then by all means." Prost gestured grandly in front of him, making a show of it.

Prost knew that his authority over Watchlight was tenuous. He'd been disliked for so many years and that wouldn't change in just a few days. He knew he would need to fight for approval, to fight for control. A thought pressed at his mind, the part of him that questioned his decision to stay with Watchlight. In theory, his pact was gone. He could leave, abandon these people who hated him.

Yet he couldn't leave.

Since possessed by Ugglyn, Prost felt he couldn't get away from this war, from this problem. He wasn't sure if killing Janis, despite that being one of his only desires right now, would solve the predicament either, but having an army of Lightbearers backing him would only help.

He hoped.

Vint snarled, then drew his sword. The sound of the steel scraping his scabbard echoed throughout the throne room. A couple of faint gasps came from those around him before they began stepping back. Only one, Neera, moved toward the squat man.

"Vint, think about this. Would it be wise to challenge Prost? You could get hurt—"

"Oh, shove off," Vint cried, pushing the woman away.

She gave him a look of annoyance, and for a moment Prost wondered if she would take a shot at him, but she backed away to a pillar.

Prost stood and reached for his sword. Just then, pressure erupted in his brain. It wasn't painful, but Ugglyn was pushing back against the barrier Prost erected in his mind. Prost paused, letting his hand hover over the handle of his sword before he stopped and stood up straight.

Prost knew what the pressure was. He breathed in deeply and let the barrier fall.

Yes! Let me show this simple man the power of Voidweaving, Ugglyn hissed.

Rather than grab his steel sword, Prost held out his hand. Somehow he knew what to expect. Silvery smoke coalesced into a broad sword, about the size and shape of the one he wore at his side. Despite its size, it felt light, almost weightless, in his hands.

Vint's eyes flickered in nervousness, but they hardened in resolve.

"Fight me, coward!" Vint said, spitting on the ground.

Prost gripped the handle of his smoke-created sword, then sucked in a breath and lunged forward. He was shocked at how fast he could swing the weapon. With no apparent weight, it flew through the air. Vint gasped, also surprised by the speed of the attack, and danced backward. Prost's blade narrowly missed the man's chest, but he stepped sideways and swung at Vint's side.

This time Vint saw the movement and created a blazing Shield of red Light.

Prost smirked, then confidently moved his sword directly to the Shield. Metal clashing on metal rang through the room, and Prost grunted as the Shield blocked his sword. Pain erupted from his wrist as his sword bounced off of the barrier.

What the—? I'm supposed to be immune to Lightbearing! Prost thought. Fear sprang up inside him at the revelation and he stumbled backward, his wrist and forearm still throbbing from his wild blow to the Shield.

You fool! You are no longer immune to Lanser's gift. That was His corrupted use of Void, Ugglyn chastised him.

You took my immunity! For what?! Weak copies of Lightbearing powers? Prost replied.

The red Shield disappeared in front of him, a surprised-looking Vint standing there. It took only a moment for the man to recover from his surprise that his Shield had worked before he was attacking in earnest with his own steel blade. Prost parried and dodged each one with relative ease, but Vint was relentless. Each time Prost attacked, Vint summoned a Shield to block the blow.

He was looking smug.

After spinning and slamming his smoke-sword into another Shield, the wall vanished, and Vint sliced Prost's shoulder.

Roaring, Prost backed up, holding the gash. Blood poured through the wound.

"Do you yield, then? Yield to this battle, yield your leadership over Watchlight?" Vint challenged.

Be calm, he can't win, Ugglyn mused.

Just then, silvery smoke wreathed through the wound on Prost's shoulder, a slight glow to the power flashing through his fingers. In an instant the wound was gone. Blood no longer stained his shirt or hands.

Prost marveled at the feeling. He couldn't help but let a smirk spread across his face.

"Wh—what, that can't be, I—" Vint said, but Prost cut him off by jumping forward and slashing with his sword.

Once again, Vint's Shield blocked the blow. This time, however, when the red Light shield fell and Vint jumped forward, Prost danced backward, his opponent's sword missing him by a handspan.

Let's show him the true power of Voidweaving, Ugglyn whispered. Prost felt the anti-god enter his limbs—not taking full control, but it was obvious he was there. It felt as if their minds aligned, each knowing the intent of the other. It felt natural, as if they'd done this before. Yet the feeling terrified Prost, for he was giving partial control of himself for something—unnatural.

The two moved together in unison, Prost's right arm extending as Vint growled and jumped forward. A dome of silvery grey smoke appeared around him, extending overhead and touching the surrounding ground in a circle. Vint's shouts were followed by the sound of metal hitting metal, much like Prost's sword on the Light Shield just moments before. Prost's mind buzzed. His senses heightened as he spun around, assuming almost full control of his body before Ugglyn whispered once more in his mind.

Be still, it's merely a Shield. It won't hurt us.

Prost gritted his teeth, particularly at the anti-god's use of the word "us." It only reminded him of the complexity of his predicament. Rather than reply to the unwelcome inhabitant in his mind, Prost spun around, slowly inspecting the smokey dome around him. The substance looked identical to what his sword was made of and to that which had just healed.

"It's useless if I can't see through it. Light Shields are translucent," Prost said.

He could hear voices through the odd Shield, though they were muffled. Prost hoped they hadn't been able to hear him speaking out loud to no one. That thought soon dissolved as the surrounding Shield dissipated. Still uncomfortable with this odd power, Prost took advantage of the adrenaline rushing through his body.

Vint stared at him, baring his teeth.

"You flout this power, yet you couldn't describe its nature before now?

Why keep this a secret? Why wait until now?" Vint asked, his brow furrowed.

Prost paused, eyeing the contender.

Before he could answer, movement caught his attention to his left. Eyes flashing in that direction, Prost barely had enough time to dodge a Conjured dagger.

One of the other hooded figures had joined the fight.

Prost thanked Lanser for his reflexes kicking in. Under normal circumstances, he'd have taken that dagger in the arm, expecting it to have no effect on him.

Give me my immunity back now! Prost demanded.

Another Conjured dagger flew at him, right as Vint snarled and dashed at him from the side. Penned in, Prost winced in anticipation of the blow. Before any such injury came, he felt his left arm move upward, palm open to the approaching Vint. Rather than fight it, Prost moved in tandem with the force. The moment it reached upward, Vint's body was wreathed in the same dark silvery smoke, and he flew backward, being thrown away.

Eyes wide, the man landed hard on his back, then slid to a stop. A sharp pain erupted in Prost's chest as the Light dagger entered there. Burning roared up his chest and into his neck as if the dagger was laced with poison. Ugglyn growled in his mind, reacting to whatever poured into his blood from the Conjured dagger. Jaw locked, Prost felt Ugglyn command the Void substance to combat the pain, to push away whatever burned in his veins.

Prost sucked in a sharp breath but didn't let the pain fog his mind. He spun on the other cloaked figure, whose hood was still up. Without seeing their face, Prost couldn't know who he was fighting. There had been at least twenty others in the room, though most of the Watchlight operatives had retreated to the sides of the room.

A Conjurer, but what else—? Prost thought.

His question was soon answered as a small ball of red Light appeared in the person's hand.

Prost's chest erupted in lightness, adrenaline rushing through him. He reacted to the danger, his mind still processing what he'd just seen. By now the burning had disappeared, along with the Conjured weapon on his shoulder. Relieved of his pain, he gritted his teeth again, watching the incoming attack.

The Destroying ball slammed into the ground next to him, the rock exploding outward and peppering his face and bare forearms. The force of the explosion pushed him to the side, but Prost went with it, crouching down and rolling over his back to land on his feet. Right as he leveled, Vint charged him once more. Without hesitation, Prost pushed his hand outward again, throwing Vint backward into a rock column. Vint's eyes widened in shock and he gasped as the air was forced from his lungs.

Now for the real fun to begin, Ugglyn mused again.

Prost's skin chilled. For now, the two worked in tandem. Neither led the fight, but each somehow knew the actions of the other. If Ugglyn moved one way, Prost followed. Likewise, if Prost reacted, Ugglyn moved alongside. At this moment, Prost felt Ugglyn tug upward on his empty left hand, so Prost allowed it. Just then, an orb the size of his head flared into existence, swirling silvery-black smoke moving inward like a cyclone. He tossed it upward, where it stopped just next to the main red orb in the room.

The moment he created it, Prost saw the Light of the red orbs dim, as if the power was being sucked inward toward this new orb.

Somewhere to the side, Prost heard Neera gasp. Resisting the urge to look her direction, he turned to the hooded man, who had stumbled backward at the sight. After a quick beat, the man stood and lobbed a new ball of red at Prost. Ugglyn guided Prost's hand upward, a small ball of Void smoke forming there. Roughly the same size at the cloaked man's Destroying orb, Ugglyn Moved the orb to slam into the approaching Light orb. A loud crack rang in his ears as a force slammed into him, forcing his top half backward. Just before his feet could come out from under him, Prost exerted his core strength to keep upright, though he still stumbled.

To his side, Prost saw a flash of Vint standing on his feet, shaking away the disorientation. The moment Vint's eyes landed on Prost, Ugglyn summoned the smoke Shield again, though this time only a half-dome.

Let's make an example of this fellow, Ugglyn purred. *Leaders shouldn't condone challenges such as this.*

The words irked Prost. He was equally frustrated with this random man joining in the spar, but he knew Ugglyn's intentions had to be more extreme than his own.

No! We can't kill to gain control! That's not— Prost thought, but Ugglyn forced his way out in Prost's mind.

Then he went numb.

No—no—no, Prost roared in his head.

Ugglyn controlled his body, forcing them to face the cloaked man. He stood shakily from where he'd been thrown backward into the wall. Prost couldn't feel anything, yet his other senses worked as expected. He stared, feeling the anger inside.

The force of the colliding Destroying powers must have pushed the attacker with more force, for he still shook. His hood had fallen backward now, dark-brown hair covering his ears and falling down his forehead. Blood dripped from the side of his head.

"You are not meant to lead, dud. Riln would never have named you his second," the man spat.

Prost recognized the man, but his name eluded him.

Ugglyn laughed, using his voice.

Prost yelled inside, trying to force himself to the surface to regain control of his faculties. He felt as if he'd been trapped in a prison and drugged to lose all senses save for hearing and sight. The normal anger Prost felt at being called "dud" was squelched by the fear of being separated from his ability to control anything.

"Then prove to me I can be defeated," Prost's voice said.

A deeper tone overlayed his normal voice, sounding as if two men spoke at once. It chilled Prost to the core to hear it. His voice sounded blank, dead. There was a time he'd sounded like that, a time when he'd first arrived at Watchlight and been scarred by Riln. He'd spent years digging himself out of that hole. For a moment Prost thought he might have glimpsed the twisted mind of the anti-god. He couldn't dwell on the thoughts long before a man's screams yanked him back to reality. Prost saw the man dash toward him, Conjured sword in one hand, Destroying ball in the other.

His face smiled, then he let out a small chuckle.

Calmly, yet more rapidly than Prost could have expected, Ugglyn controlled his arm upward, palm facing the man. The man froze in place, silvery smoke covering his whole being. The man widened his eyes in shock before his expression switched to fear. Struggling, he cursed. Prost's other hand opened upward, a thumbnail size ball of smoke forming there. Prost screamed inside his own head, panicked at what he was seeing. He'd hoped to never feel this helpless again, not after the times Janis's Lightbearing had made him lose control.

"Help! Stop this tyrant! He can't be left to—" the man tried to say.

His words were cut short as Ugglyn thrust his hand forward, the ball of smoke slamming into the frozen man's chest. In an instant, he disintegrated to dust, a whispering swish the only remaining sound as the man died.

Prost's stomach writhed at the scene. Somehow the feeling snapped something within him and he forced his way to the surface.

"No! I'm not done—augh!" Prost's voice said, Ugglyn's own will controlling him.

Then he was gone, forced downward by Prost's frantic inward tugging.

Give me control again! I must deal with that other insubordinate imbecile! Ugglyn shouted in his head.

Prost's head throbbed. Somehow pulling himself back to the surface had taken a lot out of him, though he couldn't say why.

I—am—in—control, Prost thought forcefully.

Ugglyn became silent then.

The gravity of the situation landed on his shoulders, and Prost cast about for how he could pull himself out of such a scene. Despite Riln's tyranny within the compound, he'd never killed anyone in this gruesome of a manner. He had Prost take care of such business. Still, it was never in front of anyone else, save for Prost himself and sometimes Jord.

The silence that followed should have been encouraging, but Prost didn't find it so. Calmly and collectively, he turned to face the others. Most of them had slipped behind pillars, watching with fearful eyes from a distance. Curiously, Neera stood closely to Vint, her eyes fixed on Prost, though he didn't see fear there.

Was that admiration?

Prost's chest tightened at the thought that anyone could admire anything about what just happened.

"The fog do you think you are? You're a murderer! A killer! You aren't good at anything else but—"

"Shut up!" Prost shouted.

Vint jumped, a red Shield of Light expanding outward in front of him and Neera.

Anger flared inside at the sight of the Shield once again being used against him, but Prost breathed deeply, recognizing the fury as Ugglyn's, not his own.

Prost knew he had to lie—again.

"That man was a spy for Evenir," he stated, his breath quickened from the still-present adrenaline pulsing through his being. "My words were meant not only for you but those within our compound. Whoever betrays us to Evenir will find themselves in the same spot."

Vint, hearing this, sputtered, trying to come up with a reply.

Neera put her arm outward and squeezed the man's shoulder. "Drop the Shield. He means no harm to us," she told him.

Her eyes remained on Prost the whole time. Heart fluttering, Prost stood up straighter, opting to look confident despite his complete loss of control to the anti-god moments before. Neera's gaze felt piercing as she walked closer to him.

"What is this power you just showed us? How can we have it?"

She sounded far more eager than Prost could have imagined. Suddenly, this quiet Lighter felt more foreboding than ever.

Prost thought for a moment to let Ugglyn free, even just a little to answer her questions, but he already knew the answer.

"Voidweaving," Prost said.

Neera eyed him from head to toe, then directed her attention upward.

"And it behaves like Lightbearing. Shielding, Fixing, Moving, Destroying, Conjuring—" Neera paused. "And whatever *that* is."

She pointed upward to the dark, head-sized sphere of silvery smoke swirling above. Her own Light appeared to be bending toward it, as if it was a void of some sort, absorbing Lanser's Light around it.

Her gaze shifted to his face once more. "What of Seeing? Have you this power as well?"

Prost nodded.

Neera tilted her head to the side, considering this.

"Intriguing," she commented before turning to the others. "It's obvious who the true leader of Watchlight is. Can we ever doubt his true position? Who held position immediately near Riln at all times? Who was called to journey most often to retrieve new Lightbearers? Who now communes with Ugglyn's power more than Riln ever professed to be able to?"

She turned, her eyes scanning Prost's person once more.

"He has my loyalty," she said, curtsying slightly despite her lack of skirts.

The others emerged from the surrounding pillars, forming up in a tight group around her. Slowly yet surely, they bowed in turn, mumbling words of assent or loyalty in their own way. Vint glared at them but finally turned toward Prost.

Prost took the moment to hold his Conjured Void sword in the air, somehow asserting his self-proclaimed dominance over the others.

"My lord," Vint said, "tell us more of this Voidweaving. Is this Ugglyn's intent for us to conquer Evenir and Lindrad?"

The question was forward, yet Vint's voice still held bitterness that no man could hide.

Prost paused, letting the silence permeate every bit of the cavern, before he halted his gaze on the seemingly small man. Ugglyn whispered inside him, bidding Prost to let him free once more to reign in chaos and terror.

He didn't oblige.

"It is the way we will finally gain the control we've been fighting for all these years. Ugglyn's gift will ensure victory for those who seek refuge within the ranks of Watchlight," Prost declared.

Prost's chest constricted even as he said the words. He could feel Ugglyn's approval pressing within his head, accepting the things he'd said. The anti-god continued to push for control, but Prost exerted his internal efforts to keep him down. Before, when they'd first aligned, Prost assumed he and Ugglyn wanted the same thing: to kill Janis. Yet this Voidweaving irked Prost too much. If Lightbearing was unnatural, Voidweaving was even more so.

Still, Prost could feel the thrill of the power pushing him forward, urging him to do things that were more extreme, to wreak havoc on Watchlight and Lindrad alike, to kill anyone who came against him. Prost steeled himself and gazed upon the onlookers. The moment he had these thoughts, Ugglyn slipped out of Prost's subconscious, whispering promises to him in his mind.

This time, Prost let the anti-god do so. His mind numbed as he allowed the promises to persuade him down, to let Ugglyn control him. Darkness stirred up around his mind, pulling Prost into a deeper sense of security.

"Voidweaving *can* and *will* be ours. Once I retrieve my source of power, we can conquer all of Evenir and Lindrad," Prost's voice said.

The sound of Prost's voice shocked him, pulling his consciousness from the stirring darkness inside of him. Snapping back to attention, he growled and grabbed hold of Ugglyn's presence inside his mind. That voice hadn't been his, not completely.

Stop it! Stop trying to lull me into submission. I won't give in, Prost growled in his mind.

Ugglyn's laughing echoed in Prost's mind as the anti-god slipped away.

I'll have you soon enough. One man can only fight for so long, Ugglyn said.

"How? How can we get this force?" Neera asked, bringing Prost back to the room.

He paused, then eyed the woman, trying to keep the composure on his face despite the battle he'd just fought with the possessor in his mind. Prost didn't know the answer, yet Ugglyn continued to whisper inside. Movement around him made Prost shift his gaze through the group standing below the throne. Shadows moved along the walls as the Void orb above continued to suck the red Light toward it, Neera's orbs flickering to overpower the Void.

"In time, Neera. First, we need to make sure the rest of Watchlight knows who is in control," Prost said, eyeing Vint and the others.

Prost turned and stared at the dust of the man he'd just fought, peering thoughtfully. This had the intended effect on the remainder of those in the room. A series of whispers and sharp breaths showed it was so.

"Remember what will happen to those who think otherwise," Prost stated.

Vint's gaze hardened somehow despite the already furious look he had there. He was angry, as he had every right to be, but he knew when to step back.

We'll have to do something about him. Let's just kill him now, Ugglyn considered.

There is no we, *anti-god. There is only* me, Prost insisted.

Amusement flashed in his being, a forced emotion that was not his own. Prost sneered, recognizing that the reaction would be proper for the internal battle and the external one.

His companions noticed the reaction, and silence followed. The onlookers trickled out of the throne room then, Prost watching them go with hatred.

For now, Ugglyn mused again. *For now.*

10

Marric felt like he'd fall off his horse any moment. He was vaguely aware of his surroundings as his mare cantered through the cave entrance to Terris Green, the cool wind disappearing the moment he entered the threshold of the cavern. He was reminded of the first time he arrived at Evenir's sanctuary, seemingly years ago.

No, not years. It's been only months since Avryn came to get me, Marric thought.

Marric marveled at how things had changed in such a short time. A sigh next to Marric made him turn his head to see Narinda leaning back on her own horse, eyes closed, breathing deeply.

"There's nothing more satisfying than returning home after a long and hard journey," she said. Marric grumbled inwardly at her reaction, mainly because he didn't feel like he could relate. Not only was Terris Green not his home but the air was acrid and stuffy, having little ventilation. Still, Marric did notice that it was the first time he could really relax since they'd left Wurren days ago.

Traveling had taken far longer than anyone could have expected. After three days, Marric had Seen that they'd cross paths with wild spine hogs and they had to redirect to avoid being trampled by a stampede. The detour had added a whole day's journey to their travel. After day five, they'd run into a storm that lasted hours, lightning cracking and wind blowing so hard that they had to find shelter.

Jubilation melted from his emotions the moment he thought of seeing Harmel and the others. Marric's eyes shifted to the covered body of their friend. Carrying Shrell's body had not been the most practical decision he made, but even Narinda, now the acting leader of the group, agreed that the man needed a proper burial. They'd lost many, but Shrell had been a trusted advisor to Avryn. Plus Marric had insisted.

Sorrow wormed its way through Marric's insides as he remembered seeing his friend killed the way he had in Wurren. Marric still felt he should have been able to do something to stop the man who'd done this.

Shaking his head, he focused forward. Two Evenir guards, a man and a woman, led them through the darkened tunnel until they reached a larger alcove into the base. Blue orbs of Light illuminated the larger room, a dome that extended thirty paces overhead. Each wall was smoothed and equal, the room a work of art in Marric's mind. He still couldn't fathom how Destroyers could have shaped such a place.

His gut squirmed at the thought. Marric still hadn't come to terms with his new power and he doubted he ever would. Still, he hoped that talking to Avryn would at least help him cope with the new destructive abilities. An image of the Watchlight man in Wurren flooded his mind, making him nauseous. His vision became red at the thought of his Destroying powers ripping through the man's body as if it were parchment.

"Hey, we made it. It's going to be ok," Narinda whispered.

With a start, Marric shifted his gaze to look at the woman. Over the last week, he'd connected with her on a whole new level. For that he was grateful. There was something about experiencing a common friend's death that had a way of bonding near strangers. Gone was the quiet Lightbearer who read books behind her large round spectacles, gone was the snarky librarian who seemed to stare critically at every passerby. Marric knew now that the woman was a soldier, a fighter, better than he could have foreseen.

More than anything, she was a woman who cared. They'd carried on many discussions on their way back to Terris Green, some deeper than Marric was willing to accept. Still, that they'd been together when Shrell died felt almost binding.

Nodding, Marric pressed his lips together and continued staring at her.

"I will share the details of Wurren. It's my duty to bear—" Narinda paused, concern still in her eyes.

She'd been about to mention Shrell being gone. Marric knew it, but still the pang of sadness dug deeper. Forcing back tears, Marric faced forward once more. Tears had been too prevalent in the past week. He was ready to move on, to give his friend the funeral he deserved, then look to the future as best as he could.

But what does that future hold? So much has changed; what else will change before we are truly safe? he wondered.

The guards whispered as they guided the entourage of people on their horses. Marric couldn't make out the words they said over the clopping of the hooves beneath and behind him. Admittedly, he didn't care too much to know what they discussed. At the moment he would have been more than happy to just lean forward on his horse and take another rest. But he knew it wouldn't be feasible right now.

An amazed gasp to his right pulled him back to reality. Crents stared wide-eyed at the ceiling of the domed room. The moment they'd entered Terris Green, his friend had gone silent and peered around, looking nervous. Marric couldn't help but smile at the reaction. It brought him back to the wonder and intrigue he'd felt when he first came into the Destroyed-shaped caves and tunnels. With intention, Marric tried to break away from his recently earned wealth of knowledge about Lightbearing and look at the room, covered with Lighting orbs, with the same perspective he'd had then. Thrill filled his chest as the wonder and delight returned. It felt familiar, innocent, and majestic. He was grateful they'd saved his friend, but he was even more grateful to be there to experience Crents's first time seeing the amazing structure.

The whispering in front of them intensified, and Marric watched a courier talking to the guards, who led them through another tunnel. After the hasty and unheard discussion, the man sped off in the direction they moved. His feet pounded loudly on the stone floor, the echoing joining in the cacophony of the horse hooves sounding through the small space.

At length, the group emerged on the other side of the tunnel, a few men and women rushing forward to grab the reins of the horses they rode. Marric proffered his own to a woman in a simple brown dress. She bowed to him, then indicated that he should dismount. The gesture made Marric uncomfortable. He'd not once had anyone treat him like that, but the non-Lightbearers here in Terris Green revered those with the gift, including him. Still, the treatment was unusual. He wondered if something had changed since they'd left. Marric averted his eyes and dismounted, trying not to notice how the woman regarded him like some sort of royalty.

"M'lord, Avryn be wantin' t' speak wif yous in th' war room roit quick."

The woman's accent caught Marric off guard. Her words were dripping with accent and somewhat distracted him. It sounded like the people he'd grown up with in Wurren. Marric narrowed his eyes at the girl, trying to note if he knew her from Wurren or not. His gaze must have made the woman uncomfortable, for her brow knit and she looked away.

Marric opened his mouth to apologize or just to say anything at all, but he paused, finding no words to give.

I'm still feeling out of sorts from this journey. How long will it take me to get back to normal? Marric lamented internally.

Forcing a smile, Marric nodded to the woman, then dismounted, patting the horse on the side. He never used the same horse when they traveled, but he felt he should remember this one for the next time.

"You can head to your quarters to rest," Narinda said. "I'll bear the burden of the tale of our journey to the others. I'm sure they are waiting—"

"They are," Marric interrupted her, "and no, this is also my burden to bear. He was my friend as well."

A pang of sorrow tore through his chest once again. Marric breathed in deeply, pushing the feeling away as best as he could. Narinda looked worried, but she nodded in understanding. Though he didn't know all of the woman's story, he could somehow tell she'd dealt with grief more than she would admit. There was something in her eyes that indicated she related to him.

"Erm . . . can oi git sum—'elp?" Crent's timid voice asked from behind.

A few people around them chuckled before moving to his horse. Marric turned to see the boy's face flushed. Crents stared at the ground, realizing he didn't know how to dismount. It had taken a great deal to get the boy on the horse the first time, as well as each morning. Not once had Crents ridden a horse, given the lack of any healthy mounts in Wurren most of their lives. They also frowned upon recreational riding with the work that needed to be done in the fletchery anyway.

A few men moved to aid Crents. Despite the boy's slight figure, it was an awkward sight to watch. Marric flushed just watching the two men try to extract the small boy from the saddle. In the end, they had to pry his feet from the stirrups and lift him down. Despite the numerous dismounts on their journey, Crents still hadn't learned the skill. Marric moved to the boy and put his hand on his friend's shoulder.

"It's all right, you'll get used to it. I'm sure someone will help you master riding a horse while we're here," Marric encouraged.

Crents nodded but still looked mortified. "Erm, yeah. 'S this is th' place we git t' live, then?"

Marric looked around the cavern, people bustling here and there. Some carried what looked like recently harvested vegetables from one of the fields, while others carried odd bits and bobs, likely things they'd created by their trade. It seemed busier than he remembered it being when he left, and he wondered if there was something else going on he hadn't heard of yet. Traveling through the forest had been quiet for the past week, so Marric figured he'd just forgotten how it truly was here. A few women approached from the throng and curtsied to him. Once again, Marric was surprised at their reaction.

"Sir, Avryn roit ask'd us t' tell yeh tha' 'e's waitin' fer yous in the war room," the foremost of the women said.

The woman's gaze shifted to Narinda and she bowed her head. Narinda noted this as she exchanged a look with Marric, raising an eyebrow.

So she thinks something is off too, Marric thought.

"Yes, thank you. We'll be going now," Marric replied.

"Wait! Yeh're jus' gonna leave me 'ere?!" Crents exclaimed.

He'd moved right up to Marric and grasped his arm, holding him there. Marric jumped at the sudden touch, adrenaline rushing through him, before he took a deep breath and relaxed. He'd been so on edge from their travels that any touch made him nervous.

"Someone will take care of you," Marric said before he thought of a better plan. "Miss—"

Marric realized he didn't know any of the names of the women who stood before him and he flushed at the thought.

"Yes, sir?" the foremost spoke again.

"Can you please take my friend to my father? I think that's the best place for him to be right now. Seeing a familiar face will help him get used to being here, I think," Marric suggested.

The woman curtsied once more, the other two following her lead, then they moved to gently pull Crents away.

"Pa Narim? Oi'd be roit glad t' see 'im again. When yeh told me 'e'd not died in the fire, Oi was 'appy t' 'ear it," Crents said. He continued to speak as the women led him away, but the words were lost in the large space of the cavern and the bustling noise around them.

Marric chuckled, knowing how Crents could talk forever.

"Let's go, then," Narinda said.

With a sigh, Marric stood up straight and walked toward the tunnel that would lead them to the war room. He glanced once more at Shrell's body draped over a horse. It was still covered with the tarp they'd requisitioned from the Fields of Erisdell. For a moment he wondered if he should bring it along or leave it. The thought was interrupted by a commotion near the mouth of the tunnel he'd just been about to move toward. Turning in that direction again, his eyes landed on Harmel.

Marric broke again.

For days, he'd learned to deal with the grief of Shrell's death. Marric had only cried the first day, resolving himself to be more mature and handle the sadness with dignity. Narinda indicated that he could cry if it helped, but he knew that hardened warriors wouldn't. A death couldn't rule a soldier's mind for too long before it became a danger. He'd rehearsed these things to himself the second day and finally could cope with no tears.

But his resolve disappeared when he saw the red-rimmed eyes of Harmel. Marric rushed to him and threw his arm around the man. The two stood there for a time, sobbing together. Though he thought he should feel embarrassed by his reaction, he didn't. Seeing Harmel had loosed the suppressed sadness of the past week. Through tear-fogged eyes, Marric noted that Evenir men and women stood watching them, while others walked by uncomfortably. Either they hadn't heard the news of Shrell or they didn't take well to seeing men cry.

In the back of his mind, Marric wondered how Harmel knew of his brother's death. They had been so focused on getting back to Terris Green safely that they'd Shielded themselves strictly the whole time. It worried him that Seers from Evenir must have peeked in on them at just the right moment. Yet the discomfort was swallowed by the moment.

Marric felt a warm hand press on his back and he started, the same nervousness as before taking hold. He jumped back and whipped around to see who it was.

A gasp escaped his mouth before he could stop it.

Janis stood there, looking awkward. She must have been with Harmel when he'd locked eyes with the man, but Marric hadn't seen her.

Was she just touching me? Marric marveled.

At a loss for words once more, Marric sniffled and wiped his nose on his sleeve. This made Janis wrinkle her nose a bit as she stared at the arm he'd just used. Despite wearing the same attire she always had since he'd met her, Marric could tell something was different about her. Narrowing his eyes, Marric attempted to identify what had changed. With a shuddering breath, he looked her up and down.

While he stared, Harmel moved to the horse carrying Shrell's body, his sobs echoing in the large room.

When it became clear to Marric that he couldn't identify what was different, he did the only thing that he could think of at the time. He hugged her. Even as he moved to her, he knew she would be angry. Janis didn't like being touched. She was not affectionate and didn't like seeing emotion. Marric didn't care.

Except she didn't shy away.

Marric's eyes shot open in shock as he felt the woman's arms wrap around him in a soft embrace. It wasn't a firm grip, neither was it the most comforting hug he'd had in his life, but the skin tingled under his shirt where she touched him. This felt like the most meaningful embrace he'd had in his life, and he couldn't describe why. Not wanting to prolong the moment too long, for fear of annoying Janis, Marric pulled away. He looked at her with wide eyes, but she looked away, her lips pressed together firmly.

"I'm glad you made it. I was concerned you wouldn't after what we went through in Stilten," Janis said, her head still turned away.

Though her expression was hard while she spoke, Marric focused on the fact that she said she'd been worried about him. The hug aside, even her simple words were uncharacteristic of her hardened nature as an assassin. Marric's mouth fell open in shock. Just then, Janis fixed her eyes on him once more. He slammed his jaw shut, not wanting her to see him standing there with his mouth agape.

She obviously noticed still, for she raised an eyebrow after eyeing his mouth.

Marric flushed again and cleared his throat, trying to get his bearings.

"Umm, I'm glad to see that you made it back as well. What happened for you, then, that was so bad? Did someone die?"

He loathed even voicing the question, but after the past two weeks, he realized he couldn't afford to be shy about things like this. If anything, his encounters with Watchlight and Jord, as well as Awakening as a Destroyer, made him feel more brazen. Marric wasn't convinced that the change was a good thing, but it also had proven to save him a lot of time with communicating.

Janis once again raised a brow at this, showing that she'd realized he'd changed as well.

Who hasn't changed after all this? Marric wondered.

Janis sighed and put a hand to her temple, shaking her head.

"I think it's best we talked in the war room where you can sit. You look like you'll pass out any moment. Wurren is a lot farther from here than Stilten, but we're all curious to know why you took fogging forever to get back," Janis said. She then gestured toward the tunnel they'd just come from.

Harmel's sobbing continued next to them. Marric turned to see that Harmel was hugging Shrell's covered body and shivering. Looking grim, Janis moved to his side and placed her hand on his shoulder. The man immediately reacted to the hand and stood up straighter. With a sniffle and a few coughs, Harmel wiped his face on the sleeve of his tunic before nodding to Janis.

"There ain't no reason t' sit 'ere an' cry forever. Let's git yous to Avryn to talk about Wurren," Harmel said.

He immediately reached for Janis's hand and clutched it. The woman stiffened at the touch but didn't pull away. Marric was once again taken aback at Janis's change. Before, when anyone had tried to touch her in such a way, she'd threaten to slice them with one of her daggers. Though she looked uncomfortable still, she allowed Harmel to pull her toward the tunnel leading to the war room. Narinda cleared her throat next to him and he glanced at her, catching an odd look on her face. Based on the way she looked at him, he got the meaning: *What's gotten into her*?

Marric replied with an unspoken shrug and the two followed.

People continued to bustle around, but they parted ways when they saw Janis approaching. Seeing this reaction from the other people in Evenir clued Marric in to the fact that everything hadn't changed with Janis entirely.

Still, the way they're holding hands, Marric thought, watching Harmel and Janis walk before them.

His thoughts were interrupted as he almost ran headlong into a small girl hustling by with a basket of carrots on her head. She gasped as the basket wobbled and almost tipped over. Reaching out, he caught one edge of the basket and righted it. After a moment of fuss, the girl looked up at him and gasped. She whispered something that Marric couldn't quite hear, then bowed to him awkwardly.

"Sorry, S'ren. Oi din' men t' git in yer way," she said before looking at Janis, who watched from ahead.

"Oh, it's no problem. I should watch where I'm going, that's all. I've just traveled for so long that I think I'm too weary," Marric said.

"'Ere, eat this, then. Moit jus' give yeh a bit o' steam t' 'elp yeh git to where yeh need," the girl said, handing him a carrot.

Marric smiled at her, but the girl wasn't looking at him. She was warily looking toward Janis as if she'd be in trouble. Despite the girl's nervousness, Janis shook her head and continued walking to the tunnel with Harmel.

After a moment, Marric lost sight of them. The moment they disappeared from view, the girl whispered sharply.

"Can yeh believe she's to be the new leader of Evenir? Fog me, Oi don't fink we've 'ad anyone loik 'er in charge around 'ere."

Marric started.

"What are you on about? What happened to Magness?" Marric asked.

The girl stared at him flatly. Her face sent an obvious message that he sounded like a fool asking something like that.

"'Aven't yeh 'eard? Magness kicked it in Stilten. That assassin Awakened into something else, Oi 'eard," the girl said, still in a whisper.

Marric could hardly understand why the girl bothered to whisper. Even if Janis and Harmel had been closer, he doubted they'd have been able to hear a thing. All the people and bustle around them made it so even he had a hard time hearing her. Still, he heard the most important part of it.

Magness was dead.

He opened his mouth to say something else, but the girl twisted her head as if she'd been called by someone. Before he could ask anything, she rushed off into the crowd of people.

Marric stood there, the rough edge of the carrot he held seeming more textured than it had a moment ago. He felt hollow. Janis would have told him the moment he got to the war room, but hearing it like this, offhand from one of the Evenir locals, felt like an awkward blow he couldn't recover from. He was suddenly worried about the others he'd gotten to know since arriving at Terris Green.

How many others have died? How many more have to die before we can do something? Marric thought.

His heart sped up as the frustration welled up inside. He'd experienced too much death since he'd been with Evenir. Now he'd been the cause of some. To think he'd been a simple fletcher's apprentice a few months ago. Now he was taking the lives of enemies he hadn't known existed.

Marric inadvertently squeezed the carrot in his hand, his head pounding from the news. Suddenly, a flash of blue Light exploded from his grip and the carrot exploded into pieces. The light was accompanied by a loud cracking noise, which startled Marric back to reality. A few children shrieked at the sound, and many around him stopped to stare wide-eyed at the Destroyed carrot that littered the hard stone floor of the large cavern.

Oh Lanser's beard, Marric cursed mentally.

The cavern was suddenly very quiet. Marric blushed once more and moved to follow his companions toward the war room. As he passed, he heard a few people muttering something about him. He caught the words "crazy Destroyers" and "he'll kill us all." Marric averted his eyes and hastened through the crowd, fully aware of all those who stared at him.

Somehow his emotions had gotten the better of him just then, confirming something he'd dreaded even before he'd awakened to his Lightbearing powers. He recalled learning of the different classes and pleading with Lanser not to give him the powers of a Destroyer.

The prayer must not have worked.

Every time he'd seen Watchlight Destroyers, they'd seemed insane and volatile, as if their powers controlled their mind, made them do horrid things or lose their temper. Even Avryn had moments when he'd Destroyed something in desperation during a battle. Marric's insides twisted as he continued to feel the stress and worry of knowing that Magness was dead but not knowing why. He thought of the anger he'd felt in Wurren when he'd accidentally Destroyed the man with Jord. Marric opened his hands and closed them repeatedly, trying to push away the fear and frustration, worrying that the Destroying would hurt him or someone else.

It wasn't long before he left the gaze of those in the large room behind. He soon caught up with Narinda and the others.

As they walked, no one spoke. There was an air of seriousness around them as they moved toward the war room. Harmel and Janis had stopped holding hands, and they walked in a single row to allow for passersby to pass next to them. Before long, they arrived at the library just outside the war room. Marric breathed a sigh of relief as he smelled the musty books and shelves there. A man sat behind the desk writing something furiously with a quill.

Narinda chuckled. "You all start without me. I want to see how the Lighting has been without me here to oversee it."

Marric watched as she moved to the man and tapped him on the shoulder. He yelped, his hand flipping quickly to the side, leaving a black mark across the words he'd just been focused on. He looked angry at the interruption, but his eyes opened wide and he stood with a salute toward Narinda.

The door leading to the war room was as magnificent as Marric recalled. He was immediately lost in the ornate wood carving of the many faces and images within the tree. There, right in the center, was his mother. He'd not seen any other depiction of her. That type of art was too fine and expensive for his father to afford, so he'd never commissioned any likeness of his former wife. Every time Marric saw this image, he tried to soak in as much as he could. Despite the medium of wood, the carver had managed to get even the finest of details in the woman's features. Marric guessed that the image was accurate, for he could not only see his shared eyes with his mother but the woman in the wood looked reminiscent of Magness, his aunt.

The pit returned to his stomach. She'd been the only family save for his father and he'd just lost her as well. With little pause, Janis pushed open the doors. A rush of cool air from inside the war room ruffled Marric's clothing before they settled back in place. With a slight shiver, Marric followed Janis and Marric. Narinda had finished her brief conversation with the Lighter and had joined them again.

"Oh thank Lanser, you made it back," Avryn said, beaming. He moved first to Marric before patting him on the shoulder, then the man turned to Narinda. Something shone in Avryn's eyes that Marric either hadn't seen before or had overlooked.

Avryn's gaze lingered on Narinda's face, his hand now resting on her shoulder before he breathed in and moved back to the war table.

"I understand you've been traveling hard for the past week and a half, but we must know everything that happened. Save for the moment when Janis could See you, you've been completely hidden from our view," Avryn said.

"Sir, you must understand that we had to—"

Avryn's hand interrupted Narinda, moving up in the air, palm facing her.

"I understand why you had to Shield yourselves. There's no need to apologize. Your safe return was the highest priority. Now that you're here, I'm eager to learn of the events," Avryn said.

Marric stared at the man. He'd changed somehow. The normally soft-spoken yet intense man seemed to have disappeared, replaced by an authoritative and firm figure. Avryn's gaze landed once again on Marric, if only for just a moment. Pressing his lips together, Avryn averted his eyes after a brief pause.

"Sir, the others made it to Wurren before we could enter the town. They had the boy captive the moment we arrived at his house. We engaged them immediately and were able to rescue the boy," Narinda said.

Avryn relaxed. "Yes, Janis indicated that she'd Seen the newcomer with you. Have we tended to him, then?"

Narinda nodded, causing Avryn to smile once more.

"Good, thank you for that. While I am glad to hear that the trip to Wurren wasn't a squandered journey, I fear we lost something great."

Avryn looked to Harmel, who stood to the side, his arms folded. The man was listening, that was clear, but he kept his eyes down at the ground. Harmel's eyes were still red-rimmed from crying, but his face was now hardened, as if he could think of nothing better to do than find those who had taken his brother's life. Janis stood there, close to Harmel but not touching him.

To his side, Marric heard Narinda continue to share the more intricate details of the happenings in Wurren, but Marric wasn't paying attention. His eyes darted back and forth between Janis and Harmel as he tried to understand what dynamic existed between the two. That Janis could be fond of even one person perplexed him, yet she seemed different now. Marric thought back to the hug she'd given him earlier. Unsurprisingly, Janis noticed Marric's gaze. Raising an eyebrow, she stared back at him.

Normally Marric would have looked away quickly and more than likely blushed, but right now he didn't feel embarrassed. The past weeks had been hard on him, and he knew that he'd never be the same. Instead, he held her gaze, their eyes locking on each other for a few moments before he looked down at his hands, flexing them open and closed. He gritted his teeth, knowing that at some point Narinda would get to the part where Marric had fought against Jord near Crents's home. He loathed having to share the news of his new Lightbearing power, yet he knew he could not avoid it. As if responding to his thoughts, Marric heard Narinda reach that point.

"And—well—then Marric overwhelmed the Watchlight men. I believe one of them was a friend of his," Narinda said before gesturing for Marric to continue.

Marric sucked in a deep breath and faced Avryn.

"My second-born power came to me. It was—unexpected. But I killed one man and fought off Jord, my friend from Wurren. I also discovered that Jord's second power is Seeing, which led to a somewhat interesting match," Marric admitted.

Avryn raised an eyebrow, showing that he hoped for more detail.

"I'm a Destroyer now as well," Marric blurted.

To his surprise, Avryn didn't react. Instead, the man just nodded and continued to watch him. Avryn stood straighter now and appeared far more commanding than he had when Marric first left Terris Green. The way he acted, it was almost as if he was the current leader of Evenir. For a moment the words of the small girl echoed in his mind, something of Janis being the future leader. He stretched his neck to ward off the discomforting idea, then affixed his eyes back on Avryn.

Marric nodded as he realized this was likely the reason for the change in Avryn. Someone had to lead in the interim. Determining not to dwell on this further, Marric continued.

"Jord and I had something in common that I'm not sure many have had during a duel." Marric paused for a moment, wondering why he'd used that word for the situation. It didn't feel wrong to say he'd dueled Jord, but they'd often used the term for child's play when fighting with sticks or soft fists as children. Gauging Avryn's response, and once again finding it hardened, Marric spoke again.

"We both fell into some trance; I've not experienced anything like it before," Marric said.

Marric caught a stiff movement in the corner of his eye and he turned to see Janis had straightened so she was no longer leaning on the wall like Harmel.

"A trance? What do you mean?" Avryn asked, noting Janis's reaction as well.

Somewhat distracted now, Marric tried to find the words.

"Erm—it was as if my Seeing activated, like it would within a vision, but I wasn't Seeing any past or future event. I was Seeing the very scene I was in, except a few moments ahead of time."

The words sounded ridiculous, and Marric couldn't help but look off past Avryn while the man processed what he'd said.

"I—see," Avryn replied after a brief pause.

"I know what he means. I've experienced it as well," Janis said. "When I Transformed in Stilten, something like that happened to me."

Avryn frowned.

"I've never heard of this before. Normally Seers have their visions and are incapable of functioning until they are over. Rivelen, have you heard of such a thing?"

"I 'ave, tho' t' 'asn't 'appened much to the likes o' me. Most I've 'eard it 'appening is when the Seer is in the middle o' a fight or such like," Rivelen said.

Marric started as he realized the blonde woman sat primly in a chair to the side of the room. He'd been so focused on Avryn when he'd first entered that he hadn't surveyed the room. Rivelen wore a grey gown that seemed far too fancy for a simple meeting. That's how he'd always seen her. She had an air about her as if she was annoyed at having to be here at all. This irked Marric, though he didn't know why.

"Our Seers don' offen go about wif those 'oo git the new Lightbearers, so we don' See it much. But I've witnessed it 'afore, yes," Rivelen continued.

Her words had an icy edge to them. Marric thought for a moment that he might be imagining things until her eyes landed on him. Something burned behind them. Jealousy.

Marric looked away, nervousness burning in his chest.

"The same thing happened to Jord. I know it because his eyes glowed as we fought," Marric said.

"It's fortuitous for you to have gained Destroying powers of your own. Fighting them is difficult for a new Lightbearer, and I'm glad Lanser blessed you at that very moment," Avryn replied.

Marric shifted on his feet. It did not convince him that gaining Destroying powers was a good thing, let alone a blessing from the god Lanser.

"What of the others? Were there many other casualties save for—" Avryn paused, his eyes shifting to Harmel for a moment before he closed his mouth.

Narinda spoke then.

"Yes, half a dozen others were killed," Narinda replied in a strained tone. Her eyes betrayed the pain she was trying to hide. Marric didn't know everything about the woman, but she wasn't a general like Avryn or Rivelen, so reports like this weren't something she was likely used to.

Avryn cursed and slammed his fist on the table. The sound echoed loudly through the stone cavern, making it seem more ominous to those present.

"Again and again, Watchlight is robbing Evenir of our good people. How long must we go before they end us all? We're a sanctuary for Lightbearers, a place where we can live in peace until we can someday be accepted into Lindradian society. Yet all of this means *nothing* if Watchlight continues to slaughter us."

Marric was overwhelmed by Avryn's reaction. He'd not seen such passion from the man before now. During their travels from Wurren, Avryn had only been intense in moments of danger. The rest of the time he acted laid back, calm and collected.

Once again, Marric was reminded of how Magness responded. She'd had the same air of authority and intensity. He assumed it came with the burden of leading people.

"Evenir is in danger, more than we can say. While Watchlight is still unaware of our location, I fear they will work in earnest to locate us. It would be wise of us to work on the same objective. While I dislike the idea of having to march to a direct war with them, this must end. On our terms," Avryn said, fire burning in his eyes. "First we'll sort out the matter of the new leader of Evenir, then we'll make plans accordingly."

Janis grunted at the comment, drawing the attention of the others in the room.

"There's no need to assume you won't be voted the leader; it's practically done. You've taken command as you should," Janis said, leaning back against the wall.

"That is not the way of Evenir. We vote for successors when a leader passes. It was such with Magness after Talatha's death, and it will be forever. I've taken the steps necessary to keep these people together. As her second, Magness expected me to do such, should she fall. I may be the second, but that means nothing if the vote is cast for someone else," Avryn replied.

Avryn seemed to bore a hole in Janis the way he stared at her, something short of rage emanating from his eyes. Janis did not indicate that she felt any reservations at his reaction. Still, Marric could tell something was bothering Janis, even if just a little. It was then that Marric understood that Avryn was insinuating Janis be the new leader. The thought was not only ridiculous but impossible. He didn't know everyone's intentions within Evenir, but he'd seen the way they looked at Janis. Many of them whispered and talked quietly about how nervous she made them.

Janis must have thought the same thing, for she shook her head and looked away. "The people here don't trust me the way they trust you. I don't know them and they don't know me. I've kept it that way on purpose."

Avryn maintained a diplomatic face, but tension rose in the air that was almost palpable. Marric shifted uncomfortably as he watched the exchange. Glancing at Harmel and Rivelen, Marric noticed similar reactions from them. A few moments of silence followed before Avryn spoke once more.

"You said it yourself, you Transformed. You've been called as the new Prime; that means something. That you aligned yourself with us instead of Watchlight means you should lead the Lightbearers. It's the way of things. If they won't vote for you, then I'll convince them to," Avryn replied.

This statement made Janis stiffen, her eyes locking on Avryn once more. Right as she was about to respond, the door to the war room burst open, air rushing in.

"Oi fink yeh're over-reactin' t' the news," Turrin said as he entered, with Alsry and Varith at his side.

Turrin noticed Avryn's expression and the way he stared at Janis before he stopped. Alsry and Varith followed suit.

"Is this a bad toim, then?" Turrin asked.

Avryn relaxed and looked at the other generals.

"No, your timing is fine. What is it?" Avryn replied.

Janis breathed out, folding her arms.

"No, it's alroit if now ain't the roit toim. Yeh seem t' 'ave somethin' else on yer mind," Turrin offered.

"Please, just tell me what you need," Avryn urged.

Glancing at his companions, Turrin hesitated.

"There's been a bit 'o—well, some commotion 'bout yer leadership. Got a few men in the commons try'na recruit others away from Evenir," Turrin said.

"And I must say, the words are far more persuasive than I would expect from men like these," Varith added, brushing off his brand-new-looking tunic and breeches. He wore fine embroidered clothing in red fabric, as if he was some rich aristocrat for the politicians in T'Arren Vale.

Avryn cursed. The tense air from moments ago diffused at once with the revelation.

"How long has this been going on? Why have you just now come to let me know?" Avryn asked. His voice wasn't rude, but it had an air of command.

"Erm, jus' terday, Oi fink," Turrin replied.

"I must speak with them. Insurrection within Evenir is something we can't afford right now. Infighting could cost us too much in this war," Avryn said before moving to the door and turning around.

"Janis, I think it's best if you come with me. Rumblings of what happened in T'Arren Vale have undoubtedly passed around through the group. We've been back nearly a week and they've yet to hear the account of our missions. Marric and Narinda's entourage was the last to return, so we must let them know what occurred."

Janis stared at him, likely thinking of a way to decline the invitation. To Marric's surprise, she said nothing. Her jaw was set and her eyes firm, but she moved to Avryn and nodded, opting to keep her mouth closed.

What in Lanser's name happened in Stilten? Marric wondered.

"Wait! Aren't you going to let us know what happened in Stilten? It's clear something changed." Marric paused, eyeing Janis once more before turning back to Avryn.

Avryn sighed. "Unfortunately, we must address the current problem before we can delve into that story. Perhaps we should move to the main cavern in case we need aid in the event of disorder. You can learn more about it there, then we'll fill in any details that we might have missed."

Marric knew this wasn't a suggestion, but it was Avryn telling him what he intended to do. Turning on his heels, Avryn moved to Narinda, grasping her hand momentarily, his eyes pausing on her own before he brushed past Turrin and the others through the war room door. Harmel continued to lean on the stone of the war room wall, his eyes averted downward. Rivelen made no motion to join them, but the other generals followed quickly after Avryn.

Janis moved to the door silently as well, her head held high. Marric grumbled to himself about having to stand any longer. He realized he should have sat down in one of the chairs in the room, but he'd been so distracted by the odd dynamics of the generals, and most especially Janis. He felt as if he could fall asleep any moment and his feet and bottom ached from the long journey from Wurren, but he followed, his curiosity about the events in Stilten more pressing to him than rest. As he walked, he moved to Janis's side and nudged her arm. When she looked down at him, he raised his eyebrows as if to ask what happened.

"You'll hear more about it soon," Janis replied to his unspoken question. "I'm just hoping he's planning to monologue. I'm not in a chatty mood. Especially for a large group of people I don't know."

Marric cracked a smile at the response. It was more in line with the Janis he'd known since they'd left Wurren the first time, causing him to take heart that everything wasn't completely different. He knew it wouldn't be long before they made it to the main cavern, and he steeled himself for what they'd find. After a moment, he scrunched his face up, realizing he hadn't thought to visit his father, who likely was worried sick about him. Marric decided he'd go see his father after he heard more about Stilten.

Echoing sounds reached them as they walked down one of the larger tunnels. From what Marric could tell, it was people arguing and shouting over one another. A single voice echoed above the others. It took a moment before Marric could understand what they said, but when he heard them, his stomach clenched.

"They've no roit to rule us loik this. Oi call fer new leadership! We take control of Evenir, then we take the foit to the enemy!"

The words themselves weren't what made Marric feel nervous, but the many voices that sounded to rise up to support the one shouting them.

11

The crowd bustled as a man shouted various things about the need for new leadership. Janis's senses heightened as Avryn led them into the throng with not even a moment's pause. Such brazen actions were not something she would choose under normal circumstances, but then again, nothing was normal after what had happened in Stilten.

Janis watched the man speaking to the crowd, keeping her hearing focused on her surroundings as they pushed their way toward the front.

There are too many people here close together, she thought. *How could a rally like this happen so quickly without someone being here to notice before?*

Right as she had the thought, she recalled her first days within Terris Green. She'd overheard a couple of men talking about Magness and how they needed to remove her. Cursing, Janis pushed harder through the throng to get to Avryn. She got just behind him, despite the grumblings of the people she shoved out of the way, and grabbed his arm, stopping him.

His reaction was not what she expected. Rather than turn around and discuss what she'd done, he shouldered her grasp off of his upper arm and kept moving. Either he thought it was someone else trying to stop him or he didn't want to discuss anything with her at the moment. The crowd got more raucous around them. Avryn, unabashed by the uproar, reached the table and pulled himself up onto it. Silence fell on the crowd, as if some fiend had sucked away all sound.

"Well looky 'ere, if it's not the one an' only Avryn, come to take the loiks of us over again," the man said with disdain.

Janis reached for a dagger, which she held in a sheath under her left shoulder. She thought to rest her hand there without pulling it out but decided she cared little about the worry of the surrounding people. Sliding it out, she let her right hand fall to her side, the dagger gripped there.

He stood tall, showing no signs of concern at the many people talking literal blasphemy before him, the acting leader.

"People! You know this is not the way! Evenir has lived on a compact for centuries that allows for the majority vote for leader. We've been delayed on this *only* due to the absence of many of our brethren, but they've returned. We must prepare ourselves for—"

"Oh, shove it, man! We be dun list'nin' to yer vain words. Yeh ain't the one t'bring us to victory. Watchlight needs to be destroyed. It's toim we *do somethin'* 'bout it," the man shouted, interrupting Avryn's words.

Members of the crowd, though not all of them, Janis noted, shouted agreement as he finished. Janis scanned the throng. Many faces watching the man held curiosity more than anger, though it was relatively easy to pick out the ones who agreed with the dissenter on the table. These must have intentionally been placed throughout the crowd to create a feeling of mutual agreement from seemingly random people.

It wasn't hard for Janis to see through that. This was an organized revolt, and the man on the table was the one orchestrating it all. Looking back at him, Janis couldn't help but notice how clean-cut he appeared. His clothing wasn't overall fancy, not like Varith's or Rivelen's, but it was perfectly kept and clean. His long hair was slicked back in a ponytail, his face clean-shaven. Janis assumed he was a Fixer just by how clean he looked.

Turning her eyes again, she found the closest person who appeared to be in cahoots with the leader of the insurrection, then started moving that direction. With more than a few angry glares and words, Janis pushed through.

"In due time, we will bring the fight to Watchlight. But we must do so with a plan and a well-organized assault. Rushing into a battle would be both unwise and costly for us," Avryn explained.

"Yeh're jus' as scared as Magness. We be needin' *proper* leaders to take us to victory. Loik me!" The man held up his hands, causing the various members throughout the crowd to cheer.

This action confirmed that Janis targeted one of the right people, her quarry lifting her hand with a shout. When she was mere feet away, she stepped up to the woman and grabbed her arm firmly. The woman gasped, eyes wide, and froze as Janis positioned herself behind her.

"Did he put you up to this, then?" Janis whispered in her ear.

The woman nodded but didn't say anything.

"Leave. Now, or you'll regret you came to the meeting today," Janis hissed.

The woman's face paled at Janis's words. Janis released her grip, letting her retreat through the crowd. Though Janis didn't expect it to help much, she figured it would be better than standing still somewhere.

"I have little fear of Watchlight. I've fought them too many times to fear them. Any who have accompanied me on one of our journeys has witnessed this very thing. Do you deny it?" Avryn questioned.

Murmurs flowed through the crowd like a wave. Janis knew his statement carried weight, and the reaction of the people validated this. Half listening, Janis located another man with the same confident posture and sneer. She moved with ease this time, the people surrounding her having seen what she'd done.

"An' what do yeh say we do, then? Wait longer? Sit longer? Until they come 'round 'ere and kill us all?! 'Ow many 'ave doid because o' waitin'?" the man sneered.

This statement struck Avryn hard and he paused, collecting his thoughts. His face fell slightly at the mention of the deaths. It was a well-known fact that each and every death affected Avryn. He'd proven more than once that he knew every person in the compound. He never took death lightly.

What a horrible life to live. Being worried and saddened about deaths, Janis noted, finally reaching the next man.

Then again, hadn't she changed? She recalled the moment in Stilten when she'd worried about Marric, and consecutive times she'd thought he'd never return. There was the feeling of knocking Macks through the roof and worrying for his death.

The crowd continued to murmur around them as they listened to the debate. Neither contender had swayed the crowd in either direction. Janis slipped behind her target and threatened a similar thing. Though he didn't seem as scared, he still left after hearing the seriousness of her tone.

"The deaths we've suffered sadden me to no end, but we must not let their sacrifice be in vain. If we march on Watchlight right now, I fear we'll be lost. I swear that whatever my place is after the vote, be it at the head or not, I will avenge their lives. I *will* secure the safety of our citizens," Avryn promised.

Another wave of murmurs followed. Janis felt a sincerity in Avryn's words that almost pained her. He'd always proven loyal and passionate, but the words were so confident that even she felt trust in his words. Just then, Janis noticed something odd. A faint blue Light caught her attention and she flinched, thinking it was some Light-Conjured object being used on her. When she looked more closely, she realized it was a blue line connected to her person. Furrowing her brow, she lost sight of her next quarry and followed the faint line with her eyes. Ultimately, it passed through the crowd and ended on a single figure at the back.

Marric.

Her mind buzzed. This wasn't the first time she'd seen such a thing. Curiosity blossomed inside of her. Without hesitation, Janis reached inside, letting her Seeing flow through her until her eyes glowed. Gasps sounded around her as the people closest to her noticed what she was doing. It felt odd to do something like this in public, but she'd only Seen the line once and couldn't miss the opportunity to investigate, should it disappear as it had before. Plus, she hoped that displaying her Lightbearing would potentially intimidate those around her as her mere presence seemed to do.

The line thickened, turning into a blazing rope of Light. Marric's body wreathed in a subtle but obvious aura of Light, as if he were surrounded by a swarm of insects that glowed blue.

"False promises! Yeh're all words and no action! We be needin' action, not just talkin'," the man rebutted.

Janis let the vision end, coming back to reality.

"Oh? And do you not wish to hear of the victories we've had in the past weeks? We've defeated Watchlight on several occasions, relinquishing their hold on three new Lightbearers who've come to bolster our ranks. With mere words, these victories could not have been won. Even now we have been gifted a power that Watchlight cannot account for," Avryn said.

Janis froze, understanding what he meant.

"The woman you treated with disdain and anger has Transformed into something unimaginable. She alone led us to victory against Prost and Riln. Even she slayed the leader of Watchlight, his blood spilling on the stones within Stilten."

Gasps and whispers followed. The people immediately surrounding her moved away, bunching themselves together as if she was plagued with some disease they feared catching.

"Lanser chose Janis as the Prime Lightbearer, capable of wielding every Lightbearing power to its fullest. Have we not hope? Had we not waited, planned, and plotted, Janis would not have had the time to become what she has," Avryn stated.

Janis loathed every word that came out of his mouth. Tryvv's words in Stilten echoed in her mind, distracting her. She knew she was meant for something bigger. She and Livella were the sole binds for Ugglyn's might, and whether or not she liked it, she would have to act it.

"*This* woman? The black-clad insanity? Surely yeh 'aven't put all 'ope in the loiks o' 'er. We can' be trustin' an assassin fer anythin'!" the man complained.

This received far too many agreeing whispers and shouts from within the crowd. Janis steeled herself and stood straight, realizing how many people were watching her now. She could no longer deny her place in this. Her eyes met Avryn's, and he gave her a pointed look as if to say, "Confirm my words. Show them what I mean."

Despite being more comfortable and in control of her powers, Janis still disliked displaying them too much. Still, she felt Avryn would lose traction if she didn't. With little concentration needed, Janis raised her hands and summoned an orb of Light the size of her head. In an instant, the orbs exploded outward, filling the enormous cavern with brightness beyond that of the sun. She felt a buzz within her as the Light bolstered her powers. She Conjured two broadswords, impractical in any normal fight but very impressive and intimidating to look at.

Those closest to her backed away as if she might chop them to pieces with her weapons. Janis could feel the eyes on her and it caused her skin to prickle. Attention had never been a good thing. As an assassin her purpose was to hide in plain sight, to never draw the gaze of anyone who might be skeptical of who she was and what she was doing. Resisting the urge to dart out of the crowd, Janis stood up straighter, eyeing Avryn.

What's happened to me? Janis thought. She knew she was playing into Avryn's words that she should be the leader of Evenir, but she felt she had little choice.

She laughed internally at the idea. Just a few weeks ago she'd wasted no time in reminding Magness that she was not subject to the woman's rule, that she could do whatever she wished as an independent assassin. Now Janis stood here amidst hundreds of people, displaying powers that would make her stand out for leagues. All at the behest of the temporary leader of a group she formerly didn't want to be a part of. She looked atMarric, who watched her with wide eyes. He scanned her up and down a few times, his mouth dropping open. She smiled grimly at him, then nodded, hoping that he'd get the message that they'd talk later. When she'd left with Livella and the others, her Lightbearing was still infantile and shoddy. She could only imagine what seeing this was like for Marric.

Janis's eyes met the man on the table and he glared at her. Despite the anger he held in the gaze, she could see fear hidden behind. She smiled at him. If anything, she was confident she could best the man in a fight.

"She's no simple assassin, as you so carelessly accuse. Janis has Awakened into something far more than you or I could imagine. Riln, former leader of Watchlight, was the only known person to wield such power until now. We are fortunate that the new Prime has aligned her interests with our own purpose," Avryn stated.

This irked Janis, for she hadn't fully done anything of the sort. Her Awakening had happened after she'd been mixed up in the matters of Evenir despite her protests. She hadn't come here because of interest in their cause. Still, considering what she'd learned of Watchlight, she couldn't support madness like that.

"With Riln slain, we have the advantage. We *will* take that advantage but after careful planning and deliberation. There are too many precious lives to preserve here, my friends." Avryn's voice wavered as he said the words. His compassion had to be well-known within the compound. Janis had always considered this a weakness, something that would likely get him killed someday. Yet now, Janis realized how strong it made him sound as a leader.

The whispers continued around them, angry faces standing out even more in the crowd. The followers of this fool man's cause appeared stark amongst those who now doubted the insurrection. With the crowd swayed even more toward Avryn's ideals, the man atop the table growled. He turned on Avryn and Conjured a sword of brilliant blue.

"Yeh speak words o' confidence, but where's the actin'? Show us the truth o' the words yeh speak. *Prove* yeh ain' weaker than that wench Magness!" the man shouted.

Avryn stiffened as the man yelled and rushed him. A sword flashed into Avryn's hand and he easily parried the attack. The Conjure appeared so quickly and naturally that Janis felt a slight pang of jealousy. She'd gained full command of her abilities, but she still had a lot to learn and she knew it.

Janis logged a mental note to allow Avryn to help her gain such skills. Though she still felt hesitant to use her Lightbearing too much for fear she'd become reliant on it, she had realized the importance of using her resources.

The man bared his teeth in a wicked grin, pleased that he'd forced Avryn's hand into a fight. Rumblings of surprise and fear ran through the crowd, seeing this man attack the person who led Evenir. Avryn faced the man, his Conjured sword held at the ready.

"A duel will prove nothing for you. Stop now before you regret your decision," Avryn said coolly.

The words didn't calm the man but instead seemed to rouse his anger even more. With another shout, he lunged at Avryn, his Conjured sword casting shadows on the faces of the onlookers as he stabbed. Avryn parried the second attack, stepping backward lightly on the table.

Janis had seen Avryn fight a number of times, and she knew he wasn't attacking back in earnest. Instead he parried and blocked the man's attempts, sliding around the edge of the table so he didn't fall off. His face remained calm, though Janis could tell that Avryn's opponent almost had him on the full defense. In a flash, Avryn finally took a step and attacked the well-kept man. Unfortunately, the man blocked Avryn's attack almost as easily.

The battle took on a different tone after that. Avryn's face scrunched in determination as he counter-attacked with purpose. Swords clashed as the two men battled in front of the crowd. Light flashed in the eyes of the onlookers, the Conjured swords casting their bright glow on everything in the room. No one spoke, save for a few shouts of affirmation for the man opposing Avryn.

Janis watched with curiosity. She'd fought with swords and had been trained with them, but the tenor of the battle felt different between the men. Her choice of weapon was only a sword when the moment called for it, which wasn't often. There was a type of beauty that came with the engagement that Janis could admit. Realizing people no longer watched her, she dismissed her swords. She kept the Lighting orbs she'd summoned floating above the crowd, feeling no need to pull them back.

Sweat trickled down the brows of both men as they fought fervently with each other, until Janis saw Avryn's opponent make a fatal mistake; he stepped too close to the edge of the table. The moment she noticed, she expected Avryn's next move. Avryn's mouth flicked into a slight smile as he moved in close to the man and slashed forward with his sword. The man, expectedly, held his sword up to block the forward blow, but the moment the swords clashed, the force of Avryn's weapon pushed the man's foot off the edge of the table. With a shout of surprise, he tumbled backward, falling to the floor in a heap.

With a curse, he scrambled to his feet. The damage was done. Terms hadn't been spoken for the impromptu duel, but such a blunder cost the man his reputation, and he knew it. Face reddened, he cursed Avryn and stomped off, shoving members of the crowd out of the way.

He can't be left to his own devices, Janis thought, watching him go. Fortunately, tracking people was a skill she had developed quite well. She was confident she could find him and deal with him, in whatever way wouldn't cause too much commotion.

Breathing hard, Avryn faced the crowd once more. For some reason no one had left, as if they expected him to say something else. Avryn held his Conjured sword, point down, and stared at the people watching. Rather than dismiss the weapon, he held it tight, his face red from exertion. Janis felt impressed by his show of confidence and leadership.

"This is proof of not only my skill but my dedication to the people of Evenir. We *will* be victorious over Watchlight and the other forces that may oppose us. In time, we'll have the true sanctuary that Talatha, Magness, and the other leaders promised us. Given the circumstances, I propose the vote for leader happen in three days' time. I, foremost, select Janis, Prime Lightbearer, as candidate for leader of Evenir."

More whispers and comments from the crowd.

"You! We select you as candidate, Avryn," a man shouted.

This roused more comments of affirmation, which was unsurprising to Janis. She still thought he would make a much better leader for these people than she ever could, despite her status as Prime.

Another voice spoke up, this from one of the angry-faced people who'd been planted in the crowd.

"I nominate Gallin!" he shouted.

The remaining sympathizers of the man spoke up, showing their approval. Avryn expected this and nodded in understanding. This reaction impressed Janis. She was confident that many leaders cared too much about power to allow such insubordination to exist. Yet he took the nomination with a collected response.

"Are there any others at this time that anyone wishes to select?" Avryn asked, his sword still glowing ominously at his side.

Silence.

"Let it be known that in three days' time, a vote is to be held. Should any other nominations arise, they will be valid. The news will be spread to everyone with the intent to vote," Avryn said, "after which, discussions will continue on the Evenir offensive plans. But one thing I regret to say is that we have more to deal with than anyone can understand. Something has emerged that none of us expected."

Janis clenched her jaw. She glanced at Marric, who still stood at the back of the crowd. To her surprise, he didn't look concerned or even awed by what they'd just witnessed. He focused on Avryn, his face determined. Janis knew even he'd changed since she'd met him months ago.

Loss can do that to you, she thought.

"I fear that some evil may have come into Lindrad that we can't describe. It's well-known that Lightbearing is a gift from Lanser, the god many of you worship. Over the last few weeks, we've learned that Janis and Livella hold Ugglyn's powers at bay."

Avryn paused. Janis wasn't sure if it was for effect or if he was trying to consider the best way to discuss the next piece.

"As I mentioned, Janis managed to best Riln, the most powerful Lightbearer we've known in Lindrad, during the battle in Stilten."

Janis continued to stare at Avryn, trying not to feel uncomfortable with the eyes that stared at her from the crowd.

I merely injured the fiend. Prost is the true killer, Janis thought with some disdain. In the end, she didn't care too much about how the man had died, but she couldn't help but wonder what would have happened if she'd killed Prost before he'd reached Riln.

"Moments after Riln's death, some force, some power, was unleashed on Lindrad. Though we're unsure what it means, or how powerful this might be, we fear it's connected to Ugglyn," Avryn explained.

The stunned silence that followed this statement broke quickly, cries and shouts of worry sounding in a cacophony around them. Janis took the moment to glance at Marric again, gauging the boy's reaction. His eyes were wide for a moment, but it changed into a look of determination. Janis felt even more pride at that.

"What does it mean?" a woman from the back asked.

"Do you have a plan for this?" asked another.

"How do we know what you say is true?" a man challenged from the front.

More questions echoed through the cavern, the sounds overlapping, creating more chaos among the people. Though many things were asked, Avryn locked on one question, his eyes landing on Janis.

"We know because we have our own personal accounts, plus that of many others who saw the strange happenings in Stilten," Avryn stated, pointing at her. "Janis was the closest to the event. Let us hear what she has to say on the matter."

Janis would have preferred not to say anything. In a direct conversation with an enemy or a smaller group, Janis could outwit those she spoke to. When faced with a larger group, it didn't turn out well. Even watching Avryn over the last few moments made her uncomfortable, for she couldn't understand a leader's skill in speaking wise and encouraging words to a crowd.

The eyes of the onlookers never left her, despite Avryn's continued speech and final offer for her to speak. Steeling herself, Janis continued to stand straight, her eyes scanning the crowd. She wasn't *nervous* to say anything, but she still didn't want to. For a moment she thought she ought to string together some inspiring set of words to describe the events in a positive light or to at least be more commanding with what she said. Her mind spun through the various words and structures she could use to do just that, but she decided it wasn't worth it.

"Riln died with my dagger in his neck. The man called Prost delivered the final blow in the end. Once he'd fallen, a tempest of silver-black smoke stoked up around the two men. I watched as they were engulfed in the power, and I recognized it as the anti-god himself. Ugglyn faced me twice before then, and I am sure it was his power that consumed Prost and Riln. Once the tempest dissipated, Prost looked at me with blackened eyes."

Under normal circumstances, the tale she told would have sounded like a farce, but those who had heard of Janis knew she did not have a reputation for humor. The air in the cavern took on an ominous feel, as if Janis speaking the anti-god's name invoked the power of the being. A subtle wave flew through the crowd, the change in the conversation's tenor obvious in their faces and postures. One man closest to her opened his mouth to say something but must have changed his mind, his mouth slamming closed. Noises around them either stopped or became muffled as the Light above and around them dimmed slightly. Narrowing her eyes at the oddness of their surroundings, Janis looked upward and held her hand out. She focused on the Lighting orbs she'd summoned and split them, expanding the network of Light above.

The encroaching darkness melted into the brightening Light. Returning her gaze to the surrounding people, she noted their looks of awe and shock. Janis scoffed internally. It felt theatrical and cheesy, but she couldn't help but accept that it would benefit her. If anyone had any doubts about her and Avryn's ability to combat this supposed darkness, they likely wouldn't feel so inclined now.

Janis packed away what had just happened in her mind. Though she was fairly confident that speaking the anti-god's name would not summon any part of his influence, she couldn't discount the oddity of what had just happened in the room. It was clear by the reactions of Avryn and those around them that she wasn't the only one who noticed the darkness.

"As you see, we must tread lightly until we can build the force we need. Know this, I will stand tirelessly with, or as, the new leader of Evenir to ensure the safety of our people," Avryn assured them.

Despite the oddity of the event moments before, Janis could feel the confidence and trust of those who listened. She even spotted Marric standing straighter at Avryn's declaration. Once again, Janis recognized the obvious difference in Avryn's ability to lead the organization. She was meant to work alone, to care only for her safety. Yet, she knew she couldn't return to her previous life, not anymore.

There's no use lamenting my past. It's time to move on, Janis scolded herself.

Avryn's final comment must have felt like a dismissal, for the group around them broke up quickly, hushed conversations continuing only among a few. Janis watched them leave, her eyes scanning for more signs of trouble, locking on a particular man and woman near the back. They each sneered at Avryn, who had jumped down from the table and now spoke quietly with a woman there. Narinda had slipped through the moving people to reach him. She listened carefully, her face giving Janis no indication of what might be the topic of conversation.

The man in the unfamiliar pair shifted his gaze until it landed on Janis. His brows furrowed and anger set deeper in his eyes, as if seeing her lit a fire inside him.

Janis thought that maybe a normal person might be intimidated by such a look, but she felt nothing. Instead she stared back, planting a condescending look on her face. This had the effect she'd hoped, for the anger deepened in this man's eyes. He turned away, grabbing his companion's arm and spinning her to the entrance of another tunnel. Janis had already memorized what they each looked like, but she knew she could call on the memory in the in-between later.

She shook her head, remembering that she no longer needed to rely on the in-between to get information from the past. Seeing did that more effectively anyway. A small wisp of discomfort spurred inside her at the thought of her powers but she stifled it. It was shocking to her how easily she could do that now. It had been less than two weeks since she'd fully come into the strange abilities, but they already felt familiar, like a skill she'd had for so long but didn't realize.

Marric stood where he was until more people filtered away, after which he moved to her. His forehead was firm above his eyebrows, wrinkles forming there.

"That speech was great and everything, but you never explained what happened to Magness or the other Lightbearers you were meant to retrieve," Marric said bluntly.

His tone didn't sound angry, but he was clearly frustrated.

Oh, what it was like to be a youth and wear everything on your sleeve with no trouble, Janis thought.

Janis took in a measured breath, considering how to explain. Before she could continue, Avryn and Narinda were there.

"The potential insurrection is worse than I feared. Egylven told me there are at least a hundred others who agree with Gallin. If that's true, then I'm not sure we can last three days. Still, we must send word to everyone in Terris Green, letting them know of those for whom they should cast the vote. Should it fall on Gallin, I fear we'll be at a worse fate than ever," Avryn said grimly.

The bustle of the cavern returned to normal far more quickly than Janis would have guessed. Men shouted about what they were selling, some offering labor for various projects. Light flashed left and right as Lightbearers used their abilities. One man stalked by with five heavy baskets full of some type of vegetable they'd grown here. She wasn't close enough to see exactly what they were, but she was also focused on how the baskets glowed a steady blue, floating around his person. It was an odd sight, though Janis knew it was his Moving ability.

Another woman Conjured a cloak from the same blue Light, affixing it on a teenage boy, likely trying to understand the design and measurement required for her to sew a new one. Such practical uses of Lightbearing were something Janis hadn't considered, yet people casually leveraged the abilities all around her. She made a mental note to keep the applications of the power in mind should she need them later.

"Why not take control? You are the second-in-command. Could you not proclaim yourself the leader?" Janis asked frankly.

This made Avryn chuckle, despite the circumstances.

"I could, but I don't think that would be the best course of action for myself *or* Evenir as a whole. How would people take to that? Especially after my speech just now. I touted you for killing Riln, who is well-known around here as the dictator of Watchlight. No one wants that. The best thing we can do is give them a voice," Avryn explained.

Just before he could continue, a commotion sounded from the other side of the cavern. The woman Avryn had just been speaking to rushed over there to deal with the matter.

"Egylven says outbreaks like this have been happening a few times a day. There is unrest among the citizens here. Until we have a voted leader, I fear it will continue to get worse," Avryn said.

Narinda's eyes filled with resolve and she unabashedly reached for Avryn's hand. Grasping it in a tight hold, she raised it between them, her eyes locking on his. "Though I understand your reasons for not taking command, I pray to Lanser that the majority falls on you. A man like Gallin will only tear Evenir to pieces. He only cares about power and fame, not protecting us or the compound," she said.

Marric shuffled next to her. He'd shifted his hands behind his back and was looking at the ground, his feet scuffing the stone beneath him. Janis could tell that he wanted to repeat his question but wasn't feeling so brave as to ask Avryn as he had her. With a sigh, Janis did the work for him.

"Politics aside, we owe these two an explanation. News of Magness's death spread with no trouble," Janis suggested, though it was more than a suggestion and Avryn knew it. Raising a brow, he nodded, then gestured to a tunnel to their left.

"We should speak somewhere more private, then. The last thing we need is someone hearing our failings in Stilten and using that to get Gallin voted as leader," Avryn said.

Avryn turned toward a tunnel and made his way to the opening there. Marric silently walked next to him. It was obvious to Janis that Marric didn't want to have to wait to hear the details, but he wouldn't object.

"So—are you going to leave those up, then?" Narinda asked. "I'm relatively sure that my Lighters will keep this place alight just fine."

Janis glanced up, just now remembering that she'd summoned the numerous orbs that hovered halfway to the tall ceiling of the cavern. Narrowing her eyes, Janis scanned the room above.

"I can recall them, sure," Janis offered, ignoring the obvious sarcastic nature of the woman's question.

Just as she raised her hand to recall the large spheres of Light, she paused, looking at Narinda once more.

"How far could I walk away before these disappear? Is there a limited range?" Janis asked her.

Narinda shrugged in response. "The exact distance is unknown, I believe. One Lighter can Light the whole compound, though it requires extensive knowledge of the network of tunnels and rooms. A Lighter has to study for years to be able to send out the Lights they need to throughout the compound," she explained. "Even then, we have two or three on hand and awake at all times should something ill fall upon the one Lighting the halls."

Though she hadn't asked for the explanation, Janis was grateful for it. She felt it was something she should know. The thought discomforted her more than she wanted to admit, as if the fact that she required this knowledge meant she bought into the idea of her leading Evenir. She quelled the thought quickly.

"I see," Janis said, still not reclaiming the power.

Narinda smirked at her.

"You can try to hold it, though we don't want the others getting too used to how light it is in here," Narinda replied.

Janis had not practiced much with the power, but she had used it before. Still, she was surprised at the instinct she had to reclaim the Light. She held her hands out and willed the orbs to disappear. With a slight flash, they disappeared into the air, leaving the cavern dimmer than it had been moments before. The act caused more than one grumble as eyes were forced to adjust to the dimmer Light. The orbs spaced throughout the cavern were plenty, as they had been before, but the change was somewhat depressing.

Narinda watched her with a measured gaze.

"You really came into that, didn't you?" she said, obviously amazed. "Seems like yesterday you couldn't do anything but accidentally blow caverns to pieces."

The comment was undoubtedly intended to embarrass her, but Janis wasn't affected by comments like that any longer. Not after years and years of emotional conditioning from Macks.

Thinking the man's name spurred the same warmth and sadness inside her that it had all these years. She'd tried to See him again just earlier, to no avail. Either that meant he'd allied himself with a Shielder or he'd become one himself. That, or he was truly dead.

Something inside Janis told her that wasn't true. Although she'd incorrectly thought him dead all these years, his involvement with Luden, and consequently Lightbearing in general, made Janis think that he would be too resilient to have died in Stilten two weeks ago.

"It comes with the job, I'm told," Janis said flatly.

Narinda looked confused at her words, but Janis just shook her head and moved to the tunnel. Without context, everything she did must have appeared not only odd but very disconcerting. It was well-known that a maximum of two powers could be held by any person, save for Avryn and Marric. Janis had shown more than that already.

The two women walked quietly, following Avryn and Marric. The men had moved quite a bit farther ahead, making the two women hasten their pace until they were within a few strides. It required little effort for Janis, but she was surprised to hear that Narinda wasn't out of breath despite their haste.

Janis looked at Marric's back, his dirtied and torn brown cloak dragging on the floor where the corner had been ripped off almost completely. The thin blue line she'd inspected before hovered faintly between the two of them. Curiously, Janis realized another line extended from him in another direction.

Cocking her head, she packed the memory away for later.

At length, Avryn stopped at a wooden door. Janis hadn't seen very many rooms with actual doors, most being open or covered with a cloth like her quarters. Avryn pushed heavily on the door, the hinges creaking as it swung open. He gestured for Marric to enter first, then stood by while Narinda entered. Janis paused, eyeing him. She looked from him to the door, then back again, giving him a pointed look.

Avryn sighed, then stepped in front of her.

"Still don't trust me? Don't you think you'd be over that by now?" Avryn asked. There was a tinge of humor in his tone, but Janis knew he was partially annoyed with her.

"Oh, it's not that. I trust you just fine. But if we're going to get ambushed, I'd rather be the last one attacked. At least then I could save you all," Janis replied.

She wasn't joking. Part of her did prefer to go last in situations like this unless she absolutely had to go first. Janis wasn't ashamed of the habit, but she recognized how it didn't align with a majority of people's views.

After ducking through the short portal to the room, Janis blinked. It was pitch-black inside. The Light orbs created by the Lighter on duty rarely extended into the sleeping quarters, not because of lack of ability, but mainly because of preference. Avryn had told her that should some people have different sleeping times or like to nap during the day, specifically asking the Lighter on duty to remove a single orb was not only impractical but an organizational nightmare. Thus, Lighters employed their own methods of Lighting, while others used candles.

Janis thought back to the time before Stilten when she had used a candle for her room. Even though she'd Awakened, she dared not use it for illumination on the off chance she accidentally created the wrong type of

Light. The room blossomed with a dim Light suddenly, Avryn and Marric both standing with their hands outstretched, a small fingernail-sized ball of light hovering above each of their palms. Janis felt proud of the boy for some reason.

"Narinda, if you please," Avryn said.

"Oh, yes, of course," Narinda responded before clapping her hands together softly and pulling them apart. A large orb illuminated the space. She opened her palms, the orb splitting outward into half a dozen more, then flying to the corners and sides of the room.

"Thank you. As much as I like discussions in the dark, this will suit us better," Avryn said. He turned to Narinda and smiled at her, their eyes lingering on each other for just long enough that Janis started to feel uncomfortable. Janis noted, independent of the odd moment between the two, that Avryn's speech had taken on a new tone. Not only when he spoke before the crowd but even now in private conversations. Whether this change was forced by his temporary position or if he felt like he needed to be more formal, Janis observed the shift. Finally, he continued.

"We've already talked to the other generals about what happened in Stilten. Rivelen is the most recent to hear it. Still, we'll recount the details again for you. When we arrived in Stilten, we split into three groups. I headed the one for retrieving the twin boys, Janis and Magness for one, and Alsry for the girl in the bar. When we arrived at the aforementioned location, the boys were already seated there, entertaining some smaller children. Not moments after we arrived, arrows rained down on us from above. Fortunately, Magness was wise enough to send at least one Shielder with each. While the arrows didn't pierce the Shield at first, they soon did. Our assailants used some form of poison on their arrowheads that allowed them to pierce any Light barriers. Some of our men fell to the attack, but our returned volleys kept them at bay. I got to the boys before too many of us had fallen and secured them within their home.

"Before I could sneak them out another way, I heard shouting on the road outside. That's when I saw the red Light. Watchlight ambushed us from behind, and we lost far more than I'd like to admit. Despite that, we escaped with the boys. We've already put them to work learning their skills, though they've proven great aptitude for them. As for Alsry's story, I fear it's much the same, except their quarry died to the strange poison you saw on your journey for your father," Avryn finished.

Marric paled at the mention of the poison, but he nodded in understanding. After a moment, when it seemed like neither Narinda nor Marric had any questions regarding the recounting, Avryn looked at Janis.

Steeling herself, she began sharing the events of her time in Stilten. When she got to the part about Luden and the archers with poison-tipped arrows, Narinda looked horrified. Marric, once again, just looked sick. It was understandable to Janis why the mention of the odd substance would make him react the way it did, given his experience watching Turrin almost die from it. She explained more about Luden, though that didn't hold much interest for either of them. It was obvious they wanted to know about the quarry and specifically about how Janis came to control her abilities more. So Janis skipped to that part, leaving out the visionary details with Tryvv but continuing to her battle with Riln and their eventual retreat. Marric grimaced at the part about her dagger slamming into Riln from behind, and she realized that such displays were still new to Marric. He'd been forced to kill men recently, but it took a long time to get used to violence.

She explained the details behind Magness's and the new Lightbearer's death, a small feeling of guilt creeping up inside of her. She balked at the experience, recalling how she'd not felt guilt for the longest time. As practiced, Janis quelled the encroaching emotion, keeping her face measured.

"The only reward for our journey at this point is my heightened Lightbearing. We lost many in Stilten," Janis explained. "Magness, the Lightbearer girl, my favorite dagger."

She added the last part with bitterness. Surprisingly, none of those who listened appeared offended that she lumped in the loss of a weapon with the loss of two human lives. Marric shook his head, a slight smile on his face. He probably thought her mentioning of the weapon was a joke, some form of dark, twisted humor, but she was definitely serious. Regardless, the silence that followed somehow darkened the surrounding air, not literally, but figuratively.

For a moment Janis thought to stop there but she paused, then fingered the small book wrapped in a handkerchief and stuffed into her belt. From its place there, she couldn't feel the odd effects from touching the cover.

She'd told the other generals about the book, but Avryn either must have forgotten or hadn't considered this a piece of information Janis needed to pass on. In the end, something inside urged Janis to share it.

"And another odd thing came of it," Janis continued. "Macks, my former mentor, carried this. When I—subdued him—I found it on his person."

She gingerly fished the book out and held it forward with two fingers. It was easy to do, the book being light given its size. The handkerchief fell away from the book, save for the part she used to grasp the bottom corner. Immediately, the Lighter orbs around them dimmed. It was subtle, and Janis noted that none of the others noticed.

"What does it say? I can't read the inscription on the front," Marric said.

Narinda removed her glasses, cleaned them on her shirt, then moved forward, replacing the round frames on her nose. Brown eyes inspected the book, yet they narrowed in confusion only moments later.

"I can't read it either. It's some ancient script I'm unfamiliar with, though it seems to share elements of the old language we are familiar with. See here? This is the *trilan*, it represents the t sound, and this here is the *ervil*, which is pronounced 'e.' The rest looks reminiscent of the other symbols, but they are odd combinations of them. This here—"

Narinda paused when Janis raised a brow at her. She had been thinking to tell Narinda that this wasn't the time for a full analysis of the text, but she wasn't going to say anything. The look Janis gave her must have been sufficient.

"What's it for, then? Why did Macks have it?" Marric asked, oblivious to the interaction between the women.

Janis shook her head. "I don't know. If we haven't been able to read it, I can't imagine Macks could. The man is brilliant, but so far, only Livella's been able to read the text fully."

She paused, trying to determine the best way to describe the effects it caused.

"Text aside, it causes strange sensations to those who touch it with their skin," Janis noted, offering the book to Marric.

His eyes widened and he took a step back, shaking his head. Narinda must have seen his reaction from the corner of her eyes, for she flinched as well, but in the end extended her hand and grabbed the book with her bare fingers.

The moment the woman's tan fingers touched the leather of the binding, she yelped and dropped it, the book thudding on the ground. Avryn jumped forward, holding back Narinda from the small book, which now lay between them all.

"Are you ok? What happened?" Avryn asked her.

Narinda shook her head, her face full of wonder. Even before the woman could describe the sensation, Janis was relieved it wasn't just her who experienced the odd feeling. She couldn't be sure if she'd imagined it or if perhaps she was the only one who felt it given her status as the Prime. Whispers echoed almost silently off the stone walls around them, as if Narinda touching the book with her skin caused something to awaken within the walls of the ancient mountain around them.

Janis might have thought she imagined the whispers, her limbs buzzing from the sudden heightened stress within her, but she noted the others stiffening as well. The whispers continued to echo for longer than should be possible for sound, then they fell silent.

"That did *not* happen the last time a Lightbearer touched this," Janis said. In her haste, she'd Conjured a dagger that looked exactly like the one she'd lost in Stilten. The blue Light glowed on the wall immediately next to her despite the bright blue orbs hovering around them. Avryn still stood tense between Narinda and the book, but he turned slowly and inspected the woman's hand, worry obvious on his face.

If this wasn't a more clear sign of the man's affection for this woman, Janis would consider herself crazy. A pang of jealousy rocked through her chest, but she shoved it away. Memories of Macks began flowing in, along with the memory of seeing him broken on the ground through the shattered roof of the bar in Stilten. She packed them away as easily as she did any emotions that got in her way. Even though she'd Transformed, she refused to let emotions rule her the way they did the common person. Emotions got you in trouble; they got you killed.

After whispering something to Narinda, Avryn turned and eyed the book on the ground, which no one was hurrying to retrieve. Not even Janis.

"And how many experiments have you done with the book, then? Have they all been this extreme?" Avryn questioned, his voice hard.

"I don't make a habit of handling objects that feel like they're attacking me," Janis blurted, squatting down to look at the book.

Avryn scoffed but didn't say more.

"What does it say? I can't read the front of it," Marric admitted.

Janis shook her head.

"No one but Livella can read it, as far as I can tell." She paused, thinking of Macks. "Though I've a suspicion that the man I took this from could read at least some of it. I can't imagine why else he'd have it."

Narrowing her eyes, she leaned down and touched the cover with her handkerchief-covered fingers. She flipped open the thicker leather front, revealing that the inside was made from parchment of the same blackness, bright red ink forming again on the pages. Moving closer, she inspected the actual text, noting that the symbols looked as unfamiliar as those on the front.

"Livella's ability to read it is what led me to believe that this is somehow connected to Ugglyn. She's infused somehow with whatever makes up the anti-god, so it would make sense that this book is his or at least something he's touched."

Avryn grunted.

"And when she read it?" Avryn asked, though Janis could tell by his voice that he knew the answer.

"The pillar of smoke appeared when she read it. I don't know why—"

Janis paused as she noted that one sentence, right in the middle of the page, began to move. The characters of the sentence rippled as if it were the surface of a lake that had just been hit by a pebble or small stone.

Immediately, the words transformed into something she could read. It wasn't in Lindradian but rather in the old language. Still, the characters became a script she could decipher. Inside, something whispered that she knew what the words meant.

Vilick fritlat Ugglyn ug yasnin.

Ugglyn, I call upon your attention, she translated in her mind. Her stomach twisted, curiosity tugging at her insides to speak the words aloud.

"*Vilick fritlat Ugglyn*—" Marric said before Janis jumped up.

"No!" Janis shouted, interrupting Marric's words.

Despite her speed, the book let out a vibration that made her hair stand on end. It stood open still, but the pages began pulsating, a dark silvery smoke forming around it. Marric's eyes widened, and he backed away, Conjuring a bow and arrow of Light. Avryn held his sword in front of him, the Light reflecting off of the silvery substance that grew from the book like water bubbling over the lid of a cup that had been overfilled. The orbs of Light around them intensified as well, and Janis eyed Narinda's pressed lips as she stared nervously at the book.

The growth protruding from the pages looked familiar. Janis moved closer, Avryn muttering a warning to her side. She waved off the comment and stood just over the substance. After a moment Janis realized the growth appearing from the book was growing spikes made of the same smokey substance, though these took on a more solid appearance. They all stared on, unsure what to do, waiting for something else to happen. Suddenly the apparition moved, an arm appearing on the side. The arm slapped the ground and made a sound like a human hand might if hitting rocks. Avryn cursed and pushed Narinda back behind him. Marric yelped and shot his arrow in surprise, the sharp point skittering on the floor as it flew past Janis and the odd creature.

Janis realized it was a similar creature to the one she'd seen in T'Arren Vale and didn't hesitate. Holding her Conjured dagger with her right hand, she created a ball of Destroying power and flung it at the growing apparition. Just as she'd seen it in the capital, it slammed into the creature, shattering it to pieces. A loud, high-pitched screech pained her ears, though it faded quickly.

"Lanser's beard, what was that?" Narinda exclaimed, pushing Avryn to the side with irritation.

The creature was gone, the book sitting alone on the stone between them.

"I think Marric almost summoned the rotten anti-god himself," Janis pointed out.

Marric paled, his face taking on more of the blueish hue from the orbs.

"I didn't mean to—I was just reading what I saw," Marric reasoned.

Janis waved her hand dismissively.

She furrowed her brow, realizing that at the exact moment she'd been able to read the words, Marric must have experienced the same. Though she couldn't describe why, she felt that was important.

"It's fine, just don't read it again, aloud or silently," Janis suggested, "and let's hope that didn't give Ugglyn any information about where we are right now."

12

The night felt cool and refreshing. Too long had he been stuck in the cavernous compound beneath the Hurran Mountains. Many others had tried to convince him that leaving their lair was unwise, given the importance of keeping their location hidden, but Prost didn't care. News of his quelling the rebellion by Vint and his companion had traveled the whole compound. He guessed it was the reason for the lack of force employed to keep him inside. If there were any at Watchlight who hadn't heard of his new power, they soon would.

They wouldn't dare touch you now, not with me leading the way, Ugglyn contemplated inside his mind.

Prost ignored the comment, focusing instead on the breeze that blew through the grass on the mountainside. Over the past day since fighting Vint and obliterating the other man, Prost had tried to lock Ugglyn's voice away completely. He found that the voice not only came more often but melded with his own thoughts and emotions even more so than they had before, as if using Voidweaving had made Prost more susceptible to the intruding anti-god.

"You forced your way into me. You are nothing more than a parasitic plague in my brain. You control me no more than I control the people of Watchlight," Prost said quietly.

He was aware of a few Lightbearers standing just outside the entrance to their compound, but he didn't care what they heard. With his return, it was becoming well-known that Prost spoke to himself often. It wasn't altogether surprising, for Riln had done a similar thing when he was alone. Or rather thought he was alone. Prost guessed the other members of Watchlight would assume it came with the mantle of leadership.

Give them reason to fear, that will grasp them far more effectively than anything else, Ugglyn suggested. *And get us out of this horrid moonlight. I can't stand the blue nature. It reminds me far too much of Lanser and his annoying Lightbearing.*

Prost smiled. This was why he made a point to come out during Mellan, for he knew it irked the lurking monster within. He figured if there was to be an uninvited resident inside his body, he would assert control in whatever fashion possible. The night of their return, Prost had come out merely to get air; now it had become an almost nightly ritual to disturb Ugglyn.

"Complain more and I might just set up camp out here for the night," Prost threatened.

Amusement spread through his thoughts and chest, driven by the anti-god.

It's not all light that bothers me, just that of Mellan. Stellan's red light is welcome, and Isllan means nothing to me, Ugglyn said with contempt.

There was a hint of something in Ugglyn's tone that made Prost narrow his eyes. He thought to question the voice in his mind but pushed the urge away. Even the thought alerted Ugglyn of Prost's intentions, the anti-god flaring up in anger at Prost.

Lightning flashed far away along the skyline, framing the forest below and the distant mountains. Despite his separation from the storm, Prost could feel the buzz of excitement he'd get when he was enveloped by such a torrent. He couldn't be sure if there was rain, but thunderstorms without rain were uncommon in Lindrad, the land being surrounded by the ocean. The breeze picked up almost immediately after the distant lightning flash. If Prost hadn't known better, he'd have thought they were connected.

A rumbling came from behind, the familiar sound of the stone doors opening at the behest of a lever inside. Prost didn't turn, instead holding his gaze on the storm as more lightning flickered over the mountains.

He was aware of a person coming to his side, but he didn't look over. The act wasn't intended to be a show of power, but Prost felt somehow that it would be interpreted that way by whoever had just joined him.

Since the events of Stilten where Ugglyn had healed Prost with Void-weaving, Prost had become more lax in his personal security. More than once had an individual from Watchlight descended upon him in his sleep or when they thought he was unaware. When awake, ambushes failed nearly every time, Prost's reflexes lending him the skills needed to outmatch any who attacked him.

When he was asleep? Prost found that no matter what damage the attacker did to his body, if any, he could heal through it. Thus, as he stood there, enjoying the storm, he cared little about who came to him. Should they try anything, he knew they would fail.

"Yeh spend yer evenings 'ere, wastin' time on faraway storms, when our people could fall apart any time," the voice said.

Prost recognized the straight, cold voice. Jord. The very prodigy Riln himself had chosen to visit. Even with Ugglyn's powers and the newfound confidence within, hearing the boy's chilling tone made Prost's hair stand on end. Prost held his gaze forward, not wanting to show the boy that his presence caused him any discomfort.

"I've little care for those who try to overthrow me. If they aren't killed by those who support me, then they'll die by my hand," Prost said nonchalantly.

Jord scoffed next to him.

"And wha' o' those 'oo die searchin' fer Awakenin's? Yeh don' care fer them?" Jord hissed.

Prost smiled. "They die fighting for something meaningful and receive an honor in Lanser's court," Prost said.

As usual, the moment he spoke the god's name, heat flared up in his whole body. Ugglyn always reacted to the mention of the being who'd locked him away. Prost didn't speak Lanser's name often, but he was curious about the anti-god's unbridled anger every time Prost spoke the simple word. He had yet to question Ugglyn on the real reason the anti-god despised Lanser so. Prost assumed it was his imprisonment that made him so angry, yet he wondered if there might be more to the story.

"And those who live for me will be rewarded handsomely, to say the least," Prost mused, his eyes still locked far off on the sky.

Jord remained silent then, presumably thinking about how he could respond. Prost saw movement to the right of him and resisted the urge to spin his head that direction. A fox moved from his peripheral vision, chasing something that bounded through the grass unseen. The only telltale signs of another animal was the tall grass swaying frantically in a narrow path down the slope of the mountain's base.

Another flash of blue lit up the sky, though this appeared to be closer than the others had been.

"Wha' is it tha' yeh want, then? Riln 'ad a vision fer Watchlight to take Lindrad fer 'imself. What of yous?" Jord asked abruptly.

Prost breathed evenly, unbothered by the frank question. It was something he'd thought of regularly, yet he didn't have an answer. He chose to say nothing for a time. The lull in the conversation might have appeared to some as a weakness, but to Prost, it showed that he spoke in his own time, when he felt the need to. During the silence, Jord held still, his uncanny ability to stand unmoving taught by their late leader. Even with Prost's commanding presence, he still required shifting on his feet occasionally. Yet Jord stood there as if nothing could move him.

Curbing the small sense of eeriness Prost still held inside, he spoke.

"I care little for taking over Lindrad, though I think it will come in time," Prost admitted. "Ugglyn whispers to me as he did Riln. The anti-god wishes to rule Lindrad, to eliminate Lightbearers everywhere."

Jord stiffened next to him, and it wasn't overtly obvious until Prost realized he was speaking to a Lightbearer, one wielding the very power Ugglyn wished to remove.

So he fears me or at least what's inside, Prost thought.

In the past week, Prost had revealed, in part, how Ugglyn had granted him Voidweaving, though he did not admit that the anti-god himself possessed his person. That felt like a piece of knowledge best kept for himself should someone try to exploit it in some way. At that moment Prost felt his arm twitch: Ugglyn trying his best to pry full control of Prost's faculties away from him. Prost ignored the movement and eyed Jord to see if he'd detected anything amiss. When the boy didn't react, Prost turned back to the view before them.

"Except for those who are loyal to his cause, of course," Prost explained.

His words didn't ease Jord's concerns, he assumed, for the boy still didn't relax.

"As for my own intentions, I care only for removing Evenir and its loyalists from this place. They've caused me endless grief these past six years, and I don't want them out causing more chaos. They can't be left to their own devices, lest they be successful in their attempts to gather a bigger army," Prost said.

Jord snorted next to him. "T' kill Evenir? Or t' kill the assassin?" he jeered.

Prost's chest flared, though this time the anger was his own.

The woman must die, yes, Ugglyn whispered in his mind, *for only then can I be fully free.*

Terror wormed its way through Prost's body again as Ugglyn started to take over Prost's body. Gritting his teeth, Prost calmed his anger to regain control. The result was his limbs twitching in slight jerky motions. Jord glanced at him sideways, an amused look on his face. Prost assumed the boy thought he'd struck a nerve. In part he had, but it was far more meaningful than Jord could ever understand.

When Prost's emotions of anger, sadness, or fear overcame him, Ugglyn rushed in to take control, trying to lock Prost away in his own mind the way Prost currently held the anti-god at bay. To date, Janis was the only person who had bested him in a fight more than once and still lived. It was almost a requirement for him that she die.

But if she died, Ugglyn would be stopped by nothing. Prost knew he couldn't live with that. Part of him knew that he'd need to find a way to lock Ugglyn away again before he could kill Janis. Yet, at the same time, Voidweaving, which was only granted to him by the parasite himself, was the only thing that could even the odds between him and Janis.

Something buzzed within his brain, and Prost could tell it was Ugglyn reacting to his thoughts. He'd not been sure if the anti-god could perceive every thought inside him or not, but this felt like a confirmation. Ugglyn seemed—amused.

"The woman needs to die, yes, but it is part of the design for Evenir to fall. How can we expect a person with powers like hers to not continue rallying Lightbearers to fight against us? Kill the leader, the rest fall apart," Prost said.

He laughed internally at the idea that Janis could ever be a leader. He may not know her well, but her reputation preceded her. Every employer—every person she'd been close to—had indicated to him that she was egotistic and didn't work well with others. To think that she could rally armies was ludicrous, yet it was the best and only way to justify focusing on her death as a way toward their ultimate goal of destroying Evenir.

Jord pursed his lips and turned away from Prost. The boy wasn't a trained soldier like Prost, but he knew logic when he heard it.

"So wha' do we do, then? March off t' kill them? We don' even know where they are, for Lanser's sake," Jord spat.

Ugglyn balked within Prost. Lanser's name had been spoken once more. Prost logged the memory away, noting that even someone external to himself could use the god's name to irk the anti-god. It felt like a minor victory each time.

Jord's answer was forward and impertinent, lending more information to Prost on how his relationship must have been with Riln. If their former master allowed the boy to make such comments, then he had more power over Riln than Prost thought.

Prost let his lips turn up in a satisfied smile. *And I've just robbed him of that power.*

"You forget, boy, that we have Ugglyn on our side. Voidweaving has its advantages, but there is a way, a plan, to locate Evenir when the time is right."

An evil joy emanated within Prost, Ugglyn reacting to the comment. Ugglyn had insisted that he had a plan, a way to get into the Evenir compound and find them, though he hadn't elaborated. Every moment Prost found himself alone, the anti-god took the opportunity to whisper various plans in his mind. Only sleep gave Prost respite from the voice.

But then the dreams came.

Prost breathed evenly, calming himself again whilst pushing back thoughts of the dreams that haunted him. He knew he couldn't let them distract him, especially not now. He knew that if Jord found any reason that Prost would be unfit to lead Watchlight, he'd exploit that without a moment's hesitation. It was exactly how Riln would have acted.

Do you truly have a way to find Evenir? Or are you flaunting false promises? Prost growled in his mind.

As of yet he'd been unable to intimidate the anti-god, whether because the being himself was too powerful for Prost or because there was no way to remove him. The latter of the two explanations scared Prost the most. For the third time during the interaction, Prost shoved the thoughts away, not wanting Ugglyn to dwell on the considerations.

A gust of wind slammed them in front, the grass around them waving wildly, swishing enough that it would have been difficult to hear anyone speaking next to him. Jord remained quiet, though, his eyes veiled with an almost complete lack of emotion. It bothered Prost to no end to be unable to read the boy's emotions. Riln had trained him in that skill, something Prost never even considered trying. He wore his emotions on his sleeve for the most part, but he didn't care. What Jord did, living in a false, emotionless state, was inhuman and unnatural.

What reason do you have to distrust me? Ugglyn questioned. *I have delivered everything I've promised as of yet.*

Prost grunted out loud, causing Jord to narrow his eyes.

"Yeh don' 'ave a way, then, do yeh?" Jord challenged.

Ignoring the comment from the boy, Prost spoke to Ugglyn.

You've promised little more than giving me some power. Voidweaving has its advantages, but has it stood the test of Lightbearing from a Prime? Remember, I killed Riln without your help. I'm more than capable without you.

And yet you admitted needing Voidweaving to the boy just now, Ugglyn whispered. He sounded more than amused.

Gritting his teeth, Prost pressed back.

Fog it, tell me how you propose finding them, or Lanser's might be upon you, Prost countered.

As expected, invoking the god's name caused Ugglyn to hiss loudly, retreating momentarily before anger flared inside like a fire stoked with more fuel than it needed to persist.

Before Ugglyn could respond, Prost felt a tug at his stomach, as if an invisible rope had been tied around his waist, some unseen person pulling on it with a surprising force. Prost stumbled before righting himself. Jord gasped and scanned the surrounding darkness. He must have assumed they were being attacked and promptly went on the defensive. A small orb of red Light flared into existence, hovering above the boy's pale hand.

What the fog was that? Prost asked.

The rapid anger melted away, replaced by satisfaction and joy once more.

Ah, there it is now, Ugglyn crooned. *I knew I'd find you again.*

The tugging disappeared as quickly as it had started, Prost glaring into the distance. He scanned the field of grass extending downward on the slope of the mountain, trying to determine if he'd been Moved by a Lightbearer. He reminded himself that there had been no Light around him, blue or red, that would have indicated a Lightbearer attack.

Jord still stood poised next to him, but he flashed an angry look at Prost. "Wha' was tha', then? Are yeh tryna scare the loiks of me fer no reason?"

The boy finally relaxed, but he inspected Prost with contempt, assuming Prost's behavior was some type of joke. Prost held up a palm to the boy, glaring him in the eyes and sending the message that he should stop speaking.

Before I was locked away, I stored a piece of myself in a book, a small thing. It was the best I could do at the time. Some imbecile assassin found it months ago and summoned me, though I don't think he knew what he was doing. Yet my words called to him, else he wouldn't have been able to read it, Ugglyn said.

Scrunching his brow in frustration, Prost began to ask what the anti-god meant when he was cut off.

See, there, someone read from the text, but they stopped, Ugglyn said, the satisfaction returning.

Prost inspected the oncoming storm, the lightning flashing almost continuously in the thick black clouds. When he didn't see anything right away, he felt his hand go numb, his arm flying upward. A breath caught in his throat as he lost complete control of his arm and hand. Struggling to recover from Ugglyn's immediate takeover of his limb, Prost saw that his finger pointed to a spot in the distance where a dim glow rose toward the sky. It was faint, likely only visible to them because Mellan was now covered by the oncoming clouds, but there was a mercurial pillar of smoke that glowed ever so softly. The substance lingered for only a few moments before it disappeared. Once he saw what Ugglyn meant for him to see, feeling returned to his arm. As relief flooded in, Prost let his arm down, not wanting to indicate anything might be off to Jord.

They didn't complete the incantation, else I'd have been summoned there, Ugglyn said, *or perhaps we'd be taken together. I can only guess what will happen if someone finishes reading now that we've bonded.*

The word "bonded" made Prost's skin crawl, and he suppressed a shiver. *Bond* often meant something was shared between two people. In this case, there was no feeling of mutuality from Prost.

"Evenir is that way," Prost said, guessing the meaning of Ugglyn's words.

The anti-god began whispering something else, but Prost suppressed it.

"Ugglyn planted a piece of him among them. He can sense it. That should lead us there in due time," Prost said. He wasn't completely sure the information was correct, but Prost knew he had to say something. The silence between Jord's question had already drawn on far too long. Too much hesitation and he'd lose whatever small ground he had over the boy.

Jord sneered at him.

"Yeh brag o' Ugglyn's promises, yet not one soul can say they 'eard anythin' from the source. Fer all we knows, yeh could be lyin' roit good," Jord spat. He gave his hand a flip, the small orb of Light flashing into the darkness in front of them. A bright flash of red blinded Prost before it faded, rock and dirt exploding where the orb landed ten paces away.

Ugglyn hissed inside. *This boy needs discipline. How dare he question me?*

Prost's hand numbed again, though this time the onset alerted him quickly enough that Prost locked the sensation to his forearm. Ugglyn growled, the anger at Jord's impertinence taking over, but he couldn't force Prost's hand upward, though he tried. He managed to summon a smoke-filled orb with the same metallic hue that glowed softly. A discomforting feeling wormed its way into Prost at the sight. Voidweaving had that effect on him every time, though this felt familiar.

This was an imitation of Destroying. Though he wasn't sure how he knew, Prost was undeniably right.

With Prost's attention locked on the arm, the anti-god seized his tongue.

"You'd best remember that you can die at my hand, imbecile!"

The voice that came from his mouth was not his own. It sounded like an echo of a hundred men, warping into something so inhuman that Prost's skin crawled where he still controlled it. Relinquishing control of his arm, Prost seized his mouth with his consciousness, pushing Ugglyn away. Just then, his arm, now fully numbed, lifted back in a throwing motion.

Using Prost's arm, Ugglyn lobbed the orb into the darkness in the same direction as Jord's. When it landed, the reaction was altogether different from Jord's just moments before. Mercurial smoke billowed outward in the darkness, glowing ever so softly as they watched. Rather than exploding rock and dirt, they only heard a muted whooshing sound before the smoke imploded on itself, leaving darkness once more.

Jord stared at Prost, indignation rather than fear showing there. Prost yanked the control of his limb back from Ugglyn, the feeling rushing back with intense tingling.

"I have a plan, and it will work. You'd best not trifle with me. Riln is not here to block your insubordination from my anger. Remember that."

At that he turned from Jord and inspected the sky once more. Prost was grateful for the darkness, for he could feel himself trembling, not from the confrontation of Jord or his Destroying, but from the fact that Ugglyn had taken control. Prost couldn't be sure that Jord didn't notice, but the boy did growl in frustration and walk away, muttering various curses under his breath.

The stone door opened behind Prost. Though it was quiet for how heavy the doors must be, the ground rumbled beneath his feet at the weight of the movement. Prost looked back to see Jord's back for one last moment before the doors closed behind him. The guards remained where they were, a lone red orb hovering between them so they could see their immediate surroundings.

Such brazen reactions will lose us what little loyalty we have, Prost roared in his head. *Do not take control like that ever again.*

Laughter echoed in his mind.

Or what? You have no power over me, dud.

Prost's skin tightened in his hairline when he heard the term.

Ah, it still stings, I see. You've no need to be sensitive to such menial name-call-

ing. You've been given something so much better than immunity to Lightbearing. Embrace it. Embrace me, Ugglyn whispered.

The air dropped in temperature, the storm wall approaching rapidly. Prost sucked in the air, feeling the coolness rush through his nose. The potent smell of rain accompanied his breath, and he knew it was only a matter of time before it met him. Though the lightning still felt distant, the edge of the storm was almost upon him. Even over the ringing wind in his ears, he thought he could hear the faint falling of the torrent of raindrops on the earth.

Prost's mind cleared as it normally did with the rain. His emotions calmed and he felt a stronger resolve to push back Ugglyn's oppressive force. Ugglyn snarled, a sound that made Prost's skin crawl, like that of a beast fighting for its life with froth at the mouth. A smile broke upon his lips as he realized he was winning, at least for now. He knew he still had no way of removing the anti-god from his body. Such inhabitation had not been heard of in Lindrad, save in the false stories of the priests of the Lanserian church. He recalled such tales only barely, since he'd not attended worship or studied the religion since he'd left to be a soldier years ago. His parents had not been devout. Perhaps they were now.

His chest constricted for a moment; thoughts of his parents and older brother stung. He'd left with complete disapproval from them. Since then, he'd not returned to Port Lindle, which was completely by his design. Even Riln couldn't force him to make his way back there. He couldn't face his parents. No, he wouldn't face his parents. The life he'd left behind was that of frivolity and lavishness, idleness to the point of madness.

The moment Prost allowed these memories to exert force on his mind, Ugglyn tried to come back from the deep recesses of his consciousness. Prost cleared his thoughts again, sucking in an even deeper breath. Once satisfied, he considered what he should do now. Ugglyn remained quiet, at least for the time being. Raindrops fell around him as the very edge of the storm met him from above. The guards behind grumbled in frustration at the notion that they'd be wet soon.

Prost could stay in the rain forever. He hated the idea of retreating to the dark recesses of the lair. It was unnatural for any person to have to hide from fresh air and nature for the amount of time they did. His thoughts proceeded to some of the older members of their organization, whose skin paled from the lack of sunlight. Prost could not understand anyone's drive to stay completely hidden from the outside.

Grunting, he turned sharply and stalked to where the guards stood by the door. His sudden motion caused one of the guards to yelp in surprise. The other stiffened but didn't make any noises. Once recovered, the one who yelped stood straight and forward. Each held a Conjured spear of bright red Light, which glowed in the night. He knew that each likely wielded a second ability, but he didn't know these well enough to remember what they were.

Prost's eyes lingered on the spear of the one who'd yelped in surprise. Shifting his gaze to the man's face, he noted the clear signs of nervousness, pale face, a bead of sweat trickling down his brow. It wasn't hot, and the coolness of the fast-approaching storm would have kept anyone from feeling overheated. Yet this man sweat like he'd just sparred for hours. Prost smiled with contempt, reaching his hand out and grabbing the Conjured spear with his left hand. The man cringed and closed his eyes momentarily before opening them again. He continued to stare forward as if he didn't notice what Prost was doing.

Ugglyn screamed inside. Prost wasn't sure if touching the Conjured spear hurt the anti-god or if just the thought of it tormented his possessor. Either way, he squeezed it, allowing the moment to linger, if not for the pure torture of Ugglyn, then for the growing discomfort of the man who held it.

"While a quick reflex and fast reaction may be well desired for those standing guard, you'd do well to make sure you don't sound like a frightened child," Prost said with a chillingly calm tone.

The man stared forward but nodded vigorously.

"You've no reason to fear me," Prost explained. "I'm not like Riln was. Forget whatever you knew in the past. I'm a dud no longer. Fear those who threaten our brothers and sisters and our cause. Don't flinch in the face of danger."

An air of awkwardness wormed its way into Prost's chest as the words came out. They had been far more encouraging and positive than anything he'd said in years. Before he could dwell too much longer on the uncomfortable stares of both guards, Prost pressed the lever to open the door.

"Um, thank you, sir," the man said uncertainly.

Prost considered saying something else, something that was laced with harsher words or at least a bit of anger, something to indicate that he hadn't changed from the hardened man they all knew him to be, but he locked his jaw and ignored the man's comment. He hoped that refusing to say anything to him would validate precisely the impression he wanted to make. The man cleared his throat when Prost didn't respond and faced back toward the storm.

Just then, a large gust of wind pushed Prost in the back, nearly causing him to lose his footing. The men cursed next to him, one of them holding up his hand as if to ward off the wind. Right as the palm of his free hand extended forward, a red dome of Light flung outward and hovered in front of him. Prost felt the wind die down instantly as it was redirected around the Shield.

Prost glanced at the man and nodded in approval.

Fog it, what's happening to me? Prost lamented. He felt himself slipping into something, someone he'd almost forgotten—the person he'd been before becoming a hardened, bitter soldier.

Ugglyn surfaced suddenly, hissing in anger. *You've become weak. You found strength in anger, strength in what Riln cultivated inside of you. I'll force it to come out of you if I must.*

Opting not to respond to the harsh words, Prost walked through the door with his head held high. For the first time in a long while, he realized he felt something other than anger and frustration. Even the smallest encouraging word had reawakened something within him. A memory flashed in his mind, Avryn laughing as they sat at the mess hall table within their military barracks.

He shook his head, focusing on the stairs in front of him. Prost knew he couldn't spend time looking into the past, dwelling on the way he used to be. But hadn't that been what he'd just experience moments before? Was that not a piece of the way he used to see the world and the people around him?

As a distraction, Prost focused on sensing anything outside of his mind, the feeling of his clothing on his skin, the way the stale air smelled as if there'd been no movement for years in this cavernous place, the way the stairs looked garish in the red Light of the orbs hovering above them. He lost focus on the path he took as he retreated into his mind. When his foot slapped the floor at the bottom of the long flight of stairs, he was jarred back to reality.

At that moment he felt power overwhelm him. A cold, tingly feeling swarmed through his brain until it filled his eyes. He shivered at the sensation, knowing that the Voidweaving that Ugglyn had brought with him was taking over once again. Smokey figures sitting at a long dining table appeared on the level floor around him. Despite the medium they were made of, the faces, postures, and clothing of the figures were shockingly intricate. He gritted his teeth, recognizing two of the figures as his parents. Movement to his left made him shift his gaze there. Two more figures appeared out of the smoke as if they'd just materialized from the wall of the tunnel. Longing exploded in his chest as he recognized his older brother and a younger version of himself.

Where have you two been? I hope not causing troubles for the Hildengaard family again. It wouldn't do to have another wealthy family against us. The Frillens are enough of a nuisance already, his mother's voice said, strikingly accurate as if she were in the cavern right then.

Dear, we needn't worry about them. We've far more money and guards than them. I, for one, would not care if they were causing problems for them, his father's voice crooned.

Nostalgia for not only the memory but for his former home exploded in his mind, filling in the gaps of what was not being shown in the smokey images in front of him.

Father, we've been doing nothing of the sort, his brother, Alfred, said. *If only you knew that I'd just caught Prost conversing with the cook, of all people. I merely told him that he's more important things to do than dally with the cook's apprentice.*

Though he couldn't see the reaction on his face, he recalled blushing profusely at his brother's accusation.

I'm not dallying *with anyone. I just thought it would be nice to learn something more useful than running a banking business*, Prost complained.

He'd just turned twelve, the age his father had decided to include his sons in his business dealings. For some reason he thought that starting them young would set them up for more success than even he could bring the family.

The image of his father pursed his lips as he sat up taller in his chair.

Prost, you'd do well to let the servants do what they are paid to do. You've no time to waste learning about them or their duties. As a businessman, it's important to know when hiring out for work is more efficient and profitable than doing it for oneself. Now sit and eat. I fear the food is cold now because of your tardiness, his father reprimanded.

And where is the wine? I sent Martha for it ages ago, his mother added.

Prost's younger self looked down at the ground but moved to his seat. The table was ostensibly larger than necessary for a family of four, but his father had said it was about appearances more than anything.

Now, have you both inspected the ledgers for this month? Are you prepared to recite your findings on the bank's expenses and gains? his father questioned, primly slicing a piece of steak with his sharpened knife.

Alfred spoke clearly and wisely about what he'd found. Present Prost was lost on the words being spoken as he inspected the drooping figure of himself. He remembered being so bored by the details and feeling discouraged at his father's forbidding him to learn anything practical.

Prost! Must I remind you to sit up? *A gentleman ought not to be seen with such lack of decorum!* Grilondil, his father, shouted.

Rather than defend him or speak in his favor, his mother looked down at her plate, shaking her head.

The sting of disapproval rocked through him once more at seeing the memory. The circumstances of his childhood were not something Prost wanted to dwell on. In fact, he'd blocked the memory of his upbringing once he joined the militia in T'Arren Vale.

To have a memory like this not only repeated in his mind but played out before him filled him with frustration.

Prost's younger self stood suddenly, his hands slapping the table.

What if I don't want to be more proper? We have all this money, and what do we do with it? Squander it away for our own pleasure while others are starving out on the streets, he shouted back.

Rather than get angry, his father started laughing.

And what would you have me do? Give all our funds to the poor? Give away everything I've worked for as if it was given to me with little effort? We can't save the world, Prost. We may be wealthy, but it hasn't come without sacrifices of our own. Now sit *and eat else you go to bed without supper.*

Prost's form slumped back into the chair. He remembered wanting to bring up the fight again or walk away from the table, but he had no courage then. Hopelessness was all he felt, moment after moment, as he tried to tell his parents he wanted something else for his life.

All at once, the images puffed into the air as if it hadn't happened. Not moments after they disappeared, he heard footsteps slapping the stairs behind him. He started, wondering how long he'd been standing in place during the odd vision. Turning, he noticed the guards were the same distance they'd always been behind him.

"Sir? Yeh alroit?" the other guard said, looking uneasy. "Did yeh see somethin' wrong?"

This one didn't sound as scared as the other had when addressing Prost.

"Did you make sure the door was fully sealed before you followed me down?" Prost asked gruffly. He didn't care if they had, but he knew he had to come up with something in response.

"Yeh, is roit closed up noicely. Checked it meself, Oi did," the man responded confidently.

Prost nodded, then continued moving into the main cavern. He knew that his hesitation at the bottom of the stairs, though several minutes in his mind, had lasted a mere second outside of his vision. He knew that was how Seeing worked with Lanser's Lightbearing, but he'd not considered the implications of Voidweaving and how Seeing worked.

A thought struck Prost then, and he almost paused once more to prod Ugglyn's presence inside of him, but he continued forward, not wanting to alert those following behind that something else was off. The enormous cavern was abustle, as it always was, with the black-cloaked figures of Watchlight. Riln had banned any other clothing save for black. He insisted that everyone match in likeness, if not for discipline, then for proper recognition of members of their faction during a fight. Evenir had picked up on this quickly, for during every encounter with them outside of their compound, he noted the distinct lack of black clothing in their ranks.

Save for Janis, of course. Though the woman never wore a cloak to his knowledge.

Prost disliked the rule, but it seemed trivial to change something like that now. He feared a focus on something like rules on dress would invalidate him in his already precarious position as their leader. No vote had been held, but then again, none had been held for Riln either. With his recent battle in the war room, he was confident news had spread, fear growing among the populace about what would happen to those who opposed him.

He turned right sharply and walked up the ramp to the next floor of the cavern. To his left, over a waist-high wall, stood a deep drop to the floor below. Destroyers had carved a massive cavern in the surrounding mountain, blowing tiers into the wall from floor to ceiling, marked above by at least fifty glowing red spheres of Lighting power. The throne room stood one level up from the entrance and was, ironically, the last place he wanted to go. Yet Riln had set the precedent that the leader should spend most of their time there. The men followed him dutifully until the opening to the throne room appeared. No door stood in the rectangular frame of the entrance, so privacy was not truly found in the room, but it was large enough that Prost could quietly slink into the shadows and remain unseen from those who peered in.

He paused, the men following behind him.

"I wish to be alone. Tend to your guard duties elsewhere. I don't need you here right now," Prost ordered.

The men glanced at each other before shrugging and moving off in opposite directions. Prost was relieved that they didn't argue. He'd never demanded such treatment, but Neera had insisted that he needed loyal men with him at all times, should those who disagree with his leadership try to assassinate him in the night.

Ugglyn stirred at the thought. Ever since the conversation with Neera, Ugglyn had reminded Prost time and time again how Voidweaving would protect him from any threat a Lightbearer could toss at him.

After eyeing the throne for a moment, Prost turned and walked along the pillars that lined the room up and down. At the roof of the tall cavern, at least half a dozen orbs glowed. One of the first things Prost had done was to amend Riln's rule of leaving the room unattended by the Lighter. Now it glowed brightly from the orbs above. Without Lighbearing of his own, he couldn't create even a single Light for himself to function in the cavern.

Prost stepped up to a column and placed his hand there. He felt the hard stone, remembering Riln's display of power and anger when he'd first arrived. The dagger Riln had Moved into the wall broke through the stone as if it was made of something soft, like the bark of a tree.

Considering this, Prost held up his hand and willed the Voidweaving inside of him to respond. The moment he did, Ugglyn emerged unfettered.

You can't stay away from the power, can you? Try all you might to lock me away, you'll always come back in the end.

Prost ignored the comment. He'd known Ugglyn would come out of his mental block the moment Prost called on Voidweaving, so he wasn't surprised. While he wished this didn't happen every time, he'd learned he couldn't access the power while locking the anti-god away. As he focused on his hand, an icy feeling filled his breast and spread up his arms. Resisting the urge to shiver at the sensation, he focused harder, the unseen power flowing to his hand. Once there, the mercurial smoke formed out of thin air, twirling lazily around the palm of his hand until it formed into a dagger. The weapon was nondescript and basic as far as forge work could go, but Prost knew it was as sturdy as a normal steel one.

With a grunt of effort, Prost slammed the dagger into the stone pillar. Though it didn't enter as easily as Riln's Conjured Light dagger had years ago, it broke the column with a web of cracks. Prost stood back, examining his work. His heart thrummed in his chest from the exertion of the blow. With a wave of his hand, the dagger melted into air, remnants of the silvery smoke lingering momentarily before they disappeared.

Prost took a step up to the column. For a moment he thought to leave the hole in the pillar as a type of trophy of the past, but he thought better of it. Should this pillar fall for any reason, he didn't want to be caught unaware. He placed his hand on the crack and focused once more. The icy chill returned to his chest and arm, flowing out of his hand with the same silvery-grey smoke. He watched as the smoke filled the hole created by his dagger, extending up the cracks to fill them.

The thought he'd had earlier stabbed his mind like a thorn in one's finger while picking Yarrowberries in the fields.

If you claim to be so powerful, why imitate the abilities of the very being you loath? From what I've seen, Voidweaving is merely the same powers gifted by Lanser but with Void instead, Prost blurted.

While he didn't altogether intend this to be an insult, Ugglyn clearly took it that way.

Anger flared in his chest, shocking him at the intensity.

Ugglyn screamed in his mind, causing Prost to gasp and slam his hands over his ears to block out the noise. Given the fact that the sound was in his head, it did little to help. Growling, Prost fell to the ground as he was overwhelmed by the screaming and the anger inside him.

You dare talk down to me in such a manner! Ugglyn screamed inside of him. *I can destroy you at any moment!* Prost closed his eyes and focused, trying to sort his own emotions from that of the angry anti-god within. He found shock and also a fair bit of anger of his own, though it wasn't out of control. There was resolve and—amusement.

He grabbed hold of that, bolstering it with confidence, then started laughing. He knew the anti-god's words were empty. If he'd been able to kill Prost, he would have by now.

Anger shifted to confusion, then back again as Ugglyn tried to process what Prost was doing.

You laugh, yet you know you can't defeat the woman without these gifts, Ugglyn said threateningly.

For a moment Prost didn't respond. Once he'd controlled himself, he forced a condescending thought inward.

You tout power unfeigned, yet it seems Voidweaving is bound by the same rules as Lightbearing. Don't deny it, tell me it's true, Prost urged.

Ugglyn's anger diffused almost entirely, though loathing continued to burn deep within him.

Yes, Ugglyn replied with derision. Then he was quiet.

Taking a moment to enjoy the newfound silence in his mind, Prost reflected on the information. While it was logical that Voidweaving felt like a sort of imitation of Lightbearing, it did beg the question of why. He knew trying to ask now would bear little fruit.

How long until you can find us the lair of Evenir? Prost asked impatiently.

This question must have been the right one, for Ugglyn emerged once more, slinking into his mind.

If anyone reads the words of summoning within Evenir, we'll know where they are, Ugglyn said.

The words were few and Ugglyn didn't appear to want to say anything else, so the message was clear to Prost.

They had to wait.

13

The small black volume sat on the ground amidst them. A misty smoke dome floated around the opened pages. Marric stared at it wide-eyed, then took a step back as if the substance might fly outward. Avryn still stood in front of Narinda. He held his hand backward as if to hold her from jumping forward of her own accord.

Marric looked from the book to Janis, then to Avryn and back again. The next time Marric saw Avryn, he noted a curious look on the man's face.

"That seems—familiar. Doesn't it remind you of the poison we saw Luden's men using in Stilten?" Avryn asked, looking at Marric. "The same you described in the forest with Turrin."

Janis nodded. Marric could see in her eyes that she was working something out in her mind.

"Macks had this book, for how long, I can't be sure, but he was the Seer who helped Luden send men not only to the places where Lightbearers would Awaken but also at the exact time of our arrival," Janis surmised.

Marric cocked his head, then opened his mouth to speak. Before he could add anything to the conversation, a slight thumping sound erupted in the middle of them. He jumped back once more. Like a snail retreating to its shell, the dome of silvery smoke sucked inward, disappearing between the pages of the book.

"That is—unsettling," Narinda voiced.

Janis snorted. "To say the least. I think it's safe to say that this book belongs to the very irritable anti-god himself and that Macks was in cahoots with him."

Avryn nodded and turned to Marric. His eyes narrowed.

"You had been about to say something when that"—Avryn paused, then cleared his throat—"thing happened. What is it?"

Marric's mind felt as if it was full of cotton, overwhelmed from all the new information that was threatening his ability to process anything in his brain. He couldn't recall exactly what he'd been about to say. As he considered the trail of the conversation, Janis leaned down and flipped the cover of the small book closed. Even though the smoke had retreated, closing it filled Marric with relief. She picked it up with far more confidence than Marric could ever imagine. He knew she held it between a handkerchief, but it still amazed him.

All at once, Marric recalled what he'd been about to say.

"The poison the men used on Turrin, it did look just like that, as if someone had laced smoke with some type of metal," he confirmed.

Avryn pressed his lips together, then eyed the book once more.

"How Macks came to find such a thing is unimaginable. It's a shame we couldn't have subdued him and brought him here," Avryn said.

Janis stiffened ever so slightly, but with everyone in the room on edge, Marric was sure he wasn't the only one to notice her reaction.

"Peace, Janis. That wasn't an accusation," Avryn said before relaxing and stepping out from in front of Narinda. "Removing yourself from Prost's presence safely was the right move. Still, we'll need to see what we can learn about the book and about the events that transpired in Stilten."

"Something just came to mind," Narinda said. "I hadn't thought of it until you mentioned the appearance of the substance just then. Talatha was researching something similar before she died. I've read her notes a few times and have made little sense of it. Yet I recall a particular entry about metallic smoke, or something like that. Until now, I assumed Talatha's secret research meant little to us. Though she was a revered leader, she was known to be secretive about the strangest things." Her eyes widened for a moment, then she looked at Marric somewhat sheepishly.

"Sorry, Marric, I don't mean to speak ill of your mother. She really was an incredible leader to us," Narinda added.

He furrowed his brow at the apology. Marric hadn't thought she'd said anything rude about his mother, and even if she had, he couldn't take offense. He didn't know the woman. Still, the mention of his mother's name made something fizzle within his chest, like the bubbles that exploded out the top of a mug filled with fresh ale.

After a brief moment of silence, Marric shrugged. "No offense taken," he said, at which Narinda relaxed.

"Where are her notes? It's been some time since I've looked at them myself. It might do me good to read through them," Avryn said.

Janis stuffed the small book in her belt, then eyed Avryn.

"I suppose you're going to suggest I look at them as well, then?" she asked pointedly.

Avryn gave Janis a perplexed look, then shook his head. "You are free to do as you choose. But given your current status in this war, it would be wise to do so."

"While I don't enjoy spending time with my nose in a book, I didn't learn to read as a child for no reason, did I?" she said, though Marric assumed she wasn't looking for a genuine answer. "You have these in the library, then?"

"Yes, though I'll have to make sure they are where I left them. Old Barrigon has a tendency to get his hands on everything while he's on Lighter duty. He has little common sense for replacing things when he's done," Narinda said, sounding annoyed.

Marric wasn't sure who this Barrigon was, but he knew what Narinda meant when she mentioned the Lighter on duty. He'd not yet met every one of the Lighters who worked to illuminate the compound, but it seemed that every time he talked to Narinda she mentioned the name of another one. He did not envy whoever was to take over Evenir as the new leader. There were far too many names to remember.

Flashing a glance at Janis, Marric pondered momentarily on how things would change if Janis was voted in as the leader of Evenir. He expected that she would very much dislike the responsibility, but he hoped he was wrong. Shifting his gaze to Avryn, he noted the tall man's pensive face. Avryn looked to have aged years in just a few short weeks. Though he insisted that his position as second in Evenir wasn't a heavy burden, Marric could see just how the weight of such responsibility had affected him.

"I'll go see my father, then. I'm sure he's worried sick about me," Marric said, drawing the looks of the others.

"Yes, that's probably for the best. From what I hear, the medics have had a rough go of keeping him under watch. After you didn't return for the past week, he's been trying to leave Terris Green to search for you himself," Avryn replied.

There was a twinkle in his eye as he spoke to Marric, as if he thought the idea of his father causing a commotion to be amusing. It did not altogether surprise Marric to hear of his father's actions. He'd not known Narim to be anything other than a ruckus, either out of humor or frustration. It seemed to have gotten worse with his age.

Marric didn't stay for much longer, opting to see his father as soon as possible. He left the room through the opening and turned left. After walking for some time, he came back to the common cavern where the stables connected. Many people shifted about the road as they continued their business. No other gatherings had appeared to form after the one they'd broken up earlier, much to his relief.

A man shouted to his left about his Yarrow root, a hearty food for soups, making Marric jump at the sudden noise. In just a moment the man had walked past him, seeing another figure raise his hand as if affirming his interest in buying the goods.

Nostalgia slammed into Marric's brain, and it made him sway on his feet momentarily before he recovered himself. He was reminded of the market in Wurren. The busy nature of the market in his hometown felt, smelled, and looked just like this, albeit being outside where the sun could actually touch citizens as they went about their business.

Sighing, Marric pushed the longing out of his mind and focused instead on making his way through the crowd without getting knocked over or hailed by someone trying to sell him something. At length, he made it through the crowd to the wall opposite the tunnel he'd just come from. He stared up at the tall archway leading to the narrowing tunnel, wondering if this was the right direction.

Pausing for just a moment, Marric considered how he could find where the infirmary was. When he'd been here before their trip to Wurren, he'd memorized the way to the important places such as the privy, infirmary, and his quarters. Now that he'd been gone for almost two weeks, he feared he'd lost the memory, though he expected that if he found a starting place that was familiar, he could make it to the infirmary with no trouble.

Glancing around, he thought about how those around him would react to his Seeing but shrugged it off. Filling his mind with images of his father, particularly of the bed he'd lain on when Marric last visited, he closed his eyes and focused. His eyes snapped open, full of intense blue Light. A few surprised gasps sounded behind him, but he ignored them.

How am I so brazen that I can ignore those around me? I used to get overwhelmed in the middle of just two conversations, Marric thought.

The world around him melted until an image of his father materialized in his eyes. Narim sat at a small reading table with a square wooden slat. A woman sat across from him, but she was much younger than him.

It looked to be the same room Narim had rested in when Marric first left Terris Green for Wurren, and Marric felt some pity at the thought that his father might not have had the chance or help to see the grandness of the tunnels and caverns. A wooden slab sat on the table between the two, and various pieces of multicolored rocks sat in bunches around the board. He recognized the game of Hurley-trail. Though it had been years since he'd played it, even more since he'd seen his father play it, he smiled, his physical mouth responding to the behavior of his projected Seer self.

Without watching much longer, Marric let the world spin around him until he stood just outside of his own body.

Seeing oneself during a Seer vision was not only an awkward experience but also a very disorienting one. Marric's stomach lurched as he had a brief existential processing moment before he could overcome the feeling. It was the first time he'd Seen himself externally for a few weeks. The boy he stared at, eyes aglow, now had a face more chiseled and scarred in places.

Marric marveled at the change he could see in himself. With all the rigorous travel, training, and combat, he could see that his upper arms were a bit more bulky, though not too much to fill the sleeves of the white shirt he wore. His hair was grungy and dirty, which was to be expected, considering his lack of a bath for the past few weeks. It was getting longer too, and he made a mental note to locate the barber in the compound and make a trip there.

People milled about him, though they looked uncomfortable as they walked by him. He wondered if it was because he openly used his power or if they still associated him with Janis, the terrifying witch of a person—or so they gossiped about her. Ignoring their stares, Marric let his mind-vision focus on finding his father. With a lurch, his vision sped to the right and then through a small tunnel. His vision extended forward quickly, flying through the lit tunnels. He memorized the path to the best of his ability, then allowed the world to spin again, returning to his body.

Right as he slid back into his mind, a flash of something purple caught his attention to the right. Skin prickling, he angled himself in that direction, a Conjured sword landing in his hand as if it had been there all along. A man cursed and backed away, saying something rude to Marric, yet Marric wasn't focused on that.

That looked like corrupted Lightbearing. Could it be Watchlight? Marric thought, anxiety rising in his chest.

As he scanned the crowd, his eyes paused on two brown-cloaked figures. One was a man Marric did not recognize, the other was the very fellow who'd spoken against Avryn just earlier on the table in this room. His eyes locked on Marric's for a moment before they narrowed, and the man gestured to the other to turn through the darkened entrance to another tunnel.

The man made him uneasy, but he brushed the thought aside and continued on.

With a sigh, he weaved through the merchants until he came to the tunnel he'd just gone through in his vision. Before he could move into the entrance, a couple of kids ran across his path, almost tripping him to his knees. Marric caught himself, grabbing the closest thing to him.

It happened to be the armed sleeve of a woman.

"Tha' ain' a roit proper way to grab a lady, 'f Oi say so meself," a feminine voice said sternly to his side.

Marric started and turned to see Rivelen staring down at him from above. He gulped at the sight of her and flushed as he realized he'd just used her arm as leverage. She glared at him severely, though she didn't seem as angry as Tins would get. If she had, Marric assumed she'd be shouting at him as Tins always had.

Marric grimaced at the thought of his old stepmom, now a corpse. The thought was grim and gruesome, so he let it slip from his mind, focusing instead on the pure embarrassment he felt at the moment.

"Um, sorry. I just didn't want to trip on those kids. I didn't mean to grab you improperly," Marric said, though he was confident that his bright red face would be more telling of how he felt than any words he could say.

Rivelen continued to glare at him, but she nodded.

"Yeh'd best be careful 'round 'ere. Lots of folks don' care t' watch their footin' in this place," Rivelen said. "Mind if Oi ask yeh? D' yeh know where Avryn moit be? Been lookin' right long fer 'im. Moit 'ave Seen him, bu' Oi don' loik spyin' in such a manner."

Marric's eyebrows shot up in surprise, not at the question, but at the implication that Seers in Evenir might watch anyone at any time. The unease in his stomach returned at the thought, but he did his best to hide it.

"Yes, he's that way, in one of the side rooms," Marric replied while pointing in the direction he'd just come from.

"Thank yeh muchly," Rivelen said.

She paused after thanking him, watching him.

"Are yeh alroit, then?" she asked. "Yeh look loik yeh've seen somethin' gut-rollin'."

Marric's mind roiled, trying to interpret her words. Though it took a moment longer than it should have, he shook his head.

"I'm fine. Just thought I saw some strange Lightbearing. I'm sure I'm just imagining it. We had a run-in with them in Wurren," Marric explained.

Rivelen nodded slowly but looked unconvinced.

"Keep yer head on, then. Can' be walkin' into every one round 'ere. We 'ad a run-in as well in Arivan. Oi 'ope yous were luckier than the loiks of us," Rivelen said.

Marric grimaced. That they didn't have success getting the Lightbearer there made his heart sink. His whole life he'd never dealt with death and loss as much as he had in the past few months, let alone the loss of so many teenagers. That he survived not only his own Awakening but the conflict between Watchlight, Evenir, and this other group seemed unlikely. Images of Turrin came back to him, the smokey-silver veins of poison running through his leg before Avryn Fixed it out of the man's body. Marric forced down a shiver.

"Right, yeah. I'll try to pay more attention. Thank you," Marric replied before slipping around her and entering the tunnel. He noticed that there were not many people traveling this path, and he wondered what it led to. The abandoned nature of this passage as opposed to the busyness of the cavern behind him, made him uncomfortable. Supposedly they were safe, engulfed by a massive Light Shield that kept the prying eyes of Watchlight's Seers out of their cavern, but the possibility that he'd seen some corrupted Light made him feel unsafe. He knew he'd need to tell Avryn as soon as possible, but for now, he continued his course to his father's room.

As he approached the room in the dim hallway, for the orbs of Light were more spaced out here for some reason, Marric felt intense gratitude that he could use his Seeing within the compound.

At length, he pressed open the door to find an empty bedroom. Perplexed, he peered into the dark room. As expected, there was no orb of Light illuminating the room, given that it was a place for someone to sleep. Marric had to squint his eyes to even be able to see the outline of a bed and chair from the glow of the orbs in the hallway. The table with the game stood to the side, both chairs now empty. After a moment Marric held up his hand and summoned a tiny orb of Light in his palm. Though it wasn't bright, it was piercing and steady, allowing him to see inside the room.

Marric frowned as he realized that if his father had been sleeping, he'd likely just have woken the man with the pinprick Light in his hands. Right before he could snuff it out, followed by a curse at himself, he noted that the bed was bare. Furrowing his brow, he looked in the corners to make sure that his father wasn't lurking there. Confused, Marric entered the room to look around. Under normal circumstances he wouldn't do such a thing, but given that his father used this room, it didn't feel overly inappropriate. Marric was sure he'd just Seen his father in his room only moments before, yet there was clearly no one here.

"Roit tryna scare the fog outta me, then?" a voice sounded behind Marric.

Marric yelped and turned so sharply that his foot tangled behind his other one, pitching him to the side. Fortunately, his reflexes had improved over the past few months and he caught himself on the frame of the bed.

His father stood at the door, holding a flickering candle in his hand. Marric wondered how he'd not noticed the flickering light before his father had startled him. Relief flooded his father's face as he appeared to realize who was in his room.

"*Mar*? Yer back! Lanser's beard, Oi thot yeh were never comin' back 'ere," his father said, hobbling into the room and hugging him.

Marric grunted at the force of his father's embrace, though he was pleased that Narim had regained more of his strength over the past couple of weeks. Narim pulled his son back from him and used the candle to inspect him, though after a moment he tutted to himself and set the candle aside.

"Roit pointless candle, yer Light is much easier to see boi," Narim said, continuing his inspection.

That explains why I didn't see the flickering light before, Marric noted, realizing his Light was much brighter.

"Hey, Pa, we made it back. Sorry, it took longer than we expected. We ran into some"—Marric paused, considering his next words—"trouble."

Marric winced, hoping he wouldn't cause his father more worry than he intended, but Narim appeared not to care.

"Meh, yeh made it, tha's all Oi care 'bout roit now. 'Ere sit, sit."

With a firm press on his back, Marric allowed Narim to lead him to the bed, where he sat down more heavily than he expected. The bed frame creaked when his father settled down on it as if it was screaming for reprieve from both of their weight.

"Did yeh get 'im, then?" his father asked.

There was so much hope in his eyes, so much happiness. Marric's chest panged from the sadness he'd had to endure. Seeing his father like this reminded him of how innocent and sheltered he'd been from all of this. Over the past few days, he'd managed to at least cope with the sorrow of Shrell's death and the losses sustained by their group. Coming back to

Terris Green had opened the wounds once more as he'd heard of Magness's death and of the other Lightbearers they'd meant to bring to safety.

Marric sighed, trying to not let on the sorrow he felt inside. "Yes, we got Crents. He's probably resting, but I'm sure he'd love to see you once he's settled a bit more."

Narim beamed. "Oh nah, th' boy came 'ere only just. Oi fergot 'twas 'im tha' yeh went to get. Roit silly boy 'e is but glad to see 'im, Oi was."

Marric shook his head. His mind was foggy from all that had happened since they first arrived. It felt like it had been ages, yet it had only been mere hours.

Marric nodded. "Yes, he's a Mover, like me. It might be nice to practice with someone I know. Normally, it's just me and the teacher, but he's a beginner, kind of like me."

Narim huffed.

"Beginner, yeh say? Can't be such loik. If 'n yeh were roit a baby wif the Loit, they'd 'ave not sent yeh on such a journey," Narim said. The older man noticed something on Marric's tunic and leaned in close. Without commentary, he began picking things off of Marric's clothing.

Marric blushed and thought to swipe away his father's hand but he suffered it. He allowed his father to just be his father again for a time. Although the motion agitated him, Marric tried to ignore the fussing.

"So now wha'? Yeh get to stay 'ere? No more gallivantin' round Lindrad?" his father asked, still focused on cleaning Marric's clothing.

Marric frowned. "I'm not sure what to do now. I'll want to spend some time with Crents. I didn't realize I'd missed him so."

Marric was relieved to know that the boy was safe. Even before he knew Crents would Awaken, there were times he'd longed to talk to his friend. Crents had a tendency to be overwhelming, but Maric found it somewhat endearing given the circumstances.

"Roit good, I fink. Sorry fer the startle earlier. Been walkin' more an' more t' try to get me strength back. 'Ad to run to the privy, but tha' still takes more toim than oi 'oped. Didn't mean t' startle yous such loik, but Oi din' expect no one t' be 'ere when Oi got back," Narim explained, sitting back and leaving Marric's clothes be.

Shaking his head, Marric looked around the room.

"I thought you'd have a nurse here with you like when I left." Marric paused, flushing slightly at what he was about to admit. "I—looked in on you with my powers before I came, and I was sure you were both in here."

Marric wasn't sure what he expected his father's reaction to be.

At first Narim blinked in surprise at the comment, then he busted up laughing.

"Yeh *spied* on the loiks o' me wif them Loit powers, then? Expect me t' be snoggin' wif the nurse? Roit would be fine thing that, bu' yeh ain't gonna be seeing nonc that soon," Narim said before getting lost in a laughing fit, causing him to cough in the end.

Marric pursed his lips, unamused by his father's joke, but soon he couldn't help but smile and laugh himself.

"Pa, that's not—I just didn't know my way here, ok? I had to See you to know where to even go," Marric explained, but he was blushing deeply now.

Right at that moment, someone came into the room behind Marric—the very nurse he'd Seen with Narim before he'd made his way to the room. The woman looked concerned to see Narim laughing so heartily while coughing profusely, but the moment she moved to Narim's side, he waved her away. She glanced at Marric, noted his blush, then rolled her eyes and set a small wooden bowl of something on the table next to the bed. Without even the slightest sound, she left Narim to his laughing.

Though his breath still shook from the laughter, Narim recovered from the hilarity of his joke.

"Lanser's moit, that's a good one," Narim said. To Marric's surprise, Narim picked up the bowl gingerly and began sipping the light brown substance. He recalled the stink his father was giving when Marric had checked on him before he left, fighting with the nurse to stop feeding him broth. "So what now? We just gonna live 'ere ferever, then?"

The question was valid, but Marric didn't have an answer. While he wanted to tell his father what he assumed the man wanted to hear, the news from Janis was not encouraging. A pit formed in his stomach at the thought of having to tell his father that they might not even be safe here. Giving that information to his father felt wrong, at least right now. These weren't details a man of his age should have to worry about. So Marric just shrugged.

"I don't see how we'll be able to return to Wurren, if that's what you mean," Marric replied. His heart sank when he saw his father's face fall, though the wrinkled man picked up his mood quickly in a clear effort to hide the sorrow. Narim let out a sigh, but his mouth still turned upward in a small, forced smile.

"Wurren was me 'ome fer almost all me loif. Oi can' imagine not ever goin' back t' the people there," Narim said. "Do yeh think they'll be alroit? Did anyone else get 'urt?"

Marric's mind spun. He'd been so focused on getting Crents and trying not to get killed that he'd not bothered to pay much attention to the town. After they'd left, he and Narinda had heard reports of Watchlight engaging with their companions in some sore fights, but little was said about the locals. Marric felt a pang of guilt that he hadn't bothered to see what destruction befell the people of his childhood town. He was loath to tell his father this, so he spoke generally.

"I think people are ok, though I had to rush out. We had to escape with Crents before Watchlight could stop us."

He tried hard not to wince, expecting his father to scold him for not spending more time on the people of Wurren. Narim didn't berate him. Instead the old man looked off in the distance behind Marric's shoulder, a wistful look on his face. Marric resisted the urge to look over his shoulder to see what Narim was looking at. It wasn't the first time this type of thing had happened. Since their home had burned in Wurren, Narim seemed to retreat into his mind more often.

"'Tis a wonder yer ma helped build a place loik this," Narim whispered. "Seems roit lucky tha' they found yous 'afore others killed yeh. Just like Talatha to do good fer yous even after she died."

Marric frowned, then moved forward and pushed his father's shoulder gently.

"Pa, you did the best good for me. More than anyone could have asked for. You taught me to fletch and to care for those I love. We had a good home."

"Aw tut, yer stepma was a terror. And don' yeh tell me otherwise. The wench tried to kill yous, after all!" Narim almost shouted.

Pain wracked in his father's eyes, tears welling there. For years, Narim had seemed blind to the insanity of Marric's stepmother. Now he was taking it all on himself. Marric could think of nothing to say as the man covered his face with his hands and wept softly. When words wouldn't come, Marric moved to Narim's side on the bed and placed his hand gently on his back.

"I know you loved her. I'm sorry, Pa," Marric soothed.

Silence fell around them, save for Narim's quiet sobbing that echoed through the small room. Rather than dwell on the events of what happened with Tins, Marric's mind sped through the things he'd learned from Janis. Somehow Ugglyn was involved with Watchlight, though he was shocked he hadn't thought of it already. Until now, Marric hadn't realized why their Light would be red while Evenir's shone blue. Even after Janis's encounters with the anti-god, Marric hadn't thought much about it.

His skin crawled as he recounted the conversation they'd had just before he made his way here. Marric was Lanserian, taught the religion by his father, but he'd never been an avid worshiper. Narim had been, for a time, attending the twice-weekly services in honor of the god, but that was a time before Marric was old enough to remember. Narim told him he'd stopped after his mother left them, that the services reminded him too much of her.

The wood-carved image of his mother swam into his mind's sight, and Marric almost opened his mouth to ask about her before he clamped it shut. Narinda had said something about his mother doing research about Ugglyn and Lanser, something about the seal Janis was now a part of, and he wanted to know if his father knew anything of this. Shifting on the bed frame, Marric retrieved his hand from his father's back and leaned forward, waiting for his father to recover enough for him to bring up Talatha. Though it worried him to have to remind his father of another lost spouse, Marric felt it was important to talk about her. Little had ever been said about Marric's true mother, and Marric suspected it was due to Tins always being around.

After a few more moments Narim stopped crying and breathed in shakily.

"Fog me good, Mar, Oi thought this was all past me. Oi'll be roit fine, yeh'll see." Sniffing, Narim looked sideways at Marric.

"Oi can' 'elp but wonder what would've 'appened if Talatha 'adn't left loik she did. I fink she'd be roit proud o' the man yeh're becomin'."

His father smiled at that comment, another smile breaking out below wet cheeks and teary eyes. Marric's chest filled with a thrill, knowing that his father had given him the perfect opening to ask about her.

"Tell me more about her. All you've ever told me is that she was kind and fierce, the 'type of woman to make a towering man stop in his tracks,'" Marric said, recalling the exact description his father had given him so many times.

Narim chuckled, then wiped his eyes dry.

"True that is, 'ooever told yeh that," Narim teased.

Marric rolled his eyes and punched his father on the arm, who awarded him with a false grimace and glare. After another long sigh, Narim looked down at the ground.

"'Tis roit smelly o' me t' not tell yeh more of 'er. Oi thought movin' past 'er leavin' us would 'elp us more than anythin', but now Oi realize my mistake," Narim apologized. "Talatha was—well, she was the strong one o' the family. Pretty thing she was, but more feisty than a poisonous snek. Her father was a hunter, or so she said when Oi met 'er in Wurren. She was buying wares at the market. Arrows and such loik. She 'ad the most beautiful blue eyes, 'er 'air was blonde, loik the sun. When she meant to scare summon away, she could do it wif one look in her eyes, yet Oi never seen anyone care fer me an' yous the way she did."

Narim stared off in the distance, falling silent for a moment. Marric couldn't help but squirm on the edge of the cot, the wood squeaking loudly from even the slight motion. This was already more information than Narim had given him his whole life, and it was welcome. Yet Marric had to resist the urge to skip to the more meaty parts of the question.

"When she left, moi world fell down. Oi thought she was 'appy. She loved yeh loik nothin' else, could tell boi the way she 'eld yeh in 'er arms. Yet one day, she was gone, jus' loik tha'. Left no note, made no sense fer 'er t' just disappear. She left me other notes sometimes, jus' fer fun. After she left, Oi kept the last one close t' me, the last piece o' 'er."

Narim pointed to his head, then looked sideways at Marric.

"'Love of me loif, moi love fer yeh is deeper than toim itself. Never leave me, and Oi won't leave you.'"

His father's voice changed in a way that Marric assumed meant he was reciting the note. A sting of the last part tore at his heart. Marric's first response was frustration, knowing that his father had kept this from him his whole life without ever mentioning it. Whenever his mother came up, Narim gave no information. Despite the flare of emotion, Marric forced it down, opting to bottle that up for another day. He knew his father was still hurting and he couldn't show any anger for his father, who was clearly trying to protect him.

"Pa, she left because she knew of Lightbearing. She was trying to protect us," Marric said, repeating words like those Magness had told him when he'd first arrived at Terris Green. He cursed himself for not taking the time to ask her more questions about his mother. Now Magness was gone, just like her.

Shaking his head, Narim sat up straight and stretched his back. A few cracks from his spine echoed quietly on the walls of the small stone room, causing his father to wince.

"Don' know 'ow tha' could be. We'd been married four years, and Oi seen nuffin' loik Lightbearin' the whole time," Narim said, his face now thoughtful.

When he'd learned of his mother's Lightbearing, Marric immediately wondered how his father hadn't known about it. Narim was more than observant when it came to his surroundings, and hearing that his father had been wed to her for four years prior was even more perplexing. As a child, he'd not been so curious to know the past of his mother. He'd just accepted the vague answers his father normally gave him about her before she'd left. They'd both assumed her dead, though for what reason Marric didn't know. As if reading his mind, Narim answered one of the questions Marric had.

"Oi don' know why she left. These folks make it sound loik she put us in danger, bu' Oi don' know 'bout that. Oi was too much in tending to the loiks of yous tha' Oi couldn't chase 'er fer too long. Oi tried though."

Marric put his hand on his father's shoulder once more and squeezed it comfortingly. The man wasn't crying any longer, but it was clear that talking about this was bringing back emotions long suppressed. Warding off the guilt of putting his father through the pain again, Marric stood, the bed creaking once again. He began pacing the room, trying to gather his thoughts on the matter. Now that they knew what they did, Marric assumed his mother had left because she'd gone to be with Evenir, but did Watchlight exist then as well? These were questions he would have to ask Avryn. He knew little of the man's history, but he hoped that Avryn knowing his mother would help him learn what he needed to.

"Talatha—Mother, I mean—she was the leader of Evenir," Marric said.

Narim sighed again, resting his chin on his hands.

"So Oi hear, was a roit good one too," Narim replied.

"Avryn told me she was studying something, learning about"—Marric paused, realizing he was about to delve into the subject he'd tried to keep from his father in earnest—"things that we need to learn about. Was she the studious type?"

Narim furrowed his brow and sat up. Marric bit his lip and turned away from the knowing look his father was giving him.

"Oi've raised yous long enough to know when yeh lie, Son. Yeh know, Oi always knew yeh was up t' something with Jord, even after he was gone," Narim confessed.

Marric scrunched his face up, but he kept his back to his father. If that was true, then Marric felt ridiculous at trying to keep up appearances during his escapades in the dark. Until now he'd not thought that anyone would suspect him of any foul play, not even during the time when Jord was with him. The mention of Jord filled Marric with anxiety, his eyes flashing side to side as if the red-Light-wielding Destroyer would be there to kill him any moment.

"Sorry, Pa, I didn't mean to lie to you all those years. It was just something Jord and I did—well, to help others," Marric said, turning back to his dad.

Narim tutted and held up his hand to stop Marric from speaking.

"None o' tha' now, Oi don' roit care 'bout that. If'n Oi did, Oi'dve said something 'afore, no? Now, 'bout yer mother. Oi'd say she would've learned anythin' should she 'ave the toim fer it. Never met a smarter woman, did Oi," Narim said wistfully before his expression darkened, "which is woi Oi was so confused when she was gone. She could find a way out o' any problem, Oi'm sure of it. Yet she ran."

Once again the timbre of the conversation took on a notably sour note and Marric shied away from it.

"Look, Pa, we don't have to talk much more about it. I know you meant to protect me by keeping the information from me, but now we're here, now we know that Mother was doing something else, something grander. I'm going to learn what I can about her, even if I have to ask people myself."

A thought struck Marric so suddenly that he rocked on his heels, eyes wide. Narim didn't appear to notice his son's reaction, given that he was still looking at the ground.

"Whate're yeh say, Son. Oi'm a bit toired, Oi'll admit," Narim said.

"Right, yeah. You sleep. I am glad that you're doing better. I'll come visit you again soon, once I've learned more about the plan," Marric answered.

Nodding, Narim leaned back, the bed groaning under his weight, and lay still. Marric slipped from the room quietly, not at all concerned with his father's lack of farewell. It was a wonder to him that his father even felt like saying the words he had during their difficult conversation. Feet pounding on the stone floor and echoing on the surrounding walls, Marric angled himself toward where he thought his quarters were. Though the conversation they'd just had floated in his mind, many questions unanswered, Marric had realized at the end of it that he could take matters into his own hands, so to speak. He intended to read through the notes his mother had left behind, the ones Narinda had spoken of, but his mind was too focused on his next task.

He guessed there was only one copy of the notes, and Janis likely would be poring over them any moment now.

Yet Marric had Seeing. This very idea was what had distracted him so at the conclusion of the words with his father. Not once since he'd learned and trained with Seeing had he thought to find his mother. Seeing could reach into the future. It could scale the farthest distances in seconds. Why not scour for information in the past? The possibilities of things Marric could try to See suddenly felt endless. His hands shivered with excitement, his whole body trembling with the anticipation of what he could find if he Saw into the past. His mind reeled as he thought through the possibilities as he tried to decide where to start.

As he walked to his quarters, he was so focused on looking into the past that he almost ran into a woman carrying a large stack of baskets. The moment she noticed Marric walking a mere finger span from her, she yelped and dropped the heavy load. Hearing her exclamation, Marric turned sharply, shoving his hand outward to catch the baskets. His reaction was too slow, and they tumbled to the ground. Before they could land, Marric sucked air through his teeth, focusing on the falling objects. Each basket glowed a brilliant blue and hovered just above the stone floor.

"Foggin' fool! Can't you watch where you're—" a girlish voice said before it stopped. "Lanser's might, it's *you*."

Marric couldn't take his eyes off the baskets he'd barely managed to catch with his Moving, but he could tell the voice was not that of a woman's. She sounded young, perhaps his age or younger. Forcing his mind to focus deeper, he raised the few baskets until they softly stacked on one another, sitting in the middle of the tunnel floor. Once satisfied that they wouldn't topple over, he relaxed, releasing his hold on them.

He spun to the girl and inspected her. She wore a simple grey shirt and brown skirt that came to her ankles. Her red hair was tied back in a blue scarf, the wavy locks tumbling down her back. Fierce green eyes stared at him from beneath well-kept eyebrows. Barely shorter than him, the girl stared at him with a hand on her hip.

"Well, are you just going to stare at me all day?" she said, interrupting Marric's inspection.

"Oh, Lanser—sorry, I wasn't watching where I was walking," Marric said, blushing again.

She raised an eyebrow at him, then looked him up and down.

"I hope that was the case. If you meant to bump into me just to get a good look at me, then you are a deplorable kind of boy."

Marric blinked a few times, his face slack.

Did she just accuse me of knocking her baskets to stare *at her?* Marric thought. His face felt even warmer now and he resisted the urge to turn away. Instead he cleared his throat and opted to ignore the statement.

"Um, no, I was just thinking. I caught your baskets at least," he replied. The moment he said it he felt like a fool. Not only did he speak the obvious but he did so with a face that must have resembled a tomato.

The girl didn't respond immediately but she looked amused.

"Well, there's that, yes. I am impressed, if I say so myself. If I was a Mover, I'm not convinced I could have reacted that quickly."

She moved to the baskets and crouched to inspect them. Marric looked down the hallway, trying to decide if he should just leave or wait until she was done talking to him. She hadn't outright indicated that she wanted to continue the conversation, but he feared doing something even more stupid than he already had, lest she draw more conclusions about him.

"They look fine to me. Good work. Did you learn that before you came here with the lady in black?" the girl asked nonchalantly.

"Oh, um, definitely not, no. Alsry is the one who taught me, but I've only been here for a few months or so. I think if anyone's got skill with their Moving, it's her over me."

She stared at him flatly.

"I wasn't saying you were the most powerful Mover in existence. There's no need to compare yourself to any other Lightbearers," she replied.

Marric's stomach did flips as she stood and returned her hands to her hips.

"Still, you can take the compliment if you want. A simple 'thank you' would suffice, I think."

"Oh, yeah, thank you," he said, eyeing the tunnel ahead of them.

She rolled her eyes. "You clearly have somewhere you want to be, so get on with it. There's no harm done here," she said, bending over and picking up the baskets.

His brain screamed at him to run, to get to his quarters as soon as possible, as if time was running out and he'd not have the chance to See anything before Janis or one of the others came looking for him. Yet his feet remained firmly planted on the stone beneath him and refused to take him anywhere. Heart fluttering, he cursed internally at how flustered he felt standing with this girl. Though his face no longer bore the heat from when he'd first cast his eyes on her, he still couldn't grasp the situation. It was as if his mind was full of cotton, blocking his ability to speak or even think clearly.

"Name's Miredith, in case you're wondering. It didn't seem like you were polite enough to ask, so I'll just tell you."

Her voice wasn't biting but she did sound a bit resentful still. Cursing himself, he apologized.

"I'm Marric. Sorry, I've not seen you before, I didn't expect to have run into someone—well, like you," he explained, then looked away, his blush forming again.

She laughed. "So I was right. Lots of people around here have been whispering about you and that woman. Many think you're her love interest," Miredith said, then scrunched her nose. "I think that's a disgusting idea. Aren't you like, twelve or something?"

This time embarrassment switched to annoyance. Marric would be seventeen in a few months, yet this girl was trying to tell him he looked like a child. He wasn't the largest of teenagers, but to say he looked twelve was more than ludicrous.

"I'm sixteen, nearly seventeen. What are you, eleven?" Marric accused.

The girl was clearly older than that, but he was trying to prove a point. Once again his mind screamed at him that something was wrong. Nothing was working properly in his mind, and his body wouldn't respond to him urging it mentally to walk away, to leave this girl to her work.

Rather than get angry, the girl laughed. "I suppose I deserved that one, didn't I? No, I'm fifteen, just turned a few weeks ago," she replied before standing up and sidling up to him. "I definitely didn't expect the famous multi-powered Marric to be a simple farm boy like you."

Butterflies flew within his gut. As he stood there, Miredith standing too close to him, Marric felt light-headed. With a start, his lungs let out a breath with a rush. He'd been holding his breath without even realizing it.

"I'm a normal kid, sorry to disappoint you," he said before turning away sharply and hastening down the hallway.

Miredith called after him, but he didn't listen. The moment he was not next to her, his mind apparently decided to work for him again. He shook his head, focusing on the task at hand.

What a weird girl. What did she want from me anyway? Marric wondered.

As he walked, he paid far better attention than he had been before. He didn't want to inadvertently walk into another person lest his mind get all muddied like it had with Miredith. Even though he'd turned a few corners, leaving the girl behind, he still felt as if her eyes were boring into his back, watching him walk away. He couldn't be sure that she'd stared at him at all, but she seemed the type to do that. An image of her face was burned into his mind, despite the discomfort he'd felt while standing in front of her.

She was beautiful, and only now that her stern and condescending look wasn't on him and inspecting him critically could he focus on that. Had that been the reason he'd lost the ability to think like a normal human? Shaking his head, he made the last turn to his quarters and moved to the opening to his room. The cloth looked untouched, dust settling in places, giving it a more musty look than it had when he'd left. Likely no one had thought to enter his room whilst he was away, which comforted Marric for some reason.

Without a second thought, he summoned a small orb of Light, illuminating the walls of his room. A lone bed sat in the corner with nothing else. He'd been told that chairs and desks were in short supply in the compound, given only to those with a need to write or spend time in their quarters. Mostly, Seers who needed a place to meditate would get these things. That he was a Mover, a Conjurer, a Seer, *and* a Destroyer now meant he would continue to be assigned where he'd been already, journeying to retrieve newly Awakened Lightbearers. He didn't mind the lack of furniture. He didn't want to spend much time in the dim room anyway.

Grateful that Lightbearing was becoming natural to him, Marric halfheartedly tossed the thumbnail-sized orb of blue Light upward, the orb touching the low ceiling of his room. For a brief moment he looked up and smiled, then thought of how he'd caught the baskets so easily with his Moving just earlier. Apparently, the encounters he'd had outside of Terris Green were the practice he truly needed to someday become as proficient with his abilities as Avryn and the other generals.

Marric sighed, realizing that he'd wasted even more of the quiet time he'd have before someone was likely to disturb him.

He shifted for a moment, then closed his eyes and thought of the wooden carving of his mother. Normally, Seers could only See something or someone that they had seen before in person. It prevented Seers from Seeing everything about Lindrad if they didn't know what they were looking for. Marric furrowed his brow, thinking of the odd visions that befell Seers when new Lightbearers would Awaken. Only now did he realize that it didn't match the same thing he'd been told about the power as Rivelen trained him. Packing it away for later, Marric continued to focus on the image.

Narim's words describing his mother earlier echoed in his mind. He imagined her being strong, firm, and intelligent. He imagined a form for her, a stately woman holding up a Shield of blue Light, protecting those around her. He imagined her hair being the same as his, though he couldn't be sure if that was an accurate picture. As he sat, Marric waited for the world to spin, to take him to another place. When nothing happened, he clenched his fists, frustration leaking in.

What good is being able to See the past if you can't get it to work? Marric complained internally.

Squeezing his eyes shut even harder, he focused more deeply on the wooden image of his mother. Just when he thought nothing would happen, he gasped as his whole body went numb, the world swirling with colors around him. The sensation felt wrong. Every time he'd entered a vision, he'd always had some connection to his body as his vision-mind soared to where it needed to be. This time he could feel nothing. He gritted his teeth, or at least made the motions to do so, but he couldn't tell if his mouth followed his mental command.

Soon the swirling colors coalesced into a lot of grey with some bits of color here and there. When it stopped, he found himself in the war room, though it looked somewhat different. Fewer chairs littered the floor and the table in the center had only one next to it. A woman sat there, inspecting a book on the table. The rest of the surface was covered with more books and scribbled parchment. She was tall and fit, her body covered in a green dress with a golden belt. Connected to the belt was a short sword, a pouch connected to the other side. A small wreath of leaves sat atop her brow, as if it was a natural crown formed just for her. Wavy blonde hair cascaded down her back, stopping just above her waist. She was turned away, so Marric couldn't see her face.

He could hear her whispering something as she pored over the table. Suddenly, she sat up straight and looked around the room, as if she knew he was there. Instinctively he sucked in a breath, only to find that he couldn't feel the motion at all. His mind buzzed at the lack of physical sensation. He wanted to scream as he felt like a prisoner in his own mind, but he could do little about it. Instead he focused on his vision-body, urging it to move around so he could see the woman's face.

Slowly but surely the room shifted around him as his incorporeal body moved the way he commanded it. The moment he saw her face he froze.

She looked almost exactly as the carving portrayed her. Marric took a moment to look that way, seeing the same smooth wooden doors he was familiar with.

She stood up abruptly from her seat.

Marric started, then turned back to look at her. When her gaze passed over him without seeing him, he relaxed. Internally he knew that she couldn't see him, but for some reason he still felt nervous. Whether it was because he feared facing the woman who'd abandoned him as a child or because he didn't want her to think him spying on her, he couldn't tell.

As expected, the woman found no one watching.

Deftly Talatha stood and leaned back on the table, her hands pressed on the smooth surface. A few books shifted and fell over as she moved. Tilting her head back, she closed her eyes and breathed deeply. Marric's vision-body chilled, almost half the sensation of what his normal body would experience.

He knew that motion; he'd been taught it by Rivelen and the other Seer trainers. But it was too late.

Talatha's eyes flew open, glowing a brilliant blue. As expected, an image of the woman split from her form, standing on the ground just next to the table.

"There you are," she said, folding her vision-body arms. "I thought there might be someone watching."

Marric sputtered, trying to get an apology out, though he didn't know why he would need to, when Talatha's eyes widened and her hand flew to her mouth.

"It's you," she said, suddenly moving toward him.

Marric's mind buzzed once again, a warning that he should escape. Just before he could, she spoke again.

"Marric, is it really you?" Talatha said in almost a whisper.

Without any warning, Marric started to cry.

14

Rivelen tapped her foot as she sat at the edge of the war room. Alsry and Trease sat on the other side of the room, whispering something Janis couldn't hear.

Janis glanced at them, then back at Rivelen.

It wasn't that she *couldn't* hear them; it was that she was not even trying. For now she was focused on the tall blonde Seer who looked disgruntled in the corner. Avryn and Narinda had yet to return with the next set of texts written by Talatha. For the past hour they'd taken turns reading the words aloud, but nothing was ever of interest. When Narinda had spoken of Talatha's research about the "pact" and Lightbearing, Janis assumed it would be a small volume of notes. Little did she know that it was hundreds of pages, some scribbled in a type of shorthand that only Narinda could interpret. The parts that were written in long-hand, fortunately most of it, was what the various leaders took turns reading.

Rivelen shifted in her seat and folded her arms across her chest. The red dress she wore looked uncomfortable and gaudy, an impractical outfit for pretty much any occasion save for a royal ball.

Janis snorted, drawing the attention of the other women in the room.

"Somethin' funny, then?" Rivelen asked harshly.

Shrugging, Janis walked around the war table, one hand sliding smoothly on the map that always lay there.

"Oh, just inspecting your outfits, as usual. Mind if I ask, did you travel to Arivan in that garb? If you did, I'm impressed you made it back in one piece. You look like dinner to any number of wild animals in the forest," Janis replied, lifting herself to sit on the table.

Rivelen's eyes narrowed and she stopped tapping her foot.

"Think we should all dress loik yous, then? Yeh look loik a girly man more than anythin'," Rivelen countered.

This led to a snicker from behind Janis. It sounded like Trease, though Janis couldn't be sure. Regardless of who it was, Janis remained unbothered. Such petty insults were wasted on her. These flippant terms used to describe her dress meant nothing. With no trouble, Janis smiled, continuing to look at Rivelen.

"Well, I think we can all agree that one of us is better suited to handle the harshness of life. It's clear you can't even handle the lightest of scuffles, based on how shaken you appeared when you returned," Janis mused.

Rivelen blushed at this and had just opened her mouth to respond when the doors slammed open and Turrin strode into the room. "Oi fink there's better things t' be doin' wif our toim, but Avryn wants us all 'ere, so we'll do it," he boomed.

Janis rolled her eyes. She was confident that the older man had only one volume when he spoke—loud. She marveled that he'd been successful in his career before coming to Terris Green. Only recently she'd found out he'd been a mercenary. Bravado was something he had, but lying, deceiving, and sweet-talking seemed far outside his capabilities. Yet he claimed to have been successful.

Varith, on the other hand, walked primly, as if he worried for his clothing as much as Rivelen did. Janis inspected his current getup, though she hid her disdain. He wore clothing made of a green silk, embroidered on the hems and edges with gold thread. Even his cloak, which furled out behind him, was made of the same material. It looked ridiculous, to say the least. Despite this, Janis liked the man. Since she'd been back from Stilten, she'd sparred with him occasionally. He'd proven far more skilled than she had expected.

"Ah, I see the stuffy funeral goer is still enjoying bantering with Miss Uptight. Seems we missed nothing while we were away, Turrin," Varith said, moving to the closest chair to him and settling in. The way he leaned back, his bald, dark-skinned head leaning against the stone, proved how unbothered he was.

Janis smiled, amused at how he'd referred to her.

"You're all fools," Alsry said gruffly, "wasting your time joking like this. Janis told us that the world could end, that Ugglyn's power looks to have manifested in Prost, and you all laugh as if nothing's happening! It's a wonder Magness chose any of you to be leaders here."

At first no one spoke, then a few of them started talking all at once. Right as Turrin justified their lightheartedness, Rivelen began complaining about the little information they had, while Trease talked about working together being the most important thing right now. After a few failed attempts to allow one of the three to speak first, Janis shook her head and slid off the table.

"Right now there's not much we can do about it," she said. "Unless you want to march out into the forest and walk around in circles looking for Watchlight and their compound. I'd wager you would have such success with that plan." Her tone made it obvious that she was being sarcastic, and fortunately, Alsry picked up on it.

"Joke all you like, but come three days, we could have new leadership. Fog it, we could all be demoted and replaced by any person who that fool man Gallin wants at the head," Alsry spat. "We should end him right now. It would save us trouble."

Trease grimaced at the suggestion, leaning forward in her chair. "Lass, I don' think tha' would be wise. All that'd do would be to make uprisings more likely. Can' 'ave leaders goin' round killin' people 'oo disagree, can we?"

Janis was sure that Trease was the only person in this compound who could get away with calling Alsry something like lass. It was clear the women had some friendship that existed since before they came to Evenir. Janis hadn't had time to look into each of the leaders' pasts, but she still planned to do so.

If I ever make it out of here, she thought grimly.

Since Stilten and the events there, she felt an obligation to stay with Evenir. While she didn't relish the idea of being a leader for them, she didn't feel right about leaving them alone altogether. She cursed Lanser silently for drawing her into this situation. Janis couldn't help but wonder where she'd be right at this moment had she not been threatened by Watchlight. Would she have even Awakened? Were these events caused because she'd been in close contact with Marric when he Awakened? As she thought of these things, she tuned out the other leaders as they continued the discussion of whether they were wasting their time. Tension was high in the room and it was clear in everyone's postures and expressions.

Janis kept up the appearance of being relaxed. Emotions and questions stewed within her, but it felt important not to show the way she felt inside to the others. Even if she wasn't voted in as the leader of Evenir, being recognized as the Prime Lightbearer—a concept no one here had even been aware of before now—made them look at her differently. Gone was the unwelcome assassin. Gone was the woman who made everyone uncomfortable by just looking at them. They'd treated her differently ever since she'd told them about Tryvv and the hidden cavern within Terris Green.

One of the first things she'd done once they'd returned to the sanctuary was to try to find that same hidden cavern with the Light statues. Her memory was perfect and she recalled the day as potently as if it had just happened. Yet when Janis had gone to the same dead end, there was no door. Even when she'd coerced Livella to come with her, nothing changed. After that failure, she'd tried to convince Avryn to allow her to blast her way through the wall to see if there was something behind it. Not only did he decline it but he forbade her from trying, even when she'd insisted that she could just Fix it after she was done. If the same order had come from Magness, Janis wouldn't have listened. It wasn't because she respected the late Evenir leader any less than Avryn; Janis just knew what her actions could have caused, given the lack of true leadership at the moment. Any level of insubordination could cause dissenters to rise, especially if they saw it within the higher-ups of the organization.

The conversation continued around her but Janis still wasn't listening. None of the others were looking at her, so she assumed they weren't speaking to her. She noted that Rivelen was still silent. Looking over at the woman, Janis saw Rivelen's eyes shift rapidly from Janis's belt to her face, eyes narrowing.

She was looking at the book, Janis thought.

Rivelen, despite her accent, was actually quite studious. She'd claimed to speak the way she did out of honor to her upbringing, but Janis thought it was pure laziness. Still, Rivelen was intelligent, and she could read and write as well as anyone else in Evenir. It was little surprise that she might be curious to read the black book. The idea of allowing her to touch it bothered Janis, though she wasn't sure why. She'd had similar feelings when she thought of letting any of the other generals touch the book. Perhaps she didn't trust any of them as much as she told herself she did.

The doors opened, a tired-looking Narinda entering with Avryn at her side. The woman held a medium stack of bound books, most looking well-worn.

"I apologize for my tardiness. Hiron moved the records without telling me, and then he'd forgotten where he laid them," Narinda explained. "It took me time to coax the memory out of him." Her voice sounded as tired as her face looked.

Rivelen scoffed. "Oi could've just Seen where he'd put 'em. Why bother askin' 'im? Man don't remember where he put his woife, fer Lanser's sake."

Sighing, Avryn looked at Rivelen.

"I know this is getting tiresome. We'll take a break soon. For now it seems important that we read the texts together. Taking turns would take far too long, even if some of us are fast readers," Avryn said, giving Janis a pointed look.

Janis had been one of the first ones to complain about having to spend these hours together when she knew she could consume the texts in less than half the time. Even though she wouldn't admit it out loud, she knew Avryn had a point. There were too many of them to take turns. Even if they could all read as fast as Janis, which she suspected they couldn't, it would take at least a week before they could all get up to speed. In that time too much could happen.

"Are you sure these are the ones?" Janis asked, unfolding her arms to wave at the small stack of books in Narinda's grasp.

Narinda nodded.

"These should have more of the notes I was thinking of when we saw the volume you brought with you," Narinda said, her eyes darting to the black book and away again.

It seems none of them can keep their eyes off of the prize, Janis thought.

"An' wha' if yeh're wrong? 'Ow many more d' we need to read 'afore we get what we need? Talatha didn't say nuttin' 'bout any o' this to any o' us," Rivelen complained.

"We'll only know once we try. Rivelen, bear with us for a bit longer. These should be the rest of the texts, right, Nari?" Avryn asked.

Janis narrowed her eyes at the man, noting the obvious nickname he'd just used with Narinda. She wasn't the only one who noticed, for Varith and Turrin stared at him as well, Turrin's mouth hanging open slightly, his eyes full of mirth. His tongue barely held back the joke he'd inevitably come up with. Trease and Alsry whispered behind as well, likely about the same topic.

Avryn noticed their reactions but ignored them, standing by his decision to use the nickname. Rather than react, he placed his hand on Narinda's lower back and pulled her toward the table. Jealousy threatened to sprout within her chest but Janis suppressed it. Her emotions had been more volatile, another unfortunate side effect of her Transformation. Not once had she been held like that in her life. She'd longed for Macks to do such a thing, but their work had always just been business, no matter what she felt.

There was Harmel though.

"Is there a way we can make this faster? Narinda looks like she'll fall over any moment, and I'm sure I'm not the only one who could use a reprieve from reading," Alsry said.

Avryn sighed, then looked to Narinda.

"Do you have an idea where you might find the words you thought of when you saw Janis's book?" Avryn asked.

Hearing the book called hers made Janis's stomach twist. Janis knew Avryn meant nothing by it, but it still made her uncomfortable.

"Actually, yes, I have some idea. I'm not sure why we didn't think of this before," Narinda replied.

Avryn shrugged. "When we began, it didn't feel as much like we had a deadline. Now that we've been at it for some time, I think we could all benefit from working more efficiently."

Murmurs of assent sounded around them, Janis nodding herself. Suddenly she felt as if someone was watching her. Janis tensed, trying not to alert the others in the room that she was uncomfortable. As inconspicuously as possible, Janis scanned the surrounding room. Almost instantly her eyes found Rivelen staring at her belt once more. Adrenaline began coursing through her at the sight. The look on Rivelen's face was something uncharacteristic of the woman. She looked almost hungry. Janis casually put her hands on her hips, her right hand veiling where the cover of the black book stuck out of her pants. She gritted her teeth as her skin touched the leather, sending the rippling cold up her hand and into her arm; she'd forgotten her lack of handkerchief. Janis eased her hand off the leather binding, but she kept her hand close. Rivelen's gaze on the text didn't look hostile, just curious. It wasn't that Janis distrusted the woman, but she knew how curiosity had almost summoned Ugglyn only just that day.

Gritting her teeth, she focused her attention on Avryn once more as the man settled into one of the chairs at the table. Narinda sat next to him, placing the books down gingerly and rifling through them.

"Let's begin—here, then," Narinda stated, placing her finger on a part of one of the books. Turrin groaned, placing his fingers on his forehead and resting his head backward on the stone wall. Alsry grunted and folded her arms, but the others remained quiet. Only after Narinda started reading did Rivelen stop staring at Janis's belt.

"*I spent the better part of last month in the libraries at the university in T'Arren Vale*," Narinda read in her stately voice. "*I can't begin to imagine why I didn't start my studies there, for their selection of texts is extraordinary compared to that of Stilten. Evenir believes me to be on collaboration business with the queen and her consort. While I did briefly have such meetings, with little success, I've spent most of my time here.*"

Narinda paused, pressing her lips together.

Avryn looked a mixture of surprised, confused, and angry at the same time.

"I think I recall this journey. Weren't you with her at the time?" Avryn said, turning to Trease.

The stout woman shrugged. "'Course I was, bu' Talatha din' roit le' me follow 'er everywhere and the loik. She'd go off on 'er own from toim to toim. Wouldn't even take a guard, she wouldn'."

Narinda stared off into the distance for a moment before she breathed out loudly. "I'm sure that she had good reason to keep this information from us. She was a great leader, trustworthy to the core," the woman stated, though her voice wavered.

Janis shook her head. It was impossible to keep whole faith in any leader, but at the same time it felt ludicrous that any leader could not have the complete trust of their followers. That was part of the reason she never meddled in working with others, especially after Macks. Most of the issue was her inability to trust, or at least her prior inability to trust people. Janis cracked her neck, trying not to let her creeping trust in Avryn and the others bother her too much. She could be ok with the changes in herself; she just had to accept them.

Avryn still looked troubled, but he urged Narinda on.

"*Most of the texts here are of an educational nature, unhelpful to my current objectives, but today I found the most curious of things. Upon reading a holy text, the very first recorded history of Lanser and his ascension to godhood, a small book fell from inside the pages. The leather cover and binding of the book were black as night, with ink of silvery nature so that it almost glowed.*" Narinda paused, a worried look on her face, then stared at Janis.

Reflexively Janis reached down and touched the book once more, wincing at the tingling that ran through her hand before she withdrew it. She berated herself for continually coming in contact with the odd book. Though she had little confidence that the reaction would disappear or that it would feel different, Janis felt she ought to keep trying it.

"Tha' sounds roit familiar, don' it?" Turrin spouted, resting his folded hands on his large gut.

Varith snorted. "My friend, I can't tell if you are joking or not. I've not even heard of methods of creating black parchment, let alone glowing silver ink. That, sir, sounds *exactly* like what dear Janis has in her possession."

"Keep reading, we need to be sure," Avryn insisted.

Nodding, Narinda looked down and continued reading.

"My first inclination was to leave the book be, for by merely gazing upon its cover did I note an unnatural feeling not only within me but in the very air around it. The space and stone around the text appeared to warp, as if the book was drawing everything around it inside."

Everyone's eyes were drawn to the book on Janis's person. Rolling her eyes, Janis grabbed it and tossed it on the table. Narinda yelped and pulled her book away, Avryn jumping a little himself.

The moment the small text landed, the air around it appeared to bend, as if it was being drawn into it. Colors distorted, and the Lighting orb hovering above the book dimmed. Almost instantly, the surrounding air grew cold. The shadows seemed to deepen in response to Janis tossing the book on the table.

"Oi fink it's safe to say they're the same book," Turrin commented.

Janis had suspected—practically knew—that the book belonged to Ugglyn somehow. Though she needed to know why it existed in the first place. To find out that Talatha, Marric's mother, had come in contact with it before her was intriguing. It became more apparent that the mysteries of the seal she'd been forced into were more numerous than she could have guessed.

Narinda cleared her throat. Not one person either affirmed Turrin's assessment or denied it. Janis guessed there wasn't one soul among them that couldn't admit the truth of it being the same text.

"At length, my curiosity got the better of me, and I did a copious study of the strange silvery letters. Unfortunately, most of the text is written in a reformed version of the ancient language of Lindrad. I'm familiar with the language of old, but the characters used in this situation are modified, to a degree that I can only assume it was tampered with for a purpose. A few phrases alone stood out on the page, ones I do not dare repeat or write in this record. Yet I must admit the oddity of the words. Only once I'd inspected certain pages did a few phrases change, as if before my eyes. What once appeared as unreadable ancient characters adapted in my mind to look like Lindradian as it is today."

Narinda paused, glancing at the book. Janis felt her skin chill at the mention of the words changing. Every time she'd seen it opened, certain characters changed, as if they wanted her to read them. Oddly, and she was sure of it, the pages varied each time. While it had only happened a couple of times, Janis had memory enough to know the exact pages and locations where the words adapted to modern Lindradian. She was confident that they were different.

Janis eyed the shadows. They still writhed and deepened as if the book was calling to them like a mother to her children. Shaking her head, Janis moved to the table and snatched the small volume up, shoving it into her belt once more. She ignored the icy chill that spread through her hands and up her arm, hurrying so that it couldn't pierce her as much as it had before.

"What? No mention of the way that book seems to freeze your blood from the inside?" Janis snapped.

She wasn't angry at Narinda; Janis knew it wasn't her fault any of this was happening, but it frustrated her that Talatha had a record of this very book and hadn't mentioned it to anyone.

Narinda frowned, then nodded.

"She spends a great deal of time describing the sensation, actually. That is what reminded me of the fact that she'd described something similar in her records. Not once did I think anything of what she'd written until you showed us that book."

"What does it *mean*? That's the prime question here," Alsry spouted.

Apparently, I'm not the only one getting impatient, Janis thought.

A few of the others in the room shot Janis hard looks at the use of the word *prime*, but she ignored them. Alsry, though gruff, had a point. Talatha was long-winded and had proven so with how much detail she put into each of her records. That was part of the reason they'd been here for as long as they had. Janis wished the woman knew how to summarize effectively.

"It's going to take more reading to get to that, I'm guessing. The best thing we can do is be patient. Talatha had good reason to learn what she did. She wouldn't have recorded her findings if she thought it wasn't worthwhile for us to read someday. But before we read on, I must ask, did you see the letters change?" Avryn asked.

Janis furrowed her brow.

"Yes, you were there the whole time. Or were you too distracted by something else?" Janis countered. Her eyes opened wide as she looked pointedly at Narinda.

Avryn flushed but kept his bearings quite well despite her jibe.

"I was there, and no, I was not distracted. I was focused on the book as it lay open on the floor. Not once did I see the text change, though you claim it did," Avryn replied.

"That makes no sense. How is it that the other three of us could see it shift when you couldn't?" Janis said.

Narinda cleared her throat, looking thoughtful.

"I didn't have a perfectly clear view, what with Avryn obscuring it unintentionally, but from what I did see, nothing changed," Narinda added.

Janis's chest burned with nerves. Until now, she'd assumed everyone who opened the book could see the shift in the letters, but that wasn't so. "Marric saw the change. He was the one to read it out loud, after all," Janis said, once again sliding her hand so it hovered over the book in her belt.

"Oi saw it too, jus' now Oi did," Rivelen said out of nowhere.

Avryn started, looking back and forth from Janis to Rivelen. He narrowed his eyes for a moment, as if he was considering something. All Janis could do was try to ward off the feeling of her skin tingling and crawling with the unnatural nature of this conversation. After a moment she thought through all those who'd seen the book change in this way. Janis guessed that Macks would have been able to read some of it, and it was highly unlikely the man could read any ancient text, let alone anything that had been modified.

Suddenly Avryn snapped his fingers, letting out a small, triumphant "ha.""Seers. You're all Seers. That has to be it," Avryn said. "Narinda and I aren't Awakened Seers, but Marric, Rivelen, and you, Janis, are full Seers. That can only be it."

Janis cursed herself for not seeing that before him.

"Macks, the one I took this from, was the Seer who helped Luden find Lightbearers so they could intercept them. He wouldn't have been carrying a book like this if he didn't think it valuable or useful," Janis added.

Janis felt vulnerable all of a sudden, as if having the powers of a Seer made her open to communication from Ugglyn. Of course, she knew that couldn't be wholly true, for if she was vulnerable like that, he'd have come to talk to her again. The moment she had the thought she looked sharply at Talatha's record. Before she could ask, Varith whistled softly. "And our dear late leader, Talatha, was a secondary Seer."

Avryn looked both jubilant and grim at the same time, which really felt like an impossible combination for one person. The logic was sound, and it just seemed right for Seers to be the ones to perceive the change in the words, yet Janis didn't want to accept it. "We should test it, just to be sure," she suggested. "If this is true, it could be important."

Nodding, Avryn gestured for Narinda to continue.

"The next few paragraphs are Talatha describing the sensation of touching the pages, which appears in line with what you've described." She dipped her head toward Janis as she spoke. "We can save a bit of time skipping that. Let's see—"

"Though I did not read the words aloud, once I'd spoken them in my head, I could feel a strange pull within my consciousness, as if my mind was trying to yank me into a vision. It felt reminiscent of me Seeing an Awakening outside of my volition. This I spurned with great effort, fearing that something horrible might occur. However, once I'd read the words in my mind, more sentences shifted, revealing much to me. Though they were fleeting, I read as quickly as I could before they disappeared. They wrote of a pact, a 'seal' of sorts, locking away the anti-god. The record spoke of a key, a way to release him from his prison, though I didn't get enough details to bear much understanding."

Janis grunted. "We know what the key is. I just have to die, that's it, isn't it?"

Avryn shook his head, looking thoughtful.

"But it must be more than that. You said that it chose you as a new seal for Ugglyn, yet something occurred when Riln, the supposed failed seal, died, did it not?" Avryn surmised.

An unsettling feeling distilled in the room as Janis noted the shifting of those around her. Varith frowned, looking at her as if she was the one to blame for this whole debacle. In part, she was, and though she still didn't know the ramifications of Riln dying, she didn't regret it. At least not yet. When she'd Moved the dagger through Riln's back, she expected the slimy man to pull out of it, to Fix himself with little trouble as he had the other wounds she'd inflicted. It had become a battle of energy over skill very quickly, though Riln had almost killed her more than once during the bout. Still, the real impact of his death was seeing Prost use her dagger to kill Riln.

"Whatever happened in Stilten with the odd swirling tempest could be due in part to the fact that Prost was the one who killed Riln in the end. Pulling the dagger through his gut was meant to stall him. I assumed he'd heal," Janis said, voicing what she had already thought.

"You mean to say that you *expected* the man to heal from a full dagger in his back? That is veritably optimistic, even for Fixers," Varith commented. "I could do so with time, but not quickly enough to keep me from being vulnerable to my assailant."

"I think it's safe to guess that Primes have a different sort of power, Varith," Alsry chimed in. "This whole 'seal' nonsense has created problems Evenir's not faced before. The real question is why Talatha didn't share the report with us before now. Why did we have to find out through her records almost a year later?"

Narinda winced at the comment. "Actually, years, really. This research was dated two years ago, though the most recent entries show as late as just before her death."

Alsry threw up her hands in frustration but leaned back and put a hand to her forehead, choosing not to comment further.

"Wha' else do it say? Keep on, then," Trease urged Narinda.

Face grim, Narinda continued.

"The text flowed more quickly as I followed along, as if it knew where I was trailing. I must say, the feeling of an unseen power reaching into my mind was not something I'd like to experience again."

Rivelen snorted, shooting looks Narinda's way. "As a Seer, I know wha' it's loik 'avin intruders in yer space wifout yeh knowin'. Dun it meself a number o' times," she said.

Sighing, Avryn held up a hand.

"Perhaps *less* commentary, so we can get through this part of the record," he insisted.

Narinda continued then.

"The text spoke of a power reserve, a place where Ugglyn locked a piece of

himself away, separated from his imprisoned self. While it never specified where such power was stored, I have to comment that I wonder if the book itself was some conduit or a vessel for said power. It seems the only logical explanation for why it has the effect it does on touch and why it responds to my reading. While I'm unfamiliar with the powers of Ugglyn, my studies months ago show that it's something of darkness, something of grilvanyat, *or 'Void' in Lindradian. No sooner had I realized the possibility of the book being the vessel for Ugglyn's stored power than someone walked into the library room I'd been using. I snapped it closed and replaced it soon after. While I was sure I recalled where I'd placed it, when I returned the next day, it was gone.*"

That made Janis's mind whirl. The book could not have moved on its own. Barring the unlikely possibility that it could actually move of its own volition, that meant that someone else had taken it just after Talatha discovered it. That could not have been a coincidence, especially when it came to something unusual like this. Ugglyn had communications with people in Lindrad, else Riln could not have corrupted himself and the rest of Watchlight.

"Ugglyn must have called someone to it somehow," Janis guessed.

The room fell silent, all eyes on her. Avryn looked at her, confused. She rolled her eyes, annoyed that she had to explain her thought process.

"Just moments ago we all agreed that Seers could decipher the change in the text, right? Would it be possible for him to use the same connection, the same power to communicate to Seers here? Riln was obviously in some type of agreement with the foggin' fool. It's possible he sent a Seer to get the book somehow."

"That's impossible. Why would Lanser create a power that could provide a connection to the bound anti-god? If Lanser created the seal to lock away Ugglyn, why would he create a vulnerability like that?" Alsry said.

Avryn was staring at Janis, a knowing look on his face. "You know something. No person, no matter how intelligent, could have made such a connection. It seems you've a past with this form of communication."

Janis shrugged.

"Something Riln did with me months ago..." She paused, realizing that she'd have to let them in on her "in-between" experience for this to make sense. For a moment she deliberated if it would be worth giving up that secret. But it quickly became clear that the secret was of no worth any longer, given that Seeing was her new standard of information gathering.

"Macks, who I learned in Stilten was a Seer himself, taught me to access my memory in a dream state. It is—was—a way for me to delve into the past to gather further information from what I'd already experienced," she explained.

Varith's mouth dropped open as he clearly wanted to ask something, but Janis pushed on, ignoring his gesture.

"We called it the 'in-between,' a place that isn't reality but isn't fully outside of it. Before I Awakened, I could use this. During one of my—delvings—Riln pulled me into what I believe was a Seer vision, despite not having those abilities myself."

Avryn's eyes lit up. "Yes, I recall you told me what you'd learned, but I thought it was merely a dream, not a conscious action on your part."

Janis grunted. "At the time it felt best to keep that to myself. You understand, assassin's rules and whatnot."

He shook his head, an incredulous smile on his lips.

"At this point I should just expect you to have kept information from us," Avryn replied, finally looking back at her. "Go on, what does this have to do with Ugglyn?"

A noise from the side of the room caught everyone's attention. Rivelen sat there, a shocked look on her face. Janis could almost see the woman's brain working. As the only other Seer in the room, it made sense that she would have been the one to put it together. Still, Janis gave her credit for it. She'd assumed Rivelen wasn't capable of much but complaint and fussing over her fancy clothing.

"Loik when anuvver Seer contacts yous through their spot in the vision. Are yeh sayin' that Ugglyn moit be able to *pull us in*?" Rivelen's voice raised at the last word, fear visible on her face.

Janis shrugged. "I doubt he'd be able to pull us in with too much ease. I think the only reason Riln could snag me the way he did was because I was already in the in-between."

"The connection between your—unusual access to memory and Seeing is something we'll need to put off for another day. For now we need to realize that Ugglyn may have a conduit to us via Seeing. The fact that we don't understand it makes it more of a risk," Avryn admitted.

Turrin grunted. "Oi fink we'd know boi now if 'e wanted t' speak t' one of our Seers. It's been weeks since Stilten; 'e can't know where Terris Green is, not yet," he surmised.

"Still, be vigilant," Avryn suggested, then he turned back to Rivelen. "Have you heard of any unusual contact like this with the Seers?"

Rivelen shook her head, her eyes still somewhat distant. "No, sir. Though Oi will be askin' them from now on. We've no luck foinding their base yet either. We've got to try somethin' else."

Narinda suddenly cleared her throat, and all eyes moved to her. "Umm, I don't want to interrupt, but before we move on, there is something else."

"Oh yes, what, then?" Avryn asked, turning back to the war table. He not-so-inconspicuously placed his hand on Narinda's back as she sat in the chair. His eyes held the true feelings he had for the woman, the ones he'd somehow hidden from Janis until Narinda returned safely from Wurren.

Clearing her throat, she read again.

"This takes place the next day, according to Talatha, but it's related to the strange book." Her voice changed as she began reading the account of Magness's predecessor. "*When it became evident that I'd find no evidence of the strange book from the day before, I delved into additional records. Many spoke of the connection of the three moons with Lightbearing, both ill, good, and something else called* H'ilvina't, *though I'm unsure what it means. It took me months to find the closest translation of the word, and even this is a rough one, but it means something along the lines of 'the causer of the event,' or 'catalyst,' though that bears something deeper I can't explain.*

"The few texts I'd found spoke of Ugglyn breaking free from his seal. Most spent an exorbitant amount of time discussing the terrible fate of Lindrad should this happen, but one single text spoke of H'ilvina't *as the only way to reverse the breaking, to reseal the anti-god away. I'm unsure what ritual or object this is, but it seems logical that we locate this device as a preparation."*

Narinda paused, sighing.

"That's it? What the fog is that supposed to mean?" Alsry voiced, annoyed.

The room was immediately abuzz with various conversations. Trease and Alsry fussed over one thing, Varith and Turrin another. Rivelen started speaking loudly, asking various questions about the words while Avryn tried to console her. Janis, ignoring all of them, moved to Narinda's other side, then peered over her shoulder at the text. She'd left her finger on the sentence she ended with, as if she didn't want to lose her place should they keep going.

Janis stared at the word *H'ilvina't*, mulling it over. It felt important and an odd tugging she felt in her gut validated this. She'd learned to trust her instinct with important information and it was obvious this was. Not only because of the other information Talatha had written about but also because it felt as if it had power to it. She suddenly had the urge to say the word aloud, if only to test what would happen. By speaking Ugglyn's words moments before, the air had darkened, as if it was drawing him in. It irked her to say something unfamiliar out loud, especially given how unknown everything was about Lightbearing and Ugglyn's Void. Still, the word drew her in.

Despite the surrounding noise, Janis spoke the word against her better judgment.

"*H'ilvina't*," Janis said.

The air seemed to thicken around them, an orange-colored haze appearing. Janis felt the same tug in her gut that she had before, though this time it was pulling her toward the coalescing orange Light forming there. She grasped the tabletop, holding it tightly to keep her balance. In an instant, wind gushed through the air, originating from nowhere, until it was a tempest blowing her hair around in a frenzy. Avryn's blue sword was already summoned, as were Varith's and Turrin's. Alsry stood tense, her own hands outstretched as if she meant to push the orange Light away with her Moving.

Oddly, Janis felt at ease with it.

"What in Lanser's name is that?" Avryn shouted over the wind.

Narinda stood sharply, snapping her own weapon out of her scabbard, then she looked hard at Janis.

"Another beast of Ugglyn?" Turrin yelled back.

The orange glowing air suddenly sped together into an orb, similar in size to a Lighting orb. There it hovered, the wind gushing around them even stronger.

Avryn pushed Narinda behind him once again.

"We should attack it before it gets the better of us!" Varith roared before he and Turrin, both looking resolved, started moving toward it.

Janis held out a hand to her side, stopping the men. They stared at her angrily, but she ignored them. The Light pulsed as if it had a heartbeat of its own. Her hair continued to whip around her head, and she was vaguely aware of voices but she didn't bother trying to listen. Somehow she knew that this wasn't a danger to any of them, though she didn't know exactly why. Reaching the orb, she moved her hand toward it, expecting a similar sensation to that of Lighting orbs. The moment her hand touched it, the Light flew over her head.

Screams and shouts of surprise echoed on the stone walls as the orb moved rapidly toward the door of the war room. On its way, it passed through Narinda and Avryn, who both tried to jump out of the way with no success. The Light appeared to have no effect on either of them, save for fright. The wind abruptly stopped, as if a door had been closed to block it.

"'Ow many times we gotta see the foggin' strangest things in 'ere?!" Turrin exclaimed. "Startin' to think this room's cursed!"

Others murmured their assent, people moving to right the maps that had blown off the walls. Janis didn't bother helping them; instead she focused on the wooden door where the light had gone.

"More importantly, how did it come? Why did it appear?" Avryn asked.

"It was me," Janis replied. "I know that Light somehow, but I'm unsure how or why. It wasn't an apparition of Ugglyn; that would have been the same silvery smoke, like what we saw in Stilten."

Avryn grimaced. "It's true, then. Whatever happened in Stilten happened at Ugglyn's hand. Lanser help us, it isn't as serious as Ugglyn being free."

Her insides writhed, though it wasn't from fear or agitation, merely from intrigue. She disliked riddles she didn't know the answer to. The urge to chase after the orange orb tugged at her, but she pressed it away. She couldn't keep up with it.

"I could always say the word again. I bet it would come back," Janis suggested, but it was mostly in jest. She watched as Rivelen paled and Alsry grunted. "It's a joke, relax."

"Regardless of its innocence, we should find out where it went. We'll ask around, find out where it flew," Avryn said. "In the meantime, we should look more at this black book. Rivelen, can you inspect it further with Janis?"

Janis shook her head.

"I need a break from reading. Here." She casually grabbed the book, the tingling flying up her arm like a hungry animal ready to consume her flesh, but she ignored it and tossed it on the table. Narinda yelped and stepped away from the table. The small text thudded on the table in front of her.

"I have a Light to hunt," Janis said.

15

Thwack!

Prost's sword thudded on the wooden dummy that stood in one of the sparring rooms. Most of the other Watchlight men and women sparred further away, no one daring to get close as he practiced. It had been weeks since the events in Stilten, and not one new Awakening had occurred. No Awakenings meant no journeys and no fighting. Prost gritted his teeth, sucking in the stale air through his nose and trying to imagine it was something fresher.

While he left the compound occasionally to get air, it was unlikely that he'd have the opportunity to continue fighting. He had little fear that he'd lose his ability with the long break, yet he couldn't go any longer without hitting something with his sword. He gripped the hilt of a longsword with both hands, swinging wildly at the dummy. In the hour he'd been practicing, he'd hacked the dummy into so many pieces, he couldn't count. It mattered little, for a Fixer could repair it in an instant.

Roaring, he swung the massive sword overhead, the sharp blade splitting the still dummy into two pieces. Whispers continued around him but he didn't care.

"M'lord? Is there something wrong?" a woman's voice said behind him.

Prost turned sharply to see Neera watching him. Ever since the fight he'd had with the rebel man yesterday, she'd hovered near him, admiring him in ways that made him uncomfortable. Sweat trickled down his brow, but he nodded his head.

"Nothing save for the problems of the recent weeks. I just needed to hit something. It's been too long since I've fought in an actual battle," he said, eyeing the broken dummy before shouting. "Someone Fix this fogging thing! I need another bout!"

A few stirred around him, but no one moved. Veins bulged in his neck at the lack of response. He drew in a large breath, ready to shout again, but paused.*This isn't my anger*, Prost thought.

THESE FOOLS DON'T LISTEN! You've ruined them! They'll never obey you unless you show them how you'll deal with those who don't follow your every order! Ugglyn raged inside.

Forcing himself not to close his eyes, Prost pressed his jaw together as firmly as he could, trying not to lose himself to Ugglyn's control. Every day their minds inhabited the same space, Prost felt his own consciousness melding together with the being.

He focused on the closest person to him, calming his face to not scare them away despite the rage that still swarmed inside him. Pointing, he commanded the man.

"You, fetch a Fixer," he said, his voice hard.

The boy, for he couldn't have been more than fifteen years old, jumped at the direct order, then nodded.

"That won't be necessary. I'll just do it myself," a thin man said.

The wiry man stepped up to the dummy and held his hand to the wood. Splinters flew from around them and aligned themselves back on the man-sized dummy. Prost didn't recall this specific man's name, but he looked familiar. Given that he'd roamed Watchlight's lair for the past few years, it wasn't unlikely that Prost may have crossed his path.

"Perhaps you could use an actual opponent, rather than waste your time and energy on something that won't fight back," the man suggested. He stared at Prost, one eyebrow raised. His face appeared young, though wrinkles betrayed his likely age of a man in his later thirties. Hair red, eyes green and piercing, he looked a handsome specimen for any woman around. Even now, Prost noticed a few women admiring the man from the sides of the room. Prost's chest flared with annoyance at their attention before he snuffed it out. He didn't have time for dallying with women, yet his manly instincts twinged with jealousy.

Perhaps you need a woman to release your tension, Ugglyn mused.

Keep your thoughts to yourself, Prost demanded.

Standing up straighter, Prost eyed the man before him. Prost stood a few inches taller than him and was obviously more bulky, but he knew that didn't mean anything. A man such as this could be remarkably quick and hard to keep up with.

"If you wish to be beaten at swordplay, then by all means. Know that I won't go easy on you," Prost replied, a bead of sweat trickling down the side of his face. As it fell, he watched the man's gaze follow the droplet's path down his cheek, amusement clear not only on his face but in his posture.

"You look like you could use a break, if I'm being honest," the man countered.

The comment was a play of dominance and Prost could tell. The man had just challenged Prost to a sparring match, knowing full well how long he'd been fighting the dummy. His arms already ached from the exertion of smashing the wood. It had been repaired twice, both Fixers retreating rapidly from the room fearing Prost's wrath, or so Prost assumed. Still, by declining the fight, Prost would look weak.

"I've energy to spare. Let us get on, then," Prost replied, moving to the center of the room where etchings in the stone floor formed a circular space.

This was the largest of the sparring circles. A few more half its size filled other parts of the cavern, but this was where the main sparring events were held. Even now, people listening to the exchange gathered, some running to tell their friends what was about to happen. Taking up the first position, Prost held his two-handed beast in front of him, feeling his arm muscles become taut with the weight. The man still held a smirk as he stood several paces in front of him. He Conjured two short swords, each identical, with little adornment. The red from the swords lit the floor and surrounding space, adding to the Lighting orbs that filled the cavern.

"I hope you don't mind me using these, since you are no longer immune, I hear," the man stated, still amused.

While Prost had known he wouldn't be able to keep that news away from the others in the compound, he'd hoped it wouldn't be broadcasted so forwardly. Prost stared at the swords with contempt, but shook his head.

"If they're your weapon of choice, then it seems fair," Prost said, still holding his ready stance.

The man stood there, a sly smile lifting the corners of his mouth."But one last thing, it's only right that if I'm to use my Conjured swords, you would as well. You have spoken of Ugglyn's gifted abilities, yet you share them not with the rest of us. Come, show us what *true* power you claim to wield."

A thrill filled Prost as Ugglyn heard the recommendation and snatched it up mentally as a bird would catch a fish jumping ever so slightly from the surface of a lake. Murmurs sounded around them, residents agreeing, some complaining about fairness.

"M'lord, do you think it wise after all this time—"

Prost held up a hand to Neera, who'd been standing there watching the exchange quietly. She looked worried. She wouldn't need to worry about him.

"He can have what he requests, though he may regret it," Prost said, holding out the heavy broadsword to the woman. Sighing, she grabbed its hilt, grunting as Prost released the full weight into her hands. Immediately, relief from his tense muscles flooded his arms.

It's time. Don't you try anything now, you can't have control, Prost insisted, both as a reminder for Ugglyn and himself.

Ugglyn murmured something like assent before causing a shift in Prost's mind. The cool feeling, as if icy water were running through his veins, flowed through each of his arms.

"Let us begin, then," Prost said as the Voidwoven broadsword formed into his hands. One thing he'd noticed since he'd gained the powers was that Conjuring, or whatever he did, came on differently than a Conjure of Light. Any Conjure of Lanser's Light exploded into existence, appearing in a flashing brilliance. Voidwoven Conjures grew outward, as if from Prost's limbs themselves, forming as if forged from coalescing smoke. The chill intensified in each of his palms until the sword was formed before the feeling slid inward, settling in his chest.

With a grunt, Prost dove at his opponent, the man dancing away easily from the first go. The man spun, then slashed with both blades at Prost's side. A quick slip from his broadsword caught both of the shorter blades on the flat edge. The moment the weapons touched, a loud hissing split the air, accompanied by the normal steel-on-steel echoing through the cavern. The sound surprised Prost, but he veiled his reaction.

Using more force than was likely needed, Prost shoved the man backward with his enormous sword, causing his feet to slide on the ground. With a low growl, his opponent attacked forward with both swords, each coming in quick succession after the other. Prost avoided one of the swords easily while parrying attacks from the other. As expected, they fell into a rhythm, each attacking ruthlessly for moments before it switched and the other gave their bouts. Adrenaline coursed through Prost's mind and body, melding with the icy chill that still filled his breast. The combination of the two felt like heat and cold fighting earnestly for control of the room, but neither dominating, as if a steaming cup of tea held the coldest ice cube without it melting.

As he analyzed the sensation, the man before him stepped forward, slicing Prost's arm on the sleeve. Blood slipped down his upper arm underneath his clothing. It stung, but the pain felt so inconsequential compared to past wounds he'd suffered. Suddenly, burning exploded in his arm where the Light blade had cut him. Prost's heart thudded as panic tried to set in before he forced it to calm.

Is that poison? Prost thought.

Sure enough, he could feel something spreading up his arm like flames running through his veins. He'd never heard of anyone using a substance on the blades of their Conjured weapons, yet he'd always been immune, so he wouldn't have known. Ugglyn roared in his mind, cursing Lanser's name over and over. The chill of Voidweaving gathered in his arm, pressing the feeling of poison out of his system. Within moments, it was gone.

Beware the blade of Light. It eats away at the Void, just as the Void chases away the Light, Ugglyn whispered.

The man before him cocked his head in confusion before diving forward. With a roar, Prost rushed the man, putting more strength into swinging his two-handed sword than normal. The man gritted his teeth, realizing he couldn't dodge the quick slash from Prost's sword. Instead he caught the large Void-Conjured sword with one of his own. A shattering sound echoed in the hall as the sword exploded into pieces before disappearing into the air like it had never existed. Prost heavily forced his blade into the arm of his opponent. The man shouted in pain as it cut a few inches into his upper arm, blood seeping there.

Jumping backward, the man let his single sword flip into the hand of his injured arm, which he caught deftly despite the wound. With his now free hand, he covered the wound, air hissing through his teeth.

"You laced your blade with poison! This is meant to be a spar, not a fight to the death," the man growled as he Fixed his arm. Sweat formed on his forehead as he forced the power through his limb. Prost was unfamiliar with the mechanics of Fixing, but he was sure it normally wouldn't have taken this long for a cut like that to heal.

Before he could think about it, Ugglyn confirmed what they were seeing. The Void substance from his sword pushed its way through the Lightbearer's veins as the Light had done just moments before to Prost. Movement around Prost made him suddenly aware of angry faces and hands readying their weapons. Though he couldn't be surprised at their reactions as they watched, he realized how easily insubordination would come if they observed foul play during a spar. It was considered an honorable form of exercise and practice. If a man cheated by using something like poison, it was in everyone's right to have the cheater's head.

Prost's mind flashed back to his time in the T'Arren Vale military when they'd seen this happen. He recalled viewing a spar alongside Avryn. One of the men clearly outmatched the other, but suddenly, the one with the upper hand fell to the ground, writhing in agony. The poison took him quickly, though not as quickly as the spectators took the life of the one who'd cheated.

Reading the crowd, Prost dropped his sword, the blade dispersing as a thick fog would under the sun's light.

"By Lanser's name, no foul play was employed here," Prost declared loudly.

Ugglyn hissed at Prost swearing on the god's name, but Prost ignored it. He knew an oath like that wouldn't be taken lightly; even a liar wouldn't dare use a vow like that.

Some of the spectators relaxed at his confident declaration, though there were some who still held their hands on weapons, glaring at him. Silence followed for a few moments until Ugglyn began whispering the words in his mind.

"Just as you feel the burning in your veins, so felt I even just now when you cut my arm. Lanser's Light and Ugglyn's Void are, and will forever be, in opposition to each other. By this method will we, with Ugglyn's power, be able to overcome Evenir."

Prost paused, seeing the perplexed faces around him. The man sighed as the cut closed on his upper arm, blood disappearing from the sleeve of his tunic. As expected, the Fixing would repair not only his flesh but also the clothing that was ruined.

Prost realized the words he'd repeated from Ugglyn sounded formal and stiff, something he wouldn't even dream of saying. He thought for a beat to just accept it, to mark it as a change in him since he'd taken control of Watchlight, but he thought better of it. Even Neera, who still stood as close as any might dare to stand by a couple of sparring soldiers, stared at him with slightly narrowed eyes.

"Ugglyn's power courses through me as Lightbearing does you. You've seen the poison the other black-cloaked men used on our fellow Lightbearers as well as the newly Awakened. It was a gift from Ugglyn, a way for us to defeat our enemies," Prost said as confidently as possible.

A few shifted uncomfortably, eyeing the others. There were some who looked at Prost hungrily, as if he'd promised something to them they'd been wishing their whole lives. These likely were men and women who were not blessed with the same power of Light. Prost guessed the angry ones were Lightbearers themselves.

"Our enemies wield the same Light as our own. How can we trust a leader who holds a power that can eat us away from the inside?" Prost's opponent snapped before Conjuring another sword.

Despite Prost's lack of weapon, the man stood there at the ready, as if Prost would do something completely out of bounds of the sparring conditions. Internally, he felt the urge to summon his blade again and kill the man ruthlessly. Opening his hand, the cold formed in his palm, smoke whisking through the air around it as the sword began to form.

Avryn's face flashed in his mind.

He didn't know why the image intruded his thoughts but that it did sucked his anger away. Ever since his youth, Prost had always been hotheaded and easy to provoke. Avryn was the opposite. Not only was the man slow to anger but he could intimidate a man spitting in his face with his mere presence. Prost had known that he would never be a commander so long as he had Avryn by his side, for he was what a true leader could be.

Yet he loved him. Avryn had been the closest thing to a brother he'd had since leaving home. Pain wrenched his gut as he thought of his friend. They'd been separated by time and space, the pact between him and Riln making it easy to fight Avryn over the years. Now that that was gone, the former friendship wreaked havoc inside of him.

Avryn's voice echoed in his mind: *A little humility goes a lot further than pure wrath for a man who leads. What is this? A man of the Light? There's no place for scum like that,* Ugglyn complained at the memory.

Ignoring the voice once more, Prost released the chill in his hand, instead bowing his head and putting his empty hands upward.

"The opposition is two ways. Your Light burned my veins just as the Void did yours. In time you'll see that our goals are the same. I do not intend to use this power to destroy you." Prost paused, considering his next words. He regretted having thought of them, but he knew there might be little else that could fix the current situation. "There's still much I need to learn of Voidweaving. Until now I was unaware of how it would infect a Lightbearer. Neither did I know how Light could infect me. I yield this match to you for peace."

Prost's mouth tasted of dirt. He loathed the things he'd just said, but he could feel the tension in the air melt away as many onlookers took it to heart, relaxing. His opponent watched, eyes still narrow, for a few moments before dismissing his swords. "An honorable defeat," he said, nodding. "It appears we all have something to learn of this Void power you hold. Perhaps we should stick to sparring with steel."

The tension in the air hung ever so slightly in the crowd, but people dispersed as Prost eyed them. There wasn't anger in his eyes—at least, he didn't think there was, for he felt little. He thought it was odd that he didn't feel too angry. Perhaps it was because of the inherent anger that exuded from Ugglyn at all times. It somehow downplayed any anger that Prost could feel himself. That, and ever since Riln had died, the oppressive forces of Watchlight had lessened.

Neera moved silently up to him and placed a hand on his arm. The skin there tingled, but it was a much different feeling than using Voidweaving. This was pleasure.

How long has it been since I've been touched like this? Prost thought. While he was curious, he opted not to think too deeply on this. He feared it would be too dismal.

Forcibly ignoring the growing sense of fondness he felt from the woman's gesture, he focused on her questioningly.

"You yielded," she said frankly. "I've not seen you do something that drastic in my whole time here."

She looked a combination of proud and frustrated at the same time, as if she'd held a high view of him up until this very moment. Yet even now the wrinkles in her forehead relaxed and she looked at him with approval. "You've changed since Stilten. Is this because of Ugglyn's might within you? Or is it—the absence of something else?"

Her voice changed on the last statement, as if she reluctantly shared a secret she'd been holding for years. Her eyes flicked around them to see if others had overheard what she'd said. If she hadn't reacted this way, Prost might not have understood her true intentions, but this lent him the context he needed. Prost assumed others could see the change in him; whether for the positive or negative, they'd seen it. They whispered as he passed in the tunnels, watched him warily as if he might return to his old self and backhand them as he moved closer. He'd not felt any of the normal anger he'd had before leaving for Stilten. Then again, he'd not been called *dud* or confronted by anyone save for the time in the throne room and just now.

Except one person *had* used the derogatory term, and that person —*thing*—lived inside him.

Prost once again resolved to find a way to separate the anti-god from his mind. Though even if he could find a way, he wasn't sure what he truly wanted to do. The moment he had the thought, anger rushed through him and an image of Janis flooded his mind. The passion to kill her returned to his bosom, and though he couldn't tell if it was his own desire or Ugglyn's, the feeling energized him, renewing his sense of purpose. It was a fault of his, something Avryn had urged him to overcome.

Prost didn't lose fights, or if he did, he made sure to take something from the person who bested him in a way that would make them realize they had lost in the end. Janis had beaten him at Arrant Falls, then again in Stilten. No man or woman could be left without his retribution. Prost knew it was shortsighted, but it continued to seethe within. Now that he'd gained the abilities he needed to defeat her, he wouldn't back down. Unfortunately, that meant he'd need an army, for Janis had Evenir to back her every whim.

Yes, kill the girl, that is the only way, Ugglyn whispered.

Prost gritted his teeth. Logically, he knew that by killing Janis, he would release Ugglyn. Was that what he really wanted?

"You have a plan, don't you?" Neera interrupted his thoughts. While it had only been moments in his head, he realized he'd paused and was staring into the stone wall of the cavern. A slight shift in the air cooled his brow, which still flooded with sweat. Prost wiped it away, then nodded at Neera.

"Ugglyn still has confidence that he'll be led to Evenir's base. It's only a matter of time before it shows itself. Until then, we prepare for battle."

"And what of Voidweaving? Can you grant us your same gifts?"

Pleasure filled Prost's very being at the suggestion, but it wasn't of his own accord. Ugglyn was pleased to hear the potential declaration of switched loyalty from a Lighbearer. All at once, Prost's mind ran through things he'd not considered before, things Ugglyn must be pressing into his mind. He saw flashes of Riln, Goralt, Alts, and many other Watchlight

Lightbearers. They'd begun with blue Light but were then influenced and corrupted by ideals and actions driven by Ugglyn through Riln's guidance.

Prost took the feeling inside him as a confirmation that what Neera wished was possible. That terrified Prost more than he wanted to admit. While Voidweaving himself, he couldn't help but feel a surge of adrenaline, an extension of the will and power that he felt he already had. The idea of giving this to others was disturbing. He didn't fear others, but he feared what Ugglyn's power might do to them.

Power doesn't change everyone though, Prost thought, Avryn returning to his mind.

"In time," Prost replied. "I fear we can't access the potential for others without the power I've locked away. Once I get my book, things will be different. The power can be yours, but only then."

Neera narrowed her eyes but nodded resolutely. She looked confused by his words.

With a start, Prost realized he hadn't said them. Panicked, he searched inside his body, only to find that he'd lost control of most of it. Internally roaring, he pressed back the darkened presence of Ugglyn in his mind, his thoughts becoming lucid once more. He felt his limbs again, almost immediately, but the panic remained in his chest.

"Leave me, I've some thinking to do," Prost said roughly.

Neera didn't appear put off by his harsh tone but turned and stalked away, glancing back for a moment before she disappeared down one of the side tunnels.

You dare take advantage of my thoughtful moments? Prost growled in his mind.

Ugglyn didn't respond. This made Prost even more angry. Only when the being was unwanted was he there, pressing his wild emotions and opinions into Prost's thoughts.

Once he was sure he'd achieved the control he needed, Prost slipped through the closest tunnel, aiming for his quarters. While Riln spent an unhealthy amount of time in the throne room, Prost preferred the seclusion of his quarters. Each person he passed averted their eyes, as if they'd heard he was unstable. The few who did look at him bore angry, almost resentful looks. He ignored them. They knew as much as he did that if they dared lift any hand in violence to him, it would not end well.

Opting to ignore the looks after a few dozen passed by, he focused instead on the slapping sounds of his hastening feet on the stone. Despite the smooth surface, his boots had the grooves necessary to avoid slipping. When building the tunnels, the Destroyers had managed to create a delicately rough surface. Such finesse was thought to be impossible when they'd first arrived at the mountain, but after further practice, the Destroyers of old had gained much skill. That skill had been lost, however, and Prost was reminded of this when his toe caught on the uneven transition from one tunnel to the next.

Goralt had emphasized skill with every aspect of Lightbearing, indicating that after they ruled, they'd need to teach the ways of Lightbearing to others, to enhance life as it could be with their abilities. Riln cared only for combat. Thus, the Destroyers didn't care about the details now. Instead power was found in destruction only. The bigger the explosion, the more effective in combat.

Ugglyn stirred inside, telling Prost he aligned with that philosophy himself.

At length, Prost reached his quarters. He flung back the wooden door there, his being one of the few rooms with a hinged door attached to the stone with thick steel hinges and bolts, and swept through, his black cloak billowing behind him. With a grumble, he ripped his cloak free from his neck and tossed it on the bed. Cloaks were impractical inside of the compound, given that they were meant for travel, but it had become somewhat of a habit, a sign of belonging for all the members to wear them. He sat hard on his bed, then glared at the door, expecting an attendant or other person to knock, seeking his attention.

You wish to be alone? Use Voidweaving, then, Ugglyn whispered. The way the anti-god whispered the words made Prost shiver. Having any voices in one's head would get them sent to an insane house, a place where they could be locked up and hardly fed until their untimely death. He'd never imagined he would understand how those people might feel.

Shield us. The whisper came more harshly this time. The rebellious part of Prost wanted to ignore the words, instead focus on something else entirely, but Prost had to admit that he didn't want Seers spying on him.

He held his hand up, trying to imagine what he should do, and the tingling cold spread down his arm and pooled in his palm. Though he couldn't describe the sensation, his brain seemed to click into something familiar and he knew the motions. Putting his hand outward, he imagined the wall forming. A dome of grey smoke, glowing slightly from mercurial veins flowing through it, expanded outward, launching his immediate surroundings into darkness.

Prost sighed. He could deal with darkness.

We are invisible now, even to them, Ugglyn said with too much pleasure.

With the promised solitude, Prost gently but firmly pressed Ugglyn away, hoping the Void Shield would hold. He allowed his mind to clear and focus on what it had moments before he'd retreated here. The power—it tempted, it sucked one into a void of pride, eventually leading to their falling. It happened to Goralt, it happened to Riln; would it happen to him? Ugglyn tried to surface once more, but Prost wouldn't have it, not now. Again, thoughts of Avryn swam in his mind. A man who had gained significant power yet maintained the humble air that made others envy, love, and hate him at the same time.

His eyes suddenly filled with the same tingly coolness of Voidweaving, and images appeared in the gloom. Despite the Shield veiling the surrounding area in darkness, the images he could see were clear and distinguishable, made of the same smokey substance with mercurial veins running through it.

You can't let something like this get the better of you, Avryn's voice echoed in his mind. *The tournament is set to finish in a few days. You give in straight away and you'll have little chance of getting appointed general, now or in the future.*

Hearing his former friend's words filled Prost with regret. The familiarity of the tone threatened to bring back memory upon memory of times when they'd backed each other. Prost remembered this very conversation, and he ground his teeth together.

It was the day after the voice had begun to torment him.

A smokey image of Avryn sat on the edge of a wooden bed frame, and another image, this of himself, sat across from Avryn on another bed.

Though most of the background was indistinguishable, if Prost focused intently, he could see faint outlines of other beds in the barracks. No others stood around to overhear them. It was at this point that both Avryn and Prost had made it to the top four tiers of the tournament. Sword combat was one of the final events.

But the voices had taken that all from him.

What do you propose I do, then? Ignore them? They break my concentration every moment I think of something else! his past self complained.

The face of Avryn's image contorted into something filled with pity and concern all at once.

What does it say? What does this voice want from you? Avryn asked, his voice shaking.

A number of soldiers had complained of hearing voices and those were often sent home, if not for their own safety, then for the safety of their fellow soldiers. At this point, Prost had yet to speak to anyone save Avryn about the voices.

Riln. And something about following the light, Prost said before growling and grabbing his head.

Avryn grimaced. At that moment Prost noticed Avryn's face shift to something he'd missed before, likely because at the moment his head rested in his hands. Now he saw his friend's face betraying knowledge or a familiarity with something he didn't want to tell. Prost's skin chilled. Until he'd come to Watchlight's compound he knew nothing of Lightbearing, but it became apparent, years later, that Avryn's admission that he'd been responsible for the destruction of the armory the day before was his own Awakening. Jealousy sprang up in his chest again, and this time he let it flourish, opting to focus more on what was happening in the scene before him. All at once, he could smell the barracks, the musty dirt that accompanied a few dozen soldiers resting in one stuffy room each night. He felt the occasional breeze that would slip through the crack of the tents.

The light, that—must mean something. Does it not say anything else? Avryn asked.

Prost's past self shook his head in response. He recalled how he was willing to try anything to get the whispers to stop.

You can get through this, friend, Avryn said, putting his hand on Prost's shoulder. It felt as if a phantom version of Avryn reached out and touched the present Prost. It was almost as if he could feel his friend nearby. Prost longed for his comrade, for the companionship they'd had, for the years they'd spent in the militia together in T'Arren Vale. His breathing increased as he fought his emotions. At that moment of vulnerability, Ugglyn reached out to take hold of him once more, to which Prost pressed back firmly.

Why are you showing me this? Prost growled in his mind.

A deep and eerie laugh bubbled within him.

Why, this is the very moment you were chosen. Do you not recall my whispers, then?

Prost realized then that the whispers back then sounded as Ugglyn did now. His skin chilled, far beyond the sensation he felt from using Voidweaving.

How can I expect to fight with this breaking my concentration every waking moment? Prost's past-self said before grunting and pressing his hands to his temples.

You're far more capable than most of these other soldiers, even after drinking far past your body's limit. Why not with a little voice interrupting you? Avryn insisted.

Prost smiled grimly and leaned forward to place his hand on Avryn's shoulder. *I don't know why you care so much about my success in this competition. You know it will result in us fighting each other in the end,* he said, wincing slightly as the voice inside tormented him once more. The current Prost shifted in his seat as he recalled the frustration he felt when fighting against the persistent whispers.

Avryn grinned, the smoke-figure's mouth somewhat vague but detailed enough for Prost to make out that much at least.

I'd rather it be you than someone who was trying to kill me. You know how some of the others are. They'll stop at nothing to get the prize, even if it means completely destroying the other's ability to fight on, Avryn stated before standing up abruptly. *Look, it's about time to get to the arena anyway. You've an hour before the actual fight.*

Nodding, the smoke-figure of Prost followed his friend out of the tent. The beds and figures melted into the air, the smoke dissolving away into nothing for a moment before more figures formed in front of him. One of them, a younger version of himself, stood with his two-handed sword facing another man, smaller than him but still well built. His chest burned as he recalled the last fight he'd had before leaving T'Arren Vale. Growling, his opponent dashed toward him, swinging his sword from the side. Prost's figure easily parried the blow and followed with a quick swipe to the face. The man narrowly dodged it, falling to the ground with a grunt. Taking advantage of this, Prost recalled spinning in time to slap his sword down, the flat of his blade on the helm of his opponent. The force of the blow would have knocked the man out, thus winning him the match. As the sword flew toward the downed man, Prost gasped and put a hand to his head.

Anger flowed in Prost, though this time it was his own. At the moment he would have claimed victory, the whispers pierced his attention so intensely that his head split in pain. He'd inadvertently released one hand from his two-handed sword, which went off course, missing the man's head by a finger's width.

The man on the ground, seeing something was off, scrambled up rapidly and used his own sword to land a hard blow on Prost's helmet. Prost's smoke-figure fell hard with a grunt. A phantom pain rocked through the present Prost's mind as he recalled the pain of the metal on his head. At the same time, dread consumed him as he rewatched his failure, the second to last match before he'd face Avryn for the last battle and he'd failed.

Pain and regret swirled in him as it had as he'd lain on the ground in the arena that day. The smoke figure stirred, though the groaning was the only thing he could remember. He hadn't even realized it was his own groaning. His mind was so foggy from the loss.

Anger returned as Prost recalled the experience. Unable to accept his victory as a good-standing soldier, his opponent had moved toward Prost and spit on him disdainfully.

Yeh deserve the loss, fool. No one would listen t' yeh if they made yeh general, the man mocked as he turned away.

Whether from his intense emotions or because the vision had proven its purpose, the smoke figures melted away. Prost loathed seeing the events of the day before he'd left T'Arren Vale. As much as he could, he'd pushed that memory out of his mind. It had defined him as he was today. Earlier he'd remembered his past self and how he would ruin those who crossed him. His pettiness was something Avryn tried to cure him of, yet this very experience reminded him of the deep satisfaction he would get from giving those who'd bested him what they deserved.

The smoke scene returned to him in the barracks. Prost shoved clothing in a pack with a small assortment of provisions. The smoke figure's face winced again as the whispers relentlessly pressed at his consciousness. A moment later the flap of the barracks tent flung open, another figure moving in.

What have you done? Avryn hissed, his voice frantic. *Rinal's been attacked, he can't even fight in the last match on the morrow. Please do not tell me you had anything to do with it.*

Prost watched, part of him regretting the pain he could see in smoke-Avryn's face, while the other part of him filled with satisfaction from the memory.

The smoke-formed Prost paused and looked up at the wall beside him.

He ridiculed me, ruined my career. Anything that's come to him was deserved, his deep voice declared.

Prost! You cut his hands off, for fog's sake! They'll know it was you. You'll be removed from duty and dishonored because of it, Avryn pressed, stress still lacing his words.

Doesn't matter, I'm leaving. The voices want me to travel north, Prost said.

You're leaving, just like that. What of Illiana? Avryn challenged.

Hearing the woman's name reminded Prost just how much he'd loved her.

She won't want me anymore. I didn't win the competition. My only accomplishment is ensuring that you, my friend, came out on top, Prost declared, putting his hand on Avryn's shoulder.

Avryn's form stepped away from him, his head shaking.

Not like this. This isn't how it's supposed to be, Avryn said, something veiled in his voice.

Prost's form grunted before shouldering his pack. He'd been ambitious to think that he could carry all he'd packed the entire way to Watchlight, but he remembered how soon he'd lost the pack and traveled with only his dagger to accompany him.

Yet it's the way it has to be, Prost said. He moved toward Avryn, who stood his ground, looking angry. Breathing heavily, Prost embraced Avryn, who grunted from the man's colossal form. His friend returned the hug momentarily before Prost pulled away and stalked to the slit in the tent.

You won't find happiness in retribution, Prost. Wherever you go, remember that, Avryn shouted from behind.

Live well, friend, Prost said without turning.

If you return, you won't find me, Avryn had said.

Prost paused, his breath hitching. A burning sensation wormed its way into present Prost's chest. At the time he didn't realize it, but Avryn would leave for Evenir that same night.

You can't leave, not after what you've accomplished, Prost insisted, turning back to his friend.

Avryn looked pained.

I—must. Circumstances have changed for me, smoke-Avryn said.

The burning in his chest changed to an uncomfortable twinge of pain. He'd forgotten about this moment. The anger he'd felt that Avryn was throwing it away, giving up his claim on victory, showed on his past self. Shoulders tense, he remembered wanting to shout at his friend, to tell him he was being a fogging fool.

But Avryn had Awakened. That was why he left that day.

Past Prost breathed heavily, holding back his shouts. He had been at a loss for words.

If that's what you want, then give up. I hope this isn't the end of our brotherhood, Prost said. His past self turned sharply and exited the barracks then.

The scene disappeared as quickly as the others had, leaving Prost reeling. Whatever ability this was, to be able to See things away from himself, was disorienting. Dimness still surrounded him as the Void shield held firm above and around him, but Prost accepted this. Despite the oddity of the powers, it was good to know that no Seer could spy on him. When he'd left T'Arren Vale, he did not know what life would bring. He could not have guessed what would happen to him. Emotions warred with each other inside. He was filled with regret, pain, and strange satisfaction at the situation he'd just witnessed once again.

An image of Janis swam into his mind, though no smoke figures appeared. For a moment he thought to try Seeing something but then recalled that just as his own lair was, Evenir's base was Shielded by many Lightbearers. Avryn's words echoed in his mind, the last warning before they'd become natural enemies. Despite those words, Prost seethed at the knowledge that Janis had bested him and still lived without his retribution. His hands shook from the frustration. The surrounding darkness appeared to deepen from his anger.

Prost would have his retribution.

16

Marric cried for only a moment before he gained his composure. The sensation was odd, as if he had a distant memory of feeling the tears on his face but couldn't quite feel them himself. He suspected that his body back in Terris Green, the *present* Terris Green, was experiencing the feeling. Talatha, the woman he'd heard so little about his whole life save for the past few months, stood right in front of him, and in two places, no less.

He glanced behind the woman standing before him, seeing her duplicate by the table, standing upright, a surprised look on her face while her eyes glowed bright blue. He'd heard that Talatha was a Shielder, but no one had mentioned her being a Seer as well. Marric thought the knowledge would bring him closer to her somehow, connect them on a deeper level because of their shared power, but he just felt awkward. Looking at her directly, he noticed just how deep blue her eyes were, something that was rare in Wurren. Narim had told Marric he'd gotten the eye color from his mother, stating that she'd come from somewhere outside of their little town, but only now did the knowledge seem more potent to him.

"How you've grown," Talatha said, her eyes squinting as she smiled at him. He could see the deepened wrinkles extending from the edges of her eyes, showing her aging state. Still, she looked like an exact replica of the woman in the wood grain of the door to the war room. He couldn't help but look over at the portal now, but the carving wasn't there. She'd yet to become part of the artwork. Talatha's hair was long, wavy, and blonde. She was tall and strong. From here, Marric could see that he stood at about the same height as her.

She watched his motion, furrowing her brow with curiosity.

"Are you looking for something?" Talatha asked, though she did so with a slight smile as if she thought Marric's actions were funny.

Marric shifted on his incorporeal feet. He'd never thought about what his reaction would have been if he'd met his mother in real life. For some reason he was disappointed in himself. Still, he couldn't bring himself to feel anything other than nervousness. Though his chest burned with excitement, a long since unknown scratch that needed to be itched, here stood a woman who shared blood with him yet had left him when he was merely a babe. He could see how Magness could be her sister, for they had the same eyes and cheekbones. This thought caused a stabbing sadness to return to his gut, which somehow made him feel more guilty. Should he have a better relationship with his aunt than with his mother?

"I've watched you all these years, Seen you from a distance without you even realizing who I am, yet here you stand before me. I had no idea you'd be a Seer yourself," she said, putting her hands on her cheeks and watching him longingly.

His emotions continued to roil inside of him, confusing and overwhelming him. Part of him couldn't believe he was meeting his mother, a person he'd never known, mainly from lack of information. The other part was confused and angry at why she would leave them the way she had.

The former part of him overwhelmed the other, even if for a brief moment, and he rushed to her, wrapping his arms around her. As usual, his vision-form felt nothing, save for a slight tingling where his arms and chest met her own form. Marric had been sure that his form wasn't physical, but the force of his body hitting Talatha's didn't bring him through her like he might have guessed. Normally, in visions such as these he could walk through walls and objects as if they didn't exist or perhaps existed somewhere else, but in this case, his body met something, though it didn't feel quite physical.

He focused on the sensation, accepting it as best as he could for what it was. Though it felt nothing like embracing a person, he reveled in the feeling.

"Oh, Marric, I'm so sorry I left you," Talatha said, regret obvious in her voice.

Hearing her say this made him sob again. He felt so angry at her for leaving, something he'd not thought about in all these years. He'd not realized how angry he was. It might have been easier if his father had just told him she'd died, but he'd known the truth, at least part of it. Yet feeling the "closeness" of their vision-forms distracted him enough from the anger for the moment.

"You—you're here—and alive," Marric sputtered before sniffing and shaking his head.

He felt a tingling closeness on his head momentarily and glanced upward to see that she'd moved her hand over his hair.

"This is not how I imagined seeing you again, but I'll take what I can for the moment. Until we meet again in person, I think," she replied, pushing him back.

Marric pulled back from her, confused.

"Talatha—um, Mother, I guess," Marric said awkwardly before resolving to just move forward. "We'll never meet. You died six months ago."

Talatha's eyebrows shot up in surprise before her face changed to something more sad.

"By Lanser's throne, that explains it," she replied. "I can't See into my future as far as I hoped. Seeing you was difficult enough since I knew not your grown face, but I could accomplish it by Seeing your father."

At that, she started and stood up straight again. "Narim? Is he all right? Does he live?"

Marric nodded."He's alive, but he was in rough shape a few weeks ago. Our house was burned by men searching for me. I thought it was Watchlight, but it turned out to be someone else, some other men looking for me to kill me with poison made from Ugglyn and—"

He paused, realizing he was dumping so much information that it wouldn't make much sense. Still, Talatha watched him, fondness still in her eyes.

"It's clear a lot has happened," Talatha said before sighing and gesturing to the ground. "Perhaps it's best to sit. Our projected forms shouldn't tire, but it seems proper for the setting."

Nodding, Marric sank to the ground, linking his legs together in a way a child might sit. Talatha sat down on the floor gracefully, her dress sinking through the ground as if it hung over the edge of a cliff. Seeing her clothing react that way was distracting, but he focused back on her. He knew they could sink through the floor at any moment, but for now the stone held them as if they had physical forms themselves. He made a mental note to ask Rivelen how their vision-forms did such things.

"So much has happened that I don't know where to begin," Marric said, inspecting the ground beneath him to distract him from looking at his mother's face.

"Start from the beginning, then. Well, the beginning of how you came to be a Lightbearer, I suppose. I fear that, even though time is different here, we won't have enough for you to recount your whole life."

Marric hadn't considered the time they'd have here. Each vision he'd had in the past was merely moments long, but those were often forced upon him, and he had little control over what he saw or where he went. In this case, he'd pulled himself here. He hoped that when it was time to return, his mind would give some warning that it was about to end.

"Just months ago, things were—normal. It was just Pa, me, and—well, Tins," Marric said awkwardly, looking up at his mother to see her reaction. She didn't react as sharply as Marric would have guessed.

"The woman your father married in my absence. I've Seen her," Talatha said calmly, though her eyes hardened as if she knew all that the woman had done in the past. Marric guessed she could have watched how Tins treated Marric, but he opted not to go into too many details, focusing on the more important parts of the story.

"Well, Avryn and the others came to get me from Wurren, and we had to leave Pa behind, but not before—" Marric paused, trying to determine the best way to say the next part. "Um, before Janis killed Tins."

Surprisingly, Talatha wasn't taken aback by that news. Marric wondered what might have caused such a woman to be unaffected by death, but he pushed the thought aside. His mother's eyes wandered off to some place behind him momentarily before they snapped back to him.

"Who is Janis? Did she mean you harm?" Talatha asked, still glazing over Tins's death.

"Uh, no, not at all. She's an assassin—"

This word incited more of a reaction in his mother than Tins dying. Eyes widening, she shook her head as her face shifted into something angry, almost feral.

"Watchlight sent an assassin for you?! Are you safe from them now?" Talatha questioned.

"No, she doesn't mean any harm! Tins was the actual one working for Watchlight, or so we discovered. Janis saved my life so many times. She even became some special Lightbearer or something, though I'm not sure I get what that means," Marric paused, seeing something change in Talatha.

"Special Lightbearer? What do you mean?" she asked, changing subjects again rapidly. Marric's mind buzzed with the constant shift of the conversation and his mother's intensity. He knew little of the woman, but for some reason he didn't expect her to be so intense. Her eyes bored into him, urging him to give her an answer to her question.

"The Prime or something. I don't remember how she put it. Lanser chose her for something, I guess," Marric said.

Talatha's mouth twitched upward at his words. She looked pleased, as if he'd said something she'd been waiting for her whole life. Casually she turned and inspected her body, frozen in time.

"*Yrillnan*," Talatha whispered. "What of Riln? Based on what I've learned of *Yrillnan*, I assumed it was he that held the Prime powers of Lightbearing."

Marric deflated. He'd never imagined when he'd meet his mother, but he didn't expect that if he had, the whole of their conversation would be focused on something besides him and his father. Despite his best efforts not to let her apparent obsession with whatever Janis was bother him, it got the better of him.

"Janis killed him, or I think she did at least. All I know is that he's dead, and something's going on with Ugglyn—but we aren't sure what."

Talatha paled. "But *Yrillnan* still holds. It should if this assassin you speak of is the Prime."

Marric shrugged, "I guess so, yeah."

A piercing silence followed as Talatha fell into deep thought about what he'd just shared. Marric shifted uncomfortably on the ground, though he couldn't truly feel anything, save for what his muffled senses were feeling back in his physical body. His gut wrenched at the awkwardness of the situation, and he almost sated his thirst to return to his body, leaving his mother in this state, before she sighed and turned to Marric.

"I'm sorry, Marric. This topic has consumed my mind for too long, and to have you appear in the war room only days after I've found more information about this seems more than fortuitous." Talatha grimaced before smiling again and turning to Marric. "Let's put that aside for a minute. Tell me of your Lightbearing. You're a Seer, I can see, but what of your second-born power?"

Once again, the shifts in the conversation left Marric reeling before he could compose himself. Fortunately, Talatha didn't seem bothered by his hesitation. Instead she watched him steadily, her hands folded in her lap as she sat atop the war room table.

"Actually, it's more complicated than that," Marric said, shifting again. He cursed himself internally for displaying such habits even without being inside his physical body. "I actually have three abilities—well, four, now that I came into another."

Talatha's face shifted to wonder, flashed through something that looked like jealousy, then beamed with pride.

"That is incredible! I've only heard of that once before in all my years, and I'm sure you know Avryn as well," she said.

"Yes, he's been able to help me a bit with them, since we both are Conjurers and Movers, and—Destroyers," he admitted. He suspected that if he'd been in his body again he'd be blushing, though he didn't know why.

Smiling, Talatha slid from the table and moved to him once more. He stood, not wanting to be sitting alone. She quickly put her hands on his shoulders, the tingling sensation of their closeness running through them and into his upper arms.

"That, my son, is incredible," she said, before frowning. "Though I do wish one of them had been Shielding. It would be nice for you to uphold my legacy since I no longer live."

"Oh—I'm sorry—I didn't mean—"

Talatha began laughing. She pulled away from Marric and stared him right in the eyes.

"Son, I'm just joking. How can I be disappointed? I am thrilled to hear of Lanser's blessing for you. Have you been able to train, then? Did you make it here?"

The oddity of the question struck Marric. He knew what she meant by it, for they stood in the war room within Terris Green, but he didn't have any idea how far in the past they were. Her asking if he'd made it to Terris Green reminded him of the strangeness of Seeing into the past. He felt a distant sensation of nausea as his mind considered the inquiry. Rather than take too much longer to dwell on it, he answered abruptly, his voice coming out forcefully.

"Yes, we made it," he gasped.

Talatha paused, noticing his reaction to her question, before she shook her head and continued. "Then they're seeing to your training? You have a lot of potential for greatness."

Marric's stomach twisted. Some deep part of him was irked by her comment, as if he'd been longing for her approval and pride his whole life. The emptiness of her absence suddenly felt so real, it pained him. He'd not considered how affected he might be by his mother's absence, but now it was coming back. The anger returned, and this time he couldn't help but ask.

"Why did you leave? How could you leave Pa and me like that?"

His voice was hard but he didn't feel guilty. Tears formed distantly in the eyes of his physical body. The tears must have appeared in his projected form, for his mother's expression changed to something like pity.

"Marric," Talatha said, before sighing and standing up straighter. "I had no plans to leave you. My Awakening happened years before. Evenir found me and invited me to join them, but I declined. I was only a young girl at the time. I escaped the life I'd lived near the sea and moved to Wurren, where I met your father. Not using my abilities was difficult at first, but I didn't understand them as I should have. When I married Narim, I cared more for him than some secret magic that made little sense."

Marric listened but he bristled inside. He wasn't sure what he'd expected her answer to be, but she continued to stand straight and confident. A pang of jealousy ran through him at her charisma. Turrin, Varith, and the others had described her as a powerful leader, and this only validated their claims. She stared at him, her face betraying sadness, but she appeared strong.

"Evenir came to me when I Awakened. I shunned them, told them to leave me be. I wanted nothing other than living away from the power. Lightbearing wasn't something I wanted in my life. But I was forced to use my Shield to keep me from their prying eyes. In the end, they found me. When you were but a year old, Watchlight attacked me in Wurren. I was saved by a man from Evenir—"

Her eyes became wistful at the mention of the man. There was something there, a deep-set sadness. Talatha reached down and grabbed the hilt of a sword belted at her waist. Until then, Marric hadn't noticed it. He'd been told she was a fierce warrior. Jealousy wormed its way inside him before he focused on her words, refusing to appear anything other than confident himself. Checking his posture, he mirrored his mother's stance. She didn't appear to notice.

"They would have killed you, Marric—and Narim. Watchlight gave nothing but ultimatums to other Lightbearers. If only I'd known more about Shielding, I'd have stolen away into a different town with the two of you, Shielded us from the eyes of Watchlight for as long as I could. But the damage was done. They knew my location and my face. But they didn't know about you," she explained. "I left for your safety. I didn't want you wrapped up in the nonsense of this pride war between Lightbearers."

His tears had stopped as his mind locked on to the things she said. Though he hadn't thought about the exact reason his mother had abandoned them, he'd always assumed it had something to do with protecting them.

"Why didn't you bring us with you? I still don't understand."

Talatha's hand tightened on the hilt of her sword, but her face remained stoic. The knuckles of her hands protruded from her skin at the firmness of her grip, and veins corded up her bare hand and forearm.

"That was a mistake on my part. I knew not what I was getting myself into. If Watchlight was as dangerous as Evenir showed to me, I couldn't risk dragging you into the war. Had I known you'd Awaken someday yourself, I may have reconsidered. There wasn't a day that I didn't question my decision after I left. Once I'd learned my second ability, I watched you every day, sending Lanser's blessing your way. I am grateful Lanser kept you from Watchlight's hands."

Marric shifted on his unfeeling feet once more.

"Um, they got me, at one point," Marric admitted.

Talatha's brows shot upward in shock. For a moment her confidence broke, even if just briefly. It returned as quickly as it had gone.

"Yet you live? How did you escape?" she asked. "Not once have we been able to recover a Lightbearer after they've fallen into Watchlight's hands."

Thoughts of Janis flooded Marric's mind. Until now, he hadn't considered how incredible it was that Janis had followed Prost as he carried Marric to their lair. Not only was she able to track them but she'd entered the lair without being noticed. Marric's Seeing was the ultimate savior in the end, but Janis had gotten him to where he needed to be so they could escape.

"Janis, the one I spoke of before, she found me and helped me escape. Riln tried to force me to join them or die, just as you said," Marric said.

Talatha breathed out in relief.

"This woman, Janis, does she truly bear all the gifts of Lanser?" his mother asked.

The fact that the conversation had returned to Janis was not lost on Marric, but he obliged. His anger had diffused somehow, as if hearing the genuine reasons from his mother was what he'd needed all his life. Though he hadn't forgiven her, the things she'd said made sense. Her humble admittance of error was both unexpected and appreciated.

"I don't know what you mean, but she knows she is the Prime. Now that Riln's dead, she thinks it means something more important, something about Ugglyn being free."

Talatha grunted, then turned to the table behind her. A book sat there, open to a page in the middle. When Marric had first come to his mother, she'd been reading the volume. She reached out and tried to turn the page before cursing. Though it was difficult to tell in the dim blue light of the stone room, Marric thought he saw her flushing at her mistake.

"Blasted Seer forms, we can't do anything in them, can we?" she said, mostly to herself, but at the same time the comment seemed directed at him as some type of solidarity statement. Though his emotions were shifting, he couldn't help but smile.

"It was a few pages before this, but I don't recall the exact writings. I found this book in the archives of T'Arren Vale. I'm unsure of its origin, but it is filled with religious theories and stories of the Lanserian sect. Just before it speaks of something, a pact of sorts, called *Yrillnan.*"

This time when she spoke the word, the air buzzed around them, as if a swarm of bees entered the room. Though it was quiet, he could feel the energy. Talatha tensed as if she'd noticed the same change in the air.

"The word has power, that much I know, but I don't know what it means. The ancient priests of Lanser spoke of Ugglyn's temptation and how he sought freedom by breaking the *Yrillnan,* but they are all just theories, stories passed down for years and years. If what you have said about this woman is true, then it must be correct. I'd always assumed it was Riln who bore the pact, but I must be wrong."

Talatha's eyes darted around them as if she was reading something from the air, something unseen to Marric. He didn't want to interrupt her, but the odd feeling in the room hadn't changed.

"Then I found another text, which spoke of something called *H'ilvina't.* Hildengaard, one of the priests who lived over a hundred years ago, spoke of that word as if it was some key, a catalyst to combat the forces of Ugglyn. I didn't think much of it until now. Something is happening. I've sensed it for the past year. Watchlight is getting more powerful, their Light a deeper red, but I don't know why."

His mother was speaking fast now, as if she needed to get the words out before the vision ended. Marric reached inside, feeling the power of his Light and the vision they shared. Somehow he knew that their time together was growing short. He cursed internally and faced his mother. No sooner had he locked eyes on her than a flash of red Light caught his attention to the side of the room. Looking that direction, his breath caught, his mind going numb with fear.

Standing near the wall to his right was a green-robed man, hair whiter than seemed possible, face a similar hue, eyes piercingly blue.

Riln. Panic rocked Marric.

He's dead! Janis said she'd killed him in Stilten. How is he here?! Marric thought.

"Ah, Talatha, it seems you have a guest in your visions today." His serene gaze drifted to Marric and he observed the boy up and down before making a clicking sound with his tongue. "One might think I should apologize for the intrusion, but I don't care."

Marric crouched down, his hand opening to Conjure the first thing that came to mind. His bow flashed into existence, the blue Light intense but somehow faded. Without hesitation, he nocked an arrow and launched it at the man. The Light arrow passed through with no effect. Riln stood there as if nothing had happened. He eyed Marric critically before turning back to Talatha.

"This one's got spirit, I'll give him that much. Must be a new Seer, no?" Riln said.

Talatha faced the robed man, but she didn't appear concerned, though she stood tense. Marric flushed at the comment. Until now, he'd not tried to attack someone within a vision, but he knew he couldn't touch anything. His emotions had gotten the better of him and he'd just acted. Hearing Riln's voice made his skin crawl and he wanted to cover his ears to block out the noise. Something within him warned of showing vulnerability like that. It finally dawned on Marric that he was in the past, though how far past he didn't know.

"He's not one of ours, I'm not sure why he's even here right now," Talatha replied. As if taking a cue from her own words, she turned to her frozen body, eyes still glowing a steady blue.

Riln raised an eyebrow. Marric's stomach twisted and he glanced toward Talatha, noticing that she pointedly ignored him despite their recent conversation.

"I doubt that. The boy's Light still glows blue," Riln said, looking back and forth between the two of them, "and he's here, which means he knows you."

It took Marric a moment to realize she feigned disinterest in him.

She doesn't want him to know who I am.

"Why are you here, Riln? You know you aren't welcome. Even if you continue to interrupt my visions, you'll never locate us. I've overseen the training of our base Shielders and they're far more powerful than even your prying eyes."

Sneering, Riln pointed a bony finger at her.

"Yet you've gained no ground on us, wench. You act so confident when we are tucked away somewhere your impudent Seers can't find us," Riln spat. "One of these days I'll find a way through your Shields. I find it fortunate each time I catch you in this realm, separated from your body. It gives me access to your form and immediate surroundings. Each time I find you in a vision, you reveal just a bit more."

Talatha shook her head, acting nonchalant about his claims. "I tire of this vision. I suggest you leave before you get caught up in something you don't want, boy," Talatha said, nodding toward Marric. "Know this: Watchlight has nothing to offer, if you choose not to join Evenir. This man makes false promises of grandeur."

Riln laughed. Marric's mind buzzed with nerves. He'd only met Riln once, but the eerie man's false joy meant something far darker based on his singular experience.

"I care not for this Seer boy. If he's not with you, we'll find him eventually. He'll have no choice, just like the others," Riln said, waving his hand to the side. "Submit to us, *Talatha*, or we will come for you."

Riln spoke her name with such contempt that Marric felt the urge to attack the man. He couldn't say why he felt the need to defend his mother from Riln, but the urge pressed on him. Without thinking, he Conjured a sword this time, narrowing his eyes at the pale man. Riln noticed Marric's movements, looking curious.

"He's very keen on protecting you. Are you sure you don't know each other?" Riln asked, inspecting Marric once more.

Before Talatha could say anything, the air rushed around them as if a storm had blown down the walls of the cavern. Marric's logical mind warred with his muted senses. He felt nothing but his ears and eyes picked up the sound of the rushing wind. Talatha's body, still standing stiffly at the table next to her vision-form, stirred from the strong wind, her hair whipping around her head. The paradox of seeing the room's contents fly around in the air but the three figures remaining untouched discomforted Marric.

Just next to Riln, a pool of grey substance grew rapidly until it expanded upward, forming into a shape. Marric gripped his Conjured sword, the tingling sensation his only evidence that he touched anything, and faced the pool. Talatha reached down, pulling free the sword she held in her scabbard. Marric figured she probably knew the weapon would do nothing, but it felt good to have someone else by his side.

The smokey substance coalesced into the shape of a man, tall and fit, standing within arm's reach of Riln. Marric noted how Riln stood casually, watching the forming figure with no concern. Within moments, the smoke formed into features, an older man, grey hair and a trimmed and well-kept beard. His eyes, rather than showing the normal whites, pupil, and irises, instead were filled with the same soot-colored smoke, cracks of mercurial substance writhing within.

"Ah, now this is a gathering, isn't it," the man said. His voice was sharp. Peering at Marric, the man tilted his head, "Now there's a face I don't recognize. Talatha, did you bring a new Seer into your fold without telling me?"

Talatha glared at the man, then shook her head.

"He's not one of ours," she said stiffly. "What is it you want?"

The man tsked quietly, then moved to the table. His feet seemed to glide on the stone, as if along a slippery surface. He inspected the table and the contents there.

"Still trying to find a way to lock me away, are we?" the man said casually. "Dear woman, by now you must have realized you will fail. As Riln builds my army, you'll find my power grows. Even now, I had the energy to visit you."

Talatha turned her sword point on the man. "Warble all you'd like. I'll find a way."

"Now, now, we don't need to be like that. Put your sword away. It will do nothing here. Surely a seasoned Seer such as yourself can remember that detail," he said.

Marric's stomach twisted. He didn't know the man, but hearing their conversation and seeing the way he'd come clued him in on the situation.

He gasped unintentionally, drawing the attention of the anti-god.

"Well, well, clever one, this is. I didn't even need to introduce myself for him to discover who I am," Ugglyn said. "How'd you put that together?"

Marric wanted to ask how Ugglyn was there, but he refrained, hardening his face to hide his surprise, though he felt unsuccessful. He locked his mouth shut, refusing to respond. Ugglyn raised a brow again but didn't question further.

"Knows when to stay quiet, it seems," Ugglyn mused. "Have you considered my proposal?"

He directed these words at Talatha, who chuckled. She suddenly dashed forward and slammed the tip of her sword into Ugglyn's chest. The sword traveled through him, leaving him untouched, but Talatha must have expected it, for she used the momentum to spin and kick the image of Ugglyn in the face. She jumped back, looking satisfied.

"How's that for an answer?" she replied.

Pursing his lips, Ugglyn shook his head.

"You can delay all you'd like, but I'll eventually find my way in. Just like you, I can speak to anyone with access to this place. The middle plane is an excellent medium for communication, wouldn't you say?"

This time he turned to Marric, looking at him pointedly. He insinuated that he knew Marric was there for a conversation with Talatha. Marric's mind buzzed with nervousness again.

"You can try. I doubt any of them care about your false claims," Talatha replied, sheathing her sword. "Meanwhile, I'm one step closer to locking you away."

Ugglyn sneered, and Marric took a step back instinctively.

"The bonds are already breaking!" Ugglyn spat. "You think you can lock me away? Nothing has the power to do that. Even Lanser himself has failed. He shouldn't have trusted mere humans to be the seal. You are far too easy to tempt with power and money."

Marric glanced at Riln, expecting an adverse reaction from the man, but his face betrayed no such feelings. He marveled again at seeing the man who, only months before, had threatened to kill him if he didn't join their cause. Riln must have felt Marric's eyes on him, for he looked in his direction. For a moment the two locked eyes.

Once again, no sign of recognition. Marric's head began aching somewhere distant and he gritted his teeth. He recalled Rivelen telling him how disorienting going into the past could be, but he hadn't expected to feel this way. Nausea was beginning to set in, and the feeling returned that only moments remained before the vision would drop. Panicked, he looked at his mother, longing to talk to her more, to spend time with her before the moment ended.

Talatha's mouth turned up in a knowing smile before she spoke again.

"*H'ilvina't*," she said.

Ugglyn's eyes widened in horror, his bravado dissipating momentarily before he composed himself once more.

"You meddle in magics you know nothing about, wench." His eyes flashed to the book on the table before he growled and ran at her. Talatha flipped her sword upward and slashed Ugglyn right through the chest. Of course, her attack had no effect on the intangible being, but he shouted nonetheless. Marric, seeing the exchange, Conjured arrow after arrow and launched them at Ugglyn, hoping that his Light-formed arrows would do something.

They had no effect either, though they appeared to anger Ugglyn more.

"You dare use the power of that cursed beast Lanser on me?!" he roared, turning his attention on Marric.

Marric gasped as the anti-god bore down on him, his body growing to double its height and size, the man suddenly towering over him. Over and over, he launched arrows through the hulking form, each doing nothing. His mind screamed at him to get away, yet it also advised him to stand his ground. He couldn't be hurt here.

Suddenly, a bright flash of orange light blinded Marric. It came from somewhere off to the side of his vision, and he yelled in surprise.

"Marric! GO!" Talatha's voice shouted from somewhere behind the orange hue. Her vision-form merged rapidly with her own body and she gasped from the reconnection. Then without hesitation, she formed a small Shield and pushed her hands outward, expanding it to fill the room.

Ugglyn screamed in rage, fury in his eyes as the orange Light filled Marric's vision completely. Just before the vision dropped, he saw Riln's face through the brightness, eyes filled with glee. He grinned directly at Marric, having just heard his name.

Marric's head fogged as the world spun in brilliant orange Light, every color from the vision mixing with it to become a muddy brown. Then he gasped as he returned to his body. The hard frame of his bed pressed sharply into his legs and he realized they felt sore. He had no way of knowing how long he'd been in the vision, but based on the soreness of his rump and legs, he guessed it was longer than visions normally lasted. Movement to his right caught his attention, and he jumped as an orange light receded through the wall next to him, disappearing. He furrowed his brow, recognizing the orange Light he'd just seen in the vision. Once it was completely gone, he was surprised to make out details of his room, the rough stone walls still visible despite the orange Light's disappearance.

Looking upward, he noted that his minuscule orb of Light still held its form a few handspans from his head. He marveled that he could maintain that power without being conscious. He was no Lighter, but still he'd kept it there with no practice.

All at once, the happenings in his vision came back to him, his mind whirling. He'd met his mother, something he never thought would be possible. She'd been strong, beautiful, and she had cared for him. Her death panged in his chest briefly until the image of Ugglyn rushing him pushed that away, fear replacing it.

Then the image of Riln glaring at him, a wicked grin on his face, overcame all. Something inside him warned of danger, yet Marric couldn't understand how. Riln was dead, Janis had said so.

Yet Marric couldn't help but wonder what he'd just done. Something told him that it was his fault Watchlight had found him first in Wurren. He shuddered, the complexity of time mixing in the vision making him nauseous once more. His head pounded, but he had to tell Janis what he'd learned.

Shaking his head, he pressed his hands into his legs and stood, wobbling slightly from the pain in his skull.

With a pit still formed in his stomach, he hurried through the door to find the others.

He rushed out into the hallway, only to find that they were all empty, save for the few guards roaming the hallways. They looked at him as if he was the strangest person alive. It was then that he discovered how late it was. Somehow, despite the short length of his conversation with his mother, the time had sped up back with his physical form. Marric didn't expect being sequestered in his room for so long. He was forced to retire and get sleep before talking to anyone.

17

The stone felt cold through her thin shirt as Janis leaned against the wall with her arms folded. She watched a few girls pass by, whispering to each other about the attractive boys they'd just been accompanying. Janis watched them go, resisting the urge to roll her eyes. Her teen years had not been the usual kind often experienced by women. While girls spent time twittering to each other about the best and fastest way to get married, Janis was learning how to kill or be killed by the hardened assassin Macks.

Thoughts of Macks and his tousled black hair invaded her mind for a few moments before she shrugged them off, leaving her vantage point in the cavern to find Livella. After exiting the war room, Janis had been unable to find where the orange light went. She tracked it as far as a tunnel just off the cavern she currently walked through, but no passersby had seen it once it retreated that way. As far as she could tell, the odd Light left no evidence where it touched. That wasn't altogether surprising, given that it had moved directly through her, leaving nothing behind.

She'd retired to her quarters for the night after her failed attempts to find the Light's path the day before. Now that a new day had come, she'd been using most of her waking moments retracing the Light and trying to find any other information she could.

As she moved, she resisted the instinct to slink along the sides of the room, hiding from view. Her trained senses picked up the commotion of the market within the cavern, warning her that an ambush could come from any side, but she pushed that away, part of her regretting it. She stood out among the women, being one of the few, save for the soldier women, who didn't wear a skirt or dress. Lanserian ideals, which Janis assumed was the dominant religion among the people here, suggested women be proper by wearing such clothing. Fortunately, the fighters among the women didn't follow the practice. Janis marveled that Magness could have functioned in what she wore most of the time. Then again, the woman *had* changed her apparel when they'd left for Stilten.

The memory of Magness resulted in thoughts of the upcoming vote for leader. Janis loathed the idea of being the leader of this place, yet something inside her told her that it was inevitable in some way. Even if she didn't get voted in, they'd still look up to her because of her role within the Lightbearing world. After Avryn's speech the day before, news appeared to have spread about what had happened to her and what she'd done. They'd not meant to keep it a secret, but when they'd first arrived, people only cared about their return and that Magness had been killed.

And now I've got the enigma of the orange Light to deal with, Janis grumbled internally.

Just then, a small child ran up to her, looking embarrassed. Janis stopped short of her, looking down at the small form. This caused the little girl to tremble, stepping back before she took a deep breath and stood up straight. Janis looked past her to see a woman who must have been the girl's mother standing there, hands holding a big basket of flowers. Before Janis could even wonder where the specimens in the basket originated, the girl before her thrust her hands out, holding one of the flowers.

Janis stared at it for a moment before realizing the girl meant for her to take it. Feeling somewhat awkward at the attention, Janis reached out and took it gingerly. Though she felt ridiculous doing so, she smelled the bright petals, a sweet aroma filling her nostrils. She forced a smile and nodded down at the girl.

"Thank you, that's beautiful," Janis said.

The two stood there silently for a moment, each staring as if they didn't know what to do next. Soon a few others around them noticed the interaction and paused to watch. Janis cursed softly at the attention but kept the smile plastered on. The looks on the faces around her, including the girl's mother, told her they expected something more from her. Janis knelt down before the girl and looked her in the eye.

"Did you harvest this flower yourself?" she asked.

The girl nodded, still looking terrified.

"Well, it's beautiful. Your family's contribution to Evenir is amazing. Never forget it."

The words felt awkward and almost cheesy, but they made the girl grin. She giggled and ran to her mother, turning back to wave at Janis. Murmurs came from the few who watched, some whispering and pointing, then they resumed their activities. Though Janis felt uneasy about the interaction, she gave herself credit for not being irritated with the child. She'd worked alone for all these years, but still she'd seen how leaders were expected to act. She felt like what had just happened was a win in the long run.

Feeling the urge to get out of the crowd, Janis walked swiftly to the other side of the cavern and entered one of the smaller tunnels. Traffic was heavy, given that it was the primary way to other points of interest such as the mess hall and the sparring cavern. It was there that she wanted to visit next. Most people she passed continued to ignore her, but an increasing number looked at her directly, offering greetings or nods as they walked by.

Whether the interactions were due to the previous day's events or the knowledge that she could be elected the leader of Evenir, Janis was irked by the increasing attention. Though she knew it looked bad, she began walking more swiftly, focusing on the orbs of Light hovering above them rather than at the faces passing her. At length, she arrived at the single wooden door to the sparring chamber. Even now she could hear the clangs and clatter of people training. This door hung on iron hinges like many of the main rooms and chambers. She pressed the dark wood firmly, hinges creaking loudly from wear.

The room wasn't as crowded as she'd seen it in the past, but there were a few pairs of warriors practicing. Her eyes found her intended quarry almost immediately, for the woman looked a bit awkward still with her weapon. Livella, mousy hair disheveled and dirtied from her exchanges, shouted and dashed at a man before her with a wooden practice sword. The swing was too wide and slow, her opponent blocking it easily. Janis pressed her lips together, moving to the wall opposite the two to watch. It was obvious the man with her had the upper hand, for he moved smoothly, blocking and parrying Livella's blows with ease. Livella grimaced and tried once more, this one a bit faster, but still too slow.

"Yeh need to use yer momentum t' git where yeh need to," the man said, holding his hand up for her to stop.

He moved over to her and began showing her the proper stance for battle and how to move her weapon. Janis could see that her sword had weights tied to it, simulating what a proper steel sword might feel like in her grip.

Livella looked exhausted, but she appeared determined. The man moved away again, counting to three before they started once more.

For the past couple of weeks Livella had been training within the sparring cavern every day. Though she still looked awkward with the sword, Janis could tell her reflexes were improving and that she was getting stronger. The skirt she wore, which she insisted on keeping despite its unwieldy nature during sparring, spun around her as she danced forward and backward. She hadn't noticed Janis enter the room, which Janis preferred. She suspected her presence would throw Livella's concentration.

Livella's dodging skills were on point as she slipped out of range from the man's thrust and smacked his sword away, but her attacks were slow and clunky.

She needs a different weapon, Janis thought, watching Livella stumble off balance. The man before her took the opportunity and smacked her leg. Livella cried out in pain but surprisingly didn't submit. Instead she feigned reaching down to her leg with her free hand. The moment she did, the man jumped forward. Livella crouched down quickly and swiped her sword, the movement still wide, but it caught his feet and he fell to the ground with a curse. The man had been too busy focusing on her supposed weakness to notice her attack.

Janis clapped a few times, drawing their attention.

Livella's head whipped in her direction, a blush forming as she saw who it was.

"You've improved," Janis said, moving over to them, "but I think you should train with daggers instead. Your nimble arms and legs could do better with them."

"Thank you for your suggestion," Livella snapped, "but I'd like to learn something less wimpy."

Janis raised a brow at the comment, then casually Conjured a dagger while simultaneously pulling out one of her steel ones. They felt equal in weight and balance, making Janis wonder if she'd inadvertently patterned her Light dagger after it. She paused a moment, stretching the Conjured dagger out until it was the length of her forearm, the adornments, albeit faint, matching the dagger that she held in Stilten before she'd left it.

"And how many times have you seen me best someone with a sword using my measly daggers?" Janis asked, inspecting the steel dagger in her left hand.

Livella blushed but didn't answer.

"If you refuse to use a dagger, fine, but at least take my advice. Your center of gravity is set too far forward for a heavy sword to do much good. Try a staff instead. Similar tactics work, though the weight and length could give you an advantage," Janis suggested before exhaling and throwing her Light dagger swiftly to the side. Flying end over end, the blade of the Conjured weapon slammed into a wooden dummy there, sticking in a few inches before it puffed away into the air.

"Actually, Oi fink tha's a good idea," Livella's opponent and apparent teacher agreed.

Without even asking Livella, he moved to the side where weapons were attached to the stone wall with thick iron brackets. Selecting one of medium length, he tossed it to Livella, who awkwardly dropped her sword to catch it. Janis was grateful that she caught it, even if it looked clumsy. The poor woman had been improving, but she appeared to be making more a fool of herself than anything.

"A' the ready," the blond man said, crouching down with his own sword.

Livella's knuckles showed white where she gripped the wooden staff in her hand, and she glanced at the man before her, looking skeptical. The man didn't wait much longer for her to prepare, for no sooner had Livella slid into a defensive position than the man lunged at her, air hissing through his teeth at the brisk movement. Livella gasped but moved her staff instinctively in the direction to block his blow. Rather than missing as she had before, her staff moved with ease, the wood slamming into the blade of his sword and knocking it off course.

Looking a bit surprised, the man redirected his momentum and came at her again. As expected, at least by Janis, Livella countered that attack too. It was easy to see the recognition in Livella's eyes as she realized the weapon felt more comfortable in her grip. Soon the bout became more earnest on both sides. Within a few minutes, each was panting and sweating from the exertion. Janis watched as Livella's face turned from determination with a bit of fear to confidence in her movements. The man's practice sword missed Livella's head by a finger's width before she spun, letting him fly past her so she could slam him on the back.

Cursing, he flipped around to parry her next attack with the staff. Again they sparred until both were so out of breath that the man held up his sword in surrender.

"Lanser's beard, tha' actually worked," he said, looking at Janis with respect.

"A good instructor should have seen her weaknesses and thought of other ways to amend them," Janis said, looking at Livella. "Good work. I guess we won't have to leave you behind for much longer, will we?"

Livella glared at Janis, but it was clear the look was in jest. "I just wanted to make myself useful. Now that I've got the blooming voices out of my head, I can function even with you far away from me."

Over the past weeks, they'd each left once or twice to go on scouting parties near their enclave. Each time, the voices screamed in Livella's head to be near Janis. That had apparently stopped in the last few days, or so Livella said. Whatever torments the woman experienced seemed assuaged now that they realized she didn't intend to leave Evenir to slip away from Janis.

"The next toim we 'ave Awakenin's, we'll bring yous along," the man said, nodding once more before moving to a water barrel for a drink.

Janis grabbed a cloth from a stone bench nearby, recognizing it as the sweat cloth Livella had used in past sparring sessions, and tossed it to the woman. Livella thanked her and wiped her brow, using her other hand to put her weight on the staff she still held.

"Now you just need to work on endurance. That was a good bout, but expect real fights to be drawn out far longer than that spar," Janis said, leaning against the wall.

Livella grimaced but said nothing.

"So, the great *Prime* graces us with 'er presence, eh? Watchin' 'er pet girl foit and fail over 'an over," a man's voice drawled to her right.

At first, Janis ignored the comment. It wasn't because she was bothered by it, but more because she knew the tone of the person. The condescending nature gave her pause. People who were overconfident, for whatever reason, didn't deserve immediate attention.

"'Ey! Talkin' t' yous, Janis," the man said again.

Janis turned her head in the direction of the voice, casually placing herself between him and Livella. He was coming at Janis, but she didn't want Livella in the midst of a conflict that apparently was her doing.

"You seem to be having a bad day, *sir*," Janis commented, folding her arms across her chest.

Her use of the honorific had the intended effect on him as he turned beet red, anger swelling inside of him. He pulled his steel sword free, the metallic *shing* of blade on sheath echoing in the room. Janis was well aware of the fact that the room had fallen silent at the man's comment. All eyes watched her reaction. Adrenaline started moving through her, sharpening her mind and tensing her muscles. Whoever this man was, he wanted a show, and a show they would give. Her eyes flashed behind him and she realized more people had slipped into the room. Where before there were only a few pairs of sparring soldiers, now at least two dozen mulled around the room, their eyes trained on the interaction.

Her gut warned her that something was off, but she remained calm.

The man walking toward her looked comical, his small head not matching his large and bulky muscles. His head was bald, shaved as close to his scalp as possible with blades. Save for his size, his appearance looked like that of a mere teenager. Her memory buzzed as she recalled seeing the man's face somewhere. Janis stared at him, unfolding her arms. Though she should have sheathed her dagger, she held it forward, as if challenging him to attack her.

"Yeh claim t' be a foiter, but Oi've not seen anything such loik. 'Ow's about yeh give us a show, eh?" the man said, bowing mockingly.

Janis inspected the man up and down, assessing the situation. He'd easily caught her in a tricky spot. If she declined, even if honorably, it wouldn't look good for her, especially with the vote for leader set for two days from now. While she didn't dislike the idea of becoming less popular and losing the vote, she felt like it could leave a dangerous precedent for Avryn and those not loyal to the mounting insurrection. On the other hand, if she accepted, she would bear a weight she didn't feel equipped to hold. After a few moments longer, she recognized him as one of the men in the crowd who'd backed Gallin.

Sighing, Janis pointed her steel dagger at him and waved it.

"If you must, let's get this over with, then," she said.

The man, hearing her condescending tone, growled and rushed her with his sword. Janis easily swiped her dagger to the side, smacking the blade of the sword so it went off course. Gasps sounded around them as the onlookers observed their bout. It took Janis only a few minutes to see that the man actually had standard skill with the sword. The fight felt as if it was something from a combat scroll, memorized and practiced so many times it was instinct.

You'd think someone so bold would at least be a better swordsman, Janis thought.

Rounding him, Janis slipped one of her daggers, the steel one, up the sleeve of the man's shirt, ripping the cloth. The man roared, spinning and coming at her with his short sword. While the move was still standard, it was far more rapid than Janis expected. Still, she dodged it and sliced the upper arm of his other sleeve, careful to not cut his skin, only the clothing.

At this point, the man knew she toyed with him, and his face reddened in anger. He let out a shout again before rushing her. Just as he got to her, something in her gut warned her to dodge. Urgency entered her limbs as she stiffened. She chose not to move in the direction she originally planned to avoid the slash. Just then, a dagger flipped from behind her, the blade missing her face. She cursed, dodging two more blows from the man and turning in the other direction. There, a woman stood readying another knife. Janis knocked the next dagger from the air while dodging the sword coming at her. Within moments, many others from the room had pulled their weapons and were advancing.

Ah, I walked right into that one, didn't I? Janis thought, scanning the surrounding room.

Her original opponent rushed her once more, and now that she could see her predicament, she slipped around him, slamming the hilt of her Conjured dagger into the back of his head. He fell to the ground with a grunt and stopped moving. Livella, eyes wide, backed up to the wall, holding her staff upward awkwardly. As per usual, a new fighter such as her couldn't rely on instincts through fear yet. Janis focused on her dagger, extending it outward like a spear, and swiped it outward, causing those moving toward her to dance away.

"Wha' the bloomin' spine hog are yeh doing?" Livella's instructor said to those who advanced. He gripped his own sword and moved to Janis's side. They were backed into a wall now, the door to the sparring chamber opposite them. As if validating the direness of the situation, the orbs of Light around them flickered, shadows casting on all the faces of the attackers. Five of them lunged, trying to overwhelm her, but Janis jumped backward, her back slamming somewhat firmly into the stone wall. Pain lanced up her spine and elbows as they connected with the hard material.

By now there were at least thirty other men and women, each of them glaring at her.

Gallin's retinue is far larger than we thought, Janis thought.

"Torin, stop this nonsense *now*!" the man beside her said.

"Oh, shove it, Yult, this wench isn't meant to lead us. Best if we kill her now to rid us of her weak ideals."

Janis eyed the attackers. She figured she ought to be more concerned about the fact that she was outnumbered but she felt calm. Even if she hadn't been given Lightbearer abilities, she'd still have thought up some way to get herself out of the situation. Janis recalled a few times she'd been outnumbered at least ten to one. The numbers here outweighed her chances, but her past self would have at least tried. But she was a Lightbearer now.

A few of the oncomers Conjured various weapons, mostly swords and daggers, while one particular woman created a ball of Light, small and hovering by her hand. The man who aided her glanced at her warily. Janis was impressed that he didn't look at all scared about their odds, more like reluctant to engage with the group.

Janis spoke cooly to the two people behind her.

"Livella, defend yourself. Don't bother attacking. Yult," Janis said, "try not to get in my way."

Snorting, he replied, "As long as yeh don' ge' in my way either."

With a wicked smile, Janis pushed outward with her hand, three of the closest men glowing with a blue hue before being thrown backward into the few behind them. Coincidentally, Yult apparently had Moving abilities of his own, for he made the same motion, a few others being thrown on the other side of the group. Two men launched at her, swords met with her own Conjured daggers. Slipping her daggers from under theirs, she moved forward, slicing the arm of one man. He shouted in pain, retreating back while she fought the other. Two more women replaced him, both with glowing blue swords.

Gritting her teeth, Janis barely managed to dodge all the weapons, though she could not attack them. With a flashing glance toward Yult, she saw he had similar challenges, four others engaging him.

Livella grunted to her right, but Janis could see that she was holding her own just fine. Apparently, arming the mousy-haired woman with a staff had given her a confidence she'd previously lacked. She was only being attacked by one person, most of the mob's attention being focused on Janis. Livella was protecting herself well enough that Janis didn't have to worry about her for the time being. At that moment Livella spun and slapped the end of her staff on the woman's head, knocking her to the ground. The surprised look that followed on Livella's face was far too satisfying for Janis. Within half a moment another man took the downed woman's place, fighting Livella.

We'll be overwhelmed too fast, Janis thought, pushing outward with her hand once more, the three before her flying backward. The man landed on his backside, growling, but the women recovered from Janis's Moving push quickly. Before Janis could stop it, one of the sword tips slipped into her chest. Fortunately, she'd seen it coming and moved just far enough back that it didn't pierce her heart or a lung. Grunting from the pain, Janis pushed out again, harder this time, the two women sprawling on the ground. Janis raised a hand to her chest, warmth and blue Light pooling there until the wound healed.

This action appeared to infuriate those attacking, as they came with more speed and passion. Janis quickly threw up a Shield, yelling for Yult to back into it. Despite her infancy in using the abilities, she knew how to withdraw the Shield enough to allow him in. She closed the Shield behind him. Men and women shouted, slamming their weapons into the wall of Light. Looking over, she saw that Yult had cuts and slices on his limbs and face.

"Meh, don't mind me, Oi've got it," he said before putting his own hand to his wounds to heal them.

Janis raised a brow before saying, "I don't know if it's just luck that we both have Fixing abilities or just unlucky for them."

Despite their odds, Yult laughed.

"Oi take i' yeh've been in this situation 'afore," he shouted over the angry noises of the small mob.

Smiling, Janis nodded in affirmation.

Just then, Livella let out a yelp and a loud crack pained Janis's ears. Whipping her head in that direction, she saw that the woman holding a small orb of Light before had lobbed it at her Shield. In a smooth motion, she simultaneously summoned and tossed another orb at the Shield. The crack sounded louder this time, though Janis wondered if it was just because she expected the noise.

“They'll break the Shield!" Yult yelled.

Janis eyed Livella standing there with her staff. She couldn't help but feel a bit of pride for the woman and how she handled this real application of her fighting. She bore an already purpling bruise on her face where she must have been hit with a fist or hilt, but she looked determined.

Another crack smacked the Shield.

"Lass, best be coming up with a plan fast. We ain't going to make i' much longer," Yult warned as another crack slammed into the Shield.

Janis didn't know how she knew it, but she could tell that only one more orb of Light would shatter the barrier. Even now, her energy waned at an alarming rate. She didn't recall losing energy this quickly during her fight with Riln, but then she hadn't had to hold a Shield against so many Destroying orbs.

Her mind flashed, eyes widening for a moment. Time sped to a rapid rate, images of herself and Yult splitting off in many directions. It was the type of scene that Janis expected would drive a man mad, but her mind processed it. Her eyes felt warm and she knew she was Seeing possibilities. She watched as a version of herself dashed forward, dropping the Shield and flinging a Destroying orb of her own downward. Too many would die. She saw another, Yult rushing forward while she fought with long swords Conjured by her hand. She watched herself and Yult die in the end. Possibility after possibility ran through her mind, so rapidly that she could hardly believe she was understanding them all. Strangely, none of them included Livella. A black smudge in her visions was all she could See of the woman. Lasting only a moment, she knew she had to pick one of the options quickly. She locked on one of the futures.

Even before her eyes dimmed, she spoke out.

"Livella! Trust me!" was all she said before pulling the Shield inward so that Livella was drawn out of the walls.

For the third time in such a short amount of time, Livella surprised Janis. Standing her ground with a stoic expression, Livella held her staff up higher as various Conjured objects were thrown in her direction. Livella flung her staff outward to block the objects, but she only hit a couple before the others flew true. As suspected, they went through not only her staff without any effect, but also through her body.

That wasn't what Janis was waiting for.

Just then, the woman, the Destroyer among the crowd, finally summoned another small orb, taking the bait Janis had set. Smiling, Janis reached out with her Moving and grabbed the woman's hand. A shocked expression sprouted on the woman's face as she realized she couldn't throw the orb. Instead Janis focused hard on tipping her hand to the side just enough that the orb slipped out of her grasp. Gasping, the woman tried to open her mouth to warn the others, but she wasn't fast enough. As if in slow motion, the orb landed on the ground at the woman's feet, exploding outward and throwing men and women in all directions. Those in front of the Destroyer slammed hard into Janis's Shield, bodies crushed by the explosion and the firm Light dome. Rock chips and debris flung outward, clattering on the Shield like rain. The air filled with dust, obscuring Janis's view of the room.

Outside of the Shield, she watched as Livella's body absorbed the force of the Destroying but took the brunt of the debris. She closed her eyes in pain as her face, hands, and arms were sliced by the objects flying at her.

"Ugglyn's behind!" Yult exclaimed beside her. The man rushed through the Shield before the dust had a chance to settle, snatching the woman and shoving her through the Shield.

Livella's eyes locked on Janis, and rather than anger in her eyes, Janis could see determination and resolve, even with her body covered in cuts and bruises.

Lanser's might, she's come so far so fast, Janis marveled.

"What is the meaning of this?!" Avryn's voice was heard over the groans and shouts of those Janis had just outwitted. "Seize them, *now*!"

Brown-robed men and women stormed through the dust, gathering those who had fallen to the ground in the explosion. A few tried to fight back, forcing their way toward the door, but their efforts were thwarted by the numbers who had come with Avryn. Janis, Yult, and Livella coughed from the dust in the air.

"What in the heavens happened here?" Avryn asked. He sounded more angry than Janis had ever heard him. She didn't know whether that anger was directed at her or those who attacked, but she didn't care.

"It seems we were ambushed by men"—Janis paused to cough—"who I'm guessing work with Gallin."

Avryn's expression darkened.

"How has it come to this already? I knew I shouldn't have delayed the vote for leadership. The longer we wait, the worse this will be for us and for Evenir," Avryn said, covering his mouth so he could avoid coughing himself. "This is quite the mess you've created here."

Janis looked around for a moment before raising her hands and focusing. Small bits of blue Light flickered and sparkled as she Moved each dust particle downward more quickly than gravity could carry them. Within seconds, the dust was gone from the air, though puffs of the dirt and dust still flew upward as men and women mulled around. At this point all eyes were now on her. Many looked shocked, though some looked angry, mainly those she'd just bested.

Avryn cleared his throat, "Yes, well, that'll do, thank you."

"Fog me good, Oi've no' seen a Mover do something like tha' in all me loife," Yult exclaimed, eyes wide.

Janis ignored the comment, turning to Livella.

"Sorry for using you as bait. It was the best option I could think of at the moment. I hoped they'd forget Lightbearing doesn't work on you and still attack," Janis explained.

Livella shot her a fiery stare for a moment before she laughed. "At first I wondered what in Lanser's name you were thinking, then it made sense when the Light didn't touch me." Livella grimaced as Yult yanked another piece of rock from her arm. "Though I could have done without the explosion."

"Moit 'ave been foine if yous weren' foggin' immune to me Fixin'," the shorter man grumbled, wrapping another gash on her arm.

Avryn looked side to side at each of them, looking confused.

"She used their own Destroyin' orb 'gainst them," Yult explained.

After seeing his still-confused expression, Janis delved into the details.

"I would have created my own orb, but I was too focused on keeping the Shield up. Plus, using her orb would cause zero casualties, rather than multiple."

Avryn inspected her before shaking his head. "And how many possibilities did you See, exactly?"

Cocking her head in jest, Janis shrugged. "Didn't count, maybe a hundred or so."

This time there was more than just shock from Yult. The small man let out a strangled grunt as if he was choking on his own saliva.

"Lanser's—" Though Avryn never finished his curse, he glanced around the room again before speaking. "I've never heard of a Seer having such rapid visions during combat like that. Combat visions were never a thing until now, yet you and Marric have spoken of them days apart. We'll have to ask Rivelen and the others if they've had similar experiences. For now I'll call in Fixers to mend this room."

Snapping his fingers, Avryn called over one of the soldiers who accompanied him to apprehend the attackers. The man looked at Avryn with more respect than Janis could ever have gotten from anyone within Evenir. Janis saw the same expression in anyone who faced Avryn. The people here loved him and trusted him as their leader. She couldn't imagine the vote, however skewed by Gallin's men, would fall on anyone else, let alone herself. As the man left, Avryn rubbed his forehead before addressing them.

"The vote must happen now. We've no luxury of waiting like I imagined. I'll send messengers to the various wings of Terris Green announcing the vote on the morrow. Lanser help us that Gallin hasn't reached more of our numbers than we imagined. I could not have expected an ambush of this scale happening right under our noses."

"'Twas clear they planned i'. Timing loik tha' couldn't 'ave 'appened spur o' the moment. 'Ow did yous make i' 'ere so fast loik?" Yult asked.

"Gallin's men must have forgotten that there are sympathizers in Terris Green for our cause. A woman came running for me the moment they began attacking. She'd been in here refreshing the water barrel and cleaning up. She slipped out before anyone noticed," Avryn said.

The room emptied quickly around them, men and women taken by soldiers, hands bound, through the door on the opposite end of the room. Some had to be carried for how injured they'd been by the woman's rogue Destroying orb. Janis couldn't help but pride herself on the cleverness of her actions. The floor near them had a deep crater, about six feet wide and a few feet deep. Pieces of stone and debris still littered the room.

Sighing, Janis thought back to the moment when her eyes were aglow, possibilities spinning through her mind as she considered all of the options she had. As usual, the visions had come unexpectedly. She made a mental note to talk to Rivelen about how to control the visions more. Something like that had to be possible, for even Riln himself could fight her without being consumed by them.

Glancing around, Avryn was taking stock of the damages to the room.

With a grand gesture, one fit for a regal leader rather than a loyal friend, he called a man from the other side of the room.

"We need this Fixed as soon as possible. I don't doubt that word of these happenings has already broken free from this room, but it would be best not to draw too much attention to the events. We can't have people worrying about their safety or about the potential uprising within our ranks."

Nodding, the man moved off to give instructions.

"Ah, Oi can 'elp clean up 'round 'ere. 'Tis no worry," Yult said.

He grimaced slightly as he stood, likely harboring bruises of his own from the fight. Avryn reached out and gripped the man's upper arm, turning his body so Avryn could look at him directly.

"You don't have to help. If you need to rest, then take the time to do so." Avryn spoke firmly but kindly.

Yult chuckled. "Lad, yeh know me well 'nough t' know tha' Oi won' si' 'round and watch woil others do all the work. Oi'm foin, Fixed meself just roit."

Face darkening, Yult nodded in Janis's direction before speaking once more. "Oi fink yous two need to figure some things out 'afore tomorrow," he suggested before bowing slightly and moving off to help Fix the room. Already two others had joined and were placing their hands on various parts of the floor, blue Light pulsing gently beneath their palms. Stones and debris stirred around them, glowing with the blue Light of Fixing. Most moved slowly back to their original locations, though others moved more rapidly, having been thrown far across the room.

It wasn't the first time Janis had seen Fixing of this caliber. Just weeks ago she'd accidentally blown up her own quarters and had observed similar Fixing routines performed. Her gut still twisted at the sight, despite her own use of Fixing on herself just moments before. The power was still unnatural, and seeing rocks and dust moving seemingly of their own free will was disconcerting.

"Yult's right. We've things to discuss, but we shouldn't here," Avryn whispered before moving to the door.

Though he hadn't explicitly asked her to follow, it was implied. Livella watched him go curiously before she looked at Janis.

"Umm, should I come too, then?" she asked.

"I think he wants to speak to me alone. Stay here, enjoy the entertainment," Janis joked.

Livella looked around uneasily at the Fixers doing their work. Her eyes unfocused almost instantly as she receded somewhere in her thoughts. It wasn't unusual for Livella to do that. Whenever she wasn't addressed directly by anyone for more than a few minutes, she retreated into her mind, eyes glazed. It wasn't a terrible problem to have, if you weren't a soldier or assassin, but Janis wondered if this was how the woman was before she was called to Terris Green by *Yrillnan* or if it was an artifact of her being brought here.

Janis snapped her fingers to get the woman's attention once more. Livella jumped at the noise but focused back on Janis.

"I'm impressed with what you've learned. Keep practicing and you'll be a good fighter before you know it. It'll be good not to have to worry as much about you if we take you out with us to get Lightbearers," Janis stated. "With any luck, you won't have to hide inside a bar again," Janis said with a wink.

Livella blushed, then looked down at her staff.

"Thanks for the tip on the staff. I didn't think about using something other than a sword. It just seemed practical to learn with a weapon that everyone else uses."

"At some point, you'd learn to trust my instincts for personal defense and combat. I think there was a time you didn't even think I could protect the two of us as we walked into an odd cave with glowing statues," Janis joked.

This brought a slight smile to Livella's mouth as she rolled her eyes.

"Oh, shove it, even you have to admit that was eerie," Livella replied.

At the time, it had been, but Janis shrugged in jest.

"All in a day's work. It's a survival game in the end. We will just have to come out on top, no matter what unnatural phenomenons come our way," Janis said, eyeing the doorway. "But alas, I'm being hailed by Avryn as we speak."

The man had poked his head back through the door on the other side and glared at her pointedly. Janis stood and stalked toward the open door on the other side of the room. As she moved, she had to step side to side to avoid the flying bits of debris and stone as the Fixers repaired the surrounding cavern. One girl, young compared to the others, seemed very concentrated as she held her hands aloft, blue glowing objects around her moving into their places. Janis stared at her for only a moment before looking back at her destination. Her mind marveled at how kids so young were being Awakened into this dangerous war. If she ever had the chance to talk to Lanser, she'd be sure to rebuke him for that.

Avryn stood just outside the door, greeting those who passed him in the hallway. Despite his plain best efforts, he looked more agitated than ever.

"What in Lanser's mind were you *thinking*?" Avryn hissed when she met him there.

Janis looked behind her, knowing full well he was talking to her but pretending he might be addressing someone else. Sighing, Avryn gestured for her to follow him.

The two walked down the hallway before Avryn turned sharply to a small door. As he pressed on the wooden surface, the iron hinges wailed. Avryn stood to the side and gestured her inside. While Janis appreciated the chivalry, she looked to the dark room, then back at him, raising an eyebrow. This drew yet another sigh from the man and he moved into the room. Before entering, Janis summoned a small orb of Light. She didn't expect what she saw in the room. Linens, clothing, and other storage items such as bandages and nonperishable foodstuffs lined the walls of the dark room, which was long and narrow.

Avryn noted her reaction, which she'd not bothered to veil given the circumstances, and shook his head.

"We needed privacy, and this was the closest thing to us," Avryn said.

"As long as all you wanted to do was talk. You're a handsome man, Avryn, but no one's charming me into any snogging," Janis said sarcastically.

Knowing Avryn and his propriety, she expected him to blush or even be somewhat embarrassed. Surprisingly, his reaction was neither.

"Even if I wanted to try, I'd be too late. Harmel's managed that bit already," Avryn replied.

The comment surprised Janis. For the first time in years she felt her face flush. Even if it was only slightly and she pressed the feeling away before it took too much control, she cursed herself internally. It was the first time that anyone had voiced whatever she and Harmel had out loud. Janis would admit no fondness for anyone, let alone romantic feelings, however small. Yet hearing Avryn's observation felt more potent given the situation. Avryn must not have seen her blush in the dim light, for he changed the topic immediately.

"Do you think Gallin was part of it? Or did it seem like they acted of their own accord?" Avryn asked.

Shaking her head, Janis replied. "Honestly, it doesn't matter. If Gallin wasn't involved, he'll have been told now. A man like him would only feel proud of what happened, there'd be no discipline, I suspect."

Avryn grimaced but he didn't disagree.

"If we're truly to hold a vote tomorrow, then you must be prepared for what must be done. Gallin and any who sympathize with him will have to be found and eliminated. I fear our dungeons won't be large enough if his numbers are great," Avryn said.

"We could just kill them," Janis offered frankly.

For the second time in the last few moments, Avryn surprised her. She'd have thought her comment would outrage him or at least mildly anger him. She'd just suggested killing some who were once loyal to Evenir. Instead Avryn furrowed his brow in thought. He absently Conjured a sword in his hand and let it dissipate over and over as he delved into his thoughts. She'd not seen him have any such habits before now.

"Do you truly believe that is the best choice?" Avryn asked.

"If I really did believe that, then the men and women in that room would all be dead. Why do you think I used her Destroying orb when I could have used my own? The likelihood of someone dying from the indirect explosion was low compared to if I had thrown my own."

Janis couldn't help but feel somewhat surprised by her own decision. When she'd Seen all the possibilities she had in her rapid visions during that fight, most of them resulted in the death of many or even most of the attackers. Her assassin's instincts shouted for her to follow one of these paths, to eliminate the threats before they could cause more havoc and problems, but there had been something else. Tryvv's image had appeared in her mind, only briefly, but enough to remind her of the discussion they'd had in Stilten.

Janis had changed and she had to keep changing. Death was not the only option, and it shouldn't be treated with such simplicity.

Avryn smiled at her comment.

"Why, the assassin intentionally chose not to kill? I thought I'd seen it all," Avryn teased.

Glaring at him, Janis snatched one of the Conjured swords from Avryn's hand before he could make it disappear. Eyebrows shooting high, Avryn crouched down, summoning another blade in his good hand. Janis smirked at his reaction.

"And you still have problems trusting me, it seems," she said, looking to his sword.

Avryn cleared his throat, then let both swords disappear into the air. The shadows being cast on the surrounding storage snuffed out with the swords. The man replaced his Conjures with his own Light orb and he tossed it up lightly into the air, the blue hue now showing their surroundings again.

"I trust you, to a point. Give me time; I've only just learned about your history with Watchlight and Marric," Avryn said. "But before we go into the vote tomorrow, you must know that you are ingrained in Evenir more than you can know. As the newfound Prime, people will look to you, even if it's me they choose as their leader. There's no running from your responsibility."

The words hung heavy in the air between them, but Janis masked her reaction as she ordinarily did. She didn't want Avryn to know just how grave a comment such as that was for someone with her prior life. Gut wrenching, Janis grinned at him.

"So why bring me in here? You aren't the only one to have made that point."

"Janis, if they choose you as their leader, it's in your best interest to keep me close. Name me your second. If I am chosen, I intend to name you second. The only way for you not to be at the head, in some capacity, is if Gallin is chosen. Lanser help us if that's the case." Avryn formed his hand into a claw and swiped it through the air. The gesture, while superstitious, was heavily rooted in Lanserian beliefs.

Janis couldn't even imagine worshiping a being that you'd discovered had granted strange magic to a select few and had sealed the anti-god away using random individuals. At the very moment, the only thing she felt for the being was annoyance.

"So be it," Janis replied. "But don't expect me to be accepted further than reverence. The people here will never see me the way they see you."

Avryn pressed his lips together, betraying his own worry.

"With a little luck, I'll be able to cushion that for you with me leading alongside," he said. "For now, let's get some rest. The past few days have been filled with far too much uncertainty."

Smirking again, Janis gestured grandly toward the door. "After you, then."

With a pointed eye roll, Avryn moved out the door.

Janis knew what Avryn suggested would be wise, but she had some searching to do. Now that she had the power to See into time and space itself, she thought to spend the evening using it.

Whatever tomorrow brought, she had to be ready.

18

Prost woke with a start, shivering as he lay on the cot in his small quarters. The ceiling of his room stood just tall enough for him to stand, the walls only spanning wide enough for him to extend his arms outward in any direction. At first, Riln's assigning him this room had been an obvious slight, an attack on his worth as a person, but over time Prost had learned to appreciate it. Riln hardly slept, or at least it seemed that way, but his quarters were at least twenty times the space of Prost's. Filled with lavish furniture and red adornments, it could have been the luxurious quarters of a king.

Yet Prost didn't care. Security was all he cared about. The wooden door to his room remained closed, a lock fitted firmly into the edge. There were occasions when Riln had locked him in here, but those were long past. Over time, Riln didn't care to lock him away. He must have realized Prost was unlikely to kill him in his sleep. Despite the many times Prost had considered it, he had never acted.

Until Stilten, at least.

Since he'd returned to their lair, he'd not taken any moments to consider his decision in Stilten. As far as he could tell, not one soul from Watchlight witnessed the event, yet something within warned him to be cautious.

His body continued to quiver, as if from the cold, yet the cavern stayed warm throughout the complete year of Lindrad, mainly because of the hot springs that flowed through parts of the mountain. Prost gritted his teeth, trying to control the shaking. Something itched at the back of his mind, a piece of information that he couldn't quite grasp yet knew was there. He felt as if he recognized something important but couldn't recall exactly the nature of it.

Ah, he wakes, leaving me with little time to my own devices, Ugglyn whispered in his mind.

More than the eerie sound of the voice inside, the words grated at Prost's soul. The suggestion that Ugglyn had any opportunity to do anything of his own accord terrified Prost to the core. Prost began analyzing his body, trying to get any hint of being moved while he slumbered. He slept in his normal clothing, something unusual for most, but common for him, and nothing appeared to be awry. Prost hoped that if Ugglyn had taken his body on a stroll for the night, he'd feel something in his limbs. Ugglyn rumbled with satisfaction inside of him, apparently watching Prost do his physical analysis.

I can't move you while you sleep, so there's no point in fretting about it, Ugglyn said, evidently amused.

While he appreciated the anti-god's forthright nature on most days, Prost had little trust in anything the being said. He didn't know the full history of how Ugglyn came to be, but Prost knew that one didn't obtain a status like his by being truthful.

What have you done? What do you mean by leaving you to your own devices? Prost demanded hotly.

With echoing laughter, Ugglyn retreated deep inside of him. In a moment he was gone. Prost shivered, trying not to let the idea of Ugglyn meddling with anything during his unconsciousness get to him. Prost rose and brushed off his clothing. He'd been wearing the same ensemble for a few days now and could tell that he'd need to freshen up his clothing soon. The soldier instincts in him warned that one should not be left unprepared while out on the battlefield. While he remained within the lair most of his days, he still felt that at any moment someone could try to slit his throat while he slept. Now that Lightbearing affected him like everyone else, he felt less safe than he had before.

The dim red Light from the hallway outside his door bled under the crack below, illuminating the room just enough for Prost to make out the outline of his cot. He considered spending a moment of meditation in his room before emerging, but he thought better of it. Without more Light, it was tricky enough to find the flint to start his candle. The stiffness of his body as he stood validated his findings that Ugglyn hadn't mobilized his body while he slept, yet he still felt uneasy about Ugglyn's declaration moments before.

As he pressed the door open, the first thing he saw was a person dressed in all black, holding a Conjured red spear next to them. Prost's instincts flared up, and he grasped for his steel sword, only to find that it wasn't there. Chest burning, Prost sucked in a breath, ready to dodge whatever attack came from the man. When none came, he relaxed.

"What are you doing here?" Prost demanded.

The man jumped at the sound of his voice, twisting toward him and flipping the tip of his spear upward. When he saw it was Prost, he relaxed, returning the spear to the upright position. Prost had to squint at the brightness of the red Light.

"Ah, sir. Sorry fer th' trouble. Mistress Neera sent us 'ere t' guard yous while yeh slept."

A mixture of intrigue and annoyance swirled within his gut. Neera had become fascinated with him over the past weeks, so Prost wasn't surprised to hear that she'd sent them. What was intriguing, more than anything, was the fact that the men listened. There was no set hierarchy within their ranks, yet Neera had been physically closest to him on the occasions when Prost had been challenged. It appeared that her proximity to Prost gave her an amount of prestige.

"Riln never required such guarding. Why do you think I do?" Prost growled, pushing the door further.

He immediately noticed two others behind the opening door. One brandished two steel daggers with warped blades, as if they'd been pressed hard against the anvil while they cooled. The other was Alts.

Prost's heart fluttered in his chest when he saw her. She wore a sleeveless shirt, the upper parts of her shoulders exposed, and she bore no cloak. The Watchlight tattoo on the upper part of her right arm was stark against her pale skin. Her blonde hair was braided down her back, with an orange stripe standing out against the pale strands of the rest of her hair.

"'Bout time yeh woke. These blunders wouldn't let the likes o' me in t' wake yeh right proper. 'Ad to wait ferever fer yeh," the woman said, her voice ringing high and clear.

Fog, why is this woman so attractive? Prost cursed internally, forcing his eyes to stay on her face. Every other time he'd seen her, particularly when Riln was around, he'd had little difficulty ignoring the fact that she was a strong and beautiful woman. He had had far too many other problems to deal with, such as the hate he drew from the majority of Watchlight men and women. The presence of the anti-god within him had already proven to be shaking the foundations of what he knew about himself.

That, and she was courting the insufferable Mert.

Fortunately, Alts wasn't looking in his direction. Instead she inspected twin Conjured daggers that looked like exact replicas of the daggers held by the man next to her. Even with a quick glance, Prost could see the intricate designs woven into the handle and pommel. Alts sighed, then let the daggers disappear into the air.

"Now that yeh're awake, let's git a move on. 'Ad a scoutin' party get back, and they brought somethin' yeh'll wanna see," Alts said.

Prost furrowed his brow. They'd sent a small group of Watchlight operatives a few days ago to scout for Evenir. While they had no clear instructions to stay out for longer, he didn't expect them back already.

"They failed, then," Prost said. It was partly a question but mostly a statement of his expectations of the group.

Alts glanced at him, folding her arms across her chest.

"Oh yeah, they found Evenir while yeh slept, we killed the lot o' them and made it back 'afore supper," Alts said sarcastically. "No, they got somethin' else fer yous. 'E's been askin' 'bout yous all night."

"Who? What do they want from me?" Prost questioned, suppressing the irritation at her tone.

Alts rolled her eyes, then gestured grandly for Prost to move down the corridor.

Grunting, Prost eyed the two soldiers standing next to him and moved roughly down the hall. The sound of his footsteps echoed off the empty walls of the tunnel, and Prost used the moment to wake his mind up to reality. The fuzz of sleep still hovered in his brain, and he felt he needed his full attention to deal with whatever Alts was talking about. Prost tilted his head to each side, the cracks from his neck echoing on the walls as well, as if they were part of the symphony of sounds rebounding in the stone hallway. He noticed the others following behind him, but he didn't bother to protest. Prost didn't feel the need to have anyone guarding him, but as long as they stayed out of his way he could suffer them.

"When did they return?" Prost asked.

"Just ten minutes ago. I came right away t' wake yous," Alts said.

"Do you have a summary of what they found? We've still a ways to the stable chamber," Prost said.

"I think yeh'd best wait till yeh got there t' see, but let's say summon was searchin' fer yous," Alts replied.

Prost clenched his teeth, then spoke through them. "Evenir?" Prost asked.

"Nah, they din' show up at all." Alts cocked her head to the side then, intrigued by the idea. "They're 'idin' real good, they are."

Before Prost could ask who it was, a group of men and women, bunched together around another person, came stalking up the hallway toward them. Alts exhaled next to him and rushed forward.

"What are yeh doin'? I told yeh I'd bring 'im to yous."

A few of those bunched together looked uneasy at the statement, but the one in the front inclined his chin proudly.

"Thought boss-man shouldn't have to wait any longer. Figured we'd meet you on the way," the man proclaimed. He turned and gestured to the half dozen guards so they knew to fall away from the prisoner.

The man between them wore tight-fitting black clothing. His unkempt black hair flew wildly around his head, bangs hanging down on his forehead and into his eyes. His jaw was chiseled and his stature strong, despite his average height. While unassuming for the most part, Prost's eyes still narrowed at the figure, mind buzzing.

It was the very man he'd seen on the roof of the bar in Stilten.

Ugglyn emerged from within, fury burning hot with a passion. Prost sucked in a breath at the overwhelming feeling of hate from the anti-god and he resisted the tingling in his palm. Prost could tell Ugglyn meant to create a sword from the Void.

You will watch yourself here, anti-god, Prost roared in his mind, clenching his teeth to ward off the anger that threatened to overcome his mind.

The man dares show his face here, in this place?! Kill him! Kill him now! Ugglyn shouted, his voice echoing in Prost's mind as if he spoke out loud in the stone cavern.

"Sire?" The foremost man spoke, face still impassive.

"Why did you bring him here?" Prost asked, trying to mask the anger raging inside. A thought entered his mind, a way to gain control of the situation more easily. "He aided those who ensured Riln's untimely death."

He knew it was a lie, but the reaction he hoped for came instantly. The black-clad soldiers around the man stepped outward, most drawing weapons while one summoned an orb of what was likely Destroying Light. The leader of the pack, looking angered, turned on the man and thrust his sword forward.

"Wait!" the man said desperately.

Whether from the force of his words or the desperation in his eyes, the soldier stopped, staying his blade.

"I know how to kill Janis," he stated.

Prost froze. Even Ugglyn's fury retreated momentarily at the comment.

"I taught her everything she knows. If you want to kill Janis, you'll listen to me," he said.

At a gesture from Prost, the men and women relaxed, stepping back but still holding their weapons aloft. Prost casually placed his hands behind his back, walking forward with deliberate steps. Based on the apparel of the man before him, Prost assumed he was an assassin. Under normal circumstances, Prost would think it a lie, an attempt to kill him up close. Yet the man had used her name. Prost also had a flash in his mind of Janis seeing this man on the roof. She'd been shocked.

"What makes you think I even want to kill her?" Prost said, staring at the man directly.

"Because that's what Ugglyn wants, and he's free now, isn't he?" the man said.

Chills ran through Prost and he resisted the urge to inspect the reactions of the others. While they knew Ugglyn had granted Prost some type of power, no soul knew, save for himself, that the anti-god lived. A slight smile turned up the edge of the man's face. Somehow he knew he'd caught Prost in a challenging spot, yet Prost could bluff. He doubted the man, whoever he was, knew where Ugglyn was at the moment.

"A bold assumption. I wouldn't think it wise for someone who is outnumbered not only by us but the entirety of the compound to be so brazen with his words," Prost said coolly. "It's clear you know nothing of the matters at hand. See, we've plans already to kill her. What help could you offer?"

The man's face remained determined, but something in his eyes fell at the comment. Staring at the soldier closest to him, the man gestured with his head.

"Well? Show him."

Scowling, the leader of the group reached into his cloak and pulled out a dagger, blade black as night, matching the pommel and handle. Prost knew the weapon the moment he'd seen it. Janis's dagger.

Prost moved forward and snatched the dagger from the man's hand. The leader of the soldiers tensed but didn't say anything. Thoughts of Riln danced in Prost's mind at the sight of the weapon. It was the very thing he'd used to take the life of the one who'd dominated his life with chaos. He'd left the blade in Stilten, fearing that having it with him would link him to the death of their former leader. Even now, Prost pushed away feelings of anxiety that the others in Watchlight knew he was the one who had killed Riln. Though he knew it would be difficult if not impossible to link him to Riln's death without an eyewitness. The only person who *had* seen him kill Riln was the very owner of the dagger itself, the one accused of the event.

"Why do you have this dagger?" Prost asked in a calm voice. His own skin chilled at his tone. It reminded him exactly of how Riln used to talk to him when he'd been angry. The last thing he wanted to do was to become like Riln, but the rage simmered inside of him, his own merged with Ugglyn's.

The man glared at him, resolve in his own eyes. An uneasy feeling settled in Prost's gut as he realized the man was nowhere to be seen after Prost had been thrown off the roof. The possibility that he'd seen Prost slay Riln wormed its way into his mind. Suddenly, Prost felt as if on the edge of a cliff. This unknown man stood prepared and armed to toss him off of it if he willed it. Yet the man's gaze wasn't accusatory; it was shielded, guarded by his inescapable position in their compound. Despite the man's apparent resolve, Prost could see the fear behind his eyes. Every person felt fear. Every *being* felt fear.

As if in response to his thought, Ugglyn stirred, the anger faltering just enough to tell Prost that something hid there, beneath the power and complexity of the anti-god inside him. Breathing evenly, Prost fingered the blade delicately, trying to push back his stress in order to prod at the man's knowledge.

"I have it because Janis left it in Stilten. The wench knocked me out and left me for dead. I'm lucky to have made it out alive after she blew me through the roof," the man said before looking away sharply.

The man recognized Prost. The events in Stilten would be hard to forget, and he imagined his visage was burned into the memory of this stranger.

"You worked for Luden, not with Janis. Why come to us? Your employer tried to kill us in Stilten," Prost said, his voice hardening. "I should kill you right now for what you did there."

"Wait!" the man cried. "Ugglyn, I know him. He—was the one who truly employed me."

Ugglyn's mood shifted so suddenly that Prost almost fell over when the wave of anger changed to delight.

Ah, so he's still mine, Ugglyn mused.

Tingling coolness blossomed in Prost's chest and he felt his limbs go numb. Panicked, he pressed back at the feeling, though his resistance was futile.

Do not worry, host, I only have the strength for a few moments. You'll have your control back, Ugglyn pressed, the tingling overwhelming him.

Ugglyn took control then. Prost watched in horror as his vision shrunk to a small view, as if he watched through a window from afar. He couldn't feel anything; he could only see the small range and hear the conversation echoed on the invisible walls around him.

No—no—no, this can't be happening, Prost pleaded.

The experience felt slow and drawn out, but it must have happened in an instant, for Ugglyn, now speaking with his own voice, kept up the conversation.

"So, you are still loyal to me, then, little Seer," Prost heard his voice say. Though it sounded exactly like his own, there was something deeper there, an overtone that didn't match his normal tone.

The man narrowed his eyes briefly before they widened and he bowed quickly.

"Ugglyn, by Lanser's might, you are free, then?" he said, his voice betraying his sudden fear.

The men and women surrounding the man shifted uncomfortably, pulling their weapons upward. It appeared that they didn't know what to make of the situation.

Prost screamed in his mind, tugging outward with his consciousness to regain control of his faculties. He'd harbored the fear of losing his body to the anti-god ever since he'd been inhabited by the being, but Prost had only ever lost partial control, never like this.

"Free, in part," Prost's voice spoke casually. "Unfortunately, the fiendish woman and her Voidbearer still hold me at bay from being fully restored. This man offered himself as host in the interim."

Gasps and whispers erupted in the group of black-cloaked Watchlight men and women. All but the leader in front looked horrified to hear it. The man at the forefront of the group continued to look angry. "You claim to be Ugglyn himself, when you stand there as just a man. I've been here since you came to Watchlight, *dud*. Yet you try to proclaim that you are something that you aren't? If Riln truly communed with Ugglyn, he'd have told us. Who are you?" the Watchlight man challenged, holding his sword up.

Despite his predicament, Prost seethed at the comment. This man wouldn't be the only person in Watchlight to loath Prost like this, but hearing the term *dud* drew out all the frustration Prost felt through all the years. Though he didn't know how, Prost knew that his vibrant emotions reached Ugglyn the same as the anti-god's did to him when he was in control.

"Ooh, this one's got a temper," Ugglyn said aloud. "It's clear Prost likes you about as much as you like him. His anger brews inside me, even now."

Ugglyn turned around, facing the only person who stood behind him. Alts.

Her eyes were wide as she looked back and forth between Prost and the group behind him. Seeing her shock broke something with Prost. He wouldn't have ever called the woman a friend, but she was at least somewhat loyal to him. She'd defended him, and not once had she degraded him in the way others did by using menial terms such as *dud*. Her hand flexed and a Conjured dagger appeared there. Alts looked terrified at the news she'd just heard.

"It matters not whether you believe me, but let this serve as a testament to my power," Ugglyn said.

Prost cursed internally, trying to swim to the surface of his mind, to seize control of his limbs once more. Before he could, he saw a smoky sword appear in his hand. With a growl, the small window blurred as his body spun around and slammed the sword into the chest of the man in the front. The other Lightbearers shouted, jumping backward. The one with the Destroying orb lobbed it in their direction, but Prost's free hand flew upward, summoning a dome of smoke as a Shield, the Light orb cracking against it. With a thud, the corpse of the man in front of him fell to the ground, lifeless.

"Voidweaving can only be granted by me. You think Prost could manifest these abilities himself if he hadn't agreed with me directly?" Prost's voice roared.

The irony of the statement bothered Prost more than the situation he was currently in. Not once had he agreed to be the Voidbearer, the *K'alek Tar'n* for the *Yrillnan.* He'd not chosen to come to Watchlight, to be involved with Riln. He hadn't asked for any of this. Anger, this time at Lanser and Lightbearers in general, flooded his mind. With a roar, he pressed upward with all his might, forcing Ugglyn to recede into his mind.

For a moment he felt his limbs again, though only for a flash. Ugglyn grunted, Prost's body stumbling from the internal struggle, but Ugglyn regained his control.

"Riln cared only about domination, about control, but it was because *I* whispered them to him. He always communed with me. Only now do you know from where your red Lightbearing comes. I changed your Light, corrupted it with my ideals. Riln worked to release me, and in the end, he accomplished that. I am your true leader. If you dare to oppose me, then you'll die just the same as him," Ugglyn roared. "As for you, Seer, you may remain, for now. If you truly know how to kill the woman, then you will prove yourself."

Prost saw the man before them smile slightly, then bow.

"It's been some time since we've talked, Ugglyn. I feared you'd been subdued entirely," the Seer said.

Ugglyn scoffed. "In my current state I can only do my work while he sleeps. I thought you'd gone astray, joined Evenir in the end."

At that moment Prost sensed the vulnerability in Ugglyn's control. Pressing again, Prost felt his limbs again. The window of his vision sped forward, expanding until he had the full view from his eyes. With a rush, the intense tingling sensation subsided and was replaced by the simple coolness of Voidbearing. Prost gasped, looking down at his hand where the Void Blade was still grasped in his palm. At his movement the group tensed, most stepping back as if he would lash out again, killing another random person.

"Ugglyn has gone," Prost said gruffly. "I don't know what agreement you had with the anti-god, but it doesn't hold here. Take him to the cells, lock him there until I can consider this further."

Ugglyn's protests came loudly from within Prost's head, but he ignored them. His body was filled with adrenaline from the internal fight he'd just won. The guards who held the stranger glanced warily at Prost, then back at the man.

"Take him!" Prost roared, and the group jumped to action, seizing his arms again.

They hesitated briefly before pushing the man forward toward where Prost stood. He moved to the side to allow them past him. They advanced quickly, as if Prost was going to attack them if they got too close. Right as they passed, the stranger spoke.

"Call me Macks," he said before they shuffled him off down the corridor, leaving Prost and Alts alone.

The tunnel fell silent once the group left them standing there. What remained was the sound of dripping water, somewhere off in the distance. A warm spring ran through the tunnels up ahead. It was the place Prost often retreated when he needed his thoughts to be drowned out. For a moment he was tempted to head there now, to let the loud roar of the flowing river take over so he wouldn't have to think about what had just happened.

He had become quite an asset. You shouldn't ignore his offer to help you kill the Prime, Ugglyn whispered.

Prost ignored the comment. Even he couldn't deny the fact that it would be helpful to have someone who knew Janis personally. He knew that he'd have to dig into how Macks knew her so well, but for now there were other things to consider.

"So 'e's inside yous, then?" Alts said suddenly, her voice wavering.

When he turned to her again, she tensed, her hands still gripping her Conjured daggers as if Prost was an immediate threat. Under normal circumstances, the action might have annoyed him, but Prost knew Ugglyn had just seized control and killed a man in front of them all. Glancing down at the corpse, Prost felt a pang of regret at the death. When he'd been enslaved to Riln—for that is what it truly was—Prost had been flippant about death. Now that Riln was no longer a problem, Prost's former self had been dragging itself out of hiding. Despite his temper of old, he wouldn't kill so thoughtlessly and feel no remorse.

"He is," Prost replied simply, "but I control him, not the other way around."

The declaration stood as both information transfer to Alts, who would share the news with the others, and also as a reassurance for himself. Only a few times before now had Prost felt helpless since being made into the Voidbearer. Most of those instances involved one of the "Primes" of Lanser, but not this one. Ugglyn had taken complete control of him, and even if it was only for a moment, Prost couldn't help but wonder if it was a precedent for something else.

Was Ugglyn gaining power over him? Suddenly, the idea of going to the river made sense. If he could drown out his other senses, perhaps he could figure something out from the recent events.

"Find men to clean this up, bury the body, and try to do damage control. I don't suspect that Watchlight will take well to the death of this man," Prost spat before stalking off toward the falls ahead of them.

Alts spoke as he walked away, but he ignored her. Whatever the woman had to say or ask was irrelevant right now, at least until Prost could gain more knowledge from the being inside his head. He hurried, the sounds of his boots on the stone becoming wet as they moved upward toward the flowing river in their compound. The air took on a warm quality, becoming heavy and muggy as if after a summer storm. Water trickled down parts of the incline, moving backward away from him as he trudged up the tunnel.

Soon the roaring of the river became the only sound in his ears. Even the plodding of his footfalls was drowned out by the force of the flowing water. Prost welcomed the distraction. If he were more fearful of being ambushed by dissenters, this was the least safe place, considering how dampened his hearing was this close to the water, but Prost didn't care. For a fleeting moment the thought struck him that he didn't know what would happen to Ugglyn if he were to die, but he pushed that away, not wanting to address the question.

This close to the river, the powerful flow of the water was not only deafening but also majestic to behold. Prost turned right, inspecting the wide opening in the wall. Though no Lighting orbs sat in the recess of the wall, Prost could still make out the water flowing from inside the mountain. The river, about twice his height wide, gushed out of a space in the wall, flowing down the steep decline perpendicular to the path on which he stood, before flowing under him and into the wall to his left. Though he'd never touched the water, he knew it was warm, almost hot to the touch, having been heated by whatever sat within the mountain of their compound.

Warm springs within caverns were not uncommon, but to be so close to one humbled him.

What would happen if I just...jumped in? Prost wondered.

Ugglyn's emotions betrayed amusement at that moment. Though Prost could have questioned the being, he opted not to, letting the anti-god feel what he wanted without having to discuss it with him. He could hear Ugglyn trying to say something, but Prost focused on the noise of the water to drown him out. It worked surprisingly well.

I doubt I would die, Prost considered. *We know where the river goes.*

Suddenly, the irony of his location slammed into him like a burly man with a hot temper. He recalled just months ago when they'd been chasing Marric and Janis. The Seers discovered that the two had fled down this very river. Though Watchlight knew where it would come out, they still weren't fast enough to find the two of them before they slipped into the forest. Prost wondered if the same could work for him. Could he slip out of the compound? Could he leave and never come back to deal with the problems of the pact?

Emotions within reminded him that was not a possibility. Ugglyn would always be there, and if he was truly slipping, then there was only a matter of time before Prost lost control. The only options, and Prost knew it, were to free Ugglyn or lock him away. The latter seemed impossible, so Prost returned to the idea of killing Janis.

Reluctantly Prost opened up his mind to Ugglyn, allowing the being to come back to the forefront of his consciousness.

You speak of this "work" you do, Prost urged. *What have you been doing while I sleep?*

The question was forward, and he didn't expect any answer from Ugglyn, but to his surprise, the deep voice rumbled within his mind.

I have access to another plane while you sleep, the place of visions and Seers, Ugglyn said. *I've always been able to come to Seers wherever they are. Now that I'm separated from the plane myself, being stuck within your stubborn form, I resort only to the time you enter the realm.*

Prost furrowed his brow. He'd not considered much about Seers and how their powers worked, but if what Ugglyn said was any part truth, he felt far too unsafe while he slept.

What have you been doing? Prost pressed, a mixture of anger and fear taking over.

Now, now, no need to worry. Let's just say I've got friends in many places. Ugglyn laughed.

The eerie dread forced its way into Prost once more.

19

Marric started awake, his breath catching in his throat as he looked up at the darkness above his cot. A cold sweat broke out on his body and he shivered, feeling his clothing stick to him everywhere. He'd just been dreaming of his mother, living in Wurren with him and his father. It was as if she'd been there all their life and hadn't left. They'd just been living in peace, working in the shop, when the house caught fire. The only way out was blocked by two figures, each with grey and shriveled faces, skin decomposing in places all along their bare arms. Tins and Riln blocked the way out of the house. Marric tried to use his Lightbearing to get them free, but nothing worked.

Shivers rocked through him once again as he recalled the grotesque image of Riln and Tins. The panic he felt rising as he watched the house around them being consumed in flames, the family he'd never truly had doomed to burn inside.

They're dead, they can't get to you now, Marric told himself.

Until now, he hadn't thought about how traumatized he might be after being confronted by Riln. It became clear when he'd seen Riln in the past, speaking to his mother. Tins's treatment had left trauma daily while she still lived. The thought that she might have killed him at any moment, having worked for Watchlight all along, made him shiver. Shifting slightly on his bed, he turned so he could look at the curtain that covered the entrance to his quarters. Through the cracks, he could see the unwavering glow of the Lighting orbs in the hallway. He'd been grateful that his assigned room wasn't directly across from one of the orbs, for he feared the Light would be too bright despite the brown fabric covering the portal.

Thoughts of Tins and Riln continued to dance in his mind—more than anything, the question of why Tins had waited until just then to attack him. He also wondered why Janis was sent after all, if Tins was already there to watch him for Watchlight. At length, Marric was wide awake and figured it would do him little good to stay in bed when he had yet to tell anyone of his vision last evening.

Marric jumped up, rushing to gather his things. With a grumble, he instinctively reached for the flint to get his candle started, then gave up when he didn't feel it right away in the dim light. Sighing, he summoned a miniscule orb of Light, then left it hovering above his head. The Light was small, but it pierced the darkness of his room easily enough for him to gather his clothing. While he dressed, he noticed a dull rumble echoing in the hallway outside of his door. Just then, a few voices grew louder as they moved toward his room.

"I can't believe we just have to *pick* someone without even knowing about them," a woman's voice complained.

"Yeh're jus' sad tha' we don' get a break from the chores fer a bit. Speeches and whatnot ain't good fer nothing save fer procrastinatin' a job," a man replied.

Marric heard their voices retreat, and he wanted to throw open his curtain to chase after them but thought better of it. After emerging in the lit stone tunnel, Marric could tell that the dull rumble was a large group of people. Though he couldn't tell exactly the size of the numbers gathered, he knew it must be a lot. Fussing over his tunic for a moment, he tried to walk toward the main hallway where the noise originated. It wasn't long before he was forced to slow down, given the density of the travelers moving in the same direction. Claustrophobia twisted his insides as he found himself wedged between two women. He blushed, the women's arms and chests brushing against him as they, and the collective group around them, tried to push their way into the main chamber.

Soon Marric was ushered into the large cavern, the cacophony of conversations deafening him from the massive group of people. Over the last six months, he'd grown a bit, having gained a few finger widths in his height, but he still was shorter than many of the Evenir members. By straining himself, he could hear a man speaking over the noises, though he couldn't hear what was being said. More bodies pressed inward, Marric now feeling more uncomfortable as at least half a dozen men and women pressed into his body, movement slowing as more people piled into the room.

His chest started moving rapidly as his breath sped up, the stress getting to him. Marric had no idea what drew so many people into the main cavern all at once. Before he could ask the person next to him, he heard someone shout something about the vote. When he'd last heard, the vote for leadership wouldn't be for a few more days. Had something happened to push up the actual event?

Frustrated that he couldn't hear anything above the loud noise, Marric covered his ears, trying to block out the shouts and grumbles. The dense group paused, and Marric was no longer driven forward by the flow. He could feel the air heating as sweat sprouted at his brow and dripped down his back. Until now, he'd not realized how anxious large groups of people made him. He wanted to scream, to tell everyone to back away, but he knew that wouldn't do anything. Instead he tried to calm himself, breathing as deeply as possible despite the muggy and limited air between all the bodies.

Concentrating, he focused on the room around him, then let his eyes fly open, filled with Light. All the stress and sensations from his body dulled tremendously as his vision-form launched upward. With a slight glance backward, he made sure that the throng of people wouldn't accidentally knock his body over. He didn't know what would happen if he did get pushed over, but he guessed it would pull him back to his body. The buzzing in his mind pressed inward as he saw his own face, eyes glowing bright blue, hands still covering his ears. The world twisted and spun from the oddity of seeing himself before he forced his gaze away. Just as he did, he noted a few agitated people around his body glaring at him as they inched away.

Satisfied, he turned to look forward. At the front of the massive crowd stood tables set together in a wide format, a few chairs sitting atop them. In one chair sat the man he'd seen just yesterday in this very cavern. Gallin, he remembered his name now. In another sat Janis. Her hands gripped her knees so hard that her knuckles shone white, the tendons in her hand protruding so far that small caverns appeared on the back of her hands. Even though her hands betrayed her true feelings, her face remained impassive. Marric couldn't help but marvel at the fact that her body language gave anything away. When he'd first met Janis, she was as difficult to read as a stone.

Avryn stood in front of the third chair, hands cupped over his mouth as he shouted to be heard over the crowd. His attempts remained unsuccessful as he continued to be drowned out. Janis looked from Avryn to the crowd. Suddenly, her hands relaxed, and she changed to a look of annoyance. With a casual movement, Janis summoned a small ball of light, holding it aloft with her right hand. The ball flew upward without her even making a motion with her arm. Though it was difficult to see, Marric suspected that the slight increase in the Light's intensity meant she Moved the orb. It flew silently upward until it slammed into the ceiling overhead. A deafening crack erupted as the orb, apparently a Destroying one, connected with the stone, shattering a small area. After shouts of fright, the crowd grew silent at once, so quickly, in fact, that it was jarring to Marric.

Gasps and whispers echoed as the rocks fell, Shields popping up randomly as the Lightbearers with the ability tried to protect themselves. Just before the falling debris and dust could hit the crowd, a massive Shield, large enough to cover all those directly under the damage, appeared to block it all. Marric turned to see Janis holding her hands outward. He gawked at her for a moment before he composed himself, looking around sheepishly, feeling grateful that no one could see him at the moment. Janis had always reacted so negatively to Lightbearing powers, and though he'd heard what she'd been able to do in Stilten, he still couldn't believe it. This marked twice in the past couple of days where she'd openly used her abilities without a second thought. Gone was the veiled and private assassin, Marric supposed.

Avryn shot Janis a pointed look. He must not have approved of her methods. Though murmurs and quiet conversations buzzed throughout the crowd, they no longer masked Avryn's voice.

"Citizens of Evenir! I thank you for being here today. As it stands, only those present are able to vote, as per the conditions when the organization was formed years ago. Under normal circumstances, we would allow a few days of meetings, time for each candidate to hold speeches to persuade you to support their candidacy, but I fear we don't have the luxury. Only yesterday insubordinates, allied with parties we still don't know, attacked one of the candidates during a sparring session."

Janis shifted in her seat. Her normally stone-faced expression broke, likely intentionally, as she frowned at Avryn's comments. Somehow Marric knew what the look meant. It was the first time he'd heard of any attack, since he'd been consumed with the vision in his own room, but he suspected that Janis knew who was behind whatever the attack was.

"Though we apprehended the individuals involved, they have yet to reveal their intentions. It became apparent that new leadership should be selected as soon as possible so the true and fair punishment could be applied to those who are guilty. Voting will occur today, and only today. There will be no recalls or recounts once your vote is cast."

Marric couldn't help but wonder who else was unfamiliar with the proceedings. He didn't know how long it had been since Magness had taken over the organization. His memory sparked at the realization that the last vote would have been who should replace his mother as leader. A feeling much like homesickness burrowed into his gut at the thought. He was still affected by the conversation with his mother the night before.

"Given the circumstances, however, I think it's prudent to allow each candidate some time to speak for themselves, say, a few minutes each, after which the voting will proceed," Avryn said.

A tug on Marric's consciousness startled him, and he promptly reached out to his body below. Vaguely aware of something touching his arm, he spun backward, his mind somewhat panicked to see what it was. Standing next to his body was the same girl he'd run into the day before. Her reddish hair, wavy and thick, was tied back in a ponytail with a blue piece of fabric. She wore a normal brown dress, like most of the women. He watched as she warily inspected his eyes, then shook his arm once more. Cringing at the odd sensation of being able to see her touching him and feeling it as if from a distance, he focused on his body, the world spinning around him until he could feel everything again. Gasping, the pressure behind his eyes disappeared and he turned to look at the girl.

"Uh, hi, Miredith," he said.

The girl jumped, releasing his arm.

"Fog it, what were you doing?" she asked, exasperated.

Marric couldn't help but blush, though this time he didn't have the separation from his body to mask the sensation. Miredith noticed and covered her mouth to hide an obvious smile.

"I was—I just couldn't see anything, so I was watching from up there," Marric replied, pointing upward.

Miredith looked at him as if what he said made no sense whatsoever before she raised a brow. "Clever, I guess. My mum's a Seer, but I don't think she's ever done anything like that before. I'm kind of impressed."

The girl poked him in the arm with a sharp finger, Marric squirming at her touch. "I'm even more impressed that you remembered my name," she said, grabbing his upper arm again.

The tingling intensified under his skin, butterflies forming in his stomach. His brain got a little foggy and light before he shook his head, coming back to reality. He could hear Avryn saying something, but he'd stopped listening now that he was distracted by the girl right next to him.

"Uh, yeah I guess so. You're the first—girl to talk to me since I've been here." Marric winced, realizing how silly his comment probably sounded to her. Face hot once again, Marric spun to look forward, standing on his toes to try to see over the taller people in front of him. Miredith seemed stunned next to him. He refused to look in her direction, afraid that his lack of experience with girls would embarrass him more than it already had. The girl eventually withdrew her hand from Marric's arm, but her motions were slow, deliberate. It felt as if she reluctantly moved, not wanting to stop touching him.

"—know I've been here for many years, more than most of you, I'd say," Avryn was saying. "We've grown in numbers and in strength, and I believe that we can continue to thrive as friends and family of Lightbearers for years to come. In time, we'll help Lindrad and the monarchy understand our place in society. In short, my experience in working with Talatha and my position as Magness's second puts me in the uniquely experienced position to lead Evenir."

Avryn's words hung in the air as Marric processed them. He was too stunned to do anything but stare at the back of the head of the man standing in front of him. Not once in the past few months had Avryn indicated that he'd worked so closely with his mother. His hands ached and he realized he was clenching them tightly, heat resonating in his chest, heart racing. The anger had crept up on him. All at once, whatever he'd been worried about with Miredith diffused as if it had never been there.

Apparently sensing his agitation, Miredith reached out and cupped her own palm over his clenched hand. For some reason the action made him relax. Though he couldn't explain in words why he felt so frustrated at the revelation, the feeling was potent. He suspected this wouldn't be the first time feelings around his mother would invade his mind for a while. Talking to her had rehashed so many things that he didn't know existed within himself.

"And now Janis will speak," Avryn declared before sitting down.

The taller people before Marric had shifted just enough that he had a view of whoever stood near the center of the makeshift platform. Janis stood tall and seemingly unabashed. For a moment she just scanned the crowd. The idea of Janis giving a speech to even a small group of people seemed ludicrous to Marric, but here she was, before thousands of people, ready to say who knew what.

"I think it's safe to say that you all know my past. You know who I was, who I am. Still, to clear any confusion that may remain about me, I am and will always be an assassin," Janis said frankly.

Marric squirmed, listening to her. While she was confident as she addressed them, she sounded awkward and clunky compared to the eloquent speech given by Avryn.

"But I've been chosen to be something else, something more. Brevity is, in my opinion, one of the greater traits in a person when it comes to communication, so let me say this. Lanser, against his better judgment, chose me, of all people, to be the wielder of his powers. While many of you hold only one or two abilities, I hold all seven. Livella and I," Janis said, gesturing to a mousy-haired woman standing below the table to her left, "hold Ugglyn at bay with a pact created by Lanser years ago. I hate to say that we are no longer safe from the anti-god, and while I can't speak for why you should choose me to lead Evenir, know that whatever my place is in this organization, I am the person best equipped to deal with the threat of Ugglyn."

With that, Janis pivoted on her heels and returned to her seat.

"Well, that was—unexpected," Miredith said next to him.

Marric squirmed inside. Janis had a way with words when it was obvious she held the upper hand, but that likely only happened when she was conversing with a smaller group of people.

"Yeah, she's—not a woman of many words," Marric replied.

He'd forgotten that the girl had grabbed a hold of his hand, likely distracted by the awkward nature of Janis's speech, but she tugged firmly on the grip, making him turn her direction.

"Wait, you *know* her? I mean, I know that she came here at about the same time as you, but you seem to know her better than I thought," Miredith pressed.

Marric shrugged. "Janis was the one to reach me first in my hometown. I've been with her, for the most part, for the past six months or so. I can't say that I know her *that* well," he replied.

Miredith gawked at him, and he couldn't help but notice how pretty she looked when her mouth fell open like that. His eyes wandered up to her red hair, lingering there for a moment before he let them move downward. Forcing himself to stop, he cleared his throat and faced forward, where the other man stepped up to the center of the stage.

"I have so many questions for you, I don't even know where to start," Miredith said eagerly, but Marric ignored her, pointing upward at the man who meant to speak. She rolled her eyes at his reaction and turned to watch as well.

Gallin appeared to be a hardened man. He stood taller than Avryn, his blond hair cropped sloppily and mussed in many directions. Somehow it made him look more serious and fierce rather than a fool. Marric shifted on his feet as murmurs rumbled through the crowd at the sight of him.

"Evenir is on the path to death," Gallin began, "and I know tha' yeh all can see it. I mean no disrespect t' those 'oo led Evenir 'afore now, fer they helped us be wha' we are today. But yeh can't deny tha' Watchligh' grows stronger each hour. It's only a matter o' time 'afore they march on Terris Green. The best defense is a good offense, and I fink we take the figh' t' them. We can only live in peace if we know tha' they won't pose a threat to us. I plan to lead us in tha' direction. We use our abilities to overtake Watchligh'. If wha' they've said about Riln is true, then attacking them now is the best time to do i', while they're scrambling withou' leadership."

People around Marric whispered, some agreeing with the man. Marric's skin chilled. Until now, he'd assumed that Avryn would be the most likely person to become the next Evenir leader, but based on the reaction of the crowd, he wondered how true that was.

Gallin bowed slightly before returning to his seat. Marric knew he wasn't the only one perplexed by the man's speech. When he'd seen him a few days ago, battling Avryn on the same platform before, he'd seemed so brash and unreasonable, but even Marric couldn't deny how logical he sounded.

Avryn returned to the stage as the noise rose again in the large chamber. By now, the air was hot and muggy, and Marric could feel the sweat forming everywhere on his skin. His shirt stuck to his back with it. Licking his lips, he tried not to be distracted by the horribly uncomfortable sensation. Then Miredith placed her hand on his wet back and he tensed.

Lanser! She'll think I'm disgusting! Marric thought, panicked.

Glancing in her direction, he noticed how impassive her face remained. He'd just met the girl yesterday and already she was touching him as if she was a dear friend or courting him now. His body continued to react to the girl's touch, his heart pounding faster in his ears so that he had to strain to hear Avyrn.

"The voting proceeds now. On either side of the cavern there are two short rows of tables. At the first, you will get your token to cast your vote. These are Conjured for you upon arrival and will have your name and a symbol unique to these proceedings. If any Conjurers try to create their own token, we will know they are false," Avryn explained.

Marric wasn't familiar with the politics of the Lindradian government, but he knew it was a monarchy. The king of Lindrad wasn't chosen in this way but came from birthright, yet Marric knew there was a panel of scholars chosen to advise the king in his decision-making. These were selected from the populace of T'Arren Vale, though he didn't know how that worked. To see Lightbearing used as a part of the vote wasn't altogether surprising, but it did seem tedious.

"After casting your token into the basket for your candidate, you will proceed down the hallway closest to your table. We set guards at the exits to prevent anyone from reentering and voting once more. This cavern will be closed off until the final tally is read, after which the Shield will be removed from the entrances returning to the cavern."

Conversation erupted behind Marric and he turned to see what the commotion was. A few shouts from one of the four entrance tunnels to the cavern they stood in pulled his attention that way. A flash of blue light announced a Shield sprouting over the opening to the cavern, closing it off. His stomach twisted as two more Shields blocked the way in on the others. The final tunnel had a few brown-cloaked figures gesturing to those still in the opening until it was completely emptied. Marric turned away, guessing that the tunnel likely held a large number of people who hadn't wanted to press themselves into the crowd to listen. Now they were being forced to move out of the tunnel.

"As soon as the final entrance is emptied, the Shield there will also make sure that no person may reenter to cast their vote. We will continue until everyone has chosen and the three candidates have cast our votes. Let's begin!"

Miredith wrapped her arm around Marric's again. He marveled that someone could be comfortable touching another person they hardly knew in such a way. This close, he could smell a floral scent coming from the girl's hair, likely whatever detergent she used when she bathed. The butterflies intensified in his gut so much that he thought he might double over from the discomfort. Instead he tried to breathe in the wondrous smell of her hair without her knowing. The feat proved to be more difficult than Marric expected, and he ended up choking for air a couple times when he attempted to suck in too quietly. She didn't appear to notice, much to his relief.

"So who are you going to vote for?" she asked him suddenly.

Given the concentration he'd needed to employ for the past few minutes, he didn't register the question that came from her mouth for a few moments. He blinked, trying to come back to reality.

"Oh, I—" Marric paused, realizing that he'd not thought the vote through. For some reason he'd not considered himself able to vote, having just arrived at Terris Green only recently. Though he'd lived here for a decent amount of time, he still felt new, almost like a visitor to the compound. Yet he'd been ingrained in the organization as well as any. Marric kept his face forward to mask the growing blush in his face, then shook his head.

"I still haven't decided," he finally said.

Miredith sighed next to him, patting his upper arm with one of hers.

"Well, you don't have a lot of time to think about it. We'll be up there before you know it. Everyone's moving so quickly," she pointed out.

Marric was surprised to see that what she said was true. The throng of people in front of him was moving forward at a regular pace, and Marric couldn't help but marvel that the process could be progressing that rapidly.

"Me? I think I'll vote for Gallin," Miredith said.

Shock ran through Marric at her comment. His emotions continued to swirl within him, Miredith's constant touch distracting his ability to know much else, but a small ember of anger welled up somewhere inside. Marric, while somewhat annoyed at his inability to focus, ultimately was thankful that her touch and the burning sensation within him prevented him from sounding too harsh.

"How? You truly think that he would be a better leader than Avryn, the man who's served the leader for so many years?"

Miredith shrugged, the motion tugging him toward her slightly given her tight grip on his arm.

"It's not that. I like Avryn. I would agree that he's the most equipped to lead us, but I wouldn't mind us taking some action first, if you know what I mean. Watchlight could attack any time, why not get them first?" she replied, looking down as if she was ashamed.

Just before Marric could open his mouth, another person bumped into him on his other side. Exasperated at being touched far more than he was used to, he turned to glare at whoever it was, only to find his friend smiling broadly at him.

"Mar! Can yeh believe it? I can' believe 'ow cool this is!" Crents said, beaming.

Flustered, Marric nodded, taking in the sight of his friend. The normal Crents, sheepish, shy, reserved, was apparently replaced by a well-kept boy who walked with confidence.

"Yeah, it's crazy," Marric replied. "It's only been a few days, Crents. You already look so different."

Crents smiled broadly. "Trainin's been going right good s' far, I've been told at least. They said I was a natural er sumthin'," he replied before leaning over Marric to glance at the girl there. Crents stifled a laugh before eyeing Marric. "'Oo's this? Go' a new girl?"

This time there wasn't a place to hide his blush.

"She's not my girl!" Marric said hastily, tugging on his arm in an attempt to break Miredith's iron grip on him. She held tight, apparently unfazed by his action.

"Not yet at least," Miredith replied. "Name's Miredith. I've been here my whole life. My ma and pa got married and had me here."

Marric's mind whirled. Until now, he'd only guessed that most of the people here were brought along when they Awakened. He'd seen kids and other teenagers around, but it never dawned on him that the kids may have been here since birth. Shivering, he imagined a life without easy and constant access to the outside forests, a place to get fresh air and explore.

"What's yer power, then?" Crents asked her.

"I don't have one," she replied.

A pit formed in Marric's stomach. He didn't care that she wasn't a Lightbearer, but he looked at her sharply, wondering if the question offended her. She appeared unbothered still.

"My mum's a Seer. Dad was a Shielder before they killed him." Her tone changed to a somber one, laced with a bit of anger.

Suddenly, it made sense why she would want to attack Watchlight.

"Fog me, sorry. Din' mean ter offend yous," Crents said, wringing his hands in front of him.

There's the Crents I know and love, Marric thought.

He absently reached out and patted the boy on the back, trying to console him, but the moment soon passed.

"Looks like we're about there," Miredith said, finally releasing her grip on Marric's arm.

Relief flooded him at the return of his personal space, yet his pounding chest and butterfly-filled gut longed for her to come back. He tilted his neck, trying to crack the spine there in an attempt to bring his mind back to reality. The group of people around him broke up, slightly cooler air coming through the spaces. His sweat-stained brow and chest could feel the coolness as if it were a winter breeze. He sighed in satisfaction, his two companions doing the same. It seemed he wasn't the only one tiring of the muggy air and heat from the dense crowd. Just through the few people ahead of him, he could see a sturdy wooden table with some people sitting behind them. He recognized one of them. Turrin, the burly older man, sat between two women of slight build. Next to them, he looked like a giant. His white-and-grey hair was slicked to the side and his handlebar mustache looked perfectly styled.

Marric watched as the man held up his hand, a flash of blue appearing before a small chip of blue Light was left there. Turrin handed the small item to the woman he spoke to, then gestured for her to move past the table. The women next to him were doing the same. At length, Miredith stepped up to the table, where Turrin addressed her with his deep and merry tone.

"What's yer name, lass? Seen yeh 'round 'ere bu' don' recall yer name at the moment," he said.

"Miredith, sir," she replied, curtsying slightly.

"Ah yes, yer the kid o' Ghrinelda, no?" he replied, Conjuring another chip in his hand.

"Yes, that's my mother," she replied, taking the chip gingerly in her hand as if it would break. For a moment she stared at the object, clearly amazed at holding it and feeling its physical form. Marric watched, somewhat surprised by her action until he remembered she had no powers of her own. Thoughts of the first time he felt a Conjured object in his hands returned to him and he understood her reaction.

"Fine Seer she is, must say so. Go 'head, walk 'round the table jus' there an' cast yer vote," Turrin said, gesturing.

Marric let Crents go next, Turrin's jovial tone now directed at him. The woman to the left of the general finished with her patron, then gestured for Marric to move forward.

"Name?" she asked, her tone light and pure.

"Marric, ma'am," he said.

She raised an eyebrow at him, a slight smile forming on her lips.

Turrin chuckled heartily next to her, pausing in his explanation to Crents.

"Seems 'e's aged yeh quite a bit in jus' a few moments," Turrin said.

It was then that Marric noticed that the woman he spoke to couldn't be more than a year older than him.

"I guess so. I'll just take that as a compliment, I suppose," she said, making Marric blush again. He cursed at the number of times he'd blushed in the past hour. He thought he would have been past that now that he'd gained more confidence in himself and his Lightbearing. Apparently girls had a different effect on him.

The girl raised her palm, a flash of Light announcing the Conjured chip there, before offering it to him. Turrin, not even bothering to hide his mirth, finished his explanation to Crents while chuckling about his comment to Marric and the girl.

"Take this chip, and move just there around the table. There are two voting tables behind us. You may select any, for each candidate has a basket there," she instructed, then nodded.

Marric stood there awkwardly for a moment before he realized she was done. He started, then moved quickly to the side, his foot catching the table leg and pitching him forward. He caught himself on the table, the Conjured chip slamming against the wood and causing a loud clacking sound, which drew the attention of a few people around him. The girl looked at him, worried for a moment, before she put her hand to her mouth and looked away, clearly amused. Righting himself, he moved past the Conjurers' table to see Miredith there, arms folded and eyebrow raised.

"Enjoying yourself?" she asked, looking annoyed.

"I just tripped on a table, you think I had fun with it?" he snapped. His tone surprised himself, but he couldn't for the life of him understand why she looked annoyed. He'd done nothing but embarrass himself, not her.

Miredith rolled her eyes but waited for him to come with her to the baskets. True to her word, she tossed her chip into the basket with Gallin's name hovering above it in glowing blue letters. A man sat at the table with the baskets, scratching something into a short parchment as each person dropped in their Conjured chip. Marric couldn't help but glance in the baskets when he got there. When he glanced in, however, he noted that they had hardly any of the Conjured items inside. Even as he watched, one or two of the chips disappeared with a slight flash.

He recalled his training as a Conjurer and how even the most skilled ones could only hold a handful of items in form at any given time. Marric looked at his own chip, a sinking feeling suddenly reminding him that his might disappear before he could even choose someone.

"May I see your Conjure, please?" a man asked, startling Marric. He looked up to see a brown-haired man raising an eyebrow at him, hand outstretched.

"Oh, sure," Marric replied, handing it over.

The man inspected the Conjure critically before nodding in approval and handing it back to Marric.

"Go on, then," he suggested, gesturing to the table before him.

Marric looked back and forth from the basket with Janis's name to Avryn's, his nerves taking over. With a glance toward Janis, he offered a silent apology to her before tossing his chip into Avryn's basket. Within seconds of his vote being cast, the Conjured chip disappeared. He gulped, wondering what might have happened if he'd hesitated any longer with his decision.

Following the throng of people moving out of the unblocked exits, Marric caught up with Miredith and Crents, who were locked in conversation.

"Don' yeh feel kinna bad tha' yeh don' 'ave a power?" Crents was asking when Marric arrived.

Marric gritted his teeth, looking sharply at Miredith for her response. Surprisingly, she still looked unbothered by the blunt question.

"I don't need a power to use my brain, kiddo," she replied. "Did I care at first? Yes, I was foggin' angry when I didn't Awaken, but now I live my life just fine."

Crents nodded, inspecting his hand in wonder as if he were trying to unlock the secrets of his new life.

"So who'd you end up choosing?" Miredith said. Marric looked up to see her raising an eyebrow at him.

"Um, Avryn," he replied. "I trust him more than anyone else."

The guilt ripped through Marric once again at the profession of his decision. He'd come to trust Janis so much since he met her back in Wurren, but the idea of her leading Evenir seemed a bit over the top.

"I voted fer Janis. Did yeh see wha' she did back there? Amazin', i' was," Crents exclaimed.

Miredith shrugged, leading the three of them down a side tunnel. Marric still had some trouble knowing his way around the complex network, and he hadn't been in this particular tunnel for some time, so he just followed.

"This is the quickest way back to the cavern, but most people don't know about it because they aren't small like us," she said, inspecting Marric head to toe. "Though it may be a tight fit for you, I think you could probably squeeze in."

She led them through a few tunnels, and as they moved, the space became less and less populated. At one point, they were moving against the crowd as if they were headed back to the cavern where everyone was exiting. The strata on the walls here were multicolored, and Marric couldn't help but gawk at the beauty of them. The floor began getting slightly wet, and Marric felt nervous, his memory of the large river in Watchlight's compound coming back to him. He shivered, remembering how he'd almost drowned as his Seeing led him and Janis down the perilous torrent inside the mountain. Though no thunderous sound came from where they stood now, he did hear quiet trickling. He watched as the wet floor transitioned to small streams of water that seemed to come from nowhere. This part of the network was now completely quiet, as if no one dared disturb the beautiful designs on the walls or the busy streams running along the floor in various places. He paused, looking more closely at the wall to his right. Though the wall was wet, he couldn't tell where the water came from until he summoned a tiny Lighting orb. He held it close enough to see that the water seeped out of the pores of the rock as if the tunnel itself was sweating. Small drops of water came from all over this section of the wall and combined into the larger streams by the time they made it to the floor.

"How does it work?" Marric asked, his voice echoing in the empty tunnel. Until now, they'd remained quiet, Miredith determined to lead them down this unknown path.

"Hmm? Oh, I don't know, something about the rock being porous or something. My mom tried to explain it to me, but I don't really care," Miredith admitted. "Here, this is where we squeeze through."

She pointed to a small opening that looked hardly large enough for a medium-sized animal. Marric's stomach turned.

"You want to crawl through *there*? That doesn't look safe at all. What if we get stuck?" he asked.

"Then I guess you'll die there," Miredith said frankly before kneeling down and shuffling through the opening. She disappeared almost immediately, as the Lighting orbs above didn't extend their light into the small opening. Crest shrugged, then crawled into the same hole. He slipped through more easily, as if the entrance was meant for a kid his size. Swallowing, Marric knelt down on the ground, the wetness soaking through his trouser knees instantly. He shivered. The water wasn't cold, but the feeling of being wet reminded him too much of the times he'd been in the forest during all the storms on the way to Terris Green.

Hesitating only a moment, Marric crawled through the opening, the world falling to darkness around him. His back scraped on the top of the hole and he winced in pain. Though it stung, he didn't think the scratch was bleeding. At least he hoped it wasn't. The rising panic inside him threatened to make him stop in the center, but he pushed on, hoping that Miredith was right about the shortness of the tunnel. Sure enough, it ended within a few moments of him entering, the exit smaller than the entrance. He was forced to bend down on his elbows and shuffle through the end to get out. He'd been so focused on getting out of the tiny tunnel that it took him a moment to process the loudness of the path on the other side. Just ahead, the bigger tunnel opened to a larger one full of people moving to the right.

"And now we are right at the entrance. Looks like they just opened up the cavern again. I see the people moving. Come on!" Miredith said, gesturing wildly for them to follow.

Crents shivered, looking at Marric with relief. For some reason Marric assumed the small boy would have had no trouble crawling through the space, but his reaction indicated otherwise. The two exchanged a glance before chasing after Miredith. By the time they caught up, she was slipping into the crowd of people moving into the main cavern. Holding his breath, Marric followed her into the throng. He lamented the short time he had to recover from his claustrophobia before diving back into a tight space. He gasped for air, trying not to be overwhelmed by the mugginess of the space around him, now that he was once again surrounded by so many people. A tight grip brought his attention to his elbow. Miredith's small face was peering through a couple of women to Marric's left. She looked absolutely delighted by their circumstances, at which Marric marveled even more.

Tugging firmly, she coaxed him through the barrier of people to stand by her side. Marric was about to ask about Crents when his friend slipped through the group behind him.

"We need to get to a spot we can see better. I hate being short," Miredith grumbled, pushing through more people. Most of them didn't notice the three younger teens pressing their way through, but there were some who scowled at them as if they were a nuisance.

"We're almost there. Come on!" Miredith exclaimed, still pulling on Marric's arm.

His arm tingled again, exactly where her slight but firm hand grasped him. Her grip was a bit painful, but Marric hardly noticed since she was carting him through a situation he did not want to be in. At length, they emerged on the side of the moving crowd, a few last grumbles ending as Marric pushed through. The air dropped in temperature so sharply that Marric breathed in relief, trying to take the moment to recover. Of course, Miredith didn't award him that luxury before she was pulling him again. The girl moved to the stone wall, roughly cut in this part of the cavern, jagged spires about as tall as them jutting out of the floor next to the wall.

He watched in awe as Miredith pressed her back against the wall on the other side of one of the spires and shimmied her way up. She made it look so easy that his jaw dropped.

Crents laughed next to him.

"Sheesh, she's loik a wittle mouse, she is," he said before moving to follow her example.

Marric wasn't as surprised to see Crents perform the same action, for the boy was a known climber in Wurren. Shaking his head, Marric followed, positioning himself against the wall, the spire before him. He sighed, then slowly climbed his way up the natural-looking stone pillar. Grateful that it was somehow as easy as his two friends had made it seem, he got to the top, noting that a flat platform-like structure jutted from the wall just to his left. There Miredith and Crents sat, watching him with a bit of humor on their faces.

"Yeh might wanna learn t' climb better someday," Crents said, stifling a laugh.

The two of them broke out laughing. Marric teetered on the ledge as he tried to transfer his weight from the spire to the platform. Marric chose not to address the comment but instead change the subject.

"How is this even here? I haven't ever noticed these before," he said.

"Destroying is a cool ability, but it doesn't have as much finesse as something like Moving or Conjuring. My mum told me that when they blasted out this cavern the edges were tough to get smooth, so they left a lot of them like this. You probably never noticed because it's always so busy in here," Miredith replied.

What she said was true. Every time he'd been to this cavern it was crowded with people. He looked down where his legs dangled, seeing that the ground was only about the height of two men, but his mind still fuzzed at the distance. Shaking his head, he instead focused on the fact that the small platform barely fit the three of them. The spire they'd climbed sat snugly against his right arm, and if he strained, he could see that Miredith sat at the other edge of the flat spot. He shivered, grateful he had something to lean against. Marric's eyes wandered up to find Miredith staring at him. She looked a combination of annoyed and amused at the same time.

He blushed, smiling awkwardly. Miredith's eyes flicked to Crents as if she was trying to tell Marric something, but he wasn't catching on. Instead he just stared at her with a confused expression. She rolled her eyes, then casually placed her hand on top of the hand he had extended behind Crents to steady himself. His stomach leaped to his throat and he choked. Averting his eyes from Miredith, he focused instead on the group of people below them. His hand burned from the touch, as did his face, but he pretended like he didn't notice.

"Right good spo' yeh found, Mir. I can see everythin' easy," Crents said, his face full of wonder as he looked outward.

His words rang true, for though the main platform holding Janis, Avryn, and Gallin was ten men's height away from them, they could see everything. When he looked, he saw that Gallin and Avryn were just settling back in their seats. Scanning the voting tables, he saw Janis toss a glowing chip of her own into the middle basket. Though he was too far to read the label there, he remembered it being the one with Avryn's name on it. He watched her walk back to the row of tables and hop up with ease. She remained unreadable, as usual, but Marric wondered what thoughts she could possibly have being in front of Evenir.

Avryn stood and cleared his throat. This time, shoved elbows and hushed hisses brought the crowd to attention quickly. Janis smiled, likely recognizing the crowd's unease with the idea of her tossing out another Destroying orb.

"The final votes have been cast. In just a few moments, Narinda will read out the results of the vote. For now, my esteemed friends, I am honored to have been here as a candidate. Whatever happens today, know that I will continue to serve Evenir as I have for years. I suspect that my fellow candidates would agree to the sentiment," Avryn said, looking backward at Gallin and Janis.

They both nodded, but Gallin looked unhappy about the statement. Avryn's gaze lingered on Janis for a moment, lines forming in his forehead. Marric felt a chill, sensing that something wasn't right.

He didn't have long to think about it before Narinda, hair tied back in a ponytail, her large frames covering half her face, stepped to the front of the stage. It felt strange seeing her in this way. She looked almost clerical by the way she dressed, but he knew she was a fierce fighter.

With a gesture toward Avryn's chair, Narinda dismissed him from the head of the table. The formalities of the situation felt awkward considering how close Marric felt to Avryn and Janis, but at the same time it was encouraging.

"The vote has been counted, and as such, Avryn's temporary place as leader of Evenir is no longer intact," Narinda declared in a loud voice. With a sweeping gesture, she created three orbs of Light, all about the size of her head, then let them fly to hover a few paces over the heads of Janis, Avryn, and Gallin respectively.

"The majority vote, as counted by myself and validated by three others alike, falls upon—" Narinda said, turning on her heels to face the three behind her.

Her pause, while not altogether unexpected, felt like it would draw out forever. Janis's amused look had switched to a hardened glare as she stared at the woman. Gallin sneered, as if he knew what would come of the vote. Avryn maintained his friendly smile, but Marric could see his folded arms quivering as they waited.

With a sweep of her arms, the orbs above Janis and Gallin disappeared into nothing, leaving only the bright orb above Avryn.

"Avryn Trilanger!" Narinda said loudly.

Cheers erupted from the crowd around them as the majority heard their candidate had been confirmed. Marric relaxed, hearing the proclamation and knowing that the man sitting next to Avryn had no power any longer. A few scuffles broke out in the crowd, likely from those who had voted for Gallin. They were quickly apprehended by guards wielding spears of Light and dragged from the room.

With a smile, Narinda grasped Avryn's hand and pulled him up to shake it warmly. Avryn quickly dropped the handshake and wrapped the woman in a hug. Laughter erupted from the crowd, while some whispered and murmured about the informal interaction between the new leader and Narinda. It was Narinda's turn to blush, but she didn't pull away until Avryn allowed her to. Avryn's hand immediately dropped to grasp Narinda's.

"Thank you! Thank you for your support and votes. I am honored to have been selected as your leader. I have three important things to say," Avryn said, peering over at Narinda. "It's been known by some of you of my fondness for Narinda. I wish to declare the rumors true. We've been courting each other for some time and wish to make our relationship official."

More shouts and excitement came from the crowd. Marric felt Mireddith's hand tighten on his own for a moment before it released. He tried to ignore it but only found it possible when he glanced back to see Janis, watching tight-lipped as Avryn and Narinda kissed before the crowd. She didn't look angry, but for some reason she looked like she disapproved of the announcement's timing. Gallin appeared full of hatred at seeing the display, his arms crossed. He flexed his hands as he watched Avryn and Narinda.

After a moment Avryn raised his hands to gather the crowd's attention once more. When they didn't quiet immediately, Janis raised her hand threateningly. This worked to quiet them faster.

"Many of you may disapprove of our union, especially of the timing of my announcement," Avyrn declared. "While the vote proclaims the elected leader, I select Janis as my second."

Though more subdued, there were some cheers that came from the crowd. Gallin looked incredulously between the two of them, his anger growing with the revelation. Janis sat there, prepared for it but not looking altogether happy about the situation. She stood stiffly, bowing slightly and waving to the crowd. Marric couldn't help but stare at her, noticing how awkward she appeared before them.

"There is one more thing," Avryn voiced.

Marric's stomach dropped. Something was off. He'd sensed it the moment Avryn had stood to invite Narinda up to declare the winner.

"I now wish to exercise the right of abdication and step down as leader," he said, "leaving Janis as the new head of Evenir."

Silence.

20

Janis stared at Avryn's back as he stood before her on the makeshift stage. Her chest burned in anger at hearing what he'd just said. Despite her roiling emotions, she kept her face stoic to prevent the immense crowd from seeing her reaction. When the vote landed on Avryn, she'd been able to relax, knowing that at least as Avryn's right hand, she would be able to avoid the brunt of leadership.

Then he'd dashed it all to pieces.

Her mind reeled, trying to decide what her options were. She had just come to terms with the fact that she couldn't leave this Lanser-forsaken place, but she found solace in knowing that she could glide by, slip under the attention of most of the people, letting Avryn keep his position as is. Now that he'd thrust that mantle on her, she felt stuck. Gallin, unable to mask his own emotions, looked like he wanted to rip Avryn to pieces. The man clenched and opened his fist repeatedly as he stared Avryn down.

"Many of you know that this clause was put in place when a leader felt that they were compromised in a way that would prevent them from leading effectively. Given my assistance to both Talatha and Magness, and the nature of Janis's newfound station as Prime Lightbearer, it seems best for everyone if she leads us," Avryn explained before turning in her direction.

As he did, he pulled Narinda with him, just enough that Janis met the eyes of the studious-looking woman. She looked just as shocked as Janis felt.

So she didn't know about this either? How long has he been planning this? Janis wondered.

Avryn held out a hand, gesturing for her to join him. Janis saw Gallin redirect his anger toward her, the muscles in his jaw now just as taut as he still held his fist. Janis stood confidently, continuing to hide her shock and anger. The silence in the room was palpable to the point that Janis wanted to slip away to avoid the confrontation. Her bootfalls echoed from the table throughout the cavern as thousands of shocked faces watched her move. Looking outward, she caught the attention of Marric at the edge of the cavern. He sat atop a small plateau next to the Wurren boy he'd just brought back and some girl she didn't recognize.

His eyes were wide and he shook his head in disbelief. A look like that may have been discouraging to her former self before she'd become a hardened assassin. It showed doubt and a bit of pity. Even if Marric wasn't an open book, she could have guessed what he thought about all of this. With a slight start, she noticed the same translucent blue cord of Light that ran from her chest over the crowd and into his own person. A second blue cord ran from her off to the right, but before Janis could determine where that led, she was at the head of the stage. Her focus changed and the blue lines disappeared.

"While I am more than surprised, I accept your decision, and stand ready to lead Evenir to their peaceful future," Janis said loudly.

The words rang hollow in her chest. They didn't even sound anything like she would normally speak. Drawing on all her observations of Avryn and other leaders addressing their followers, she tried to adopt a similar way of communication. To help herself feel less like an imposter, she decided to create a persona, something that she could use as a disguise to hide the hardened assassin she was on the inside.

Breathing deeply, she smiled, imagining the woman she'd pretend to be to lead Evenir. She imagined Magness, wearing a stylish yet practical dress, sword strapped to her belt. She imagined her hair bound behind her head to show her face, showing her womanhood but keeping it reserved to show her strength.

"As indicated by Avryn before his unconventional announcements, I must select a second to be the leader in my absence," Janis said loudly.

Avryn's words echoed in her mind, and she looked over at him. He still held Narinda's hand tightly in his own palm. He smiled at her, eyebrows raising while giving her a slight nod. She knew what he was asking. This was why he'd told her to name him her second. It wasn't because he thought she could actually be voted as leader, but because he assumed he would be and then would abdicate the role to her.

Resentment formed in the pit of her stomach. Avryn's image flipped back and forth in her mind, his hair now pitch-black, face chiseled and holding in a wicked grin. The man standing there was Macks, the man she'd loved, the man who'd betrayed her in the end. Avryn's face returned to her mind's eye. He now looked confused at her pause. Her mind screamed at her to trust Avryn, to follow his instructions and name him her second.

"I name Harmel"—she paused, realizing that she didn't know Harmel's surname—"as my second-in-command."

The moment the words left her lips, Avryn's face fell. He stared at her wide-eyed for a moment before pressing his lips together determinedly and then nodding curtly. Changing his face to joy, he turned to the crowd. Now whispers and conversations ran through the cavern as people heard her words. The crowd began parting near the right side, and Janis could see a man moving down the aisle created by the many bodies. Janis's head swirled but she continued to hide it. Everything was happening so fast that Janis felt like she was watching a dream. She eyed the onlookers, wary of their reactions as Harmel proceeded toward the platform.

Her brain cursed at her, asking what she was doing and why she'd chosen Harmel to lead with her. She had no idea if the man had the same leadership and political prowess that Avryn had already proven. Janis realized she did not know if Harmel had *any* experience with the matter whatsoever. Despite the doubt and anger that swam inside her, Harmel's firm stance and stoic face seemed to bring her some consolation.

"Oi accept the post," Harmel's voice rang throughout the cavern.

He then broke out in a massive grin and turned toward Janis before speaking quietly.

"Ugglyn slag me, tha' was unexpected," Harmel said, then he wiggled his eyebrows. "Looks loik yeh get t' keep me 'round fer quite a while, don' yeh."

Janis continued to force her smile, pretending to chuckle at Harmel's joke as she realized thousands of eyes watched them. Then she reached out her hand and shook Harmel's own beefy palm. Right as their hands connected, Janis spotted movement behind Harmel as Gallin jumped from his seat. Time slowed down as Janis took in the information. In Gallin's left hand he held a small blue orb of intense Light. Instincts told her exactly what that meant. She shoved Harmel to the side, seeing Gallin's burning gaze locked on Avryn and Narinda just in front of her. Without hesitation, she flung her hand outward, a Shield springing up between Avryn and Gallin. She simultaneously Conjured a dagger in her hand and lobbed it at the roaring Gallin.

It all happened so fast that the surrounding crowd didn't have time to react before Gallin's orb slammed into Janis's Shield, the explosion flashing in everyone's eyes and a loud crack echoing on the stone walls. Right then, Janis's dagger slammed into Gallin's chest. Eyes wide, he fell to the ground in a heap. Cursing, Avryn let Narinda's hand go and rushed toward the fallen man. Janis dropped the Shield quickly, then ran to Avryn's side.

Gallin lay on the table there, grunting as he reached for the Conjured dagger protruding from his ribs. Blood pooled on the table below him as his eyes danced wildly around the room. A commotion sounded in the room, and Janis looked to see that blue flashes of Light cropped up here and there as scuffles began in the large crowd. Sympathizers of Gallin, Janis guessed, saw the altercation and decided to start an uprising.

"Harmel! Get men down there to subdue them all!" Janis shouted at her now surprised second. Face determined, Harmel nodded and jumped off the table, shouting orders to people around them.

"He can't die! That would not look well for either of us!" Avryn shouted over the rising commotion around them.

Janis nodded resolutely, knowing what Avryn meant. Without hesitation, Janis created an orb of Light and let it fly just over their heads. Based on the injury, she anticipated it would use quite a bit of energy to Fix this wound. She grabbed Avryn's left hand, shocking him for a moment before she gestured to Gallin's outstretched body. His face was pale and he looked clammy as he lay there, gasping for breath. Janis had intentionally missed his essential organs, anticipating the ill effects of his death. Despite that, she could tell they didn't have much time before he was lost.

"Together," she said before pressing her free hand on Gallin's chest. Avryn followed. Janis could feel a slight pulsing from the hovering orb over their heads. The same tingling sensation she'd felt when she touched a Lighting orb ran through her hands, enhancing the effects of her Fixing. Their joined hands glowed brightly and pulsed with the same rhythm as the orb above them. The open hole in Gallin's chest knit itself together, the blood disappearing from his chest. Somehow the Fixing extended downward, the blood disappearing from the table, leaving the wood there as perfect as if there had been no substance to stain it. Finally, the man's shirt sewed itself back together as if the fibers had never been separated.

Energy drained from Janis, not so much that it exhausted her, but enough that she noticed. Avryn shivered slightly next to her, and she assumed he experienced similar things. Gallin gasped and opened his eyes, face now full of terror rather than the anger he showed before. With a flick of her hands, she Moved the man over onto his stomach and Conjured a rope, the fibers visible but glowing with blue Light. Using knots she could only have learned from master-assassin Macks himself, she tied Gallin's hands.

"Watch him, don't let him go anywhere," Janis ordered Avryn.

Avryn nodded, but his tight jaw and narrowed eyes showed the betrayal he clearly felt at her orders. Even if she'd named him her second, he still would have had to listen to her instructions, but she suspected the request stung more than if he was in the position.

Janis rose to her feet, calling back her Lighting orb with a careless gesture. Ever since she'd come into her full abilities in Stilten, she could feel the well of power inside of her, as if it had always been there but hadn't been fully accessible to her until she knew how to reach it. Finding the first scuffle, she leapt off the table, vaulting toward the fighting men and women. With a quick motion, she Conjured a club, slamming the short weapon into the face of a dirty-looking man holding a Conjured sword of his own. He fell with a grunt, his sword disappearing as he fell unconscious. Right as it did, Janis noticed that the blue sword had taken on a purplish hue.

She didn't have long to dwell on that as another person, this one a woman, shouted and slammed a steel sword down toward her. The blade missed its mark, scraping on the stones. Another woman nearby shouted in fright. Janis dodged another blow, careful to throw a Shield upward as the attacker's blade flew wide, almost hitting an older man watching in horror from the side. The sword skidded off the solid Shield before Janis held up her hand and Moved the weapon free from the woman's hands. Janis took the attacker's surprise as an opportunity to jump forward and slam her in the gut with her fist. An elbow to her head made the woman drop the rest of the way.

Conjuring more ropes, she dropped them on the bodies.

"Tie them. Make sure they won't be going anywhere," she ordered a couple men nearby. With a start, they jumped to, grabbing the Conjured ropes and tying the two attackers.

Though she'd not Conjured so many things before, she could tell somehow that she couldn't create ropes for every one of the usurpers. Even now, she had a sense of how far away she was from the rope that held Gallin. Cursing, she looked up to the stage, where Avryn held the former candidate in an upright position. She wanted to shout to Avryn to Conjure his own ropes, but a rough hand snatched her upper arm. Hissing through her teeth, she spun to stab the attacker with another Conjured weapon when Harmel yelped.

"Lanser's bu', 'tis *me*, love," Harmel shouted.

Janis relaxed but tried to pull her arm away. Harmel held firm, but his face showed nervousness at his actions.

"Jus' sayin', yeh can' foit 'em all. The others 'ave it just foin, lookie," he said, pointing around them.

Sure enough, the scuffles were ending rapidly as the organized members of Evenir restrained those who had attacked. Within moments, the shouts, flashes of Light, and clashing weapons ended, though the commotion did not. Janis gritted her teeth, drawing the leader persona within her to emerge and sort this all out. She imagined the woman, the leader of Evenir, with her face and hurried to her spot at the head of the table. She knew she wouldn't easily draw the crowd's attention without something louder, so she shouted and created hundreds of Lighting orbs. The Lights zipped upward, hovering everywhere in the open spaces of the wide cavern. Though still unconventional and not nearly as effective as Destroying the ceiling, the action brought the crowd's attention.

"I know this has been an unexpected turn of events for all of you, and trust me, it's the same for myself. The best thing we can do is move forward together. I've seen Watchlight and the man who undoubtedly stands at its head. I've fought him before and defeated him. I promise that I can do it again regardless of whatever abilities he's acquired," Janis said. "If anything, know this. My years as an assassin have taught me plenty about survival, and I intend to make sure Evenir survives the coming days as I have my whole life."

There were many around her who nodded, murmuring in assent. She let her silence stand in the air, wanting her words to sink in. Janis couldn't be sure if her voice carried to the back of the crowd, but messages like this had a way of spreading rapidly. One thing she could not deny was her status as a famed and dangerous assassin throughout Lindrad. There were likely many here who disliked her for that very reason, but she refused to believe they couldn't find merit in the fact that she'd been successful. Fortunately, it appeared that her words were settling on the crowd. A man shouted out from somewhere, cheering her name. Her immediate reaction was to tense, ready for another attack, but when she realized it was someone agreeing with her, she relaxed.

That appeared the catalyst for more shouts and cheers for her short yet confident speech.

Raising her arms, she kept her head held high. Her head screamed at her to run, to hide. She longed to be watching from the crowd, slinking through the dense group of people and doing background work for the person who stood at the head.

I can't be that anymore, Janis told herself. *Tryvv told me things need to change, that I need to change. I'd better start somewhere.*

Though her chest still tightened at all the eyes that watched her from the crowd below, she exclaimed again. At first she was drowned out by the cheers and shouts, but the people quieted quickly at the sound of her voice.

"Citizens of Evenir! The best thing you can do today, and for the next week, is return to normal. Our Shielders will continue to block Evenir from Watchlight's view. They cannot find us before we find them," Janis said. She didn't even know if the words were true, but she assumed they were considering the fact that Watchlight hadn't invaded them yet.

"Those apprehended will face trial and sentencing within the next day. For now, please live your lives as normally as you can," she pleaded, then waved her hands in dismissal.

The crowd broke into hundreds of conversations, the sounds echoing loudly on the stone walls and ceiling of the cavern. As people filtered out of the cavern, Janis noted Harmel ordering those apprehended be gathered at the wall to her right. She thanked Lanser that he'd already proven capable, more so than she might have thought. He'd always been a silly man but not just once had he shown his hardened nature in precarious situations.

Trying not to appear too eager to leave the stage, Janis lingered before turning to look at Avryn. The man stared at her, his mouth slightly ajar.

"That was—very unexpected," Avryn said.

He still didn't look pleased by what had just happened but he didn't look overly angry.

"I guess you have time to settle down now that you've been relieved from your responsibilities," Janis blurted. She didn't even try to mask the annoyance that she felt at his betrayal.

Sighing, he pulled Narinda tighter to his side.

"Janis, I couldn't have told you what I was planning. If I had, you'd have fought me, you know that's true," he pleaded.

She knew it was true. If he'd suggested abdicating his role to her, she'd have likely argued, finding some way to ruin his plan before he could go forward with it. Still, the sting of the decision would be fresh for some time.

"It's done now. The best I can do is try not to make a fool of myself as I figure out what in Lanser's name to even do here," Janis said, nodding to Narinda. "But why would you announce your courtship at the same time? Aren't you concerned it would make you look weak?"

The move was bold for more than just placing the mantle of leadership on her. Because he started with his intent to marry Narinda, it appeared that he abdicated his leadership for a woman more than anything else. Whether that was true or not, Janis didn't care, but that's what it would seem to all those present.

Avryn shrugged.

"I don't care what they think, though I think you are judging the people here a little too harshly. They know me and my political skills. Honestly, I'd be more concerned about you. Though I hadn't discussed my plans with anyone, I suspect there will be many who will be skeptical of you not picking me as your second," Avryn said, raising an eyebrow.

Janis scoffed.

"You know I'm not scared of anyone who might disagree with my choices." Her eyes landed on Harmel, who was now ushering the prisoners through one of the side tunnels. "Plus, Harmel has proven himself more than once, I think."

Nodding, Avryn followed her gaze to their ally, a smile forming on his mouth.

"He's a good pick, even if I think there were some other motivations in selecting him as your second," Avryn said.

The words slammed into her like a massive ocean wave. Almost staggering, she stared daggers at Avryn, her chest now burning with embarrassment and anger combined. Her brain came up with more than one biting remark to offer back to him, but she chose not to say anything for fear of someone listening. She'd just put on the show of her life, being nothing like her normal sarcastic self, and she'd keep that front until she could decide what her next actions would be, now that he'd locked her in this leadership role.

"I know of what you speak, but I assure you, no feelings save duty and preservation were employed in this decision," Janis said. Technically, that was true. Other than Avryn, Harmel and Shrell were the only other men she'd gained some semblance of trust with. Now that Shrell was dead, she couldn't have imagined naming any other person her right-hand man. The other generals had yet to prove that they wouldn't betray her.

Then why was her chest burning as she watched him?

Avryn closed his eyes, submitting to her commentary, before shrugging. "Well, that's that. I—"

Janis raised a hand, stopping him.

"You aren't relieved of your duties, soldier." She intentionally used the word because she expected it would annoy Avryn. Sure enough, he narrowed his eyes at her. "I would be loath to lose your skills and knowledge completely by having you step down. You will come to the war room now to discuss what's next with the other generals."

Looking somewhat annoyed, Avryn nodded.

"Lanser's might, do you plan to always talk like that now? I wouldn't have thought the power would get to your head that quickly," he teased.

Janis grinned.

"Let's call it a little payback for the scene you caused. You've put me in a pretty terrible place, you know. I can't run, neither could I abdicate in the way that you did. I didn't have much of a choice to take it," she said, glaring back at him.

This time he grinned heartily. "That, my dear, was the point."

Rolling her eyes, Janis found the closest person and gestured him over. The man stared wide-eyed at her, not moving at first. Sighing, she gestured again, more emphatically this time, and the man jumped, running to her.

"I need you to deliver a message to the generals. Tell them to meet me in the war room within the hour. It's time to make plans," Janis said.

The man nodded profusely before turning and rushing away. Janis relaxed, seeing that most of the people weren't watching her as closely now, though some gave her side glances as they moved about the cavern. It would take time for things to get back to normal, but Janis felt she could leave the procession without too much concern.

"Are there any other ridiculous clauses I need to know about in this supposed treaty set up for Evenir?" Janis asked idly as she moved past Avryn.

He and Narinda joined her as they started toward the tunnel that would lead them to the war room.

"Oh, I'm sure there are a lot that would make you roll your eyes, but we'll save that for another time," Avyrn said, jumping lightly off the table. Narinda stepped off after him, landing easily. She immediately turned and slammed a hard fist into Avryn's arm. He cursed, jumping back and rubbing the spot she'd hit.

"At what point did you think it was fogging ok not to tell me your plans?" Narinda said, looking angry.

Janis stifled a laugh, slipping off the stage and around the confrontation.

Avryn sputtered.

"Now, see here, I didn't mean to make you—ouch!" he exclaimed as Narinda slammed another hard fist into his shoulder.

"I would have thought you could be more romantic to me before declaring your intentions so publicly," Narinda complained. Janis admired the woman for her forward statements.

Avryn grimaced. "Unfortunately, I admit that wasn't technically part of the plan, but it seemed proper given the circumstances. I think more people were aware of it than we think, so I wanted to clear the air lest someone take it the wrong way when I abdicated the leadership," Avryn replied.

"And I think all that did was confirm the likelihood of Narinda being the reason you gave it up," Janis blurted before turning her back and hastening toward the cavern.

Avryn stood in stunned silence as Narinda harrumphed and followed Janis closely behind.

"I'll never understand men," Narinda said.

Janis chuckled. "Trust me, I know what you mean."

Her thoughts wandered to Macks before she pressed them out. Janis was vaguely aware of heavy footfalls following them, but she ignored the sound. She suspected it was just Avryn trying to catch up to their rapid pace rather than any immediate danger. Janis was grateful that Narinda didn't continue the conversation, for she had to think up what to do now that she was in charge of the whole of Evenir. Even just hours ago she'd not entertained the possibility of even coming close to where she was now. She'd assumed she was safe from getting the majority vote.

Narinda soon fell back to walk with Aryn, apparently forgiving the man for his massive public confession. Janis felt a little envious at their ability to let go and be together, but she berated herself. She wasn't meant for relationships. If she had, it would have worked out in some way with Macks. As if on cue, Harmel shouted from behind.

"'Ey! Wai' up fer me!" he called.

Janis didn't bother slowing down. She gritted her teeth, anticipating his cheery disposition and ridiculous jokes.

"Fog i', Janis, why'd yeh keep walkin'?" he asked, his breath coming out in loud puffs as he made it right beside her.

"You're young. I didn't think you'd have any trouble catching up," she replied.

His reaction, of no surprise, was to laugh.

She had the sudden and strange urge to embrace the man. The assassin in her screamed a warning, telling her not to trust him. No man was capable of loving her, it said.

"So wha' is the plan? Now tha' yer stuck wif me all the toim," he said, falling in step with her pace.

Janis pressed her lips together, painfully aware of the admiration that glowed in his eyes.

"I'm hoping we can figure that out together," Janis said, turning forward to get her intrusive thoughts to end.

"Fair 'nuff, I can ge' behind tha'."

They soon reached the outer library to the war room, the sofas empty. One man, this one Janis hadn't seen before, sat at the only desk in the room. Narinda stopped to talk to him, Janis catching slight echoes of the conversation. As his eyes inspected the books of the small shelves before her, she thought of the strange black volume she'd found with Macks. Having carried it for weeks, it felt strange not to have it at her belt. Still, the chaos of the past two days had led her to forget about it for a moment. Now the lingering feeling of protection for the book returned.

Before she'd left to chase the strange orange Light, she'd given Alsry and Rivelen permission to take it somewhere in the sanctuary to study it more. Janis marveled that it was only a couple days ago that the orange Light had exploded from the nether. Janis pushed on the wooden doors to the war room, her hand ironically falling directly on Talatha's face carved into the grain.

She tensed as she saw movement within the room, and she instinctively Conjured a dagger in her free hand. Laughter sounded from the room.

"Yup, she actually 'asn't changed, 'as she?" Turrin joked.

Two others laughed alongside the jovial old man, though one of them was more subdued than the other. Alsry and Varith stood near the war table with Turrin. They watched her with amusement as she walked into the room.

"Eleven years of living for myself, trying not to die, can't be quelled by the mere proclamation of leadership. If you didn't notice, it's not what I wanted anyway," she admitted, flinging her dagger at Turrin, whose amused expression melted to panic as he tried to dodge the incoming Conjure. Janis let it snuff to nothing just a few feet from the man.

"Lanser's name, yeh're still crazy as ever," he exclaimed, breathing hard and holding his chest for emphasis.

Alsry looked less than impressed. "You might try to create a better impression for us, since we are your closest council," she said.

"Oh, you know I wouldn't have let it hit him," Janis replied. "If I'd wanted to hurt any of you, I'd have done it already."

By then, Avryn walked into the room. He looked curiously at the flustered Turrin, then eyed Janis as if to say, "What did you do?" Janis replied with her own look, then turned back to those who waited.

"I don't have plans to demote any of you, though I guess I probably could if you don't like the way I do things," Janis remarked casually, to which Alsry scowled. Janis had had the distinct impression ever since she'd arrived here that the dark-skinned woman cared little for her, which Janis didn't mind at all. She'd found it was easier to get on as an assassin when people didn't want to be near you. Now she had to address the treatment directly.

"Given that I am new, are there any rules in the treaty about how many generals I may have?" Janis asked, looking at Avryn specifically.

"No, there isn't anything in there," he replied, still looking displeased with her behavior.

"Well then, the first thing I'll do is to appoint you to that role, Avryn. Is there a necessary ritual to solidify this? Do I need to place a sword on your shoulder or anything?" Sarcasm dripped from the words.

Avryn rolled his eyes before speaking. "No, that should be fine. I'll accept it if you wish, though we'll need to rearrange the companies of soldiers a bit if you intend on having me lead a company like the other generals."

Janis imagined the clerical work that must be involved with something like that and balked at even having to address it. Still, she held in her feelings to not cause any more issues with the generals. Fortunately, before she could respond to the suggestion, Trease and Yult, the man who'd been training Livella the day before, walked into the room.

"Sorry fer bein' late. We tried ter find Rivelen but din' find 'er quick. I sent a few scouts round 'bout t' tell 'er t' come righ' away," Trease explained.

Avryn spoke then. "Hopefully she makes it sooner rather than later. I fear we have much to discuss with—"

He cut off as Janis cleared her throat. Eyes widening, he pressed his mouth closed and nodded curtly. While she was mostly amused at the fact that he tried to step up and lead the meeting, she was even more tickled to see his frustration with the fact that she could silence him that way. She felt he deserved it for dropping the problems on her without revealing his intent. Janis let them sit in silence for a moment, taking the time to look each of them in the eyes. Of all the people present, only Varith and Trease gave her a direct look. Though Janis suspected they didn't approve of her leading anything, she at least had respect from them. The others either looked away or shifted uncomfortably as she gazed at them. Harmel, of course, grinned in his childish way.

After inspecting the others, Janis paused, then stalked over to the door silently. Her footsteps echoed in the room. Flinging open the door with more drama than necessary, Janis spoke clearly out the door, hoping that a courier would be outside. Sure enough, a young boy, perhaps only eleven, sat on the sofa looking around the room distractedly.

"Please find Marric and Livella and tell them to come to the war room at once," Janis said. The boy jumped as she spoke, snapping to attention and standing at the ready. His eyes took a moment to refocus on her, and as she raised a questioning eyebrow at him, he paled, likely realizing he hadn't heard her request.

"Er, Marric—yes, an' 'oo? Sorry, was a mite bit distracted," the boy admitted, his pale face growing somehow whiter.

Janis wasn't even mildly annoyed at his reaction or the fact that he had to clarify. Instead, she plastered on a smile, trying to adopt the persona she imagined of leader-Janis, poised and patient.

"Livella, the woman with mousy hair who you often see muttering to herself. The one immune to Lightbearing," Janis finally said. At the last words, the boy brightened, nodding profusely.

"Ah, yeah, tha' one, as yeh wish," he said before bolting out toward the main cavern.

The Lighter sitting at the desk there was trying to discreetly observe her by glancing over the tome he read, but he snapped his eyes away when Janis looked at him. She'd been aware of his gaze the whole time but waited until then to return it. His reaction represented what she imagined a majority of Evenir thought of her being their leader.

"May I speak, miss?" Avryn said as Janis closed the thick wooden doors.

"Oh please, there's nothing stopping you," Janis remarked, moving back to the table.

"With all due respect, do you think it wise to bring them here? Livella has proven to be volatile with her emotions, and Marric is still too young to be involved in politics," he said, looking around the room. Based on the number of nods he received, Janis guessed that most of them agreed with Avryn that the two shouldn't be invited to the proceedings.

Janis didn't care.

"I appreciate you speaking your mind, but need I remind you that there is more at stake here than just organizing a bunch of supplies and people? No one can deny the fact that something larger is going on. We believe Ugglyn may have broken free from whatever hold was on him. Now that the problem of leadership is out of the way, it makes sense that we talk about dealing with the anti-god," Janis replied.

Avryn's mouth dropped open, but he said nothing. Whether or not those present liked it, Janis wasn't illogical with the assessment, and they wouldn't protest that. She walked to the closest stone chair and sat facing the war room table. A few others followed her example and sat in the chairs nearest them.

"Ever since we read that strange text, which we all know must be from Ugglyn, there have been a lot of bizarre things happening. It's probably best if I take more time to look at it myself. If I'm this Prime for Lanser, then it has connections to me and Livella. Though I don't expect to learn anything new, I have to try. Next, we need to prepare our soldiers for battle. We can deny it all we want, but it's only a matter of time before we'll have to confront Watchlight. The best thing we can do is make sure it's on our terms," Janis said.

The generals watched her warily, though a couple looked somewhat determined. Turrin, having recovered from his shock, watched her with resolve, nodding as she spoke. His white hair, though disheveled on the side, looked perfectly slicked everywhere else. His matching white beard reminded Janis of his many years of experience.

Janis's mind reeled at what to do next. She felt ill equipped to handle such a large organization, not to mention the fact that she frankly didn't want to. She knew if she ran now, if she tried to step down, more of Gallin's men would come out of the woodwork and try to usurp whoever had to step up at that point. While she didn't have innate relationships with many people here, she recognized, at least tactically, how bad it would be if Evenir fell to civil war while Ugglyn was on the verge of breaking free.

Thus, Janis was forced to behave. She began deconstructing the problems in her head, reacting the way that she would if she were on her own. Time felt as if it slowed down momentarily, and she was vaguely aware of her eyes glowing. She let it happen, images of people and situations merging into her field of vision as if they were apparitions themselves. Somehow she knew that, while they could see her eyes glowing, the others in the room would slow to a crawl, that what would seem like hours for her would be seconds for them. One by one, Janis thought through their predicament, the leading of the organization, the problems they'd faced until now, and how she would deal with it if she were alone. Finally, her eyes dimmed, and she spoke firmly.

"Turrin, I need you and Alsry to lead the combat training of the soldiers. What that looks like and how it's done, I'll leave to you. I've seen you both fight and am confident that you will get them ready. Start immediately. Train anyone who is at least eighteen years old," Janis ordered.

They nodded, though Alsry looked angry at the command. Janis was surprised to not hear any disagreements about the age for training, but she proceeded.

"Trease and Yult, we need to reevaluate our defenses. Seeing how many fights broke out earlier leads me to believe that there are more defectors hidden among us. All it takes is someone with a silver tongue to increase that number to a situation we can no longer handle," Janis warned. "And make sure we have enough Shielders to hide us from Watchlight Seers. I can't help but shake the feeling that we are being watched."

"Yeah, no issue, we can do tha'," Trease agreed.

Yult nodded, his arms folded over his broad chest.

"Varith, how's our stockpile situation?" she asked.

Varith raised a brow, then leaned on the table. "We're fine on that front. Though I've not been historically the one to procure the supplies, I am familiar with those who have been involved. I'm guessing you want me to check and make sure we have enough weapons for our soldiers?"

"That's the main of it, yes. Unless we've already been training those who are eighteen, I suspect we'll need more weapons to arm them," Janis replied.

Varith waved his hand dismissively. "Oh fine, I'll do that. I could be more useful elsewhere, but I'll do as you ask."

"Narinda, I'll need you and Rivelen to join me as we look into the book a little more. There has to be something there that can help us know how to deal with our favorite anti-god. Collect every bit of writing from Talatha and bring it here," Janis said. "I don't love the idea of having to study more, but we need to find something."

Janis looked around the room, frowning to see that Rivelen still hadn't arrived. Her mind returned to the wary look that the Seer general gave the black book when they'd been inspecting it days ago, and Janis felt a lingering feeling that something was wrong.

Just then, the war room doors burst open to reveal Livella and Marric standing there. Janis noticed the same blue, nearly translucent blue line that attached from her to Marric. Oddly, Janis noticed a similar connection from herself to Livella. Knowing she didn't have time to analyze it much longer, she put the thought away.

"Thank you for coming," Janis said to the two. Marric looked at her with something that appeared to be pity, then nodded. Livella, aside from wearing the standard brown cloth dress and apron, had a staff attached to her back. Janis couldn't help but feel proud of the woman for carrying it around.

They each muttered something affirmative, then moved into the room, though Marric continued to look at her cautiously, as if he was concerned about her.

Janis ignored the thought, doubt creeping into her that she sounded ridiculous talking like this. In her mind's eye, she pressed the leader-image of herself, dressed much like Magness did, back into her subconscious. She told herself that she was just playing the part of leader; she was just being someone who the others needed to see. Each time she lost focus of what she had to at least pretend to be, her mind fuzzed and she felt silly commanding the others. Her eyes met Avryn's, and she spotted surprise there. He clearly didn't expect this from her either.

"You two," she said, pointing to the newest arrivals, "will join us in looking at the black book."

Marric looked terrified to hear it but mumbled something in agreement.

"You're a Seer, like Rivelen. The more eyes we have on the black pages, the more likely we'll be able to find anything in them. And it's obvious why you're needed," Janis said, pointing to Livella. "You've already shown you can read what's there."

Livella ostensibly looked unworried about Janis's ask, but Janis wondered if the woman was putting up her own front.

"Where is the book, then?" Janis said, turning toward Narinda.

The woman fussed with her large spectacles, clearing her throat.

"After you left me with the book, Rivelen and I took to studying it. Though we found nothing, she insisted on taking it back to her quarters to try something, though I do not know what," Narinda explained.

Dread settled inside Janis. For the second time since coming to the war room with the others, she recalled the way that Rivelen had been staring at the book. The persona Janis pressed upon her own mind shattered, the assassin Janis coming through as if she'd never been hidden.

"Fog it, you let her have the book *alone*?" Janis almost shouted.

Narinda, appearing a little nervous about Janis's reaction, looked from her to Avryn.

"You gave me no reason not to. She's been a general for years in Evenir. She's as trustworthy as anyone else here. Just because *you* have some differences you clearly need settled with her doesn't mean we have to emulate your behavior," Narinda replied.

Janis resisted the urge to shout.

"Then where is she?" Janis said finally.

Narinda opened her mouth, then paused, furrowing her brow. Janis cursed, then turned away from them. Her gut warned her that something was off. Rivelen was known to be tardy but not like this. Her mind locked once again on the image of Rivelen inspecting the tome fearfully just days ago. Even then Janis had thought the woman's reaction was unusual.

Focusing on Rivelen's face and elegant yet impractical choice of clothing, Janis let her Seeing take over as her eyes filled with blue Light. She couldn't believe that just weeks ago she was loath to even come close to such a power. Now she used it almost flippantly in the company of others. Though her brain screamed at her not to make herself vulnerable with people around her, she trusted Avryn and Harmel enough to stop anything that might come at her.

The world solidified into a fast-moving image of Rivelen riding a mount through the forest. The night was almost upon her, Stellan's red light forming above the trees. Rivelen looked terrified as she whistled and kicked her horse to run faster. Janis cursed, opening up her field of vision to look around her. Three others rode alongside her, a woman and man in Evenir brown robes, neither she recognized, then another man wearing black clothing.

Janis recognized this one. It was the very man Evenir had captured months ago, just after her own Awakening. The man sneered as his lone ponytail of black hair flapped in the wind around his shoulders. The group careened through the trees, dodging them here and there. Though they'd left some time ago, they appeared to be avoiding the pathway and made their own through the trees. While perilous, there was only one reason they'd take that course of travel.

They feared being followed.

Janis's mind reeled at the reason Rivelen would flee the compound with the Watchlight prisoner when it hit her.

He's taking her to Prost, Janis thought.

Right as she made the connection, Rivelen looked down at the pack tied to her saddle. Flipping the cover up, Janis caught a glance of the small book that had already caused so much trouble for her.

Rivelen looked around in terror, then gestured to one of her companions. The horses slowed to a trot, and the man next to her raised his hands outward, a Shield of purplish Light flying outward.

Then her vision went dark. Her incorporeal form felt as if it was moving very swiftly before she landed back in her body with a jolt.

"Fog it! She's run!" Janis shouted.

The others in the room looked at her, Narinda turning pale.

"What? How can you be sure? I—"

Janis didn't even bother listening to her. Instead she abandoned all memory of the charismatic-leader persona she'd clung to. Still cursing, she let her instincts take over.

"She's taken a Shielder; I can't See her anymore, follow if you can," Janis shouted hastily before rushing out the doors. Those behind her protested, but she ignored them.

The assassin was back. She had a traitor to capture.

21

Prost awoke with a start. For the third time this week, he had the feeling that he hadn't been in control of his body while he slept. Gritting his teeth, he skipped the analysis of his muscles and instead went to the source.

What have you been doing?! Prost roared in his mind.

Ugglyn growled in response. *I've work to do. Stop waking up and ruining it all.*

Rising from the bed, Prost realized he'd slept fully clothed, cloak and all. He hardly recalled what might have made him sleep in that manner, but he brushed it off.

We need to send men to retrieve someone, Ugglyn said suddenly.

Finding the request odd, Prost shook his head. As he exited the room, he noted the two guards who Neera religiously insisted be stationed there. Every time he saw them he was reminded of how little he trusted anyone in this compound. His mind locked on the assassin he'd spoken to the day before and he moved toward their dungeon.

I said send men to the forest. There are people I must see soon, Ugglyn pressed in his mind.

Once again, Prost ignored the voice inside, walking more swiftly.

Pain suddenly lanced through Prost's brain as the same cool, icy tingling flooded his head.

Cursing, Prost leaned against the wall, the cool stone there bringing some lucidity to his now foggy mind, but not enough that he could recover.

Try as you might to ignore my call, you will *listen to me!* Ugglyn roared in his mind.

The guards standing behind were suddenly there next to him.

"Sir, are you all right? What happened?" the one holding a Conjured spear asked. His face bore scars in a few places, most mild but enough for Prost to see that this man had seen battle. The other looked hardly old enough to grow any facial hair.

"I'm fine," Prost growled. "Still recovering from sleep."

The tingling intensified in his head, then pooled in his eyes, making Prost cringe from the discomfort. It didn't hurt, not like the pain that had just shot through his brain moments ago, but it didn't feel natural. Images formed in the air around him, just like they had the day before, showing him smoke-like statues of people, though these moved. A woman rode on horseback, face panicked as she pressed forward. Wisps of trees and brush formed and disappeared around her, suggesting to Prost that she rode swiftly through the forest. Another image appeared next to her, and rage filled Prost's chest.

Mert.

Scowling, Prost righted himself, using the firmness of the stone wall next to him.

"Anything we can do for you?" the same man asked.

Prost was hardly aware of their presence. The smoke images continued to move, ignoring any other physical object that shared the same plane. Even now, trees formed and sped through the two soldiers who stood before him, neither indicating that they could feel it nor were even aware of what was happening. Watching curiously, Prost saw the woman, one who looked familiar, reach down and open the pack at her horse's side.

Ugglyn purred in his head. *That's a good girl. Finally succumbing to my call,* he whispered.

Gritting his teeth, Prost suffered the vision for a few moments more before he pressed back in his mind, the tingling feeling receding from his eyes and head. Disappointment rocked his insides, though the emotion wasn't his own.

"I'm fine," Prost growled out loud before continuing. "Get me a contingent of soldiers. We've one of our own to save."

The men exchanged a curious glance, neither moving right away.

"Now!" Prost ordered.

This time the men moved instantly, the older-looking one pointing down the corridor where Prost had been moving. When the two had left him, Prost righted himself. He stalked down the hallway, trying to stand up straight lest any other passersby see him feeling tired. Frustrated that he'd slept all night but still felt exhausted, he made his way as quickly as possible to the dungeon. Of all the people he'd hoped to see with one of these Voidwoven visions, Mert was not one. Prost wasn't surprised to see that the man still lived, for he knew that Evenir killed none of their prisoners. Yet he still had hoped to hear of the demise of the irritating fool.

Amusement filled his chest, Ugglyn apparently finding joy in how much Prost despised Mert, but Prost shook it off, pressing his mind once again to get the anti-god to submerge back into his subconscious.

Soon, Prost arrived in the dungeon. Save for many pairs of guards lining the hallway, no other doors or obstructions blocked that way to the cells. Lining each of the walls, thick iron gates sat firmly in Destroying-blasted holes barring small cells. He hadn't been here when the dungeons were built, but Prost would have preferred to add extra physical measures to the hallway. Riln had instructed and trained each of the guards to kill anyone on sight if they tried to escape. To him, information-gathering was less important than a hostage dying.

"Where is he?" Prost asked one of the guards. The woman, clothed in the customary black pants and tunic, pointed gruffly to the third gate on the left.

"In there, been mutterin' t' imself all noit, 'e 'as," she said, sounding disgusted.

Even now, Prost could hear slight echoes of mutters and speaking. The sound felt eerie considering the circumstances. Prost didn't believe in anything ghostly or supernatural, but the echoes sounded all too reminiscent of Ugglyn's voice constantly in his head. A dim red Light shone through the gate, casting shadows on the hallway and the gate across from this one. Moving just before the entrance, Prost squinted at the bright red Light that emanated from a small orb hovering there. The Lighting orb was tiny, perhaps the size of a thumbnail, but the power that came from it caused Prost's eyes to burn uncomfortably. With a smooth gesture, Prost raised his own hand, summoning a large orb of swirling smoke, which he held up before him. At once, the Light orb nearest them snuffed into nothing. He let the Void orb disappear then.

The assassin fell silent.

"You say you know Janis, yet I know nothing of you or your history. Tell me, *assassin*, why you care so much about her." Prost's voice echoed in the stone cell.

Chuckling echoed back.

"I never said I cared about her, I only said that I knew her and could help you kill her," the man replied. "I also recall telling you my name, so if you'd please use that, I'd appreciate it."

While somewhat impressed, Prost's insides twisted at the man's brackish behavior.

"You act so bold, yet you know I can kill you if I want to," Prost mused, grabbing the bars firmly with his hands. The cold metal felt refreshing against his palms. He focused on the feeling, using it to aid him in keeping Ugglyn's constant pressing on his mind at bay.

Macks laughed again. "I chose assassination as my profession. You think I'm afraid of dying? A man like me expects to only live a certain number of years. Fortunately for me, I'm always too useful to kill."

The bravado of the man took Prost by surprise, but he knew Macks spoke the truth. Janis had proven more crafty than he had expected. Any edge he could get over her might be worth it. For a moment he thought back to Riln's intent to draw her to their side. Having her involved with Marric's Awakening was intended to be the "in" needed to convince her to use her skills in Watchlight's favor. Prost couldn't help but wonder—if he'd just left her alone, would she be the thorn in his side that she was right now?

"What can you tell me about Janis? What makes you think you know enough about her to kill her?" Prost questioned.

Through the slats between the iron bars, Prost thought he could make out a sly smile.

"I taught her everything she knows," he replied.

"Are you suggesting that you were some sort of mentor for her? Is there really such a thing with assassins? I thought you learned your slimy skills on your own," Prost jibed.

The insult apparently didn't offend in the way Prost meant it to, for Macks just shrugged and continued on as if nothing happened.

"Found her practically dying in the streets when she was a teenager. Didn't plan on teaching her anything until I saw her swindle a shop owner out of a loaf of bread without any trouble. That behavior had to be rewarded, don't you think?" Macks mused.

Anger filled Prost at the comment. At this point, he didn't think Janis deserved any amount of reward or respect. Prost slammed his hand against one of the bars, the sound echoing in the cell and the surrounding hallway. Macks winced, shifting only slightly but enough that Prost could make it out in the dim Light.

Ah, he fears dying, even if he claims he doesn't, Prost thought.

He had half a mind to leave the man rotting in the cell until he starved to death. He found that no matter how much of a show a person put on, they would buckle in the face of hunger. No person, in his experience, had faced an empty stomach and been completely confident in themselves.

We need him, Ugglyn pressed. *Let him free. He means no harm. Besides, I'll just mend whatever wound he attempts to inflict on you.*

Prost, not wanting to budge, tried a different tactic.

"Why come here? You hate the woman so much that you would kill her? Years of training didn't bind you together in some odd mentor-protégée way?" Prost asked.

Macks went silent for a moment before shuffling slightly, just close enough to the bars that Prost could make out his face.

"I work alone," the man said, ice in his voice.

Prost understood the message, but the coldness of his gaze lent him far more information than Macks likely intended to give. There was something there, but Macks would never admit it. Still, the fire in the man's eyes was something Prost could trust more than his words. As an assassin, he could likely mask whatever emotions he wanted to. It was just something they learned. But no man could fake that burning hatred.

"Besides, she took something of value from me, something I fear will get me killed if I can't return it," Macks said. His voice quivered, just enough that Prost knew he was afraid.

"What's so important that you would kill for it? I thought assassins cared little for things and more for the money itself?" Prost asked.

Ugglyn raged within him for a moment before the emotions leveled to something more benign, like annoyance.

I know of what he speaks, Ugglyn whispered inside. *Let me speak.*

"Assassin, speak, or I'll *make* you," Prost threatened.

"A book," Macks said, hesitating, "of the anti-god."

Prost's skin chilled at the words. He recalled Ugglyn insisting that he go back to Stilten, that he mount a rapid attack on Evenir, even though they knew only a general location of their lair. Somehow Prost knew that this is what Ugglyn wanted.

Intense tingling ran through his limbs, and Prost tensed. The anti-god pressed outward, the sensation much like Prost's veins filling with a burning solvent. Then everything went numb. His consciousness didn't recede into his mind like it had a few days past, but this was uncomfortable enough. He gritted his teeth until he couldn't feel those either.

"Yes, you are still mine, aren't you?" Prost's voice drawled, though now it sounded like another deeper voice was layered over his own.

Macks's eyes widened and he bowed suddenly.

"Master!" he said, shaking visibly now.

"I've watched from within this pawn, but he refuses to give me control, for now." Prost shouted in his mind, pulling on his own consciousness, trying to gain control again. He thrashed inside, trying to grasp hold of something.

"I'm—sorry, I didn't mean to lose it—" Macks sputtered before Prost saw his hand move in his peripheral vision.

Ugglyn stopped him from speaking with a raised palm.

"What's done is done," Prost's voice intoned. "You were not the only Seer I worked with while in the middle plane. Even now, a pet Seer just like you travels to meet us."

Prost's field of vision changed as Ugglyn turned to the guards stationed to the side.

"Open the cell, let him free," Ugglyn ordered.

The man watched with shock on his face but nodded. Prost wondered if the news of Ugglyn inhabiting his body hadn't spread as quickly as he thought it had through their ranks. Fumbling for the cell key, the man dropped the ring with a clang, reaching down and shakily retrieving them.

"Sorry, Oi'm tryna 'urry," the man said, finally grasping a single key.

Surprisingly, Ugglyn didn't appear altogether too annoyed. Still shaking, the man opened the cell, Macks still bowed down on one knee. Prost continued to search within for something that he could grab hold of. Just then, he felt it. One of his fingers felt chilled as his hand grasped the bar there. Seizing the feeling, Prost pressed with his mental might, trying to regain control of his fingers.

"Oh get up, you idiot, I won't kill you," Prost heard his voice growl, "at least not today. We will ride to meet those who bear what I need, then we'll return and—"

Something snapped within him and the feeling of his body returned with an overwhelming rush. Gasping, Prost's vision filled with darkness for a moment before his sight returned. Prost's view of the dungeon filled with smokey figures, a vision coming on unexpectedly.

I told you not to do anything foolish, Prost, Avryn's voice echoed in his mind.

He saw two figures, one a younger version of Avryn, the other a version of himself. Recollection slammed into him as he recalled the conversation. This was long before he was plagued by the voices in his head, and Avryn had Awakened to a Lightbearer unbeknownst to him.

They had it coming, Prost growled, grunting as the shadow Avryn wrapped cloth tightly around his upper arm.

Prost, there were five *of them. Did you really think you could teach them a lesson by yourself?* Avryn questioned.

What is the meaning of this vision! You waste my time! Let me out now! a third voice roared. Prost recognized it as Ugglyn's, but he was so entranced by the memory before him that he just ignored it.

I can handle myself, Prost's past self replied.

Prost watched the scene, nostalgia tearing away at any anger or fear he'd harbored over the past few weeks. He remembered this experience as if it were yesterday. Just before this, some others had been grouping up against some of the newer recruits and were threatening them. From the moment he joined the militia of T'Arren Vale, there had always been types like that. The more tenured soldiers called it "initiation," but Prost knew it had nothing to do with that. While he suffered it as a new recruit himself, the moment he gained enough combat knowledge and strength, he never tolerated it. Prost had, against his better judgment, stepped in when five of his companion soldiers took it upon themselves to enforce the supposed initiation.

Avryn sighed, the sound echoing in his mind as if from a distance.

I know how you feel about the initiation, but there's not much we can do about it, Avryn replied.

Prost's past self scoffed and turned angrily on his friend. He winced as the cut he bore on his upper arm twinged.

You would rather just sit there idly and let the idiots get away with it? The only reason they do it is because they feel inferior to most of the other soldiers. When you can't win the normal fights, you take it out on those you know you can beat, Prost said hotly.

Avryn cinched the cloth tighter, making Prost gasp in pain.

Oh, it's not that bad. If I hadn't come, you'd be without an arm, Avryn said.

Though the details of the smoky figure representing him didn't allow for Prost to see it, he recalled grinning at his friend.

I think part of me knew you'd come. You can't resist teaching inept soldiers a lesson, Prost joked.

Avryn shook his head, sighing again. *And there you are, once again knowing me all too well. Well, they got what they deserved in the end.*

This time they both laughed, which eventually turned into Prost wincing and cursing as his arm ached from the pain.

Are you sure you don't want to go to the infirmary? They'd be able to do a much better job of it than I can, Avryn said, grimacing at the work he'd done with Prost's wound.

You know how they respond to infighting, Prost replied. *They'll turn a blind eye when no one's there to see it, but if I go, they'll insist on knowing what happened. I've worked too hard to be kicked out now.*

Prost had been in the militia for years at that point. Though Avryn was newer, the two had become fast friends.

Fine, but don't complain if you end up dying from infection tonight, Avryn said, punching Prost in his good arm.

Prost sucked a hissing breath through his mouth, the blow still causing a jolt of pain in his injured one.

He watched, entranced by the events before him. While he couldn't say he enjoyed the random visions that came to him, this one caught his attention in a way he couldn't have expected. Since leaving the militia in the capital city, he'd been forced to come to terms with his decision, knowing that he had little choice. Either he ran or they would have discharged him for mental instability. Yet seeing this memory caused an aching within him so deep that he thought he'd burst. He'd faced Avryn more than once since they'd aligned themselves with opposite objectives, but each of those times Prost had numbed himself to the memory of their former friendship.

This one ripped through him.

If I die, then you'll be exposed as the shoddy medic I've always known you to be, Prost grumbled.

The joke caused Avryn to roll his eyes again.

Prost tensed as he remembered what came next. The smokey version of Avryn put his arm around Prost's shoulders, leaning in. As if a phantom was there within the room, the present Prost felt the touch of the arm. With no warning, tears started forming in Prost's eyes before he stubbornly choked them away. He unfocused his gaze from the images before him and checked to make sure those present couldn't see what was happening. To his surprise, they still appeared frozen in time, as if the vision stopped normal life from continuing while he observed.

If you die, then I'll have a rough go of finding anyone else to relax with, Avryn said. *By befriending you, I've isolated myself pretty well from the others.*

The smoky version of Prost nudged Avryn's arm off his shoulders, and Avryn leaned away at the reaction, mock surprise on his face.

Oh, come off it, you know well that everyone likes you. I don't get why you bother being anywhere near me. I'd probably do best on my own anyway, Prost replied.

And yet again, the dramatic Prost I know so well, Avryn mused.

This time Prost slugged Avryn, though there wasn't much in it because Prost recalled the sharp pain preventing from using his full strength.

For a moment Prost just watched, reveling in the memory, until he realized that Ugglyn was silent. Just moments ago the anti-god had been roaring in his mind to be set free; now he was nowhere to be found. The icy feeling dominated Prost's body, focused in his eyes. Until now, the feeling, while intriguing, had been uncomfortable and almost painful, but now it felt familiar as it combined with the past sensations and emotions of the memory.

Prost's past self paused, eyeing Avryn.

I am grateful for your help, Prost said.

He remembered how agonizing it had been to say the words. Prost was anything but humble, likely because of his wealthy upbringing. He'd been haughty and lazy, and still was, about how affluent his family had been, which was part of why he left them. Yet the learned behaviors of the ego couldn't be easily shed by simple combat training.

Wow, thank Lanser you actually have some semblance of a conscience, Avryn replied, sounding amused. *You're welcome. Now try not to do anything stupid for at least a few weeks. I fear we're getting too much attention.*

At those words, the smokey figures faded. As they did, Prost noted movement just behind them. Macks, the assassin, began moving again as if the odd vision Prost witnessed had not frozen him. The guard who'd opened the cell stood there, eyes shooting back and forth between Prost and Macks. Emotions still lingering from the vision, Prost cleared his throat, trying to focus on the facade that nothing was amiss with his mental state.

"As you can see, Ugglyn has graced us all with his presence. Yes, the rumors are true; he lives inside. But let's not dwell on that," Prost said. "As for our journey, well, as he stated, there's work to be done. You will go with us to retrieve our companions."

An image flashed through his mind of the woman he'd seen in one of his smoke visions. While he'd been somewhat distracted by the presence of

Mert, he had overlooked the fact that she must have been from Evenir. He'd known that Mert was captured and assumed they had brought him to Evenir's lair, wherever it was. It was unlikely that the man escaped of his own accord, which suggested that either the woman or one of the other companions came from there.

Which meant they could find Evenir.

Prost suppressed the urge to rejoice in the thought. Taking advantage of Ugglyn's absence in his mind, Prost thought of Avryn and their former friendship. Now that Riln was gone, the only thing keeping him from leaving this place was the being inside him. He doubted there was any way to extract Ugglyn from himself save for one obvious path.

Prost would kill Janis and be rid of the monster.

"Guard," Prost said suddenly, causing the man to start at his level tone. "Change of plans. We won't be sending a small contingent to get these people. Inform Neera and Jord to prepare our army for departure as soon as possible. We'll need supplies and tents for the long haul."

The guard stared at him, unmoving for a moment, before Prost glared even harder.

"Is there a problem, soldier?" Prost asked, though his voice was void of any annoyance.

Jumping, the guard moved off to follow his orders.

"With all due respect, won't it take longer to bring an army?" Macks asked behind him.

Though Prost knew little of the man, he knew assassins, so the words meant for groveling sounded more condescending than anything. Prost turned slowly to the man.

"Combat for assassins is much different than for armies, but one thing you probably agree on is that the element of surprise can give a person the upper hand. I have reason to believe that someone who once allied themselves with Evenir will be with that entourage. If we take our leave urgently, we can meet them and they can lead the way to slaughter Evenir."

Though Prost had little intention of truly killing every Evenir member, he felt he had to put up a front. He didn't think Ugglyn would be so merciful to say that he only intended to kill one person. Janis was, however, the only mark that mattered in this case.

Macks watched him, looking deep into Prost's eyes. When he'd first arrived at the cell, Macks wasn't scared of him, but the moment Ugglyn showed himself, the assassin's tune had changed drastically. Prost intended to use that intimidation to control him.

"And since you'll be coming with us, I suspect you'll have a lot to say about Janis and how we can kill her more easily," Prost said. "I also suspect you know what will happen if you've misled me in boasting the information you have."

With that, Prost gestured to the man. Normally, he'd have stalked out before the others in the group, but the last thing he wanted was an assassin at his back. Moaning sounded from the back of the hallways where some of the other prisoners lay. Prost guessed they had heard him release the assassin and were now vying for their own release. He had half a mind to let them go, for he didn't care about anything here anymore.

He had the distinct feeling that this might be the last time he would set foot in the lair, for if he left, either he would die or Janis would and he would be free.

22

Marric thought of Janis running out of the war room, a sinking feeling in his gut. She'd rushed out so quickly that only Avryn and Turrin were able to keep up with her, or at least he hoped they'd been able to; they'd been the two closest to the door. The conversation ended immediately, no one having anything else to say. Within a few minutes, they all trickled out of the room with the understanding that they would resume Janis's orders come morning.

Now Marric sat at a table between Narinda and Livella, the latter making him uncomfortable. Glancing sideways at the woman, he couldn't help but compare her to Prost, who still haunted his dreams. The scarred face had imprinted itself in his memory more than once, the earliest being when Jord had been taken by Watchlight. Marric had tried to put the events of Jord's kidnapping out of his mind, but thoughts of the boy crept up again. Marric had been tempted occasionally to try Seeing his former friend, but he knew that would do little good.

Narinda shuffled next to him, her face deep in the cover of one of his mother's records. He'd just finished explaining his conversation with his mother, and they'd all become quiet for a time.

"I'm sorry, but is anyone else having trouble focusing?" Livella said, leaning back in her chair.

Looking up from the page she was poring over, Narinda fixed Livella with an uncaring gaze. "You must not do much reading in your free time," she guessed.

This made Livella blush, though Marric didn't know why. He didn't find it embarrassing not to enjoy reading as a pastime. He didn't do much of it himself. He wondered if it was a woman thing.

"I'm having a hard time focusing with Janis and the others gone," he admitted.

Narinda pursed her lips, clearly unhappy with his confession. "For a new leader, I must say that's not the most responsible of actions, but it is what it is. Can't you try Seeing them?"

Shaking his head, Marric grabbed the closest book to himself and began flipping the pages idly.

"No, I suspect Janis is Shielding them," Marric said, "or at least I assume she is. I can't See anything about them at all, just blackness."

"Well, that's at least one thing they are doing wisely," Narinda said before taking the book from Marric. "Tell me again what your mother said in the vision."

Marric sighed. He'd told her at least three times since they'd come together this morning, and he'd begun tiring of the message. Still, he folded his arms, recalling the image of his mother. The moment he visualized her face, he had to resist getting choked up. He was grateful he'd lived most of his life without too much trauma from his mother leaving, but that seemed to appear with a fury now that he'd spoken to her. Focusing on the task at hand, Marric recounted the events with as much detail as he could. When he'd finished with the more menial parts, he stopped to think for a moment.

"She seemed very obsessed with Janis and the balance, which we've already heard about, then she mentioned the strange word that you already knew." Marric paused, straining to remember it.

"*H'ilvina't*," Narinda reminded him.

"That's the one, but what does it mean?" he asked.

Narinda shrugged, her eyes still focused on whatever record she'd been reading. While she watched the page, a couple people walked through the small room to the shelves lined along the far wall. Livella watched them warily, as if they might turn and attack without any warning. Narinda didn't even notice them come in. When they'd decided to begin this morning, Marric somewhat hoped they would do so in the war room, but Narinda insisted that she couldn't be in that stuffy room any longer. It seemed ironic for her to call the room stuffy, since the whole of the compound had little ventilation and could be described the same. In the past hour, he'd come to terms with their more public location for study. The two strangers grabbed a few books, then turned and walked out of the room, whispering and laughing about something.

"People ain't gonna bite yeh, hun," a voice said from the sofa on the other end of the room.

Livella started at the sound, then nodded to indicate that she'd heard.

The woman who sat there was by far the oldest person Marric had seen since being here. A majority of the people were younger or at least middle-aged. Though Marric didn't know why, he'd not spotted many older people at all. The woman here looked to be in her seventieth year, though he could only guess.

"Oi don' mind that yeh booted me off me spot, but if yeh're gonna be roit bothered by any sound, Oi moit go crazy," the woman said.

Given that there was only one table in the small room, Narinda had appropriated the space for them to study. Since she was the head Lighter, Marric guessed that it was well within her right to do that. She said that Lighters could do their work from anywhere in the compound, but having them in one place made it easier to track who was scheduled to take over at any given time. Marric watched the woman, smiling. He'd never known his grandparents, but he guessed they'd be something like this.

"I'm sorry, Tilda. If you'd rather, we can move into the war room to give you back your space," Narinda offered.

The old woman waved a hand dismissively, turning back to her book. "Oh tut, no worries 'bout that. Oi'm doin' just foin, Oi am," she replied.

Her white-and-grey hair was pinned up in a top bun, tightly wound and well-kept save for a handful of strands that escaped. Face riddled with wrinkles, her brown eyes were deep set within the folds of the bags under her eyes and the skin folds around them. Somehow this made her seem even more kind. She was squat and rather large, which Marric assumed would make her very comfortable to sit next to.

Perhaps I'm dwelling too much on the loss of my mother again now that I've seen her.

Narinda moved on quickly from the conversation and was poring over another description.

"Here, Talatha annotates something from another historical record. It doesn't mention the same word in the ancient language, but it does say something about the catalyst." The woman read on. "*And so it shall be that Ugglyn be set free by the ego of man, for no man can forever escape the evil save by the catalyst alone.*"

Marric grimaced. Narinda had told him that using the ancient word had summoned an orange Light, much like Lightbearing, that rushed through Janis and out of the room. He recalled the same thing happening when his mother used the word in his vision. While Lightbearing now felt like second nature, he'd only been accustomed to the Light of red and blue. There was something unnatural about the orange, yet at the same time it seemed very familiar to him.

"And here, three months earlier, according to her dates, she cites the catalyst once more but from an old children's rhyme," Narinda said before reading through the small song.

"*The darkness calls and with it sleep, guard your tongue, guard your sheep. When Ugglyn's free, your old life missed, unless you find the catalyst.*"

Livella scoffed at the words, drawing the attention of both Marric and Narinda.

"What does this even mean? It's all just a bunch of nonsense. Isn't there something else I can do? I'm not even helping you with any of this," she said, standing roughly. As she did, she bumped a pile of books, knocking them to the ground. The leather-bound volumes hit the floor with a series of thumps.

"Oh, Lanser's might, I'm sorry," she said, bending down to pick them up.

Narinda pursed her lips in disapproval but watched as Marric moved to help gather the things that had fallen.

"What would you rather be doing, then?" Narinda questioned.

"Sparring or at least practicing. I still feel useless in a fight, and this isn't helping me to feel any better," Livella grumbled.

Tilda spoke up from the couch.

"The war o' words can off'n outwit even a t'ousand swords," she said, her croaky voice light and lilting.

Livella scowled, but Narinda seemed to appreciate the words.

"Whether we like it or not, Janis is in charge of Evenir, and she asked us to put our heads together to figure this out. If you aren't going to help, then at least sit there and be quiet. I'm happy to pretend you did something useful, but I won't lie to her about you leaving if it's what you choose to do," Narinda threatened before looking back at the page.

Marric watched the whole thing feeling awkward, then he focused down at the book he held. His mother had drawn three moons and labeled them. Though she didn't have access to colored ink, for that was only available to the rich, she'd labeled each of them after the moons in the night cycle. Next to each of the names, she'd written the color of that moon's light.

Marric's skin chilled. He didn't know how he'd not seen it before.

"Orange light," he said, lifting the page to look more closely.

"Hmm?" Narinda asked.

"Stellan, Mellan, Isllan. I never thought much about their light until now," Marric said. "Does it mean anything?"

"What are you on about, then?" Narinda asked, glancing over his shoulder.

Livella paled, then looked up as if she'd be able to see the sky through the stone. It was morning, so none of the moons would be up at this time, but being inside the tunnels and cavern gave one the feeling that it was always night, so Marric could understand the reaction.

"Look. Stellan is red, Mellan is blue, and Isllan is orange. I wouldn't have thought about it much until—"

"Foggin' brilliant," Narinda said, sliding the book from Marric's grasp so she could look more closely. "It's a wonder no one has made the connection before now."

Marric shrugged. "Probably just like me, they didn't think anything of it because there's no orange Lightbearing."

Narinda leaned back in her chair. "Now we just have to figure out if it means anything."

The three sat silently, losing themselves in their own thoughts. Light snoring sounded from the couch, and Marric looked curiously to find the older woman had dozed off. He glanced at the orbs of Light above them, wondering when they'd flicker out. It had happened before that the Lighter keeping the network of stone tunnels lit would doze and they'd flicker off. Somehow these remained strong and unwavering.

Marric shifted in his seat, not wanting to be disrespectful but also genuinely curious to know how this was happening. Fortunately, Livella proved to be more brazen with her communication.

"How are the Lights not going out?" Livella asked.

It took a moment for Narinda to come out of her thoughts, but when she finally did, she looked at Livella with confusion. "How do you mean?"

Livella pointed, eyebrows raised.

Following her gaze, Narinda smiled in understanding. "Ah yes, Tilda is one of the oldest known Lightbearers to Evenir. We've learned that once you've practiced your powers for many years, it becomes second nature, possible to hold up even when you are unconscious."

Marric marveled at the idea. Though he didn't expect that Moving or Conjuring could be of much use when he slept, the thrill inside him made him hope that someday he could learn the same thing.

Picking up on his expression, Narinda nudged him in the arm. "I know what you're thinking, but yes, there are practical applications of even your powers if you were sleeping. Think about if you Conjured any items of use for those traveling with you, but then you needed to rest. Say they were cooking with a pot you made, but then you drifted to sleep. You can imagine how helpful it would be for that pot to not disappear."

The example was clearly used in jest, based on Narinda holding her hand to her mouth to stifle a laugh, but it demonstrated the usefulness well enough.

Livella folded her arms. "Wouldn't help me any."

The air soured immediately with the comment, and the three lapsed into an awkward silence once again. Marric could understand why someone might be upset about being without Lightbearing, but he wondered if she was even more upset about the fact that even Fixing couldn't work on her. She still sported the bandages on her arms and cuts to her face from the attack in the sparring room days ago. He imagined it must be frustrating to see everyone else healed within moments, only to know that you had to wait for your body to heal naturally.

"Perhaps it's time for a break," Narinda suggested when it was apparent that they wouldn't recover from the grumpy comment. "We've been at this for hours."

Sighing in relief, Livella rose immediately. "I'm heading to the sparring room again. If I can't be of use anywhere else, then I might as well keep training. I'm going crazy without being able to breathe fresh air."

With that, she promptly left.

Marric watched her go, observing the way she held the staff strapped to her back with one hand, as if she might need to draw it at any moment. She acted far more confident in contrast to the way she was when they'd first seen her come to Terris Green. He couldn't help but wonder what differences had come to him now that he'd been with the group for a few months. An image of a scrawnier, quieter boy being thrown into a war seemed amusing, yet that was what he was. It was amazing what almost daily training could do to someone like that.

"I could tell the moment Janis asked her to join us that she wouldn't last long," Narinda said, pushing her glasses up on her nose.

Smiling awkwardly, Marric was too sheepish to admit that he understood where Livella came from with respect to the studying. He could read, yes, but he didn't prefer to sit for hours reading books that held little interest for him. A snort from the other side of the room brought his attention there as Tilda woke herself up from her surprise slumber. Afraid that he'd be stuck in a conversation now that they were taking a break from studying, Marric excused himself quickly and left the room.

He was so focused on his thoughts and the wall next to him that he didn't see the person standing just before him. The moment he saw the flash of red in his peripheral vision, he gasped and stopped, narrowly avoiding a collision with the girl.

"That would have been the second time you ran into me," Miredith said, putting her hands on her hips.

Marric flushed but he didn't look away. If he intended to be more confident in himself, he'd have to face his problems directly.

Not that she's a problem, but—

Just from seeing her, his heart began racing and he began sweating. Cursing under his breath, he righted himself and stood as straight as he could.

"If you stand right in the path of people walking, you should expect to be run into like this," Marric pointed out.

Miredith's mouth twitched in a sideways smile. "Cheeky today, are we?"

Marric blushed deeper.

"Oh, come off it, it's fine. You are right. I *did* put myself here so that you'd notice me. I think if I just walked on by, you'd not have noticed me at all. Is that what you were trying to do, by the way?" she asked, folding her arms.

He thought for a moment, feeling somewhat intimidated by the girl's forward nature. Then he matched her posture and stance.

"I've just got a lot on my mind, that's all. What are you up to, anyway? Doesn't your ma need help with her business and whatnot?" he asked, trying to deflect the conversation from himself.

Shaking her head, Miredith relaxed her arms, evidently not noticing his obvious mimicking of her actions. "Nah, she gave me a break. I figured it would be great to show you something."

Marric furrowed his brow. Hearing that she was looking for him specifically was both terrifying and exciting at the same time. His chest continued to burn, but he tried to ignore it, hoping that she couldn't tell how flustered she made him feel.

"Come on, it's just down this way. I bet you've never seen this before," Miredith said, grabbing his arm and tugging him along.

Just as the day before, Miredith led him confidently through the hallways, weaving in and out of people as if they weren't there. Ironically, those they passed ignored her as if she weren't there, but their eyes lingered on Marric as if he was some anomaly that they couldn't understand. He focused on the girl's back in front of him, trying not to let the stares bother him too much. He'd always known Janis to be a fascinating person, but he didn't expect her to draw this much attention to him by mere association.

At one point, Miredith led him down a hallway Marric had never been down. He couldn't track exactly when that happened, for he was too focused on following to have noticed. Yet the hallway strata took on a more vibrant color, which tipped him off that they'd wandered somewhere he'd not been. The flow of people slowed but not enough for him to feel comfortable looking upward to see where she was leading him.

Suddenly, a thought occurred to him that if he truly wanted to be more confident, he'd have to face the attention at some point. Steeling himself, he looked up, preparing himself for the looks and inevitable gossip of those around him. Sure enough, two women passed, eyes locked on him as they leaned in to whisper to each other. One pointed, unembarrassed about the fact that she was watching them. He smiled and nodded, then followed Miredith closely. He soon lost sight of those staring as he got caught in the beauty of the stone. Most of the tunnels and caverns were the same grey stone with bits of brown here and there, but this stone looked to have been painted by multicolored dyes of some sort. Stripes and twists of colors flowed downward on the stone, as if a waterfall of color had flowed, then froze there for all time. He reached out and ran his finger along the stone, shocked to feel that it had been smoothed.

Miredith didn't bother looking back at him, neither did she slow her pace. Marric gasped, seeing how far ahead she'd gotten, and rushed to keep up. Fortunately, there were no turn-off points from this tunnel. Soon he saw an opening in the tunnel ahead, the soft glow of blue Lighting orbs coming from within. He guessed there must be a more concentrated amount of the Light for it to be glowing so brightly where they walked.

Marric's eyes widened as they entered another large cavern, perhaps only a fourth of the size of the main cavern of the compound but wondrous just the same. Most of the large room was filled with a lake of dark water, emphasized by the bright orbs of Light hovering all over the ceiling. The still water reflected the orbs above, creating the illusion that the water extended deep below with the same glowing orbs at the bottom. Marric was struck by the beauty, then felt himself get slightly dizzy as vertigo caught hold of him. Shaking his head, he turned back to Miredith, who hadn't even stopped to enjoy the wonder.

Catching up once again, he asked, "What is this place? Where is this water coming from?"

Most lakes and ponds he'd seen had clear inflows of water, such as a waterfall or a river, but in this case, the water stood quiet and still, no water coming into the pool.

Miredith shrugged. "Oh, something about a spring. I don't remember all the details. I think it bubbles in from the bottom from somewhere in the mountain. It's pretty warm too if you touch it."

Marric had noticed the air become thicker and warmer as they moved through the tunnels. He just hadn't put much thought into why. A slight steam rose from the water's surface as if the water indeed harbored heat within.

"Am I allowed to? It looks like it's been undisturbed forever," Marric noted, seeing the still nature of the water.

"Yeah, you can touch it. Normally, you'd see all sorts of kids bathing and swimming. I guess they're all busy today," Miredith said.

The narrow path they walked ran around the entire room. Here people walked slowly as they traveled to and from the only other exit from the chamber. Before Marric could ask where that led, Miredith disappeared from his side vision. With a start, he turned to see where she'd gone but he couldn't tell.

"Down here," came Miredith's voice from down by his feet. He peered downward to see her face within a slender hole in the wall just at the base.

Marric's stomach turned as he saw just how narrow the opening was. Not only that but a small yet steady flow of water came from the pond to his right through the same opening. He quickly scanned the rest of the pathway around the large lake, trying to see if there were other outlets for the water, but this appeared to be the only one. Marric could hear the trickle of water bubbling within the hole where Miredith waited.

"Are you coming or not?" the girl asked.

He couldn't say why, but this didn't feel like something they should be doing. Yet he felt compelled to because of his uncanny fondness for her. With a glance to the few adults who ringed the room on the other side, Marric sat down next to the stream of water, trying to figure out how he could get through without getting his clothing wet. Unfortunately, that proved impossible, given that the flow extended to either edge of the opening. Gritting his teeth, he slid through the small river of water until his legs entered the hole. Nervousness burned in his chest and arms as he dangled his feet, trying to find the bottom of where Miredith had stood just moments before. The water saturated his backside and legs instantly and he grimaced. With a prayer to Lanser, he slipped through the hole, though not as easily as Miredith had. Still, he didn't get stuck like he feared.

His boots hit hard ground almost instantly, even before he had made it all the way through the opening. Relief flooded him. He marveled at the new sight. They'd entered a small cave, barely tall enough for Miredith, too small for him to stand up straight, also filled with water. The trickle of water through the opening filled a smaller spring, hardly twice his height wide. The water came right to the edge of most of the small chamber, save for a half dozen feet of clear stone where they stood. It was hard to see all the details, given that this room was devoid of all Lighting orbs. Still, the blue glow filtered in through the hole they'd just used enough to adequately see.

"Uh, here, let me do something about the darkness," Marric said, creating his minuscule Lighting orb.

"This is one of my favorite places to come think," Miredith said, sitting down with her knees to her chest.

Marric followed her example, letting his orb hover above their heads so he could settle next to her using both of his hands. The water here wasn't as still as the larger lake above them. Light ripples moved along the water as the bubbling flow from his left fell into the water's edge.

"How does it not fill up all the way?" Marric asked, suddenly nervous that they would get trapped in here and drown.

Miredith shrugged yet again to his side. "I'm not sure. I don't know much about nature. All I know is that a lot of parents tell their kids not to come here. The hole's too small for most adults, and they don't want something bad to happen to their kids without them being able to help."

Marric nodded, thoughts of drowning kids entering his mind before he shook those off.

"My ma doesn't love me to come here, but she doesn't know how often I do," she said, leaning her chin on her legs.

For a moment the two just sat, listening to the bubbling water and watching the reflection of Marric's orb above. Marric's mind wandered from the anomaly of the pond and he soon found himself thinking of Janis and Avryn. He didn't know the details of their journey, only that Janis was in such a hurry to leave that Avryn had followed. He hoped that more than just the two of them had gone after Rivelen.

Why would she take that book? Marric thought, remembering the oddity of the black tome.

After a few minutes, Miredith spoke again.

"What does Lightbearing feel like?" she asked suddenly.

Marric started, having been lost in his thoughts.

"Uh, well, it depends, I guess," Marric replied, pressing his lips together and facing away from her to hide the awkwardness of his response.

"Start with Seeing. You can do that, right?" Miredith asked.

He nodded. "Yeah, that's the one that I've had to deal with the longest. I Awakened to Moving and Conjuring too, but Seeing has a way of coming to you when you least expect it. I couldn't handle the visions at first."

Miredith watched him with a wistful expression but she didn't interrupt. Instead she raised her eyebrows, expecting more. Though he'd not known her for more than a few days, he felt like it was uncommon for her not to have interrupted him while he spoke. Clearing his throat to get hold of the nerves worming up inside of him, he looked out at the small pond.

"Um, Seeing just feels like my eyes are being stretched open for a moment, then you get disconnected from your body and sent—well, wherever you are going in the vision. Once you're gone, you can't really feel what your body does very well. At least it just feels far away," he said, still feeling awkward about her asking such a question.

He'd never enjoyed being the center of a conversation, but if he were to try to wiggle his way out if it now, he feared offending the girl. Even more perplexing was why he was so nervous to do that. Marric instinctively reached out to grab a small pebble or rock to throw in the almost still water, but his hands grasped at the smooth grey stone, nothing loose to grab a hold of. Realizing his distraction tactic didn't work, he Conjured a rock instead.

Miredith gasped next to him and he started at the noise.

"Sorry! I've seen Conjuring all the time. I just don't normally get so close to it," she said, moving so she was slightly in front of him. "The tokens at voting are really the only thing I've used. Mind if I hold it?"

Marric squirmed but he handed her the stone he'd just created. Over the past weeks he'd become used to the fact that Conjured objects felt and weighed very much like the real thing. As the weight left his hand, he Conjured another in its place. The facets and ridges on this stone looked exactly like the first, as if Marric only had one image in his mind of what a rock must look like.

He made a note to work on his creativity. While it probably didn't matter in the practical sense, he figured that Conjuring could be enhanced with some imagination.

Miredith flipped the stone over in her hands. It was only about the size of her palm, but the details were surprisingly accurate for a standard rock.

"That is the foggin' oddest thing I've ever felt. It's just like a real stone," she said, tossing it back and forth in her hand. "What happens if I throw it?"

Marric shrugged. "Probably what happens to a normal rock, I guess," he said.

With that, Miredith threw the rock with a grunt. It slammed into the wall on the opposite side just above the water where it broke into a few pieces, the shards falling into the water with a splat. Marric released the Conjure as it sank into the depths of the pond.

"Wait, this is *perfect*," Miredith said. "I've always wanted to know how deep this thing is."

She held out her hand expectantly, and Marric, raising a brow, handed her the new stone.

"Don't let it disappear," she ordered, then pulled her hand back. Before she could toss the stone, she angled herself back toward him. "Um, I forgot to ask—you did do that on purpose, right? Or can you not keep it Conjured for very long?"

In the dimness of the blue Light, Marric saw the confident girl's face turn slightly pink. His chest blazed at the reaction. The fire-headed girl had seemed nothing but confident and strong-minded. To see her flush like this in front of him endeared her even more to Marric than she had already. Eyes wide, he took a moment to process her question, realizing after a few beats how awkward it probably was that he was just staring at her.

"Oh, yeah—no, it's fine, I can hold it," he assured her.

Nodding, she concentrated, then tossed the rock right in the center of the pond. The ripples of the splash moved outward, the small waves reflecting the tiny orb of Light that hovered above, creating a masterpiece of art that Marric almost got distracted by. Forcing his eyes away, they watched as the bright blue Light stone sank about ten paces deep, then came to a stop.

Miredith sat back, looking disappointed.

"Fog it, I was hoping it was deeper," Miredith said, folding her arms across her chest.

"Why is that?"

Miredith made a tsking sound with her tongue, then looked at him flatly. "I was hoping I could swim down there and find a way out of this place."

Marric stared at her, trying to understand what she meant. "Wait, you want to *leave*? I thought you liked it here." He paused, realizing that she'd said nothing of the sort. He'd just assumed that. If her mother and father were truly Awakened Lightbearers, then there wouldn't be a safer place for them. He'd just guessed that Miredith liked living in the safety of the compound.

Sighing, she moved a lock of her curly hair over her ear and looked up at the orb he'd created. Marric squirmed in his seat, realizing how uncomfortable it felt to sit down on the hard stone in the short cave. He couldn't help but feel like he'd done something wrong or asked a question that was out of line.

"I don't feel like I belong here," she finally said.

Marric opted to stay quiet.

Miredith stretched her legs, then faced Marric. Her green eyes locked on his, reflecting the Light above, and his breath caught in his throat. For a moment he didn't breathe, until he was forced to let out the breath, lungs screaming for air. Unfortunately, nothing seemed to get past Miredith and she raised a brow at him.

"You ok there?" she asked. "You know breathing is kind of necessary."

Marric flushed, not even having the time to turn away to hide his reaction.

"I just—don't know what you mean," he said finally. "Your parents are safe here. Their Lightbearing could get them into trouble somewhere else."

"Didn't work for my dad," she said, still looking at him.

Marric cursed himself in his mind.

"I'm sorry, I didn't—oh, fog it—I forgot." Marric couldn't even put the rest of his apology into words before she raised a hand.

"I wouldn't expect you to remember everything about me. We just met, no harm done," she replied. "My dad died years ago, and I've had to come to terms with it. Still, I can't help but feel that even they are disappointed in me."

The gurgling of the water flowing from the larger lake behind them seemed to get louder as Marric processed the words. He hadn't thought about what it would be like to have two Lightbearing parents but not have gifts of your own. His father, of course, didn't have any powers, even though his mother had. Marric recalled asking Avryn if the magic was hereditary, but he'd been told that it was not as far as they could tell. Marric awkwardly reached out a hand to console the girl, who had now rested her chin back on her knees, but he stopped, not sure if his touch would be received well. Instead he pulled it back and laced his fingers together to prevent them from quivering any more.

"What does your ma think of it?" he asked sheepishly.

Miredith shrugged. "She claims she doesn't care, but I know she's disappointed. I'm nearly fifteen and haven't Awakened yet. It's not going to happen."

Marric opened his mouth to respond before Miredith turned sharply toward him. "And don't try to tell me I'll just be a 'late bloomer.' It doesn't happen. You're the first kid over thirteen to Awaken since, well, probably Avryn, honestly."

Marric's mouth snapped shut as he realized his attempts at comfort were foiled.

"Anyway, there's no point in dwelling on it. I'm stuck here, you're stuck here, and we'll just die here like the rest of everyone. Maybe I can at least convince my ma to let me train with the sword so I can go on expeditions to get new Lightbearers. I'm getting so bored in here."

Even though he wanted to try to console her more, he knew nothing he would say could change her circumstances. Even now he was getting antsy without exploring the outside, without smelling the fresh air and seeing the sun.

"Maybe we should train together," he suggested. "I still have a lot to learn."

Miredith's expression brightened at the idea. "You think they'd let me?"

"I don't see why not. I'll talk to Turrin to see what he says."

Miredith smiled, then nodded.

"You never told me about the other ones. What's it like to use your other powers?" she asked.

With the conversation turned back on him, the tight feeling in his stomach returned, but he focused on Miredith instead. He smiled and launched into the best explanation he could think of for what Lightbearing felt like while his mind slipped back to Janis and Avryn. Though he assumed Janis Shielded them, he would still have to try to See them when he got a moment.

For now he just wanted to enjoy the company.

23

The underbrush rustled as Janis kicked her horse into motion, pressing it faster than she would normally push a mount. While she knew the animal couldn't keep the pace for the entire journey, she wanted to close the gap between her and the wretched woman as quickly as possible. Janis had found that using her Fixing on the beast helped it regain some of its energy, mending the torn tendons and tired muscles from the rapid pace. Rivelen's face loomed in Janis's mind, her expression blank yet clearly intrigued by the black book they'd inspected days before.

Avryn cursed behind her as she pulled the reins of the horse to dodge an oncoming tree and he had to scramble to lead his horse to do the same. The horses of her four companions barreled behind her as fast as they could to keep up. They'd been traveling all night, following the tracks that Janis could easily pick up. Though they had to slow for a moment to Fix their horses a few times, the pace continued. Janis knew her horse could only take so much more; even now she could feel the animal tiring.

She allowed her eyes to fill with Light, imagining Rivelen's face just as she had in the war room. Where normally her vision would spin and she'd separate from her physical form, this time nothing happened. The woman's Shielder was still hard at work.

Grateful that Rivelen didn't have the instincts to not leave an obvious trail, Janis released her power and focused back on the path. The group had intentionally ignored the pathway that sat twenty paces to their right, probably trying to avoid being followed, but in doing so, they'd left a more obvious path. Foliage sat crushed in multiple places where the hooves of the horses had trod. Branches had broken from riders sitting atop their mounts. Even if they'd stayed on the path, Janis was confident that she could track them, especially given the lack of rain, but this made it so she could hardly make a mistake.

"We're going to have to slow. Fixing the horses isn't a sustainable solution," Avryn called from behind her.

She grimaced, knowing it to be true but not wanting to admit it. With a sigh, she pulled on the reins to slow the animal. Still breathing hard, the horse moved to a slow walk. Janis could almost sense the relief from the animal or perhaps she imagined it.

Four sets of hooves followed suit, switching to nearly a crawl.

"Blast i' all, yeh tryin' to kill us? Or yeh tryna kill the horses?" Turrin complained.

Janis knew she drove a hard pace, but the urgency in her was drawing her forward. Even now she felt the tugging at her gut that something wasn't right.

"If we hadn't left Rivelen alone with the book, this wouldn't be a problem," Janis reminded them. Though her tone bore no hardness, the words alone were biting enough to cause Avryn to scoff.

"She's been with Evenir for years. There is no way Narinda could have known her intentions," Avryn said, defending his love.

Still, Janis didn't feel any anger. She couldn't be angry at anyone but herself. Janis had seen Rivelen's reaction and known something was off, but she did not expect the former general to take off with the most important asset she had against the impending release of Ugglyn.

"I think we're getting closer," Janis said, ignoring Avryn's defensive words. "When we find them, we need to make sure to get the book first. Any retribution you want from Rivelen is not worth our quarry slipping away."

Nods and murmurs of assent sounded behind her. Avryn looked as if he would blow an artery, angry at her declaration, but he didn't challenge her.

"She'll need t' be punished fer this, yeh know that, right?" Turrin said, apparently being the only one not afraid of Janis.

"I can assure you, she will," Janis said, the twisting in her gut reminding her of the real problem. "But if that book slips out of our grip, then I think we'll be in an entire world of hurt."

Avryn furrowed his brow, his anger diffusing at her repeat mention of the odd tome.

"What is it? Why should we be so concerned about the record falling into Prost's hands?" Avryn asked.

The question was valid, but Janis still felt bothered to have to explain it at all.

"I believe Ugglyn is inside Prost," she said bluntly. "And that book has been touched by whatever powers the anti-god has."

Avryn's brows shot up at the revelation.

"You truly think that Ugglyn has possessed Prost? If that were true, don't you think he would have come for us in all his glory?" Avryn asked, his voice incredulous.

"Not unless he needs something from that book," Janis said, facing forward in an obvious attempt to not have to look at those who followed her.

The others remained quiet. Either they didn't have anything to say or they didn't want to interrupt the argument. Janis took the moment to look upward, inspecting the Shield that followed overhead. Avryn had insisted that they bring another Shielder, even though she was confident that she could do it herself. He clearly didn't trust her Transformation as much as she did. At the time she hadn't bothered arguing, for she only cared about leaving right away. Whatever responsibilities came from leading Evenir were second to this. She could hear a horse's hooves padding in the moss and underbrush, moving closer to her mount.

"And this is all worth leaving our sanctuary without a thought?" Avryn said quietly. "You are the new leader of Evenir. You can't just run out on your people like that."

His words held a bite to them that was unusual for the man, though he'd changed a lot in the recent weeks. Janis guessed the death of Magness drove much of this change. Admittedly, she wasn't bothered by it. Even with his newfound hardness, he was kinder than most soldiers with his skill and practice. Still, the words struck her more deeply than she wanted to admit. She felt the weight of leadership. Even though she wanted nothing to do with it, she wouldn't shun her responsibilities. Janis knew what this journey looked like. She had run through the tunnels at breakneck pace, flying past the citizens in the hallways as they gasped and shouted in shock. She had taken a few moments to mutter some quick consoling message to some in the stables, ordering them to pass word, but that was it.

Do they already think I've failed them? she thought. If she ended up dying from this little escapade, then it would be a failure.

But she knew she had to try.

"Some sacrifices are meant to be made. Yes, I could have come up with a plan or organized a following party, but how long would that have taken? Hours? A day? Every minute we wasted in Terris Green allowed Rivelen to get farther away. I don't know the members of Evenir well enough to say there is a better tracker than myself, so I just acted. I'll clean up the pieces when we get back," Janis said. "I left Harmel to keep things running in the meantime, so that's at least something."

Surprisingly, this had been the most conversation they'd had since they left Terris Green the night before. Save for the few words she'd given to those back at the sanctuary, Janis had only been focused on leaving. She recognized, in part, that running off on her own doubtless wasn't the wisest. Janis was grateful that Avryn was bold enough to chase after her, ordering people to grab quick supplies and follow her. He'd rounded up three other soldiers, all Lightbearers in some fashion, and Turrin had invited himself. Even with the recent changes in leadership, Avryn commanded enough respect for people to pay attention. When people saw them rushing through the caverns, they probably didn't have a second thought about who really was in power at the moment. Harmel had been less than thrilled about her intent to leave him behind, but he had enough—or perhaps more—respect for his responsibilities, enough to let her leave.

The image of Harmel's disapproving gaze formed in her mind. He'd made it clear that he understood what she was doing and why she had to leave, but it frustrated him that he had to stay. He'd more than once been overly concerned for her safety, so much so that it baffled her. At the same time, the warmth of her fondness for the man filled her chest. She'd not once attempted to court any man, especially since the whole Macks incident, so she balked at the idea of even trying. Still, she was growing used to Harmel's protectiveness over her, despite his annoying jokes and ridiculous grin. She was brought back to the moment as Avryn nodded, his face still angry but more resolute.

"While I disagree with your actions, I will support you in this. Infighting will only get us killed in the end," he said, looking forward. "What do you propose we do when we reach them?"

Janis thought for a moment as she imagined the scene. She recalled Seeing those who accompanied the tall blonde woman. Rivelen had helped the Watchlight man escape, and Janis knew him to be a Conjurer. From what she remembered, he was a Destroyer as well. That would complicate things. Rivelen was a Seer, they had a Shielder, and there was another man with them, one she didn't recognize. She assumed it was another Lightbearer Rivelen had wooed into joining them.

"The best I can come up with is having the others engage with her extras while you and I find her directly. I'd prefer to take her alive, but the book is the priority," Janis replied.

Avryn locked his jaw, clearly unhappy with the mention of Rivelen being killed but wise enough to know how real the possibility was. The sun shone high overhead, the yellow light filtering through the canopy above. Janis appreciated traveling through the trees since it kept the air cool and moist for them despite the heat of the beating sun. She knew it was about time to stop for food, but she wouldn't give any of them the luxury of waiting for long. A few minutes was all they needed to nibble from packs of rations they'd grabbed on the way. There would be no time for hunting and cooking until they were on the way back, presumably holding the object that threatened to rock the balance in Lindrad.

As if hearing her thoughts, Turrin's voice sounded from behind. "'Ey, when we gonna eat? I'm foggin' starvin'," he complained.

Janis pulled her horse to a stop, listening to the gentle breeze that constantly rustled parts of the forest. She scanned the surrounding forest, noting the direction Rivelen's party had traveled and making sure that nothing followed them. They'd seen a spare spine hog here and there, but since the animal wasn't prone to living in packs, she didn't anticipate any ambushes like they had months ago on their way to Terris Green.

"Here is as good as any," Janis said, motioning behind her for the men and women to grab what they needed.

She kept watching the trees and brush around them, waiting for any sounds or even slight movements. A few longbirds flitted through the trees above, their long, sinewy tails flowing behind them like wriggling worms while they flew. These particular ones were blue with red beaks. They called to each other in song, something that brought her back to the times she'd had to travel alone in the woods. Longbirds were one of the more helpful animals in the forest. Myths claimed that they watched over those in the forest, warning them of danger when it was near.

Janis knew better. The animals were merely skittish, sensing emotion from other creatures around them, changing their tune to warn one another of the harsh feelings emanating from anything hostile. The song these two sang as they flew was the careless one they normally had.

This was one of the more useful things Macks had taught her over the years. Watching the birds flit through the branches until they disappeared, she turned as Avryn touched her softly on the arm.

"Round three of our favorite dried rations," he said, offering her some dried apples and pork.

She took them, nodding in appreciation, and began eating. Janis wasn't one to complain about the food, as was often the topic of conversation for those who traveled long distances. Having to eat was an inconvenience to her, along with sleeping and using the privy. She did not understand what merited the jokes and silliness around dried meals. They gave her enough energy just fine.

The others stretched out behind her, one man even lying on the soft ground for a moment to stretch out his legs. Quiet conversations ensued between her companions, occasionally interrupted by the telltale booming laugh of Turrin. If the recent longbirds hadn't sang their normal tune, Janis would have scolded the man for being so loud, but they didn't appear to be in any danger.

Thoughts of Macks brought her back to the man, and she figured now was as good a time as any to try to See him. Steeling herself for the chance of witnessing his eyes once again, she allowed her Seeing to take over. Eyes filling with bright blue Light, she felt herself separate from her mount, her senses dulling to almost nothing as the world spun into blurs of color. Almost at once, they sharpened into the image of Macks, grimly looking out over a prairie mountainside. Next to him, Prost sat atop a black stallion wearing his usual cloak but also mail. A steel helmet was tied to the saddle next to him.

While seeing Macks did shock her system, more distracting was the army that stood around them, all mounted and wielding armor and weapons of their own. Her chest, distant, hardly palpable to her, constricted at the sight. She didn't know the true numbers of Watchlight's ranks, but what she saw looked like a formidable group.

"How long should we stand here, unguarded?" Macks asked, his green eyes peering off into the setting sun.

"Just until they See us coming," Prost said.

Janis knew immediately that something had changed within the man. He looked to be his normal, hardened self, but there was something there. Uneasiness plagued his eyes, a discomfort she couldn't describe.

"The woman should See that we will meet them soon, with enough force to guard them," Prost said.

"Sure, but there are other prying eyes. I've had to Shield myself from—certain people ever since Stilten," Macks said, looking around uncomfortably.

She scoffed, realizing that was why she hadn't been able to locate him. More than once she'd tried to find him with her Seeing, but he'd been dark. He'd developed Shielding abilities she didn't know about. Macks still wore his usual assassin's garb. His hair was still the same pitch-black cropped mess it always was. He still bore the scars on his brow from the fights they'd been in together. Yet Janis realized something fascinating.

He looked terrified.

Not once in her time with Macks had he exuded anything but charisma and confidence, but the man who sat before her looked weak. Sweat beaded on his head and his gaze darted to Prost and away. She narrowed her eyes, trying to figure out what made the man so nervous. Then the air shifted, and something felt wrong.

Looking back at Prost, a jolt flung through her like her dagger slamming into a solid sheet of metal.

Prost stared at her, his eyes filled with a grey mist, almost smoke, laced with silver streaks. He smiled.

"Said prying eyes have already found us, I see," Prost said, but his voice sounded different. It sounded as if another deeper voice echoed in line with his normal tone.

The voice sounded like Ugglyn's had when she'd seen him weeks ago.

Skin chilling distantly in her actual body, Janis stood straight, somehow feeling that she should appear confident if he could See her. She caught sight of movement just below her and looked down in shock to see that somehow, overlapping her vision-form was the same smokey-grey substance that filled Prost's eyes. Her mind screamed in panic that he had her, but she felt no pain. Whatever power he used looked all too similar to the arrows laced with whatever poison Luden's men used. Until now, she'd not thought about the possibility of the poison being associated with Ugglyn. She moved her hand upward, taking a page from Harmel's book and grinning widely.

"Hey, it's been a long time," Janis said casually.

Prost's smile melted into a frown, showing that he clearly could hear and see her. Apparently, he didn't enjoy her banter. Yet she knew he couldn't get her here.

A flash of purplish Light to her right drew her attention to see Rivelen there, eyes wide as she observed the army.

"Blastin' fog, what are yeh doin'?!" Rivelen asked, shooting a look at Prost. "Bringin' an army out like that, yeh're gonna be found!" Her eyes showed some amount of recognition. As one of Evenir's generals, she would, of course, know Prost and his reputation. "I don' answer t' yous, only t' Ugglyn. Where's he?" she asked, voice shaking.

"Do you not recognize me? We've been chatting for so long, I thought you would at least recognize my aura," Prost drawled.

Macks looked confused, hearing Prost's words but not understanding to whom he spoke. All of a sudden, his eyes filled with red Light and his jaw hardened, his gaze immediately landing on Janis.

Fury filled her, as if his Seeing her reminded her of all the things he'd done to her in the past.

Well, this is turning into quite the party, isn't it? she thought.

The sun was setting in whatever vision this was, and Janis got the sense that this event had happened the night before. Looking over at Rivelen, she lamented the fact that she couldn't gaze upon the woman. Even now she tried but failed. Her instincts told her that Rivelen was still protected by a Shield. Janis didn't know if the Rivelen she now saw was from the same time as Janis or the same as the past events she now watched. Her gut wrenched distantly as the time meshed, her mind almost unable to comprehend the oddity of the joint group.

"I care not if Evenir Sees us, even if they recognize the landmarks. We'll have long slaughtered the lot of them once you lead us to their base," Prost drawled.

He winced as if he'd felt some internal pain. Janis furrowed her brow, noticing the shift. His throat growled softly, holding something back. Janis continued watching the man as his wicked smile returned and he focused back on Rivelen. Rivelen didn't seem to notice the change, as it was only brief, and Macks was still watching Janis warily.

"Fog it! She's 'ere!" Rivelen said suddenly, drawing Janis's gaze.

"Don't worry yourself with the wench! She'll have little effect on the army I bring to you. Now, *show us where you are*," Prost urged, the echo in his voice more prevalent now that it displayed anger.

"I can'! She'll See us if we—"

"Woman! Show us now, or *I'll* kill you when I find you first," Prost roared.

Macks and the soldiers immediately surrounding them winced at the anger. More than one head turned to watch their apparent leader with perplexed looks. To them, it probably appeared that he spoke with himself, for even Macks wasn't speaking back to him.

Rivelen cursed, then disappeared.

Janis knew her moment would soon be lost. With one last wink at Macks, Janis focused on the memory of Rivelen's face. At first she felt the same force blocking her, and the world spun to blackness. Then, out of nowhere, the scene formed quickly in her view. Rivelen sat on her mount, hand held out to the man next to her. Janis assumed he was the Shielder she'd brought. The man was tall, his face gaunt and pale as if he hadn't eaten in days. His hair was blond and came down over his ears like a mushroom. She made a mental note of what she saw, hoping to ask if Avryn knew the man.

Her mind reeled as she tried to figure out just where they were. Without landmarks, it would be practically impossible to know how close they were.

"Jus' a bi' longer, steady," Rivelen said.

An idea struck Janis and she launched her vision-self into the air, the canvas of trees rushing past her. The sun shone brightly above her, proving that they were in the same time once again. Resisting the urge to close her eyes, Janis reached through the narrow connection through space to her body somewhere out of the vision. She focused on the feeling of her lips together and the muscles within. Struggling, she opened them and spoke out loud. It was odd feeling like she was saying something and not hearing her own voice with her ears. She mouthed the command, slowly at first, then more quickly.

Nothing happened.

She cursed, looking down through the canopy. The translucent Shield began to form in the air below her and she knew that she would be out of time within moments. Just as the vision faded, her connection to Rivelen's location lost, a lone blue sphere, small yet piercing, soared over the distant trees to her right. Her head snapped that direction. Janis took one last look at the sun dipping to one side of the sky before her vision went dark. With a start, her mind focused back on her mount in the forest.

Thank Lanser that being in a vision feels so much like being in the in-between, she thought.

"What on earth was that for?" Avryn asked incredulously. His eyes darted wildly around them as if he expected an ambush out of nowhere. "Anyone could have seen that Lighting orb for leagues around us."

Janis ignored his words. She was just glad he'd received her message before the vision failed. Admittedly, she was surprised he'd followed her command to toss an orb as high as he could.

"Keep up if you can" was all she said before kicking her horse into a run again. The animal grunted in protest but obeyed her command, rushing through the brush once more. Wind and branches whipped into her face and hair, stinging her cheeks and nose where she could not dodge. Over the loud clomping of her horse's hooves, she could hear the others following her.

Looking up, she took stock of the sun, searching for the mental image she'd gathered from her vision. They were only an hour away. She thanked Lanser for how the horses were able to keep up such a pace but knew that it would come at a terrible cost to them. Though she could Fix their tiredness and muscles, she feared they may age far more from this journey than they should.

At length, she was forced to slow once more, but she knew they'd catch up to Rivelen's group soon. All of a sudden she felt as if she was being watched. Cursing, she flung her hand upward, Shielding herself with a lone blue dome of Light. The prying feeling disappeared as quickly as it had come.

Soon, Avryn and the others came crashing through the trees.

"Gee, lass. Yeh moit wanna stop runnin' off like tha'. It's not leaderly loike, if yeh know what Oi mean," Turrin said, panting from the stress of the rapid ride.

Avryn shot the older man a pointed look, but Turrin looked away furtively. Janis didn't care that he called her lass. She realized that other people's personalities, however weak or strong, couldn't affect her if she just ignored them.

Janis matched Avryn's energy, staring at him as if she was boring into his soul. That got his attention and his head pulled back in shock at her reaction.

"They are just an hour away. Prost is bringing an army. If he gets to her first, their next destination is obvious," Janis said, choosing to leave out the details.

Avryn's eyes widened and he spat to the side.

"How do you know this? I thought you couldn't See her?" he questioned, obviously irritated.

Janis gritted her teeth, knowing how much she didn't want to have to give all the details. Instead she opted for a summarized version. "I Saw Prost. I think he's possessed by Ugglyn. Rivelen appeared and eventually showed where they were. I needed *you* to send up the Light so I could see their position from ours."

Avryn blinked at the response.

"Clever," he said, "but why would Rivelen do this? I still don't understand."

"Ugglyn said he's been tempting her for some time. He can connect with Seers. It's kind of his thing," Janis said.

"*What*?" Avryn barked.

"It's a long story. I'll tell you if you can keep up," Janis said, kicking her horse to move faster. It had just been a theory before, but now that she'd Seen firsthand how Ugglyn, in Prost's body at least, had spoken to her directly in the vision, she knew it had to be true. Any Seer was in danger of his temptations.

Thoughts of Marric flew into her mind and her stomach coiled. She hoped he wasn't being drawn in by the Void.

Janis couldn't believe that she hadn't seen it before. The look in Rivelen's eyes when she'd seen the tome was hunger, longing. In fact, Janis had recognized it the moment she saw it. She just didn't understand how it applied in this situation, so she'd discarded the possibility.

Janis led the group rapidly through the forest. They didn't bother trying to be quiet, for they knew they had little time to catch up. She wished she knew just how far away Watchlight and their army were from their position. At first Janis explained how other Seers could interact within a vision. It was difficult to yell over the noise of the horses' hooves and the rustling of the trees, but she tried anyway.

Hoping that Rivelen and her group hadn't spotted the beacon Avryn had sent up in the air, Janis followed the trail with a passion, a thirst for the prey. They rode for hours, the horses needing continuous breaks, even more than before now that they'd been traveling for longer. The trail became more and more clear, showing just how close they were to their quarry.

Janis spotted movement ahead and pushed her horse forward with one last go. She rushed forward, ahead of the others in the group, when she spotted a brown robe rushing through the trees. Gritting her teeth at the noise she made as she rode, she pushed through two enormous trunks, then cursed. A translucent purple Shield sprung out of nowhere, blocking her way. Janis cursed again, yanking on the reins roughly until her mount skidded in the soft soil below. When she saw she wouldn't be able to stop fully, she dove from the creature, rolling in the dirt until she ran into the tree, her momentum finally stopping. The horse didn't have the same luck as it slammed into the barrier.

Jumping to her feet, she saw the barrier and touched it. Janis looked left and right, trying to find the Shielder who'd created the wall when it disappeared. Rustling to her left made her dart in that direction, where she saw a brown-cloaked man running through the trees. Reacting quickly, she threw her hands outward, the man's body glowing blue as he was thrown sideways into the bushes. Janis heard him shout in surprise before he vanished in the thick underbrush.

A new Shield sprang up, this one flickering from purple to red every few moments. At that point, Avryn and the others had caught up.

"What in Lanser's name—" Avryn said before Janis talked over him.

"Turrin, break the Shield, knock the fool out so we can bring him back to Terris Green," Janis ordered.

The older man nodded, then jumped from his horse.

Pivoting in the direction of the tracks, Janis took off on foot, hoping she wasn't too far behind Rivelen and the other two. Avryn called after her, but she didn't have time to wait for him. Soon he was upon her, his horse moving alongside. A hand extended from the horse. She grabbed it and let him pull her onto the creature's back.

"You won't catch up running like that," he said as he kicked the horse into motion once more.

Janis thought about the Shielder behind. How long ago had he separated from the others to create a distraction? She knew that if she was in a similar position, being pursued, she'd have done the same thing.

The man's sacrifice wasn't worth it. He'd only been able to buy Rivelen a few moments.

Avryn followed the path surprisingly well as he guided the animal through the forest. Janis could see the broken branches and bushes clearly, the pathway obvious.

"They separated from the Shielder," Janis said suddenly.

"What are you on about?" Avryn asked.

"Just keep riding!" she said before allowing her eyes to fill with Light.

The sounds of the rustling plants around her faded away, as did the feeling of the horse below her. She felt light as her body whirled in the colors of a vision beginning. As she focused on Rivelen, she didn't feel the same force blocking her as she had so many times. Sure enough, the scene around her formed into another part of the forest, shouting and panting from a couple people.

Rivelen looked determined as she pressed her way through the tight arrangement of trees and foliage. Her hair was disheveled and dirtied from the hard travels. The red dress she wore, wildly impractical for traveling, made her look even more awkward with rips and dirt smudged all over. Apparently she didn't take the time to Fix her clothing. Probably wise, considering their pursuers. Janis couldn't help but feel amused at the sight, considering just how perfect Rivelen always kept herself in Terris Green.

"Yer goin' too slow! Git yerself up 'ere and Move it all," Rivelen's voice commanded.

"Yeh may 'ave saved me from tha' wretched place, bu' I don' repor' t' the loikes of yous," another voice spoke back. Janis spun in her mind's eye to see the skinny man who'd been captured months ago. A ring of steel protruded from his nostril, and his long ponytail was no longer the lone hair on his head. Fuzz sprouted amid the longer tail of sleek black hair, making the hairstyle look even more ludicrous than before.

Though he argued, he pressed his hand outward, a slight glow emanating from them as the branches and bushes also glowed with red Light. Rivelen shouted at her mount until he scuttled through the foliage. The man continued Moving things out of their way so that they could move quickly through the challenging terrain. He had to angle his horse, so he was slightly behind and to the left of Rivelen so he could get a good sight of the plants he needed to Move. The method was awkward and looked uncomfortable, but ultimately, their horses could travel without too much trouble.

Janis berated herself for not thinking of the same thing. They'd managed to catch up, but at the expense of their horses tiring far more than they could have if she'd been Moving obstructions out of their way.

“Those yeh left won’ last long, not against ’er," the man shouted, his face still concentrated on the way ahead.

"They don’ need t’, jus’ long enough fer us to get over th’ hill," Rivelen said, pointing forward.

Janis saw the ground rising rapidly where the woman pointed. Launching herself upward in the vision, she lost the ability to hear what Rivelen and the man were saying, but she could see the rise coming upward sharply until it created a bluff extending far to the left and right for leagues. Just beyond the rise, an army of black-clad men and women rode thousands of horses. Though she couldn’t see where Prost rode ahead of the pack, she knew he was there, and with him Macks.

Her mind buzzed at the sight. They would be too late if they didn’t hurry. Turning in the other direction, she saw that the vast forest extended in every direction. Thick green canvas of trees and branches created a beautiful scene that she wished she could enjoy for more than a moment. Instead she squinted, trying to find any evidence of where she and Avryn rode behind. Janis’s hopes fell when she couldn’t see anything. She moved her vision-self back downward, following closely behind Rivelen and the man.

Then she noticed something off. There had been three others riding with Rivelen when she last saw them. Eyes widening, she fled the vision as quickly as she could. The moment her eyes focused on Avryn’s back, the horse screamed and collapsed beneath them. Janis slammed forward into Avryn’s back, the two rolling on the forest ground in a tangle.

Janis was the first to recover, though Avryn wasn’t too far behind.

Spinning in all directions, Janis tried to find what had caused the horse to pitch forward. Breath coming in fast spurts, she tried to focus on everything and nothing at once. Leaves rustled in the breeze blowing through the trees, and Avryn’s own gasping and the horse’s whinnying sounded loudly in her ears.

A branch crunched quietly to her right, and she turned sharply to see a brown-clad man. He flipped his hands outward toward her, blue Light shimmering from his palms as something flew in her direction. Janis cursed and dodged the projectiles. She heard thumping as the Conjures slammed into a trunk behind her.

In a flash, she jumped to her feet and rushed the man, who created two more daggers to toss in her direction. Slipping side to side, she pushed her hands outward, Moving the man's body backward until he slammed into the trunk behind him, grunting. Before she could move closer, the man's hand flung upward, a blue Shield forming out of thin air. Janis pressed her heels into the dirt and sticks below her, rooting herself just in time to avoid running headlong into the barrier.

Cursing, Janis dove to the ground as the man lobbed another knife in her direction.

Rolling to her side, she created a Destruction orb and slammed it into the lower half of the Shield. The crack echoed in the trees around them and made her ears ring. The Shield held, but she somehow knew it would fall soon. Before she could create another orb, the man expanded the Shield, knocking her in the side and making her roll through the brush. Gritting her teeth against the pain of the sticks and rocks beneath her, she tried to recover but couldn't until the Shield stopped growing.

"Janis!" she heard Avryn say from somewhere to her left. "You have to go on! Find Rivelen and get that book back!"

His words met her with a powerful force and she nodded, jumping to her feet and weaving through the trees away from the Shield. Another crack echoed in the forest, and a wave of relief washed over her. In her haste to best the person, she'd forgotten that Avryn was well-equipped to handle a Shielder-Conjurer combination Lightbearer. With a glance over her shoulder, she skidded once more to a stop, eyes wide.

The previously blue Shield was now flickering to purple, red, then back to blue. Though she didn't know the man behind the Shield, as Avryn more likely did, his garb showed that he wasn't a Watchlight prisoner who had been released by their traitorous general. Seeing the color of his Light fading to red at least confirmed that the man no longer deserved to be a part of Evenir.

Avryn cried out, pulling Janis back as she wanted to aid him, but he shouted once more over the conflict.

"Go! Now! I've got this!" he shouted.

She spun on her heels and rushed up the hill toward the last quarries.

Janis hadn't been able to get a good idea of how far she'd been from the two escapees, and she gritted her teeth as her chest burned. She'd had years of practice running and gaining stamina, but running headlong up a hill like this was enough to wind even the most fit of people. Weaving through the trees didn't help her move any more swiftly, but still she pressed on, Moving what she could out of the way.

A flash of black caught her attention ahead, and she smiled, knowing that it wasn't part of the fabric of the forest canvas. Before she could revel too much in the sight, her body grew rigid, a slight red tinge glowing on her skin before she flew to the side, her body slamming into a tree and pitching her to her knees. She cursed as her arm throbbed from the impact and her stomach clenched from the sudden change of direction. Still, the power that had grabbed her released her when she landed on the ground.

Fog it. Forgot he's a Mover, she thought grimly, tossing her hands upward and summoning a Shield. She stood steadily, ignoring the pain radiating through her body and head, and pressed through the trees.

Janis felt a tinge of something, a pressure on her Shield that was ever so slight and part of it glowed red before disappearing.

She knew then the man was trying to press her back with his Moving. Smiling, she continued, marveling only slightly at how the trees and shrubs passed through the Shield as she walked through the confined space. Janis had seen this work before but hadn't taken the time to truly focus on the fact that certain things could pass through the Shield when others couldn't.

Deciding it probably had something to do with the threat to the creator of the Shield, she continued running, close enough now that she could see the full person of the black-clad man. A few paces further up and to the left stood Rivelen, eyes wide, staring back at her.

"You didn't think you could get away from me that easily, did you?" Janis teased, shouting over the sounds of the forest.

"Kill 'er!" Rivelen shouted, terror in her eyes.

Janis pressed forward, closing the distance between them, when a loud crack echoed right before her. A powerful force pressed her back and she realized the man had thrown a Destroying orb at her.

They locked eyes for a moment and he grinned evilly.

"Yer Shield won' last ferever," he said with satisfaction, creating another orb. Rather than throwing the creation, he merely opened his hand, the orb flying at her as if it had a mind of its own. Janis tried to shift to the side, but the orb moved too fast, hitting her Shield with another resounding crack. This time Janis could feel her Shield weakening, and she knew that it would fall with the next bout.

Janis watched Rivelen's brown cloak disappear into the trees, a sinking feeling in her gut. In a snap decision, she eyed the man before her, who'd created another orb, and dropped her Shield, throwing her hands forward. His body glowed blue and, with wide eyes, he was flung backward, the orb slipping from his grasp. Landing on the ground where he'd been moments before, the orb exploded, rocks, leaves, and branches flying everywhere from the force.

Janis was pelted by the debris, any exposed skin on her person stinging from the barrage. For a moment she thought she'd killed the man with his own power or at least knocked him out, but her body lurched backward as he grasped her with his Moving. Grunting, she rooted her feet enough that she didn't go flying like she had before but not enough to remain there. She slid back a few paces, teeth clenched. Her foot caught on a branch as her body slid and she almost pitched backward before she threw up another Shield.

Immediately after, another orb smacked her Shield, the sound hurting her ears once more. Expecting another orb, she held her Shield strong, knowing it could take a few more hits before it broke, but nothing came. Scanning the surrounding forest through the translucent Shield proved difficult, given that the scene warped in the Light. Frustrated at herself that she didn't have perfect instincts with her new abilities, she pressed on.

Janis guessed that she'd be able to kill the man easily if she'd had more practice with her Lightbearing.

Though her eyes didn't pick up the evidence of his movement, she heard the rustling of the trees and brush, the sound of someone retreating. She cursed again, dropping her Shield and rushing up the hill, not directly after the man but somewhat parallel. Janis knew if she followed precisely behind where she thought he'd gone, there was more of a chance he could reach her with his Moving ability.

Her heart thundered in her chest as she pressed up the steep incline, dodging branches and using brush as cover. The sun still shone high overhead, but the thickness of the canopy above left the forest floor dim enough that she had to strain to see the ground in front of her. The trees just before her glowed a subtle red, and she cursed, diving to her face before an orb collided with the middle of the tree a few paces ahead. It exploded, leaves, branches, and splinters flying everywhere. Resisting the urge to create a Shield, she let the barrage of nature hit her like the rain in a massive storm. Janis knew that using her Lightbearing would give away her location and she didn't want to risk it.

Holding still for just a moment more, she moved as quietly as possible to the right, toward where the attack had come from. She paused, realizing she could hear shouting.

"She's no' there! Oi swear Oi got her with tha' last one," a man said angrily.

"Rotten luck 'avin t' leave the Shielders behind," a woman's voice replied.

Rivelen. Her voice sounded unfamiliar, strained even, and then Janis recalled the hill she'd just trekked up. Though she didn't know the general well, she suspected that if the hill was challenging for Janis, it would be even worse for Rivelen.

Janis slinked through the trees, surveying the space between the trunks where she could hear the two speaking. A gust of wind made their voices disappear for a moment, but they came back quickly when the leaves calmed down.

"—do yeh s'pose we git down there? Oi can' fly, can yous?" Rivelen was asking.

"Yeh mean yeh didn't figure that out already? Why did yeh bring us this way, then?" the man shouted.

By now, Janis could see them through the trees. She held her breath, though she suspected the blowing of the brush and leaves above was enough to mask her sound. Watching for only a moment, Janis jumped from behind the tree and thrust her hands outward, catching both figures with her push of power. They each glowed blue and flew backward, Rivelen yelping loudly. The man landed hard on his back and rolled over his shoulders before settling on his face. Rivelen slid to the edge of the cliff that Janis hadn't realized was right behind them.

Moving swiftly, she ran at the downed woman, hoping to overtake her. Before she took a few steps, Lightbearing shoved her to the side and she rolled to her left with a grunt, tossing up a Shield to release the Mover's hold on her.

Janis gritted her teeth at the quick succession of Destroying orbs that slammed into her Shield, each blow weakening the barrier until it fell abruptly from the power. She rolled hastily to the right, narrowly dodging the next orb that exploded where she'd been moments before. Another Shield up, Janis could feel the energy draining from her. Expecting the orbs to come flying once more, she eyed the cliff just behind Rivelen, who was now recovering from Janis's hasty Moving.

The next set of Destroying orbs slammed into her Shield, but this time Janis shrunk the Shield so it was just around her person. As they fell, the explosions kicked up rocks and dirt, which pattered along her barrier. Putting all she could into the Shield, she walked as swiftly as possible to the right and toward the man. As she'd hoped, he matched her movements, mirroring her steps, which angled him toward the cliff. His face was dirty and his dark eyes looked determined. She grit her teeth, instincts pushing her to kill him when her mind warned her that she needed to bring him back as a prisoner.

If I could just kill him, my life would be so much easier right now, she thought.

Janis took a moment to note the hideousness of this man. His single, thin black ponytail traveled from the center of the top of his head down his back, the rest of his hair a few finger widths long. The moment he reached where Janis wanted, she dropped the Shield. Unfortunately, the man was waiting for this opportunity, and he threw his hands outward, pressing his Moving on her body. She created another Shield and his force left her suddenly.

I can't reach him with him Moving like this, she thought, trying to stay calm. While she thought, he barraged her with more orbs, fortunately missing more than hitting her narrow Shield. Still, a few slammed into her barrier, cracking loudly and drowning out the forest sounds around them.

She knew she had little time before her Shield would give out and she couldn't keep standing there taking the attack. Without thinking, she did the first thing that came to mind. Pressing outward with her hands, she shoved.

Her blue Shield sped outward, slamming into the now wide-eyed man in front of her. With a shout, he flew backward over the edge of the cliff.

"No!" Rivelen screamed as the man plunged downward and out of sight.

Janis smirked, grateful that her snap decision had worked. While Rivelen was distracted, Janis rushed her. Just then, Rivelen spun back, eyes widening. With a quick snap of her hand, she reached to the pouch at her side and pulled something out, her face scrunching in what looked like pain. Holding the black tome aloft, she threw it outward over the edge of the cliff. Janis's stomach sank as she watched the very quarry she'd been after fly over the edge of the mountain. Though she hadn't reached close enough to the edge of the cliff to see them, she knew Prost's army awaited at the bottom. Teeth clenched, Janis reached out and focused on the flying book. To her relief, her Moving grabbed hold of the small book, the black covers glowing blue with her Lightbearing.

Rivelen glared at her. "Yeh can' 'ave it! Tha's the master's work!"

Eyes full of fire, Janis braced herself for whatever Rivelen would use to attack her. While she knew the former general had no combat Lightbearing, she still carried a sword at her side. Rivelen spun on her heels and, without warning, leapt off the edge of the cliff, grabbing the black book with her hand and falling to her death. Janis cursed, the book ripped from her power's reach, and rushed the edge of the cliff.

By the time she reached the drop, she watched, anger and disbelief swelling within her, as Rivelen's body, now wreathed in a dingy grey smoke, floated slowly to the ground.

Averting her eyes, she looked down to see Prost atop his horse, hand outward toward Rivelen. Next to him sat Macks. She gritted her teeth, seeing her former mentor there with Watchlight. All she wanted to do was slit the man's throat and leave him rotting on the forest floor. Janis then locked her gaze with Prost, who grinned evilly.

24

Prost held his hand outward, guiding the descent of the brown-cloaked woman before him. He grunted in frustration as he realized he'd lost control of his limbs once again. Only moments ago, they'd watched a man fall to his death; his broken corpse still lay on the large stones at the bottom of the rocky cliff. He hadn't seen who it was, but he suspected, and secretly hoped, that it was Mert.

The other members of their army watched with a mixture of shock, horror, and worry on their faces as Prost guided the Evenir deserter downward with his Voidweaving.

No, not his. Ugglyn's.

He struggled internally, fighting to control his body once more, but it had little effect. The only thing he could feel was the intense tingling he experienced when using Voidweaving.

Stay down, dog, this is power beyond your control, Ugglyn roared in his mind.

Before Prost could argue, the tingling stopped as rapidly as it had come. Taking his chance, Prost pushed back to the surface of his mind, Ugglyn's anger rising within his breast. Ignoring the feeling, Prost noticed that the woman had softly alighted on the stones below but wasn't moving. Ugglyn continued to fight for control, leaving Prost's body quivering from exertion.

He angled his gaze upward, his eyes landing on someone standing at the top of the cliff. His insides froze, a mixture of terror and anger swirling inside him as he noted the woman staring at him from above.

Janis.

Narrowing his eyes, he smiled wickedly up at the assassin, knowing that the deserter she'd been chasing was now in their hands. Though he couldn't see her well enough from the distance, he thought he saw her glare back before another man joined her at the edge.

Long hair, large frame, confident stance. Even from here, Prost could recognize Avryn. Ugglyn roared in anger as a strength flooded Prost, pressing Ugglyn deeper in his consciousness. Just as remembering Avryn had aided Prost's escape of Ugglyn's control before, seeing him like this helped Prost gain a stronger footing.

Alts cursed, dismounting and running not toward the woman but instead toward the black-clad man. Prost's chest constricted at seeing the shock on her face as she knelt next to the man who'd just fallen to his death. Her actions confirmed the identity of the now dead Watchlight man. He had no remorse for Mert.

"Vint, go get her, *now*," Prost ordered. The stout man glared at Prost but moved his mount quickly forward.

Vint waited until the last moment to dismount and inspect the woman. "She's unconscious, looks like."

Bring me what's mine! I can sense it, just there! Ugglyn hissed inside his mind.

Locking his jaw until the echoing voice faded, Prost shouted to Vint. "Does she hold anything? Bring me what she has."

From afar, Prost could see Vint lean down and ruffle through the woman's unmoving form before standing up, a small book in his hand.

He cursed suddenly, dropping the book with a shout. "The fog is tha'?" Vint cried out.

Prost's senses heightened and he tensed, the reaction putting him on edge.

The fool! Tell him to ignore the feeling and bring me the text, Ugglyn emphasized again.

Before Prost could convey the message, Vint had already used the edge of his cloak to gingerly grasp the corner of the book, looking at it warily.

Prost furrowed his brow, confused at the significance of the book. Still, a thrill sprang up inside him, Ugglyn's excitement practically bursting from within. Forcing his gaze away from the approaching man and book, he eyed Alts, who wept over the body of her dead lover. Prost felt a twinge of regret for the woman's loss. He never cared for the man that lay dead, but there was something for the woman who cried over him.

As the book approached, clutched tightly in Vint's cloak-covered hand, Prost felt an increasing fear rising within his chest. For the past week Ugglyn had been speaking of whatever this was as if it were a child, cherishing it and wishing it would never have left his grasp. Now that it was right before him, Prost wanted to throw the thing away or even destroy it. The thought crossed his mind, and even though he would have no idea how to do such a thing, Ugglyn pressed sharply on Prost's consciousness, a pain erupting in Prost's head.

Don't even consider such foolishness, lest you wish to die quickly, Ugglyn growled within.

Before Vint made it back to him, the woman stirred on the ground. Prost held up a hand, stopping the approaching man. Vint narrowed his eyes, then spun back toward the woman, pulling his sword out. She stirred slowly at first, then rose on her hands as if she'd just woken from a deep sleep. Prost's gut tightened, anticipating some type of trick, a ploy to get an assassin close enough to him to kill him.

Ugglyn laughed inside.

Never you worry, my friend, this woman is all mine, Ugglyn declared.

While the anti-god's word's should have been encouraging, all they did was sink a deeper feeling of despair within Prost.

Bring the book to me, now! Ugglyn shouted.

Prost couldn't help but wince at the loudness of the voice in his head, drawing the attention of those closest to him. Jord in particular glared at him, his brows furrowed as if he suspected something. The idea that the pet child of Riln stared at him irked Prost still, as it had for years. Before it was simply a minor annoyance, even if the stare made him uncomfortable, but now he knew he wasn't immune to Lightbearing anymore and he half expected a Destroying orb square in the back someday.

Ugglyn continued to curse and shout inside Prost's mind, so much so that he was forced to hold out his hand, requesting the book.

"Forget the woman," Prost said. "Bring the book to me. She won't do us any harm."

Vint hesitated only a moment before walking backward to Prost. Internally, Prost knew it was probably wise to be so wary of the woman on the ground. If she came from Evenir, as Ugglyn professed, she couldn't be considered anything but a possible threat to them. Before long, Vint stood before Prost, his back still to him. He reached over his head, holding the odd black tome closer for Prost to grab.

The hunger grew within Prost, Ugglyn's desire bursting forth as if he'd never wanted anything more in his life. Gritting his teeth, Prost reached out and grabbed it with his bare hand.

He instantly regretted it.

A bursting tingle ran through his arm, so cold it hurt. He gasped, wanting to release the leather-bound book, but his hand was not his anymore. Panicked, he shook his arm, trying to drop the object, but soon the tingling ran through his arm, freezing it in place. Sinister laughter erupted within his mind. Prost shut his eyes and covered his ear with his only free hand, trying to drown out the horrid sound echoing through his head. Prost tried to shout, to ask for help, but Ugglyn clamped his mouth shut, refusing him the ability to get aid. Even if he'd been about to voice something, Prost knew no one could help.

What is this madness? What are you doing to me? Prost roared inside.

Ugglyn continued to laugh, the tingling having reached Prost's chest and now spreading through his other limbs.

Before the fool Lanser sealed me away, I managed to put a piece of my power into this very book. I've been wanting to get my hands on it for years, plotting and tempting Seers to do my bidding. I finally found one willing to use it to summon me, Ugglyn mused.

Prost suddenly realized the significance of Macks, the man who sat on his mount just to his left. He turned his head, finally noticing that all eyes had moved from the woman and were now on him. Fear shone in the black-haired man as he and the others watched whatever power came from within the book taking over Prost's faculties.

I should have killed him when he first came, Prost growled.

Ugglyn hummed within.

Even if you had, the damage was done. I've been working on that woman for months now. Little did I know how easily this tome would have fallen into Evenir's grasp, Ugglyn said.

"Sir, are you all right?" Vint asked, looking over his shoulder warily.

Until then, Prost didn't realize that he'd been grunting and gasping as the power ran through him. He still wanted to plead for help, to scream in pain, but his mouth was still frozen, teeth aching from the firmness of his set jaw. Finally, the tingling having consumed every part of him, it wrapped his whole head, encasing him entirely.

Something snapped within him and he felt himself fall downward until he landed in a dark place, a large window showing what he could see through his eyes.

No—no—no, Prost thought, panicking.

"I'm doing just fine, thank you." Prost heard his voice echo through the odd chamber as if from afar. He detected the change immediately. There was an overlaying echo of a deeper voice, Ugglyn's voice. Vint turned completely around, likely detecting the change in their leader's tone, but he said nothing.

What have you done to me? Prost shouted outward into the darkness.

He remembered this place; he'd been here just a short time ago, back in their lair. Prost shivered, knowing that it meant Ugglyn had full control, just as he'd been working toward all this time.

"It's been far too long since I've been so close to freedom, hundreds of years, in fact," his echoing voice sounded.

Vint's face turned pale, and suddenly, the woman on the ground in front of him didn't seem to concern him. Instinctually, he turned to Prost and bowed his head slightly. The look on his face was something between wonder and horror.

"It's yous, then," Jord said next to him, his own expression hard. "Yeh're finally free?"

Ugglyn tsked loudly before addressing them. "Oh, not fully free quite yet. I've still got work to do, but now that I've had part of my power returned to me, the real war can begin."

Macks shifted uncomfortably in his saddle next to Prost. His jaw was held firm, but there was something deeper in his eyes. Fear.

"You've done well, my subject. I'll admit, when you were the first of my servants to find the book, I thought you'd fail," Prost's voice warbled. Macks stiffened next to him, the fear spreading to a quivering of his whole body. "In part, you did fail, but in the end, I finally have what's mine."

Everyone went silent then, the air growing tense. Only recently had they even learned of Ugglyn's inhabitance within Prost's mind, but now they could see the truth. Prost hadn't been in control for a long time, not fully, and now Ugglyn had the reins.

"What of Prost, sir?" Neera asked, her brow furrowed.

"The nuisance still lives within me, but his dormancy will eventually put him into a long-term slumber," Ugglyn said, grinning.

Prost's eyes widened at hearing the revelation. Somehow he could see his body, a form of himself within this dark place. He wore simple brown clothing, pants and a rough tunic, and he couldn't feel anything save for emotion, the primary one currently being terror. Staring out at the burly man before him, Prost felt a pang of regret, knowing that of the people near him, Neera was the one to ask where he was. He'd detected that she'd become more fond of him over the past weeks. Despite his disinterest in such a relationship, he had grown somewhat accustomed to it.

He tried to turn his head to look at the woman, but his neck failed him. How easily he relied on such instincts, yet now he could not satisfy any of them.

Thoughts of Avryn, his last and only true friend, danced in his mind, and Ugglyn hissed loudly, the sound echoing within the cavern of his mind prison. Even though Prost couldn't feel or control his body, he still somehow knew that the sound came from within. For just a moment feeling returned to his limbs, and Prost stretched his fingers outward, his eyebrows raising slightly before Ugglyn pressed him down.

None of that nonsense! This is my form now, and you'll be better off staying down there, Ugglyn's internal voice scolded him.

Yet Prost couldn't ignore the fact that thoughts of Avryn, as they had in the past, pushed against the power of the anti-god. Confidence burst in his chest, but before he could gather more thoughts and memories of his friend, a fog slammed into his mind, dampening his ability to think. His form swayed as if in a trance and he was forced to just watch, unable to think much at all.

"Wha' of me, then?" A woman's voice sounded in front of them. In the relative chaos of Ugglyn assuming control, he'd forgotten that the woman was there. She now stood tall, her hand on her side sword wavering visibly. Vint turned back to her, holding his weapon at the ready should she jump forward and attack.

"At ease, Vint," Ugglyn's echoing voice said. "That's no way to treat the woman who did this all for me."

The blonde woman looked uneasy, looking at Prost with trepidation. "I did nothin' fer the loiks o' yous."

Prost's insides squirmed at the nerve of the woman, but the only emotion he felt from the anti-god was amusement.

"Ah, but can't you see it? My face may be different, but my aura is the same," Ugglyn mused, bowing his head slightly before returning his gaze to her.

Inspecting him for another moment, her eyebrows shot upward when she made the connection.

"I'm sorry, sir. I din' knows i' was yous," she sputtered, trying to get her bearings.

Prost saw his hand move upward, waving in a nonchalant way, a gesture to glaze over the hardness of her comment.

"In time I'll have my true form back. Until then, I have to use my resources. Now, shall we get to the business of your reward? You still want it, I presume?" Ugglyn asked.

The woman's eyes widened and she nodded, stalking forward warily, her hand still on her side sword. Vint glared at her but stepped aside to let her pass.

Something stirred within Ugglyn, the amusement gone and replaced by something pure, something so dark that Prost gasped from the intensity.

Hatred.

"Rivelen, isn't it?" Ugglyn asked as the woman stepped up next to his mount.

She nodded, eyeing those that sat on their mounts around them.

"Good, now before I give you any such gift, I need you to tell me where to find your little sanctuary," Ugglyn demanded.

She nodded but looked concerned.

"'Ow did yeh want me t' tell yeh? 'Tis right complicated to git there," she said, eyeing the soldiers that sat on their mounts behind and next to him.

"Don't mind them, and don't worry about telling me anything," he said. Prost watched as Ugglyn extended one of his strong hands outward, pressing the tips of his forefinger and middle finger on the woman's head. Suddenly, smokey images exploded from the woman's mind, decorating the stone wall before them. Ugglyn hummed in satisfaction as the smokey scene, mostly of trees and forest canopy, sped forward in an odd dreamlike fashion. Prost, though still feeling foggy within his own mind, watched with fascination as the vision flew forward until it hit the terraced mountains of the east. Eyes wide, Prost witnessed the vision reveal an entrance just beyond one of the small falls near the center of the long mountain range.

"There you are," Ugglyn purred. "After all this time."

Prost's stomach dropped but not from fear. For years Watchlight had known Evenir to be a threat but had no evidence, no thoughts of where they could be housing their large numbers. He'd never thought that they'd be in the mountain range to the east. It seemed logical. Watchlight's lair had been created from Destroying powers into the mountain's heart; why wouldn't Evenir have the same thoughts?

"That's it, thank you," Ugglyn mused, adorning a fond look on his face. "Do you truly want the power of the Void? Do you really want to turn your back on the very god who bestowed the wretched powers of Light upon you?"

Jord's head snapped at Prost, his eyes narrowing. Prost knew the boy was clever, but he was grateful that someone else had noticed Ugglyn's choice of words. Ever so slightly, Jord turned his mount until he fully faced

Prost's form, his hand retreating to just below his waist and to the side. He created a glowing orb of red, almost imperceptible in the bright light of day. Given that the sun was almost directly above them, any Lightbearing was masked by the even brighter orb high above.

Part of Prost hoped that Jord would throw it, kill the being who took control of his body, but he knew that even if the power ripped his form to shreds, Ugglyn would probably be unaffected. Prost knew little of the being, but he suspected that killing Prost would only force Ugglyn to find another host.

Still, seeing the wariness of Jord validated that wrongness of the situation before them. Watching with more unease than anything, Prost eyed the others, the ones he could see through his narrow view. Something clicked in his mind and he realized, fear striking him, that the hatred he felt emanating from within wasn't his own but Ugglyn's. Not for the woman, but anger for the mention of Lanser, for the Light the god had given all Lightbearers.

"I do wan' i'," the woman said, face resolved.

"Wait! M'lord." Neera's voice sounded to his left.

Anger flared within Ugglyn at the interruption. He turned Prost's head in that direction. Neera's eyes were wide and hopeful.

"This power, the Voidweaving you wield. Bestow it on me, as you've promised this woman," she said.

Prost felt sick. He didn't love her, neither did he share the fondness she apparently held for him, but he couldn't believe what he saw in her eyes. Obsession. There was a hunger there, a desire so deep that it infused Prost with an unsettled feeling. The anger emanating from Ugglyn shifted to amusement, then to a sick satisfaction.

Neera slipped from her mount and stood next to Rivelen, the Evenir deserter tensing as she approached.

This one's worship of me is amusing, I have to say. I'll take any opportunity to cull Lightbearers I can, Ugglyn's words echoed in his mind.

Prost knew something was wrong, but he couldn't do anything about it. He didn't love these people, but knowing Ugglyn's true intent filled him with fear.

"So be it," Prost heard his voice say.

With a flourishing gesture, Ugglyn lifted the black tome upward, the pages falling open. Prost couldn't help but marvel at the writing that appeared out of nowhere, written in glowing silver letters as if by an invisible quil. He saw the words but couldn't read them, for they were in the old language, something he'd never bothered to study since he'd skipped university for the militia.

"*K'alek Tar'n yrillnan griltnan ulivar von triltan*," Ugglyn said, his and Prost's voices twirling together and booming loudly against the rock cliff's face twenty paces before them.

Mercurial tendrils of something, almost like squirming snakes, sprung from the pages of the book he held. Hovering there for only a beat, the substance spun on the women, the tips pointing downward like a curious animal before it dove straight at them. Rivelen screamed, throwing her hands upward to block the tendril but to no avail. It slammed into her chest, the entire thing disappearing easily within her. Neera stood there, reverence in her eyes as she allowed the tendril to disappear into her own chest with a slight grunt.

Prost felt sick.

Soldiers shouted in surprise, some drawing their weapons as they all watched Rivelen, wide-eyed and terrified, convulsing where she stood. Her eyes filled with dark smoke, minuscule tendrils of the same silver substance weaving through the darkness. She smiled slightly, looking at something distinctly before her features twisted into a painful expression and she screamed wildly, her hands shooting to her head. Dark veins shot outward from her eyes and filled her face. Soon they covered her whole body, wrapping her from the inside until she fell to the ground, unmoving.

Neera didn't appear to notice the woman's reaction. Her dark-skinned face looked stark against the pale stone wall behind her as she looked upward, her eyes filled with the same mercurial smoke. She was smiling, then she started laughing.

All of a sudden, her mouth twisted downward in pain, face stricken with panic.

"No! Not this!" she screamed. Neera reached up to her head, tugging at her thick black hair before screaming loudly and falling to the ground.

A wave of confusion and fear spread through the soldiers closest to the scene.

"What in Lanser's might did you do to them?" Vint demanded, sheathing his sword and dropping to Neera's level. He felt for a pulse but found none.

Prost heard his voice humming as Ugglyn stared down with his eyes.

"It appears they were both unworthy of the Void," he said, clicking his tongue.

It was a lie. Prost knew it was. The hatred he'd felt from Ugglyn before he'd unleashed whatever power he had on them revealed the truth. He never intended to give them anything, he knew that he would kill them. More of Ugglyn's intentions were revealed, as if Prost could hear the anti-god's thoughts and desires. Prost suddenly knew how Ugglyn felt when he'd been deep within Prost's mind. He must have been able to hear every one of Prost's thoughts, know every one of his intentions.

Casually scanning the other Watchlight members, thousands upon thousands of soldiers, many mounted and some on foot, the sickening satisfaction of the women's demise ran through his being. Ugglyn wished it upon all of them.

"The power of the Void only chooses those it deems worthy, I've found. I fear the Light within these two rejected the gift I tried to give," Ugglyn said, feigning sadness. Prost cursed, shouting internally at his possessor.

"Do yeh intend to kill us all like tha', then?" Jord spat, pulling his hand upward to reveal a Destroying orb.

Ugglyn turned to the boy. "Now, now, let's not be too hasty. If I'd wanted to kill, don't you think I'd have done it already?"

Jord hesitated but already his action prompted more soldiers pulling their weapons from sheaths, others Conjuring various weapons and creating Shields.

"Please, let's calm down. I don't intend to gift the Void to anyone who bears the Light. Your gifts are different, potent, more so than my Void, in a way."

Prost saw his hand move upward and once again marveled at how he couldn't feel any of it; he could only feel the burning satisfaction and hatred from Ugglyn's mind. A ball of smoke formed in his hand, similar in size to Jord's but made from swirling mist and silver veins of power.

"As in the past, the Void is a gift meant only for those who haven't had the favor of Lanser. I hoped my return meant the Void could quell their Light and instead give them my power. It seems that is—still not the case. Know this—I am grateful for the gift of your loyalty, Lightbearers, and would do nothing to break your trust. I promised Riln, as I am promising you today, domination over Lindrad. I can't do that without you. However, given that Evenir has many Lightbearers of their own, I plan to give us an —advantage."

With a quick motion, Ugglyn tossed the orb onto Rivelen's corpse. The moment it collided, it sank into her soundlessly, disintegrating her body into grey dust. Prost's mind, still foggy from the dampening effect Ugglyn had lain on him, sharpened at the sight.

Whispers and conversations broke out around him as people saw what he'd just done. Ugglyn immediately lifted his hand and summoned another orb, preparing to do the same to Neera's body.

"Please, don' do tha'. I think she needs a proper grave," Alts said to the side.

Waves of conversations continued around them as news of what they'd just witnessed passed to the whole of the army. Seething anger flared up at the interruption, but Ugglyn gazed at the woman standing below his mount. He hadn't even noticed her return from the side of her dead lover.

"I'll bury 'er meself," Alts said. Though her eyes were still tear-rimmed, she was determined. Prost was impressed at her resolve to stand up to Ugglyn in such a way. Fortunately, the anti-god ultimately agreed, his anger fusing with amusement enough that he smiled wickedly.

"Do what you will, but we will not wait for you," he said, pulling the reins of his horse taut to spin the beast around.

Ugglyn held up his borrowed hands, trying to quiet those who watched. Though many of the soldiers still held their weapons and conjures aloft, they didn't move to attack.

"There is but one more thing to take care of, now that my text has been restored to me," Ugglyn said, holding out his hand again.

Tension rose in the air among those closest to him, and Prost could see the distrust in their eyes. From inside his own mind, his field of vision moved until it fell on Macks, the man who'd been accompanying them.

"I fear I've no use for you any longer," Ugglyn said casually.

The assassin's eyes widened and he threw his hands upward, likely trying to create a barrier, but before he could, Ugglyn's orb entered his chest, the man letting out a scream of pain as he turned to dust.

Weapons flashed, but Ugglyn held out his free hand, summoning a Shield of shadows that domed around his whole person. Though his vision was cut off from those around him, Prost could still hear the shouts of anger and fear from what they'd just seen.

"Put your weapons away and trust me. That man had no right being among our ranks. He was an assassin, a hired hand who cared only for his self-preservation. It was because of him that we had to wait so long for me to get this power back. I've no quarrel with any of you," Ugglyn shouted through the hazy smoke dome.

Waiting just a beat, Ugglyn waved a hand and the barrier dissipated. To Prost's surprise, no one attacked right out.

"Now, watch as I raise your comrades, your non-Lightbearing counterparts, to a higher status. I will lend them my aid so they can stand and fight side by side with you until we defeat Evenir."

The soldiers shuffled around them. Prost could see the sweat dripping down the faces of the men and women nearest him, and he longed to feel the heat of the sun as they did. Experiencing life with sight and sound alone felt empty. Though the tension in the air was still thick, no one moved on Ugglyn. With a satisfied smile, he looked down at his book again, the words appearing once more.

"*K'alek Tar'n yrillnan griltnan ulivar von irilialin grenvar!*" he read, shouting it loudly this time.

Just as before, power emanated from the small tome in his hands. Prost watched as hundreds of tendrils, the same silvery snakes, flung outward, pouring out at an incredible rate as they flew through the air. The sky became a smattering of mercurial snakes, glinting in the sun high above. Somehow the presence of the odd entities made the wind increase, the air buffeting the clothes and hair of the massive army around him. Shouts of intrigue and wonder came from the soldiers until the first tendril snapped downward, colliding with the chest of a Watchlight woman there. She collapsed with a cry of surprise. Soldiers erupted into chaos as more tendrils dove into the large army as if they were eagles diving on their prey.

Shields popped up everywhere as Lightbearers desperately tried to protect themselves from whatever force was upon them. Men and women batted at the mercurial tendrils attacking from above, their Conjures or steel swords missing the extremely mobile entities. A sinking feeling settled into Prost as he watched, feeling the intense satisfaction of Ugglyn mix with the dread that pressed from his own mind.

"What are yeh doin' to them?" Alts cried from behind.

"I'm helping them realize their potential," Ugglyn replied, a smile spreading on his face.

Jord cursed suddenly as one of the tendrils flew past his head, narrowly missing as it slipped into the chest of the unsuspecting man next to him. The man screamed, tearing at his chest, his hands doing nothing to extract the tendril that had entered through his mail shirt.

Ugglyn turned his attention to the man, watching with satisfaction as he gasped, then held his hand out, a Void sword appearing in it. Perplexed at the event, the man stopped shouting and instead stared at the weapon in his hand.

"I'—burns," he said, but he didn't appear in any pain. "Wha' is 'appenin'?"

Laughing, Ugglyn leaned forward on the horse, smiling broadly at him.

"How do you expect us to gain the upper hand without some advantages of our own? I never intended on keeping Voidweaving to myself," Ugglyn explained. "I've simply raised an army."

Prost's insides twisted at the revelation. Ugglyn had veiled his intentions this whole time, yet the being had been able to decipher every thought that flowed through Prost's mind. Now that he could see the intentions of the anti-god, he wanted more than ever to get him out of his body. Looking upward, Ugglyn and Prost watched as hundreds of the flying tendrils of power flew through the air in every direction.

And Lindrad will finally be mine, Ugglyn thought.

~

Janis cursed as she ran down the steep hill. She'd seen Prost again, but he seemed—different. The theory she'd had before about the man and his connection with Ugglyn was confirmed. The look in his eyes wasn't the same. She'd faced Prost enough times to be able to read his expression; though he would think he veiled his emotions, he was like an open book.

And he'd just killed Macks.

When Macks had aligned with Luden, using his hidden Seeing ability to hunt and murder Lightbearers, Janis had been shocked that he was still alive. Learning that he'd run off to join with Prost was a new low.

Until he'd been dusted. Her stomach twisted and her mind cried out, sorrow longing to burrow its way into her chest at watching the first man she'd loved die in front of her. No, she wouldn't say love. She couldn't admit that to herself. Janis knew a part of her was sad to have seen him die. The other part knew he deserved the death. She shook her head, packing the event away in her mind in favor of figuring out what needed to happen now.

"The army is much larger than I expected," Avryn said breathlessly as they moved down the hill. "We have to warn Evenir and hope that we have enough time to prepare."

"They'll know every way in," Janis surmised, concentrating momentarily as she used some thick roots to step down the steep decline with quick steps. "Rivelen knew everything about the sanctuary, didn't she? We have to assume she told them where Evenir is in visions already."

Avryn grimaced next to her, then nodded. "We're dealing with an insurrection of our own, and now a general is betraying us? How did this happen so quickly? She knows everything about Terris Green and the soldiers we have organized."

"Then we'll have to make some snap changes," Janis replied as she took the last step down the steeper parts of the hill. "How far away is the horse?"

She realized with a start that Avryn had left the traitorous Shielder since he followed her to the cliff's edge. Seeing her expression, Avryn shook his head.

"I didn't leave the man alone; don't panic. I knocked him out and left him with the others. They managed to catch up with enough time for me to leave him apprehended in their hands."

The longbird's song echoed through the trees, indicating the apparent lack of danger. Grateful once again for the natural warning system, Janis turned sharply to Avryn.

"Find the others, tell them we have to leave immediately. I have to contact the Seers in Evenir to let them know of our arrival and that the army is on its way," Janis said.

Avryn's shoulders slumped. "And how do you expect to do that? You know the Shielders are working overtime to veil the sanctuary."

Janis pressed her lips together. "Their Shields are focused on the entrances to the sanctuary, correct? I wouldn't be able to See anyone or anything near them, but I should be able to at least See, even if unclearly, one person."

It was partly a question but mostly an explanation of the thoughts flowing through her head. She'd not tried to See anything within Terris Green before, but she knew they didn't have much of a choice. If they were going to warn Evenir of the incoming army, they couldn't very well send any carrier birds. Janis didn't even know whether Evenir had any of the creatures trained and on hand.

A pit formed in her stomach at the reminder that she knew so little of the organization, yet she'd been made the primary leader over them. Avryn fell silent as they walked, a show of deference to her idea. Avryn wasn't a Seer himself, so he couldn't give much indication of how he thought her attempt at contacting Evenir would work.

"You go on, find the others and tell them we need to mount up and get back as soon as possible," Janis ordered. "With an army of that size, they won't be able to travel quickly enough to keep up with us. It may give us a day or two to aid in the preparations."

Avryn glared at her. "With all due respect," he replied, though his tone didn't bear much respect, "I'm not leaving you alone."

He Conjured a shimmering sword of Light and stood his ground, raising a brow at her.

Rather than argue, Janis just rolled her eyes and concentrated on what she needed. As usual, the forest surrounding her melted into a swirl of colors, the work of art turning into a muddled mess. Though she didn't know the names or faces of any other Seers within Evenir, she knew of one.

Marric.

Even if she'd been aware of who the other Seers were, she wouldn't have even tried contacting them. After the Seer general, the very person tasked with training the other Seers, fell prey to whatever Ugglyn offered her, Janis feared that the others may have also been tempted. It couldn't be coincidental that both Macks and Rivelen, Seers themselves, had aligned with Ugglyn. Janis could see the pattern.

At first the vision didn't form into anything of use. The colors spun and swam in her eyes for longer than they normally did when she used her Sight, but finally it started to form into something. She could see the boy, his features and body still obscured, standing still in the swirl of colors. Straining mentally, Janis could feel that she was pressing through some force, something attempting to keep her Seeing away. Other Seers had described the feeling, and she recalled Avryn saying that weak Shields couldn't prevent a Seer's Sight, but they could muddle it.

After some mental force, Janis felt the Shield give way, and she could See Marric sitting on the edge of a pond of sorts, cavernous stone walls all around him. Her stomach clenched in her body distantly as she found herself back in the stifling stone walls of Terris Green. While she didn't revel being in the open all the time, she had been refreshed with their traveling through the forest, despite the reasons for doing so. Janis immediately noticed that Marric wasn't alone but instead sat with a girl, hair red as fire, freckles adorning her face so much that her skin almost looked a light brown. Whoever she was, she was clearly fond of Marric, for she clung to his arm and laid her head softly on his shoulder.

Janis inspected the room for a moment, realizing how dim it was. A single Lighting orb, likely Marric's given the small size, hung in the air over a small pond of water. She wondered what the point of such a room was but didn't dwell on it for long.

She watched the two sit for a moment before she realized she didn't know how to get his attention. Marric had told her before that he'd been able to pull a Seer into a vision, but he hadn't said anything about how. Urgency pressing at her mind, she hovered her odd vision-form closer to Marric. Even though she knew her hand would pass through him, she flung her palm at his face, using the most practical way of getting a person's attention. The moment her hand passed through his head, he gasped, sitting up straight.

Adrenaline pressed through her body at his reaction, and even though her physical form was distant, she could feel the wave through her body. She jumped back over the pond, crouching low, her eyes scanning the small cavern for danger. Marric's eyes filled with Light and a second version of him, clothed the same as the body Janis could see with the girl, sprung outward until it hovered above the water like Janis's.

It took a beat before his eyes focused and he stared at Janis curiously. His eyes widened at seeing her crouched in such a way and he held out his hand, a sword forming from the Light.

"What's going on? Are we in danger?" he asked, spinning toward the hole in the wall where water trickled in.

"No, I'm just on edge," Janis replied, standing up straight.

Marric turned back to her and relaxed as he spotted her doing the same. He held on to his Conjured sword, and even though she suspected he knew it would do no good in this vision state, she still respected his defense mechanism.

"There's something I need you to do. I could have gone to the other Seers, but with Rivelen having just betrayed us, I didn't want to risk giving the wrong person information," she explained.

Marric nodded slowly but said nothing.

"Rivelen's dead. Prost brought an army of thousands, and he now knows where Terris Green is. It's clear their intentions are to march on the sanctuary immediately. I need you to find Harmel and warn him, tell him to set up defenses everywhere. We have to assume that Rivelen told them everything about the sanctuary."

Marric paled suddenly, a stark difference from the red it had shone just before.

"How long?" he asked, leaving Janis proud for the third time. Rather than dwelling on the fear of the revelation, he cared about the details.

"With the size of their army, it will take them time to move through the forest, perhaps three or four days. I'll try to make it back before then, but—"

Janis! Something's not right! Get back here now!

Avryn's voice echoed in her mind distantly, as if she could hear it with her normal ears but at the same time couldn't. Marric furrowed his brow at her pause, but it was clear he couldn't hear Avryn's echoing voice.

"Something's wrong, I need to go," Janis said suddenly. "Tell Harmel to get ready for the attack immediately."

"But—" Marric began to say before Janis waved her hand, the vision melting into the swirling colors. Her gut wrenched and she readied her mind for a fight.

The moment the colors formed into the forest backdrop around her, she snatched the daggers in her hip hilts, holding them outward.

"No, not down *here*," Avryn hissed. "Look up there!"

She averted her eyes, looking through the narrow bits of sky they could see through the canopy of leaves above. For a moment Janis only saw the moving leaves of the massive trees until she saw a glint of something in the blue sky above.

"What in Lanser's great name?" she whispered, seeing what Avryn meant.

Something flew in the sky, something unnatural. Though she couldn't make them out well enough, given how high they were in the sky, it was clear they weren't a normal part of the Lindradian skyline. One of the entities meandered lazily along the sky, giving Janis a good view.

It looked like an eel made of metal—silver, to be exact. Wriggling through the air at a slow pace, hundreds of others flipped and swam past the other, moving in the direction of the mountains in the east. Janis's chest constricted as she realized these came from the direction of the cliff behind them. Cursing, she spun on her heels and rushed back up the hill, her already exhausted legs screaming at her as she pushed through the pain. Avryn called to her, but she ignored him.

The steepness of the climb and the frustration from her mind that she was retracing her steps was suppressed by her desire to see what Prost had done. Even though she didn't know what hovered in the air high above, she knew it had something to do with the book. It couldn't be a coincidence; Janis knew it.

She could hear the brush shuffling and branches cracking behind her as Avryn trundled through the trees after her. Flashing blue Light and shadows on the trees in front of her told her that Avryn had Conjured something in his defense. She knew it would do little good, for there was no way Prost and his army had scaled the cliff that quickly.

Still, she followed Avryn's example by gripping her daggers tightly in preparation. At length, she made it to the top of the steep incline, stopping just short of the immediate drop before her.

The scene before her made her blood run cold.

The same silver eels, or whatever they were, flipped and spun through the air, though there were far fewer down below. Still, she witnessed one slip silently into a screaming woman, who doubled over, a dome of smoke forming rapidly around her like a Lightbearing Shield made of shadows. Silvery veins of power rippled through the dome momentarily until it disappeared. All around, Janis could see others wielding weapons of the same substance, while others' eyes were filled with the shadows. Screams and shouts echoed in the air, and Janis realized she'd heard them as she ran but hadn't registered it given her breakneck speed.

The urgency intensified in Janis and she knew they had to get back to Terris Green. Avryn stumbled next to her, panting loudly.

"What in the blazes were you—" He stopped, seeing the scene below, then cursing, continued. "What is going on down there?"

Janis grimaced. "Something of the Void. They look like reverse Lightbearers."

It was the best way to describe what she saw, but her thoughts on the matter melted away as she locked eyes with the scar-faced man, an evil smile on his face. He held the pitch-black book in one hand and a smoke sword in the other.

Something dark and cold sat in that gaze. Though she could only watch from afar, Janis could tell that Prost was gone, overcome by a darker essence.

25

Marric gasped as he felt his limbs more potently. The moment Janis had left, his vision-form melded back into his body instantly, emotions wracking his chest almost painfully. He could still feel the burning desire in his chest, emanating from Miredith's grasp on his arm and her head on his shoulder, but now a fear rocked him.

Miredith sat up sharply, looking at him curiously. "What happened? Is everything ok?"

He shook his head but needed a moment to find the words to speak. Marric stared at the lone thumbnail orb he'd created, focusing on the Light it spread throughout the small cave. His chest pounded from nerves as he took in what he had to tell Harmel.

"Janis came. She told me something. I need to find Harmel right now," he said, jumping up so quickly that his head ran into the lower part of the cave wall. He cursed, holding his throbbing head for a moment while the pain subsided.

"What did she say? What's going on?" Miredith said. "I saw the Light in your eyes for only a second before you gasped like a madman."

He shook his head. "No time, I need to go. You can stay here. I'll see you later."

Marric looked at her apologetically, then rushed to the small opening back to the cavern with the larger lake. The moment he reached the entrance, however, he paused, realizing that he didn't remember how to navigate Terris Green. Miredith had led him through places he'd never been and he knew he'd get lost trying to go on his own.

Seeing his pause, Miredith folded her arms, looking at him skeptically. "You remember the way out, then?" she asked.

He responded by shaking his head and stepping aside from the opening. She rolled her eyes, then moved to the hole and climbed through easily.

He was surprised to see that the larger room was more filled with people moving in and out busily as they went about their business.

"Are you going to tell me what's going on? You look like you're going to be sick at any moment," Miredith said, standing just outside the smaller pond room.

Marric pressed his lips together, knowing that Janis preferred he not say anything to anyone about her message but also knowing Miredith to be a stubborn person. He opened his mouth to respond but closed it quickly as a man and a woman, each carrying closed baskets of something, walked up to them. Marric reached out and softly pulled Miredith by the arm to the side away from the lake in the middle of the room so the strangers could pass.

"I'm not supposed to tell anyone," he hissed when they'd moved far enough away.

Miredith folded her arms again, lifting her chin. Her hair flipped backward, the red strands glinting in the soft blue light of the orbs overhead. She stood there saying nothing but her message was clear. She wouldn't be taking him anywhere until he told her what Janis had said. Scoffing, he shook his head.

"Fine! But don't you go telling anyone yet until I can find Harmel," he said.

She smiled, a triumphant look on her face as she leaned in expectantly.

"An army is coming from Watchlight. You know Rivelen, the woman who ran away?"

Miredith gave him an annoyed look. "I've been here longer than you. I know most everyone."

He grimaced at her words, feeling silly at not thinking of that.

"She told them where we are, and they are on their way," he said.

Miredith cursed, for once holding her words inside as she spun on her heel and began running toward what Marric assumed was the entrance they'd used on the way in. Unfortunately, with the newfound busyness of the cavern, they moved in the opposite direction of the flow of people. Marric blushed, keeping his eyes down as they slipped by a half dozen perplexed people in what appeared to be the wrong direction. Once, Marric almost slipped into the depths of the horrifyingly still water in the center of the large cave. He shivered, his mind creating images of creatures hiding in the deep black waters below.

Miredith appeared to have no problem traveling along the narrow pathway, even as she weaved in and out of those moving toward them. More than once she was given a stern look, Marric's blush deepening as their critical gazes landed on him.

Fortunately, they exited the cavern quickly enough that Marric could hide behind the walls of the tunnel just outside the lake room, though he could somehow still feel the annoyed faces boring a hole in his back.

"When will they be here?" Miredith asked as she continued moving down the hallway.

"Days, that's all I know. Janis said they would try to be back before the army arrives, but I'm not sure that'll happen," he explained, still unsure why he was giving more details to this girl.

With a grim expression, Miredith sped off quickly, the revelation of the timing apparently motivating her even more to find Harmel.

"He's probably in the main cavern; that's where most people are during the day," she said.

Marric thought of Harmel and how he'd been named second. It felt fair that a good man like him should be rewarded in such a way, especially after the death of his brother. Marric's stomach turned, sorrow constricting his chest. He'd not forgotten Shrell's death, but the sadness of it had been drowned out in the overwhelm he'd felt for the past week. Every once in a while, like just now, the memory of his friend came back to him and he resisted the urge to sob.

The pathway Miredith took them along was far quicker than Marric expected. At some point as they rushed through the stone tunnels, Marric began to recognize various places until he knew exactly where they were. As they entered the cavern, the thunderous sound of feet shuffling, hundreds of conversations, and rations and wares being sold flooded his ears.

"Look around! He could be anywhere," Miredith yelled over the throng.

"It will take too long; we have to ask someone," Marric suggested, but Miredith was already slipping through the crowd, apparently uninterested in what Marric had to say.

He paused, watching her disappear into the throng of people. For a moment he thought he should have followed but then realized he could find Harmel more quickly without wandering around the crowded room. Focusing on the sensation of entering a vision, he felt his eyes expand and he knew they glowed with blue Light. His vision-form separated from his body, hovering just over his head, when he thought of Harmel's face. Immediately, his incorporeal form shot through the air to the other side of the cavern, where he saw Harmel in a conversation with a man and woman. Spinning around, he could see the steady glow of his eyes from his vantage point over the larger crowd. Satisfied, he allowed the room to melt away into colors and blurs until he stood back in his body.

"Yeh alroit there? Oi thought Oi was 'bout to knock the loiks of yous over, Oi did," a man said just next to him.

Marric started, noticing that the man carried a large pallet of something on his head, the square wooden platform at least four times as wide as the man. When Marric didn't respond right away, the man raised his eyebrows at him questioningly.

"Oh, I'm sorry. I was just looking for someone, but I found him right over—"

His words were cut short as piercing screams echoed throughout the cavern. Marric's chest constricted and his blood ran cold at the sound. He instinctively Conjured a bow and arrow, spinning around to find the source of the screams. By then, more shouts and screams echoed in the large stone room. Movement above made him snap his attention upward. Silver tendrils of what looked like shiny metal wove in and out of each other lazily near the ceiling. Furrowing his brow, Marric tried to get a good look at one of them but couldn't because they moved too quickly. He was struck with fear as he spotted one of the tendrils snapping downward directly at him. He gasped, nocking his arrow and aiming. With practiced precision, he let the arrow fly, but the tendril flipped over, avoiding contact with his weapon. Before he could Conjure another, the tendril flew just past him, the air rushing past his ear.

"The fog—?" the older gentleman exclaimed before the pallet on his head came crashing downward loudly. Leather waterskins, woven baskets, and other handmade goods spilled on the ground. Marric spun toward him, cursing that he wasn't a Fixer who could mend whatever injury the spindly silver tendril had caused. With his bow still in his hand, he moved to the older man and helped him up.

"Wha' 'appened t' me?" the man said, holding his head. He held his head up, looking upward, and Marric gasped. The man's eyes were filled with grey smoke, metallic spindles of something moving within.

Marric backed away, his breath catching in his throat. Chaos erupted in the cavern as Shielders, Conjurers, and Movers used whatever means they had to block themselves and those around them from the strange attack from above. Realizing he didn't know what had just happened and that he didn't want to be near the man with the odd smoke-filled eyes, he dashed through the chaotic crowd toward where Miredith had disappeared. Bodies slammed into him multiple times as men and women tried to defend themselves. Someone's foot came out in front of him and he tripped on it, the momentum pitching him forward momentarily until he righted himself.

"Marric!"

Miredith's voice called from somewhere ahead and relief filled him. Through the undulating fabric of noises, he could barely spot Miredith's bright red hair.

Bless that hair, he thought, pushing forward. He was forced to let his bow disappear in order to press his way more fervently through the crowd, and soon he found himself right next to Miredith.

"What are those things?" she asked, her expression surprisingly resolute considering the situation.

"I—I don't know, but they're attacking people," Marric said as he watched another tendril disappear into a woman's chest. She screamed, crumpling to the ground. Immediately, a dome of dark grey smoke appeared around her, like a Shield made of darkness rather than Light.

"I can see that! We need to find Harmel *now*," Miredith reminded him and he nodded, grasping her outstretched hand as she pressed forcefully through the throng. Another glint from above drew his attention there, and he saw another tendril diving directly at them. Cursing, he pulled his hand from Miredith's and Conjured a sword. Focusing intently on the movement of the entity, he tried to time a swipe over his head, hoping that doing so above would prevent him from accidentally skewering one of the Evenir citizens. At the last second, however, the tendril switched course, slipping easily into Miredith's back.

The girl fell forward, shock on her face.

"No! No-no-no," he stammered, falling to his knees next to the girl.

He shook her back, trying to rouse her, and she looked up far more quickly than he anticipated.

"Miredith? Are you all right?" he gasped. His vision blurred and it took him a moment to realize that tears were forming in his eyes. Wiping them away, he helped Miredith sit up. Her eyes were still wide and she shivered.

"Something doesn't feel right," she said, staring at the ground. "I feel—cold. Like a winter storm is brewing inside of me."

She grimaced and held her hands to her chest. The moment she moved the hand, something appeared in her palm. Gasping, she jumped to her feet, looking in shock as a perfectly crafted sword made from swirling shadows formed, the same minuscule silver tendrils swimming throughout it.

"What is happening—?" she asked, looking over at Marric for an answer.

His world was spinning and he couldn't find the words. Slowly his mind reminded him that he was meant to deliver a message to Harmel.

But all he could think about was what just happened and what it meant for the incoming army.

~

JANIS KICKED HER HORSE, shouting for it to move more quickly through the forest. The moment she'd seen the things flying above, she'd rushed to where Avryn had left the horses. Though she wished they could have stayed together as a group, they didn't have enough horses for all the party to rush back, given that they now had two traitors tied up to bring back to the sanctuary. At first she'd thought to just kill them for their treason, but Avryn indicated that they probably should be more lenient. Something about being too harsh in her first days as the appointed leader. Instead she, Avryn, and Turrin had rushed ahead to help Evenir prepare for the coming army. It had already been a whole day since she'd witnessed the strange silvery tendrils flying in the air.

Lightning flashed above in the darkening sky, and she grit her teeth against the harsh wind. Even in the thickness of the forest, the weather buffeted them. Throughout the majority of their chase after Rivelen, the weather had been perfect—not a cloud in the sky, or at least from what they could see through the leaves and branches above. Now that their urgency was even more intense, the storm chose to follow them.

"We can't keep moving at this pace!" Avryn shouted over the storm.

She knew he was right, but her gut told her that they needed to get back soon, not just for the preparations but because of another idea that had come to her as they ran.

"The horses will have to last! We can keep Fixing them, giving them bursts of energy," Janis suggested, pulling her horse to a slowed pace so they could move through a particularly thick set of shrubs.

"While I am worried about the horses, I'm more concerned—"

A clap of thunder high above drowned out his last words. The air tensed with energy at the nearness of that lightning. Janis put her head down instinctively, waiting for another clap of thunder for only a moment before she pressed on.

"We're hours away," Janis replied, continuing her push. Though they couldn't make the horses run, she knew if they kept rushing, they had a chance of making it before the storm.

"Yes, I know that, but we won't do any good if we're killed," Avryn pointed out.

"Oh, i' ain' tha' bad, is i'?" Turrin shouted over the noise.

Janis couldn't help but roll her eyes. Of course the jovial man thought this was fun. He hadn't said anything of the sort, but his choice of words and the way he said them spoke loads of what he was thinking. The older man reminded her all too much of Harmel.

Her stomach flipped at the thought of her newly appointed second. If she had any intention of trying to stay away from the silly man before, she had little hope now. Janis's mind reeled at her decision to give him the position. She really didn't have much choice, given that the only other people she knew well enough in Evenir were Marric, who was too young, and Avryn. If Shrell still lived, she wondered, would he have been her choice?

"We press on," Janis decided, pushing her mount forward through the trees. While their pace was slow, she knew that she'd rather risk the storm than waste time waiting.

A flash of blue Light reflected off the trees in front of Janis and she tensed, her instincts telling her that it didn't come from the right place for it to be lightning. She spun around just in time to see a Destroying orb slam into the trees ten paces before her. Cursing, she dropped low against the horse's mane and summoned a Shield to block the three of them.

"S'all right, 'is only me, see?" Turrin shouted over the wind.

She stared at him incredulously at the insanity of what he'd just done.

"Wha'? Yeh said yeh wanted t' git back 'afore long, so let's git back, then," he said.

Slightly confused, Janis looked to Avryn, who sat with a serious look on his face.

"We can't do that! They'll know the exact way to our sanctuary! You want to lead them there easily?" Though even as the words left his mouth, his face betrayed the realization that it didn't matter anymore. "I rescind that comment. If that's what you wish, we can make a path for ourselves."

Janis nodded her head resolutely. It sounded brutish and admittedly far beyond her normal preference when traveling through the forest, but she had come to terms with the fact that she was a Lightbearer now and the leader of Evenir. She had to stop living and thinking like an assassin eventually.

Turrin pumped his fist in the air, clearly excited about the allowance.

"Wif the free o' us, we can ge' through the forest righ' fast, methinks," he said, creating another orb.

With that, Janis focused again on the trees before her, creating her own orb of Light. With a hesitant sigh, she lobbed the orb, aided by her Moving for better precision, so it slammed into the trunk of the largest tree. Another blue Light flung from behind, followed by a third. In seconds, the obstacles before them disappeared to splinters and debris-littered ground.

Before long, the three carried on a pace three times that of their former one as they fell into a rhythm of Destroying and galloping through the forest.

Hope sprang up in Janis as she realized they'd be back in Terris Green within the hour. She hoped she'd find them prepared for the Watchlight onslaught. Janis trusted Marric, and she didn't doubt Harmel's ability to organize, but part of her still warned that if Rivelen had gone astray, there could be other Lightbearers who'd fallen prey to the temptations of the anti-god.

And if there were more betrayers, she didn't know how they'd outlast the army coming for them.

Lightning cracked overhead, announcing the impending storm. Prost flinched at the sound, lamenting the fact that he couldn't have sensed the storm if he wanted to. Ever since he'd been suppressed in his own mind, he could experience nothing but sound and sight and the obtrusive emotions of the volatile anti-god that controlled him.

Ugglyn fumed inside, knowing that his revenge was being delayed by the elements.

"Are yeh crazy? We 'ave t' git somewhere safe from the storm. We can' travel in it loik this," Alts complained next to him.

Ugglyn fixed his gaze upon her, and Prost couldn't help but feel the same burning desire he had before losing control of his faculties. Fury stoked up a fire from Ugglyn at the conflicting emotion from Prost.

Keep that passion to yourself. You're already a plague enough for my goals, Ugglyn roared inside.

The fog that held Prost captive continued to press upon his mind, making it difficult to process much, yet strong emotions of his own provided some semblance of lucidity. As the dull fog pressed upon his mind, Prost focused on the trees around them, lit up by periodic lightning and the steady blue glow of the moon behind the clouds. Even then, red orbs of Light hovered everywhere, hundreds of them, to light the way through the forest.

"A little rain won't do us any harm," Ugglyn said haughtily, "and if you think that it will be a problem, perhaps it was better for you to be left at the lair, waiting until Evenir came to get you."

Alts scowled at him. She wore her emotions on her face, something that Prost knew was inadvisable for a warrior such as her, but the fact that she did was a bold move that made him like her even more.

Before the desire could burn up again, the fog pressed inward on his mind. Prost grunted from the effort but eventually gave in.

"No, sir. I'll be fine," she said, though the fire burned in her eyes.

Movement to their right made them snap their attention in that direction. Ugglyn sat upright, apparently unbothered by the approaching person.

"They're a bunch of crazies, they are! Foggin' fools are going to get themselves killed," Vint complained from afar. Alts released her Conjured daggers the moment she realized who it was coming toward them. Jord, riding just to Prost's left, held a Destroying orb he'd created in his defense from the sound.

"How do you expect us to help them see when they just shout at us, cursing us like animals?" Vint complained. He reached up, nursing a cut on his arm. It wasn't deep, but it appeared that if he hadn't been fast on his feet, it could have been a severed arm.

Ugglyn raised an eyebrow. "Having trouble with the Voidweavers, I see?"

Vint scoffed. "Trouble is a nice way of saying it. They curse us every time we get close, telling us that the Light is a plague to them. Why ask us to make sure they're keeping pace with the group when they want us far away from them?"

Sighing, Ugglyn turned forward, pointedly not looking at the man he addressed.

"Leave them be, I will guide them myself," Ugglyn said.

Vint scowled, then turned around and gestured to another man there. The soldier reacted quickly, moving to Vint's side to Fix the wound in his arm and tear in his shirt.

"How do you expect to do that? The gift you gave them, they're all smoke and darkness, so they can't see a thing in this din. The clouds may be lit above, but that canopy is too thick," Vint surmised.

Ugglyn looked lazily over to where he could sense the thousands of new warriors he'd created. Though the connection was still weak, he knew it would grow in time. The past days had proven sufficient for his bond to them to strengthen enough that he could guide them. Through the trees, he could see their dark forms moving, some on foot, others on horseback, a few spotty Lighting orbs hovering high above.

"Call the Lightbearers back. These men will be fine on their own now," Prost's own voice said, Ugglyn's echoing voice overlaying it eerily.

Vint stared at him, then looked from him to Jord, then back again. The glance indicated something dangerous. Prost had lied about Riln's wishes, never having been made the former leader's successor, but many looked to Jord as the de facto leader. Given the circumstances, Prost was able to curb that for the most part, asserting dominance over the younger boy, but things were slipping, and Prost knew it.

Fury burned within Ugglyn once again at the thought of the Light-bearing around him. He eyed the orb hovering above Jord's hand before swiping his own through the air.

"Put that horrid Light away, we've enough of it above, we don't need more of it tainting the area around us," Prost heard himself hiss at Jord.

The boy narrowed his eyes at him but didn't move. A strong desire to kill Jord filled Prost and he gasped inside, the strength of the hatred, even though it wasn't his own, pushing through the suppressing fog in his mind.

"If you're so scared of it, why bring us?" Jord asked.

An impish grin formed on his face, the fire within Ugglyn stoking to such a high level that Prost buckled under the emotion. Despite the raging emotions within, Prost could hear Ugglyn's even tone.

"Fine, keep it, if that's what you want. The Voidweavers are still infants, new to their powers. If we're to triumph over these petty Lightbearers of Evenir, we'll need all of us," Ugglyn spat.

Though the words indicated working together, the tone of his words carried something deeper, something that Jord could clearly sense right away. Ugglyn would work with them, but only because he felt he didn't have a choice.

Something stirred within Prost's mind and he shivered. Ugglyn reacted to the same feeling, looking over to where the large group of men and women traveled parallel to the main group. With a start, Prost realized he could sense them. As if they were small pinpricks of energy, a dark shadow from a distance, Prost could sense all those who'd been hit with the Void tendrils the day before. Until now, he'd not noticed it, but the connection was more potent than before. Ugglyn smiled at the realization.

An uneasy feeling settled inside Prost as he realized there were more connections, distant, yet becoming stronger and closer as they traveled.

He'd seen the tendrils flowing outward through the sky but hadn't thought about where they were or what they did. Prost desperately pressed at the fog that kept him suppressed, trying to find any emotion that could pull him upward. An image of Avryn flashed in his mind, a memory, foggy, but becoming clearer every moment. As if a beacon in the darkest storm, he saw Avryn and himself, poised with their swords in the arena in T'Arren Vale, grins on both of their faces. Immediately, the brotherhood, the feeling of belonging with his brother-in-arms, pushed the fog away from his mind. Prost gasped as he could feel his arms and his fingers, which he flexed. Ugglyn roared in his mind, shouting for him to stop.

"Not—safe—for you," Prost managed to say out loud. Jord's eyes snapped to Prost, his hand tightening around his orb.

The pressure inside his mind intensified, pulling him back within the confines of his mind, the speed of the change making him feel nauseous. Vint, Alts, and Jord exchanged glances, their attention only being pulled away by the sound of another man approaching.

"Sir!" the man called from the shadows of the trees.

Ugglyn sat straighter in the saddle, flexing his hands open and closed for a moment to regain his composure from Prost's sudden intrusion.

"What do you want?" he snapped, his voice coming out impatient. Prost smiled with satisfaction. Even though he'd only gained control for a moment, it was enough to fluster the anti-god. The effect didn't last long however.

"How long until we get there? The men are restless."

Prost couldn't help but notice the odd tone of the man's voice. It sounded as if he was not really there, as if he was in a trance of some sort. Despite the man's arrival, the tension didn't ease in the air, or at least Prost assumed so given that he couldn't feel anything except Ugglyn's emotions. Jord's tense muscles were the best indicator.

"This blasted storm is making things difficult," Ugglyn protested as the lightning cracked above, "but I think within two days, or one if we are fortunate."

The man grimaced as if this was the worst piece of news he could have received. "Why did you ask these *plagued* Lightbearers to accompany us? With the new Voidweaving we have been given, we can manage without their aid," the man said.

Vint scowled at his words. "If you want to walk in the dark, then go ahead. Don't complain to us if you stub your toes or stumble your horses."

Fury exploded within Prost and he gasped at its intensity. Despite the emotion, Prost could hear his voice, even and normal.

"I wasn't sure when your abilities would come to fruition, but I see that they are nearly there. The Lightbearers will back off, no need to worry about them any longer," Ugglyn assured him.

The man bowed his head, the trancelike sound still thick within his voice. He stood there momentarily before he glared pointedly at Jord with his Destroying orb. Without hesitation, he summoned a Void sword, the dark blade swirling with the smoke it was made from. Prost's insides lurched at the sight. Until a few days ago, those had been abilities that he thought were unique to him. Now that there were thousands of others with the same gifts, Prost realized how wrong they felt.

The irony wasn't lost on him. For years Lightbearing had felt unnatural and wrong, even with him being immune; now this new power bothered him in a different way.

Vint drew his sword, and Alts Conjured her daggers in response to the man's action, and the four had a stare-down. The same odd feeling he'd noticed earlier stirred within and Ugglyn spoke.

Calm yourself, now is not the time for infighting. There will be plenty of that later, his deep voice echoed. A pulse of something shot through the air, unseen to anyone save for the two who shared a body, until it washed over the man. The newcomer sucked in a loud breath, then relaxed, the sword disappearing from his hand with a puff.

"Return to the others, and beware of the fog," Ugglyn ordered. "Keep pace in this direction, watch the Lights from afar, and follow along."

The man nodded, a blank expression in his eyes, before he turned and stalked off toward the others.

"What the fog was that about?" Vint said, glaring at Prost. "What's got them all fired up?"

It was clear he wanted an answer from Ugglyn, but the being didn't offer one up.

"The lesson you've learned today is to stay away from the Voidweavers for now. Things will make more sense when we get to Evenir's lair and start killing them one by one," Ugglyn replied instead.

Alts grunted. "Tha's easy fer yeh to say. Yeh're gonna send the lowly ones in first, don' righ' care if'n they die fer yous."

The woman's comments earned her a steady gaze from Ugglyn. Though the fire burned within him, he once again masked it all with his expression. "I've gotten you this far, have I not? Trust me; in the end, our crusade will be successful. The addition of my Voidweavers will lead us to the victory we've been working on for years."

Alts threw her hands in the air, not believing his words at all but not having anything to say to it. Vint continued to watch Prost with a measured look, and Jord just looked away, his hand still holding the orb. After a few moments the boy lobbed the ball outward, the power connecting with a tree with a loud crack. Ugglyn winced at the pain from the flashing light, his eyes flickering toward Vint and Alts to see if they noticed his reaction.

The mental suppression hadn't returned to his mind, and Prost pressed hard against his captor. Ugglyn resisted easily, pushing Prost's measly attempt back.

If Voidweaving is really the way to win this, why is it that you couldn't create something unique? Prost teased. *Voidweaving is bound by the same restrictions as Lightbearing. They'll detect it easily.*

The fiery hot anger redirected from his companions to Prost, causing him to gasp once again.

Prod all you want. We can and will overtake every Lightbearer. The Void was patterned after Lightbearing, but it bears the exact qualities needed to kill them.

Satisfaction roiled through his chest at the thought of overtaking Evenir. Prost gasped as the suppressing brain fog slammed into his consciousness, forcing him downward.

As his consciousness was lost to the darkness within his mind, Prost felt despair at knowing that they neared Evenir's sanctuary. The hope he held in seeing Avryn once more snuffed into nothing as he fell into a sleep.

26

The rain slammed into them, cold water seeping into every seam and crack of Janis's clothing and provisions. She gritted her teeth against the torrent and tossed another Destroying orb into a large tree. It exploded easily, as if it hadn't been there at all.

"There it is!" Avryn shouted over the torrent.

Lightning boomed directly above them and Janis's hair stood on end at the realization of just how close the lightning was to them. The rain and wind hadn't begun until ten minutes ago, when their rapid pace was forced to slow. She'd been soaked within seconds, the wall of rain hitting them hard and fast.

Turrin grunted loudly and flung one last orb that cleared the way to the waterfall before the entrance to their sanctuary. Janis expected to feel something like relief at making it back to the safety of their stone caverns and tunnels, but she knew that they were no longer safe.

As they moved out of the trees, the wind snapped into them even harder, causing her black cloak to flap wildly behind. She had half a mind to open the clasp at her neck to rid herself of the ghastly piece of cloth but she held it firm. Just then, an arrow snapped past her head, disappearing into the brush behind her. She cursed and almost dove from her mount before Avryn held out his hand.

"Don't move! They're trained to kill you if you try to flee or attack," Avryn shouted.

Her insides screamed for her to run or dash directly at the waterfall, but she held back. Avryn Conjured a sword in one hand and summoned a Lighting orb in his other hand. Though small, the blue Light pierced the night.

Over the din of the storm, Janis could hear a shouting and halted conversation before half a dozen men, all bearing bows and crossbows, stepped out from behind the falls.

"Fog me good, you're back!" one of the soldiers said, dropping his weapon.

Avryn sighed and moved his horse through the clearing, the other two following his lead.

The man at the front of the grouped soldiers waved his hand, telling the others to put their weapons down. Avryn grinned, his sopping hair strung in strands down his cheeks and sticking to his back. Janis watched uncomfortably as the two men embraced for a moment before pulling apart. Another crack of lightning above reminded her that it would be better to get out of the storm rather than observe from afar. The three travelers stepped carefully behind the waterfall and through the stone entrance behind. It felt like ages since she'd set foot indoors despite having only been gone for just under a week. She admittedly wasn't thrilled to be back. Musty warm air met her and she couldn't help but crinkle her nose. Just through the stone doorway, two dozen men and women stood at the ready. At the forefront stood soldiers with spears and swords, while a few paces behind them were archers. A few held weapons Conjured from the brilliant blue of Lightbearing, while the others held weapons of steel. In the small space, only twenty paces wide, then tapering off to a narrow tunnel after, the array of defenders looked uncomfortable and cramped.

Still, seeing them brought a certain amount of peace to Janis. Normally, only a few guards stood at each entrance, and the fact that more were stationed here meant that Marric had been able to deliver the message to Harmel.

The soldiers all saluted her, standing stiff and formal. Her gut twisted at the treatment, wishing that they'd return to their hardened and critical gazes. At least when she was just the unknown assassin she got the reactions she'd been used to for years. When people were scared of her, even if they despised her, it was something she could deal with. Despite their formal reaction, she could see doubt in their eyes. Something else was there in their expressions, as if they were agitated by something more than her mere presence. For a moment she thought to ask them what was wrong, but the urgency of the coming army and the task she had set her mind to would have to come first.

Trust me, I feel the same way about this arrangement, she thought grimly, nodding to the soldiers and locking eyes with them one by one until she moved past. She couldn't help but curse Avryn internally for putting her in this situation, but there was nothing she could do about it now except move forward.

"Have there been any signs of attacks from Watchlight as of yet?" she asked the man who escorted them through the throng of soldiers.

He shook his head, pausing to let her walk first through the next entrance into a larger tunnel.

"None yet. Harmel didn't give us any idea of how long it might be until the army arrives. Our scouts are watching adamantly from above, but the storm is making it hard for them to see anything," the soldier reported.

"What of the Seers? Are they scouring the surrounding areas for any signs of trouble?" Avryn asked, drawing the attention of the soldier. He looked warily at Avryn, then back at Janis, as if he was afraid to undermine her authority by answering the question.

Resisting the urge to roll her eyes, she gestured to the man to answer.

"Um, yes, they are watching, but I think that Watchlight will probably have Shielders blocking the way. I don't think the Seers would see much if they were close," the man replied.

Janis hadn't considered the fact that the normal scout arrangement could be enhanced by Seers. She still didn't understand the ins and outs of Lightbearing enough, let alone how to use the knowledge to properly lead an organization of thousands.

"Well, at least they haven't seen glowing domes of Light. If they were close, a red glow would give Watchlight away quickly," Janis surmised.

Avryn looked impressed. The conclusion was apparently beyond what he thought she was capable of. Janis felt both proud and annoyed at his reaction. If he truly felt that she'd be the best person to lead Evenir, he ought to expect more of her. He pressed his lips together, allowing her to take the lead in the conversation.

"The main army is still at least a day's time out, if not more. The storm will be holding them back, but with the intensity of the throng out there, I think it should end quickly," she said. "What we're looking for is parties that Watchlight may have sent ahead of time."

The man nodded, eyeing Avryn once more before clearing his throat and continuing down the tunnel.

"The other entrances have defenses in place, but with the recent events, our numbers are fewer than we hoped they would be," the man replied.

Janis stopped, making the two men who followed stop abruptly, Turrin cursing.

"Wha' in the blazes? Did yeh ferget 'ow t' walk?" Turrin grumbled as he slipped around her.

Something was off. She'd sensed it the moment they had entered the tunnel network behind the waterfall. The soldiers appeared nervous about more than just her being back at the compound.

"What happened?" Janis asked, leveling her eyes directly at the soldier who led them.

He looked suddenly nervous, his eyes flicking to her sides, inspecting the rough edges of the stone walls and the Lighting orb that hovered closest to them.

"Oh, they didn't tell you, then. I'd have thought that they'd have sent a communication to you or something," he said, wringing his gloved hands before his chest.

Though her mind screamed at her to shout at the man or at least give him a good punch to make him focus on her again, she gently put her hand on his shoulder. The gesture felt awkward, but she'd seen both Avryn and Magness do it in different circumstances. Trusting the envisioned "leader" version of herself, her touch caught the man's attention. He glanced down at her hand for a moment before matching her gaze. She could both see and feel his body tense at her motion.

"Something happened a few days back, something—unnatural," the man explained, sweat beading on his forehead. It was clear that he wasn't thrilled to have to be the one to deliver the news. "Some strange things flew through the sanctuary, silver things, like snakes. They attacked people and gave them strange abilities of darkness. Harmel ordered us to take them all to the prison wing. It took almost a day to round them up, but we think we've got them all."

Though his words were likely meant to make her feel better about the news, she felt nothing of the sort. Janis's mind returned momentarily to the time Avryn had pulled her back from talking to Marric. The silver tendrils of power flying overhead had come here. When she'd first seen them, she thought there was a possibility they were flowing toward Evenir, but she didn't think too much at the time about what it could mean.

"How many?" she asked frankly.

The man blinked at her, still frozen from her tight grasp on his shoulder guard. She assumed he thought she'd ask a different question and that's what caused him to pause.

"We didn't number them all quite yet, but at least a thousand, if not more," he said, his face paling, but not from the news he'd just delivered. Sensing that he might wet himself, Janis released his shoulder and stalked through the next large stone archway into the main cavern. As usual, the room teemed with life and conversations, though it was clear they were more subdued than usual. Tension hung in the air, and Janis now realized why. Her mind pressed her, urging her to do what she'd been wanting to for days. This had to come first.

"Take me to them right away. I have to see what you are speaking of," she said.

The man nodded, then scurried through the room, Janis and Avryn following his heels. Janis paused, then turned to Avryn. "I need you to find Harmel and Livella. Tell them to meet me at the dead-end tunnel nearest the war room within the hour."

Avryn furrowed his brow. "What could you possibly want with them there? That's not the most private place to meet if you want to discuss the coming battle."

Janis was grateful that he didn't seem bothered by her order at all, even though he questioned it the way he did.

"I'd find them myself and go there right away if I didn't feel like I have to see what's happening in the prison ward," she replied. "Besides, it will give you more time to see Narinda."

Janis assumed the man was itching to see his lover and assure her that he'd returned safely. The emotionally masked face of the former, though temporary, leader of Evenir was gone now and he grinned broadly.

"I'll use the time to the fullest," he assured her. "But really, why do you want to meet there rather than the war room?"

She smiled. "I've got a god to talk to."

Avryn's expression fell, his eyes widening as he processed what she'd just told him.

"And something tells me that it won't be as easy as I think it will be," Janis said.

~

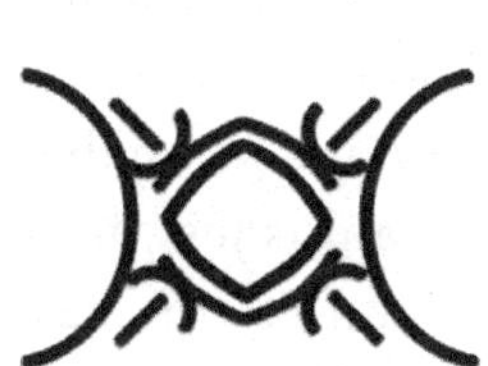

MARRIC WALKED ALONG THE CORRIDOR, his mind counting the Lighting orbs they passed along the way. He felt his nerves buzzing, making the muscles in his arms and hands shake. Narinda looked at him reassuringly as the two moved toward the prison ward of the compound. Until now, he'd not even wondered where the ward was, neither had he any intentions of going there himself, but the recent events had changed that.

Miredith was there.

In the short time he'd gotten to know the girl, he'd grown far more fond of her presence than he wanted to admit. Now that he hadn't seen her in two days, he was worried for her. At first he kept the worry to himself, but as preparations continued throughout the compound, and as he was forced to stay in the war room studying with Narinda, his mind had become increasingly obsessed with seeing the girl again. When he'd brought it up with Narinda earlier in the day, she'd assured him that it wouldn't be wrong for him to try to see her. With her clout as a general, she figured the guards would let them in. Livella had been with them, but when they mentioned going to visit the others affected by the unusual events a few days before, she'd grumbled something about needing to get away, then disappeared as if she wanted to be far from them.

"Are you sure this is a good idea?" Narinda asked him, her eyes worried. "You look like you'll pass out at any moment."

He cursed himself internally for his emotions being so obvious.

"I just—don't know what to expect," he replied.

His mind hoped that Miredith wouldn't have changed, that whatever this power was that gripped her hadn't taken over her mind, but then he thought how ridiculous that was. She'd Conjured something, but she seemed the same as always. Quick-witted, fiery, and generally obtrusive to his personal space. But he hadn't had much time to be with her before she was taken away with the others and put in the ward.

"Fortunately, the prison ward is just the same as any other one of the tunnels, so we aren't walking into a terrifying castle dungeon or anything of the sort," she replied, looking forward, "but something tells me that's not what you mean."

He shook his head, confirming her suspicions. Marric could agree that prisons that normally held fugitives or vagabonds were scary enough. They only had a few cells in Wurren, but they were deep in the earth beneath the town hall and had little light. Once he'd snuck down there with the mayor's daughter, when they were barely waist-high. He shivered at the memory of the deep, dank darkness.

This prison ward was different, and though he'd not been there, he had Seen it before. When Livella arrived he'd watched Magness and Janis enter the cell blocks, and he'd caught a glimpse of what they looked like before his Seeing stopped working. Thoughts of Magness caused his chest to constrict, life seeming so much more fragile than it had before the leader died.

"I've Seen it before, using my Lightbearing. I'm not nervous about that, just—" He paused, not sure how to continue.

Narinda half smiled and nodded toward their destination, which came into view within moments.

"Let me talk to the guards; they'd probably just dismiss you without allowing you to say anything," she said.

Marric nodded and pulled back slightly to let her take a small lead down the narrow stone walls. Narinda walked confidently as she usually did; her large spectacles must have slipped down her nose for a moment because Marric watched her hand move up to them.

"Ho there. We seek entrance to speak with one of the prisoners," Narinda said, walking right up to one of the guards.

The guard shifted on her feet, the spear she held in one hand grasped tightly. Marric could see how white her knuckles were from the pressure of her grip. His stomach flipped as he wondered what could be making her so uncomfortable.

"'Oo are yeh lookin' fer, then?" the woman asked, eyeing Marric, though she didn't spare him too much of a glance before she was all eyes on Narinda.

"A girl named Miredith. She is one of the individuals affected by—well, whatever it is that happened yesterday," Narinda said. Narrowing her eyes momentarily, the woman flashed one more glance at Marric before nodding.

"Fair 'nuff, bu' yeh'll 'ave t' wai' a bi' fer the Destroyer to come back. He dun takin' a break righ' now," the woman replied.

Narinda frowned.

"There's none of you on duty who can get us through the entrance?" Narinda asked.

Marric was grateful that he'd Seen Janis and Magness enter the prison ward some months ago; at least he knew what to expect.

Clasping her hands politely before her, she nodded, then looked at Marric.

"'Fraid no', they on break righ' now. Should be back in ten minutes or so," the guard replied.

"Fortunately, I've brought one with me," Narinda said.

The soldier looked confused for a moment before Marric's companion gestured to him.

"He can get us through the door, no problem. I presume you have at least a Fixer on hand to repair the entrance once we're through, no?"

Still looking warily at Marric, the soldier-woman nodded.

"That's him, then, is it?" the second soldier asked, pointing at Marric. Though Marric didn't know what exactly the guard meant, Narinda apparently picked up on it.

"Yes, that's the one with the three Lightbearing powers. He just picked up a fourth, fortunately, for us today," Narinda said matter-of-factly.

Marric's insides twisted as everyone's eyes fell on him, the guards looking at him curiously. He'd tried to forget the Destroying powers that had come to him in Wurren, and he hadn't had any reason to even touch them since he'd left his hometown. He peered down the circular entrance to the prison ward, seeing how it ended twenty paces down in a solid oak wall, iron studs protruding from the round edges and pounded into the thick stone walls.

"Tha's lucky fer you, then. Well, go on," the guard replied, still staring at Marric warily. He hadn't immediately noticed the lack of the guards' staring eyes until now that they actually bored into him.

Narinda didn't seem to notice his unease, smiling and gesturing for him to go into the tunnel. At the other end, a lone guard stood with a Conjured spear in her hand. She gave him a severe look before glancing behind them at the guards standing outside the hallway. The entry guard nodded, giving them permission to continue, and the woman standing before the wooden wall walked stiffly away from the barrier. A few paces away, she spun on her heels and held her hand to her mouth.

"The door's coming down!" the guard shouted.

Marric jumped at the declaration, his skin tingling as adrenaline rushed through him. He'd been so lost in thought about what he had to do next that he hadn't expected the shout.

Marric stood before the wall, sweat dripping down his back. His heart pounded in his ears as he shakily put his hand on the wood. It looked to be made of oak, firm and clean as if it had never seen any wear despite how long it had stood blocking the way. The fact that it was Destroyed and Fixed repeatedly yet still looked brand new was not lost on him. He cursed Lanser for giving him the very power he wanted to avoid, wishing instead that he'd been blessed with Fixing.

Narinda raised a brow, questioning his hesitation.

"Is everything all right? You do have the ability; I've seen you use it before, back in Wurren," Narinda pointed out.

He nodded. "Yes, I'm just trying to remember exactly how to make it work."

Marric cleared his throat, uncomfortable at his lie. Whether Narinda detected this or not, she didn't show but just stood there patiently. He remembered the feeling, the warmth that spread through his hand as the Destructive Light pooled in his palm. It felt the same as Conjuring yet so different at the same time. Trying to focus on the pleasant aspects of the terrifying ability, he placed his hand firmly on the wood.

Gritting his teeth, his heart pounded faster and harder in his chest. Marric focused on the warmth in his palm, concentrating the power there until, before he could even prepare for it, the wood exploded forcefully forward, dust and debris flying everywhere. Marric let out a yelp at the suddenness of the explosion. It took so little energy to make it happen that he hadn't been fully ready. Blushing, he hoped beyond all hopes that no one had heard his reaction. He didn't know how many Destroyers lived in Terris Green, but he didn't get the sense that yelping when using this ability would be considered positive.

Narinda coughed lightly, then stepped up to the broken barrier.

"That worked well, didn't it?" she said, stepping easily over the larger pieces of wood. Realizing he hadn't let his hand down from what he'd just done, he looked at his feet, embarrassed, and folded his arms.

On the other side of the now broken barrier, two men stood with their hands on their side swords. They hadn't drawn the weapons and they looked relatively at ease, but Marric assumed they were trained to be on the ready for anything. One of them smiled brightly, waving with his free hand, while the other leveled a hostile gaze at Marric. Their eyes locked and the man shook his head, turning to the side to let the two pass.

"Did you need me to take care of this, then?" Narinda offered, gesturing to the pile of broken wood and splinters.

"Nah, i's alroit, Oi fink. Desree's got the Fixin' in 'er," the joyful guard said, pointing back the way they came.

Before Marric could even turn to look at whom he pointed at, the debris at their feet glowed brightly, wreathed in blue Light, spinning and rushing past their feet and bodies to repair itself behind them. Marric had seen Fixing before; he'd even Seen the very wall before him Fixed like this, but he couldn't help but marvel at the restorative power. Jealousy wormed its way into his chest at seeing the wall Fixed. Narinda didn't stay long, instead slipping through the moving bits of wood and continuing down the long stone corridor.

The final pieces of wood slipped into place, the sound somehow the reverse of the explosion, then settled into stillness.

Realizing that Narinda had left him behind, Marric spun around to follow her, blushing once again at the cackling of the guard. Fortunately, no words were offered in jest of Marric's reaction, but the laugh was enough to make Marric feel like a complete child.

"With how many were affected, I fear that it might take us some time to find the girl," Narinda was saying as he caught up with her. She either didn't notice his delay or didn't bother mentioning it.

"Is there an easier way to find her?" Marric asked as they approached the cross-tunnel.

Immediately before them stood a cell made of iron bars, the metal melded somehow into the wall.

"We can try asking one of the guards, but more than likely, they won't know. There are a lot of people in Evenir, after all. Even I don't know every person's name," she said as they finally reached the next tunnel.

Lighting orbs hung in the air near the top of the walls and they were spaced much farther apart than they were in the main caverns. Every twenty paces, directly under one of the orbs, stood a guard. Marric shivered at how dim it was here. He'd gotten used to living underground, but the din of the prison ward made his skin tingle with unease. The prison tunnel extended left and right, with no end visible from where they stood. Each way turned slightly enough that Marric lost sight of where the tunnels continued.

"Foggin' darkness, I'll never understand why we have to leave this ward so dark," Narinda muttered, bringing her hand upward and creating a large orb of Light. "As far as I know, it's never been different. Something about keeping the prisoners in the dark as a form of punishment. What about the guards? Do we have no regard for them?"

Marric furrowed his brow. It was clear that the woman was passionate about the sparse Lighting in the tunnel. He had to agree. Now that the area immediately around them was better lit, he felt less uncomfortable with their circumstances.

"Well, while I'm here, there will be none of this nonsense," she said, extending her hand until her lone head-sized blue orb split into at least a dozen before flying to either side. The orbs moved seemingly of their own volition, positioning themselves between the normal Lighting orbs that stood there. Marric flinched at the sudden increase in Light, his eyes having adjusted to the dimness from before. Though he appreciated the Light, it seemed that she'd slightly overdone it, the orbs being more frequent here than even in the main caverns.

Forced to squint through the now-bright tunnel, Marric moved to the closest guard. The man looked bored, and for some reason this made Marric feel guilty, though he didn't know why. It wasn't his fault the man was stationed in the prison ward.

"Excuse me, I'm looking for a girl named Miredith. She was one of the people affected by the—silver things," Marric said awkwardly. Ever since the odd event days ago, no one wanted to talk about what had happened, as if by talking about it they would bring it all upon themselves again. Fortunately, this guard didn't seem to care about it.

"I don't know where one specific girl is. Just walk around, you'll find her," he replied, leaning back against the wall and resting his head there. For someone meant to watch prisoners, he seemed far too lax to be effective.

Marric opened his mouth to continue the conversation, but the man shifted the hood of his cloak over his face, indicating that he was no longer interested in talking.

Narinda scoffed. "You're really going to do a lot of good here if someone breaks out of their cell."

Marric's skin chilled at the confrontational comment. Putting her hands on her hips, Narinda stared down at the man, her words taking a moment to sink it. Once the man realized she'd been addressing him, he stood up straight, pulling his hood back and glaring at her.

"Do you suppose you'd do better? Do you want to be stuck in the dank dungeons of this place?" the man challenged.

Narinda shrugged. "If that's what I was asked to do, then yes. Besides, I gave you some extra Light. Enjoy it while you have it."

The man glared at her, then grunted, leaning back and folding his arms. Marric's hopes fell as the man clamped his mouth shut. He'd hoped to at least get some direction from the guard about where to look, but it didn't seem like he'd be willing to talk any longer.

Narinda stood up straighter and stalked past the man, flicking her wrist and pulling back the orbs she'd placed nearest him. His person plunged back into the dim lighting from before. He shook his head and rolled his eyes, obviously bothered but not willing to admit it. Gritting his teeth, Marric looked at his feet as he moved past the soldier.

As he and Narinda walked, they could barely see into the cells, the only Light available to those inside filtered through the iron bars of the gate.

"We'll have to figure out the best way to find her," Narinda said, eyeing the next guard stationed down the corridor.

They proceeded down the tunnel, quiet conversations echoed around them from the cells full of the affected Evenir members. Marric gulped, trying not to stare at them. No one called out in anger, but tension was high. After they'd passed a half dozen cells, Marric heard a quiet gasp.

"Marric?" Miredith's voice echoed on the stone to his left. His skin tingled everywhere when he heard the tone and he spun toward the cell.

"Miredith? Is that you?" he said, moving closer to the iron bars.

"Yes!" she hissed. "I wondered if you'd ever come see me. I've been in here forever!"

The complaint made Marric grit his teeth, but he didn't want to dwell on it. From outside the cell, it was hard to see inside, but based on the echoing conversations and Miredith's shuffling, the cell sounded to be bigger than he would have expected. Squinting to see farther, Marric could make out at least a dozen others lounging on the ground or stone furniture within. He could barely make out a stone table, melded into the ground as if its legs had molded over time into the floor. A few stone chairs were scattered in the empty spaces of the room. His sight didn't reach further in, but he assumed there was even more space near the back.

"I'm sorry, I've not been able to come," Marric admitted, but his words sounded hollow. "We're trying to get ready for the coming army and—"

He wanted to say they were studying records to figure out what *H'ilvina't* meant and how they could use it but then remembered she wasn't involved in those conversations.

"Forget that, is the army almost here, then?" she asked.

All conversations around her ended, the following silence almost more piercing than the echoing sounds of men and women chatting behind her. Miredith didn't appear to notice or she didn't care. Chest burning, Marric tried not to dwell on the fact that all the unseen eyes in the darkness of the cell probably watched him, waiting for a response.

"It's hard to say, but probably within the next couple days. We still haven't heard from Janis or the others," he said, wincing as a few conversations and grunts came from that revelation.

"Th' bloomin' assassin left us fer dead, we all know i," a man growled from the back. "She don' wan' nuttin' wif us. Never did."

A few others joined in, affirming the same belief. Once again, guilt wracked Marric's chest, as if he was the one at fault for causing their disbelief in the new leader. Marric jumped as a bright flash shot over his shoulder, a large Lighting orb slipping through the bars and flitting to the roof of the cell. Squinting, Marric's eyes had to adjust to the new brightness before him. A few of the people inside cursed at the new Light, covering their faces quickly.

"Could you at least warn us first?" a woman's voice came from behind Miredith.

"No," Narinda said, her face resolute as usual. "I didn't want to give the man accusing the new leader of abandonment time to hide his face."

The man in question was shorter than Marric would have guessed. His short brown hair connected to a stubbly beard, full and deep brown. His dark eyes inspected them with a hardness that couldn't have come from a few days in the cell.

"I don' 'ide from me convictions, girl. I stand by wha' I said," he replied, folding his arms.

"If you have any hope of leaving this cell, then you'd best stop that nonsense," Narinda warned. "We came not only to see the girl but to see how you are faring. I understand it's not comfortable, but I can provide more Light for you if it's what you wish."

Miredith shook her head wildly, squinting at the Light for a moment before turning away and facing Marric. "Actually, we can see really well considering the dimness. I think it has something to do with whatever happened to us." She pointed to the Lighting orb. "So can you turn that off, please?"

Narinda started, and for the first time in a long time, she looked embarrassed. She flicked her wrist and the orb disappeared, the citizens inside sighing and groaning in relief.

"It's like my eyes are enhanced. I can see in the dark really easily; it's been useful down here in these rooms," Miredith said, looking back at Marric.

For a moment he got caught up in her eyes, large and green, staring back at him. An explosion echoed suddenly down the tunnel, making Marric's hair stand on end. Narinda tensed next to him, her hand slipping to the handle of the sword at her waist. Even the lax guard behind them snapped to attention, a Conjured spear flashing into existence in his hand.

The three faced the tunnel they'd just come from. Marric knew it was impractical to think that it was something or someone hostile coming, but talk of the enemy and the odd abilities Miredith and the others had obtained had put everyone on edge. Marric didn't even realize he'd Conjured his bow, a Conjured arrow nocked and ready.

He jumped as a black-clad person sped around the corner toward them.

"I don't have time to wait for a Destroyer or Fixer, I need to hurry—"

Janis paused as she saw the three Lightbearers poised and ready to attack her. She immediately fell into a defensive stance, twin Light daggers appearing in her hands. Marric's breath caught, the thrill of seeing her back in Terris Green almost overcoming him.

"You're back!" he shouted, letting his weapons disappear into the air.

The assassin's dark eyes inspected him, then Narinda and the guard, before she relaxed and started laughing.

"I should stop being surprised to see you in situations like this, Marric. You're getting more bold than you ever were," Janis said. "How'd you get in here anyway? They said their Destroyer was off duty."

Marric grimaced and Janis's face took on a knowing look.

"Ah, that's right. Isn't that useful?" Janis said, her eyes glinting at Marric.

He could hardly believe she stood before him. That last communication he'd heard from her was when she'd Seen him in the cavern days before.

"I presume you're here for the same reason as me," Janis surmised, letting her weapons disappear as she walked lithely over to them. Janis moved to stand next to Marric, and recognition flashed on her face. She glanced down at Marric, then back at Miredith.

Whatever thoughts ran through her head, Marric guessed it had something to do with the fact that the girl she'd seen with Marric days before was on the other side of the bars.

"What's your name?" Janis asked, looking at Miredith.

"Miredith," she replied, her measured gaze on the taller woman.

"So you were one of those affected by the attack?" Janis said.

Miredith nodded, then gestured over her shoulder with her thumb.

"The whole lot of us were. Figure we're unlucky, but at the same time I've always been jealous of Lightbearers," the girl replied.

Marric was astounded by her answer, so forward and blunt. Then again, Miredith had always been that way, so why would now be an exception?

"I can imagine," Janis replied, her eyes once again scanning the group of people in the darkness. "Do you know what it did to you? Have you been able to learn of the attack's effects?"

Miredith stepped back from the bars, her hands opening up in front of her. Darkness deepened in the air around her open palms until suddenly a basket, woven from the shadows and slivered with minuscule silver tendrils, appeared in her hand.

"I have no idea what this is, but it looks a lot like Conjuring to me," Miredith said, her eyes tracing the trail of one of the silver tendrils worming through the basket.

Janis stared at the object, something running through her mind. For a moment,Marric wished he could know what she was thinking, but as usual, the woman's expression was too hard to read, at least for him.

"The properties are quite unusual, I must say," Narinda said, leaning in next to Janis.

Without warning, Janis reached through and grabbed hold of the basket, her hand wrapping around the handle. Air hissed through her teeth as she pulled her hand back, shaking it as if she'd been hurt. Marric and Narinda tensed at her reaction.

"What happened? Are you hurt?" Narinda asked.

Janis shook her head, then eyed the others in the cell.

"No, but it felt similar to something I felt when touching a certain book," Janis replied.

Narinda's face paled and she looked away.

"What in Lanser's name does that mean?" Miredith asked, looking from Marric to Janis a few times.

At first Marric didn't understand her words until he remembered the black book they'd looked at together a few days ago. The very book that Janis had rushed to retrieve when she'd realized Rivelen had escaped with it. His tongue itched to say something, to ask how it was all connected, but the way Janis had clammed up after touching the odd, dark Conjure alerted him to the fact that she probably didn't want to discuss it here.

A grunt from behind made Marric turn that direction. He eyed the guard, now leaning back against the stone wall with his arms folded, apparently less than thrilled about the things he was witnessing. Marric would have thought having visitors like this would have been a nice break in the monotony of his standing, but apparently, that wasn't true.

"I can see now why you were assigned here, your attitude must be what earned you prison duty," Janis said dryly, not even turning to the man.

His eyes widened before a hardened look marred his face, his jaw locking tightly.

"The other abilities—tell me about them," Janis said to Miredith.

The girl shrugged, her wavy red hair falling from her shoulders as she did so. "As far as we can tell, they're the same as Lightbearing. Some can make a Shield, some have eyes that fill with the same stuff, whatever it is. We've seen it all, except Fixing." gulped. "No one wants to try hurting themselves to prove that one out."

Janis nodded. "Whatever power this is, we should be cautious, but you seem unaffected otherwise."

Janis finally stood up straight and looked to the bored guard behind her. His angry eyes fixed on her, and Marric could tell he wanted to say something sharp.

"Release them. I don't see any reason to have them stuck in here when we have an army practically upon us. We'll need every able-bodied person fighting for us in this battle."

Marric stared at her. Yet again, the assassin he'd barely met and come to know had surprised him.

Narinda cleared her throat. "Is that—wise? We hardly know the extent of what they can do and if their minds are addled in any way."

Janis nodded to the guard, then turned to Narinda.

"As much as I agree with you, I've seen the army that's on the way. We can't afford to have this many of our own locked away when their ability to fight doesn't appear impeded."

She paused, then looked into the darkened cell. "Lanser knows what's to come in the next day."

The way she said it felt far more heavy than it should have, as if there was some veiled meaning that Janis hid from them. Without another word, she walked back toward the entrance to the ward, her boots clicking on the stone floor. Somehow the temperature seemed to drop in the tunnel and Marric shivered. He eyed Miredith from the side, noticing that she still held the odd smoke-Conjure she'd created.

"I guess we get to spend more time together, then," Miredith said brightly. She noticed Marric's hesitant stare at the basket, then bit her lip and let it go.

Marric certainly felt some relief at knowing his friend would be free to go, but something settled inside his gut that made him nervous, for both her and the rest of Evenir.

An explosion echoed loudly up and down the tunnel as Janis Destroyed the wall separating the rest of Terris Green from the prison ward.

"Come on," Narinda said. "Let's get these open."

The guard, still annoyed by Janis's comment, grumbled and Conjured a shimmering key to unlock the cell.

27

Janis rushed away from the prison ward, her mind processing the information she'd seen. While she hadn't questioned every one of the imprisoned, she felt she didn't have much of a choice but to let them free. She also didn't have the luxury of spending too much time in the ward, testing all those within. It was as if she could *feel* the army on its way, though she suspected that was imagined.

As she rushed down the hallway, the people she passed watched her warily, some attempting to talk to her, others just stepping aside with looks of fear or wonder. Her reputation within the compound was already set weeks before now. No other woman of her age walked around wearing what she did, and she wagered her constant serious expression was enough to make them run away screaming. Despite the present urge to act like a better leader, she only cared about one thing.

She had to try to talk to Lanser.

The idea had struck her while they traveled back. Rivelen, Riln, and perhaps many others had been tempted by Ugglyn somehow, and the only explanation was that they were Seers. Janis herself had Seen Ugglyn in a vision. Marric told her how Ugglyn had appeared to him even in the past—once again, in a vision. It only made sense that Lanser could be contacted in a similar way.

Janis sped around the corridor. The Lightbearing orbs above seemed even brighter now that she'd left the dimness of the prison ward. Judging from the size of the army that was coming for them, she didn't think they would arrive sooner than the next day. Urgency pressed on her mind, making her speed up her course through the network of stone passages.

By the time she arrived at the dead end, she was relieved to see Avryn, Harmel, and Livella waiting for her. They all watched her with curious expressions as she rushed toward them.

"What is all this about, then?" Avryn asked, looking around curiously. "Don't you think it would be wiser to have our conversation somewhere more private?"

Janis ignored the question momentarily, looking to Livella, whose eyes widened as she inspected the dead end. Following the woman's gaze, Janis's eyes fell on the solid wall of grey stone just behind her three companions. It was there that the doorway had opened to them, granting access to the hall of statues made from Light.

"You remember this place, don't you Livella?" Janis asked.

Avryn furrowed his brow, looking back and forth between the two women before folding his arms before him. "Do you plan on answering any of my questions? I really don't think we're safe from watching eyes and listening ears."

Janis faced Avryn, who looked far less patient than he used to act. Something about losing the mantle of leadership had opened up a new part of him. Admittedly, Janis thought it was refreshing to see the man behaving more human rather than like an eerily perfect person. Livella trembled next to her, wrapping her arms around herself and staring at the blank wall.

"When Livella first arrived here, we were pulled by some unnatural force to this very spot. That was when we saw the statues and Tryvv, the last Prime to have lived before Riln."

Avryn's expression darkened at the mention of the late leader of Watch-light, but he relaxed his arms, looking at the wall.

"Magness told me of that and she said you claimed to have been gone for a time, when to her it was a mere moment," he said. "What does this have to do with anything?"

Janis pressed her lips together determinedly.

"I'm going to talk to a god," she said.

Harmel laughed. "Why am Oi not surprised t' hear yeh say somethin' crazy loike that? Leave it t' the lass t' think o' somethin' o' the loikes."

Avryn didn't appear thrilled by his companion's reaction, instead looking at Janis severely.

"Don't you think that if that were possible, someone would have already tried it and documented it? What makes you think that the being himself would have anything to do with us?"

Janis shook her head. "Just because you haven't read any records of someone contacting him doesn't mean others haven't tried. Have you honestly read every text in Lindrad?" She raised a single eyebrow dubiously.

Sighing, Avryn placed his hand on his head, running his fingers through the length of his hair. "Fine, but what do you hope to accomplish?"

"I believe Ugglyn was in direct communication with Rivelen and who knows who else, which tells me that there has to be a way to reach Lanser. He's the one who started this mess in the first place, isn't he? With any luck, he'll know what *h'ilvina't* is and what it means for us."

Livella paled at the words but didn't say anything. Janis knew the first experience they'd had going into that place had been more than terrifying, but in theory it shouldn't be any more dangerous than it had that time. Something itched at the back of Janis's mind, though she couldn't describe what it was or what it meant. Though it seemed a fairly practical idea to try to contact the very being who'd gifted Lightbearing to Lindrad, she wondered why the others thought her crazy.

Something inside her warned her as well.

"Just stay close by in case something goes wrong," Janis said to Avryn and Harmel before grabbing Livella by the wrist and practically dragging her to the wall.

After only a few steps, Livella wrested her arm away from Janis, looking at her defiantly. Janis spun on her, ready to make chase should the girl run away, but she didn't. Instead she stood there, back straight, and glared at Janis.

"I'm not a little girl, you know. I don't agree with this plan, but I also recognize that I don't have any other ideas, so I'll come along with it," Livella practically growled.

Janis smiled slyly, somewhat proud of the fact that Livella had been able to pull her arm away and was standing up for herself. Janis could see Livella's frame getting stronger and more chiseled, but she was glad that her training had also brought harder resolve and a capacity to stick her chest out.

Nodding in approval, Janis moved to the stone wall.

"Do you plan to just walk through the wall, then?" Avryn's voice echoed from behind. He didn't sound angry or even like he was making fun of them, but it was clear he didn't agree with them taking the time for this.

Janis's impressions of his opinions were validated when Avryn continued. "I think our time would be best spent getting the warriors ready for the assault, don't you? Chasing the wind like this isn't going to get us anywhere."

Without turning back to Avryn, and without even feeling too annoyed, Janis called back. "Last I recall, you made me the leader without even consulting me first. That means you get to stand by and listen to my silly notions whether you like it or not."

Avryn blushed but nodded, knowing he was defeated.

Naturally, Harmel let out a booming laugh, amused at her response to Avryn's grumblings. Avryn crossed his arms and grunted, but he didn't say anything else.

"Let's at least talk about what you've already done while they're busy touching walls," Avryn said, turning to Harmel. Their conversation became more subdued, but Janis had already stopped listening.

"The last time we came here, nothing happened when we touched the wall," Janis said, looking at Livella as she put her hand on the firm stone, "but I have a theory that it might make something happen this time."

Janis immediately detected something in Livella's eyes. She looked like she was afraid to say something. Grasping her hands before her, Livella turned from the wall and inspected the two men, who were still busy discussing the preparations for the coming army. Janis didn't allow the silence to last for long before she reached out, grabbing Livella by the arm.

The woman jumped and reached back to her staff, gripping the grain of the wood firmly, though she immediately relaxed.

"Sorry, I'm just on edge," Livella explained, blushing slightly.

"Clearly," Janis replied. "But I hate to say that now is not the time to be reserved about anything. Honestly, whatever you're hiding—and I know you're hiding something—it will have to wait."

Livella nodded, then turned to the wall. Janis assumed the woman had some argument, but she didn't voice any of it. More than likely she agreed with the fact that the coming army was more important than anything right now. Livella put her hand on the wall next to her own, and Janis braced herself for something to happen. Nothing did.

Livella cocked her head, glancing at Janis with a dubious expression.

"I'm going to try something, just hold it there," Janis said.

She breathed deeply, then let the Seeing take over her. Eyes widening with blue Light, she suddenly felt a rapid tingling in her hand. It wasn't the uncomfortable cold tingling of Ugglyn's book, but it still shocked her. Something similar must have happened to Livella, for she yelped, almost pulling her hand away from the stone.

"Don't move! Keep it steady," Janis ordered but without any anger inside.

A rumble sounded distantly in the cavern, the sound so deep that it vibrated through Janis's hand and into her chest. She grimaced, her senses heightening and adrenaline rushing through her brain. Unnatural sounds like that often had that effect on a trained assassin.

Livella remained rigid next to her, but Janis didn't get to look at her before the same symbols they'd seen months before appeared on the wall before them, though something had changed. The symbol before Janis was still the same glowing blue, but the one before Livella was darkened, as if it was made from grey smoke.

It was the same substance the girl had woven the basket from in the prison ward. Janis tried to recoil, but she sucked in a sharp breath when she realized her hand was stuck to the wall, as if secured there. She tugged, trying to get her palm away from the rough stone, but when she found she was unable to, she flipped out her free hand, Conjuring a dagger. The familiar grip of the handle felt comforting in her palm. With her arm still secured to the stone, she spun on Livella, her breath catching in her throat.

The woman's eyes were filled with dark smoke, the substance extending outward past her eyes as if it trailed in the wind. Livella grimaced, her arm moving as she tried to pull her arm away.

"What the fog is going on?" she said, turning to Janis with a tight jaw.

"How long have you been hiding this?" Janis asked frankly, her hand tightening on her dagger.

Livella's eyes widened, causing the smoke trails to extend farther. She paled, her gaze snapping from Janis to the men to the side. It was then that Janis realized the men had gone quiet. Inspecting them, Janis saw that they'd frozen as if time had stopped, just like when Magness had followed them to this same spot weeks ago.

"Something silver slammed into me while I was walking away from the main cavern. No one was around, and the pain I felt was so fleeting I didn't think much of it," Livella admitted. "Until I started Seeing things and doing things."

She sounded embarrassed, as if she wanted to crawl in a hole and hide forever. Though the sight was unsettling, Janis didn't sense any danger. Just like the girl in the prison ward, the strange dark abilities didn't appear to have warped Livella's mind in any way. The fact that Livella paled when she was discovered indicated that she was still the same.

"Fair enough. With any luck, it'll be to our advantage when the army comes," Janis said, turning back to the wall. "The more immediate concern is what did we just do, and how do we get our fogging hands away from it?"

Livella opened her mouth to respond but instead gasped. Janis spun back toward her, but before she could see anything, the world melted away. Her stomach lightened and she felt as if she was falling a far distance. She clenched her teeth, darkness enveloping her before suddenly, she felt her feet hit something firm. Through a dim light, she could see a stone pedestal, about the height of a man in diameter, extending in a circle all around. Janis sighed as she pulled her hand back, the stone wall no longer present.

Livella was nowhere to be found. More terrifying—she couldn't sense her real body. Every vision she'd entered before had left her tethered to her physical form. But this was different.

Though she could see the stone beneath her feet, Janis couldn't tell where the light was coming from. It was as if the moon shone above, but there was no orb indicating that she was outside under a night sky.

After a moment, Lights coalesced before her, forming into the tall woman Tryvv.

"This has certainly never been done before," the grand woman observed before folding her arms. She looked as if she wanted to scold Janis.

"At some point you'll realize that I'm an unpredictable person," Janis spouted, facing the ethereal woman. She noted that Tryvv wore the same long robe as she had when they first met, the tail of the back trailing into nothingness as if she was connected to something invisible.

"And yet you've been chosen, so we must move forward regardless," Tryvv pointed out. "Why have you come back?"

"Ugglyn's almost free," Janis said frankly.

Tryvv's face fell, her eyes wide.

"Impossible. The pact is still in place, is it not? Did you kill the Voidbearer girl out of mere annoyance?" Tryvv sounded angry and her face shone with the same emotion.

Though Janis's insides twisted in warning at the anger, she reminded herself that the dead woman couldn't or at least shouldn't be able to hurt her. Still, she opened her right hand, feeling the warmth of Conjuring pooling there just in case she needed to Conjure something in her defense.

"I'm not the fool who did anything. The other Voidbearer killed his Prime and made something happen. As far as I can tell, he's been possessed by something, some darkness. Does that sound familiar?" Janis asked.

Tryvv immediately looked guilty, but she cleared her throat, looking above Janis into the distant darkness.

"Even if that happened, it shouldn't matter. Your pact is still in place," Tryvv said, her voice wavering ever so slightly.

The woman appeared hardened, the way she had when Janis first saw her weeks ago, but she didn't seem able to hide her underlying emotions today, and for that Janis was grateful. It was so much easier to work with people when you could read them like an open book. Janis followed the woman's gaze, seeing that there was still blackness all around her, as if they were in the starless sky.

"You know something?" Janis said, turning back to her. "I don't have time to play games. This has happened before, hasn't it?"

Though Tryvv still looked away, her gaze flickered just slightly.

"Tell me," Janis ordered, a Conjured dagger forming in her hand. Though she knew it wouldn't really be able to threaten the image of Tryvv, somehow she knew it would make her seem more intimidating to be holding a blade.

"Even if I could speak of this, I know few details," Tryvv said, her voice hard.

"Tell me what you know," Janis insisted.

When Tryvv didn't speak immediately, Janis took a step forward. Cognizant of the edge of the platform before her, she stepped within inches of it, the air turning colder as if she was moving toward a wall of ice.

"Or did you want Ugglyn to be completely free—again?"

The last words were a gamble. She didn't really think the anti-god had been truly free, for if he had, she assumed Lindrad wouldn't be as it is today, but the words must have struck something within the former Prime, for she flinched and looked at Janis.

"It has happened once, when the twins were called as Prime and Void-bearer, but I *told* you I don't know details," Tryvv insisted.

"Then let me talk to Lanser, since he's supposed to know everything," Janis replied, her voice even.

Tryvv gasped. "You can't! Not one soul has Seen Lanser, and I shan't allow you to either."

Something burned in Janis's chest. She didn't like being told she couldn't do something. With a grunt, she flung the dagger through Tryvv's forehead, the blade passing through without any effect.

"I don't care about formalities. This is more important than anything," Janis said, forming a Destroying orb in her hand. Without pausing, she flung it at Tryvv. While she assumed nothing would happen, the woman screamed as the orb exploded, a flash almost blinding Janis in the near darkness. Her stomach clenched as she took in what just happened, but Tryvv was shouting.

"You insufferable woman! I can't prevent you from whatever wrath you incur upon yourself at this point," Tryvv roared before she disappeared into the darkness.

Janis thought she probably should have been more concerned about those words but she didn't care. At this point, she had little respect for the god who had dragged her into this mess. Her impertinence was likely to get her killed, but she didn't have time to worry about that at the moment.

When nothing changed immediately, Janis gazed off into the darkness, her mind flipping to where Livella was right now. The last thing she expected from touching the wall with the Voidbearer was being separated. She'd hoped they'd be able to access the same odd statue room as before, but this was proving far more interesting.

A flash in the darkness brought her back to the present, and she stepped back as she was temporarily blinded by the flashing of a blue Light right before her. Before it could even form into something visible, a man's voice boomed loudly, echoing as if she was in a cave.

"Who dares disturb me like this?"

Without hesitation, she had the daggers back in her hands. She gripped the handles firmly, scanning left and right, just past the brilliant Light forming in front of her. Her instincts told her to run, to hightail it in the other direction, but she held firm.

Even if she could run, there was nowhere to go. She had already noticed the distinct lack of connection to her physical body when she'd entered this vision.

The Light finally formed into a man dressed in a grand robe, the sleeves large and puffy, the bottom extending downward past whatever feet might be hidden beneath them. Not being able to see just how tall the man was irked her, for she didn't feel like she could size him up accurately. Her eyes wandered to the stranger's eyes and she froze.

Ugglyn's face stared back at her.

With a grunt, she flung her dagger directly at the face of the man, knowing full well that it would go through without any effect but still hoping that something might change this time. The man sneered and folded his arms.

"Ah, the very Prime who defies all expectations. It's bold of you to demand my presence, given the fact that you don't even want the power you have right now," the man said, raising an eyebrow.

Whatever anger he'd felt before seemed to have dissipated, replaced by what Janis guessed was amusement.

"How did you get here? I'm looking for the source of Lightbearing, not whatever curse you've inflicted on my people," Janis spat, readying herself by Conjuring another dagger. Her use of the word "my" when referring to the people of Evenir was not lost on her.

The glowing man before her raised an eyebrow.

"Of what are you speaking? I've done nothing of the sort," the man said, his face displaying more fury now that she was accusing him.

"You've managed to tempt away one of our Seers, but you won't be able to convince me to do anything for you, not like Riln," she said. Janis shifted on her feet so she could get a good look all around her while still keeping her eyes on the floating god before her.

"What are you—" The man's eyes shot open in understanding, his face becoming less angry and more intrigued. "You've Seen him, the one called Ugglyn."

Janis nodded, her gaze measured. She locked on the usage of a third-person pronoun, doubt entering her chest. If this wasn't Ugglyn, was it really Lanser?

Eyes shifting up and down his person, she noted subtle differences. This man was dressed in a robe, not the fine-fitting clothing from before. His face carried less anger and more intrigue. He wore his hair a bit longer, not like the image she'd seen of Ugglyn in the war room.

He sighed, the anger disappearing altogether.

"This is a first in history, I have to say. Not once has a Prime set their eyes on me directly," he said, looking proud for a moment before his face became serious once more. "Tryvv isn't happy with the way you treated her."

Janis shrugged. "I thought she was dead. Not much I can do to hurt her."

The man waved his hand dismissively, looking above her head. "It's a matter of pride, I think."

His expression hardened before he spoke again. "I've no idea why you've come, but I'm dealing with the death of the former Prime. He's causing quite the ruckus for us at the moment, and I don't have time to converse with humans, even if you are the living Prime."

Dealing with the last Prime? Janis thought. *Does he mean Riln?*

"What? Didn't Tryvv fill you in on what I told her? I would have thought she'd have the decency to share what I came for," Janis replied. "Are you not watching what's happening in Lindrad?"

Lanser locked his jaw, his words coming out strained. "What happens in Lindrad is of little concern to me. I can't change events, after all."

The words slammed into Janis. What did they mean? The darkness seemed to thicken around her, though she suspected it wasn't truly happening, just the effects of the apparent god's nonchalance.

"You're the god, the one who created Lightbearing, are you not?" Janis challenged. "How can you sit back when Ugglyn is practically free and act as if you don't have a care in the world?"

Lanser's image flickered, and suddenly, he flew to hover just before her face.

"I don't care! I've done my time on that cursed world! I'm only tied to it by default because of the power I *found*. I didn't ask for this, just like you! You think I chose to become this ethereal being? Incapable of dying and moving on to the afterlife? No! This is a curse that I wish I'd never brought on myself."

Janis's stomach dropped. Her mind struggled to process the things he said, for they didn't make any sense. She'd never been Lanserian, save for when she was a child and her parents forced her to church, but the very god they worshiped was standing before her and complaining. Her insides burned in fury. Whoever this god was, he was acting like a child.

"What about Tryvv, Riln, the other Primes? If you didn't pick them yourself, then who did?" Janis demanded, her muscles shaking from how tight they were. She glared at the god, anger continuing to swell inside.

"Unfortunate bystanders, like yourself. The power itself picks the Primes; I don't."

He spun around, looking off in the distance. His image began to fade slowly into nothing before Janis cursed, creating a Destruction orb and flinging it into the back of the image. Like with Tryvv, it exploded, the man roaring in pain.

"You dare attack me like this!" A brilliant sword of blue Light appeared in his hand and he held the tip to her neck.

Janis stood firm, though her stomach clenched in fear. She stood there with the tip inches from her neck, unsure if the Conjured weapon would affect her in this odd realm. Taking the gamble, Janis moved closer to the blade, letting it touch the skin of her bare neck. Though her chest constricted with anticipation of feeling a cut in her flesh, no such feeling came. With a sly smile, she moved into the blade, nothing happening.

"Bah!" Lanser growled, letting his sword disappear. "What is it you want from me? Why did you come here to bother me so? I've enough problems dealing with that fool Riln, and I'd rather not deal with another mortal at this moment."

"Answers," Janis replied immediately. "Ugglyn is practically free, and it's clear that you are the only one who knows anything about how to seal him away."

Lanser's face contorted into something akin to pain and worry and he grasped his hands before him. Janis was unimpressed with the so-called god's temper already, and now he showed further weakness so readily in his expression.

He's acting like a mere human, Janis thought, disgusted.

"Ugglyn is not what you think," Lanser replied.

Resisting the urge to be unreasonably rude but still frustrated with the vague answer, Janis grunted, folding her arms.

"I think that's fairly obvious, considering you wear the same face. Who is he?"

Lanser sighed, a silence following her question that seemed to echo somehow in the dark space.

"He is me," Lanser finally said.

Janis dropped her arms in shock, taking a step back from the man. She almost Conjured her daggers once again but refrained from doing so.

Something told her that if she infuriated the being once again, he would close himself off without giving her more information.

After a brief pause as Janis allowed him time to think, he spoke once more. "Ages ago, I can't even seem to remember when, I stumbled upon something, a stone bearing a precious power. What you now know as Lightbearing. I showed my friends and my family, but no sooner had I showed them than they wanted it for themselves. I found I could only access the power if I held the stone in my hand. Afraid for my safety, I ran with it, escaped into the recesses of Lindrad. Yet somehow the power in the stone called to people, for I couldn't get away. In my last effort to keep the power from others, I smashed it."

Janis watched the god shift in the air, clearly uncomfortable with the information he was giving her. Finally, after another silence, he stared at her with fire in his eyes.

"Something fractured in me then. I felt the power engulf me, turn me into a Lightbearer, but at the expense of half of me splitting off. Ugglyn, he called himself."

Lanser shivered, wrapping his arms around himself. Seeing the god so many Lindradians worshiped acting this way humanized the being far below his famed status.

"Ugglyn escaped, professing to take control of Lindrad, yet I was urged by the same force that Awakened me to seal him away, to conquer him who reflected the darkness inside of me. Yet I couldn't. Instead I ran back to those whom I cherished and loved."

"You just let him *go free*?" Janis exclaimed. "If that's the case, then how did we get here? This doesn't add up."

The god winced, looking away even further.

"Weeks after the incident, Awakenings began in my town, and I soon heard of them all over Lindrad. Whatever I'd done, I'd begun a cycle of Awakenings, both to Light and to Void. Seeing the power Awaken in others broke me, made me realize I was no longer special. I knew I had to face him, for the power inside urged me to seal away the darkness, but I couldn't."

Lanser's eyes widened, though he still looked away from her. Scowling, Janis moved so she stood at the edge of the stone pedestal, the darkness falling away just inches from her feet. She stood tall, forcing the god to look her in the eyes. It was obvious he was keeping something from her, and somehow she knew what it was related to.

"What is *H'ilvina't*?" she asked bluntly.

The man's expression changed to fury and he flung his hand outward, the gesture moving through Janis's face but causing no harm. She knew she'd struck something important.

"Tell me what it means," she ordered, following his gaze as he shifted, trying to get away.

"It is the sacrifice *I* was unwilling to make," he growled, "and I will never regret my decision. I *did* conquer the darkness from within me. I came up with my own way, a pact, a seal to lock away the very thing that wouldn't force me to make the sacrifice. It worked, oh, it worked. As long as the Prime and Voidbearer did their part, Ugglyn would be sealed forever, and I could die in peace."

Lanser's tone changed to bitter.

"Little did I know that it would cause me to live in a middle place. It was then that I found I would be cursed, as would all the Primes, not to be able to die, not to move on to the next life. We find ourselves bound to the same in-between where Seers find their vision. Though their visions are only temporary; they can return to their bodies when they end."

Janis's stomach dropped. Whether his choice of words was intentionally charged to slam into her or not, mentioning the exact phrase "in-between" made her insides twist. Noticing her reaction from his peripheral vision, he spun on her, a satisfied smile on his face.

"And now you see the same fate awaits you upon death. Why the power chose you to uphold my pact, I can't say, but you'll be subject to the same fate as the rest of us. It's too late for you."

Janis clenched her teeth. She'd not considered the afterlife, what it would be like, but hearing the man speak of wherever he was now as a curse wasn't encouraging. She glanced outward into the surrounding darkness, the information coursing through her mind. Anger burned within her, but she knew that directing the feeling at the god would be fruitless; it was clear he didn't care about this. After all, she'd had to force him to give her any amount of information.

Instead she repeated her question, more firm this time.

"What—is—*h'ilvina't*?" Janis urged, pausing between each word.

Lanser growled, spinning on her again.

"What's done is done. Nothing you say or do will stop this cycle. I cheated the sacrifice and suffer the consequences; now you will too!" he roared, swiping his hand in the air until a Destroying orb appeared in his palm.

Janis froze, summoning her own. With a flick of his wrist, the orb flew at Janis. While the Conjured weapon had no effect, she'd seen how her Destroying could affect both him and Tryvv. It didn't appear to injure them too badly, but they weren't alive like she was. Air hissing through her teeth, she jumped backward. The orb barely missed her and exploded on the platform behind her. The stone cut in half, the severed section falling away into the darkness.

"Tell me what you wouldn't sacrifice. Tell me before Ugglyn is fully free!" Janis yelled, lobbing her orb into the man's face. He shouted and barely dodged her attack.

"Never!" he shouted again, throwing another orb. This broke another fourth of the stone platform, leaving Janis with little to work with. In a desperate attempt to learn something, Janis dove at the god, wrapping her arms around his chest. The maneuver felt more than awkward, and her feet left the stone platform, but to her surprise, she didn't fall into the darkness. Instead she felt the strange sensation that she was near someone, but not touching him. It felt wrong. She squeezed her arms tighter, hoping she didn't fall away.

"Get off me!" Lanser roared.

Unsure if this would work, she reached up and touched the god's head, trying to See something.

Janis's stomach wrenched as she felt herself spinning. Lanser and the platform disappeared, images forming from Light in the darkness around her. Suddenly, she was somewhere else, a town on the edge of the sea. She didn't recognize it, but somehow she knew she was in the distant past.

Lanser stood at the frame of a small mud-created hut, the street around him filled with similar squat huts. He watched longingly as children played and flitted down the dirt path. Suddenly, his face fell and he held his head as if he was in pain. A voice echoed in the air around her.

Face the Void! Face it now or all is lost! it echoed.

Lanser locked his jaw but recovered. Somehow Janis knew he'd been plagued by the voices for months.

You must make the sacrifice! the voice called.

"I won't!" Lanser shouted, throwing his fist in the air.

The images of the people around him paused, most staring at him with confused expressions.

"I'll never do it. He's gone. Ugglyn is locked away. He'll never be free if the pact remains," Lanser said, breathing hard as he leaned down, supporting himself on his knees.

Something caught Janis's attention to her left and she looked to see a woman there. She was beautiful with long flowing hair, her eyes round and curious.

Janis's breath caught in her incorporeal throat. This woman wasn't formed from the same blue Light but instead glowed brightly orange. Lanser's eyes caught sight of the woman and he smiled fondly.

"You'll always be mine. I'll keep you safe, my love," he said.

The world crashed down upon Janis, Lights disappearing, darkness crushing inward, leaving Janis alone with the now screaming Lanser still in her grip.

"How *dare you*! Begone!" Lanser shouted, shoving her off.

She fell downward into the abyss, her stomach clenching with the drop. Her head exploded in pain, and suddenly, she felt her back hit something hard. It took her a moment to see the stone tunnel above as her eyes focused, but when she did, relief flooded her.

A gasp sounded next to her, making Janis leap to her feet. She relaxed when she saw Livella lying on the stone ground next to her. That relief didn't last long as she noted the terrified look on Livella's face.

"What happened?" Janis asked, leaning down to grasp Livella's arm. When the woman didn't respond to her touch immediately, Janis's chest constricted, thinking she'd gone mad or something of the sort.

Finally, Livella's eyes refocused and she jumped at seeing Janis standing so close to her.

"He's here" was all she said.

Janis's whole body vibrated with adrenaline as she took in the words.

"What do you mean? The army?" Janis asked, but her mind was spinning with so many questions.

Livella nodded grimly. "They'll be at Terris Green within the hour." She shivered once more.

"How do you know? Did you See something—" Janis had been about to ask using the odd Void powers the woman had but refrained, remembering how much she didn't want to see more of the power displayed.

Nodding once more, Livella spoke with a trembling voice. Despite her obvious fear, she reached back and grasped the wood grain of the staff she wore secured to her back. Jaw tightening, she looked at Janis directly.

"I'm not sure what you Saw, but I was forced to face Ugglyn himself. He wears a different face now, and he was formed out of the shadows we've seen from the people affected by the same odd powers as—well, me," she admitted, finally taking the moment to stand up.

"What did he say to you?" Janis asked, realizing that if Livella had been in a vision for the same span of time, the conversation must not have been short.

Shrugging, Livella pulled her hand back and fidgeted with her hands. She pressed her lips together, looking away from Janis and remaining quiet. The body language indicated reluctance to share. Impatience burned in Janis's chest, but she remained calm for fear of pushing the woman away.

"I trust you now; you need to tell me," Janis said frankly, but even as she spoke the words, they burned in her mouth like bile. It wasn't that she didn't mean them, it was just that the last time Janis admitted to trusting someone, he'd abandoned her for dead. Pushing the thought away, she affixed Livella with a fierce gaze.

"He said—a lot of odd things." Livella winced, then continued. "That he and Lanser were the same, that he only wished to align Lanser's purpose with his own."

Livella paused, then looked at her.

"He was trying to convince me to kill you, saying that doing so would allow him to be lenient on those who remained after he was released from his prison," Livella said.

Janis knew it was a lie. Fortunately, it appeared that Livella agreed with the assessment that it was a front for what Ugglyn truly wanted. Janis's mind whirled with all the things she'd learned. She wanted to focus on what she'd just learned about Ugglyn being constrained to the "in-between," the state she'd learned to access before being a Lightbearer herself. Months ago, when she'd Awakened, she knew there was some connection between her learned ability to enter the space and Seers; little did she know that Ugglyn and Lanser themselves were kept in the same realm, whatever it was.

Livella noticed Janis's expression change and reached up to touch the woman on the arm. Her skin burned where the woman touched her, but she resisted the urge to slap her hand away, instead looking up at the woman with a resolute expression. Footsteps sounded suddenly behind them, Harmel and Avryn now released from their frozen state.

"Wha' in the blazes, yeh're back already? Been gone fer a mite moment only," Harmel said, appearing behind them.

Janis furrowed her brow. "Unfortunate side effect of the vision. You were frozen."

Harmel looked confused, looking back and forth from her to Livella.

"Yeh touched the wall, an' then jumped back gaspin' roit away. Fog near though' yeh were 'urt," he said, worry showing on his face, "Bu' then yeh jumped up as if nuttin' was wrong."

He reached out and grasped her hand. Warmth weaved its way up her hand, making her chest burn with a desire that she had tried to keep at bay for so many years. The urge to pull away screamed in her mind, but she resisted, focusing instead on the pleasure she felt at the touch. As if surprised that she didn't recoil or even try to pull away, Harmel squeezed her hand.

Fogging fool, how did I become so fond of someone like him? Janis thought, remembering all the foolish jokes and stories she'd had to suffer when they traveled anywhere. Yet despite his goofy grin, she could see a hardness in his eyes. This was a battle-worn soldier, someone who'd been in service to Evenir for so many years. There was a story behind the man's strong mind and bulky figure, and for the first time since she'd met him, she actually wanted to know it.

Janis suddenly felt sad that she'd not taken the time to learn more of Shrell before he'd been killed. For a moment they stared at each other, the world going quiet, until Avryn cleared his throat.

"I hate to disturb whatever moment this is, but we must know what happened," he said.

"The army is here," Janis said first, making Avryn step back in shock. "Or they will be within the hour, according to Livella."

"How can that be?" Avryn cried. "They should still be half a day away."

"*How* isn't the important thing right now; instead we need to prepare for them," Janis replied. "And I've just learned some disturbing information from our supposed patron god."

Avryn's brows furrowed in confusion, and Janis took a few moments to recount her tale briefly.

"Lanser's might," Avryn whispered, then grimaced at using the name. "The ill timing of this information—"

He trailed off, shaking his head. Janis didn't allow the man to recover from his thoughts before she moved on. "Harmel, we need the other generals stationed at the various entrances. Keep Trease and most of her Shielders at the main entrance, but send at least three to the other entrances."

Harmel looked worried. "Oi've got 'em evenly split roit now. Yeh mean to pull 'em back?"

Janis nodded. "If Ugglyn is anything like Lanser, and apparently they are the same, he'll be too brazen to think of tactical advantages. He'll just want to force his way through the front."

Harmel nodded.

Another thought came to her then. "Have Marric stand at one of the side entrances. I don't want him *near* any fighting."

The man's face twitched upward, a slight smile forming. Janis hadn't fully admitted her fondness for the boy, but she couldn't let him die, not like this. Somehow he'd become something akin to a brother in the time since she'd met him.

Avryn looked somewhat worried. "Permission, then, to spend a few moments with my wife?"

Livella and Harmel started at the word, but Janis remained impassive.

"You have twenty minutes, but I expect you to rally the soldiers by my side in the main cavern, along with you, Harmel," Janis said.

"Wai', yeh done gone an' married withou' tellin' me? Yeh old spine hog," Harmel said, punching Avryn in the arm.

Avryn blushed slightly but nodded.

"It didn't seem prudent to let it stay any longer. When you rushed out on us all a few days ago, I hadn't had the chance to tell you that we'd previously had the ceremony performed. The chaos that ensued from the announcement of Rivelen fleeing made it escape my mind."

Hearing about the marriage made something twist inside Janis, and she chanced a glance at Harmel. Whatever feelings she had for the man, she didn't know if they were deep enough for something like a marriage. Never had such a commitment come to her mind since Macks had betrayed her.

"Blimey ol' S'ren, good on yeh fer makin' it 'appen. After all this, moit we expect some little ones runnin' about?" Harmel said as they moved down the hallway.

Avryn blushed at the comment but shook his head. "I've hardly the mind to think about that right now, especially given the Void-filled Prost charging our base as we speak."

The comment pressed something on Janis's memory and she paused briefly, causing the others to stop their advance.

"What is it?" Avryn asked.

"Lanser said something, I think it's related to *H'ilvina't*," she replied, cracking her knuckles. "The fool wouldn't tell me anything; he's as worthless as the biggest coward in a fight."

Avryn furrowed his brow. "I still can scarcely believe what you've shared. How could the very god we've worshiped for who knows how long be nothing more than a man trapped within some in-between world?"

Janis knew the lamentation wasn't meant to be a challenge, but she still wondered if what she'd said was true. The affirmation that Lanserian as a religion seemed misguided was not a comfort for her. Being proven right in this matter only troubled her more. Shouts rang out from down the tunnel, making Janis snap her attention there.

"They're coming! The scouts far out have spotted the army!" a voice echoed down the tunnel.

While the shouting continued, Janis and Livella locked eyes. It wasn't that Janis mistrusted what Livella claimed to have seen, but hearing that their scouts had spotted something only proved the truth.

"This is it, then," Avryn said.

Harmel clapped his friend on the shoulder. "'Twill be alroit, I fink. We've got the lass on our side after all."

Rather than focus on the attention Harmel had just sent her way, she ignored the comment, looking at him directly.

"Get the companies ready as we discussed when I first arrived. I'll join you in the main cavern in a few minutes. Livella, I think it best if you stay on one of the side entrances. While you've been training well, I don't think it would be wise for you to die at this moment. I'm unsure what that would mean for the pact."

Livella pursed her lips, clearly displeased with the order, but nodded.

Harmel saluted her formally, then started to run off, Livella following. He paused, then suddenly spun around and ran back to her, a determined look on his face. Once again her instincts warned her to defend herself, and Janis raised her hand to smack the oaf coming at her but she held back.

Harmel's hands grasped both of her arms in a firm but gentle grasp, then his lips touched hers. Heat flared up in her chest, a conglomeration of emotions swirling in a manic frenzy. She ripped her arms out of his grasp and swung her fist at his face. Harmel slipped back just enough for her first blow to miss, but her left hook caught him on the jaw, making him stumble backward.

Then he laughed.

"Tha' was moity worth it, Oi'd say," he said, feeling the welt that was already forming on his cheek. With a wink, he ran off down the tunnel.

Avryn watched with his mouth slightly ajar, his eyes moving back and forth from where Harmel just ran to her. "That was—"

"Forget about it," Janis interrupted. "We've more important things to deal with."

Avryn shut his mouth, nodding in affirmation.

Janis's lips still tingled where she had only moments before felt the warm, rough lips of the man she'd started to love. Her mind screamed at her not to trust him, not to fall prey to another foolish man who would ultimately betray her, but her desires flared inside. Trying to clear her mind, she focused on what she'd seen in the vision before Lanser had sent her away.

"Before Lanser sent me away, I saw something that seemed important. I believe it had something to do with *H'ilvina't*," Janis said.

"Why wait until now to say something?" Avryn asked.

Janis opened and closed her fist, a nervous energy filling her breast where once before there was a surprising burning passion. She hadn't wanted to talk about it in front of the others. With her growing fondness toward them, particularly those she'd been forced to journey with in the past few weeks, she didn't want to admit to them what she suspected about *H'ilvina't*.

"I trust them as much as I trust you; that's not the issue here," Janis said, assuaging what she assumed were the concerns flowing in Avryn's mind at her waiting to share this information, "but I fear they may be involved in some way."

Her stomach clenched, thinking once again of the feeling of Harmel's large palms grasping her upper arms, pulling her in close for a kiss.

"Lanser mentioned a sacrifice—one that he was not willing to make in order to conquer the darkness," Janis continued, "then I saw a woman. The whole vision had been made from Lightbearing, as if a Conjurer created the whole scene before me, but she was different."

Janis finally pulled the hand she hadn't realized she'd been hiding behind her back, her palm now tired from how hard she'd been clenching it.

"This woman was made from orange Light," Janis said.

Avryn's eyes widened.

"Like the Light we saw when we first mentioned *H'ilvina't* in the war room," he said, looking determined. Avryn bowed his head, running his hand through his long hair as he considered the information.

"I think he loved her, Avryn," Janis admitted. "I couldn't be sure if she was his wife or just a lover, but the way she looked at him in the vision, she meant something to him."

Avryn grunted. "This whole time I was imagining this *H'ilvina't* to be some artifact, some object to use to bind him away, but you're suggesting it's a *person*?"

Janis nodded.

"But how are we supposed to find that person?" he asked, voicing the question that Janis had herself.

Images of all those she'd come to love flew through her mind, and her chest constricted at the thought that any one of them might be someone she had to sacrifice.

"It was someone close to him," Janis surmised, "so it only makes sense that it would be someone close to me."

Avryn's jaw clenched and he slammed his fist into the stone wall.

"Fog it all, we don't have time for these games," Avryn said. "I'll think on it more. For now I need a few minutes with Narinda before Prost arrives."

Janis nodded, then the two rushed off down the hall as apprehension, something that had become all too familiar in the recent months, wormed its way into her chest.

28

The waterfall before them thundered loudly, pounding in Prost's ears. Satisfaction bubbled within Ugglyn as he stood before the army, gazing upon the newly revealed lair of Evenir.

At long last, I've finally found the foe who has fought against me for all of my existence, Ugglyn mused internally.

Prost didn't know why the anti-god hadn't voiced the same sentiment out loud. It felt as if he was taunting Prost, boasting about something that would make him feel inferior.

He already felt inferior.

The fog on Prost's mind wrapped him heavily, making it hard for him to comprehend much of what happened, save for what he could see and hear with his own eyes and ears. He couldn't even appreciate the beauty of the falls, pouring from a river through the terraces of fields far above on the mountain. The sight of it rivaled the prairies of their own lair far to the west of Lindrad.

"What are we to do now?" Vint asked to the side.

"That's simple," Ugglyn crooned, Prost shivering internally at hearing his own voice still overlayed with the deeper tones of the anti-god. "We break our way in."

Despite the wonder of the falls, they could see the shimmering outline of a Shield behind the layers of water. Doubtless Evenir wouldn't have exposed the entrance to their lair by using such a bright lit Shield, so Ugglyn assumed they knew the army was here. In his haste, he'd hardly thought about the sentries and watchmen that would have spotted an army of their size leagues away, but Ugglyn wasn't worried. Many would die today, and he cared little for them save for the death of one specific person.

Thoughts of Janis swam in his mind, the images swarming the nearly dormant Prost within. Seeing the woman's face enraged Prost. She was the sole thing lying between him and his freedom. Freeing Ugglyn surely meant releasing him from the bonds of his captivity. Ugglyn laughed, causing the Watchlight soldiers around him to jump.

"Yeh expect t' jus' run in? Tha's a sure way t' ge' us all killed," Jord spat.

The boy sat forward in his saddle, his jaw tight with nerves. Ugglyn might have been annoyed at the boy's comment if he weren't so glad to be here, finally hemming in the enemy and preparing to destroy them all.

"I may not know the full size of their army, but I'm confident that ours is much larger," Ugglyn replied. "You've little to worry about."

The scowl deepened on Jord's face but he opted to not argue.

"Yer orders, then?" Alts asked.

Prost gazed on her, seeing the sorrow that still seeped from her eyes. The guilt of Mert's death a few days prior still lingered in him. While he didn't like the man at all and had felt some satisfaction at seeing the fogger dead, Prost lamented how it affected Alts. Given his circumstances, he couldn't do anything to console her.

"Jus' blast the way in?" she asked, squeezing the reins of her horse tightly.

The soldiers nearest the group tensed, shifting in their saddles and whispering to each other. While their numbers were great, no one relished the idea of running headlong into the middle of a mountain where any number of traps could be laid.

"That's what the expendables are for," Ugglyn said quietly, almost a whisper. Jord tensed again, glaring at Ugglyn before he looked to Vint and Alts.

Ugglyn breathed in deeply, the sound drowned out completely by the falling water. He tugged at some force inside, Prost feeling the same pull.

Immediately, Prost could feel them. Every soldier touched by the Void power was connected to him, and he knew that the anti-god could command them. The group of soldiers, thousands of men and women, snapped to attention a hundred paces to their right. They'd stayed clear of the Lightbearers for most of the trip.

The moment the Shield is down, rush the entrance. If you die, you die in the honor of the Void and my cause. Ugglyn's thoughts radiated with a pulsing rhythm, the dark cords of energy invisible to the eyes of everyone save Prost and Ugglyn.

The army straightened, the energy and message washing over them as Ugglyn pulled on their minds.

"Destroyers, clear the way of the Shield. The Voidweavers will take care of the rest," Ugglyn ordered.

Jord cracked his neck, still narrowing his eyes at Ugglyn, but he nodded, then summoned an orb. Alts created one of her own, a half dozen other soldiers around them preparing their powers.

"Get us in there *now*!" Ugglyn shouted, impatience rocking him that they hadn't already started.

With a grim look, Jord lobbed his orb, the power slamming with a loud crack into the blue Shield beyond.

Then as soon as we get in there, the real fun can begin, Ugglyn whispered, making Prost shudder.

~

THE EXPLOSION ECHOED through the cavern around them, men and women shifting on their feet nervously. Janis had done all that she could to rally and bolster the morale of their soldiers, but once they'd caught wind of the size of the army that was upon them, there was little more she could do.

"Hold steady!" Avryn shouted over them. "Their numbers may be many, but we have the tactical advantage!"

Janis had placed Avryn in charge of the main command, recognizing that he'd led military operations far more than she had. Still, she'd come up with a few clever tricks that wouldn't have been a part of Avryn's military training.

She eyed the platforms they'd Conjured to hold the Lightbearers just above the entrance before them. At least a dozen Shields stood along the narrow tunnel coming into their base. Watchlight would break through, but it would take time and energy to do so.

Trease winced next to Janis.

"Me Shielders can' 'old 'em back too long, they've many Destroyers in their ranks, Oi fink."

Janis nodded. "You instructed your Shielders not to expend themselves too much, correct? Trying to Shield them off for too long will render them useless if they lose their vitality."

Trease nodded. "Aye, Oi did jus' tha', but wha' will the Shields do then?"

Janis smiled slightly. "Give them the impression that we're only on the defensive."

Save for the small bands of men and women she'd placed at the entrances, most of their army was here in the main cavern. Given the fact that they'd received no communications from the sentries or single Seers stationed at the other entrances, she guessed that Prost's army was only coming from the front.

More booming thundered from the entrance tunnel, followed by glass shattering, the sound of Shield after Shield falling.

She sighed slightly, knowing that Marric was safe at one of the side entrances. Glancing sideways, she noted Narinda, her sword drawn next to Avryn. Apparently, he'd tried to get his new wife to join Marric at the side entrance, but she wouldn't fall for that. Though she hadn't been a part of the strategic conversations, she knew the main fight would be here, and she wanted to be a part of it.

Janis locked eyes with the woman, and Narinda's eyes crinkled at the side, her smile far more joyful than Janis thought it should be at this time.

"Your Lighters are ready, yes?" Janis said.

"Ready as ever. Our Light will be bolstered the moment they break through," Narinda replied.

Soldiers shifted all around them, the sound of rustling feet and clothing echoing amidst the loud explosions and pounding.

"Spare your Shielders the strength," Janis said finally, looking at Trease.

"Milady? Yeh can' mean t' let them in easy loike, can yeh?"

Janis smiled mischievously. "Of course not."

Trease furrowed her brows but nodded, shouting the order to the Shielders.

Avryn locked eyes with Janis, looking confused. "You can't be serious. I know they have the means to make it through eventually, but at least let them expend their energy in doing so," he urged.

"Avryn, you know full well how little energy Destroying takes. They'll take more than us in a struggle of might with Shields and Destroying."

He grimaced, but having the same ability himself, he couldn't deny the fact that sending a wave of Destruction used far less energy than holding a Shield. Janis waved up to the soldiers stationed on the Conjured platforms above. Alsry stood there with them, looking down upon Janis and the others. It was easy to spot the woman from far below with her dark skin and coarse black hair. Alsry nodded, then began speaking to those with her.

"On three," Janis suggested.

Avryn sighed, then began the count.

She immediately felt relieved to have relinquished control of the main armies not only to Avryn but to the respective generals.

"One," Avryn said firmly, his hands gripping his Conjured sword.

Janis eyed the rest of the cavern. Varith and his Fixers were stationed off the side, prepared to heal those who took too much injury during the fight. Among them they'd set both those of Light and Void. They'd discovered that the Void power could Fix, and though she was still reticent to trust them, Janis couldn't deny the invaluable nature of more potential healers.

"Two," Avryn said.

Janis released the dagger she held in her hand, instead focusing on the Shield-covered opening before her. Another Shield shattered, the sound washing over them as it echoed even more loudly in the cavern.

"Three!" he shouted.

Right then, the Shield just before the entrance disappeared to nothing. Sounds of yelling and roaring exploded through the narrow opening, indicating that those at the front of Prost's army had seen the disappearing barriers.

"Steady," Janis said, though the tension rose rapidly in the whole cavern. Soldiers crouched and grimaced as the sound of many soldiers grew louder from the entrance.

Gritting her teeth, Janis flung her hands outward, creating orbs of Destruction as her hands moved. The moment they left her palms, she pressed them forward, Moving them rapidly until they flew directly down the entrance. With her precise use of Moving, the dual orbs lit the narrow tunnel, disappearing rapidly through the hole. Within seconds, they exploded, soldiers screaming in pain and terror as the tunnel crumbled in on those who advanced.

"What in the name of Lanser are you doing?" Avryn said, looking at her with wide eyes.

"Improvising," Janis said, leaping off the tables on which they stood and running to the tunnel.

Soldiers watched wide-eyed as she advanced alone toward the entrance. This was part of why she wanted to relinquish the control of the army to Avryn. Part of it had been that he was far more experienced in military organization and orders, but the other part was that she didn't want to be focused on anything more than facing the man to blame for all this.

She knew he wouldn't come first through the tunnel, but she wanted to be prepared just in case he did. Instincts told her that whatever this Void power was, he would be wielding it in earnest.

Janis reached the opening, gesturing those closest to them to back up, giving her room to work. They did, though many with surprised expressions.

She could hear Avryn cursing behind her, but the sound of his voice remained quiet, which meant he was respecting her orders to stay behind and keep everyone in order.

Dust billowed out from the tunnel before her as the debris continued to settle loudly twenty paces into the narrow passageway. Her army continued to shuffle, steel echoing as swords were drawn, soldiers whispering to each other about the coming fight.

Janis Conjured her daggers, listening for the expected sound of Destroying power blasting through the obstructions she'd put in the army's way. She narrowed her eyes when no explosions came. Suddenly, the stones blocking the way of the tunnel disintegrated, disappearing to a grey dust. Her chest constricted at the almost silent destruction of the stones right before her eyes. Though her mind didn't comprehend what had just happened at first, the approaching men and women holding orbs of dark mist alerted her to the situation.

The Void power.

She cursed, realizing that she should have expected this. The few black-robed figures at the forefront of the group ran directly at her, shouting things she didn't understand, before they lobbed their orbs at her. Air hissing through her teeth, she flung out a Shield, the brilliant barrier appearing in a dome before her and extending upward. The orbs slammed into her barrier, but nothing happened. Janis's stomach twisted in surprised apprehension as the presumed orbs of Destruction disappeared harmlessly into the Shield. Though relieved, Janis spotted a few orbs that landed just short of the Shield, hitting the stone floor.

A circular area, about the width of her shoulder, disintegrated into dust, the newly formed crater filling with the material.

Note to self: don't let those touch you, Janis thought.

Her brain processed what she'd seen, realizing that it was still Destroying power, just less explosive.

Looking up, she locked eyes with Alsry and nodded.

Extending her Shield outward, Janis moved with the barrier so that it was just before her.

Take the bait, come on.

Dozens of black-robed men and women poured through the entrance, pooling in the area in front of her Shield. They glared at her, and the man at the forefront locked eyes with her.

"Your Shields are useless against our might," he said, his voice sounding on the stone walls.

Evenir's soldiers remained quiet as they'd been instructed. Though she wasn't an experienced soldier, she knew how a display of emotions could alert an enemy to your weakness or terror. By remaining quiet, she hoped the enemy would see strength and resolve.

Janis couldn't help but smirk. "Based on what you've got going for you, I think my Shield will hold just fine. Unless you plan to burrow your way through the ground," Janis said, grinning annoyingly.

The man growled and launched a volley of his Void orbs, all of which disappeared on her Shield with no effect. During their spat, more black-clad soldiers slipped into the area cavern, still blocked by her Shield.

Need as many as possible before—

Her thoughts were interrupted as a man walked through the others, his hand raised with an orb of Light.

"We'll use the Light, then," the man said, his jaw hardened.

Janis pulled her Shield back even farther, hoping to coax as many as she could into the area, knowing that this would likely be their only chance to surprise them. As she hoped, more poured through the opening. The man she'd spoken with narrowed his eyes, before they widened and he looked up sharply.

"From above!" he shouted suddenly, but it was too late.

The moment he started looking up, Janis had already gestured to Alsry, who shouted the order. Conjured stones and boulders, brilliant blue destructions rained down on the Watchlight soldiers. They screamed as the barrage of stones, arrows, and other Conjures slammed into them. Sounds of dying men and women filled her ears, making Janis grit her teeth. She'd killed for years for her profession, but her work didn't include such grisly scenes as this.

Movement within the confined area created by her Shield made her step back. They watched as a dome of smokelike energy erupted outward, the following Conjures slamming into it harmlessly. Stomach tight, Janis held her Shield firm momentarily as the Conjurers above continued their attack.

Without warning, a dark orb flew from the top edge of the shadow dome, slipping almost silently into the platform created by the Conjurers above. The platform disappeared instantly, the half dozen soldiers screaming in surprise as they plummeted to the ground below. Cursing, Janis raised her hand to try to stop their fall but wasn't successful. Bones crunched and soldiers cried as they slammed into the stone below.

Before she could command the aid, Varith's Fixers were on the scene, mending any who had survived the fall.

Janis spun on the second platform to see Alsry rushing the others off as quickly as possible. Most were halfway down the Conjured steps when another orb disintegrated their platform as well. The only person remaining was Alsry.

With a shout, the dark-skinned woman free-fell through the air, but her descent stopped suddenly as Janis reached out with her free hand, Moving her down slowly. The distraction was sufficient for a Light orb to slip from the shadows, cracking against her Shield and making her wince as energy drew from inside her. She dropped the barrier, instead launching her own orb of Destruction at the Void Shield.

Another crack and the Void barrier buckled, disappearing to nothing.

Mangled forms of Watchlight members littered the ground where previously they'd been crushed by Conjures, but more soldiers poured in through the hole. Janis Conjured her daggers, the feeling even more comforting now.

"Archers! Now!" Avryn ordered.

Unsurprisingly, the barrage of arrows, both Conjures and steel-tipped, ricocheted off the Void Shield that appeared instantly.

Before Janis could prepare another Destroying orb, the Shield disappeared, revealing more soldiers behind it. They were funneling down faster than Janis would have guessed.

Janis's eyes fell on a familiar face and her chest tightened.

Prost stared at her now from the front of the group.

UGGLYN'S BEING WARMED with satisfaction, seeing the stooped assassin with her glowing daggers, trusting in the protection of a power that would soon prove to be her downfall.

He had to admit, the army and organization they'd managed to muster in the short time was impressive, but Ugglyn knew it wouldn't be enough, not with the things he'd planned. A whirling sword of smoke appeared in his hand, the tingling, almost burning sensation a welcome feeling after hundreds of years being locked away with nothing but his emotions to accompany him.

He couldn't help but smile. Should he catch a blade this day, the sensation of actual feeling would prove far worth it in the end. Even if that was the case, his Voidweaving would mend the wound almost instantly.

Though the moment was brief, Ugglyn took in the scene around him. Soldiers clad in thick hides and mail armor stood everywhere in the large cavern. Given the circumstances, he wasn't surprised to see that their lair looked similar in nature to Watchlight's far in the west, but then again, what other options did one have when using the same stone medium and Destructive powers to build a network?

The sound of air swishing came from above, and Ugglyn flipped his free hand upward, the Void barrier that appeared blocking the successive rain of death. Darkness fell on him and his company as the dark Shield blotted out the Light of the orbs. He could see easily in the dimness, though the closest Watchlight Lightbearers grumbled at the darkness created.

A man close to him summoned a minuscule Lighting orb, making Ugglyn hiss in anger. "Put that infernal poison away!" he shouted, making the Lightbearers, however few they were currently, jump at his reaction.

The man hesitated, and when Ugglyn flicked his sword tip toward the man's neck, he gasped, letting the Light disappear.

Glorious dimness returned, and Ugglyn almost sighed. He had little trouble seeing well in the darkness, and he knew that his Voidweavers were the same. Similar smiles of satisfaction adorned their faces around him.

Soon Evenir's archers would be incapacitated by the mingling of his warriors with their own. With a shout, he forcefully pushed his hand upward, the Void barrier launching outward as it expanded toward the Evenir soldiers closest to it.

"Advance!" Ugglyn roared, hearing his voice marred by the man in which he resided.

He flexed his free hand, still reveling in the ability to actually *feel*. Though he disliked how his voice and mind were tainted by the man who now lay dormant within his mind, he couldn't help but relish the fact that he could now experience life again.

The moment his Shield fell, he winced at the bright Lights from above. They almost burned his eyes, the Void within him shrinking back at the presence of the power brought by his weaker half. Thoughts of Lanser plagued his mind, and he searched for the only one who could finally give him the retribution he needed.

Janis crouched twenty paces ahead of him as men roared and shouted, weapons of Light and dark Void flashing in the air as the two armies clashed in the midst of the large cavern. His eyes barely landed on her face before she was gone from his view, slipping through the fighting soldiers until she appeared out of nowhere. Ugglyn grinned, flipping his sword upward to block the two Conjured daggers she held tightly in her grip.

Hissing rang in his ears as the three weapons collided, the opposite energies reacting. With a grunt, Ugglyn pushed the woman back, her heels skidding on the stone.

"And so it begins, the fall of the Lightbearers as one," Ugglyn mused, jumping forward with his large sword and swiping at Janis.

Though she dodged easily out of the way, his blade sheared through two men who fought with Lightbearing, one red and one blue. Ugglyn felt no remorse as the two cursed Light wielders crumbled to the ground, bleeding out with cries of terror.

Janis's eyes widened slightly but only briefly as she slipped into range of his sword. Tightening his grip on his blade, he swung it outward, trying to follow her movements but unable to with the larger sword. The woman slipped through his slashes, slicing with both daggers. Though he dodged one, the other cut a shallow mark on his wrist, burning pain flaring in the wound.

He shouted, then flicked his sword easily back toward her. Ducking rapidly, she managed to slip once again through the trajectory of his large sword, though once again, his sword cut through a few others fighting near them. Their screams of pain fell on his deaf ears.

As she moved backward, out of his range, she threw her arm upward in something that was obviously a signal to someone. Light erupted in the air around them as Lightbearers launched orbs of blue Light, tripling the amount that already shone on the ceiling. Ugglyn shouted in pain as his eyes were overwhelmed by the Light. Men and women cried in surprise, Voidweavers of both Watchlight and Evenir shrinking back away from the Light.

Janis's eyes narrowed with resolve, a look of satisfaction on her face. With a grunt, Ugglyn threw his free hand upward, and orbs of dark energy as large as the Lighting orbs above flew outward. Though he only created a dozen, they absorbed the blue Light nearest them, dimming the cavern around them.

Pulling on the connection he held with the Voidweavers, he sent a wave of mental commands, Watchlight members around him standing up straighter and holding their hands upward. An orb exploded at Ugglyn's feet, rock stinging him in the face and eyes. He stumbled backward as the force pushed him roughly. Glaring through the now dust-filled air, he locked eyes once again with Janis, who flung another orb right as his face.

He dodged, the blast flinging a couple of Watchlight members behind him into the walls, their heads cracking as they fell dead to the ground. Ugglyn's orbs faltered above as he was forced to let his hand drop. Before he knew it, Janis was there, her dagger slicing his hand clean off with a quick blow. Eyes wide, he watched as the hand holding his sword fell to the ground, the weapon disintegrating to nothing. As blood poured on the stones, Ugglyn cried out in pain and flung his other hand outward, a Shield forming to block her next blows.

Janis barraged him with Destructive orbs immediately. The moment his barrier fell, he pushed outward with his power, the woman's body as well as a half dozen other soldiers from both sides being wreathed in shadows as they flew a dozen paces, his Moving energy pushing them away.

Grinning, he held up his stump, tingling forming there intensely. He watched Janis's reaction as his hand formed from shadows, coalescing into flesh. Feeling returned to his hand as he Conjured another weapon, this one a short sword.

Janis recovered and moved to dash inward toward him, but by then, his unspoken command had reached the Voidweavers within his band. Hundreds of Void orbs flew upward, absorbing the Light and dimming the whole cavern as if it was now twilight. Pockets of Light and darkness moved about the cavern as Lighters struggled to keep their Lights formed and Voidweavers likewise struggled.

Yet Ugglyn didn't care. He only cared for his quarry.

WARNINGS ROCKETED through her mind as she watched hundreds of the same odd Void orbs soaring through the air above them, the cavern now as dim as if the sun was setting. Janis didn't have long to dwell on the turn of events before Prost dashed toward her, now holding two short swords made of swirling smoke.

She dodged, then parried both attacks, his movements far faster and more frenzied than they ever had been when they'd last fought. Even when the man had faced her, he'd never opted to use weapons such as these. This, plus the new manic way of fighting, validated Janis's thoughts.

This wasn't Prost.

The wicked purple scars practically screamed at her as the man's forceful grin came within a handspan of her face, their weapons locking together with a continuing hiss.

"Lanser's gift will not save you this day," Prost said in a near whisper.

Her insides twisted at hearing the voice. It was Prost's after all but laced with the same crooning tone, the same deepness of the anti-god she'd unfortunately seen more than once.

He pushed firmly with his swords, his strength more than her own, forcing her to move lightly on her feet to avoid being knocked over. The moment she righted herself, she slipped out of reach of his swords, taking the moment to glance over at Avryn. Soldiers fought and fell all around her, steel and Conjures colliding with clangs and hisses from Lightbearing connecting with the Void substance. Lights flashed from above as the Lighting orbs warred on their own with the dark orbs attempting to siphon the Light away.

"Keep them steady!" Janis heard Narinda shout behind her.

Prost's dual swords whipped through the air, the swish still loud enough for Janis to hear given how close they came to her face. Gritting her teeth, she dodged them one by one. Stepping into his reach, she dodged his right sword, used her dagger to parry the other, then sliced outward with her free dagger. Her chest constricted with surprise as she felt the knife hit resistance, the sharp blade cutting somewhat along one of Prost's purple scars on his face.

Roaring from the pain, Prost jumped backward, narrowly avoiding her next thrust with the same dagger.

Janis tried as best as she could to veil her surprise. The maneuver she'd just performed was not uncommon, and she recalled using the same method on Prost previously yet she'd reached his flesh nonetheless.

Her stomach dropped when she heard Prost's roar turn into frantic laughter.

"Ah, the sting of Lightbearing warring with the Void within. There's something sweet about knowing that as your Light poisons me, so shall my Void poison you," he taunted, the cut on his face filling with the smokey substance of the Void. Within moments the wound was gone and he grinned.

Though the idea revolted her, she had a suspicion that he'd suffered the blow of his own accord, as if to prove his point. The air sweltered around her as the fighting continued intensely. Whatever ventilation they'd set up in creating this place was not enough to deal with the fighting of thousands of people. Sweat poured over her brow and she took a moment to wipe it away. As she did, she heard Prost's feet shuffling quickly and a grin spread on her face.

He'd taken the bait.

Judging from his position, she knew where he'd be coming. Even halfway through wiping her brow, she ducked, the swish of his sword flying over her head, the other coming dangerously close to her side. Still, she dodged that one and threw her shoulder into the now very close Prost. She felt her bones press firmly into his chest, the man grunting from the pressure as he stumbled backward.

Her gut twisted, her instincts warning her of something. Unsure why, she stopped executing her attack halfway through and tried to pull her momentum backward. No sooner had she abandoned her maneuver than a dark orb of energy slipped between her legs, the floor melting away to dust. She cursed and backed away before she fell into the newly formed crater.

If she'd not moved, that would have connected with her chest.

Prost laughed again.

"You are a crafty one, aren't you? I must say that of all the times to finally get my freedom, I'm glad it's you I have to face. I fear that other Primes would have proven far too easy to kill," he said with a wicked grin.

Janis didn't award him an answer, instead tossing a dagger at his face. He tilted his head so it missed by a hair, but Janis was already creating another weapon. She flung her other dagger while creating a Destruction orb in her hand. With as much finesse as possible, she melded the orb into the form of a dagger, something she'd learned from the late Prime Riln himself.

Fearing to strike the people behind him, Janis flipped the dagger downward, aiming for his legs. With a grin, he held out his hand, and her dagger was wreathed in the dark energy of the Void. Twisting his wrist, the dagger flew just past him and into the back of a Watchlight Lightbearer. The explosion ravaged the man and half a dozen other soldiers, both Evenir and Watchlight.

Prost laughed again.

"I fear that trick is too old to work on me. I'm far older than you can imagine," he said.

Her gut twisted, seeing the immediate death of not only the Evenir soldiers but those allied to him. As her mind processed what had just happened, Ugglyn launched his own attacks, Conjures of smoke and orbs of his Destructive power moving at her. Rather than dodge them all, she created a shimmering barrier, the dome of Light covering only her person.

Those deaths had been her fault. She knew that using Destroying in this space was not safe; there were far too many soldiers packed around them. Still, he'd directed her Destroying weapon into one of his own. He hadn't bothered to aim correctly even when he probably had the chance to do so. She thought of his sword cutting through those around him, both soldiers for her cause and his own.

He had no regard for anyone.

The burden of protecting everyone became far heavier on her shoulders at the thought.

Prost continued to Conjure and Move his Void-created objects at her as her Shield held firm. Unlike Destroyers with Light, his own Destructive power disappeared almost harmlessly on the barrier.

"Come now, you don't presume to hide behind the Shield all day, do you?" Prost crooned. "Here, let me provide some—motivation."

With a flick of his wrist, one of his orbs flew to his right, colliding with the back of a woman wielding a Conjured sword. She disintegrated in moments, the dust of her corpse sifting to the ground.

Janis gritted her teeth, immediately dropping her Shield.

Prost raised a single eyebrow.

"Well, you are far easier to persuade than I thought. You truly care so much about these people?" Prost asked, throwing more orbs of energy, melting half a dozen others, some from Watchlight this time.

She flung her hands up, a Shield extending outward, though she focused on making it a reverse barrier. A dome now extended over her and Prost, the wall nudging dozens of warriors around them, who cried out in shock.

"Curious," Prost said, looking around at the dome. Despite his attempts to hide it, she could see the wince of his eyes at the brightness of the dome's Light. He prodded at the nearest wall, his sword hissing loudly as it connected, then he tossed a small orb, which disappeared against the barrier.

"Your quarrel is with me," Janis said firmly.

He smirked. "You'd risk your own life by trying to hold a barrier while fighting me? Seems ill advised."

She knew what he said was true, but she still felt nauseous at the needless death he'd already caused. Janis knew it wasn't driven by Prost himself, though she knew he was no stranger to death. Staring directly at his eyes, she reminded herself that this wasn't the man she'd faced before, merely a construct of him possessed by Ugglyn.

He sighed. "Well then, let us begin."

He rapidly Conjured his swords and dashed directly at her.

~

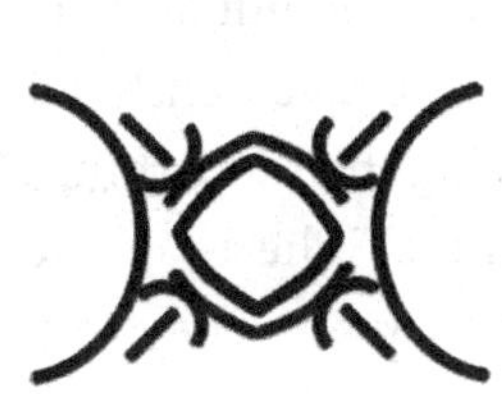

Marric's mind reeled at all that was happening. Seeing the black-clad army pour through the entrance to the main cavern was terrifying enough, but now a large Shield took up a huge portion of the center, constricting the battlefield for both enemy and ally.

Janis had stationed him at the side entrance, telling him that his Seeing ability was needed when the attack came from that direction.

He was realizing now the real reason she'd put him there. Men and women fell, both those of Watchlight and their own, and he was forced to watch it from above. His vision body hovered near the ceiling of the cavern. Seeing hadn't been that difficult when he'd first watched, but now the odd dark orbs floating around disrupted his view. Every time he moved near one of them, he felt as if he was fading away, the energy pulling him in like a deep hole with rushing wind.

Marric guessed Janis didn't want him watching them, hoping that he'd be distracted by the potential attack from the side entrance. If that's truly what she thought, she didn't know him well.

He cursed as a Void orb came so close to him that he felt the pull of the energy. A burning sensation filled his mind, the Void presence feeling wrong. With a grimace, he pulled himself back to his body, the burning disappearing from his mind as he fell back into his physical form.

Marric must have made some noise, though he hadn't realized it with what had just happened.

"Are you ok, lad?" a soldier asked nearby. "You gasped something awful."

He shook his head. "I'm fine. I think they're taking the brunt of the army in the main cavern."

The soldier furrowed his brows, looking down the tunnel that would lead them there. Miredith reached out and grabbed his arm, her grip tightening. Livella, who Janis had conveniently added to their ranks, glared at the wall, as if she was realizing the same things he was.

"What's happening in there?" she asked, her eyes wide.

"Watchlight is in Terris Green. They've poured in by the thousands, and soldiers are dying in droves," he said, feeling nauseous. "They need help."

"We've orders to stand here, and that we will," the commander said.

Marric gritted his teeth, knowing that he was the only Seer they'd left with this company of soldiers. He'd wondered why there was more than one Seer with each of the band save his own.

She is a crafty one, isn't she?

Yet he didn't care. If an assault were to come from this entrance, Marric knew it would have already.

"I'm going to help," he said, standing quickly.

"But sir—"

"You can't stop me," Marric said, sure of himself. Though he wasn't of any rank, he hoped that his prestige as one of the rare Lightbearers who'd

Awakened with three abilities was enough to make them not resist too much.

"Aye, but what if another attack comes?" the commander challenged.

"Send a messenger," Marric suggested before running down the tunnel.

Two other sets of footsteps echoed around him, and he spun to see both Miredith and Livella following behind. Marric stopped suddenly, his feet scuffing the stone beneath his feet.

"Where are you going, then?" he challenged, eyeing Miredith.

The question was posed to both women, but he didn't feel like he had grounds to challenge Livella given her position. Still, she was the one to respond first.

"Do you think I'm all right with Janis trying to keep me from the main fight as well? I haven't been training for the past month for nothing."

Miredith, seeming mildly annoyed that Livella had spoken first, folded her arms before giving Marric a knowing look.

"I don't really care what you have to say; I'm going to follow you whether or not you like it."

Marric locked his jaw, wanting to give some retort that would keep them away, but he eventually shook his head, defeated. Miredith looked satisfied, as if she'd just won a battle.

"Besides, I can probably get you there faster. You still don't know your way around this place," Miredith continued, moving past Marric.

Though he didn't want to admit it, he knew she had a point. He exchanged a look with Livella, and the woman shrugged before moving off to follow the red-haired guide through the tunnels. The soldier behind them called for them, so Marric quickened his pace, not wanting to have to deal with convincing him of their intentions. Apparently, the other two thought the same, for their feet shuffled more quickly.

"I think we probably shouldn't take the main tunnel to the cavern. If the army has advanced past the main room, that is probably where they'll head," Miredith said, turning toward a smaller side tunnel.

Marric's mind flashed to the Shield Janis had created, encapsulating her and Prost away from the others. His chest constricted at the thought of her having to face Prost alone. Something had changed about the scar-faced man, and it was more than the Void abilities he'd displayed. Immediately, the image of men and women disintegrating to dust at the hands of Prost's abilities pressed into Marric's mind and he felt sick. Instinctively he Conjured a sword, earning him a raised brow from Miredith as she saw the steady glow appear behind her.

"You think we'll get attacked right now?" she asked, but he responded by shaking his head. She looked amused.

"I just don't want to be caught off guard," he replied, though a blush threatened to engulf his cheeks. Fortunately, his statement was met with a nod from Livella, who reached back and pulled her staff free, her hands gripping the grain of the wood firmly.

Miredith's mirth melted away as she saw Livella prepare for the oncoming fight and she furrowed her brow.

"Erm, ok, you're right," she replied, holding her own hand open until a dagger formed from the shadows. She winced as the weapon came to existence. "Fog, that's uncomfortable. It's like my hand's lost feeling save for the burning sensation."

His stomach twisted at the mention of how it felt to summon the blade. He wagered it was something akin to what he'd felt when he touched the book. That seemed ages ago, but he realized it was less than a week. Rivelen's betrayal stung him, as he imagined it probably did the others.

It struck him that he didn't know what befell the woman. He'd not seen her come in with the army at the forefront of the sanctuary.

"We're almost there," Miredith said, leading them down another small tunnel. "Sorry, Livs, you're going to have to duck here."

Marric started at the nickname she'd used for the mousy-haired woman, but Livella didn't even react. Instead her eyes grew somewhat distant, as if she remembered some far-off memory. "My father used to call me that," she said before blinking and returning to her normal hardened gaze.

Sounds of shouting and steel clashing echoed on the walls around them, making Marric's chest buzz with nerves. He thought for a moment to Conjure a shield of some sort but realized he didn't have any training with one and it would likely just get in the way.

"Are you sure about this?" Miredith asked, pausing just before the ceiling got lower.

Though his mind screamed at him to run away, he nodded resolutely.

Miredith sighed but pressed on, disappearing through a narrow entrance. He realized he recognized the way; it was the same they'd taken after the initial vote for leader. Ducking through, he was aware of Livella bending down to squeeze through the lower opening.

As if a blanket was removed from their head, the sounds intensified, ricocheting off the walls as if coming from all directions. An explosion rocked the cavern, the sound making Marric wince at the din.

Maybe this wasn't the best idea, he thought grimly as a man screamed and fell to the ground before them.

A Watchlight soldier, black-clad and wielding a weapon of dark smoke, stabbed the Evenir man through the chest, his last breath leaving him. Marric froze, the scene only paces away causing nausea to assault him. His eyes locked with the enemy soldier who advanced on him. Before the man could move any closer, Livella was there, slamming the wooden staff over his head.

He crumpled to the ground before Marric.

"That was far more satisfying than I would have expected," Livella said, smiling grimly at Marric.

Two more soldiers advanced on Livella, having seen her attack on the other. She spun, parrying a sword with her staff and stepping backward. Marric's mind locked on the situation and he pressed his free palm outward, Moving both men backward, shocked expressions on their faces. With more force, he pushed them farther until they knocked into another pair fighting behind them.

It was then that he realized he didn't know what he was supposed to do. When he'd seen the fighting, he just knew he wanted to help, but with what?

"Find Avryn," Livella suggested as if reading his mind.

He nodded, then scanned the crowd in hopes of seeing the general fighting. Miredith screamed in fright next to him, and he spun to see a soldier running at them from behind. As he readied himself to Move the woman away, Livella was there, her staff connecting with the glowing red sword of the soldier.

"Go! Find him now!" she said, pushing her attack with frenzied motions.

Marric watched with admiration as she pressed the woman back with her staff, then Moved the woman away, her body wreathed in Void.

Without thinking, he reached out and grabbed Miredith's hand, pulling her toward the commotion. His gut wrenched once more at the thought of moving directly into the fray, but he held the tip of his sword forward. Most of the soldiers around them were too busy to notice, but he got shoved once or twice as they walked.

An Evenir man fell with a grunt in front of him, and Marric barely managed to put his sword up in time to block a Void sword coming at his face. The force pushed him backward, his wrist twinging with the blow, but he flicked his sword, letting the enemy's blade fall away.

Adrenaline filled him and he thrust his sword, the soldier dodging away. His hand left Miredith's and he focused on fighting this soldier at this moment. The man lunged, Marric turning just in time for the ethereal sword to just barely miss him before flicking his sword upward into the exposed arm of the man.

Marric's sword cut into the man's flesh and his stomach turned at the blood that dripped on his Conjured weapon. Looking away, he threw his shoulder into the screaming man until he fell to the ground. Though he felt sick, his mind took over and he stabbed the man directly in the chest, the resistance of the man's flesh on his blade.

Shaking his head to regain lucidity, he reached back and grabbed Miredith's hand once more. The moment he started moving, however, a familiar face stopped him in his tracks. Youthful eyes, close-cropped brown hair, and an evil deep within his eyes.

"'Ullo, ol' friend," Jord said with a satisfied grin.

29

Ugglyn growled as the assassin slipped a dagger through his swords once more, slicing a gash in his cheek. The stinging immediately spread through his face, the Voidweaving mending the wound before the Light could poison more of his veins.

"You're more cheeky than I expected," he said, glancing upward at the barrier.

She grinned, then jumped forward. This time he didn't allow her to get close. Stepping sideways out of her reach, he extended the length of both swords, making them longswords instantly and causing Janis to have to move backward defensively. Seeing this, Ugglyn pressed the attack, the feeling of the borrowed muscles straining a warm welcome.

Two hundred years without a physical form was grating and he reveled in nothing more than feeling human once again. The only thing stopping him from being fully free was the insufferable woman before him.

Janis once again slipped from his next attacks easily, acting as if she wasn't struggling in the least.

"You must not have spent much time practicing in your prison. A bit rusty, eh, old man?" the woman crooned, flicking another dagger at his face.

He dodged it easily, this time taking a page from her book and flinging one of his void swords at her. He pressed it forward with Moving power, sending it careening at her face. Eyes widening, she ducked just in time for it to slip over her head. Raising his now free hand, he pushed outward and the assassin's body cloaked in shadows slid backward into her own barrier with a heavy thud.

Grunting with exertion, he held her against the Shield as he walked forward. Determination in her eyes, Janis positioned her own hand outward just before Ugglyn felt a force shove him backward. He lost his hold on her, and she dashed to the side in time to miss his next Moving assault.

Before he knew it, she was behind him, swinging both daggers down at his back. A barrier of Void erupted in the air just in time for her weapons to glance harmlessly off of it. Given that she'd leapt in the air, her momentum kept her going, and she slammed face first into the Shield, grunting from the blow.

Amused at her blunder, Ugglyn dropped the Shield and spun, running the blade of his sword against her midsection, the sharp edge cutting in deeply. She shouted in pain and stumbled back, her large Shield falling around them and appearing around her.

Though she stood behind the barrier, he could see the pain in her eyes and the panic from the Void poisoning her blood.

"Stings, doesn't it?" Ugglyn taunted. "Just as your Light poisons me, so does the Void worm its way through you."

A steady glow emanated from within the Shield, and Ugglyn knew that she was Fixing herself. Part of him was annoyed that she could Fix herself just as easily as he could, another part was satisfied that he'd found a worthy opponent.

"I brought a little something for you," he said, reaching down to his belt and yanking the pitch-black dagger free. He dangled it in the tips of his fingers. Janis stared at him, anger burning there as he teased her with the very weapon that had been used to break him free. The weapon she'd lost. Despite her anger, she didn't drop the barrier. Shaking his head, he slipped it back in his belt.

He knew he could do little to break through her Shield, but taking advantage of the dropped barrier around him, he flung a Destructive orb at the closest three soldiers, one of them his own, and they disappeared to dust.

Though she said nothing, he could see the panic once more in Janis's eyes at seeing his needless killing. Before he could strike down more around him, heavy boots slammed into the ground next to him.

He spun on the sound, raising his swords.

Then he lost control.

Ugglyn felt himself drop into the mental prison almost instantly as his eyes landed on a man with light brown hair cascading down his head and over his shoulders. Piercing blue eyes locked on his own.

"Avryn," Prost murmured, feeling his limbs come back to him.

This can't be! Stop this, you fogging fool! Ugglyn roared in his head.

Prost had been dormant, completely lost in his own mind, the fog surrounding his consciousness keeping him from processing anything he could hear or see from his own eyes. Then everything was back. His chest constricted at seeing his friend.

"Avryn, it's you—"

Before he could say more, the man lunged with a steel sword, forcing Prost to block the attack with his own sword. The tingling still ran through his hand as he used the Void-Conjured sword. Where it was unpleasant before, Prost couldn't help but revel in the fact that he could feel anything.

"Wait!" he tried to say before Avryn brought his sword around.

Trying not to be aggressive but needing to protect himself, Prost dodged and parried each attack, backing up to where he could see a blue spherical Shield behind him. His memory snapped to attention and he remembered seeing Janis barricade herself. Cursing, he turned to avoid having her at his back. It was just in time as her Shield fell, forcing him to face not only Avryn now but Janis as well.

"Stop! He's gone! I need to talk to you—"

Avryn lunged again, but Janis hesitated, to Prost's surprise.

Despite her hesitation, he felt movement at his belt. Looking down in shock, he saw her black dagger slip from its place, wreathed in blue Light. It flipped into her hand and she grinned in satisfaction.

Anger flared within, and Prost knew it was mostly Ugglyn's, though his own mixed with it as he dodged Avryn's attack once more, pushing his hand outward. Avryn's body flew backward, covered with the Void.

As he used the power, Prost could feel himself slipping inward to his mind and he blinked roughly, trying to return lucidity to his thoughts. Janis watched curiously, her own daggers raised, but she didn't attack. She'd now hidden the black dagger somewhere on her person, still wielding only her Conjures. Prost wanted to kill her, the memory of how she'd tossed him off the roof in Stilten still stinging, but he couldn't move. Though he could feel his muscles, he could feel Ugglyn resisting.

His open hand held Avryn in place with Void, but he knew it was causing him to slip. He focused once more on his friend, feeling Ugglyn's embrace weakening as he stared, but Janis broke his concentration as she threw more Conjures at him. Cursing, he dropped his hold on Avryn to dodge them.

Avryn dashed forward, attacking in earnest, Janis by his side. Prost wanted to tell them to stop but realized he wouldn't be able to say anything. Even now, the memories of Ugglyn striking down both enemy and ally to provoke them entered his mind. Forced to back up, he threw up another Void Shield, and this time Prost felt himself drop downward, imprisoned once more in his mind.

No—no—no, he begged. But it was too late again.

The mental fog pressed in before he remembered Avryn, focusing on the man's face.

Prost could hear himself laughing, but it wasn't his own voice any longer.

"I think it's about time we make things more interesting, don't you?" Ugglyn said, his voice once more combined with Prost's.

He pressed outward, his Shield expanding forward and slamming into the two warriors who faced him. Janis kept afoot, but Avryn flew onto his back, clearly unprepared for the blow.

With a fluid motion, Ugglyn slipped the tome from his belt and opened it. Words scrawled themselves sloppily across the black pages and he read aloud.

"*Filring Ugglyn trillar y'rivnan vull*," he shouted.

Prost shrunk inside as he could feel the dark connection pulling on those around him. Once again, he could feel every person touched by the Void, both within and without the cavern. A pulse rocketed through the connections, making every one of them stop as if they'd lost their minds. Both Watchlight and Evenir Voidweavers alike paused as Ugglyn took control. Black pools of ooze coalesced on the ground throughout the cavern, pulsing upward as creatures pulled themselves free.

~

JANIS'S MIND REELED. The fighting hadn't stopped, but it had quieted to an eerie degree. Her eyes flashed about, taking in the new threat. Her hair raised on her neck as she watched hundreds of creatures appear like the one she'd fought months ago in the war room and in T'Arren Vale. Without hesitation, she flung a Destroying orb at one, the creature screaming in pain as it exploded into nothingness.

"What in the fogging fog is that?" Avryn said, righting himself quickly.

"Ugglyn's got more tricks than I expected," Janis admitted.

Movement behind her alerted her to a threat and she dodged, a Void-Conjured sword barely missing her. She stepped to the side, making to slash with her dagger, but paused.

It wasn't an enemy.

The woman, dressed in a mail vest but wearing a brown skirt and hat, stared blankly at her as she swung her sword once more. Janis shuffled back, confusion wracking her. A Void orb barely missed her, landing on the ground near her and disintegrating another crater. Gritting her teeth, she flung up another barrier, blocking more attackers from all sides.

"What's she doing?" Avryn said, protected now by the Shield.

The assassin within mocked her, teasing her for going against her own instincts to leave those touched by the Void in the prison ward. She hadn't listened, trying to put on her leader persona and focus on the impending threat. Now he controlled them.

Lightbearers and soldiers cried out around her as their friends turned on them, Void abilities now directed at any around her. She watched as a Watchlight man sliced the throat of a red-bearing Lightbearer, the man slumping to the ground lifelessly. Another Evenir man stabbed forward, an Evenir soldier crumpling to the ground.

"Soldiers! Defend yourselves! The enemy is among you!" Avryn shouted.

Though the order was wrought with much confusion, the fighting increased once more, and Janis could see the Lightbearers no longer stood dumbfounded.

Janis knew they didn't have much time and her mind returned to the words she'd shared with Lanser. Those with Void abilities slammed their weapons into her Shield, but none had any effect. Her brain screamed for her to drop the Shield, to go and aid all those around her, but she didn't know what to do next. A snarling Void creature, shaped like a crab with spikes protruding everywhere, leapt on her Shield, claws snapping wildly at the barrier. More joined in, fighting along the mindless men and women gripped by Ugglyn's power.

"You have to let me out!" Avryn shouted. "We'll be overwhelmed unless we get out of here."

"You'll die in seconds if I do that," she countered. Her strength was still there, but she knew Shielding herself wasn't the answer. Even if she could hold it indefinitely, it wouldn't help end this fight.

She recalled that when she'd learned that Ugglyn's powers resembled those of Lightbearing, she'd thought she knew the limitations of them. Now he'd summoned a whole slew of creatures and was pulling on the consciousness of soldiers on both sides. But just before this happened, something had changed in Prost. She knew logically that Ugglyn had taken control, but for a moment there he wasn't the same. He almost sounded as if he was begging for help. Whatever that meant, she didn't have time to dwell on it. Thoughts of Lanser flooded her mind at how the two men were the same. As if struck by lightning, an idea slipped into her mind.

"Prepare to run, get everyone to safety. I mean *everyone*," Janis said, a new connection to Lightbearers, both those wielding red and blue, entering her mind. As if a new door opened, countless connections spread from her mind, and she could feel them. Every Lightbearer, near and far—she could feel them. Allowing her eyes to fill with Light, she could see strings of Light pouring outward from her chest. Cords of blue tied her to every Lightbearer in the room. Some were tinged with red turning purple, but she could feel them.

Forcing a calm energy outward, she felt a pulse radiate through them, pressing outward. Avryn gasped at the sensation. She could feel a connection to every Lightbearer, as if they were somehow an extension of herself. The thought might have terrified her if it didn't feel so natural.

"What's happening?" he asked, turning to her. "You're doing something."

She shook her head, indicating that now wasn't the time. Eyes still aglow with energy, she flung her hands outward, her Shield exploding to the sides and throwing all those, creature and human alike, to the ground. Sucking in a deep breath, she flung her hands outward, pools of Light appearing throughout the cavern. From each of them sprung a duplicate of her, hundreds of Janises Conjured into reality. They immediately drew weapons of Light, attacking the nearest creatures of Void and soldiers controlled by Ugglyn's power.

"Impossible!" Prost said, eyes widening.

"Go," Janis said to Avryn and watched him dash off.

The cords of Light were still visible from her body and she started, seeing that one of the cords stood out among the others. A thick orange cord of Light, singular and strong, connected her to Prost, standing behind his shrinking Void barrier. She followed the line through her chest, seeing that it passed through Avryn, stopping at one final person.

Her stomach dropped.

No, she thought, not wanting to accept what she was seeing.

The cord stopped in Marric.

~

Chaos erupted around him as Marric slipped out of reach from Jord's next orb. It slammed with a crack into the rocks, debris flying everywhere. The moment he'd seen his friend, Jord's eyes filled with the ominous red Light. Marric had been forced to do the same, his mind heightening once more to the odd state of present-future.

They'd fought evenly, each only managing to scratch the other with their weapons. Though Jord wielded a sword of steel, Marric's Conjured sword had been sufficient in defending himself. Sweat poured down his face as he lunged at Jord once more, the boy easily dodging it and attacking with his own thrust. Marric could See it before it happened and he dodged easily.

Then something slammed into him from the side.

He cursed as he pitched to the side, landing hard on his hands and knees. Looking up, his eyes met with something unnatural. The wriggling form of some darkened creature moved toward him, mouth snapping. He cried out, throwing his hand outward with a wave of Moving energy. The creature flew backward, slamming into the back of an Evenir man who held an orb of Void, the two tangling into a mess.

Heart racing both from the fight and the unexpected creature, he turned to see who'd knocked him over.

Nausea slammed into his gut.

Miredith stood with blank eyes, her irises no longer green but instead filled with smoke, the silver tendrils within.

"Miredith?" he asked, but she lunged at him, a sword appearing from nowhere as she slashed outward. Gasping, he barely dodged her attack.

"Stop! What are you doing?!" he asked.

She advanced on him, her eyes still blank. Just before she could slice at him again, something rocked him once more. A pulsing energy, intense and hot, filled his whole body. He gasped once more, then watched as another form slammed into the girl. She struggled and squirmed, fighting with the black-cloaked figure of Jord.

Marric's mind spun. He couldn't believe what he was seeing. Mind warring but his eyes still filled with Light, he spotted Miredith's blade shrinking, the sharp knife slipping into Jord's side. Without thinking, he dashed forward, grabbing her wrist as the very thing happened that he'd seen. Surprised by the girl's strength, he forced her hand back enough for Jord to disentangle himself from her.

Now freed herself, Miredith kicked outward, her foot colliding with Marric's gut. He grunted, stumbling backward as a Watchlight woman and Evenir man came to stand by Miredith, their own irises filled with the same shadow.

"What's happening?" Marric said aloud.

"Did yeh feel tha'?" Jord asked, breathing hard next to him.

Marric nodded, his instincts warning him about Jord standing next to him. As if some energy had taken hold of his mind, Marric felt no more enmity toward his friend.

Jord gritted his teeth but continued facing the three people before them. "I—I don' fink we're meant to figh' anymore," he said through his teeth.

Marric stole a brief glance backward and staggered.

Hundreds of Conjured forms of Janis battled creatures like the one he'd seen just before. His mind reeled and he felt light-headed at the battle raging around him. Tearing his eyes away, he focused again on Miredith, who serenely jumped forward, her teeth bared.

Jord parried her attack, and Marric blocked the one that came from the entranced Evenir man. Eyes still filled with Light, Marric matched pace with Jord, as if they'd been fighting together for years. Though still confused about what was happening, he trusted the odd peaceful feeling that overcame him moments before this.

Marric, hoping to buy them more time, pressed firmly outward with his Moving, shoving Miredith and her companions backward with a rush.

"Wish Oi'd gotten tha' one, roit useful i' is," Jord said, backing up as Marric shoved them again.

"Why are you helping me?" Marric said desperately, ignoring his friend's wistful comment.

Jord furrowed his brow, then ducked as he anticipated a Void orb flying overhead.

"Don' roit know, though' somethin' was off the moment that fool led us ou' of our lair," he said, glaring over Marric's shoulder to where Janis fought with Prost.

Marric followed his gaze, his jaw dropping as he saw Janis whirling through the air with her daggers. Her own eyes were filled with blue Light. She dashed at Prost, who parried her attacks almost as easily. Upon closer inspection, Marric could see the scarred-faced man's eyes filled with the same thing as Miredith's.

"Look ou'!" Jord shouted, and Marric ducked as the Evenir man's Void spear flicked over his head. Marric spun and slammed the hilt of his sword into the man's gut. Another sword slipped around the man's back and sliced Marric's arm. He gasped in pain as intense burning rushed into his veins.

As the Evenir man fell, Miredith came into view, her eyes still blank. She jumped forward, trying to land a blow, but Marric could see them coming. The burning intensified in his arm, distracting him somewhat from the girl.

"This is foggin' ridiculous!" Jord shouted as he created an orb of Light and lobbed it at the Watchlight woman he fought. It cracked against her chest, then she was gone, exploded to nothing.

Marric's stomach twisted and he barely dodged Miredith's next blow. Stomach turning, he glanced at Jord's angry face, a frenzied fear filling him. Did he really think that his former friend had changed just like that? The thought sounded foolish, but then again, the peaceful feeling that had overcome him had been strong.

Jord, still looking angry, ran toward Miredith, raising his hand and creating another orb. "Tha's enough of tha', then."

"No!" Marric shouted, then pushed the boy back with his Moving. Jord's eyes widened as the orb flew over Miredith's head, exploding on the ground. Marric winced as rocks slammed into the side of his face and he opened his eyes just in time to see Miredith dash toward the surprised Jord and slam the tip of her blade into the boy's chest.

Marric's world spun. It all happened so fast that he couldn't process what just happened. Jord's eyes widened and he gasped for air. Miredith, still entranced, pressed the blade in farther. Finally getting his wits about him, Marric leapt to his feet and slammed the hilt of his sword into the girl's head. She collapsed like a doll, her eyes closing as she fell unconscious. Jord gasped for air as his life drained on the stone beneath him, and Marric felt so confused. When he'd first seen Jord, there wasn't even the possibility that his friend would come back, but there had been a small moment, a glimmer of hope that they could be reunited.

Falling to his knees by his friend, he watched as Jord, face full of terror, stopped moving.

Movement behind him tugged at his consciousness, telling him that he was still in danger, but his mind was screaming, sorrow filling his very being. For the second time in four years, he lost his friend.

The sound of wood splitting against a man's head shocked Marric out of his stupor and he spun to see Livella panting, her staff broken in the middle.

"Oh, fog it all," she complained, then held out her hand to Conjure another one. The air warped around her hand until another staff formed from the shadows.

Marric's skin chilled and he jumped to his feet, aiming his Conjured weapon at the woman.

"Back off! Or I'll gut you!" he threatened.

Livella appeared confused until she looked at her Void staff. Then she rolled her eyes.

"Oh, come off it, I'm not mindless like the others," she said, reaching forward and grabbing Marric's hand. He didn't recoil, for his eyes still filled with the odd Seer Light that allowed him to know danger.

"H—how?" he finally asked, but Livella shrugged.

"I don't have time to figure that out. I just came to get you," she reported. "The Lightbearers are meeting at the other end of the hall, so we need to make it there."

A creature came roaring at them, but Marric swiped his sword, cutting it in two.

"Nice one," Livella said, pulling him by his arm.

They ran, weaving through the Janis figures and creatures fighting. Explosions still rocked the cavern, and Marric could see where they were headed. He remembered Miredith and wanted to go back, but Livella refused him, pulling him harder. His arm burned, the feeling still crawling up his arm, but the adrenaline kept his mind lucid.

A half dozen soldiers with smoke-filled eyes blocked their way, some with Conjured weapons, others with hands outstretched, warning that they could summon some other power. Livella cursed and put her staff forward. As the soldiers advanced, cries of war sounded behind them, and Marric watched as a woman, clad in Watchlight black, stabbed outward with her red daggers. Her blonde hair was streaked with blue and tied in a tight braid. Alsry came with her, shoving the men and women away, their bodies glowing blue.

The path was clear in moments. With a brief pause, the two women nodded to each other, some mutual understanding passing between them as they ran with Marric to the entrance to the closest tunnel, where a Shield moved out of the way for them. Trease stood behind the Shield, her face determined.

"Barely made it, yeh did." She eyed Livella warily. "Still got yer mind, then?"

Livella nodded. "Can't say why, but yes."

Most of the others in the inlet gave her a wide berth, but Trease just nodded.

"Now tha' the Wathlight Lightbearers aren' tryna kill us, the Void fighters can' break the Shield."

Sure enough, Marric could see the mind-controlled soldiers lobbing Conjures and orbs at the Shield, but all bounced off harmlessly.

"Marric, you ruined a perfectly good tunic," Varith said, suddenly appearing out of nowhere. He pressed his hand firmly against Marric's arm, making a pain shoot up his bicep. Marric cried out until Light pulsed under the man's hand. Warmth moved up his burning arm until it was consumed fully.

"Fog it all, whatever poison their weapons are laced with is *not* easy to deal with," Varith complained, sweat dripping down his head. Even though Marric knew the man hadn't been fighting, he could see that he was exhausted.

"Incoming!" Trease shouted, making those around her move back as she pulled the Shield up for another small group.

"Blast it all! This is far more complicated than I expected," Avryn said, ushering the last few people in, then following behind.

"Avryn!" a woman's voice called from behind, and Narinda rushed through the crowd to embrace Avryn firmly. "I thought I'd lost you when you were fighting that man."

Avryn smiled grimly. "I can hold my own against Prost; I've always been able to."

His face took on a troubled look at the mention of Prost, and Marric wondered if the man was having memories of times when they'd been allies, even friends. Marric's eyes brimmed with tears at the thought of his own former friend. He'd just watched Jord die at the hand of the very girl he'd started forming a bond with.

Shaking his head, he focused on the fight before them.

"We've got to help her," Marric insisted.

Avryn's jaw hardened, but he shook his head. "I fear there's naught we can do. That fight is her own."

"Oi! Move yer tails! Comin' through!"

Harmel pushed roughly through the crowd in the tunnel, coming to the edge of the Shield. "Lemme through. I'mma go 'elp."

Harmel started to walk through the Shield until Avryn grabbed the man's arm.

"That will do little. You'll only die," Avryn insisted.

Harmel tugged his arm away, then faced Avryn, his eyes filled with tears.

"Oi wasn' there t' 'elp me brudda, Oi sure as Ugglyn's behind ain' gonna lose me girl," he said, rushing out of the Shield.

Avryn cursed but let him go. "The fool!"

After a beat, he rushed through the Shield himself, Conjuring a sword.

Marric's stomach fell as he watched two of his friends run back into the throng.

30

Ugglyn growled, his muscles feeling tired. After two hundred years of being locked away, bodiless, he was wildly disappointed in the frailty of the body. The assassin dove for him, throwing a dagger at his head, which he easily Moved away. She landed within arm's reach, slashing with the Conjures she'd created mid flight.

He created a barrier of Void, blotting out the Light of her daggers and everything else with the deep shadows. With a grunt, he commanded the creatures nearest him to attack her. Half a dozen of the crab-like creations launched themselves at her, chittering loudly. Janis cut them down easily, then exploded the last four. A few addlebrained soldiers from both Evenir and Watchlight shuffled at his command, but she dispatched them easily.

She's a force you can't reckon with, Prost pressed.

He hadn't lost complete control of his mind, though the mental fog was pressing in.

You know nothing! She only bested you before because I wasn't with you, Ugglyn assured the man.

Prost recoiled at the comment, a lingering fear and frustration at his lost scuffles coming back to him.

Ugglyn watched with annoyance as Janis easily bested the soldiers but refused to kill them. He launched a barrage of Void orbs at her, but she dodged them, though he could tell she was slowing down. Her face was paler than normal, and he could see her chest heaving as she tried to take in air.

As he stepped backward, blue Light versions of herself came at him from all sides, pressing inward. He cursed, then tossed Destructive Void orbs at them. Two disintegrated into nothing silently, but a third slipped forward and slammed into his head. Pain lanced into his neck and his vision blurred, but he Moved the image away just in time to block the real Janis's next stab.

With a grunt, he Moved her through the air until she landed on her feet, shuffling them to keep from falling backward.

"Janis!" a man called from behind.

Ugglyn looked behind her to see a man, burly with close-cropped hair, running at her. Janis turned briefly to see him, then grimaced, gesturing for him to go back. Taking the moment, Ugglyn launched a spear at the man. Cursing, he watched the exhausted Janis fling a Shield outward, blocking his attack. Ugglyn took the moment to throw a dagger at her, the blade slipping easily into her leg. She shouted in pain, collapsing.

With a satisfied smile, Ugglyn held his hand up to deliver the final blow with a large Destructive orb, when another man staggered in front of her.

Ugglyn's body froze.

This—is—mine! Prost's voice screamed.

Prost could feel himself again. Seeing Avryn standing before him provided the rapid lucidity and control once more. Ugglyn roared inside, trying to seize command of his limbs, but the two fought. What resulted was an awkward dance, each trying to move an arm here, a leg there.

Avryn stared at him, confused, then raised his sword to attack.

Ugglyn forced Prost's hand forward, shoving Avryn back.

What is it with that man? Ugglyn shouted, struggling against his host.

Prost felt it again as he looked at his friend, righting himself from the Void push. There was something about Avryn that pulled him out. It had for months. A hope sprang forth in Prost's mind that he could finally be free.

~

PAIN FLARED in her leg as she pressed her hand against her thigh. The void dagger had dissipated, but the poison worked its way through her system. She was aware of Avryn standing between her and Ugglyn, and she allowed him to buy her time as she knelt to Fix her leg. Energy fled from her as she pushed against the odd substance in her leg. Her mind swam and she thought she lost consciousness for a moment, but suddenly she was back.

"Aye, lass, are yeh alroit?" Harmel said.

"You almost got yourself killed, you dolt," she said, but the man grinned.

"Ah, S'ren saved us, don' yeh worry 'bout tha'," he said.

Though she still felt annoyed, she was relieved that the man hadn't been killed. Desire broiled in her chest and she pulled the man forward, pressing her lips firmly against his. The assassin in her cried out, telling her she was making a mistake trusting this man, but the passion burned too deep. Feeling his stubble and strong lips against her own brought more lucidity to her mind and she pushed him away.

"Well, Oi could die a 'appy man now, Oi could," Harmel said, causing her to roll her eyes.

She used his arm to pull herself up, then spotted Ugglyn. Janis couldn't understand what she saw. Prost shuffled awkwardly across the floor as if he were a puppet being controlled by a drunk puppeteer. Conjuring her dagger, she moved to attack, but Avryn held out his hand.

"Something's wrong, he's unpredictable."

As Avryn said it, Prost's hands created various things, weapons and orbs flinging outward in no pattern whatsoever, Void Shields appearing and disappearing without control. Creatures screamed as they melted into pools of shadow and reformed, chittering as they fought the Conjures of herself.

"Die! You wretch!"

Janis's chest tightened as she turned to see Livella rushing Ugglyn, her Void staff held high.

"Stop her!" Avryn shouted, and Janis rushed to intervene, but a half dozen Destructive orbs landed at her feet, making her jump back to avoid being melted to nothingness.

Prost's form snapped to attention suddenly, his hand shooting outward. Livella's staff froze midair as she tried to slam it into his head.

"Ah, the little Voidbearer created by my other half," Prost's double voice mused. "If I can't kill the wench I want, I'll make do with you."

Janis dashed forward, watching as Prost raised the woman so she hovered above the stone ground, but before she could make it, Ugglyn thrust out his free hand, orbs scattering in her direction. Janis cursed and dove away from the danger.

With a flash of his hand, Prost reached to his side where a steel sword hung that he'd never drawn, having favored his Void abilities. The metal screamed as it was pulled from the sheath and shoved directly through Livella's chest. With a flicker, one of the orange cords of Light appeared briefly to Janis, then disappeared as she died.

Avryn screamed, dashing forward to stop the scene, but Ugglyn left his sword in the woman and lifted a Shield around them, darkness engulfing them. With a shout, Avryn slammed his hand into the barrier, his Destructive power exploding loudly against the wall. Immediately, the barrier fell to the power, the shadow dome disappearing. When it did, Livella's corpse lay on the ground, and Prost chuckled.

"It wasn't the Prime, but it'll do just fine," Prost's echoing voice roared, then he laughed and darkness exploded from within him, throwing Avryn backward thirty paces. Janis grimaced and pulled the man toward her, his body glowing blue. He gasped for air.

"What's happening?" he asked, the three watching as a whirlwind of shadows engulfed Prost's form.

"He broke the seal," Janis said, her eyes looking into the distance. "He's breaking free."

"Fog i' all," Harmel cursed. "Wha' now?"

Janis's mind spun through everything that had happened. She'd called on powers she'd not known she had, sending a command to all Lightbearers near her. She'd Conjured versions of herself to battle whatever creatures Ugglyn had called forth. Yet the one power she needed, she couldn't figure out.

"*H'ilvina't*," she whispered, her mind flipping back to the orange cord of Light that connected her, Prost, and Marric. "I have to sacrifice him."

Dread poured through her chest. An image of her killing Marric, his eyes going dead, filled her mind and she shrank away. She couldn't do it. There had to be another way.

"What?" Avyrn demanded.

"I know what I have to sacrifice," Janis shouted back.

Avryn's eyes widened and he gestured wildly to the swirling torrent.

"Well, what is it?" Avryn said, clearly stressed.

"Marric," she said, her chest constricting once more.

Avryn's eyes widened.

"No—"

It made sense. Everything was coming to her. Marric's Awakening had come just before her own. He was gifted, more so than any of the other Lightbearers. She'd only Transformed when she realized how much she cared for him, as if he was a long-lost brother. It had changed her, made her realize there was more to life than living alone. Janis understood now that his Awakening had ushered in her own.

"It's him," she said again.

"Bloomin' arse, are yeh sure?" Harmel asked, his face paling.

Janis recounted her thoughts, telling them as quickly as possible what she'd discovered. She focused on him once again, and there it was, the orange cord of Light from her chest toward the tunnel covered by the shimmering Shield. Though he was obscured, she could feel him, like every other Lightbearer, only stronger. Almost on instinct, she sent a pulsing message through the connection.

Come to me.

~

MARRIC GASPED SUDDENLY.

Narinda stiffened next to him, putting her hand on his shoulder. "What is it? Are you all right?"

He nodded but stood frozen in place.

It came again.

Come to me.

Janis's voice echoed in his mind, and he felt a warm sensation urging him forward. He snapped his attention toward the hovering Prost, a looming darkness forming rapidly. After the third pulse, his feet moved. His mind screamed at him of the danger, but he felt warm, comforted.

Marric was vaguely aware of Narinda tugging on him, trying to keep him back, but he shrugged off her grip and rushed through the Shield. A wave of warm air hit him, making him shiver. It seemed to be exuding from Prost's form, which now appeared to be vibrating with some dark transformation.

Everything—will be fine, he thought.

His feet moved one after the other, his eyes now locked on Janis as she stared at him grimly. He realized Harmel and Avryn were arguing with her about something, but he couldn't focus on that very long before he was mesmerized again, the warm tugging stronger than anything.

The moment he arrived there, the sensation stopped.

"No. There's another way, I know there is," Avryn said.

Marric stared at the man, confused by what was being discussed.

"There isn't," Janis urged. "I know this is it. If we don't act now, Ugglyn will be free."

Tears dripped down Janis's face, and Marric stared, his mind not comprehending what was happening. Marric looked at each of them in turn, seeing tears welling in Avryn's eyes as well.

"Foggin' Lanser. Fog 'im to pieces," Harmel exclaimed.

A firm grip pressed on his shoulder and he turned to see Janis's lip quivering, cheeks stained from tear trails. He wasn't prepared for her next words.

"You are *H'ilvina't*," she said before taking a deep breath. "I have to—sacrifice you."

Marric's chest constricted with fear. He felt his feet call to him, warn him to shuffle away to safety, but another wave of warm comfort hit him. Somehow he knew it was from Janis.

The conversation he'd had with his mother suddenly made sense. *H'ilvina't* was the way to end this. Ugglyn could be locked away again, but only if he let Janis take his life.

It seemed cruel, and every bone in his body rebelled against the idea, but he locked his jaw resolutely and faced Janis again.

His view of her became blurry as tears of his own filled his eyes but he nodded, not knowing what else to say.

Clenching her teeth, Janis Conjured a dagger and raised it upward. Terror wormed through every part of his being, yet he couldn't help but smile.

Janis was crying. She was crying for him.

"It's okay," he said with a quivering voice. "It's okay."

Marric was saying it more for himself than anything. His thoughts switched to Miredith and how he'd never get to court her. He'd never get to say goodbye to his father or Crents.

At least he'd die among friends.

The swirling shadows suddenly exploded outward, knocking them all down. Marric stood up slowly, pushing against the blowing wind. He could see Prost's body hovering upward as the shadows engulfed him. Janis finally righted herself next to him, the dagger still gripped in her hand.

"It's time," she said, turning toward Marric.

With a pained look, she raised her hand and plunged it toward his chest.

Avryn's hand shot out, grabbing her by the wrist and stopping the blow. "Sacrifice me."

Shocked, Janis shook her head, trying to understand what was happening. Her mind swam as adrenaline left her. She'd expended too much energy in the fight. Marric quivered before her, but she could feel the constant pulsing comfort she sent through the connection.

"What are you saying?" she shouted.

Avryn's eyes shone with something, a light of understanding and apprehension all at once.

"You said it yourself. Three powers of Lightbearing, Awakened at the same time as the Voidbearer and Prime—" He paused then, tears forming in his eyes. "Someone close to them."

Janis furrowed her brow, her mind finally catching up.

Avryn had said it was rare to Awaken with more than one power. So far, they only knew of two living Lightbearers other than Primes. The picture painted itself in her mind as if drawn by the hand of an invisible artist. Avryn had Awakened days before Prost had become the Voidbearer, which presumably occurred the same day as Riln, just like Livella and her.

Then it was there. A cord of orange Light, though weaker than the one to Marric, connected her to Avryn, then up toward Prost.

"But you didn't know Riln—" she said.

Tears dripped from Avryn's eyes now, but he held her shoulders firm.

"Not Riln," he said.

Janis hadn't realized how deep Avryn and Prost's friendship had been. Avryn spoke so little of their previous bond and they'd fought on occasion before, but she could see now the pain in his eyes. She thought she'd seen the same look in Prost's eyes when he saw Avryn, but she'd chosen to ignore it, focused only on Prost's evil side.

"Do it before it's too late," Avryn said, handing his Conjured knife to her.

Her mind screamed at her, told her to find another way. Though her love for Avryn wasn't as deep as it was for Marric, or Harmel, in another way, she still cared for him. The pulsing comfort she'd been sending to Marric ceased and he slumped, sobs now making him shake. It broke her. She couldn't kill him. Locking her gaze with Avryn, he nodded curtly. A different kind of sorrow hit her. Not for the loss of a little brother, but the loss of a great friend.

It all felt too overwhelming. For a moment she thought she'd just let it happen, let Ugglyn free and deal with the repercussions with her friends.

But then her assassin's instincts for self-preservation kicked in, and for the first time in a long time she was grateful for it. Breathing hard from the shock, she gripped the handle of the dagger.

PROST WATCHED in horror as the swirling smoke spun around him. He couldn't feel his limbs, he could just see and hear the whooshing of the wind. Ugglyn laughed maniacally as the Void ripped through his body. The only thing Prost could feel was pain, burning pain as he felt his soul being ripped to shreds.

It's done, I am finally free! The seal is broken at last!

The fog was lifted from his mind, but Prost wished it was back. He groaned internally, knowing that Ugglyn's freedom didn't also mean his own. Not once had he considered that the freedom of the anti-god would mean his demise.

Though he couldn't feel it, his mind told him that tears formed in his eyes. He had no one to blame but himself. It was his idea in the first place to bring the army right away and kill Janis.

Thank you, vessel, for giving me what I needed to finally be free, Ugglyn said.

The creatures of the Void sped upward, infusing themselves in Prost's body, each one wracking him with more pain and anguish.

Through the torrent of shadows, Prost spotted four figures standing close to one another. Prost focused on them, seeing Janis standing there, holding a Conjured dagger. In front of her stood Avryn. Prost's mind locked on the figure, the familiar longing of friendship tugging at his chest through the pain. He just wanted to see his friend once more. Prost had been freed from Riln's grasp, only to be locked away again.

All hope he'd had in restoring their friendship was gone. He gazed upon his friend, his brother, once more as the darkness pulled in at his vision. Then he watched Janis shove the dagger into his brother's heart.

Noooo! he screamed, watching Avryn's eyes roll back in his head as he collapsed to the ground. Despair somehow wracked him through the pain of Ugglyn's release, tears pouring down his face, though he couldn't feel them.

An orange Light erupted from Avryn's chest as he fell, slamming into Janis's form. A blue Light, more intense than anything he'd seen before, exploded from her, blinding him instantly.

What is this? No. This can't be! Augh!

The pain eased off of Prost's consciousness, feeling returning to his limbs. Warmth spread along his arms, hands, filling his every being.

Fixing.

It was exactly as others described it when they told him of it. Somehow this Light was Fixing him.

He could feel the tears now wetting his cheeks, the saltiness falling in his mouth. Of all the sensations he noticed, one stood among them all.

His mind was quiet.

~

JANIS GASPED as her chest heated up intensely, burning so hot that she felt feverish. It wasn't an uncomfortable feeling, though it felt intense, as if a furnace burned within her breast. The Light overwhelmed her eyes, and Harmel disappeared. Avryn and Livella's bodies disappeared.

She stood on a stone platform, much like the one she'd stood on when she spoke with Lanser, though rather than darkness around her, there was Light, as if the sun filled every inch of the space around her save for below her feet.

Blue Light formed on the white canvas before her, a woman, somehow old and also young, appeared in the air.

"You have achieved the Ascension," her voice echoed. It sounded as if it was hundreds of voices overlayed with one another.

"Who are you?" Janis asked warily, her own voice muffled as if she was underwater.

The woman smiled. "I am no one, yet also everyone," she replied.

Janis hated riddles.

Before Janis could rip into her for giving an unhelpful, vague answer, the woman spoke again.

"I represent the Lightbearing within you, a gift from the creator of this world. It was set forth to protect the world from evil, yet the man who found it was unworthy. He unleashed the darkness upon us all," she said. "For years, the Ascension has been denied by pride, by an unwillingness to do what needed to be done."

Janis's chest tightened. She saw her hand thrusting forward into Avryn's chest. She felt his blood on her hands, the despair filling her chest. Tears filled her eyes and she balled her fists, wanting to scream.

"Why? Why did that have to happen?"

The ethereal woman before her looked at her with a sad expression.

"The power unleashed by the man was meant to be harnessed by one who was willing to love, willing to sacrifice. He cheated the trial and was punished for it. But you prevailed."

Janis didn't feel like she'd prevailed at anything. She wanted to know everything, to demand answers about where the power came from, why she was chosen, but she got the distinct sense that the woman wouldn't give her any answers. Instead she focused on the only thing she could think of.

"If you answer me anything, tell me this. Why Riln? Why give an evil man such power?" Janis asked.

To her surprise, the woman smiled at her.

"A risk was taken to prevent Ugglyn's release, and the risk failed. Riln and his brother were corrupted. By Awakening Prime powers within him, we hoped to turn him back to the Light. We failed," she replied.

Janis's skin crawled as the woman used "we," as if she spoke for a collective of people despite the fact that she stood alone. More questions flooded her mind, but once again, she had a sense that she'd get answers to none of them. The assassin inside her scoffed at the situation. More than anything, her past self couldn't fathom how any entity could have hoped to change Riln. That man had been evil through and through.

"What now?" she asked, her jaw hard as she pushed down the sorrow inside.

The woman smiled, hovering lower so Janis could feel warmth emanating from her face.

"That is entirely up to you. This power was hidden, waiting for one to find it and accept its burden," she said.

Janis scoffed. Even though she'd come to accept the power, she still shied away from it. She could feel it within her, stronger than ever. Somehow she knew that it was more than just the seven classes now. She felt transcendent, immortal.

She didn't want it.

"Take it back, take it so I can go back to living with those I love," Janis said.

The woman's face fell as she listened.

"If that is your wish, then so be it, but the burden is yours to decide on whom to bestow the source of Lightbearing. Know that Lanser's failings in the past opened Lindrad up to the unspeakable evil. You have conquered it, but by giving it to another who may fail, the Void could return."

With a disappointed look, the woman faded away. Janis watched as images of Tryvv, Prileen, and even Lanser faded into view just before her. They each smiled happily as they turned, fading once more as if to follow the woman who stood before Janis. Suddenly, Livella and Avryn were there, smiles on their faces.

Guilt constricted Janis's chest and her jaw locked. Tears flooded her eyes and she cursed herself, pent-up emotions breaking free after a decade of suppression.

"I'm sorry," she whispered, but neither image said anything. Instead they each gave a slight nod, then disappeared into the distance with the others.

They finally get to move on, Janis realized.

Seeing the last of them fade, Janis called to the strange ethereal woman, hoping for her to return.

But she didn't.

Janis stood there, the stone pedestal beneath her feet cold to the touch. Somehow she knew she could do anything, be anything, but all she could think about was getting rid of it all.

An idea formed in her head and she locked on to it. Focusing inward on the well of power, Janis pushed her hands outward, her eyes glowing fiercely with the blue Light. Heat grew in her chest, almost to an uncomfortable point, then she screamed, shoving her hands outward. With an explosion of Light and heat, the power within her split into seven orbs, the Light piercing her eyes, before six flashed off into the distance, disappearing into the white canvas before her. One single orb, bright and piercing, flew back into her chest.

Her eyes drooped and she fell to the stone pedestal unconscious.

31

Marric sat on one of the soft chairs just outside of the war room, contemplating the past few days. His mind ran through the images he'd witnessed at the end of the battle. Heart racing, he recalled watching Janis plunge her dagger into Avryn's chest, a strangled scream escaping his mouth as he watched his friend fall to the ground in a heap.

He and Avryn were both *H'ilvina't*. Not once had he even thought he would be a part of it all. His conversation with his mother had taken on a whole new light. Suddenly, the orange Light that had disturbed their conversation made sense. A subtle pulsing in his temple reminded him of the headache forming. It was all too much.

"You're still thinking about it, aren't you?" Miredith asked, placing her hand on his arm.

He started, having almost forgotten that the girl was there with him. Ever since he'd seen the destruction in the main cavern and witnessed the countless deaths, his mind had been too addled to function normally. Based on the sad air around them, he knew he wasn't the only one affected. Before he could even answer, he recalled the image of Avryn lying on the ground. That thought quickly pulled him to another image of Jord's body, an addlebrained Miredith pulling her sword free from his chest as he died on the stone.

Chest constricting, he had to look away from the girl, who somehow didn't remember the event at all. Marric didn't hold it against her, but for a time he'd feared he wouldn't be able to look at her the same. She knew something had happened, but he didn't have the heart to tell her what she'd done. Sighing, Marric smiled wanly, trying to focus on the more positive aspects of what had happened.

"I'm not sure I'll ever forget it," he said, tears forming in his eyes. He sucked in a staggering breath, held it for a time, then released it slowly. "I guess we can be grateful that the whole cavern mended itself. I've never seen so much Fixing energy in one place before."

Miredith pressed her lips together firmly.

"I don't think anyone ever has," she admitted.

Immediately after Avryn's death, an intense blue Light had exploded outward, so bright that it blinded everyone. By the time it had cleared, every inch of the cavern was repaired as if the battle hadn't even happened. The only indication that any fight had occurred were the corpses strewn across the floor. Marric shivered at the eerie sight. Somehow without the evidence of a struggle, seeing the bodies lying there motionless haunted him, as if some wraith had stolen their souls instantly.

Miredith squeezed his arm. "Everything will return to normal—someday. I hope you know that."

He grimaced. "I somehow doubt that. You still have your powers after all."

She furrowed her brow, looking at her hands for a moment before creating a small image out of Void shadows. The figure, a small statue of herself, formed in her hand and she winced.

"I'm not sure what to make of that," she admitted, "but I don't think we have to worry about me losing my mind anymore. Something tells me that Ugglyn won't be a problem."

Marric nodded. Every one of the people touched by the Void energy had kept their abilities granted by Ugglyn, though most of them shied away from it. Marric shivered, grateful that he wasn't accursed with it. Movement at the other end of the cavern caught his attention.

His chest constricted as he saw Narinda, dressed in her usual garb but wearing a violet shawl over her head and face, a sign of mourning. Grief rocketed through Marric again at seeing the woman. Though he didn't understand how she might feel, every time he thought of her, let alone *saw* her, he was reminded of her and Avryn's marriage days before Avryn's death.

Miredith followed his gaze, then looked down at her feet, her face flushing slightly. Since he'd known the girl, he realized that most things didn't bother her, given how frank she could be with her commentary, but in times of intense emotion, she shied away.

Much like Janis.

Looking away from the grieving widow, Marric's mind pulled him to thoughts of Janis, still unconscious, even though days had passed since the actual fighting.

Hoping to take their minds off the sorrow for a moment longer, Miredith changed the subject.

"Going out at night is very strange now. I don't think any of us were aware that there was a time in history with only one moon," Miredith pointed out.

Marric chuckled. "I'll admit, it makes me uncomfortable. I've only been outside once since everything happened, and I don't know that I'll ever get used to the one moon out *all night*."

The two shared some quiet laughter, but it was free of mirth. For the past months, Marric thought the extent of the surprises he'd encountered had hit their maximum, but the past few days had proven that it was a folly to think so. His simple life as a fletcher's son felt ages away, and in reality *was* ages away. Narim, somehow more vital after the explosion of Fixing energy, had happily taken to fletching once more for the soldiers and hunters of Evenir. He'd even found a lovely woman, similar to him in age and widowed by her soldier husband years ago.

Imagining his father settling down with a woman made him smile. It wasn't that Marric hadn't thought they could live their lives here, but seeing his father adjust in that way was encouraging. Learning of his first wife's fate was apparently cathartic, allowing him to finally move on.

"So what will we do now?" Miredith asked, her question lingering for a time.

Marric sighed. "I don't think we have to worry about Watchlight, now that they're living with us," he replied. "So—normal life, I suppose. Maybe we can try to live lives outside of this compound."

The idea sounded preposterous. To think life could be anything close to normal seemed humorous to Marric. Yet every member of Watchlight, as far as they knew, had marched right to their sanctuary. After the strange, peaceful presence pressed through them all, enmity between Lightbearers had almost ceased. Harmel, overwhelmed at seeing his friend dead before him and having to make decisions of his own accord given Janis's unconscious state, had ordered all members of Watchlight imprisoned for the time being. From what Marric heard, they barely had enough space for the numbers in the ward. The generals spent most of their days conversing with those put there, releasing them after pledges of loyalty, which came easily now.

A messenger burst through the door, interrupting all conversation. Marric's chest tightened at the man's manic entrance and he stood quickly, knocking his knees on the small table just before the chair. He winced but focused on the man.

"Master Marric, sir, Oi've been sent t' tell yous tha' she's wakin' up now," the man said, his breath staggering from his rapid pace.

Eyes widening, he turned to Miredith, who waved him off.

"I don't get the feeling she would want me there, she doesn't even know me. Go ahead," she said.

Marric sped off, hope blossoming in his chest that Janis was alive.

Prost sat in the stone chair, staring at his hands. He'd been put here after the events days ago, and they'd ensured that he was alone. For days it felt like all he'd done was sit and look at his hands, yet somehow he didn't even care at all.

Because everything was quiet.

It felt like ages since he hadn't had to worry about voices in his head, then Ugglyn had taken him completely over. Prost felt numb remembering the past few weeks, then realizing it was all gone; everything was finished.

His mind recounted the events of a few days before, the intense warmth, the bright Light that slammed into him. He couldn't help but laugh at the strangeness of it all, yet despite the comfort he found in being freed from the demon, he still bore a hole in his chest.

Avryn was gone.

All the memories he'd recounted prior to coming to Terris Green, all the times he'd remembered with his friend, now felt like daggers to his mind. After he'd been released from Ugglyn's hold, he'd seen Janis lying on the ground. Anger now flared up in his chest, a mere remnant of what he'd felt after witnessing her killing his friend, the last hope he'd had of returning to normal, returning to the past.

Though he'd been revitalized in whatever blast came from Janis, he was no match for Harmel, who defended Janis easily.

Now he was here, trying to piece together everything that had happened.

Soft knocking echoed through his cell, which he shared with no one. Prost looked up through the dim Light, the only orbs of Light coming from outside the gate.

"'Ey." A woman's voice echoed on the stone walls around him.

"What do you want?" he said, his voice coming out angrier than he actually felt.

Alts didn't appear to mind.

"They still 'aven't let yeh out, huh?" she asked.

Prost didn't answer. He knew she was just trying to play nice. Not looking up, he clasped his hands firmly together, still marveling at the fact that he could control his faculties once more. The cool, wet air around him felt more of a comfort than it probably would have before he'd lost control of himself. Silence followed her question, time drawing out.

"'Ow long was 'e in yeh?" Alts finally asked after some time.

Prost's jaw hardened. He didn't want to admit that he'd lost control, that he'd succumbed to the fury-driven being.

He shifted in his chair, looking sidelong at the woman standing outside his cell. "Since Stilten."

She whistled softly. "Did a right good ol' job hidin' it, yeh did. Wouldn't o' guessed it meself."

Heat flared in his chest, the reminder of his internal struggle and ultimate failure infuriating him. Ever since Ugglyn had fled, his former tendencies toward anger had returned, much to his chagrin. He knew people didn't change that quickly, but he'd hoped it would be different for him. Holding his breath momentarily, he diffused his anger by focusing once more on the death of his friend. The burning turned to a hollow sadness.

It wasn't the healthiest way of coping with his quickness to anger, but he would use what he had for the time being.

"I fought him as long as I could, but in the end he was stronger," Prost admitted, his tone bitter. He turned away, hiding his shameful face from the woman who he assumed no longer thought him strong.

Surprisingly, she didn't challenge him.

"Yeh've been bearin' a burden all by yerself. Seems unkind that life would treat yeh such like," Alts said.

Her words distilled on his mind. At first he didn't register them, then they slammed into his chest like a boulder being lobbed at him by a Mover. His breath caught, eyes watering as an emotion he'd not felt for too long wormed into his chest. Not once in the years after he'd been scarred beyond comprehension had he shed any tears. Now as he thought of Avryn's death and Alts's present, albeit minor, understanding of his burdens for the past ten years, he couldn't help it.

Hands covering his face, he wept, embarrassed beyond all belief that he would show such emotion in front of anyone, let alone the woman he'd been fond of for years but never pursued.

"I'm sorry. I didn't mean t' make yeh upset," she said awkwardly, then

Conjured a dagger. The flash of Light caught Prost's attention, given that it cast a blueish hue. Breathing deeply, he composed himself enough to look out the metal bars at the weapon she'd created, his eyes widening.

"But—how?" he asked.

Alts looked sheepish, fingering the tip of the blade before holding it up.

"Strangest thing, it was. When the Void ones turned on us, we was all overcome by something weird, some peace. I 'eard it in me 'ead, clear as lightnin'. The woman told us to be still and band together. Can't say why, but me Light's been blue since," she admitted, pressing her lips together.

Prost was speechless. After he'd been overcome by the Light, they'd snatched him up quickly, pulling him roughly to the cell without seeing anyone else. Alts licked her teeth, unsure what to say next.

Squinting, she peered into the cell, and Prost guessed she was trying to get a closer look at him. A gasp escaped her lips, making Prost's skin chill. He leapt to his feet, throwing his fists up before his face if there was some threat coming from around him.

"Fog it, sorry," Alts said. "There's nuttin' there, see? It's just—yer scars. They ain't there."

Prost's eyes widened before his hands flew to his face.

He'd been so wrapped up in the past few days that he'd not thought about the wave of Fixing energy that had washed over him, but as he put his hands to the sides of his nose, he felt nothing but soft skin. Prost traced the line where the scars had been with both hands, marveling.

So it did work on me. I'm not immune anymore, he thought.

Feeling dizzy, he slumped to his chair, waiting for the world to stop spinning so quickly.

"Lanser's bottom, never thought I'd see the day yeh didn't 'ave the scars," she said, pausing for a moment. "Makes yeh wonder what I saw in that scrawny Mert."

The words hung in the air between them, Prost taking a moment to process them. Though her voice still stung with pain, he realized that she'd just complimented his appearance. For the first time in ages something stirred within his gut, his desire to be with her intensifying.

"Oh—thanks," he said, keeping his head down.

Before she could say anything further, footsteps echoed in his cell, announcing a few others coming his way.

"Why, hello there," a man's voice said. "Enjoying your newfound freedom? I must say, the blue Light suits you."

Alts grunted, then let her Conjure disappear.

"'Twill grow on me, I'm sure," she replied.

Prost finally looked up to see a dark-skinned man with a shaved head, a shorter brawny woman with brown hair and fair skin, and another woman with even darker skin and coarse, thick black hair.

"We're to take you before the other generals to question you," the dark-skinned woman said. "I'm Alsry, Mover and general."

"Trease," the other woman said, waving slightly.

The man rolled his eyes and folded his arms. "I suppose it's prudent for you to know us before we try you. I'm Varith, Fixer."

Prost eyed the man's grand appearance, his clothing fancier than anything he would have guessed practical in a humble cave-dwelling group like Evenir. Hearing that he was a Fixer explained it all.

Prost stood up straighter and he took a couple steps closer. "What makes you think I deserve a trial?"

Varith laughed. "The very question I had myself."

The shorter woman, Trease, punched the man in the arm, earning her a cry of pain.

"It's only fair yeh git a trial yerself, we roit gave the others a chance." She grimaced. "Well, we're tryin'. There's so many of yous."

The other woman continued staring at him, something smoldering behind her eyes. It wasn't necessarily anger, but it was something deep, something unforgiving.

"We've come to get you now. If you attack us or try to escape, we're to kill you right away," Alsry informed him, "and given your absence of scars, I'd wager you are no longer immune to Lightbearing."

Though he wasn't entirely sure if that was true, he just nodded in understanding.

"Well, let's get on with this, I've more important things to do," Varith said.

~

Janis's eyes shot open, wincing as she stared directly into the Light of an orb above her head.

"Oh! Sorry about that," a woman said, lifting the large orb away from her face and letting it hover upward toward the ceiling.

Before Janis could ask what was happening, a heavy chest landed right on her own. Panicked, she pressed upward with her arms, gasping when she felt how weak they were.

"Though' yeh died!" Harmel's voice said desperately in her ear.

She finally relaxed her struggle when she realized it was just him. Soft lips pressed against hers, and a fluttering exploded in her stomach and chest, a comforting warmth flooding over her like a broken dam. Janis closed her eyes, reveling in the moment for a time before she pressed him gently off of her. This time he responded.

"Glad to see you too," she admitted, then looked about the room. She was in her quarters, the small room empty save for Harmel and the woman.

"We've been Fixing yer body fer days, bu' though' yer brain addled to a point yeh wouldn't come back. Looks like it was worth it," the woman said, smiling brightly before turning and leaving the room.

"Let me guess, I've been unconscious for a while," Janis blurted, making Harmel laugh.

"Seem to be doin' that a lot lately, 'aven't yeh?" Harmel said, before his expression darkened. "What do yeh remember?"

Feeling light-headed still, she moved to sit up, pressing her hands against the frame of the small bed until she was upright.

"I killed Avryn," she said, her throat tightening up. Clearing her throat, she gained composure once more before continuing. "Then I was taken somewhere."

She quickly recounted the events for Harmel, who watched with a curious expression.

"Not sure what t' do with tha' information," he admitted.

Just then, another person rushed into the room, slamming into her just as Harmel had done. Janis grunted, but this time she didn't try to fight it. She recognized Marric before he'd even reached her.

"You're ok! I can't believe you're ok!" he said, pulling back enough for her to see the tears falling down his cheeks. Janis winced, the awkward feeling of being near strong emotions pressing into her.

"Just in time too," Harmel said. "We're about t' do the trial fer Prost."

Janis's mind reeled. "He lived?"

Harmel nodded. "Seems right unfair tha' 'e'd live when Avryn 'ad to die."

An uncomfortable air settled on the room at the mention of Avryn's demise, and Janis looked at Marric, realizing he didn't know anything about why she'd killed him. A stab of regret struck her chest, but before she could answer, Marric sniffled and shook his head.

"Harmel told me—that—that you had to either kill me or him," he admitted, jaw set, "—that Avryn agreed to it before you killed him."

Janis nodded but the sorrow continued to hollow out her chest.

Marric sighed. "There's been too many deaths of late. I hope we can move past it."

Though part of her hoped it to be true as well, Janis couldn't forget the countless Watchlight members who inevitably still lived. She knew as long as Watchlight members existed, they wouldn't be safe.

As if hearing her thoughts, Harmel put his hands on her shoulder. "Watchlight is no more. Whatever yeh did back there, yeh blasted the anger roit outta them. They're joining our ranks now."

It seemed impossible, yet Janis remembered the connection she had to them, to every Lightbearer near and far. She remembered the pulsing command she'd sent outward of peace. Whatever power she'd called on had worked. Prodding inward, she sought the same power she'd felt from the Ascension, but it wasn't there. Janis knew she'd given it away. She knew she needed to tell the others of what she'd done, but now wasn't the time.

"Let's move, then. I wouldn't miss this for the life of me," Janis said, moving slowly off the cot.

PROST'S HANDS were tied behind his back, tight cords binding them there. He hadn't resisted even once as they'd bound them together, but his captors had still pulled them as tight as possible, pinching the skin. He couldn't blame them. The events of the past months couldn't have left any good impression on these people.

He wondered why they hadn't killed him right away.

Prost sat in a chair in a round room. A stone table at its center stood empty. On one side of the room sat a wooden door, carved with the most beautifully intricate image of a tree, faces amidst the leaves. A half dozen people sat inside, staring at him roughly. Even though he'd just arrived, he felt as if they'd been sitting there for hours, sizing him up.

For a moment he thought to ask what they were waiting for. He suspected they had no reason to delay his execution but then thought the better of it. While he had no drive to continue living, he didn't want to make his situation worse.

So they sat in silence, something Prost had taken for granted until now.

The doors opened suddenly, three more figures walking through. Prost recognized the man; he'd been standing next to Avryn and Janis when his friend had died. Marric, the boy who'd seemingly started this whole mess, was with them.

Prost's eyes landed on Janis, and a frantic anger settled inside him. It wasn't anger at her for anything practical, save for his ego at how she'd bested him more than once. He veiled it, pressing it away. The more he thought about it, he had no reason to hate her, not anymore, now that he was free from Riln and Ugglyn alike.

"Oh, thank Lanser we can begin," Varith said, sitting up. "I was beginning to be bored of watching him sit there doing nothing."

Alsry grunted, her arms folded before her. Trease and another man whose name Prost didn't know exchanged looks.

"Can we 'urry up, then? Kill the bloke an' git back t' life as it were," the unnamed man said.

"Be quiet, Turrin," Janis said, her voice clear and strong. "I've my own reasons to want this man dead, but there's been too much needless killing in the world these days."

The comment stung Prost and he knew she'd worded it that way on purpose. Though his past self tried to bring up anger inside, he pressed it away again, knowing he deserved it. He couldn't help but be overwhelmed by one simple thing: he was free.

"What do you have to say for yourself?" Janis said, moving closer to him.

Prost tensed, waiting for her to attack him, but she didn't.

"I won't try to plead my case, if that's what you're looking for," Prost said firmly.

Janis narrowed her eyes, looking over his shoulder. "You've committed a lot of wrong in your life," she said, then her face became more solemn. "But so have I."

Her words caught Prost off guard, his breath increasing. Whoever the woman was, the assassin he'd employed months ago, this was not her. Prost couldn't profess to know Janis well, but even when he'd fought her, he could tell they had things in common.

"I've reason to believe you didn't do the things you did of your own accord," Janis said, looking directly at him.

"I—don't know what you mean," Prost said, a nervousness rising in him.

Janis looked him up and down, her arms relaxing at her sides.

"I saw your struggle in the final moments of our fight. You were fighting Ugglyn, weren't you?"

The question was so forward that Prost opened his mouth in shock. He shouldn't have been surprised that she'd noticed, but at the time he hadn't been very much aware of who was watching. When he didn't respond right away, Janis sighed, then turned her back to him.

"You had as much choice in this as I did, as Livella did. I can't help but think what would have happened if I'd turned to Ugglyn like Riln. Would Livella have rebelled? Would she have left?"

Silence pierced the air as Janis stood there, eyeing the others in the room. No one dared speak.

"The voices in her head wouldn't have let her. That became clear the first time we were separated," Janis said.

The woman commanded the space, something Prost would have not thought possible. Whatever change had been wrought in her in the past weeks, he couldn't fathom it at all. Every eye stared at her, some hard, some in wonder. Janis had changed.

But so had he, he hoped.

"It's for this reason I extend a full pardon of your acts," Janis said.

Prost suddenly felt nauseous.

~

THE GENERALS SITTING before her exploded in conversation, sounds echoing off the confined space of the war room. Normally, she could ignore the echoes of every little sound, but now, along with the conflict warring in her own mind, she shouted for everyone to stop.

Surprisingly, they did. Janis stared at each of them in turn, taking the moment to assert her influence over them, something she didn't feel she'd been able to do in the past. The only difference now was that they'd all witnessed the events, at least most of them, just days before. Her stomach twisted as she pushed down the strong desire to bury her fist into Prost's face, now that he was bound before her. Another wanted to use her dagger instead of a fist.

I'm not that person anymore, Janis thought, focusing on the leader version of herself making hard decisions.

"While I don't expect any of you to understand where I'm coming from, I do expect you to listen rather than act like children," she said, snapping her hand backward and pointing at Prost. He stared back at her, eyes focused.

"Did any of you know this man before Watchlight? Did any of you have the chance to hear how Avryn spoke of him?"

The question didn't fall on deaf ears. Turrin gritted his teeth. Varith looked down at his feet. She suspected that it had spread throughout Evenir that Avryn thought Prost his greatest friend before all of this.

"We all saw what happened. Ugglyn is no more," she said. The revelation seemed impossible, yet her gut told her it was true. "The seal is no more. Whatever darkness wormed its way into Watchlight doesn't exist, at least not in the same way."

Prost shifted in his chair behind her, telling her of his discomfort.

"Avryn died to end this, to end the struggle between Lanser and Ugglyn. Don't you think it would honor him if we spared the life of the man who was dragged into this mess as much as any of us? Did any of you choose to Awaken? Did you choose your fate?"

Silence still. Though Turrin met her eyes, his own brow furrowed in frustration.

"Yeh mean t' let the man live among us? The fool 'oo killed so many o' our own? Oi won' 'ave none o' it," he said, shaking his head.

Janis felt amused. "I don't mean that at all. The moment we're done here, I'm kicking him out of our sanctuary with orders that if he comes back, he'll be executed immediately."

This managed to calm down the others, though Alsry remained the most stone-faced of all. Marric looked sick as he glanced back and forth from her to the man tied behind her.

Turrin sat back heavily, shrugging. "Seems fair t' me. Git the fogger outta 'ere."

Varith sighed. “If you insist. I have little enmity toward the man. I feel no need to defend him, as you are, but I won’t argue.”

Janis eyed the others, Trease nodding curtly. She looked to Marric, raising an eyebrow. Pointing to himself, he looked at her with arched eyebrows.

“Me? Why do you want to know what I think?” he asked.

She smiled. “I regret to say that we have the need for a new general.”

Eyes wide, he looked at the others, who smiled at him. Turrin laughed, clapping the boy on the back.

“Well, what say ye?” the man boomed.

Marric pressed his lips together, then nodded, affirming her wishes. Janis knew he was young, but she couldn’t deny how he’d grown and that he would soon be a force himself. Like Avryn.

Alsry glared at her. For some reason Janis felt nervous. She wasn’t scared of the woman, but it was clear Alsry didn’t approve of the idea. Still, Janis knew she could technically do what she wanted; she didn’t have to ask for approval. Yet somehow it felt important. She’d been declared leader days ago, but since then, she’d spent most of her time either absent or unconscious. Winning the trust of the generals was an important step.

“Fine,” the woman replied, “but if he so much as comes within twenty paces of here, I request to kill him myself.”

Janis smiled.

“And so you shall.”

PROST STARED in disbelief at the tiers of terraces in the mountain around him. He never thought he’d be able to experience their wonders ever again. Trapped within the confines of his own mind, he’d not remembered what fresh air felt like, smelled like. Closing his eyes, he breathed in deeply, the fresh scent of morning air cooling his nostrils.

They'd let him go. Immediately after the proceedings, they'd taken him to the stable room, given him a horse and provisions, then let him go. His mind fixated on an image of Avryn, his former friend, watching him go from the tent. He'd thought that would be the last time they saw each other, and he wished their last moments would be different.

And they had, but they'd fared far worse.

Tears welled in his eyes as hc remembered facing Avryn, possessed by Ugglyn in earnest, killing needlessly and threatening Lindrad. Then Avryn had died, the last image of his former friend one of horror and darkness. Guilt overwhelmed Prost. He wished he'd been able to do better, to be better. Avryn's words echoed in his mind: *Revenge will never set you free, only forgiveness.*

He sighed, once again reveling in the beauty of the world around him.

The clopping of horse hooves brought him from his reverie, and he spun, fear seizing him that one of the Evenir generals had changed their mind, coming to end him. He didn't think to defend himself, only prepare for his demise.

"Couldn' let yeh go alone," Alts said, approaching on a horse.

The fear melted into surprise, and he stared at her.

"Why?" Prost asked.

She shrugged. "Tired o' livin' in a cave, thought it best to be with a friend."

At that, she kicked her horse to motion, moving past him.

Prost had no idea where he would go, but somehow he knew he could deal with it. Deal with the trauma, deal with the pain, deal with the loss of his friend and all the things he'd done. And now he wouldn't be alone. Alts spun in her saddle, giving him a sly smile. His chest fluttered, a warmth rising in his cheeks that hadn't for years. His prior inhibitions about courting the woman were now gone with Ugglyn's seal.

"Are yeh comin'? I don't reckon' they'll let yeh sit there long 'afore they change their minds and come git yeh," Alts said, her voice muffled as she rode away.

Hope burned in his breast as he kicked his horse into motion, following Alts.

I'll honor you someday, Avryn. Your death won't be in vain.

~

JANIS FINGERED THE MAP, Harmel and Marric behind her. The other generals had exited, opting to be the ones to escort Prost from their caves. Her mind reeled, yelling at her that she'd made a mistake letting the man go, but she pushed the thought away. Somehow seeing him without the scars had made her see him in a new light. She'd spotted his struggle, she'd seen the reluctance many times in his eyes. She knew Prost never wanted to be involved, but he had to, just like her.

And she felt she should honor Avryn in some way. As much as she wished she could move on, let the friendship she'd only just realized disappear with the sorrow, Janis knew her mind couldn't let it go. For once she was fine with it. She would hold the memory of him with gratitude for him and for all he'd done for her.

"Tha' was mighty generous o' you," Harmel said, moving to her side.

She scoffed. "I wouldn't count on it happening too often."

The man slid himself right up to her, pressing his hand into hers. Fingers tingling, she allowed him to lace his own fingers with hers. Stomach wrenching, her mind once again shouted at her, telling her to pull away, to not trust this man. Closing her eyes, she pressed the voice away firmly. Though in this moment she felt naked without it, she appreciated quieting the assassin inside, finding reprieve. She didn't want it gone permanently, for it had saved her too many times in a fight, but for now she could just enjoy the company.

"Thank you," Marric said finally, "for doing that. It somehow feels like a gift to Avryn, now that he's gone."

Janis nodded, then turned to him.

"And I'm sure you'll be able to bear his legacy, given that you are now the lone Lightbearer who Awakened with three powers," Janis said.

Marric shifted where he stood, a blush forming on his face. Janis resisted the urge to laugh, knowing it wouldn't help the boy.

"What now though?" Marric admitted.

"I don't think we'll be dealing with Awakenings any longer," Janis said. "I think I broke the cycle somehow when I sent the power away."

Marric furrowed his brow. "What does that even mean? You still have your Lightbearing, don't you?"

Janis nodded, Conjuring a dagger in her free hand.

"I don't mean that," she said. "I mean the power that I tapped when the Ascension happened. It was more than the seven classes. It was what I used to create the images of myself, and what I used to control all of you, in a sense. Whatever power I managed to master, it didn't seem safe to hold it together, so I split it."

Harmel started next to her. "Wha' do yeh mean? Yeh broke it?"

Smiling, she diffused the fear that seeped into his voice.

"No, just severed it. I don't think any person should have to bear the burden of that much power, so I spread the burden and kept only a part. The power I felt in that moment, just before Avryn died and just after, was an enhanced version of Lightbearing. You saw the Fixing portion yourself. Just look at the sanctuary; everything's Fixed."

Marric stared off into the room, marveling.

"Well, what Ascended part did yeh keep, then?" Harmel asked, squeezing her hand.

"The only part that felt natural," she said, her eyes filling with Light. "Seeing has been somewhat of an old friend for too long to let go."

And she Saw it. Lindrad spread before her eyes, every thing, every person, every place, exposed before her as she took it in. Though she thought it wouldn't be as necessary to use the power as before, she couldn't help but marvel at the stronger version of the ability. Being able to See hundreds, thousands of things all at once made her feel all-knowing, more powerful than ever.

Perhaps now she'd be able to learn to relax.

"Oi guess we can focus on tryin' t' integrate wif the world again, no?" Harmel said.

Janis rolled her eyes. "What else would we do? There's no more Void to conquer. No more Watchlight to give Lindrad the wrong impression about us."

Harmel chuckled, then pulled her close to him, his hand wrapping around her waist. She kept her vision on, watching Harmel embrace her from a hundred different angles, reveling in the moment as she finally let go. He kissed her, and though her eyes were closed, she watched Marric's blush deepen. He covered his eyes, then slid from the room, not wanting to be part of their private moment.

For once Janis let her mind turn off almost completely.

EPILOGUE

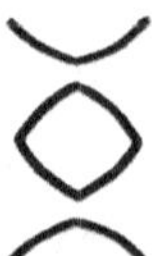

Brilinda sighed, grasping the closest fish to her and slicing it open. The flesh severed in half, entrails of the creature spilling out, just waiting for her to extract them. When she'd first been employed by her father, he'd insisted that she be the one to gut all the fish, thinking it best for her to learn to be more grounded. He'd always thought she spent too much time in her own thoughts, imagining wild things, creating stories in her mind.

Now he had her slaving away in his kitchen.

Her father, Truval, was the owner and cook of the largest tavern in Arivan. She would rather be out, swimming in the sea, living life carelessly as the young adult she was, but her father would have none of it. Her mother eyed her from the other side of the kitchen, noticing that she'd stopped her work of gutting the fish, and Brilinda immediately started working again.

"I wouldn't let your father see you losing yourself in your thoughts. You know how he gets when he thinks you're wasting your life away in your imagination."

Brilinda shook her head. "Well, I've got to do *something* interesting. This work is more boring than sitting in church all afternoon while the priest goes on about Lanser and his wisdom."

"Brilinda! You know better than that!" her mother scolded her. "If you'd rather go out on your own, earning your own keep, then leave."

Brilinda rolled her eyes, then cut into the next fish. Their customers inevitably ordered the delicacy for at least one in their party. Her father's recipe was becoming more famous in Arivan and even through Lindrad. All it meant was that she had to gut more fish and prep them for cooking. She had other jobs, of course; it wasn't just the fish, but her father made sure she was the only one to do it. Even when the other cooks offered to help, he ensured Brilinda alone handled the fish.

"Don't you wish something else would happen around here? Don't you want to know what else there is to see in this world?" Brilinda asked wistfully.

Her mother scoffed but didn't answer. A couple of the other cooks looked at her with smiles on their faces, but no one spoke.

"Apparently, I'm the only one who cares about leaving this town," she said, finishing the last fish for this order, then wiping her hands on her apron.

"Bother, I've forgotten to get the herbs drying outside. I'll be back, can you take this over?" her mother asked, pointing to the cauldron of stew hovering over the hearth. Brilinda shook her head, then plodded over to the food, stirring it wildly.

The moment she touched the handle of the ladle, a flash of blue Light caught her attention through the window to her side. She looked out, seeing the waves of the sea splashing on the rocks just next to their tavern. Narrowing her eyes, she shook her head, thinking herself insane.

Another bright flash caught her attention, and she turned in time to see a steady orb of blue Light flying over the sea in her direction. Her breath caught in her throat, a strangled scream starting to escape when the orb flew through the open window, slamming into her chest.

The air left her lungs and she gagged, trying to catch her breath, when suddenly it was there again, and she gasped, her mind begging for air.

"What in the name of the fog," she said, holding her chest.

An image of a woman, made entirely from Light, hovered before her, smiling brightly.

And so you've been chosen. Use the gift wisely.

Brilinda stared, wide-eyed, as the woman disappeared. Blue Light exploded from her chest, bathing the whole kitchen with it. The other cooks screamed, running from the room, but Brilinda just stood there, watching it all unfold. Warmth exploded in her chest, as if she was enfevered, spreading to her whole body. She watched as the Light bathed everything, furniture and food alike. Before her eyes, the entrails of the fish, glowing with blue Light, slipped out of the bucket she'd thrown them in, reaffixing themselves into the flesh of the animal they'd come from.

One by one, the fish started flopping around on the table as if they'd never been killed.

"Fog me good," Brilinda whispered, jumping away from the fish that had been dead moments before. The walls sprouted with branches and leaves, pressing inward toward the tables.

At that moment her mother walked into the kitchen and screamed, leaping backward as a new branch growing from the door frame slapped her in the face.

Brilinda smiled, not fully understanding the implications of what was happening but realizing that her life would finally change.

Loved it? Hated it? Please leave a review!

ALSO BY DAN KENNER

www.dankenner.com/books

Epic Fantasy

Shielded: A Prequel to The Lightbearer Chronicles - Get the Ebook **FREE** at www.dankenner.com/free

Awakened: The Lightbearer Chronicles Book One

Transformed: The Lightbearer Chronicles Book Two

Ascended: The Lightbearer Chronicles Book Three

Young Adult

Sunfire

Middle Grade

The Search for Silence

A Voice in The Noise

The Thundering Echo

ABOUT THE AUTHOR

Dan lives in rural Idaho where he happily lives with his wife, six children and numerous goats, chickens and a cat named Wilma. Aside from writing, which he'd happily do full time, Dan spends most of his time outside in the homestead he built with his wife. When he's not writing, he spends his time with his nose in a fantasy or sci-fi book.

You can connect with me at https://www.dankenner.com